MARY READ:

SAILOR, SOLDIER, PIRATE

by

Cherie Pugh

Available at:
maryread.weebly.com
Amazon
Kindle

ISBN: 978-0-646-49250-6
© 2008 Cherie Pugh

Edition 8

Acknowledgements:

Thanks to Captain Brian Otter and the crew of the Nordvag for my voyage through the West Indies in 1986, where I re-discovered this story.

Thanks to Sarah and the Tricycle Theatre for vital support while I completed the London research.

Thanks to Karen and George for my survival that Winter.

Thanks to Peter LeFevre for essential assistance with historical records and pub lunches.

Thanks to Gail Saunders, Nassau's Director of Archives, for her detailed information.

Thanks to Marleena van Laathem for generous translation services in Breda and the use of her family name.

Thanks to the people of Bellingen for their steadfast support.

And thanks to Russell for constant technical advice, and for making sure my wildest dreams come true. This novel is for you, and the Adventurer in us all.

I have quoted from the following sources:

Captain Charles Johnson's "A General Historie of the Robberies and Murders of the Most Notorious Pyrates", British Library, London, 1724.

"Barlow's Journal of His Life At Sea in King's Ships, East and West Indiamen and other Merchantmen from 1659 to 1703", ed: B.Lubbock, British Library, London, 1934.

"The Life and Adventures of Matthew Bishop, 1706-10", British Library, London, 1744.

"A Journal of Marlborough's Campaigns During the War of the Spanish Succession 1704-11", Sergeant John Deane, ed: D.Chandler, British Library, London, 1984.

"Memoirs of the Life and Gallant Exploits of the Old Highlander, Sergeant Donald MacLeod, 1700-1720", ed: Fife. British Library, London, 1724.

"A Compendious Journal of all the Marches, Famous Battles, Sieges... 1708-1713", Sergeant Millner, British Library, London, 1714.

"Wits, Wenches and Wantons", E.J.Burford, London 1986.
"The Life and Adventures of Mother Ross", Daniel Defoe, 1928 edition, British Library, London.

"The odd incidents of their rambling lives are such that some may be tempted to think the whole story no better than a novel or romance; but since it is supported by many thousands of witnesses, I mean the people of Jamaica, who were present at their trials and heard the story of their lives upon the first discovery of their sex, the truth of it can be no more contested, than that there were such men in the world as Roberts and Blackbeard, who were pirates."
Captain Charles Johnson, "Robberies and Murders of the Most Notorious Pirates", 1724

"The first decades after the removal of King James in 1688 were in certain senses the most revolutionary in English history. This was the period of bourgeois revolution transcendent, of individualism and capitalism, of traditional controls removed, of the enclosure movement run rampant. Right and wrong were to be negotiated...Property became King."
Juliet Mitchell, in Daniel Defoe's "Moll Flanders", 1978.

CONTENTS:

Prologue: Adrift

We were eight weeks out of Ostend, and all but becalmed, wallowing in the troughs of the long Atlantic swells. The Trade Winds had failed us, we were on quarter rations of mouldy biscuit, and the rancid water was all but gone.

The Dutch Fleet we'd set sail with had lost us weeks before in a squall, and the dying First Mate swore there were fearsome pirates all along this latitude. When I asked if the English Navy were not patrolling these waters, he declared them too busy trading throughout the Caribbean for their own profit. The bloody flux had whittled away at us since we left the Canaries astern, and now with the scurvy upon us, those who were not dying fast, raving and shitting blood, were dying slowly, weak and woeful, losing teeth and eyesight. The First Mate raved that we'd make Charles Town on the next breeze, but death loomed over our stricken vessel, and the next morning we dropped his corpse into the sea, the Godless dog of a Captain not granting it even the courtesy of a winding sheet, sharks upon it as it hit the water.

I thought 'twould be a quicker, cleaner death, to drop overboard after him, and cursed the day I had let him sign me on. Yet the grey despair that had beset me following the death of my Dutch spouse, after four hard years of love and hatred, had left me with so little care for my own existence, that anything had seemed preferable to another Dutch Winter.

When the First Mate had smacked a rum down in front of me, in a damp tavern in Ostend, and waxed lyrical on the luscious beauty of the Caribbean, of turquoise seas and tropic heat, I had felt my fog-bound soul lift. He had parried my disgust at the merchantman's wages by claiming that with Queen Anne's war over, sailors were begging for bread all over Britain. Then, instead of returning to England to search for my mother, I had let his thin promise of a warm and distant land beguile me onto this deathship.

The Captain had baited me for an Englishman ever since we first sailed, berating the First Mate for signing me on. He had boasted of fighting the English as a boy, remembered every squabble over colonies that our two sea-going nations had ever engaged in, and spat a list of English atrocities at me. I told him I'd spent my youth fighting to keep his homeland free of the French, and had nothing to show for it but scars and empty pockets. He had cursed the English as traitorous dogs for their sudden withdrawal from that war, and I had cursed the day I'd joined his crew.

By noon, the sun beat down hotter than Hell itself, and I could no longer ignore the pleas of the dying men for water. The fat Dutch Captain had declared it a waste to help them, yet he was still in his cabin, immersed in his vast lunch and bottle of wine. I knew 'twas almost time for his daily ritual of the noon sighting, yet was sure I had time enough. With the eyes of the surviving Dutch crewmen hard upon me, I approached the water barrel, scraped out a full dipper, and crept over to the five men lying raving in the thin shade of the luffing mainsail. Ignoring my own fevered need, I dared give them only a sip each, though they begged me hard for more.

Then the Captain's roar spun me straight into his fist, and I was flat on my back, my head ringing with the force of the blow. Instantly, I was on my feet, and reaching for the blade he'd already stolen from me. My speed and fury made him step back, blustering. "Fool of an Englishman, this is not London, where every servant wears a sword and thinks himself better than his master. On my ship, I have the sword, and I am King!"

I knew that as soon as he overcame his fright, he would kill me. He was the only one aboard consuming a full ration, and there was none who could stand up to him. He would string me up off the yard-arm and watch me dance, and any protest would be mutiny. I thought to make a shambling run for my sword, hanging up in his cabin, and at least die fighting.

Then the lookout yelled: "Sail! Two to the north, Sir!"

The Captain spun away from my glare, and strode off to find signal flags, for without the help of these distant vessels, there would soon be none left to sail this stinking tub for him.

For an instant I thought I must swoon, and staggered to the gunwales for a bucket of sea water to cool my aching head. The ocean was so deep it looked purple, and it was strange to me that it came up clear in the bucket. My thirst raged, and I wanted to fall into the ocean, and swallow until I drowned. I dumped the bucket of water over my head, and my mind cleared.

Cookie yelled that dinner was ready, and I dropped below with the others, into the foetid heat and darkness of the forecastle. I messed with two Dutchmen, the third dead a week now, and one of the others very shaky. I could not stop myself from calculating how much more we would have to eat if he died today, though 'twas more likely that they who would be sharing my dinner, once the Captain found his courage.

When the maggoty mess of old biscuits was dropped in front of us, I was glad of the darkness, but still closed my eyes to eat the squirming mouthful. Compared to this, even the rats were starting to look toothsome. Then we held our cramping bellies and grumbled together in something like fellowship, while one old sea dog did his best to give us a song. My mates had a Dutch stubbornness that kept them steady under this hard oppression. I didn't dislike them, yet I knew I would give all their lives for a cool, foaming tankard of ale.

Then the water bell sounded, and we climbed back on deck, the whole crew gathered about the barrel, waiting in terrible anticipation for the Captain to dole out the precious, stinking water.

When he ambled over, full of scorn for our crawling need, I avoided looking him in the eye for fear he'd see murder, my fingers longing for the uncompromising rasp of steel.

And then I was afraid of my soul's fury, and remembered all the grim tales I'd heard of ships found adrift, all sails set and no hands aboard. For once killing begins, who can stop it? I'd seen enough of war to know that evil has its own impetus.

So I waited with the rest of them for the half-full dipper, praying to the God who had abandoned me that the Captain would not dash my water to the deck. Some swallowed it at once for the blessed relief of wetness, and then eyed the rest of us greedily. I sipped mine slowly, relishing the taste, the way the water slicked over my dry tongue and down my throat. Then it was gone, my thirst seemed greater than ever, and there was nothing for me to do but take the helm, and watch for a breeze.

The rest of the crew had abandoned their fishing lines, to stare at the two sails to the north of us, both vessels clearly visible now. The young midshipman muttered that they were headed straight for us, and they'd be sure to give us a barrel of fresh water. I thought too that the approaching ships would tell us how far from Charles Town we were, and then this slow torture might seem to have an end to it. The Captain raised signal flags, and by the change of the next watch, I was amazed to see how fast they were arrowing in on us.

"Look close", the old sea dog muttered, leaning on the gunwales next to me. "Me thinks me old eyes see English colours."

"Englishmen?" I stared until I too saw the English flag at her masthead. My heart soared, and I instantly resolved to stow away and work my passage home amongst my own countrymen.

"They make more of this breeze than seems possible", the young midshipman muttered.

The old sailor at my elbow nodded. "Aye, look at 'em schoon. They're island vessels, swift an' shallow. Won't see sails like 'em nowhere but 'mongst the Malacca pirates o' the Indies, who're always swift to attack, and faster to run."

He pointed out their mainmasts, set well back from the long, narrow bows, and the long, curving sails meeting the wind like the wings of a bird, sending the vessels flying atop the waves rather than ploughing through them. The smallest was a single-masted sloop, and the old Dutchman called the two-masted vessel a schooner. By sunset, we could clearly see their English colours fluttering brightly from the maintops. Our crew was eagerly crowding the starboard side, praying they would come upon us before night fell, no oaths against English traitors now.

Then both vessels struck their English colours, and in their places they raised the skull and crossbones. The air was filled with mad drumming and the shrieks of the damned, the sloop's rail crowded with demonic black men howling the most hideous oaths. Then the schooner sent a shot straight over our bows. One voice rang out clearly over the din: "Drop ye sails and surrender instantly, and we'll give ye quarter. Resist us, and ye'll feed the sharks!"

"Dear God, pirates!", whimpered the unmanned Captain, white-faced and stricken with terror. "Say nothing against me. I was never unfair!"

Not one man would meet his eyes, yet I could not scorn his terror. We had all heard tales of the abandoned cruelty of these renegades when faced with a Captain condemned by his own men, though 'twas said they would not touch a common sailor's seachest.

Yet the English command to drop the sails had not been understood by the frightened Dutchmen, and the schooner lay off our bow, her guns leveled at us across the rolling waves. Fearing a battle that we could not win, it was I who unwound the sheets from the belaying pins, and dropped our luffing mainsail hard to the deck. The pirates then swung their sloop alongside us, threw grappling hooks to hold us fast, and poured aboard. We were helpless before we'd even thought to grab a musket. I was frightened, yet I could not help admiring their seamanship.

The pirates were fearsome, some truly black men, others with blackened faces, all of them bearing cutlasses, muskets, and pistols, and cursing hard. From amidst these ruffians, an elegantly bearded young Irishman stepped lightly up to our quaking Captain, his hand on the hilt of a rapier. Doffing an absurdly feathered hat, he made a graceful bow. "Captain o' this tub are ye? Before the Devil, man, ye made a wise choice surrenderin' so fast." He raised an eyebrow at the Captain's desperate miming. "What, no English? Yet someone understood enough to drop yer sails." His sharp eyes swept over us, and knowing that the crew were about to push me at him, I stepped forward, snatched my cap off, and made the best bow I could, under the circumstances.

"Mark Read at your service, Sir."

"Sir me no Sirs, Sirrah, for we are all but men here at sea, until we are bones. I am Captain Sam Bellamy, and that pretty schooner is handled by Captain LeBoose, a Frenchmen with no love o' the English or the Dutch. I take it this fat fool is yer Captain. By yer bruised face, I'd say he's also a cruel bastard."

His merry grin convinced me he was more a rascal than a rogue, yet I still would not condemn the Dutch Captain to his mercy. "'Tis more the bad food and lack of water that has done for us."

"I swear by the Devil, any man who joins our Company has his fill o' fine victals and wine, and oranges fresh from Bermuda. And there are no tyrants to lord it o'er the freeborn. Think on it lad, yer skinny enough. Now, what's the cargo, and where's his cash?"

My wits struggled with the sweet memory of oranges as the Dutch crew were herded down into the forecastle, and bolted in. "I know nothing of the Captain's money. The cargo is mostly wine from the Canaries, Holland lace, and Delft blue china."

The brigands immediately tore into our hold, and

12

began passing our cargo to the sloop.

"All o' which we can sell for a pretty price to the Governor o' Saint Thomas", Captain Bellamy gloated, "though the wine we'll drink ourselves, eh boys?" A crate of Madeira was handed up, and bottles liberally passed around. Bellamy pulled the cork out of a bottle with his teeth, and gallantly offered it to me. I declined but he insisted. "Nay lad, yer almost done in, and ye'll need the strength o' the wine to see ye through a nasty business. We don't want ye swoonin' away on us, just as he tells us where his hoard is stashed. Come now, I ask ye sweetly, take a wee drop."

I sipped, and then, under the pirate Captain's urging, sipped again. The wine exploded in my blood, and I suddenly felt almost equal to the drama. "Aye lad, that's better. I like ye lad, I'll tell ye straight. Ye should run with us. Now, as to the money, they always carry sufficient to fill the hold with sugar and rum for the return voyage. Tell the fat whoreson that whether I let me mates tickle it out o' him, or he tells me freely, I'll not leave without it."

I explained this to the scowling Dutch Captain, who protested he had nothing. Two burly pirates then hustled him into his own cabin and bound him to his chair, whereupon a handsome, yellow-eyed mulatto tied a fuse around his red face. "Tell him we'll burn his eyes out if he won't tell us where the money is", he hissed at me.

I did as I was told, the Dutchman cursed me, and the mulatto grinned and lit the fuse. He screamed like an animal as it sparked its way around his face, and babbled of a compartment in the floor by his bed. Bellamy cut the fuse, and at my directions, the pirates tore the floor up. A heavy sack was dropped clanking onto the Captain's table, and Bellamy poured out the gold, to the pirate's loud huzzas.

The Dutchman cursed him, and Bellamy struck him hard across the face, still bound though he was. "Aye scum, ye'd cheat the men o' the food they need to survive the voyage, just to keep a few guilders more for yeself. Keep yer curses to yeself too ye dog, or I swear by the Devil I'll give

13

ye to me mates to sharpen their knives upon!"

I saw my rapier then, hanging above the Captain's bed, and when I buckled it about me, I was again filled with courage and hope. Bellamy laughed. "A duellist, eh?" He passed me another bottle of the Captain's wine. "Ye can't stay here, and wear that. Ye'll have to join us lad, for a free life and a merry one. There are no tyrants on our ships. I am Captain only because the men see that the wind loves me, and because I'm always first aboard in a fight. Nay lad, don't deny me for this filthy barge and a cruel Captain! The Brethren o' the Sea are the best men afloat, our vessels the fastest, the West Indies trading the richest, and our crew the merriest of all the Companies out on the account." His twinkling blue eyes looked straight into my soul. Yet I shook my head, and he shrugged, thinking me a coward.

As we stepped back onto the deck, the sun finally dropped into the sea, stars filled the sky above us, and the pirates lit smoking torches. Bellamy called down to those in the hold, and when they shouted back that she was almost empty, he ordered them back aboard their sloop. Then he turned to me again. "This is yer last chance, Mark Read. We are well manned, and have no need to force ye, yet ye'd be a fool to deny me. We've all agreed to stay together until we've five hundred pounds in each pocket, and then we're bound for the Bahamas to make merry with the boys and the booze. Come, we'll celebrate our good fortune tonight, with wine and dance. What say ye, lad? 'Tis either that or Death, for yer fat Captain will not forgive ye his ticklin'. He'll drop ye overboard for sure."

"In truth, I care little if he does."

"That's the lack o' food speakin'. Come man, another swig o' wine. And remember, life can begin anew out o' nothin'. This is it lad. Meet yer fate squarely. Run with us."

"I cannot, Captain Bellamy, though I'm tempted by your kindness. 'Tis not the merriment I'm afraid of, 'tis the killing. I'll tell you frankly, I've no taste for cruelty, and little greed to spur me on to murder."

"Murder, what murder? Did ye see any murder done here today? Wasn't it neat, tidy, business-like? Do ye think yer crew more cowardly than any other, just 'cause the haul was the poorest? They all surrender fast enough when they see our numbers, and a whisper o' pain is enough to make us rich men. The tyrants we tickle always favour us by embellishin' our cruelties, so they don't look such cowards, and that helps terrify the rest into a quick surrender. Come now Mark Read, would ye always be a slave, or would ye be free?"

"I have been rich and poor, my own master, and the slave you see me now, yet I have never been a thief."

"Yer a good sort o' fool, lad. The rich use God as a cudgel to keep ye poor and workin' hard, while they take whatever they want, callin' themselves honest because they have made the law to cover them like a blanket. We steal from them with no cover but our courage, and the Devil take the hindmost. We sell the finery cheap to the Governors of all the colonies, who will not buy expensive goods direct from Europe. 'Tis the London merchants who truly hate us, and spur the Navy on to hunt us, though they are too busy convoying ships for a quarter o' the cargo.

"As for murder, have we not all fought, by land and sea, because they told us their wars were just? And did we not kill for them without a pang, for the pittance they offered us? Aye, ye were there, and it sickened ye, I can see that it did. We may still fight, yet 'tis only when we must, and then only for our lives. We may be thieves, yet we are honest about it."

The handsome young mulatto who had organised the torturing of the Captain hauled himself out of the hold and swaggered over, his gold earring and yellow eyes glinting in the light of the torches. "It's done, Sam. Time to cast off", he drawled, eyeing me slyly. "Have you found us a new mate?"

"Nay my dear Paul, he declares he prefers death at the hands of that fat Dutch Captain."

The young rogue looked at me hard, and shrugged.

"You're blind, Sam. This is no man. This is only the husk of a man. His heart is already dead."

Sam Bellamy nodded. "You are correct as usual, Paul Williams. Then there's nothin' for it. Clap a pistol to his head, and he can consider himself a forced man. We'll buy him a rum and a whore in Nassau, and he'll not find life so worth the losin'. Take him aboard, I'll help with the last o' the booty, and we'll cast off."

"I said I'd not go with you! My conscience does not allow it!"

"What can a suicide speak o' conscience? Nay lad, 'tis a mortal sin to reject life while it still bubbles in yer veins. Ye've one last chance to snatch at it again, and prove that ye deserve the agony o' labour that brought ye into this world. Run with us lad, ye've nothin' to lose."

The mulatto aimed his pistol squarely at my chest. "You're forced, man. Fetch your seachest. We're leaving this pitiful tub."

I dropped down into the stench of the forecastle, reassured the worried crew that the pirates were leaving, and the Captain was alive. They asked me what I was about, and I told them the pirates would have me, though 'twas sore against my will. With their surly eyes upon me, I packed my hammock into my sea chest, and bidding them farewell, hauled it feebly up the ladder. Williams shook his head at me in scorn.

Bellamy only laughed. "The rapier speaks for him, Paul. I swear by the Devil, he'll be the worst of us within a week. Now, LeBoose must be impatient for news, and we should be well away before dawn."

I shook my head when Williams again turned his pistol on me. "Don't bother with that. I have no great wish to join you pirating, yet I can see life has left me no choice. I'll join you freely, if I can freely leave."

"Sign the Articles that cover this cruise, and you're a rich man and a free one at the end of it. Until then, you're one of us, sworn to stand true to the Brethren."

16

I nodded, ashamed at the sudden lightness of my heart. "Aye, I'm one of you. God help me."

I stepped aboard the crowded pirate sloop, my sword at my side and my seachest on my shoulder. I knew that though I had lived twenty-five years in this hard world abiding by my conscience, that was over now. I had fought bravely in Queen Anne's Navy and Marlborough's Army, and had done my best to earn an honest living when the war was over, yet now I was an outcast. As soon as he made port, the Dutch Captain would swear a deposition against me for piracy, and chances were, I'd end my days dancing on a rope. Still, I knew enough to show none of this regret to the pirates. I had made my choice, and must now live with it.

How had a woman as honest as I come to this?

PART 1: ENGLAND 1692-1705
Chapter 1: My Beginnings

I was born a bastard, though I was thirteen before my mother told me the truth of my father. And that was only because she felt she must warn me of the horrors of the world. He had been a Bristol sailor, with my black hair and blue eyes. She met him when she was lost in the grief of early widowhood, with nothing to show for her marriage but a sickly boy child, a few shillings, and an empty bed. Her dead husband's mother had given her a guinea at his memorial service, for her grandson's sake, and told her to write. Yet knowing she had always been seen as an intruder into that family, my mother was too proud to confess she was unlettered, and the old woman returned alone to her big house in London.

My mother said she started drinking directly after the memorial service, fighting the finality of it, refusing to believe that the storm that had swallowed her husband alive off the coast of Africa wouldn't spit him out again in Bristol, as merry as ever. She would weep all night, sodden with bad gin, and do penance for the drinking all day, muttering Hail Marys on her knees, her babe wailing in his cot.

She met my father when she fell down drunk in front of him one sticky Summer night, outside the gin shop. Her child howled, and in her misery she joined him, unable to rise and no longer wanting to. My father lifted her gently to her feet and insisted on buying her a meal. When she talked of her dead husband, my father told her to curb her hopes, that she must think of her boy and make a future for them both. He spoke of sharks that could swallow a man whole, of the ravenous wild beasts of Africa, and the savages that would kill a white man on sight, thinking them all slavers.

She was dying of grief and loneliness, and when he told her she was young and beautiful, she saw the night in his hair, and the sky in his eyes, and hoped to find comfort in his arms. At first she hoped she had found a friend, then she hoped she had found another husband. As her mind became free of the gin and despair, she thanked God on her knees for sending her a good man.

One month later she told him she was pregnant. She woke the next morning to an empty bed and the price of my abortion on the dresser. She tried to steel herself to have me poisoned in her womb, a threat to the survival of herself and her baby son.

Yet in her heart, she was convinced I was her penance for having sinned, and she did not dare ignore God's wrath in case He did something worse to her. Part of her wanted to die of shame, yet she had already survived so much, and she had her child to think of. She knew that she was doomed to prostitution if she stayed in the sailors' slums of Bristol, yet her father had not answered her petition for money, and she could not face him, pregnant again, and her husband not two months dead.

Instead she went back to the parish she was born in, the only one bound to give her poor relief, and threw herself on the mercy of the Priest, as a respectable sailor's widow. They housed her in the squalid poor house across from the church, with the vagrants, old widows and village idiots, all sleeping like dogs in the filthy straw on the floor, living on scraps and stale beer begged from the tavern.

With the Priest's help, she wrote once more to her father, then, desperate to get herself and her baby out of this pest-house before her pregnancy started to show, she hired herself out to a nearby farm. It was Autumn, and all hands were needed to bring the harvest in, the only time of the year when anyone could get work, and everyone would eat well, even women able to make a shilling a day. My mother was taken into the kitchen, and she made herself useful, and tried to be cheerful, her sickly baby squalling in a wooden box at her feet while she kneaded bread and chopped wood.

She also tended the ailing great-grandmother upstairs, a frail shadow of the Amazon she had once been, yet still

19

strong enough to bully them all into Church and pious living. This old matriarch appreciated my mother's pretty face and gentle hands, and insisted she stay on after the harvest. Her pregnancy was obvious by the middle of Winter, and the indignant farmer, declaring that she would be almost useless to them, would have thrown her and her sickly son out into the snow, but for the old lady. She insisted on having my mother for her nurse, and refused to hear anything against her virtue, truly hungry to see one more baby born before she died.

I was born with the Spring thaw of 1692, the sour farmer's wife wrestling with my groaning mother on the slate floor of the kitchen, the men banished to the barn for the day, my half-brother howling to hear his mother's groans. I was born as bouncing as a lamb, and for this my mother gave thanks. She called me Mary after the Holy Virgin she loved so much, hoping that this would help balance out my illegitimacy in the eyes of God.

Yet when her son died only a month after, she knew she was unforgiven, for she could not repent my birth, and had looked for my faithless father in my black hair and blue eyes. Utterly shaken, she turned to the village Priest, and confessed everything. He was above understanding her, and berated her for cherishing her dead husband so little, that the first sailor who came along had gotten her with child again. He demanded that she do penance, on her knees, in front of the whole village. She refused to publicly pronounce herself a harlot, though she had done it privately often enough, so he did it for her. The shame of that Sabbath never left her, me squalling at her breast, while the Priest horrified the villagers with his account of her sin.

Immediately, the women shunned her, and the men mauled her, laughing at her protests. To protect herself, she moved us into the old matriarch's room, nursing her so tenderly in her last, gasping days, that the farmer's wife finally declared we could stay.

I grew up tied to the huge apple tree in the front yard,

with the dogs and cats and birds for company. My mother helped with the rough work of the household, laboured over her Bible, and stayed away from the village and the Priest. She lived in fear of true poverty, of hunger, of illness, of being unable to raise me without prostituting herself.

I was an adventurer from an early age, strong from the generous farm food, daring to go wherever the big boys went, and so furious if they denied me, that they would carry me along like a puppy, fishing me out of rivers when I fell in, and laughing at me if I couldn't get down from the trees I climbed. I knew the names of all the dogs, where the fox had her lair, and how to talk to the bull. Yet 'twas the horses I loved best, for their great strength and quick intelligence, and even the farmer's vicious stallion would let me scratch his ears.

The farmer's wife was rough with me, yet in the evenings, she would tell us all wonderful stories of elves and goblins, fairies and demons, dragons and witches. It seemed that everything could be suddenly transformed into something else, and the greatest adventures happened to the most ordinary people.

I had just made my fourth year, when she decided I was old enough to earn my keep. She set me scrubbing the kitchen floor, and when I rebelled, she beat me with a stick of firewood. My mother came back from the milking to find me sobbing into a bucket, making pathetic attempts to scrub for fear of another drubbing. She gathered our meagre belongings into her shawl, and without a word to anyone, we walked away. She had saved every penny the farmer's wife had ever paid her, yet there was still not enough to fill her hand.

My mother knew then that only desperate measures would save us. She remembered that her dead husband's mother lived in London, and praying to God that she was still alive, decided to find her and trust to her mercy.

She had often told me that if I'd had any sense, I'd have been born a boy, and cursed the lot of women, born to slavery and shame. When she asked me that morning if I thought I could be a boy, I felt it to be an honour, and insisted it would be easy. When she told me that we would start a long walk to London that same day, I knew that all my wishes had come true, for London was the greatest city in the world, a golden place of Kings and Queens. My mother took our bundle on her shoulder, while I skipped ahead.

After many miles, we met an old pedlar with some boys' clothes for sale. He made much of me going from a child's skirts to breeches, and offered to cut my curls off, tying what was left behind my neck with a leather thong. I swaggered along, truly delighted, for as a boy, no one would make me scrub floors. I'd have a horse and an adventurous life as a highwayman, and pour gold into my mother's lap.

Despite our sore feet, we walked long into the night. When I could walk no more, my mother sat us down under an oak, to rest. We watched the full moon rise immense and silver over the dark forest, and she told me I was a boy now, and my name was Mark. I believed her utterly, not doubting such magical transformations, thinking men and women differed only in the clothes they wore, and the work they did. Soon after, a passing farmer offered us a ride on his cartload of potatoes. When he complimented my mother on her sturdy son, the magic seemed complete.

The dawn brought a dismal drizzle. My mother asked a farmer's wife for food and shelter, in return for help with the milking, and she was kind to us, and gave us immense bowls of hot porridge. When we set off again, our pace was slow, for my legs were short. When I could go no further, she carried me slung in her shawl, and though we were often offered rides in passing carts, her feet were soon blistered and bleeding.

By the next morning, we were faint with hunger, and that afternoon, in desperation, she waved down a crowded coach, and spent our last shilling to crouch with me atop it, terrified at its speed.

We pulled into London at dusk, the bustle and confusion leaving me wide-eyed and staring, even in my exhaustion. Everyone seemed to be making as much noise as they could, our coachman bellowing, "Make way there you poxy dog!" Another answering, "Mind Milady's coach you filth!" A woman sang, "Oranges, oranges, who'll buy my sweet oranges?", and another screamed, "Thief! Catch that boy!" An old man with a barrow bawled, "Oysters fresh from Gravesend", and a young man on a bridge shouted out the latest ballad on Dutch King William.

And after the noise, 'twas the stench that assaulted me. Open gutters ran through the streets, where women emptied chamber-pots, and men pissed on rotting fruit and dead cats. Horses rotted where they fell, and even atop the coach, the sour stench of the crowd was nauseating. My mother must have felt it too, for when she hugged me to her, I could feel her heart thumping through her brown serge dress; and when she whispered to me not to mind, but be brave, and never lose heart, she might have been talking to herself.

The coach set us down in Cheapside, at dusk, in drizzling rain. My mother refused the coachman's offer of a bed for the night, though we were very tired, and taking her bundle on her back, and me by the hand, she pushed through the crowd. At every step, men stared rudely, some calling her names I did not understand. She held her head high, refusing to look at them, and asked any decent-looking woman for the way to Covent Garden.

We walked past the half-built dome of Saint Pauls, and over the stinking gutters of Fleet Street, to the crowded Strand, where gentlemen in fat curly wigs sauntered slowly down the darkly lit avenue, their hands on their sword hilts, and their eyes on my pretty mother.

As the night thickened, we saw fewer she dared talk to, and we were soon asking dreadful women with red blotches on their cheeks and mouths, who screeched insults at us, their breasts falling out of their bodices. My mother started to hurry, almost dragging me along, though I was weeping with exhaustion. The narrow, dark street opened into a crowded Piazza, lit with torches.

A pleasant-faced young woman asked if we wanted to buy her roasted potatoes, and I wept when my mother refused, as we had no money. My mother asked the young woman if she knew Mistress Read of Covent Garden, a pious old lady, whose family had lived here since Cromwell's war, when this was a respectable neighbourhood. The young woman regarded us sceptically, yet when my mother insisted that we were related to the lady, she nodded, told an old lady to mind her stall, and swinging me up onto her hip, and snapping rude answers at anyone who said anything nasty to us, she strode off through the crowded Piazza. I decided I liked her, and let my head drop to her shoulder. Soon we were at a huge door, which she rapped on with a great door knocker, and then she handed me back to my mother, and wishing us luck, hurried back to the Piazza.

A bent, smelly old man eventually opened the door and thrust a dim candle into our faces. Before he could slam the door on us, my mother quickly explained who we were. He ushered us in, and with no expression on his face at all, led us up the wide staircase. The house was dark and gloomy, and smelt as musty as the old man. The paintings on the landing were of dark, haughty people, in enormous wigs. My mother stopped before one of them, and the old man mumbled that it was the old master. "My husband had just that look", my mother said sadly, and I thought I saw some emotion cross the old man's face, though it might have been a flicker of the candlelight. He knocked on a door at the top of the stairs, and asked my mother to wait while he prepared the Mistress.

Quickly my mother tidied me, trying to smile, and asked if I remembered I was Mark Read. I nodded, and she hugged me and said if it got difficult, I was to cry and demand my bed.

The old man soon waved us into a grand room, lit

only by a small fire in an enormous fireplace, and a smoking candle by a big red chair. I did not see the tiny old woman, covered with shawls, until she held her arms out to me. I went slowly over to her, and she took me in her arms, smiling at my mother through her tears. "He is a fine boy. You have done well, my dear. 'Tis good to see you both."

My mother fell to her knees and kissed the old woman on the cheek. "I didn't know where you were. We risked everything getting here. I thought we would starve...", and to my horror, large tears rolled down her face.

The old woman picked up a small bell and rang it until the old man appeared. "Ashley, bring two large glasses of the best Madeira, and a drop for the boy. And some cake." He soon returned with a tray, and my mother wiped her eyes, sipped the wine, and tried to smile. The cake eased my hunger, and the wine made me sleepy, so I curled up in my mother's lap. The old woman sighed. "He was the last of my children to die, and my favourite son, and it took me so long to recover from my grief. Then you could not be traced."

"You tried to find us?"

"Earnestly."

"Yet you hated me when I married him."

"You were no match for him in the worldly sense. He could have had that heiress, you know. Still, he would have been proud of this boy. Let me help you both."

"If I had known of this, I would have come sooner, and we would have been spared years of suffering..."

"Then let us be friendlier than we have been. I am old and ill and lonely. Although I am not rich, I should have enough to end my days on, and I can help you and the boy. Did you call him Thomas, after his father?"

"No. He is Mark, after my father."

I realised they were talking of me, and opened my tired eyes. The old woman smiled sweetly. "I am your father's mother, Mark. Will you call me 'grandmother'?"

"Yes Grandmother."

"Are you tired?" I nodded. "Then I will have Ashley

put you to bed."

I shook my head and clung to my mother. "He'll be frightened to go anywhere without me. I'll put him to bed, and then we can talk some more."

My mother followed Ashley up another flight of stairs, to a room with a huge bed in it, a canopy making it a dark and secret place. My mother promised to join me soon, tucked me in, kissed me, and told me not to forget I was her own brave boy. The full moon leaned into the room when she blew the candle out, and for once my dreams of adventures seemed less fantastic than the strangeness of life itself.

The next day, I rose with the sun, as I always did, and careful not to wake my sleeping mother, used the chamber-pot, pulled on my breeches, and crept down through the sleeping house, in search of breakfast. In the steaming kitchen, a fat woman pulled my cheek, called me a bonny lad, and warmed bread and milk for me. I stayed chatting with her about her aches and pains, family troubles, and reliance on the Lord, until a bell rang, and she told me my mother was awake, and if I was strong enough, I could carry up her breakfast tray.

My mother was anxious when she first saw me, yet pleased that I had managed my boys' clothes without any assistance. I explained that all the buttons were at the front, and that I had talked to the cook all morning, and she had believed me a boy.

"You must talk only a little, and not about yourself, or your tongue will run away with you, and you will give us away. The less time we spend here the better. The old lady raised five sons, and will not be fooled for long. I will say that the air here is bad for you. You must cough a lot."

"Will we go back to the farm, then?"

"No. I swear it. We will never go back there."

Mother spent longer than usual getting ready, brushing her red-brown hair with the heavy silver brush on the dresser, fussing over her dirty dress, and exclaiming sadly over her ruined shoes. By the time we were in the parlour, the old lady was being helped in by the butler, one hardly less feeble than the other.

We all said good morning and I coughed, as my mother had told me to. "Mark's chest has always been an enemy to his health. I thought I would lose him last Winter with the lung fever. I fear the bad air of London will injure him if he stays too long."

The old lady looked stricken. "I hoped you would stay, and be companions to me."

"I want nothing more, yet Mark needs to be climbing trees, flying kites, fishing...not running through the foul streets of this city."

The old woman sighed. "Since he's all you have, you must take care of him. And you must let me help you. The widow of my oldest son has an inn on the Brent River at Stonebridge. She may be able to offer you a decent position."

"It sounds promising. Yet perhaps this woman and I will not like each other. She might treat me as a poor relation, to be pitied and slaved. And what can I hope for the boy? He needs so much more than I have been able to give him."

"Something can be arranged. Yet I must see the boy regularly. Stonebridge is so close to London, that 'twould be a simple thing for you both to visit me. I will write to Susan this morning. Now, 'tis time for tea." She rang her little silver bell. "Mark, the cook's nephew has been told to take you to the Tower to see the lions. Would you like that? And for you, my dear, at least one new dress. Can you sew? Then you need only buy material and lace. And shoes. And here's a guinea for the boy. Come child and kiss me. I am sorry I can't go with you. My doctor forbids me to heat my blood more than is necessary, dear man that he is. Ah, Ashley, tea now please."

The cook's nephew turned out to be an arrogant, carrot-topped ruffian of thirteen, who scorned the prospect of squiring us about town. I could see my mother wondering

27

how much use he could be in the important project of buying material for her new dress. When he led us straight into the bustle of Covent Garden Piazza, the broad, open space, dark and full of harpies the night before, was now a mass of colour and sunshine. Fruit, flower, and vegetable vendors were vying with each other to see who could shout their wares the loudest, and everyone, from Lords with swords and full-bottomed wigs, to street sweepers, were haggling for their produce. Most of the stall keepers were pretty young women, who answered sharply or smiled, according to the bargain offered. My mother earnestly warned me to beware of the coaches that bowled past the railings, raising the dust, and sending stray dogs flying.

A man was standing on the corner singing a ballad on some plot to assassinate King William, and calling for the burning of Papists. When I loudly asked my mother what a Papist was, a patched and painted whore screeched at my innocence. My mother glared at the punk, and told me they were Catholics, who didn't honour our new Dutch King, but the exiled King James.

"And who do you honour?" the punk demanded rudely.

"God", my mother replied, and we walked away, holding hands tightly.

Then I saw the young woman who had helped us the night before, talking to an old orange seller. I called out to my mother, and we went shyly up to her. She was all smiles, and they traded names. She was called Meg Pridden, and was married to a bricklayer. The old woman was Mother Garth. Meg said she was expected at her father's bird stall in James Street, just off the Piazza, and I immediately asked to go and see the birds. We set off together, my mother explaining to Meg my grandmother's plans for us.

"Aye, you're right not to bring the boy up in this stinking city. 'Tis a pit of evil. 'Tis a crime to rape women, so children are violated instead, many knaves believing that a virgin will cure the pox. And every day women and children

28

are enticed onto ships, and stolen away to be sold as slaves in the colonies. Aye, the country is safer, and at Stonebridge you'll be close enough to visit London, and still have the advantage of the trade. If you want cloth for a new dress, this is the best city in the world for it. There are mercers in Russell Street who will make a dress up for you, and another in Bedford Street behind the church, where I get the cloth for my own gowns. The woman there will treat you fairly if you tell her I sent you."

We walked into the bird market, and I was immediately entranced by the colours and songs. An old man called out: "Canaries from Germany, white, mottled, and grey. Give your sweetheart a song to start the day! Hello Chuck, you're late. Who's your pretty friend?"

"This is the woman I told you of, father, the one I found amidst the ruffians in the Piazza last night. She's Jane Read, kinswoman to old Mis'ess Read in King Street."

"Your daughter was so kind, Mister Garth. I don't know what I would have done if she had not helped me. And if you could, Meg, would you spend the day with me, helping me choose the things I need? For else, I will surely be cheated. And lunch would be my treat."

"Oh, go on father. You know I've worked hard of late. And business has been more than good, despite the rain. Besides, Sally hasn't been out of Covent Garden for weeks, and the boy is just her age."

"I'll make it worth her while, Sir. She'll not be out of pocket by me..."

"I've never been able to resist the pleas of a pretty woman. Against two I am helpless. Enjoy yourself Meg, 'tis not often you meet with an honest woman in these parts. And here...buy Sally a treat for me." He tossed a silver coin at her, and she caught it easily, and tucked it into her bodice.

We made our way back through the market to the orange stall, and with a word to her old mother, Meg bent down and pulled out a girl of my age, gold-haired and blue-eyed and pretty, who was sleeping on a rug under the barrow.

She sleepily kissed her grandmother, who put an orange in each of her pockets, and we were immediately hauled off by our excited mothers.

In Bedford Street, crowded with the well-dressed and fashionable, I could see that my mother felt lowered by her poor appearance. Yet Meg stepped boldly into the mercers, and pushed through the other shoppers, to curtsey with a grin to the fat proprietress. "You look well today ma'am. That colour truly becomes you. I pity the poor doctor, indeed I do! Now here's a country friend of mine, who I wouldn't let shop anywhere else. She needs material for at least one dress, and clothes for the boy."

The women talked calico and dimity, day dresses and petticoats, before the fat mercer started gossiping of our dear Queen Mary's inability to produce an heir to the throne. Meg snorted that this due to the King's more manly interests, and the women sniggered. The mercer thought the Queen must be jealous of her sister's success, and Meg pointed out that Princess Anne's sickly child was unlikely to live to ensure the Protestant Succession.

"And there's our bonny Prince Jamie, dining with his father at the King of France's table", sighed my mother.

This was too treasonous for the mercer. "Old King James would have given us to the French priests to rule."

"And instead Dutch William uses England to pay for his war against the French, and makes soldiers of all our sons", Meg noted.

"And if he loses the Netherlands, we'll be ruled by French priests yet", the mercer insisted.

Bored with them, I dove under a table after Sally, where we frankly inspected each other's faces. Then she gave me an orange, my first, which was so delicious that I thought it a great favour. I let her wipe her fingers on my breeches, because she didn't want to dirty her dress.

"My mama says I'm to have a new blue dress. I've grown out of this old one."

"I'm to have breeches and a green shirt. I like to

climb trees. You can't climb trees in a dress."

"There aren't any trees here."

"We're going to live by a river."

"When I get big, I'm going to sell oranges."

"When I get big, I'm going to have a horse."

Our mothers called for us, and laughed when we popped out at their ankles. Then the women turned their attention to me. "Something strong and dark for the breeches", my mother murmured, "and for shirts..."

They draped material over me, until my mother finally announced her satisfaction, and grandly pulled out our guinea to pay the bill. Then she gave her parcels to Carrot-top, and told him to run home and leave them in her room. Having got rid of him, she then declared the hard work over, and said 'twas time to see the lions.

Meg led us back into the Piazza, then down the Strand, where the fine coaches bowled past so quickly, we had to run across. We picked our way down a stinking alleyway, past a swarm of beggars claiming injuries from the Dutch wars, to Salisbury Stairs, and the wide, brown Thames.

Meg bartered with the boatmen, insisting on a good price, and we all clambered into a little red boat, and rowed out into a river full of dead rats and floating turds. My mother asked in horror if this water was pumped into the houses for people to drink, and Meg laughed and told her that most houses had a cistern on the roof to catch rain water, and only the poorest drank from the Thames. It was choked with water traffic, most of it small boats like ours, carrying people of all qualities from one set of stairs to another.

The boatmen were a foul-mouthed lot, shouting insults at each other, and at their rivals' passengers. They demanded to know who our fathers were, and Meg yelled that that they were pox ridden vermin, and she knew what their wives did while they worked all day. Our boatman laughed, showing only the black stumps of his teeth, and Sally shrank into me with horror, so I hugged her.

31

The sight of London from the water was marvelous to me, with its imposing skyline of church spires and domes and grand houses right down to the river banks. The tide was with us, and soon the covered way of London Bridge loomed over us. For an extra penny, Meg persuaded the boatman to shoot the bridge, and he grinned and shoved us straight into the swirling water that ran in wide tunnels under it. My mother clutched me to her, and with our ears full of the roaring sound of trapped water, we were sucked between sturdy pillars, and shot out into the sunlight on the other side. I was in the guise of a boy, and felt honour-bound to make no sound, and the boatman winked at our superiority over the women, who had all cried out in fear.

And then we were in the Pool of London, tiny amidst the looming hulls of the great ocean-going ships. As the tide was favourable, many were unfurling their sails, heaving in their anchors, and drifting slowly down to load at the docks, or further down to Gravesend and the open sea. The boatman saw my fascination. "Eh, lad, these ships be goin' all o'er the world, to Africa and the Americas, China an' the South Seas. An' all kinds o' queer things the men on them will see, and all kinds of adventures they'll have. Some won't come back, and some will make their fortunes, yet they'll all see the world."

"When I'm big, I will see the world", I announced.

"And what will become of me?", my mother protested. "Will you leave me behind in my old age and not take care of me?"

"There's the Tower!", Meg exclaimed. There were many towers, not just one, all grander than anything I had ever imagined. Meg said they held the Mint, the Crown jewels, all the King's cannon, and important prisoners. She spoke of Kings and Queens and Princes who had lost their heads there, of Colonel Blood's attempt on the Crown jewels twenty years before, of Anne Boleyn's ghost, and the legend of the ravens. We made our way towards the first tower that guarded the causeway over the moat, pushing past fashionable gentlemen out ogling the ladies, past the punks and drabs who ogled the gentlemen, past fiddlers and pie men who ogled the punks, through an archway and into the Lion's Tower. In a damp, sour-smelling vault, we saw the great beasts lying in tiny cells, their huge, maned heads resting on sturdy forepaws, their golden-brown eyes surveying us sadly. They did not look at all dangerous, and I wanted to put my arms about the most wretched, though my mother held me hard.

Outside we found a pie man, and lunched on the bank of the Thames, watching the ships load at the docks. Then Sally and I played that we sailed to Africa on one of those ships, and I was a ferocious lion that ate her, despite her pitiful cries for help. Finally the afternoon clouded over, and we were all glad to walk back past the bridge, where a more sombre boatman agreed to row us back up the river.

That night, I told my mother that I wanted to stay with Grandmother in Covent Garden and see Sally every day. "We can only stay because the old lady thinks you are her grandson. We will try our luck with her kinswoman. She never raised her sons, and may not discover you for a while. Meanwhile, we'll live a little better, and save some money against the day you are discovered. The old lady is ill, and may well leave you something if she dies, maybe even this house, and then you could live in London and see Sally every day. You would like that, wouldn't you? So be a good boy again today."

It rained all that day, and we sat in the parlour, my mother stitching away, while the old woman spoke of her dead sons, how fine they had been, and how she had loved my mother's husband best, which made them both weep.

"If you marry again, your new husband..."

"I will not marry again, and no, please don't tell me I am young and pretty. I will not have another man simply to keep me, and I've never seen another I could love. And, after all, you did not remarry."

"I was left comfortably off after years of marriage

33

with a family of boys. You are left with nought but one child and myself. And you were a widow so soon. 'Tis not healthy for you to be so alone. You look melancholy by nature..."

"A good husband would be a boon indeed, and a bad one a curse. And before you marry him, there's no way to tell one from the other. Even your son promised me he would go to sea no more, and then once we were married, he could not stop himself. And I was too young to be left alone, pregnant and waiting for him to come home, and too young to hear of his ship going down, with the son he had never seen sitting on my knee. Yet enough of that. He was a sailor before I married him, and he was one after, and I should have known what those promises are made of."

The old lady went off to rest, and my mother and I spent the rest of the day exploring the musty old house, looking at fading pictures and dusty furniture, my mother dreaming of living there one day.

The next day was Sunday, and we went to church, and I was bored and couldn't sit still. My mother smacked me hard in front of everyone once the sermon was over, and I was sent to bed without supper. The next day Sally and I played all afternoon in the kitchen, under the eye of the generous Cook, and the next morning a letter came from the country, saying we were welcome to visit. My mother finished my new breeches, and we packed everything into a trunk the old lady gave us, and she cried when she kissed me goodnight.

Chapter 2: The Coach and Horses

I was still half asleep when my mother carried me downstairs, and I don't remember the walk to Cheapside, with Carrot-top carrying our chest all the way to the Harrow coach. I awoke just as we bumped past Tybourn, and saw a sun-blackened, crow-pecked corpse hanging from the gallows, before my mother covered my eyes.

Then we swept around and up the Edgeware Road, our coach swaying sickeningly as it lurched through potholes, the passengers cursing the driver. The stench of London's dunghills regularly filled the coach, and a student nursing a hangover disgorged his breakfast out the coach window, turning us all green. We were held up by packhorses loaded with bales, and then by flocks of sheep being driven to the Smithfield markets.

At Paddington Village, we turned off the Roman-straight, busy Edgeware Road, onto the lazier, twisting, Harrow Road. It was almost mid-Summer, the fields we passed were full of wheat rippling in the wind, and the farms looked prosperous, their fruit trees heavily burdened.

A northern yeoman began abusing the Lords taking our common land. "When they have cut down the great forests, dyked the fens, and enclosed the commons, there will be nowhere for an ordinary man to grow his wheat, and graze his cow."

There were murmurs of agreement.

"The Diggers warned us how 'twould be", a thin old man mused. "Everywhere we look, walls close off the best land, and foresters and cottagers are turned out to starve. 'Tis now a crime for a poor man to gather wood from a forest, for the forest now belongs to the manor."

The student insisted that the greater produce justified our loss. "We will never see another famine in England!", he declared.

"Nor a free man who's not a Lord", growled the

yeoman. "To feed his family, a man must now slave for those who took his land, or take to the road with a pistol..."

"Then he should hang Sir, for the law supports the common good..."

"Huh!", an old soldier sneered. "Tell that to the young man forced to enlist to fill his belly. Enclosure may have made England rich, yet 'tis all spent on foreign wars."

The student flared up. "And if we let them have the Netherlands, do you think the French would not take England next?"

"Why would I give a toss", the yeoman snarled. "Since our own Lords gave England away to a Dutchman."

We rolled into the village of Holsdon and stopped to let the thin old man down at the Crown. Then we wound our slow way up Green Hill, and down towards a sunny river, lined with willow trees. It was not until coachman bellowed "Stonebridge!", that I realised we were there.

The Coach and Horses was a pretty, white-washed inn, with an ivy-covered porch, and attics under a thickly-thatched roof. It stood by an ancient stone bridge, with orchards and meadows green along the gentle river. I loved it as soon as I saw it, and knew it would be our home, despite my mother's sudden nervousness and swiping at my face with a clean 'kerchief. I remembered too that we wouldn't be allowed to stay unless everyone believed me a boy.

The coachman announced a short halt for lunch, and the passengers eased themselves from the cramped coach. The postilion handed down our almost empty chest, and an old man with a bent back unhitched the sweating horses, and led them through a gate. We followed the coachman through the ivy-leafed doorway, into the cool darkness of the inn, where his passengers seated themselves at great trestle tables. A big boy and girl brought pitchers of cool ale, and trenchers of bread, butter, and cheese, while a large woman in a big white cap proffered roast fowl to those who could pay for it.

My mother stepped up to this Amazon, and dropped

a demure curtsey. "Mistress Susan Read? I am Jane Read, who our mother-in-law wrote you of..."

"Bless my heart, you are here already! Welcome my dear, welcome!", and she enfolded my mother in a great embrace. She turned to me next, and when I stepped back, overawed, she chuckled and examined me with her quick brown eyes. "Ah, what a beautiful boy. He must be the pride of your life, my dear. I never had one o' mine live, not past a year or two. Is it Mark, then, sweetheart? I am your Aunt Susan. Don't be afraid of me. I am big, yet I am soft. Come and kiss me." I did as I was told, and liked her wonderful smell of ale and cows.

"Are you famished my dears? Sit and eat. I wasn't expecting you quite so soon, yet I am glad you are here. We have so many travelers passing from London to Harrow, and if they come once, they come again. Good food, good stables, and no beasts in the beds. And so I have my hands full!"

I took an apple, and she suddenly bellowed: "Before Grace, child? For shame!" The passengers had their plates loaded, yet they hesitated long enough for this brown giant to press her palms together devoutly. "Lord, blessed be Thy name. I thank Thee for bringing my kinswoman and her child safe to my house. I pray that we will live in harmony under Thy loving hand and eye. I pray Thee protect the travelers that go out from under this roof, and bless them in their endeavours, Amen."

The passengers and my mother murmured 'Amen', so I did too, and was rewarded with a bright nod from my new aunt. "You can see how busy we are, with only Old John to take care o' the horses, and these two scallywags to plague me." She winked at the boy and girl serving the passengers, and they grinned at her.

Aunt Susan then tallied up what each in the room had eaten, and extracted coins from all of them, but for our surly coachman. She flirted terribly with him, until even he laughed. When they had all left, she gave a great sigh, and let herself down into a huge chair, a tankard in one hand, and a chicken leg in the other, her eyes on my mother.

"The next coach is soon due", she announced. "And we have a lot to talk of. I have a proposition for you, my dear. Over the road is the worst-run farm in the parish. 'Tis leased from the squire by a stupid old man, and makes not enough to pay for itself. I would like to take over the lease, and provide the inn from its produce, perhaps enlarging the dairy. Yet I am only one lonely, harassed, widow woman, and have not the time to run a farm as well as this inn. If you ran the farm, I would pay its rent in return for produce, and you would have the rest to sell to London merchants at the market in Kilburn. What say you?"

My mother smiled sweetly. "Why, I say you are an astute business woman, Sister Read. You could offer travellers cheaper food than anywhere else on the Harrow Road, and I would be left with only the dregs to sell. What say we combine the inn and the farm as one business, you managing one, and me the other? I am well learned in farming, and could easily supply the inn with only a few men to help with the hard work. We could split the profits from both ventures at the end of the year, paying the rent for the farm out of what we have both made. That way we would be looking out for the best for each other, and not fall out, as most partners do."

"Jane, Jane, and you call me the business woman! I own this inn, and have worked hard to build up its reputation. I can afford to rent the farm and pick my own manager. All you are putting in is your labour. We could not split half-half."

"In your position as an attractive, wealthy widow, there would be ugly talk in the village if you took on any man as manager, unless of course you married him. You need a competent woman. Someone you could trust. Even if you take the farm rent from the inn's profits alone, you would still prosper, and you would have more time to relax with an ale, since Mark and I would also help with the inn."

"I like you Sister Jane. A pretty woman with a quick mind is an asset in this business. What plans do you have for the boy?"

They both turned to consider me, and I announced through a stuffed mouth: "Horses!" I swallowed quickly and explained. "I want to look after the horses. Horses like me."

"You'll have to feed the chickens and ducks and milk the cows", Aunt Susan informed me sternly. "Yet, if 'tis horses you love, Old John will be glad of the help. Go out the back to the stables, take him this tray, tell him I sent you, and do all he bids you without complaint."

I moved carefully towards the door, determined not to drop the plate of food and the heavy tankard of ale. Old John was a scrawny, bent, mean old man, who constantly chewed on a plug of tobacco, and spat everywhere. "I am Mark Read", I told him. "Aunt Susan says I am working for you now. She says I must do everything you tell me. I like horses." I gave him the tray of food, and he glared at me, and sat down on an overturned bucket.

"Do ye now? An' what does a shrimp like you know o' horse flesh?"

I recognised the challenge, and knew he thought me too young, yet I was already four, and had been magically made a boy, so I stood my ground. "Horses like me. They know I like them, and they let me feed them and pet them."

"Oh do they ?", he sneered. "Let's see you wipe down that stallion."

I took a cloth and a bucket, and whistling a horse song, sidled up to a great, long-legged, elegant beast, with nervous eyes. I told him I was his friend, and standing on the bucket, began stroking his shining blackness with the long, firm arcs I had learnt on the farm.

The old man nodded. "You'll do, boy. A little firmer to ease his muscles. This one's only here for an hour, and though as fine a piece o' horseflesh as you'll ever see, he's been worked too hard. See how his ears droop and his eyes roll? When they're like that, watch they don't bite out o' sheer vengeance. I've walked him about to cool him, and now we'll put him in a box with a bucket o' gruel and a pint of ale."

"You must feed a horse accordin' to how long he is stoppin' for. We don't over-water those that are expected to gallop within the hour. Those stoppin' the night go into the stables, where we treat 'em well and charge their masters a fortune. If they are stoppin' for more than a night, we turn 'em out into the back paddock, at reasonable rates. And if I ever catch you leaving that gate undone, I'll take a horse whip and beat you. Mind me now."

"I'll work hard and keep the gate shut and won't be beaten", I told him firmly, and on that understanding, I worked with him all afternoon. More and more horses arrived, and needed caring for, and Old John scowled at the coachmen and riders, seeming to hate them for their hard use of their own beasts, often arguing that a horse would need more time to recover than its master thought.

When the rush was finally over, my mother called me, and told me she was going with Aunt Susan to see the farm, and possibly the Squire. She wanted me to stay and help Old John, and though I was tired, I agreed, and they were both pleased with me. Aunt Susan helped Old John hitch the old cart-horse to a dainty blue trap, hauled herself in and took the reins, standing like Boudica in her chariot, while my mother sat demurely in the back.

Once I'd waved them out the gate, I swept all the dung into a pile for the garden, and then Old John gruffly hinted that if I was tired, I could nap. First I explored the inn, happy with the low ceilings, thick beams and whitewash. Everything in it was sturdy and functional, made of wood or pewter, to be used over a long time by a great many people. There was nothing that a child had to be careful of, nothing dangerously fragile, as at my grandmother's house, and I knew the place suited me. I introduced myself to the thin, quiet woman in the kitchen, who told me that I had come to a good house, asked if I was one of God's children, and gave me a handful of strawberries from the garden.

I found Tom chopping firewood, and he looked at me as though I were an insect, told me to call him Mister Tom, and then relented, and asked me if I played marbles.

"I've never played before. Will you teach me?"

He looked horrified at the suggestion, and I knew that he would not have spoken to a girl at all. "You would have to run errands for me", he decided at last, and when I promised to be useful, we shook hands, and he gave me one to practise with, and demonstrated the necessary flick of the thumb.

With the beautiful glass stone safe in my pocket, I went inside and up the stairs, and found the big girl making beds. She was Betsy, and she had long curling chestnut hair, dimples and green eyes. She cuddled me and called me duck, and took me to a small room where my mother and I would be sleeping, with a window that looked over the orchard to the river. She threw a blanket over me, kissed me, and told me to sleep, and I curled up happily, amazed at the richness of my new life.

And so began my happiest years. My aunt convinced the Squire to lease the farm to my mother, guaranteeing the rent from her own earnings at the inn. "He tried to refuse us as we are both single women," she informed the household later, her head high. "Yet I told him that we are both widows, which is different, and that as he has been leasing the farm to a fool for years, he could hardly object to me, since I have the most profitable business in the parish."

I worked hard, mostly around the stables, carrying grain, drawing water, and polishing harness. From Old John I learned everything about caring for horses, the illnesses and remedies for each season, how to tell a showy, useless animal from one with spirit, and a good-natured beast from a biter. I heard his protests against horses ruined by bad riding, and sometimes Old John would have my aunt make some fool an offer, and we would nurse an animal back to health,

41

and add it to our own stable. I learnt to ride well, and dreamed of one day having my own horse to go adventuring on, like Dick Turpin on Black Bess.

Tom was my champion and encyclopaedia. He knew everything about the river, where it was shallow enough to wade across, where it ran swift and dangerous, where the Mad Monk had drowned himself, and where the water nymphs hid in their deep pool, waiting with long, cool fingers to drag little boys down into their cold embraces.

That first Winter, my mother took in a family who walked in off the road, half dead of cold and starvation, and these people she found she could rely on. There was a small, kindly woman who kept the cows, a thin, unhappy man who made the cheeses, and their three big boys who did the hard work of the farm. My mother was then able to spend more time helping my aunt with the inn.

Every few days throughout Summer and Autumn, she would deliver the produce the inn needed. On Thursdays we would be up before the sun to load our red cart with the garden surplus, hitch up the cart-horse, and roll along to the Kilburn market just as the sun was coming up. We loved these journeys together, just the two of us, stopping at every house to sell our produce, from the small dairy farm at the bottom of Green Hill, to the tavern at Churchend, where our grey-stoned church stood amidst great spreading elms.

We always rested the horse at Chapel End, where some Catholic had secretly erected a shrine to Our Lady to protect travellers, which no one dared take down in case of bad luck. My mother would often lay a flower there, and say a prayer for her dead husband, and I prayed for him too, thinking the brown-eyed man in the portrait at my grandmother's house was my father.

We then rolled on to Wilsdon Green, to trade with the leering tavern keeper at the Spotted Dog. Mape's Lane, with the Manor House on one side, and Mapesbury House on the other, brought us back to the busy Edgeware Road, where it ran through Kilburn. My mother would have to coax our old horse through the London traffic, until she turned into the paddock next to the Cock tavern, where the market was held.

I often got down at the new row of brick cottages, to follow the cold stream as it meandered through the sheep fields, and past the ruins of the old Abbey. My ramble always ended at the Bell tavern on the outskirts of the village, where the kind, hunch-backed woman talked travellers into drinking the milky well water, claiming it was healthful. I then followed the stream to where it turned and flowed under a bridge, just before the toll-gate. There everyone had to stop to pay for the upkeep of the broad and muddy highway, some grumbling that the money was really spent on beer at the Red Lion. Travellers descended from their coaches to eat and drink at the busy taverns, and crowded into the marketplace. There were Gentlemen of the Road working between Kilburn and London, and sometimes a coach would pull in, the passengers shouting for a magistrate, the coachman urging the constable to whistle up a mob to hunt the highwayman down.

The marketplace was crowded with carts piled high with local produce, guarded by sturdy farmer's wives smoking pipes, and selling everything at a good profit to the London grocers. I had no friends my age at Stonebridge, as Churchend, the nearest village, was too far away for an easy walk. I also avoided the village boys, as they splashed naked in the river every afternoon in Summer.

At the Kilburn market I played with the children from the nearby farms, defending them against John Tanner, the bully whose father leased Oxgate farm. John was big for his years, and like all bullies, a true coward when challenged. That was how I made a friend of Bill Helier, who lived on a small farm in Nisdon, not far up-river from me. Once, we agreed to wake at dawn on Midsummer's Day, to separately follow the course of the Brent, and meet halfway. We found an old willow tree, and almost every afternoon, once the rush was over, I would slip out with my fishing rod over my shoulder and meet him there. Bill was a quiet boy, yet would dream the most fantastic adventures, usually involving dauntless courage against the damned French, and Captain Kidd the pirate.

'Twas the Franklyn twins who convinced me that girls were vile. Their father was the Kilburn vet, physician, surgeon, and occasionally, legal adviser, and they thought that put them on the same level as the Manor girls. One market day, they mocked me with having no father, and I pushed their faces into the mud of the Edgeware Road. My mother was furious, and threatened me with skirts. I was strong and brown and active, and it shocked me to remember that I was not a boy. Yet I could not believe that she would endanger both our livelihood and my inheritance from my grandmother.

"Why have I so carefully saved all my tips and the market money, child? This is fraud, and we might yet have to run for it, or face Newgate."

"You forgot I was not a boy, too."

"Sometimes I forget. Yet I would rather have you in skirts than fighting like a savage. For God made you a girl, and if there is one slip on your part, all this is over."

Chapter 3: The Parish

The responsibility for our deception lay heavily on my shoulders, and made me somewhat solitary. There were many afternoons when I climbed Brondesbury Ridge, and spent the day watching the clouds, glad to be alone.

Yet I was not the only one hampered by our deception. My mother's success with the farm meant she was now a good catch. Rumours of my grandmother's wealth began to circulate, and many speculated on the will of my childless Aunt Susan. One after another, the substantial men of the parish came to drink my aunt's ale, and admire my mother. They gave me shillings, called me a young rascal, and asked if I wanted brothers and sisters. I thought them repulsive, and though my aunt insisted that my mother sat and talked to them, I was glad she never let them escort her to church on Sunday. Whenever my aunt was particularly insistent on the merits of a particular suitor, my mother would retire to her room, pray loudly for the soul of her missing husband, and my sentimental aunt would weep and desist.

The maidservant, Betsy, was also my friend, though we kept our games secret. While we made the beds, Betsy would play the great lady and I would bow gracefully and make up to her, and she would giggle and curtsey. The local boys were wild for her, including our Tom, yet she scorned them all. Then, the Summer I turned seven, my aunt dismissed her, which I thought most unkind, for she was going to have a baby. She would not say who the father was, though my aunt slapped her to make her tell. Tom offered to marry her anyway, and was beaten up by the local toughs when he tried to stop them calling her names. Betsy then declared that she would marry no one, and that was when my aunt called in the Squire's sisters.

When we first moved to Wilsdon, our local squire was Sir William Roberts, who was fat and merry, and died suddenly, riding drunk to hounds. He had no sons, so his cousin, also called William, inherited the estate. The new Sir William was very proud of his elegant wife, and very keen on improving the village flock. Yet our farmers ignored his pleas to keep the worst of them off the common, and only let the best breed. They had not forgotten that his grandfather had enclosed the best of the common ground, pulling down ancient cottages and ejecting families that had always lived there, to extend the estate of Nisdon House. And this land was now being sold to provide a generous allowance for his handsome younger brother, Thomas, and dowries for his five sisters.

Sir William's five sisters were very different. Sara, the oldest, wrote and travelled and took her time marrying. Margaret hardly ever left the estate, having been the long-suffering martyr to her dead father's whims for too long. Mary kept her eye on the poor, and piously married the vicar's son. Eleanor wanted to marry a Duke, since she was beautiful, and her pride matched that of her elegant sister-in-law. Edith was the plain, quiet one, who people went to if they really needed help. These five sisters ran the parish, making everything their business, and letting none be poor and idle. One of the things they could not bear was unmarried mothers burdening the parish with their bastards, and when Betsy refused to marry Tom, Aunt Susan called the ladies in 'to talk to the poor wayward girl'.

Worried for Betsy, I hid under the window to hear what they said. Pious Lady Mary, proud Lady Eleanor and plain Lady Edith, were shown into my aunt's parlour, and after much shaking of heads over the lewdness of servants, they called Betsy in. She was humble, yet stubborn, and insisted she would neither name the father, nor marry Tom. My aunt pointed out that Betsy had not been born in the parish, and they had every right to move her on before the child was born. I thought of the pregnant Virgin Mary being turned away from the inn , and knew this was wrong.

Yet Betsy merely shrugged, and said she'd not starve,

no matter what they did. Furious with her sang-froid, Lady Mary hissed that she'd have her stocked and whipped as an example to the other village girls.

"Then I have no choice", she stated stonily. "I'll break me vow and tell ye. 'Twas no village lad who got me with child, Miladies. 'Twas yer own brother. 'Twas Thomas." The ladies were dumbstruck. "Oh, I know he won't marry me. I doubt I'm bearing the first of his bastards. Yet he loves me. He told me so." With a whimper, Lady Edith denied it all, and so Betsy pulled out a purse and poured ten golden guineas out onto the table. "That will keep me until I have the baby, and then he will take a house for me in London." She looked at them and there was a slight curl of contempt on her pretty mouth. "Don't worry Miladies, I will keep me mouth shut. Me own name may be trampled in the mud, yet there will be no gossip about him." Lady Mary started screaming terrible names at her then, and Betsy ran upstairs to bundle her things together. I caught her on the landing and hugged her, and told her I would pray for her and her child, and she hugged me back, weeping now, and made me promise not to break young hearts when I was big.

"Yet you'll live a fine lady...", I protested, confused by her misery.

"Don't tell those bitches. He loves me not a fart. He told me so when he paid me off." I promised to keep her secret, hardly understanding what she meant, and in tears, I watched her run to beg a ride from a farmer headed for London. She turned and waved to me as the cart disappeared up the hill, and then she was lost to us.

That night, my aunt lectured me on the evil of sin, the wiles of the Devil, the French pox, bastards, and the temptations of bad women. I saw my mother flinch at this, and she spoke softly of how easy it was for a man to betray a woman's innocence. My aunt flared up, insisting that Betsy be utterly blamed for her pregnancy, because sin had first come into the world through the weak-willed betrayal of God by a woman.

47

I took Betsy's fate hard, and longed to run away to London and find her. Then, soon afterwards, my grandmother insisted on enrolling me in the vestry school. Despite my protests, I was doomed to ride to Churchend three afternoons a week, to spend long hours with the boys whose families could afford to have reading, writing and counting drummed into their heads. The inn was full of pamphlets and fraying ballads bought from pedlars, the London newspapers, only a day or two old, and many ancient and wonderful books, most left by those who couldn't pay their bills. Yet though I hungered to solve the mysteries of the alphabet, I was afraid of the vicar.

For Father Hawkins was an austere, upright, learned man, almost completely without compassion, and always ready to cast the first stone. His sermons belaboured us with his conviction that all but himself, and perhaps his unhappy family, would burn in eternal Hellfire if we sinned, even unintentionally, and did not repent. Like Saint Paul, Father Hawkins would take no nonsense from anyone when it came to the sins of the flesh, and made no bones about prying into the beds of his erring flock, since it was our souls that he was struggling to save. He urged us to live as though God was constantly watching us, and after his sermons, he would accuse people in front of the whole village of the crimes he had discovered, and they would have to do public penance, or be excommunicated. It was he who inadvertently informed me that a woman should not wear that which pertaineth unto a man, and by this I felt particularly condemned. The boys called him Hawkshit, and hated him for his arrogance and his cruelty. He would beat us with a leather strap for anything that smelt of disobedience, screaming at us to submit, sure our devilish souls would be purified by pain.

Of course when we began reading, it was the Bible we started on, and this made it easier, as most of us knew large sections of it by heart, from evening readings at home. Even my mother, who could not write, could stumble through her Bible.

I learnt to read faster than the boys, and I could already count and do simple sums from market days with my mother. It was writing that I found most difficult. It was easy when we used chalk on slate, yet when we used the crude duck quill pens I made great blotches trying to copy the scriptures. Hawkshit would call this blasphemy, and whack me so hard over the head that my brains rattled. Then my hand would start to shake in fear of the next blow, and the blotches would be worse than ever.

One day I rode home, determined to never return, to find that my mother had a letter from my grandmother. Proud of my ability to decipher the old lady's scrawl, I read out an invitation for us to visit her, since she was feeling poorly. My mother still feared my discovery, so every time we went to London, we went in fear of highwaymen, for we carried money that she secretly deposited in a bank.

We had kept up our friendship with Meg and Sally, seeing them every time we went to visit my grandmother, despite the old lady's disapproval of this lowly connection. Sally had grown into a marvelous girl, with a spirited disposition and a wicked sense of humor, and she was the only girl I counted as a friend. The Garths, Sally's grandparents, had continued to sell oranges and birds in Covent Garden, and through them, we were able to trace the Priddens from one cheap room to the next, as Sally's father ran from bailiffs and debt collectors. He was a bricklayer by trade, yet drank heavily, spending all of his earnings, and sometimes all of Meg's, drinking rum with the sailors at Wapping. They were living off an alley in Saint Giles when the bailiffs finally found them, and took everything they owned, right down to the sheets.

Meg had refused to live with her husband after that, and despite the girl's heartfelt protests, she had apprenticed Sally to a seamstress in Duke's Place. We found her in a dark attic with fifteen other women, all bent over elegant satin dresses with aching eyes and sore heads. They stitched from

49

dawn to dusk for scraps from the main table, and two shillings a month.

It was clear to both of us that she could never stick with sewing long enough to finish the seven year apprenticeship that the Garths had paid for, at such great sacrifice. She had begged them to let her sell oranges instead, but her mother had declared that she was too pretty not to end up a whore, orange girls having the reputation they did. And in truth, she was lovely to look at, being all white and pink, with big blue eyes and thick golden hair. She knew it too, yet didn't try her flirt's tricks on me after I mocked her the first time.

That Sunday, old Mister Garth told us of the burning of a witch at Saint Albans. Someone had seen the muttering old crone step away from the shadow of the church spire. My mother was horrified, and that evening, when my lonely grandmother again asked if I could stay with her, she insisted that the country was much safer than London, where an old woman could be burnt alive for muttering. My grandmother was sure they'd found a true witch, for the Lord would have saved her else, yet she had heard that many had been hurt by the crush of the crowd.

When we returned to our peaceful life at Stonebridge, I was happier, for I could see that Hawkshit was nothing compared to the ogress that Sally slaved for, all day, every day. I made a great effort, and by my eighth birthday, had taken over most of the Bible reading in the evenings from my aunt, whose eyes were failing.

The beginning of Summer saw Princess Anne finally lose her sickly eleven-year old son, the Duke of Gloucester. The Princess had endured seventeen pregnancies in an attempt to produce Protestant heirs to the throne, all of which had ended in miscarriages or dead children. My mother and aunt wept for the poor woman, and bemoaned the likelihood of a civil war when Dutch William died.

"Old King James will be sure to try again for the throne for his bonny son", my mother moaned. "

50

"Aye, but the Stuarts always look to France, and England would never stomach a French invasion, let alone a Catholic King", my aunt insisted.

"Better we forget the Stuarts, especially as we have Princess Anne to inherit the throne when William dies."

"She'll have no child to follow her", my mother noted. "If young James would renounce Popery, he could be her heir."

"And what guarantee would there be that he would not return to Popery once he was King? No Jane, the German Hanovers are also related to Charles the First, and they are Protestant."

"I'd rather be ruled by our rightful Prince than some fat German…"

"Dear God, you speak like a fervent Jacobite!", my aunt exclaimed, half laughing.

"I am an old-fashioned woman", my mother protested righteously.

"You refuse to be ruled by a Catholic, but don't complain of the perverted Dutchman who rules England now, as long as he keeps out the French."

Summer unfurled like the brightest of banners, the farm prosperous, the inn popular, and I thought that nothing would interrupt our happy lives.

Yet in the midst of the Autumn harvest, the whole parish was struck by smallpox. The poorhouse was the source of it, and Lady Edith took it from there to the manor. She lived through it, though she was badly scarred, yet Sir William's six-week-old son and only heir died of it. I lost my only friend, Bill Helier, who slipped quietly away, still dreaming; and I almost lost my aunt, who lived only because of my mother's devoted nursing.

Then, as Winter started, when everyone else was either buried or recovering, Sir William himself came down with it, and died two months after his baby son. On an icy December morning, the rooks cawing dismally in the great elm trees that sheltered our huddled gray church, the whole parish gathered to mourn the Squire. He was interred in the floor of the church, his younger brother presiding, his sisters weeping, Lady Elizabeth like graven stone.

Hawkshit read from Deuteronomy: "If thou wilt not observe to do all the words of this law that are written in this book, that thou mayest fear this glorious and fearful name, the Lord thy God, then the Lord will make thy plagues wonderful, and the plagues of thy seed, even great plagues, and of long continuance".

Afterwards, the parish gathered in the graveyard and wondered what kind of Squire handsome Thomas would make. My aunt said nothing of the trouble he had gotten Betsy into, and I kept my mouth shut, though I thought him foolish for not marrying her, as she had been so sweet, and so pretty. Then Winter came on hard, the snow making traveling difficult, and only the local farmers came to drink at the tavern, and ogle my pretty mother.

In Spring, the new Squire came to collect his Lady Day rent for the farm. My mother had gone for a walk and was late, and he sat impatiently in the parlour, bored with my aunt's chatter. I was playing with the soldiers Tom had carved for me for my ninth birthday, trying to be quiet, so that I wouldn't be told to go.

I heard my mother come in, and restrained myself from rushing to throw my arms about her, as I usually did. We heard her voice in the passage, musical with all the songs she had been singing, and then she stood in the doorway, her arms full of Spring blossoms, her nose smudged with pollen, and her cheeks flushed to find the Squire already there. Then he was on his feet, helping divest her of the flowers, warbling on about the Goddess Flora, while she apologised profusely for her tardiness, unable to see that he was too busy looking at her to listen to her. My mother untied a bag from around her waist, paid the rent, and asked if the old tenancy agreement would still stand. The Squire said nothing about raising the rent, and insisted on buying her an ale, and having her sit, uncomfortable and

52

tongue-tied, at his elbow. He raved on awhile about the beauty of the season, then bowed, and took his leave of her, promising to return the next evening.

He came every evening that week, insisting that my mother pour his ale, and sit with him. I saw my aunt's complacency, and demanded to know why she did not tell my mother about Betsy. She shook me until I promised not to mention a word of it, then she repented of her temper, and said that young gentlemen lived like that, and 'twas behind him now, and if my mother played her cards right, we would end up in the manor house.

Suspicious, I took to following him in earnest on my free afternoons, watching him carefully while he rode about the forest, or fished in the Brent. When I finally caught him emerging from the forest on Brondesbury Ridge with a woman on his arm, I was all triumph. Then I heard her laugh, and realised it was my mother walking with her head on his shoulder, his arm around her waist. And I knew why my mother was happy and laughing that Spring, and that when she took her afternoon walk, she was meeting him. I also knew that Aunt Susan would have been horrified, and I prayed nightly that she would not get pregnant, since she could not marry the Squire, because I was not really a boy.

Yet soon the whole parish knew of the Squire's interest in my mother, saying sly and grinning things to her at the market. She would lie, and look at them as though they were fools. Then John Tanner, still the worst of the village bullies, waited until we emerged from lessons in the vestry, to loudly accuse my mother of whoring her way into the manor house. I tackled him, diving under his guard, so that he went over with me on top of him. Winded by his fall, he failed to protect his face, and I flattened his nose and blacked both his eyes before Hawkshit pulled me off him.

He demanded to know what it was all about, and before anyone else could say a word, I asked if I could speak to him alone. I then told him that the Squire was making determined efforts to waylay my mother, yet she would have nothing to do with him, for she was still waiting for my father to return to us. I told the priest that the whole village thought my mother either sinful for attracting the Squire's notice, or foolish for not bedding him at once.

The priest called me a brave boy for defending my mother's honour, and I asked him to defend her too if any should blacken her name to him. When he agreed, I felt we were a little safer, yet I should have known he would take too much upon himself. He spoke against whoremongers at the next Sabbath, glaring at the Squire, my mother's face drained of blood, and I knew that the whole village had interpreted the priest's words the same way she had.

For almost a month, my mother ceased her afternoon walks, and made excuses not to see Sir Thomas when he called in the evenings. My aunt was exasperated, convinced my mother was half-mad to talk of her missing husband, and only I knew that it was my fault that she could not marry him. I also knew when she started walking into the woods with him again, and that it would only be a matter of time before their secret would be public knowledge. I went to her then, and suggested that I go and live with my grandmother, where I had a good chance of not being discovered, so practiced was I in my deception. She would then be free to marry Sir Thomas, if she wanted to.

At that she wept and hugged me to her, declaring she would not lose me to a city as sinful as London for anyone, yet 'twas hard for her to live without a man, and when I was older I would understand, and forgive her. She began speaking wildly, insisting that the gamble with my grandmother hadn't paid off, and it was time for us to take our money and run, so that I could start learning to live as a girl. I protested in horror at the suggestion, refusing to lose the privileges of boyhood, and she wept then, insisting she had blighted both our lives by this fraud, and that I was a monster, neither male nor female, and it was all her fault.

At the word 'monster', something broke inside me, and I fled into the forest, though the wind was rising and the sky looked ominous. By the time I had gone to ground and wept my heart out, the storm was upon me. I turned for home, yet though I knew the forest well, the screaming wind lashed branches in my face, the lightening struck a tree close by, and I stepped off the path, and was lost.

Out of my head with terror, I ran wild through the mad night as chaos erupted about me. And then I heard my mother calling me, thin and high against the howling wind. When she clasped me to her, cold and wet, she swore she would never say such things again, and together we turned against the tempest, to fight our way back home. That night, one of the worse storms that had ever hit England broke over us. By midnight great oaks were crashing to the ground, and the river began to rise under the torrents of lashing rain. The barn roof was wrenched off, and my aunt's cattle panicked and many drowned. In the Pool of London, the storm wrecked three hundred merchant ships and fifteen men o' war, and drowned six thousand sailors.

After the great storm, something like peace settled over us at the inn, though all the travelers brought news of the world-shaking events astir in the great world. Just before my tenth birthday, the General-King Dutch William went hunting in Richmond Park, where his horse stumbled on a molehill and threw him. He only broke his collarbone, yet he was an old man, tuberculosis set in, and he died. He had been an unpopular King, brought in by Protestant nobles to keep the French off our shores. 'Twas known Princess Mary had wept at their wedding, fifteen and lovely and married off to a man who was happiest in a war camp surrounded by his favourites. We had forgiven him when she died, for he had wept openly at her funeral.

Now her sister, Princess Anne, was to be Queen, and there was general rejoicing that England was once again to be ruled by one of our own, even if she was old and dowdy and barren. I hoped to witness her Coronation, yet my aunt insisted we'd need all hands to keep the beer flowing in the inn, and I had to hear the glorious details from Sally, who saw her pass by in her coach. My mother prayed that her reign would be as glorious as that of Good Queen Bess. When our new Queen declared that a woman with child could not be hung until the babe was born, my aunt swore that having a woman on the throne would make England as civilised as King Arthur's Camelot.

Shortly after Dutch William's death, Old King James died in exile in France, and his sixteen year old son begged King Louis for recognition as James the Fourth, rightful King of England. War with France was already looming, for the mad Spanish King had died leaving his empire to Louis' grandson. This meant that all of Spain and France and Flanders would be under French rule, leaving all European shipping entirely at their mercy. This was something the English and Dutch could not stand for, so they proposed an Austrian Prince as ruler of Spain instead. King Louis then invaded the Netherlands from Spanish Flanders, and there was war with Dutch William. Young Prince Jamie was all the excuse King Louis needed to declare war on England, and this roused the anger of us all, even those who believed that James was 'King over the water'.

We had barely become accustomed to the news, when a traveler rode in and insisted on buying all of us a rum, to toast the magnificent luck of our Navy. Hearing a rumour that they carried a three year hoard of gold from the New World, Admiral Rooke had chased twenty-two Spanish galleons from the New World into the protection of Vigo Bay. On the twelfth of October, the fastest of the English and Dutch ships had crashed through the boom, into a merciless fire from both shore and ships. Ormonde had attacked the main fort with two thousand soldiers, and Rooke forced the Spanish Fleet to yield. They captured over three thousand tons of gold and silver. Our new Queen had the silver minted into coins stamped with her stern and uncompromising face, and 'Anna Dei Gratia, Vigo', which I knew meant 'Anne thanks God for Vigo.' Convinced that she was destined to fight the mighty French, she put her favourite, the handsome, courtly Lord Marlborough, in charge of her Army, and after a great deal of wrangling on the part of the other allies, he was accepted as war leader.

After Vigo, Tom took the King's shilling and enlisted with a troop of local boys, all eager to join the British troops gathering on the blood-soaked battle fields of Flanders.

My mother wept a little, yet I thought he looked wonderful in his red coat, and I knew he was glad to march off and leave the thought of Betsy far behind him. My aunt gave him a haversack of food, and insisted that he write to us each Christmas, to let us know he was well. We never received word of him after we waved him away, and though my mother mourned him, I thought him too busy becoming a General to leave time for writing letters to a couple of women.

Then, just after my tenth birthday, Sir Thomas died. It was so sudden that rumours swept the Parish, and most of them involved my mother. People said that he had killed himself because she would not have him, or that his sisters had done it because my mother had finally said 'yes', and they would not be disinherited by her babe. Overnight, my mother grew old. She talked distractedly of sin and retribution, she stopped eating and became thin and pallid, and I would wake to find her kneeling in tears at all hours of the night, trying to pray. My aunt tried to comfort her, but since she shied away from knowing the truth, she could say nought to help.

I did my best, and told my mother that God would not condemn her, since she would have married the Squire if not for me, and then there would have been no sin. She would not listen, and raved of him burning in Hell, and I knew then that her mind was disordered by her loss. I was frightened that she would go to the Priest, and in confessing that she had been fornicating with Sir Thomas for years, my secret would come out. Hawkshit would be horrified to find that the boy he had taught to read and write was a sinful daughter of Eve, and would hound us through the Parish, send us to Newgate for fraud, and we would hang. I told her we should run away with the money we had saved. To my horror, she fell to her knees in the field, where any could see her, praying "Hail Mary, full of grace, the Lord is with thee. Blessed art thou among women, and blessed be the fruit of thy womb, Jesus Christ. Holy Mary, mother of God, pray for us sinners now, and at the hour of our Death..."

I saw that I would have to take charge of our lives if we were to avoid disaster. I knew that her grief was worse because she could not speak of it to anyone, and decided she must make a confidant of Meg Pridden. I told my aunt how worried I was for my mother's mind, and that a week in London might distract her from her cares. My aunt, trying not to put two and two together, for she loved my mother, and would not believe her a harlot if she could help it, urged her to go. Five days later, we were on the Harrow coach, my mother blank-eyed and miserable, and me relieved, and looking forward to seeing Sally.

In London, my grandmother insisted that my mother see her own doctor, and had Ashley bring up some of the best Madeira for us. In the morning, I dragged my mother around Covent Garden, until I had found Sally and Meg Pridden. Yet, as soon as they saw us, I had Sally weeping on my shoulder, swearing she could not endure life under that tyrant of a seamstress; and my mother had Mis'ess Meg crying on her shoulder, as her husband had finally lost patience with poverty, bailiffs and his wife, and volunteered for a Regiment of Guards. Meg had snatched up his vice as all he had left her, and was drinking hard. My mother did all she could, recognising her own old misery, trying to make Meg see that she must pull herself out of her grief for the sake of her daughters.

Yet Meg had decided that Sally was too pretty, too headstrong, and bound for whoredom. It was as though she knew that Sally's beauty was their only way out of poverty, and beat her instead of ruining her. Sally went to stay with the Garths rather than go home one night, and Meg arrived at her work the next morning in a drunken fury, calling her a whore, though she was only just eleven, and smashing into her with a broom handle. The big seamstress easily threw the drunken Meg down the stairs, whereupon Sally kicked her hard for her tyranny, and ran to help her mother. She then threw herself on the mercy of the Garths, and I found her that afternoon, one eye swollen badly and her lip cut, happily selling oranges with her grandmother.

Sally told me of the whale she had seen stranded in the Thames after the great March storm, and of how the Londoners had crowded to see it, and hacked it to pieces for souvenirs. To me it seemed that everything of importance was happening in London, and I longed to live there too.

Meg and Sally's problems moderated my mother's grief, and she went to the priest at Saint Paul's churchyard, whose sermons of love and redemption we had both taken to heart. He must have heard some terrible things confessed to him in his time, and his kind words comforted her. When we returned to Stonebridge at the end of the week, she was eating and sleeping again, and not weeping and praying so much. Yet her gaiety seemed lost to us.

Old John died, and when I took over the stables, my schooling stopped, though every spare moment found me with my nose in a book. I had soon read every book in the tavern, and though I often swapped with travelers, I loved to take the coach for London with the box of books I'd finished, and bargain for more with the booksellers in Saint Paul's churchyard. I came away with the notorious plays of Aphra Behn, the Godless philosophy of John Locke, and the lives of famous criminals, including Captain Kidd, who had been hung the year before, a notorious pirate and a public hero. I was young, and some of what I read meant nothing to me, yet I grew to understand more of the world than most children. I was often lonely, for I dared not take another friend after Bill Helier's death, yet I was proud of having tricked a whole parish into granting me a boy's privileges.

Sally was my only friend, yet at twelve she was a

hardened flirt. A great success with the Covent Garden traders, and sharp-tongued with the local rakes, she claimed she was offered vast sums for her virginity, boasted of the dancing classes that she paid for out of her own pocket, and of the rich Jewish boy she had met there, who was heir to a great fortune, and mad for her. She made her life sound terribly exciting, though I knew she was worried sick over her mother's hard drinking.

That August, we heard of the daring march of the whole English army to the Danube, to relieve Austria from the threat of French invasion. For the first time in living memory, the French suffered a complete defeat, after furious fighting at the battle of Blenheim. Lord Marlborough was lauded, not just for winning the battle, but also for the brilliantly organised march, where bread awaited the soldiers at each stage, and their boots were replaced as they wore out.

I was amazed to find Sally unconcerned as to whether or not her father might have been in the thick of that glorious battle. She was more worried at the prudish Queen Anne's attempts to reform the stage. She claimed to know all the actresses in Drury Lane, and when Mistress Barry herself bought oranges from her, and admired her clear voice and quick wit, Sally declared she would be an actress when she grew up. I thought it a marvellous idea, yet told her not to tell her mother, who thought actresses even more whorish than orange girls.

I was past thirteen when I first bled, and convinced I was dying from some inner wound, frantically ran for my mother, and was confounded to find myself acclaimed a woman. My mother was determined. "You are capable of bearing children. 'Tis time you stopped pretending to be what you are not. We will take our savings and start a new life where no one knows us, and you can start wearing skirts, and learn to live the life of a young woman."

My shame was soul-stopping, and I had to protest. "I cannot do that! What about grandmother's legacy? And our life here? And what could we tell Aunt Susan?"

"We missed our wager on the old woman. And if we explain this to anyone, we will both end up in front of the magistrates. I was a fool to let it go on so long. You must accept the truth of what you are, and you are no boy."

"I can't be a girl. I can't think like one. You want me to change right before your eyes, and 'tis not possible. I don't know how to wear skirts, and curtsey, and lower my eyes and look modest. Next you'll want me married!"

"You are a woman, and your name is Mary, and one day you must marry and bear children of your own. 'Tis the way of the world, child. I knew this was a mortal sin all those years ago. It has cost me nought but grief to keep it going so long after 'twas necessary, all for the hope of that kind old woman dying. 'Twas wrong of me. I let you turn into something you are not, thinking you were a child, and there was time to change you back. Now it must stop."

"I won't be a girl! You can't make me." Yet I saw the determination in my mother's face, and knew that as far as she was concerned, some barrier had already been passed, and she would not let me rest until I put on skirts. I had no choice, I saw it clearly. To remain who I was, I would have to run away, to leave Stonebridge, and make my own way in the world. Perhaps when she missed me, I could beg her to let me be. Until then, London was my best bet, for 'twas large enough to hide anyone, and I could seek my fortune there on my own terms. When the bleeding had finally stopped, I packed a few of my belongings into a bag, and went to bid farewell to my mother.

"You must be mad child. You are too young to be alone in London!"

"You have been telling me all week that I am no longer a child. And I won't be alone. Sally is there."

"And you will pretend to be a man, against all my wishes?"

"I will. A woman's life is too narrow for me. I won't blight my life by beginning it as some man's servant, wife, or whore. If I could apprentice myself and learn a trade..."

61

"Don't expect me to pay for it. And your grandmother won't either. You mustn't think you can live with her, without me telling her the truth."

"You must go to London to do that, since you can't write a letter, and you won't tell Aunt Susan the truth, for fear of the magistrates."

"We have enough money to leave together, now. Come child, life as a woman is a fine thing..."

"Your own life argues against you."

"You know nothing of my life, child." And that was when she told me the full story of my birth, and her own sin. My horror then was complete. I could only think of Hawkshit snarling from Deuteronomy that a bastard shall not enter into the assembly of the Lord. I wept to think of the suffering I had brought upon her, and thanked her for our survival.

"Yet at what cost child? You growing up a boy, and me consigned to life without a husband? Truly, I am indeed punished for my despair." Not entirely understanding, I told her that she was the best mother in the world, and she begged me to try and live female.

"I cannot. 'Tis not a life I have been bred to. I do not know how to giggle, and look coy, and keep my reputation above all, because no man wants to marry a harlot. I do not know how to flutter my 'lashes, and look admiringly at idiots, and pretend to be ignorant. I do not know how to evade the clutches of skirt-chasers by any means but a blow. Women are supposed to be helpless, and beautiful and silly, and I am none of those things..."

"Your Aunt Susan is none of those things, and she is a woman for all that."

"She would've been happier as a man."

"I will not let you continue your fraud, Mary. 'Tis a sin, and it rests on my shoulders. I will come to London and expose us both, if I have to."

"If you do that, I will not speak to you again, not even if we stood at the gallows together, and you begged me for forgiveness. You started the fraud, yet I will continue it. I am Mark Read. I do not know this Mary you speak of."

She swore I had no choice and that she would tell my aunt if I insisted on staying a boy. I saw that she did not understand that I could not change sex at her behest, and that she did not believe that I would really go. Then I heard the whistle of the London coach rolling in, and packed a few clothes into a bundle. On my way out of the inn, I shoved in her tatty old Bible as a way of taking her with me. As the London coach rolled away from the inn, I leapt aboard.

At the last moment, she saw me, and ran after us, calling for the coach to stop. Unaware, the coachman shouted and whipped the horses up the hill, the Summer sun blazing down on abundant fields of golden corn. She fell on her knees in the dust, holding out her arms and screaming for me. I looked away, trying to hide my tears, unable to bear the sight of her grief, and unable to stay. I never saw her again.

Chapter 4: Covent Garden

For the first stage of my journey, I bowed my head and wept, praying that my mother would accept my need to live as I must, and not betray me. As the coach rocked further down the Harrow Road, I counted the shillings left from paying the fare, and began to doubt my ability to survive London alone. I could not live with my grandmother in case my mother carried out her threat of exposing me. I would have to earn my own living, and though I was well-skilled as an ostler, I had no references to my character and abilities, and few friends to help me gain a post. I thought then of my true father, the sailor with my blue eyes and black hair, of whether he was still alive, and why he had been so heartless as to abandon us.

'Twas dusk by the time the coach bumped over the cobblestones of London, and I remembered the attention paid to lone women on the streets at night, and was glad of my boy's clothes. As I pushed my way through the crowd towards Covent Garden, the difficulties of carrying on my deception without a confederate struck me with renewed force. I looked like a bumpkin, yet could hardly go to a tailor to be measured up for new clothes. I knew that the only person I could turn to was Sally, yet, while I trusted her friendship, I wondered if I could trust her discretion.

I had planned to go straight to the Garths' lodgings, yet as I pushed my way through the Covent Garden throng, I heard Sally call my name. I turned and looked for her, yet could not see her until she grasped my arm. I gaped, and she put her hands on her hips and laughed at me. "Good God, Mark Read. Do pull your chin up. Where's your mother? Don't tell me you have run away to wicked old London on your own!"

She was patched and painted, with her golden hair in ringlets, and her bodice low over her breasts. She looked eighteen, though I knew her for fourteen, and she was shockingly beautiful.

"Who's the yokel", a young cit in full wig, lace and sword demanded, wheeling drunkenly over from an orange stall and taking her arm. "Damn it Sal, you can't go picking up pretty boys when you're out on the town with us."

Sally laughed at him and his even drunker friend. "This is Mark Read, my country cousin. Why don't you buy us both an ale, and tell him what a good girl I've been?"

"Damn it Sal, don't think you can bamboozle me. This is no cousin of yours. And if you think I'm buying ale for a rival..."

I stepped forward, catching my breath. "Gentlemen, I am no rival, I assure you. Sally and I are...distant cousins, and have known each other since we were children. I have come down from the country to see her and her family, and have only just stepped off the coach. But Lord, Sally, where did you get this rig? You look... wonderful, yet..."

"I know, not in the least bit respectable." She laughed again, though not as carelessly. "These two gentlemen buy me dinner most nights, in return for nothing more than my company and a kiss or two. 'Tis terribly naughty for me to have anything to do with them, I know, but they are a great deal of fun. Now come on, don't be prosy, this is Charles, and this is Henry. They are studying law at the Inns of Court. Now you two, I must speak with my cousin this evening, so he must dine with us, or I am forced to leave you."

Charles nodded his head, and Henry bowed, and I made my leg as gracefully as I could, inwardly cursing my rough appearance. "Well Sal", Charles demurred, "if he really is your cousin, we'd be happy to take him with us, and buy him an ale. Yet with you so fair and him so dark..."

My stomach's growl decided me. "Gentlemen, the pleasure is mine, and I thank you for taking such good care of my scapegrace cousin for me. I only fear that your enjoyment of the evening will be spoilt by my rusticity."

"Oh Lord, nothing of the sort", the younger one, Henry, insisted politely. "And if you're after a new suit, I'll give you the name of my tailor, an excellent man."

"Yes, damn it, do come and dine with us", Charles echoed, more sincerely. "You can amuse us with stories of what this goddess was like as a brat."

I told them she was still a brat as far as I was concerned, and as we moved off through the crowd, she took my arm, and deliberately pressed against me, as revenge for my comment. Feeling the absurdity of the situation, I resolved to tell her my secret as soon as I could.

We ended up at the Half Moon Tavern, a rowdy, semi-respectable place, run by Jacques le Bec, a taciturn French Huguenot. Charles ordered beefsteak, potatoes and ale for all of us, and Sally entertained us with scandals of Old King Charles' bastards, masked ladies and actresses. Charles and Henry moaned about the Duke of Bedford clearing all the brothels near the back gate of Bedford House in Charles Street, including the Cock, their favourite house of resort. Finally, Charles went off to order more ale, Henry staggered out to relieve himself in the gutter, and Sally and I had a chance to speak freely.

I told her that I had quarrelled with my mother, who threatened to tell my grandmother the cause, so that I could not stay with her. I explained that I had only a few shillings, and must find a post as an ostler quickly, for I was not going back to Stonebridge.

"Don't tell me you've been naughty, Mark. I won't believe it. It wouldn't be like you to get some poor country wench with child and run off."

"'Tis not that, I assure you. Yet I can't tell you here. And what are you about, kissing such idiots. How can you bear it?"

"I'm not on the game, if that's what you're implying. I still sell oranges with my grandmother. I don't see my mother, since she's still trying to drink herself into an early grave. My little sister Jenny takes care of her, and has taken over my apprenticeship. My father hasn't been heard of since he volunteered, and the only reason we haven't had to take

66

responsibility for his debts, is because no one can find us."

"Don't you miss him?"

"Not in the least. He was a bully and a fool. You're lucky yours died before you knew him."

"Yet if I had a father, I might have someone to advise me on how to make my way in the world."

"You're well-schooled and virtuous, always with your nose in a book. Surely you can look higher than stable hand! 'Tis not the work for a gentleman. Don't forget your grandmother's inheritance."

"If my grandmother finds out why I quarrelled with my mother, there will be no inheritance. Horses are what I know best, yet I have no references."

"Follow my advice, throw yourself on your grandmother's mercy, giving your version of the quarrel, and make the most of your time with her until she hears the scandal from your mother. You can at least get a new suit out of her, and a guinea or two. If you play your cards right, you could even get enough to buy a place at college, and then work your way into a law firm, like these idiots. I will keep my ears open for you, you may be sure."

"It seems hard to use her kindness and then run. Yet I think I have to. I should see her before she goes to bed, and before I've had too much to drink. Will your benefactors mind if I leave so soon after they've fed me?"

"They'll be glad to have me to themselves."

"In that case, I'll stay. I don't like either of them enough to leave you alone with them."

"A girl has got to do what she can for fun."

"We'll argue about it tomorrow. I'll find you in the market." I bowed to Charles as he returned, making my apologies, and he was glad to excuse me.

My grandmother was already abed when I reached the house, yet a surprised Ashley let me in. I asked after a non-existent letter announcing my visit, shrugged and blamed the post. When I awoke late the next morning, the house was already stirring. Dressed in my poor suit, I cozened the cook into letting me take breakfast up to my grandmother.

When the old lady saw me, she let out a cry of delight, and I hugged her frail bones, wishing, not for the first time, that I really was her grandson. She was surprised to see me, and full of questions. "I came down last night", I explained. "Ashley said you didn't get my letter. Here, eat some of this warm toast. The thing is, Grandmother, I've quarrelled with my mother. 'Tis over my future. She wants me on the farm, and I have larger ambitions. Let me pour you more tea. I am fourteen, well-read, and I write a clear hand. I thought I would ask your advice, and live in London for a time, if you will have me."

"My dear boy, this is a great joy. I always thought you should stay with me and enjoy London properly, yet your mother always fussed so over your health. Perhaps you could go into service for some great man..."

"I had thought of starting as a clerk somewhere."

"These are good times for men of ambition and learning. Yet, a little more schooling could see you rise more easily. I'll see what I can do. Yet first, you must see a tailor."

"My friend Sally Pridden was a seamstress. I thought to ask her to make up something for me."

"The orange seller's granddaughter? A wild piece, my dear."

"She's not wild, just high spirited. And she'll know how to get me a good deal on a suit."

"There is no room for high spirits in a lady, my dear Mark. And that baggage will talk you into the more ridiculous fashions! Lord, those wigs! So big, they have to carry their hats in their hands! You may ask Ashley to give you five guineas towards your town expenses, and I'll expect you back for luncheon at one."

I stepped out into the Piazza, with a heavy purse tied about my neck, and soon found Sally calling out her wares. She caught sight of me pushing through the crowd, turned and spoke to her grandmother, filled a basket with oranges, and set off towards me through the crowd. On our meeting, she dropped the basket, gave me a kiss, and then gave the basket a little kick.

"You carry that. We'll try and sell some down by the Bridge, or perhaps we'll go as far as Saint James. Though I'm almost ashamed to be seen with you, you look such a fright."

"I have a favour to ask of you, Sally."

"Just one? Name it, and if it can be done, it will be."

"I need time with you alone, in private, to talk."

"You must be the only man in London who just wants to talk with me. Is it the great secret of why you quarrelled with your ma? Oh, very well then, no one's at our place now." We made our way through the stalls of flowers, fruit and roasting nuts, with Sally stopping regularly to flirt and sell oranges, exchanging the gossip of the theatre with some, and the scandal with others.

"You know a great many people here", I murmured.

She noted my disapproval and laughed. "I know whores and pimps, thieves and poets. Mother Whybourn goes to church here every Sunday, the best of her girls with her, all quite respectable, and not a glance for even the most handsome of men, and yet she's London's biggest bawd."

We turned into a narrow alleyway that ended in a dark courtyard off Bedford Street. There was a man lying prone on the cobbles, an empty bottle in his hand, his badly shaved head exposed, and his wig lying in a pool of his own vomit. Sally stepped nimbly over him, and into a doorway, extracting a key from a thong around her neck as we mounted the stairs. She unlocked the Garths' door, and locked it again once we were safely inside. Then she pulled a dark bottle out from under her grandfather's pillow, and poured a dirty mug half full. Taking a swig, she sighed, and passed it to me. "Now, tell me this great secret of yours."

"'Tis something I should have told you years ago, Sally, and I'm sorry I didn't take you into my confidence sooner. I've known for some time that I could trust you with it, yet if it gets out, then I am undone, and in Newgate."

"Oh what nonsense! You're no highwayman, I'll lay money on that. What could you have done that is so terrible?"

"'Twas my mother who started it, to convince the old woman I was her grandson. I'm not fourteen, and a boy, Sally. I'm thirteen, and a girl."

She stared at me for a full minute, her chin hanging as much as mine had done the night before. Finally she shook her head decisively. "I'll not believe it unless you strip. And if this is some kind of joke..."

I sighed, dropped my coat, pulled my baggy shirt off, and seeing her unimpressed by the smallness of my breasts, undid my belt and dropped my trousers.

"Holy Mary Mother of God! A girl! Well then, dress yourself. I'm convinced. Is this what you quarrelled with your mother about?"

"She says I'm too old to keep this up, and she wants me to live as a woman."

"Have you always lived as a boy?"

"Since just before we met."

"What fun! How do you get away with it? I know, you wear my dress, and let me wear your trousers. I bet I make as good a boy as you do..."

"Don't make a joke of this Sally. I've never worn a dress. I'd feel stupid."

"Well, if you want to learn how to wear one, you'd have no better teacher. And how can you know what it is to be female unless you've tried it? You can't mean to go on with this masquerade."

"I don't know. Can't you see how hard it is for me? I know I am really a girl. I was christened Mary. Yet I have been raised a boy, and every grain of sense I have insists I stay that way. As a boy I can go where I wish, at whatever time of night, without fear. I can work at anything I can turn my hand to, the wages are better, and I won't have any master trying to get under my skirts all the time. I can look any man in the eye and speak my mind, without having to pretend I think he's God..."

"Enough. I can see the temptation. Yet 'tis fun being female and making the fools run after you, Mark, I mean Mary. You could try it."

"You are very pretty, and I am not. I don't know how to make them run after me, and I don't want to learn. 'Tis not that they don't interest me, but they don't interest me that much."

"You have no curves, and you're terribly brown, but black hair is the fashion, and those blue eyes of yours will slay them. How long is your hair when not tied behind? Well, 'tis thick and curly enough, and will fall easily into ringlets. I say you will be pretty enough in a dress..."

"Sally, that is not what I need. I need you to measure me for a decent suit, and to sew it for me, since I can't see a tailor. Can you appreciate the difficulties I face? And even if I do find work, servants share beds, dress in the same rooms..."

"You must stay with that doting old woman and her near-sighted butler as long as possible. And I will help you get new clothes. Here's my old sewing box. Hold still and I'll measure you up. Yet only on the condition I also make you a dress. You must try being female every now and again, just for practice. Think of the convenience of being convincing in either clothes. If you wanted to walk out on a tavern bill or a month's rent..."

"Sally!"

"Oh, you just wait until you've lived around here a little longer, anything will seem possible. Really, you've had such a limited education."

"You can't even read!"

"No, but I can get my dinner free every night by fluttering my 'lashes."

"You're all vanity and flirtation! I can't believe you take pride in those idiots..."

"How jealous they were of you. Really, you're pretty

enough for a woman, but you're a very handsome boy."

"I wish you'd have nothing to do with them."

"They're harmless and useful, and sometimes fun. They take me to see a play once a week, too. You must come with us next time."

"Yet they only do it because they think you might..."

"Bed them? Well, that is the point of flirtation, is it not? How squeamish you are. Don't worry, I'm not losing it to anyone as poor as that. Oh don't look shocked, I've had some very generous offers for my maidenhead, yet so far, none have included marriage. You'd better watch out for yours too. There's many that fancy boys more than girls around here. Could you imagine their surprise when..."

"Sally, stop it!"

"How can I measure you when you twist about so? And do stop being such a Puritan, I'm only jesting."

"I really need your advice on how to get on in the world. I thought of an apprenticeship, but I don't know if I could stay undiscovered for the seven years necessary to finish it. My grandmother mentioned college, and I've always wanted to increase my learning..."

"A woman studying in college, only fancy! Susannah Centlivre, the playwright you know, she who had such a success this year with 'The Gamester', she told me that she was picked up and taken to Cambridge by a young student when she ran away from home. She studied fencing and philosophy, yet she only stayed a few months before she was under suspicion. And I heard of a girl in Cheapside who apprenticed herself to an apothecary, and she lasted two years before they found out. They stocked her, and she spent a fortnight in Bridewell, and then the apothecary took her back as his assistant anyway."

"I could not bear the humiliation of Bridewell."

"Don't take on so. Unless we were stocked and whipped and beaten regularly, we wouldn't be as willing to be their wives, mistresses, servants and sluts. Mother of God, Mary, I feel I can say anything to you. We may be the only free women in London, and look how different we are. I will be a great actress, and you could be a playwright!"

"I've no talent for boasting and starving. Yet I've always thought I could be a lawyer. I was the best student in the parish school, and even Hawkshit said I had ability..."

"Because he thought you a boy. If he had known you a girl, he'd have called you a freak against nature, and performed an exorcism. There, you're all measured up. We'll go and buy material from the mercer's on Bedford Street, not forgetting enough for a dress. I know a tailor who can make a suit to these measurements, and I'll stitch up the dress myself, even though I hate the work, because I love you. And don't worry about money yet. Trust to luck, and we'll see what turns up. If your mother informs against you, you can always hide here, or with friends of mine. You'll make your fortune yet...Mark."

"You're a true friend Sally. I knew you were the only person who would help me. I won't forget it." She hugged me, put my awful hat back on my head, and we left to look at material in the mercer's shop. We agreed on nothing. Sally wanted me much finer than I thought necessary, and I told her that I was not going to ape the gentleman just to please her vanity.

"This is London, Mark Read, and no one cares whether your father was a lord or a farmer, as long as you look like you have money. If you want to be part of this city, to go to the theatres, to Saint James, to sermons at the cathedral, to eat well, to speak your mind to all, and order on credit, then you need to dress well. Why, on Sunday afternoons, most footmen dress finer than their masters. You are masterless and free, so make the most of it. It probably won't last long."

"On credit?"

She sighed. "You don't have to pay for all this now. Pay for it when you get yourself a position."

"But grandmother gave me the guineas..."

"You will also need new shoes, a sword, a decent hat,

a couple of fine cambric shirts..."

"A sword! I can't even use one."

"Everyone carries one. And if you don't know what to do with one, well neither do half the swells in the Piazza. You could always take fencing lessons, though. And I will teach you to dance."

"I don't need either."

"Mark Read, you know next to nothing of life, and I know more than I need to. We are only young and carefree for such a little time, and you don't even know what fun is. Trust me. The worst that can happen is that you'll have to dress as a girl to escape the bailiffs."

"Sally you're impossible."

"And you have no idea of the latest fashions. Come on Mark, let me order for you. Trust me."

"What choice do I have."

"None at all. I'm your only friend in the whole wide world, and a better one than you deserve. I like this for the suit. I wonder, while I'm at it, if I should order one for myself. I still fancy myself as a young lad about town, ogling the sluts and the actresses. Here's a strong calico in your favourite green. How about that for a dress?"

We bought the material, which I paid for, much to the relief of the mercer. Then we made our way to a tailor, where Sally gave over my measurements, and went into a long, detailed discussion of just how long and full the skirts of the coat would be, how wide the shoulders, what colour the waistcoat, and how tight the breeches. I thought they would never have done, and this I promised to pay when it was completed to my satisfaction, which the tailor said would take two days at the most.

We walked through the crowded, stinking streets of Cheapside, and found many of the articles that Sally considered to be indispensable for a gentleman second-hand. I walked out in a stout pair of boots, with a sword that made me feel as though I owned the street. I agreed on a couple of shirts, but refused to buy a full-bottomed wig, much to

Sally's chagrin, and eventually had to claim the necessity of my hair, in case I did dress as a woman.

Sally then dragged me back to the Half Moon Tavern, and after hunting through the crowd, pushed me towards a lanky young man, sitting quietly in a corner with a pipe and an ale. "Captain, fancy finding you here! Have you forgot me already?"

"Mistress Sally, certainly not. You are as lovely as ever. Will you introduce me to your young friend and dine with me?"

"This is my cousin Mark Read from the country. He has finally come to spend his inheritance in London. His grandmother is old Mistress Read in King Street. I'm afraid he has need of you, Captain. For although the priests taught him to read, and he knows a Bible backwards, he has never handled a sword."

"Well now, that's a terrible disadvantage to a young man with pluck. Only the clergy don't carry swords. And how would you defend your fair cousin if someone offered her an insult?"

"I'm sure my cousin could defend us both better than I could", I protested, and the young Captain grinned. Sally stomped hard on my new boots and we all laughed.

Yet the thought of swordplay had grown in me through the day. It seemed such a daring, necessary art for a young man making his way in the world. In the end I told the Captain I'd be pleased to study with him.

The Captain smiled. "Mistress Sally knows where I lodge. Shall we say every afternoon at two, for two shillings a lesson? We'll know if you have any ability by the end of the week. Then a lesson once a week, and regular bouts with some of my other students, and you'll be dangerous within the month." I looked at Sally, who nodded imperceptibly, and I agreed at once to the Captain's terms, and paid him in advance for the first week.

He then ordered us a pie and ale each from the proceeds, which I thought most generous of him, and he and

I launched into a full discussion of Marlborough's campaign in Flanders. The Captain had been on that daring march to the Danube, and had helped beat the French at the battle of Blenheim. There he had taken a nasty sabre cut across his ribs, and absconded, sure that his luck was over. He had fallen in with privateers in Den Haag, and sailed with them back to England, and now lived as a deserter, to be shot if taken.

I was entranced by his story, and when he suggested that we begin fencing lessons that afternoon, I was happy to agree. We turned down a side street into a foul maze of alleys, filled with surly rogues and drabs. The Captain noticed my uneasiness. "You are right to be wary here, young Mark. This is the Bermudas, and many of my neighbours are in a more desperate case than I am. Half of London knew when Claude Duval, the highwayman, lived here, yet they didn't dare come and seek him. They waited until he went to the Hole-in-the-Wall on Chandos Street, where he was dragged out by a dozen armed constables and half a dozen magistrates, bundled into a coach, and hanged two days later at Tybourn. We had always found him an honourable man, so to protest his loss, we carried his body back in a great procession, and buried him in Saint Paul's Churchyard. Oh yes, discretion is necessary if you flout the law and wish to escape the rope.

"Now Mistress Sally, I won't have you unchaperoned in a bachelor's apartment. Why don't you go next door and see if you can cheer your mother?" Sally shrugged and left us, and while I was glad to find one acquaintance who treated her with respect, I was horrified to think of Meg Pridden in this terrible place.

"Well young Mark, let's have a look at your sword. A rapier, eh? Well, that was lucky. You are slight as yet, and should use speed rather than strength to kill your man. If a giant wielding a broadsword takes you on, split his heart before he raises his blade. Never fight fair, boy, unless you want to die young. Now, hold the pommel between your thumb and forefinger, curve your other three fingers underneath for balance, and keep it close to your wrist, with a straight line from elbow to sword tip. Keep your weight in your arse by bending your knees, and keep your feet further apart. Now, right foot forward, left foot behind. Left hand up, behind your head. En garde! Keep your back straight. Good. If your footwork is clumsy, you'll fall. Now, look alive! When you retreat, use a longer step to get out of danger faster, then short quick steps to parry for the lunge."

The Captain drilled me mercilessly for an hour, and when I was forced by my aching muscles to stop, he suggested I join him for a hot bath at the hummums, in the basement of the Piazza Tavern. He saw my hesitation and shrugged. "You can still get a bath for five shillings, if you ignore the whores. 'Tis just the thing after a hot bout of fencing." I declined politely, remembering that I was supposed to have lunched with my grandmother, and dashed back to King Street.

When she saw me in my finery two days later, my grandmother forgave me for forgetting our appointment, and declared I was the prettiest boy the family had ever bred, and must catch me an heiress. She asked if I had spent all she had given me, and when I swallowed my conscience, lied and nodded, she told me to ask Ashley for a guinea every week. I wondered what she had sold, yet she laughed at my guilty face, and gave me another kiss. No letter came from Aunt Susan, and my mother did not arrive furious on the doorstep, so I hoped she had decided to let me be.

Ashley then opened my grandmother's dusty library, and I read every morning, and practiced swordplay every afternoon. I was quick to learn, and by the end of the week, I knew I was good. I learnt parries and counter-parries, and the lunge, and soon I could flick the point of my rapier to where it needed to be. At the end of the month, the Captain stated that I was a natural swordsman, and insisted on buying me a drink to celebrate.

I spent most evenings with Sally and her wild set of

young rakes. Still pretending I was her cousin, I quickly gained the reputation of a Puritan, for I would not enter a brothel with them, and scowled if they spoke coarsely of women. Also I drank little, not trusting myself after seeing how silly Sally became. Indeed, I lost count of the number of times I half-carried her back to the Garths' lodgings. Her family had known me for so long that they trusted me to be a brother to her, and were glad I kept her company in the evenings.

I particularly liked her grandfather, old Mister Garth. He had always been a quiet man, yet Meg's drinking weighed upon him heavily, and there was a sadness about him now that only Sally's laughter could dispel. Jenny, a plump, brown dove of a girl, meekly continued with Sally's apprenticeship, and after a week or two, Sally could mock her for her love of me, and make us both blush.

I was out rollicking with Sally after a play one night, Henry, Charles and a few others with us, and me a little drunker than usual. Desperately needing to relieve myself, I squatted down between two coaches in the gutter, only to have a coachman suddenly leap aboard one of them and drive it off. Luckily I was about to stand to secure my breeches, my shirt hanging out over my arse, for Charles saw me, and thinking it vastly amusing that I did not stand to piss, brought me to the attention of half of London. I pretended I was too drunk to stand, and as they were all worse off than me, they accepted it.

Then Sally heard a ballad on a girl who ran away to sea, and sailed around Cape Horn, pissing out a horn, and we felt we had a clue to equipment vital to my deception. We talked about it for several days, and eventually decided on a short cow horn, the sort used to carry tobacco in, comfortably wide at one end, with the point cut off. Sally covered it in soft leather, and attached broad straps, and I found it worked well. I had concluded long ago that people saw what they expected to see, and knew that if I pissed into a gutter once or twice, no one would ever doubt I was a boy.

78

Sally also told me of the sea sponges that the whores in Covent Garden used to sop up their monthly bleeding, and as contraceptives. She brought me a handful, and I was thankful for an alternative to the stinking rags that I felt sure would eventually give me away.

By Winter, and I had become used to my life as a young gentleman, when Ashley carried a letter from my aunt to our breakfast table. My grandmother asked me to read it aloud, and my first glance confirmed my worst fears. I lied, and said it was written at my mother's behest, and that she begged me to forget our quarrel and return to Stonebridge to receive her blessing. I told my grandmother this was a great relief to me, for I disliked being estranged from her, and asked leave to return to the country for a week. My grandmother agreed, and I ran upstairs, and read my aunt's letter properly.

She cursed both my mother and I for fraudulent impostors, even though my mother was indeed who she claimed to be. My mother had fled the parish, and had not been taken by magistrates, and I thought she must come directly to London to find me and collect her savings. Aunt Susan wrote that she too was coming to London, and I could see how cruel this was going to be for the old lady, and wept at the pain I must cause her. I thought of telling her the truth myself, and begging her forgiveness, yet let my fear of a whipping in Bridewell deter me.

Chapter 5: The Fall

I packed a trunk, slipped out the back door, and made my way through a chill wind to the Captain's room in the Bermudas. I told him some story of outrunning the bailiffs, and though he did not believe me, he made no objections to keeping my trunk, and offered me a share in his bed if I needed one. I then donned my worst suit, and traipsed about all the big houses in the area, seeking work with horses. I had no references, little presumption, and no success. At the end of the day, I sought out Sally at her grandparent's place, and begged her to keep an eye out for my mother, and hide her from my aunt and her constables.

I could tell that Sally thought less of me for seeking a menial position, yet I had been living so high on the town, that I had only a few shillings left from that week's allowance, and I needed to hide. She shrugged, and left me in front of a small fire with Jenny, while she scouted about her acquaintance. Jenny tried cheering me, yet I was desperate when Sally finally returned. She told me that an Irish woman by the name of Kate O'Neil was looking for someone to tend her stable. "She's a good woman, I've known of her for a while, yet...you're such a Puritan. She runs the brothel above her husband's lottery office, at the Lord Blakeney's Head, next to the magistrate's court."

I dashed off into the gloomy evening, praying fervently that the position would still be open, and that Mistress O'Neil would be kind. When I reached the Lord Blakeney's Head, I found a tall, thin, shabby man with a melancholy face, and no wig on his stubbled head, huddled on the step. I assumed he was a patron, and hat in hand, asked if this was Mistress O'Neil's house.

"Did you run all the way, boy? What Devilish enthusiasm. And you so young to be so dissolute. Take me as your warning child. A peer of the Scottish realm, a man of good family, brought up with sound principles. See where low company and bad living has brought me, and take my example to heart."

"I am here after the position of stable hand, Sir."

"Oh Lord, really? And I in such a perfect mood for reproaching sinners. I suppose you are as innocent as you look."

"I was raised in the country by a pious mother, Sir."

"And do you say your prayers, boy?"

"Yes Sir. Especially that I might find a place."

"'Lord let me not be poor lest I steal', eh? And does he listen? Not to me. I am one of the Devil's own now, and your shining innocence is a reproach to my blackened soul. Kate! There's a lovely young boy here to see you."

"Send 'im up Mordin'ton. An' make sure 'e wipes 'is feet!"

I wiped my feet, thanked Lord Mordington, and mounted the steep staircase to find the owner of the broad Irish brogue. Much to my relief, Kate O'Neil looked solid and sensible, a respectable white matrons cap over her brown ringlets, her neat dress covered by a clean white apron. She looked me quickly up and down, asked me if I could do with something hot to drink, and told me to follow her to the kitchen.

I followed Mistress O'Neil through the quiet house, and was disappointed to find it so commonplace. There were many rooms off the long corridor, each clean yet threadbare, and lacking any attempt at glamour. We went down the back stairs to the kitchen, where six women sat eating, some of them only half-dressed, all painted and patched and dirty.

"Oh, 'e's so pretty, do come in lad", one of them called, her lips and cheeks as brilliant a red as her eyeballs in the white powder.

"He's so young Hetty. Do him for free."

"How many shillings have you, child? We aint cheap you know. Exceptin' Anne, and she's poxed."

"Poxed yeself ye low harlot. Keep a civil tongue in your head or I'll rip yer wig off!"

81

Kate O'Neil glared at them. "Finish yer food, all o' ye. 'E's come as a stable 'and. Sit 'ere, boy, an' I'll get ye some stew. Ignore these bad women, they're only tauntin' ye. As soon as more'n two of 'em open their mouths they start fightin'. There may be honour among thieves, but there's none among whores."

The women broke into a babble of objections and counter-accusations, and Mistress O'Neil bellowed for quiet. "Now boy, we don't run a fancy place, and there's nothin' here that the magistrates next door have to shut their eyes at.

"No floggin', no sodomy, no sellin' o' false virgins…" Hetty began.

"Just whores and rakes", Mistress O'Neil snapped. "The wages are two shillings a week on top o' bed and board. The coachman who runs the stable is a hard ol' bastard, yet 'e knows 'is work. Ye don't 'ave to get up early, yet the nights are late, and for that ye have all o' Sunday off, since I keep the Sabbath. We won't have ye workin' drunk, ye must know how to keep yer mouth shut, and ye must not think you can lay hands on these women for nothin'."

"That's fine by me Mistress O'Neil. I've been desperate for a place, and you'll not find me ungrateful."

"What's yer name, boy?"

"John Smith."

"Oh, John Smith is it? Very well then, no questions asked."

"Aint he sweet! Jus' like me little brother what died."

"Leave him be Hetty, he's a virgin, ye can tell by his blushes."

"Well girls, now ye've decided ye like 'im, I'll take 'im to meet Jonas. 'E won't be so easily won over, boy. Ye'll have to work to please 'im."

We stepped out the back door into a walled-in courtyard with great gates at the back of it, and the stables on the right. A big, solid man was combing the mane of a sturdy bay mare. He nodded curtly at the Mistress, and raised an eyebrow at me.

"Jonas, this 'ere is John. 'E wants to be a stable 'and."

"Do ye know the work, boy?"

"Yes Sir. I've worked at an inn and know horses."

"We'll see. You can leave 'im wi' me, ma'am. Now boy, let's unnerstan' one annuver. I'm a 'ard man, an' care more for these beasts than any folks I meet. Exceptin' the Master, Mister Dillon, who I've known since 'e were a lad. I'll not 'ave you shirkin' yer work, nor oglin' those painted sluts upstairs. You're to 'ave the 'orses fed an' watered by the time the 'ouse wakes at noon, then we 'itch up the coach and take the bitches ridin' roun' Sint James, lookin' for customers. We take 'em to the play every night, an' often drive 'em back with their gulls. An' if you see a man ye know, or hear a name, don't remember it to speak of."

"If the Master is Mister Dillon, Sir, who was the man on the front step? Mordington? He said he was a Lord."

"That's the fool who married the Master's sister, Miss'ess Mary. She 'elps the Master run the gamin' tables, and that's where she met 'im. E's run through 'is fortune on those tables, and now she feeds 'im, and 'e works for the Master. An, let that be a lesson to you 'gainst gamblin', boy."

"Yes Sir. I must say Sir, that I don't like the women who work upstairs. I prefer horses."

"If you prefer 'orses to 'arlots, we'll get on. Now, you polish the two coaches every day. Mordington takes out the pair o' bays, as they are gentle. I drive the two black mares, as the older one can bolt, an' kicks if ye get behind her. We drive the whores all over town, with you standin' behin', ready to jump down to open doors, an' 'and down the sluts like duchesses. Then we wait for 'em in the sleet and snow, walkin' the 'orses to stop 'em from freezin'. If there's a brawl, you jump in with the rest of us, for we must keep the place quiet an' 'ave no complaints brought against us, so the magistrates aint forced to close us down. The Mis'ess is a Papist, and closes the place on Sunday to pray to 'er idols, so that day's yer own. We live above the stables, where I've put up a curtain, so we live almost separate. Don't bring no one

83

to visit, and don't wake me wi' careless noise."

I was relieved we lived so private, and thought the position would suit me well. I worked with the taciturn coachman all that afternoon, helping him ready the horses, hitching them to the coaches, and handing the hags in, all dressed up in their paint and finery. Mordington took the reins, and I jumped on the running board as we pushed through the narrow alleyways, and finally out onto the busy Strand, where I held on tightly in the cold wind for fear of falling under the wheels of the coach directly behind.

We turned past Charing Cross, past the grand houses of Pall Mall, and turned in through the gates of the park. It was too late in the season for the fashionable, and I wondered what the prudish Queen Anne would say if she left Saint James Palace to see these hags hanging their breasts out the coach windows, and calling out to any who looked at them.

At the canal, gentlemen rode over to flirt, and I was kept busy opening coach doors, and bowing them out, my elegant leg earning the loud approval of the whores. The women competed with each other in audacious flattery, the gentlemen smirking, and promising to take them home from the theater. As we rattled home through a bitter wind that night, I resolved 'twas better to be a man, and freeze outside the coach, than be warm inside, and a woman such as those.

Kate O'Neil and her husband's sister Mary, were sensible, pious women, with none of the bitter frivolity of the whores. Mary Dillon was a pretty girl, younger than her sister-in-law, yet with a will of her own. She refused to answer to her title of Lady Mordington, and although she was always sitting in her Lord's lap and kissing him, trying to cheer him up, I could see that she knew him for a hopeless case, and felt guilty for his low condition. When his allowance came from his family, or if he was tipped a shilling for some humiliating service, a wild look would come into his eye, and he would dash for the gaming tables, desperately optimistic, sinking into melancholy when the money was gone, and abusing himself terribly for his selfishness.

Once I found him weeping for his mother, and when I asked him why he did not take Mary and go, he looked on me with his eyes full of an infinite sadness, and told me that he was too base for his good Scots family. He was invariably polite to all, since he claimed that he was the most beastly of men, and he called Mary his angel and saint.

Kate O'Neil was less happy in her marriage, despite her husband's great success with his lottery and gambling rooms. Peter Dillon was a small, quiet man, who never left his faro tables. All sorts came to lose money to him there, from Lords to their lackeys, and I often saw him in quiet conversation with the worst of men, and suspected he was involved in many underhanded dealings.

Yet living with the taciturn Jonas suited me. Most of my work was in the courtyard, I went into the house only for meals, and Jonas would slap the whores if they were rude to me. Indeed, everyone seemed to feel free to beat them. Mis'ess Kate had a hard hand if they fought amongst themselves, or if they drank too much, or objected to some particularly disgusting client. While I was there, Hetty was finally thrown out for insulting a regular customer, Anne was sent off to Mistress Bennett's clinic in Knightsbridge to have her pox cured with mercury, and Joan was tied up for four days to prevent her drinking.

As the bitter Winter turned to Spring, the solid meals saw me even taller, with broader shoulders from the hard work. Sally wheedled news from Carrot-top, and reported that my aunt was still there, nursing the old lady. I assumed the constables had my description, and prayed earnestly that she might live, so that I would not be a murderer.

Every Sunday morning, I would visit the Garths, hoping to hear news of my mother, for there had been no word since my aunt's letter, and I was now as fearful on her account as Sally was for Meg. The Garths would insist that I share breakfast, and then they would leave for the morning service. Sally would then pour me a hot tub of water, and I'd quickly sponge the week's dirt off, and change into my best clothes, while she regaled me with the latest scandals.

When she finally considered herself fine enough, I'd don my sword, and we'd stroll in the park, keeping an eye out for my aunt. We'd then meet Sally's latest flirt at the tavern of her choice, she would charm him into buying us lunch, and then we'd go out on the town.

Then one mid-Summer dawn, Sally shook me awake in my cot above the stables, crying. Her mother had just died in Jenny's arms. I comforted her as best I could, and sat with her weeping family to watch over Meg Pridden's wreck of a corpse. After the funeral, Sally swore that she would not grieve for someone who'd drunk herself to death, when she had aged parents and daughters to support.

Yet she began drinking to excess with an older, harder crowd, including many Officers, who were hailed as heroes for liberating Flanders from the French. They showered her with money and made her crude offers, and I could not be there every night to carry her safely home. They had some measure of caution for her, for she had a wicked tongue and a fast slap, yet they respected her not at all, waiting for her to give in and turn whore. Winter came down hard upon us again, with Sally talking of Captain this and Colonel that, as though there was nothing in the world worth knowing but a redcoat.

Then, just before her fifteenth birthday, she started talking of a Colonel Peter Honeywood, a Lord, she said, and rich. That Sunday I met him, and he did indeed act as besotted with her as she had boasted, buying her everything she asked for, and treating her with a politeness that did him credit amidst the rest of the ruffians. He was not a young man, but tall and handsome, with a military bearing, and pale blue eyes that stood out in his brown face. Sally told me that for the first time she was tempted to let someone set her up as his mistress, yet Colonel Honeywood did not make the proposition, and Sally dreamed of a more respectable offer. I pointed out that Lords only married orange girls in ballads, and threatened to tell her grandparents that she was going to throw herself into the arms of an Officer, and expect marriage after.

"You need not be so prudish, just because you're so afraid of what you are."

"Afraid!"

"Too afraid to wear that dress I made for you. All that beautiful work wasted!"

"'Tis not fear but caution."

"We can lock the door."

"And have your sister suddenly banging on it, and me in skirts! I think not."

"So I must ensure their absence for at least a day before you'll wear my present?"

"At least a day."

"Then, next Sunday is the day, for they're off to my aunt's wedding in Surrey, leaving me to mind the oranges."

I spent all week dreading Sunday, and arrived at the Garth's to find Sally still abed. I scolded her, but she declared that when she married Colonel Honeywood, she would never get up before noon. Then she pulled the dress out, in triumph, and I had to agree with her over the nice contrast of overskirt and petticoat, and admire the ribbons and lace, and thank her. She banked up the fire, and insisted I bathe in perfume, making me scrub my hands until they hurt, to get the dirt from under the nails. Then she leant me one of her own shifts, and black woollen stockings against the lingering Spring cold. She wanted to lace my waist, and I refused, for I was thin enough. She stamped her foot, and cursed me, yet let me be when I didn't submit, for she was wild to see me in her dress. The green skirt, with its deep ruffles, went over the shift, and the petticoat with its panniers and laced up bodice went on last.

I felt awkward and silly, and suddenly did not know how to walk, or sit down. When Sally laughed at me, I began trying to pull the silly thing off, but she stopped me, and hushed me, and showed me my reflection in her mottled mirror. To my amazement, I saw a slim, dark-haired maid, with my own stubborn jaw, and my father's blue eyes. I was not beautiful, certainly not with Sally sharing a mirror with me, yet I thought myself not too bad.

Sally made me sit in front of the mirror while she did my hair, binding my wet locks in old rags to make them curl into fashionable ringlets. Then she built up the fire again, and while my hair dried, she made me walk up and down, criticising my stride until I minced properly in the narrow boots she had bought me. She had the most trouble teaching me to curtsey. "No, not like that. They'll think you're a man dressed as a woman, and they strip Mollies here before they are stocked and stoned. Mind you, if they have a witness who can swear to penetration, 'tis the death sentence rather than a spell in the pillory on Hart Street."

"You're a wild Bedlamite to think we can get away with this."

"And you are a cautious Puritan, and sometimes I wish you really were a boy."

"How do you expect me to keep this up if you start flirting with me?"

She told me to pretend that I was Mark Read's sister Mary, which would explain the resemblance, and make them treat me with some respect, since Mark was already known as a swordsman. "You are a simple, sweet, country maid. Make them treat you as such", Sally advised me.

"How do I do that without boxing their ears?"

"Look away from them if they offend you, and pretend to leave if they get too bad." When she was finished with me, she unwrapped my hair, and the curls made me seem much more female. Then she threw her grandmother's black shawl over my shoulders, for it was cold outside, took my arm, and bullied me down the stairs.

I took one look at the crowd in the Piazza, and my courage failed me. Convinced I looked like an impostor, I stopped, my fingers feeling for my sword hilt. It was terrible to feel less convincing as a female, than a male, and for an instant I knew not what I was. For the first time, it was I who insisted on a drink, and Sally laughed and led me towards the Half Moon Tavern for an ale. It was a relief to me when no one in that familiar crowd took any notice of me, since all eyes were, as usual, on Sally.

When we walked in, Sally saw her Colonel at a table with some of his army cronies. She assumed he had been waiting for her, and when we walked up, she was all smiles. He bowed gracefully, his hand on his sword hilt, first to Sally and then to me. "Radiant loveliness", he murmured, kissing her hands. I could see that she accepted the compliment as nought but her due. She introduced me and I curtseyed, studiously avoiding his eyes, yet he accepted me for what I appeared to be, kissed my brown hand, and complimented me on my absent 'brother'.

"My cousin is an innocent from the country, and I would not have her shamed by rough company", Sally clearly informed the Colonel, hoping to dampen the leers of his Officers. Colonel Honeywood then introduced me to them, and made a point of favouring a new face, one Colonel Macartney, newly over from Flanders. He was a burly man, nearer forty than thirty, with the assurance of a man born to command. Though less handsome than his friend, he had a charming smile, yet when he bowed and kissed my hand, his twinkling blue eyes made me blush.

Then a jovial, fat soldier, the butt of many of their jokes, grabbed me about the waist and tried to pull me onto his knee. Instantly, Colonel Macartney's sword was at his throat, and as the lout unhanded me, Macartney pulled out a chair, and sat as close as he could. "You must forgive the fool. We are simple military men, and have had a rough season. That some have forgotten that not all women are strumpets does not surprise me, as I too had almost forgotten what it was to meet a young woman of virtue."

I was embarrassed and thanked him awkwardly, and he turned to Colonel Honeywood. "My dear Peter, you told me your friend Mistress Sally was lovely, and truly I have seen none in London to equal her. And yet here is her quiet friend, the only woman I have met in London virtuous enough to blush. I have had my fill of coarse soldiers, and would rather talk to these young ladies somewhere quiet, over supper, and take them to the new play."

Colonel Honeywood gave him a quick look and turned to Sally. "We've taken a room at the Rose, and then we're to see Farquhar's new play. It would be a charming evening if you would both accompany us, my dear."

She demurred a little. "Virtuous women do not enter private rooms in Covent Garden taverns."

"You can expect no nonsense from us", Colonel Macartney assured her. "I'd rather spend a fortune on an innocent woman's smile than a groat for a whore's favours."

Sally was eager, and I was anxious to escape the crowd, so we took the Colonels' arms, and left their cronies leering after us. I hesitated at the door of the Rose, aware of its terrible reputation, yet Sally was all smiles, and I trusted the gentlemen we were with.

There were a couple of well-dressed men with paper, pen and ink by the door, and they eyed Sally and I easily as we entered. "'Tis the marvellous thing about Covent Garden", one was saying. "Every house from cellar to garret is inhabited by nymphs of such different orders, from punks to toasts of the town, that every man can find something to suit his pocket, whether he be a labourer or a Lord." They seemed to recognise Colonel Honeywood, and bowed to him. He nodded sternly, and did not stop to introduce us.

Colonel Honeywood found the tavern keeper, a red-faced bear of a man, and bespoke a private room. He led us up rickety stairs, to a small room with a warm fire. "Those were Addison and Steele, at work on the Tattler", Colonel Honeywood muttered to Colonel Macartney as they climbed the stairs. "No man is safe from their wit."

"Addison is hardly in a position to rail at other men's faults. He is kept by the Countess of Warwick, is he not?"

90

"Aye. And before her husband died too, though he ran through her fortune first in revenge. She's told Addison that if he stops drinking, she'll marry him next. She's a beauty, and all he has to recommend him is his wit."

"He's lucky indeed. He wrote 'The Campaign' for the Whigs, and though 'twas a load of romantic twaddle, it made a hero of our Marlborough."

"Steele is a lucky bastard as well. He was only an army Captain until a couple of years ago, and then married a rich widow with estates in Barbados, who died only eighteen months later. They say he's run through it all already, though, and is permanently in debt to Addison."

The Colonels sat us down at the table, and Colonel Macartney sat so close to me, smiling into my eyes, that I felt half-suffocated. The wine soon arrived, and we toasted the Queen, Marlborough, and their regiment.

Macartney began asking me details of my life, and I answered briefly, and insisted on hearing his own history. "I am Belfast-born, Mistress Mary, the eldest son of a merchant family. When still a boy, I joined the Scots Guards, and they were good enough to promote me to Lieutenant-Colonel. I raised my own Regiment of Foot in Scotland two years ago, and have been in all the Flanders campaigns, fighting under the great Duke of Marlborough."

"You were with him in the march to the Danube?"

"I was indeed, and truly Mistress Mary, if he had asked, we would have followed him to Hell and back. We are the best fed army on the field, the best clothed, the best booted, and the best armed. He leads the charge, old as he is, and for that the men call him Corporal John, and rush to his heels to protect him."

"Blenheim was far to go to seek a battle", Sally commented.

"We were boiling to get to grips with the French", Colonel Honeywood explained. "They were avoiding battle whenever possible, circling around us and running if we looked like meeting them. The cowardice of the Dutch

Generals, our supposed allies, forced us into sieges, much to the relief of the French. Yet Marlborough knew that we would win if it came to a battle, and when the Austrian Emperor begged him to save Vienna from the French, he seized the opportunity. He marched us two hundred and fifty miles to the Danube, and when we found the French, we destroyed them. 'Twas the most glorious day of my life, and one of the most glorious in England's history."

"Ah, how I would have loved to have been there!", I exclaimed, and they laughed.

"Nay child, the battlefield is no place for any woman, unless she's Kit Ross herself."

"Kit Ross?"

"A mad Irishwoman who joined the army seeking her husband. She fought as hard as a man until she found him, then became the sutler for his Regiment."

"A woman fighting in the army! I don't believe it!" Sally exclaimed.

"'Tis true enough", Macartney assured her. "I've seen her meself. And 'tis not that unusual to find a woman when the corpses are stripped after battle..."

"This is hardly a subject fit for the ears of young maids", Colonel Honeywood objected. "Come, raise your tankards. To England!"

"And to England's soldiers!", Sally returned, and we drained the tankards again.

"Aye, when we are not fighting, we are taking beautiful women to see the plays we have written."

"You do not write plays, surely Colonel?"

"Farquhar was at the battle of the Boyne at thirteen. He's a lieutenant of Orrery's Grenadiers now, and has been recruiting in the country. 'The Recruiting Officer' is a soldier's play indeed."

The chicken came, and more wine, and we grew merry, and I became more used to my pose as a woman. When we had eaten and drunk our fill, Macartney bawled down the stairs to find the time, threw money on the table, and we dashed off to the Drury Lane theatre.

It took up most of the block, and was surrounded by a crowd of beaus and bloods, masked women of fashion on the arms of rakes, and drabs looking for gulls. There were quarrels breaking out, as the coxcombs rushed to be nearest the stage and the actresses. We sat in the second tier of box seats with the ladies, above the aristocracy. Footmen occupied the highest tier, called Olympus, and competed with the coxcombs in the pit for heckling and wit.

Macartney pointed out the Duke of Richmond, called Richworld, one of old King Charles' bastards by Louise de Keroualle. He sat next to the Duke of Saint Albans, who the same King had sired on Nell Gwynn. Mother Whybourn was pointed out to me, as the most famous of the London bawds, procuring both for rich men and women, her eyes flicking over the crowd in search of talent, her arm in that of her young lover. The theatre became noisier and warmer, and the men with us more jovial, the wine in all our heads. Colonel Honeywood urged Sally to join the stage, and whispered something in her ear that even she blushed at, and Colonel Macartney laid his arm over my shoulders, so I did not dare meet his eyes.

The play finally began, and soon the whole theatre was in an uproar, laughing at the jokes, calling answers back at the actors, the wit of the pits often drowning that of the stage. The play concerned a young heiress who dressed as a man and enlisted in her hero's Regiment, when her father forbade their marriage. The hero spent his time chasing women, and leaving them pregnant, or seducing peasant girls with promises of marriage. Country bumpkins were obviously considered fair game by these city folk. The heroine was lauded for her lack of jealousy and her virtue, which I thought made her an ill match for the hero, who advised against love and constancy. The joke was that she won him in spite of himself, due to her wit and virtue.

Any ribaldry was greeted with gusts of laughter, and when the heroine appeared elegantly clad in tight breeches, there was almost a riot. Several gentlemen leapt for the stage, to be beaten off by boys with staves. When the play ended, there was a stamping of feet and a roar of applause. Farquhar was called for, rubbish was thrown at the hecklers, and after a lewd jig, we crowded outside with the rest.

It was dark and cold, and Colonel Honeywood threw a link boy a shilling to light us back up Brydge Street to the Rose. The Colonels ordered more wine, the best I had ever tasted, rich and red as blood. Sally soon had us rolling with laughter at her imitation of the actress.

"She is marvellous, George!", Colonel Honeywood exclaimed. "A woman with wit is the wife for me."

"A maid of beauty and wit belongs to a better man than you Peter, yet marry her if she'll have you. You'd do better with her than with the dull, mercenary women who've been throwing themselves at your fortune these last ten years."

Sally laughed, yet I saw the ambition in her, and prayed for her good sense. A fiddler appeared, and I was whirled wildly about the room by Macartney, my head reeling with the wildness of the music. Yet when I sat down again, my head was still spinning, and I thought 'twas time to end the evening. I caught Sally's eye, and she slipped off Colonel Honeywood's knee. "Time for us to be home", she announced.

"Not yet, my darling girl, come and sit back on my knee. I swear I'm half in love with you, and I can't have you break up the party yet." I saw the way Sally looked at him then, her face flushed and her hair dishevelled from dancing, and she did not try to hide her admiration.

Then a rush of nausea hit me. Colonel Macartney grabbed my elbow and hurried me to the door, and as I started to heave, he pushed an empty slops bucket in front of me. Relief that I had not made a mess was soon followed by shame at the foulness, yet Macartney waited patiently for me to finish, and then politely wiped my face with his 'kerchief. My head was still spinning, and I needed to lie down, so he

94

pushed open the door to the next room, and helped me collapse, half conscious, onto a stinking mattress on the floor. Darkness swept over me, and I remember feeling grateful when he started unlacing my bodice so I could sleep more comfortably. Then, when he started on the rest of my garments, I realised his intentions. All strength gone from my limbs, I could do nought but mutter pleas for my youth, and push ineffectually at his hands. Yet my horror was soon drowned in a wave of roaring darkness, which carried me away.

When I awoke the next morning, the first thing I saw was his naked back, and the first sound was his drunken snoring. Disbelief stunned me, and it was not until I staggered to my feet, and saw the dried blood on my thighs, that I understood what had happened. I wanted to cover my nakedness more than anything, yet I looked on my women's clothes with abhorrence, and instead, took his shirt and breeches, and shaking with nausea and shame, hauled them on, and ran.

When I reached the brothel, the whole place was in an uproar, Mary Dillon screaming in Mistress Kate's arms, the whores fluttering about in tears, and no one to notice my grief. I found Jonas currying the bay mares, and he informed me brusquely that Lord Mordington was taken for debt to Newgate, after a gambling spree in which he had sworn that he owned the Lord Blakeney, and lost it. He set me to a thorough wash and polish of the coaches, while he tended the horses in the stables.

I spent the whole day drowning in shame, recalling the drinking and dancing and ribaldry, and my disgust was as much for my own foolishness, as for the debauched man who chose to rape an unconscious virgin, rather than pay a woman of the town. I saw the whole evening with different eyes, and wondered if it was a common ruse to have the fat soldier be rude to women, so Macartney could 'protect' them. I was most thankful that my mother was not there to ask if I was still honest, for although I knew she would not blame me, I knew enough to blame myself.

Towards evening, the constables arrived, and Peter Dillon and Jonas barred the doors and gates, declaring us closed. When Sally knocked on the small door of the courtyard, I was the only one still there, and quickly let her in. I could tell by her over-brimming delight that she knew nothing of what had happened to me, and I could not tell her. She spoke of Colonel Honeywood as her lover, and was confident that he would marry her, and too joyous to see any of my misery.

That week, I grew thin and pale, with dark shadows beneath my washed-out eyes. I could no longer sleep, yet so feared to lose my place, that I drove myself onwards, working hard to ease my torment.

The next Sunday, Sally looked less happy. She insisted we walk down to the river, though the wind was icy. We sheltered at Blackfriars stairs, watching Newgate prisoners board ships, indentured servants for the Americas. She muttered that she had not seen Honeywood since he had lain with her, that he had changed his lodgings, and she did not know how to seek him out. I suggested that we ask the Captain, and although she hesitated, thinking he would guess the cause, I persuaded her to trust him.

We sought him out in his usual corner of the Half Moon Tavern, yet found Sally's soldier comrades instead. They were crowing over a Guardsman who had been taken in bed with three women. In court, the soldier had pleaded that he had undergone enough punishment in satisfying the demands of three women, and had been freed. The women had been sent to Bridewell, to be whipped.

The fat soldier caught sight of Sally, and grinned at his mates. Before I could pull her away, he tugged a purse from his coat and threw it to her. She did not understand, and they began to snigger. "For your services, from Colonel Honeywood", the fat man declared.

Sally turned pale. "This is an ill joke of yours", she declared, trying to brazen it out.

"Nay, the Colonel has been called to Flanders, and would never leave his whore's bills unpaid."

The crowd seemed delighted to witness Sally's humiliation, yet I had my rapier on me, and when I drew, they were suddenly quiet.

"Nay, boy, put it away", the fat man urged me, still grinning. "There's no point in defending lost honour."

"The only people with no honour are the Officers of your Regiment", I stated clearly, knowing he would have to fight me. He got to his feet, anger making his broad face red, and with an effort, his sabre was out.

Then the Captain was behind me. "Keep your eye on him!", he hissed. My wits cleared, and the heat of anger gave way to a cold resolve to kill the fat fool. He kicked back a bench to give us room enough, and then he attacked, slashing for my throat, sure I'd retreat. I sidestepped, not risking my finer blade on a parry, and as his arm went wide, I stuck my rapier straight through his broad chest.

He fell dead at my feet, and the Captain grabbed my arm and raced me away into the Bermudas before the crowd could follow us, Sally at our heels. I did not come out of the shock until the Captain prised the bloody rapier from my clenched fist, and poured brandy down my throat. "Well done, lad. A marvellous thrust, a classic lunge! They will talk of this in Covent Garden for at least a week."

And then I was weeping in Sally's arms. "Nay, Mark, you were wonderful. Never has anyone stood up for my honour, but me. I've never been so proud in my life. You were right to kill that pig. You were right to do it, Mark! And with all my heart I thank you for it. They made a whore of me, and you redeemed me. Yet you are too well known to escape being dragged before a magistrate."

"Few people know where I work."

"Are you sure you can trust them to hide you? Then come, we will go now, in case they come looking for you here. I can't go home either, since this story will be at my grandparent's place within the hour. I will stay with you tonight, and we will talk and think."

I wiped my face and we crept through the alleyways together, past Bow Street, and through the stable gates at the back of the Lord Blakeney. I told Jonas that I'd killed an Officer who had insulted Sally, and the constables would be looking for me even now. If anything, he looked pleased at the news. He insisted that Sally dress in some of my spare clothes, wind her long fair hair up under one of my old hats, and help sweep out the stables, pretending to be someone just hired off the streets for the afternoon. We worked together, and when Jonas took the whores for their drive, he left us there, and we had a chance to speak privately.

"What a fool I was", Sally muttered. "Believing he loved me because I had already given him my heart. I just hope the bastard hasn't made me pregnant." I had not considered this, and my head reeled with horror. Sally would not go back to live with the Garths, and for a month, she lived in the stables with me. We were both relieved when we bled, yet after another few weeks, Sally muttered of sores on her privates. I urged her to see a medical student she knew, and he confirmed it. She was poxed.

She disappeared, and for another month I lived with the fear that they would fish her corpse out of the Thames. Her grandfather came looking for her, begging me to tell him what had happened. Yet I shook my head at his grief and said nothing. I tried to pray for her, and could not. The Faith that had kept me warm in this cold world was gone, and a hard black stone was left in its place.

In the first week of Spring, Sally turned up at the Halfmoon Tavern, dressed in the latest fashions, having sold herself to the infamous Mother Needham for the mercury cure. For months, she was sewn up and sold as a virgin over and over again, until she declared she could stand the pain no longer. Then Mother Needham introduced her to Colonel Charteris, known as the rape-master of London, and he abandoned her in Bath when she flouted him. She had made her way back to London, and now earned a living by

98

charging apprentices half a crown for half an hour in a rancid room in Drury Lane.

Through all of this, she avoided me. When I begged her to give up the life, she laughed, as hard as the rest of the world, and said this was what she'd been born to. I became slovenly at my work, no longer caring for anyone's approval, and Jonas eventually threw me out, with nought but a bundle of fine clothes, my mother's Bible, and my rapier. I pawned my good suit, and wandered down to the Pool, watching the ships load and unload, weeping for my lost mother, and my lost friend, and my lost honour.

When a gentleman in a sensible wig and a gold-trimmed blue jacket approached me, I dashed my tears away and stared into the distance. Yet he stopped and laid a broad hand on my shoulder.

"Have you nowhere to go, boy?" His eyes were kind, but not overly so.

"Nowhere."

"And no friends?"

"None, Sir."

"And not a shilling?"

"No more than will feed me for a day or two."

"And do ye know how to use that rapier by yer side?"

"'Tis why I'm here, Sir."

"Then follow the sea, boy. We need lads who are strong and brave, to sail the finest ship in Queen Anne's Navy. I am Captain Mitchell of the Dreadnought."

"The Dreadnought! In truth Sir, I would sail with you gladly."

"I like the cut o' yer jib, boy, I'll tell ye that straight. Me cabin boy has let me down an' we sail on the morning tide for Gravesend. If ye suit me, I'll put ye in his place. No relying on the Navy for starvation wages, eh? I'll see ye right meself."

"I am at your disposal, Captain Mitchell."

"An' yer name, boy?"

"I call myself John Smith, Sir."

He shook his head. "Running away, are ye? Well, 'tis no business o' mine. Make yer farewells, for we ship out before dawn."

"I have none to make, Sir."

"Then follow me, John Smith, and I'll buy you an ale and a pie in Wapping before we ship out."

PART 2: THE NAVY 1706-1708
Chapter 6: The Dreadnought

I hastened after the well-dressed, rough-spoken Captain Mitchell as he strode through the evening crowd, scattering hawkers in his wake, so that I knew he was indeed Commander of the Dreadnought. In the thick crowd, I lost sight of all but his sensible black wig, and raced to his boot heels just as he marched into a sailors' tavern in Wapping. As if he repented of his earlier kindness, he ignored me once he was comfortable in the best chair in front of the smoky fire, a hot rum in his fist. I curled up on the floor as close to the fire as I could get, for the Spring nights were already cold. A skivvy banged a pint of ale and a pie down in front of me, and I was so humbly grateful, that I swore in my soul to serve the Captain always. I listened to the stories he swapped with the sailors drinking around us, stories of high seas and hard passages, of the Bermuda Strait and the African slave trade, of pirates and press gangs, and the intrigues of the Navy. The rough sailors seemed to know the Captain well, and every nod of deference to his gruff opinion strengthened my hope for my new life.

The sailors talked and played tenbones and smoked their long pipes, until the old clock struck midnight, and they agreed that the tide was on the turn, and 'twas time to ship out. The Captain threw the busy tavern keeper a gold piece, and she wished him fair winds, and reminded him that if he saw her Johnny, to send him home.

"Aye, but warn us first if the old bastard's on 'is way", a handsome man with a yellow beard called from the corner. "'E always wos a jealous whoreson, and it 'as bin six years!"

"Keep yer fat mouth shut, ye guzzlin' pig! If ye don't show more respect for the woman who slaves her fingers to the bone to keep ye in drink, ye'll sleep in the streets where ye belong!"

We exited to the sound of a rising brawl, and strode

to the docks, to where the wherries were moored. Ours was piled high with barrels of provisions, rope and canvas, sailors tying down the last knots, while others farewelled their sweethearts. The Captain ignored the weeping women, and ordered all aboard and cast off. I took my place in the prow, the boat moving under me, most strangely. The sail unfurled, the wind bellied it out, and we slid out into the wide brown Thames like a water bird rising.

As I turned to farewell the city where I had suffered so much, the moon came out and lit up the dome of St Paul's like a beacon, and I took it for a sign that I was indeed choosing well, to step out boldly into a new life, away from the hard recklessness of London. I wept as I prayed for the well-being of my mother and Sally Pridden, and was thankful to find some sorrow that was not for myself. I had not had to throw myself in the river, to drown rather than starve, yet I knew the simple happiness of my childhood belonged to the past. I would not dream of single-handedly saving the ship, or bravely rescuing Captain Mitchell from drowning. Just to serve him would be enough.

"Nay lad, don't ye grieve", a skinny old sailor mumbled. "Ye've started yer man's life now, so sup this back." He passed me a bottle of rum, and I sipped, feeling its fire burn through me. I wiped the tears away with my sleeve, and resolved then to master my fate. I had chosen the life of a young man alone in the world, and it was only when I had reneged, that disaster had struck. I resolved then never to don skirts again, but to live as a cabin boy on the Dreadnought, fighting for Good Queen Anne against the greedy might of Papist France.

Vessels of all sizes sailed with us down to the sea, their Captains regularly bellowing for the change of tack, their sailors echoing the orders, the water carrying every sound clearly. Yet the many months of distress and sleeplessness had taken their toll of my spirit, and in the warmth of this newborn hope, I let the hush of water against our hull lull me to sleep.

The harsh cry of a crow woke me to a grey dawn. We had tacked close to the bank, and I saw the bird savaging a rotting corpse in a dangling cage. The Tybourn gallows had already taught me the cold rigour of the law, yet this curdled my guts, for how could one's soul rest if one's body was nought but a horror for carrion to feed upon? The old sailor shrugged his bony shoulders, passed me a hard piece of brown bread, and muttered that there were pirates gibbeted all the way along the Thames.

"Damn yer eyes for fools" a hard-faced tar growled. "Without that, we'd all go a-rovin'." The Captain sat upright in the stern and ignored us, his hat over his eyes, the collar of his thick coat over his ears, evidently deep in thought.

By low tide, we were through the marshlands and moored at the dock in Gravesend, hauling the cargo from the wherry into the Dreadnought's longboat. The old tar insisted we keep all the weight low, and balanced port and starboard, for there would be a strong breeze rising with the tide. He was right, the wind rose, and I tried to contain my fear of the deep water. The longboat was much bigger than the wherry, yet her lines were longer and we hoisted more sail, so that once the Captain gave the command to cast off, the wind sent us skimming across the mouth of that broad river, past the oyster beds, all the way to Longreach. I was in the prow again, the salt spray lashing my face like a Baptism, my fear lost in awe as I first saw the sea.

At Longreach we skimmed past many ships, out into the rolling swell of the outer harbour, where the men o' war always moored. We came past the bow of an elegant frigate, and I saw a ship like a floating castle, her massive hull bearing double tiers of cannon, the men swarming over her like ants.

Then the ship's trumpeter spied us, and blew a long blast, alerting the ship's crew to the approach of their Commander. Captain Mitchell adjusted his hat on his wig, and adopted an expression so severe that I understood his true high standing in the world, and was humbled that he

103

should stoop to save me from the cold streets of London.

Then the glory of the Dreadnought overwhelmed me as she loomed over us. We dropped sail, Captain Mitchell shouting for block and tackle from the mainyard. Then he clambered up a rope ladder, nodding at me to follow him, me with my bundle in one hand, and my rapier in the other. The old sailor chuckled and almost ran up the ladder, his seachest on his shoulder. I put my bundle over my arm and my rapier between my teeth, and climbed up carefully, alert to the scars of battle smashed into her weathered oak.

When I finally stood on her wide, rolling deck, I felt that I was home, and that the Dreadnought knew it too. It seemed a chaos of shouting officers, and chanting sailors, the rigging alive with them bending sail to spar, many black men among them, abandoned slaves, pressed by the Navy.

Captain Mitchell watched as dozens of sailors heaved the first load of our precious provisions aboard, while others stowed the casks and barrels below.

Captain Mitchell nodded his satisfaction to the hard-faced sailor, and then ordered me to follow him, and bring his trunk. Somehow I hauled it as far as a small door that led aft from the quarterdeck, where he turned and grasped it himself, probably afeared I would drop it down the steep stairs. I was impressed by the grandness of his quarters, the stern gallery all polished oak panelling, the solid table and fixed benches well carved, the windows covered in green velvet. The two quarter galleries, one his sleeping place, the other his own lavatory, were only slightly less grand.

I saw the lavatory as a great advantage, for it would be easy for me to slip the bolt of the door, and use the chamber-pot myself. He showed me my alcove, a sort of dog kennel that I would have to go into on all fours for fear of knocking my head off. He said I'd have to share it with another boy, and dread of discovery again took hold of me. I stowed my rapier under the old canvas mattress, and threw my small bag down as a pillow. Captain Mitchell frowned, then picked up a blanket from the foot of his bed, and tossed

104

it at me. When I tried to thank him, he cut me short and explained my duties.

I was one of four boys who were his servants, two to attend him on each watch, while the others slept in the kennel. Between the pair of us, we would take care of his clothes, bring his meals from the Cook, tidy the galley without disturbing the charts on the table, and wait on his guests without repeating a word of their conversations. If we were not directly needed, we'd join the watch. This was the first I had heard of work other than waiting on him, yet when he grunted that I should befriend the Cook, I answered that I would rather learn to sail the Dreadnought, than skulk in the galley.

"Don't be stupid. His scraps will keep you alive."

Inwardly resolved, I forbore further argument, and he showed me where to stow his gear, watched me busy for a while, a half-smile on his face, and then asked if I thought nought of pay. I gaped at him, and he shook his head at me wryly. "You've all the advantages of a volunteer seaman, though you're nought but a grummet. You'll share in any bounty, you'll not be transferred between ships without your consent, and you'll be paid at the end of the season, seeking cash for your ticket at Guildhall. This is all you'll see until then." He threw me a coin, and returned on deck, leaving me to tidy his gear away as quickly as I could.

I wiped a salty dampness from the brass instruments I found by his charts, marveling to hold the tools that would see us safely over the great seas. I took the opportunity to study the charts, and soon traced our course south from London, right to Longreach. The Captain had even made a little cross in the midst of the bay, and written the date, April 15, 1706. I then made the Captain's bed, swept the dust from the floor, and went to seek further orders.

The Dreadnought's decks were swarming with working men and boys, all watched by barking Officers, one of them now brandishing a cane over the bare backs of the men heaving at the capstan. Others stood ten foot apart,

105

tossing enormous sacks down the line, each enough to knock me over. I felt like an odd thumb, and could not see the Captain anywhere.

When I saw a freckled, red-headed boy sorting fishing lines, I walked over and smiled diffidently. He nodded with the superiority of a working man, yet let me help untie knots and wind cord. My abashed silence piqued his curiosity. "Ship's boy are ye?"

"Captain's servant. John Smith's the name."

"Captain's servant, eh? Me too. Bill Search." He stopped unwinding knots and shook my hand.

"Is he a good master?"

"Oh the Captain's fair enough. Hard on loafers and shirkers and whiners. And he has a partnership with the Purser to milk our provisions allowance, so we sure as Hell don't eat well."

"He steals our food?"

"Hush, not so loud. The Purser buys the worst food he can, and divides the money left over with the Captain. Last year, a man was given thirty blows for speaking out against it, so keep yer mouth shut."

"What do you do?"

"I'm one of the topyard boys. See how the masts have great poles going across them, holding the corners of the sails up? Well those are the yards. I go right up there, climbing the ratlines to the top, and furl the sails to trim the ship to the wind."

"It must be like climbing a tree."

"But the tree whips yer head about in hurricanes of wind, the wet canvas smashes against ye, the ropes burn yer hands when ye grip 'em, and if ye don't hold on, 'tis a dead man on deck, or a drowned man in the sea ye'll be. We topyard boys go up in all weather, yet I'm the only one who'll go out on a yard in a storm and never flinch."

While we sorted fishing lines, he bewildered me with the names of everything we could see. "The mast at the stern of the ship is the mizzen, the tallest is the mainmast, and the

106

foremast is that nearer the bow, with the bowsprit jutting out ahead. The sails are all named after the masts, so mizzen-sail, main-sail, fore-sail, and then the jibs and flying jibs come off the bow..."

"Slower, 'tis all so new..."

Bill grinned a trifle maliciously. "All a grummet needs to know is how to stay in the Captain's favour."

"I want to know how to sail this ship into battle against the French and win. I think she's marvellous."

He grinned and clapped me on the back. "Ye'll do. Tell the Captain ye want to learn the ship. He'll put ye with Old Tom Pullen, the carpenter, and ye can ask me anything ye want as well."

"I did not expect there to be so many men aboard. 'Tis like a small town."

"There's only about two hundred aboard now. We're due five hundred more men from the press gangs. That's how many we lost last year."

"Was there a great battle?"

"Aye, 'gainst cold and damp and bad food. Those that sail without their health don't last long. Of the twenty of us boys, five are well-born, hoping to become Admirals, and even they sicken fast. The whole ship's Company is divided into two watches, one with the First, one with the Second Mate. The First Mate's a hard bastard, always angling for promotion, an' he cares not how many of us he kills for it. The Second Mate's a gennulman's son, an' sure of promotion, so he looks out for us. Watch changes every six hours, 'cept in bad weather, when we all turn out to man the pumps, sometimes only half an hour after we've turned in. Sometimes we're up for days and nights, working to keep her off a lee shore, the waves crashing into us, sleepin' in wet clothes in wet hammocks, one shoe off and one shoe on. 'Tis a hard life, but a grand one. 'Cept the food."

"Have you ever been in a battle?"

"We are a Ship o' the Line. That's the Battle Line, boy. We sail under the orders of the Admiral, guns primed and ready to blow holes in the French bastards, who think they can subdue the pride o' the English and force a Papist King on us!"

"Yet he's Queen Anne's older brother."

"Not bloody likely! They say he's a common bastard, smuggled into the Papist Queen's chambers in a warming pan to ensure the Catholic Succession! Only a Jacobite could want such a fraud to rule us."

I retreated with something I had heard my aunt say. "I like Queen Anne. She's not grand, but she leaves her people to their own consciences."

"To die for her is the best we can ask for. 'Cept that if we live, we might make it to Admiral. Sir David Mitchell and Sir Cloudesly Shovell were cabin boys once. And once a cabin boy crept aboard an enemy ship and scuttled her and won the battle. I'm soon to be made an able seaman, and then I'll be Mate, then Captain, and one day Admiral..."

"Admiral my arse!", interrupted a bigger boy, sneering. "You'll have to help Old Tom mend some chests first. He's calling for you."

"Aye aye, Pete. This is John Smith, Captain's boy and newest grummet. Wants to learn the ship." Bill showed me where to stow the ordered fishing tackle, and dashed off, and I decided I liked him despite his bragging.

The big boy ignored him. "I'm Pete Swallow, the oldest of the ship's boys. This is my second year, and I'll be made an able seaman in a few months. I run the ship's boys, and you answer to me, do you hear?" I thought that it was more likely that I would answer to the Captain, yet I agreed with Pete anyway, that seeming safest. "The Captain only needs you for part of the day. For the rest of it, he'll assign you to the Purser or the Cook."

"I'd rather 'twas sailing work. I don't mind it being harder. I want to learn to sail this ship."

"You're a bit on the small side for a sailor. And you don't know how steady your sea legs are yet. Shit off the heads in fine weather, they are there at the bows. Use the

108

bilges at the bottom of the ship in a storm. We piss and heave up over the side. Make sure 'tis the lee side or the wind will blow it all over you and the deck, an' the Boatswain'll beat you."

"What? Beat me?"

"Oh aye, didn't ye know? We're the lowest of the low, us ship's boys. We get the worst work and the worst food, and if we step a foot out o' line we're caned. The oldest sailors swear we'll have no wind if a boy isn't whipped every Monday, just after prayers, so the week begins with one of us being beaten for the sins of all the rest. Then he is made the dog of the week, and must clean the shit off the heads, and any other filthy work the Boatswain can think of. Most often, 'tis the last aboard, which is you boy."

"No one should be whipped without deserving it!", I objected. Yet 'twas the chance of having my shirt stripped from me before the entire crew that horrified me.

"All the boys get it, but only once a year or so, since there's so many of us. Look." He pulled up his shirt and showed me fresh welts. "Once I'm an able seaman, they'll need an excuse to do this to me."

"I'd jump overboard first. To suffer such injustice..."

"Only the best of the topyard boys avoid it. Unless you make the Boatswain angry. Lord, my father used to beat me every day. If I say a word to the Boatswain, he'll beat you tomorrow. I bet you cry the first time."

"There won't be a first time. I'll be the best of the topyard boys, and not get beaten."

"Lord, you're a strange one. Every sailor on this ship has felt the cane when a boy, and the lash when a man. Aye, a good whipping, that would make you think nothing of a beating. The Captain is King of our little world. Mostly, you're placed on half-allowance, that's no meat and beer, boy. That'll starve you into quiet. Yet if you're too drunk to turn out for your watch, then you're tied to the mainmast and flogged. He'll duck you from the main yardarm for stubbornness, laziness, going ashore without leave, and

109

sleeping on watch. If you thieve, you run the gauntlet between the whole crew, armed with knotted ropes. And for even skylarking in the rigging, and playing the jokes that they call knaveries, we are paid with the Boatswain's rod Monday morning and made Lord o' the Heads. Come on. Before they see us idle, I'll show you how she looks below."

We dropped below, and I found huge baulks of oak overhead, the planks of wood secured with great bolts, and sturdy knees of timber. I saw she was a tough old ship that had survived many a storm, and would survive many more. I put my hand up to feel my way through the gloom of the corridor, and it came away sticky with pitch. Pete explained happily that the ship was so tarry, that the spark of a hammer, or the snuff of a candle, could turn us all into a great blast of fire.

There were three decks, the first crowded with huge iron guns on carriages, the gunpowder room, and the Officer's quarters. We then explored the orlop deck, containing another tier of cannon, cabins for the petty officers, and berths where the sailors slung their hammocks and kept their chests. Every sailor shared his hammock, turning out for his watch as the new man turned in. Pete told me that on no account must I ever touch a sailor's chest. 'Twas all he had in the world, and he'd kill me for it. The worst berths were in the forecastle, which pitched and tossed the most when the ship was at sea, yet all the berths were dark and damp and reeked of piss. "If it gets too wet, we kip 'tween decks, in store rooms, or sail lockers, about the cannon, or in any spare corner we can find. She's an old tub, and leaks terrible through every seam, the salt making what gets wet, stay damp. Yet you'll not wake in a puddle with a dead rat floating in it. The Captain's cabin is the driest on the ship."

"He gave me a blanket."

"He's softer than he lets on. He has to keep the pressed men cowed down somehow. Yet he started as one of us. As a ship's boy. And he can sail the Dreadnought better than any of those bastards promoted over him for being better born."

"Have you ever been in battle?"

"Of course I have! Last year we skirmished twice with the Frenchies."

"Only twice?"

"We have to find them first, and then 'tis not often that either side will risk losing ships in a Battle Line. Mostly we convoy merchant ships about Europe, protecting them from the Dunkirk privateers." I was disappointed, having imagined a battle at least once a week, yet I was too pleased with the Dreadnought to foresee anything but glory.

We heard the chants of working men, and came upon a gang of them stacking stores into the black hold below us. The hard-faced First Mate soon had us hauling at lines, while he damned our eyes for sluggards.

When the Boatswain blew the note for dinner, I saw that the Captain had been watching us, and hoping this had earned me his good opinion, I took the opportunity to beg to be trained for the topyards. To my surprise, he flatly refused, and ordered me to help the Cook. But I begged again and he shrugged and told me to die in whatever fashion I pleased. Then he ordered the First Mate to get Old Tom teaching the ship's boys their river discipline straight after dinner.

After a mouthful of mouldy bread, rank cheese and watery ale, for which every man cursed the Steward, the ship's boys went to find Old Tom. He was seated by the bow, smoking a rank pipe, out of the way of the ship's confusion, and mending a seachest. He was the old sailor from the wherry, and amongst all the young faces, he looked ancient, yet his glance was keen. "Ho boys, want to learn to sail this ship do ye? If ye learn badly, ye'll die young. A caning for each lad that can't do a bowline with his eyes shut by tomorrow morn. Watch me now. This is the one knot ye can trust yer life to. No, through the loop. That's it. Now do it ten times. No fool, around and through."

We sat there desperately tying bowlines, while Old

Tom regaled us with stories of exotic seas and gallant ships. He told us of hunting the Spanish treasure ships in 1702, and storming the defenses of Vigo Bay. "Aye, the Queen got the gold, and had her fat head stamped on it. We sailors got the tobacco, and have loved our pipes ever since." At this, most of us resolved to get hold of a pipe somehow.

In that first month aboard, while still moored in the river mouth, Old Tom taught us all we needed to be useful at sea. We learnt the names of the most obscure sails, where they were kept, and how they were attached to the masts, that ropes were called sheets, and that if I went up onto the Officers' quarterdeck, I'd be whipped to the bone. I thought the skinny old man remarkable, and believed him when he said he could smell storms coming.

The schoolmaster was a poor fish, who moaned at being snubbed by the pretentious prude of a parson, who were both more concerned with insisting on their rights as gentlemen, than in carrying out their duties. The schoolmaster ignored me once he found I wrote a better hand than he did, showing us nought of navigation but a bad drawing of a compass rose.

The Gunner, a grim giant of a man, spent two afternoons a week teaching the whole ship the use of small arms. I liked the heavy weight of the musket, and the sharp smell of gunpowder, yet could not hit the mark. To deflect the Gunner's wrath, Bill boasted that I was a duelling man. The Gunner scornfully insisted that I fetch my rapier and show them my paces, and I had to parry and lunge before all the crew. To my surprise, the Gunner told me I could show the bigger boys my paces, and found more patience with my poor marksmanship.

Bill said we'd spend half our time moored somewhere, doing such drills and caring for the ship. We worked hard through those weeks, resting on Sundays and holy days, and Bill said to make the most of the full nights of sleep and the poor food, for 'twould only get worse. After supper the Captain would order the ship's musicians to strike up the fiddle, fife and drum, and the sailors would do the hornpipe, and sing shanties and ballads of ships long gone. Once I had proved myself a fast learner and industrious, the Captain ignored me, and though he was never a tyrant, I found myself trying harder to please him, seeking but one word of praise.

I offered to clean the lavatory every morning, thus making it safe for me to perform my own ablutions. In the first week, I took a chisel and soon loosened a small board behind a cupboard in the lavatory. In the alcove behind, I concealed my purse with its few coins, and a bag of sea sponges that Sally had given me, to hide my monthly bleeding. When I bled for the first time aboard, I was worried that some might smell the blood upon me, yet in truth we stank so much by then that I was safe. I thought Bill was the only one likely to discover my secret, and his open contempt for the poor spirit of girls made me very careful. Eventually the bad food left me so thin that my monthly bleeding stopped.

In truth, I thought myself blessed, and might have rested in ignorance of the Navy's harshness a little longer, if it had not been for the pressed men. They came on board by the hundreds, sullen slaves, snatched drunk from taverns and brothels, and sober from merchant ships. Now they were without any right to their lives or deaths, scorned by the regular sailors, working unwillingly at the heaviest tasks in the ship's waist, under the distrustful eyes of the Officers. The pressed men were always talking mutiny, and would jump ship at any opportunity, yet if any of them survived their harsh treatment, and learned the ropes, they could work their way up to able seamen, and despise the newcomers in their turn. "Our good Queen can make ten Lords in a day, yet it takes more than five years to make a good sailor", Old Tom Pullen insisted. Bill swore that of the six hundred men aboard, four hundred would be dead of hunger and cold by this time next year. I could not envision it, so it did not frighten me.

113

Chapter 7: Powder Monkey

We spent a month loading the Dreadnought with powder and provisions, and then on the third of May, in squally weather, the Captain gave the order to weigh anchor. The fifty strongest men heaved at the bars of the capstan, forcing it to turn, pulling the muddy chain aboard link by link, until the massive anchor broke free of the bottom, and was dragged up the Dreadnought's side. Sails were unfurled from the yards and sheeted home, and an easterly wind bellied them out. Beneath us, the great bulk of the ship's hull trembled, and came alive. Sailors grinned and heaved on the sheets, and broke into song.

"Don't you see the ships a-coming?
Don't you see them in full sail?
Don't you see the ships a coming?
With the prizes at their tail?

Oh! My little rolling sailor,
Oh! My little rolling he,
I do love a jolly sailor,
Blithe and merry might he be.

Sailors they get all the money,
Soldiers they get none but brass.
I do love a jolly sailor,
Soldiers they may kiss my arse."

The Captain hid his grin, and the Boatswain called up the entire Company, to divide the watch. The First Mate sent his best man to starboard, and the Second Mate sent his to port, until the entire crew was divided in two. Bill and I were called by the First Mate, while the Captain's two other boys were with the gentlemanly Second Mate. When we were bid to choose a mate from the other watch, a cabin boy nodded at me, and it was he who would tumble into my bed when the watch was changed, and I was roused up.

When I saw I'd be partnered with the freckled, stalwart Bill Search, both in taking care of the Captain and tending the topsails, I was over-joyed. Still at attention, Bill gave me a wink and I knew he'd done it for both our sakes.

When we were told to choose our messmates, Pete elbowed his mate and nodded at us. I was glad of this, sure I could trust them to save me something if I was called away, or ill. Bill said that if I was injured, he would tell my family, and when I told him that there was none to care if I lived or died, he tried to smile and said he also was alone in the world. "Then we should be brothers", I told him, "for I am sure you can rely on me." He clasped my hand, and declared himself honoured, and the world seemed warmer.

The Captain ordered the Purser to give every man a can of beer and a biscuit to stay our stomachs till the kettle boiled. Then the First Mate called the dog watch, and Bill and I were sent racing up the ratlines to study the gray horizon. We saw all the other ships of our squadron shadowy about us, and I was filled with pride to be part of such a great force. Nervous on account of the poor visibility, the First Mate bellowed constantly for soundings, urging us to keep our eyes peeled, or he'd have our skins.

Then the trumpeter blew the change of watch, and Bill and I slid down the shrouds to report for a sea sermon about the mainmast. The Chaplain led us in earnest prayers for Her Majesty, and for all Christian souls out upon the perilous seas. The night watch was set, and Bill and I ate supper and curled up together in our kennel to sleep. At midnight our mates woke us to the sound of the Boatswain's whistle, and we could feel the rolling of the Dreadnought as she came out into the Nore. After cold hours trimming sails, the First Mate trying to make the most of decreasing winds, we stumbled shivering to wake our mates, happy to take their warm places in our kennel. Before I fell asleep, Bill said that if the sky was clear come dawn, I'd see the coast of

France. Yet when dawn came, the weather was thick with drizzle, and I could see nothing on either side but the leaden sea, rolling out endlessly to a gray horizon.

The heaving and settling of the open sea caused me some uneasiness, yet I had none of the vomiting and lassitude of the other landsmen. Most recovered within a few days, and I never suffered from it again, causing even Pete to call me a true sailor. The days continued drizzly, and we were kept busy, even if it was not our watch. There were always repairs to make to the ship, sails to be patched, and decks to be caulked with hemp and tar against leaks.

I was soon scrambling aloft with the best of them, prancing along the yards to furl sails, half drunk to feel the clean, salt wind on my face. Bill liked to hang by his knees from the cross-trees and feel the blood rush to his head, though I thought this mere bravado. I settled into the ship's busy routine, finding the Captain easy enough to please, our orderliness suiting each other.

My only trouble was the constant temptation of the Captain's library. I knew I'd be whipped as a thief if I did not ask him before borrowing one, yet it took some time for me to gather my courage. One morning I told him I could read. He raised an eyebrow at me, and I muttered that I'd only a Bible. He stared at me, and I lost my nerve and babbled that I would care for a book of his with my life, and never avoid work, but just read a little at a time, when it wasn't my watch, and I wasn't needed elsewhere. When I'd finished, certain I'd lost his good opinion, he threw me his battered old copy of 'The Voyages of Odysseus', warning me that if I was late for a single watch, he'd order the Boatswain to take my skin off. I thanked him profusely, and though he shrugged, I thought I'd surprised him as much as he'd surprised me.

I pondered this old story of the wandering soldier at length, astonished at the gods and goddesses of those ancient days and far lands, at their whims and hatred and power. I thought Odysseus a true hero, and admired his cunning, yet his fascination with the dreadful Circe worried me, and I

117

disapproved of him being so untrue with Calypso, when he expected Penelope to wait faithfully for him at home.

Once we had spent a few days rolling in the Nore, our food worsened. We ate beef that had lain in salt for so many years that it seemed less likely to be meat than the leather of the Captain's boots. Our Purser stinted meanly with the ship's boys, and we were lucky to get fourteen ounces to the pound, the Purser claiming that the other two went in scraping the worst of the mould off the bread and cheese, though 'twas always served to us foul and sound together. Yet Bill warned that 'twould get worse still, and made me eat it all. He said 'twas that or nothing, and as we were young and growing and working hard, we ate fast and washed it down with a pint of watered ale. When one butt of the twelve tons of beer that we took aboard was staved in, 'twas looked upon as a disaster by crew and Officers alike. It happened on a Monday morning, and instead of a ship's boy being beaten, they hauled up the sailor who had tied the useless knot, and whipped him unmercifully.

The next day, an Officer came aboard with the arrears of bounty money and wages owing the men from the year before. The Navy was always backward in paying its men, leaving them nothing to take home to their families after months of hard work, so they had no choice but to sign up again. If they were unlucky enough to be transferred from one ship to another, as often happened if fever left a ship short-handed, then they would spend fruitless months at the Navy Office begging for the pay they had earned. I was lucky in being a hired servant, for the Captain had to give me a ticket for my wages every quarter.

One of the boys was in much worse circumstances, having signed on a seven year apprenticeship to the First Mate, who always kept his wages, and told him that he was bound, and must obey. How he had survived this for years, I do not know, for he was the butt of the ship, and often caned for all our sins on a Monday. I despised him as a sniveling, whining thing, much like a half-starved dog. His was the first death, and I thought it odd that almost the entire ship's Company turned out to see his shrouded carcass tossed into the sea.

Shortly after, fifty marines came aboard, the soldiers who fight aboard ship, and Pete said we would soon sail. At dawn the next morning the Captain gave the order, and we weighed anchor as the tide turned. I expected to sail straight against the French, yet instead we made our way slowly around to the Downs, to the rest of the Fleet. After the Chaplain read the usual sermon, we took aboard another boatload of pressed men, and one was whipped for foul language to the First Mate. Bad weather set in then, as Old Tom had predicted, and for four days it rained and blew at us, all hands praying that the anchors would hold. This was the first bad weather I had seen at sea, yet despite the rolling of the ship, I kept my stomach, and watched in some satisfaction as others ran for the gunwales.

Through those days of dampness and drizzle, the black-bearded Gunner taught us the thirteen manoeuvres that comprised the drill for the ship's guns. Full of bravado, I volunteered as powder monkey when no one else would, though Bill shook his head. As powder monkey, I carried the heavy tubs of powder from the gun room, to the eleventh gun on the starboard quarter, as it was needed.

Soon after, an Officer from our squadron rowed over and called loudly for Captain Mitchell. Within half an hour, the Second Mate blew his whistle, and formed the whole crew into battle lines. The Captain strode out of his cabin attended by the strange Officer, both of them drunk. "Men, we have great news! Purser, break open a barrel of rum and give every man a dram. We toast the Duke of Marlborough's great victory over the French! On the twenty-third of May, he forbore engaging in the usual French siege, and instead, he charged the French army at Ramillies, and with English redcoats in the very thick of the battle, cut them to pieces. The whole of Flanders has declared in favour of the Allies, and French fortresses fall every day with barely a fight.

119

Bruges, Damme and Oudenarde are already ours. Now Marlborough needs our help to take the port and fortress of Ostend, to ensure his supplies from England. Gunner, take your crew and fire fifteen cannon."

We gave three loud huzzas for the Duke of Marlborough, and when the Purser came with the rum, I raised my mug and drank to his glory. With the unaccustomed heat of the rum coursing through us, we fired the ships great guns, one after the other, from bow to stern, in a terrible thunder that obliterated thought. By the time our gun was to be fired, black smoke had filled the gundeck, and the Gunner put the flaming match to the powder, almost blind. The cannon's blast sent it recoiling its own length, smashing back against the breeching that held it, my guncrew dancing fast out of the way. The huff of fire from the touch-hole burned pock-marks in the beams overhead, and I understood why I had to fetch powder a little at a time, and why the bucket had to stay carefully covered.

The next day, the Captain ordered me to invite the Officers to join him for dinner, and told me I'd be table servant. When I had brought in the pork and peas, and poured the wine, they toasted Lord Marlborough with a solemnity that negated the rivalry between sailor and soldier. The Second Mate could not contain his respect for the brilliant General. "Marlborough wanted Ostend in the year three, and the Dutch refused him help. They preferred to take a percentage of all the goods we were transporting through the Netherlands, even though 'tis their own damned swamp of a country we are fighting for."

The Captain leaned confidentially over the table. "I heard that the Dutch commander, Cohorn, ignored a direct order to threaten Ostend. He took his Cavalry on a pillaging excursion instead, taking ten percent of the forage to sell for himself, and used his influence at the Hague to justify it. They'd rather make money than win a war, even against their French invaders." The Englishmen shook their heads at this cowardly evasion of the chance for a good fight, damned the

Dutch and the French, and poured themselves more wine.

On the thirtieth day of May, the lookout hollered, and suddenly the horizon was full of ships. The Admiral, Sir Stafford Fairburn, was sailing in with the rest of the Fleet. As soon as they moored, an Officer on the Flagship bellowed through a speaking trumpet that there had been an Allied victory in Spain at Barcelona. Spain was a less important front than Flanders, so the Captain ordered thirteen guns fired, and left for the Admiral's ship.

We assembled just after the change of watch the next day. "We sail with the Fleet for Ostend, to blockade it and bombard it. The Allied Armies will attack from the land side with fifty battalions, and a hundred squadrons of horse. The Duke of Marlborough needs Ostend as a route for supplies from England, and 'tis vital for our Army that we take it fast." The Admiral's Flagship loosed its foretopsail, making the sign for the Fleet to sail. "To the capstan with the pressed men, weigh the anchor, we sail for Ostend!"

We let out three great cheers, and leapt for the lines, and never had we shinnied up faster. As the sails filled, the sun shone out, and so did our hearts. After months of drudgery, to be finally heading out to battle, the whole of the English Fleet about us, was truly glorious. That evening, I was more particular than ever in the Captain's cabin, and in the morning I blacked his boots until they shone. I saw him as a great man, occupied by great thoughts, and silently vowed to prove my valour in the coming fray.

At dawn we were seven leagues off the sunlit Calais Cliffs, and by evening the entire Fleet was anchored off Dunkirk, the setting sun gilding the steeples of that privateer haven. In the middle of the night, we set sail north, and were anchored off Nieuport for a last Captain's conference on the Flagship the next morning. That afternoon, we all sailed for Ostend. I had expected a castle on a cliff, but found a great star-like fort, set on low ground, a graceful spire rising above billowing clouds of smoke. The rolling hills above Ostend were covered with great lines of our men, each representing a battalion, their batteries of field cannon already spitting fire at the fortress.

The Fleet began to form the Battle Line, and after a frightened prayer from the Chaplain, the Captain urged us to remember our drills, and to acquit ourselves like true English sailors. He then ordered: "Down chests and up hammocks", and we cleared the ship for battle. Pete had the honour of hanging our colours from the poop, we topyard boys furled the lighter sails to keep them safe, bulkheads were fortified with blankets and hammocks to reduce splinters, and Old Tom readied oakum and sheets of lead in case we were holed. After we'd gulped our food and beer, the cook-room fire was put out, and the Captain ordered the great guns to be cast loose and loaded.

I was ordered below, and only realised that this was no drill when the Gunner ordered that the hatches leading to the hold be locked. One of my guncrew told me 'twas so we had nowhere to run. "Yet that would make a man a deserter!", I exclaimed.

"Aye lad, yet 'tis a hard thing not to run from Hell." When the planks about the guns were sprinkled with sand, he said 'twas to stop us slipping in our comrades' blood, and I thought he was trying to frighten me.

Then the trumpets blew, the drums rolled, and we swept onwards, the Fleet strung out ahead and behind us. The Gunner explained coolly that we had taken our place in the Line, and we would come about and deliver our broadside, well within the range of the Ostend guns. Despite the pounding of the guns ahead, I felt wonderfully brave. Then the ship before us was badly hit, the screaming of her men sounding clear over the water.

The Gunner ordered the gunports opened, and we pushed the massive guns so their muzzles were well out, and tied the breeching so the recoil would not kill us. Then the Gunner ordered me amidships to the powder room. I carefully filled my first small bucket with the heavy black grains and fitted the lid, and then ran to stow it by my gun.

Then, as the great guns of Ostend blasted about us, the Gunner muttered a quick prayer to Saint Barbara for all our souls, and we answered 'Amen' with all our hearts.

Then the Second Mate screeched as the plumb-line dropped to no more than five fathoms, the Captain bellowed the order to come about, and ready the starboard guns for our broadside. Through the large, square gunport, I saw the beauty of the sunlight on the waves, and found my courage no greater than my fear. My guncrew pulled the caps off the touchholes, poured powder onto the cartridges in the guns, and when we heard the trumpet blow the war cry, the Gunner signalled, and one by one, our own guns finally answered the Ostend batteries. Each explosion shook the mighty Dreadnought in the water, thick smoke billowing about us, until it was our guncrew's turn to fire.

I covered my ears against the blast, and then heard the Captain bellow the order to come about, and ready the port guns. Every other ship had fired only one broadside, and the Gunner cursed him for a cold bastard, which was the first time I'd ever heard that surly giant mutinous. He then shouted at us to ready the port guns, and fast. Yet the breeze would only bring us about slowly, leaving us entirely exposed to the Ostend guns.

"Damn him and his murderous ambition!", one of the men moaned, and the Gunner struck him across the face and threw him at his guncrew.

I dashed off for more powder as my guncrew moved to port, glad of my set task amidst the smoke and terror. As I grabbed a bucket of powder, a great crash sent the whole ship reeling, and when I staggered from amidships, it was to find that a cannonball had smashed through the deck, sending murderous splinters into my guncrew. Two men were grievously wounded, one mortally, for his leg was quite broke in two, and the blood was pumping from him freshly red. A sharp elbow to my ribs set me running to help drop the wounded men into the hold below us, where the surgeon's mates laid them on sails. Sailors insisted that each

123

man wounded must be attended to in turn, regardless of rank, and I knew that by the time the surgeon saw him, the man with the busted leg would be dead.

Then I was too busy tamping and loading, desperately trying to remember the entire gun drill, cursing myself for not having paid attention to any but my part in it. I could see nothing of our course, for smoke still poured out our gunports, and I badly wanted to run, yet knew I was doubly trapped, for we were still creeping about, our sails luffing. Then they filled, the ship turned broadside on, and the Captain bellowed his orders. "Take your aim Gunner! We sail when the last gun is fired!"

The Gunner laid his bearded face on the cool barrel of the first port gun, one eye closed, an arm raised in the smoky hold, and then he yelled, the gun blasted, and he was already at the next one. Our rate of fire must have been the fastest in the English Navy that day. We fired our gun, and as the blast sent us reeling, a terrified boy came staggering out of the thick, black smoke. An Officer slapped him and threw him back at his crew, and then drew his pistol and roared that the next man leaving his post would be shot.

Then it was over, though my ears were ringing so badly, I could hardly hear the cheers of my mates. I laughed and wept to find the survivors of my guncrew clapping me on the back, the Gunner praising us all for our steady courage. The hatches were unbolted, and as we poured on deck, the Captain and his officers saluted us from the quarterdeck. Bill leapt forward with the rest of our mates, pounding me on the back, delighted to see me safe. I knew then that, noble or beggar, we were all at sea together, death as likely to take one as another. The Dreadnought was nought but a rotting hulk of wood without our united courage, and all, from cabin boy to Captain, felt it strong and sweet that day.

The Dreadnought swept out of her pall of smoke, and then we could see the terrible damage done to her, the mizzenmast down, the foremast badly hit, and the rigging in shreds. We stood off with the rest of the Fleet, the Captain ordering the readying of the guns and the powder returned to the armoury, before Old Tom took charge of repair crews.

We anchored on dusk, with strict instructions to keep our eyes open for French boats breaking the blockade. When we gathered about the mainmast to give thanks for our preservation, I could clearly see the damage done to the fortress, for there were great rents in the walls. One of her batteries had fallen silent, and I soon understood that this was down to us.

In the last of the evening light, the Captain returned from the Flagship seething with anger. I fetched a hot dinner for him from the Cook, and he ate while his Officers made their reports. Then he poured rum for himself and the First Mate, and told him he'd been severely reprimanded for risking the Dreadnought. The First Mate declared he'd made them all look like damned women, and they drank damnation to cowards. When the bottles were empty and the First Mate had left, the Captain fell onto his bed in his clothes, dead drunk. I pulled his boots off without waking him, and threw a blanket over him against the chill of the night.

Yet the moans of the wounded men and the hellish reek of gunpowder made it impossible for me to sleep in our cramped kennel. Bill finally growled at me to get out, and I made my way out into the cool sea air, to find the Second Mate's watch asleep on deck, to escape the ship's stink. I slipped quietly between the sleeping men, climbed the ratlines as far as I could, and watched the fires of Ostend burning. And then I had to admit to myself that I had always thought the choice was death or glory, and I had never considered the screaming and the stench of hot blood.

Though it was the clean air I craved, the cries of the wounded soon drew me back into the stink of the hold, partly to see if I could do anything to help them, yet also to face the truth of my first battle at sea. One man from my guncrew was already wrapped in torn sailcloth. The other had half his face in a bloody bandage, and though pale as death, he was conscious.

"Can I get you anything?", I asked him softly.

"Not unless ye can fetch me back me eye", he rasped. "I'll be wearin' a black patch for the rest o' me days. I hope me girl likes it. 'Tis seven shillings a week and the pest-ridden hospital at Rochester for me for a time. Yet, oh God, the pain!"

"I'll see if I can find you rum." I knew through the gossip of the ship's boys, that the surgeon had drunk himself into a stupor that night. With most of the men on deck, I guessed 'twould be an easy thing to creep into his cabin. I found him snoring, reeking of blood and rum, a half empty bottle clutched in his hand. I gently pulled the bottle from him, took a swig myself, and hiding it awkwardly under my shirt, I returned to the wounded sailor. He gulped the hot liquid greedily, draining what was left, and then sighed, blessed me, and slept.

Soon after, the whistle blew for the change of watch, and I helped bring down the topsails. We were given a grand breakfast, and then, after a short prayer, the dead men went into the sea. Then the Purser auctioned their clothes before the mast, the proceeds intended for their widows. I bought a thick wool coat for two shillings, for I had great need of it, yet it always felt strange to me to wear it.

The Dreadnought was too badly damaged to sail in again, and we set to repairing her, the men gossiping over the Captain's double broadside, and arguing whether the Admiralty would promote him, court martial him, or ignore him. The bombardment of Ostend continued all that day, many ships being hit in the return fire from the fortress, and I saw flames aboard one.

The next day, the return fire from the fortress grew less as their batteries were wiped out, and upon the following dawn, the land forces attacked. For us, all seemed over, some ships leaving on convoying missions, or returning to England, the rest of us crowding the decks to

126

watch the lines of soldiers descend on the outworks of the fortress.

Then it was over, Ostend taken, and the Duke of Marlborough had the port he wanted, and open communications with England. The French walked out of Ostend with honours accorded them, this being the usual bargain struck when a fortress was ceded. The Spaniards from the garrison declared themselves for Charles the Third, the Allied contender for the coveted Spanish Crown. As soon as Ostend was taken, fifteen sail of transports came in from England, full of stores and reinforcements for the Duke of Marlborough, and I told myself that our suffering was the price we paid for the liberty of Europe.

Chapter 8: Cabin Boy

The Fleet continued to break up, the weather worsened, and the men grumbled to share our beer with ships that had lost stores during the siege. As soon as Old Tom had the Dreadnought seaworthy, we set sail for Hollesley Bay, and I was set to polishing the Captain's brass. Though I had learnt a little of the price paid for glory, 'twas still tedious to return to such mundane chores.

The next day dawned in thick, squally weather. Old Tom insisted on having a detail of boys to caulk leaks, and he kept us at it even when the grey dampness turned to drizzle, and we shook with the cold. At the end of our watch, Bill and I fell into our kennel, half dead but for Pete cadging hot water off the Cook, and mixing our dinner in it to make a sort of soup. We had just sunk into a miserable sleep, our skinny limbs huddled up together for warmth, when we felt the rhythm of the Dreadnought change. I tried desperately to sleep, yet there was something of battle in the way the great ship flung herself at the sea, only to be thrown back. It was almost a relief to hear the Boatswain's whistle, and the fear in his cry: "Up every hand nimbly or we perish!"

Bill, a sailor to the bone, scrambled up as soon as I did. We emerged on deck into a howling gale, and the First Mate immediately grabbed us and thrust us at the mainmast. "Furl the topsails, and nimbly you bloody monkeys. She's over-canvassed and could roll us all under!" And up the ratlines we scrambled into the merciless teeth of the wind. As we edged our blue toes out onto the footropes strung below the yards, the helmsman edged the Dreadnought away from the wind, the frozen sails luffed and showered us with ice, and we grabbed fistfuls of the cold canvas, hugging it to us as we lashed it to the yard. And all over the Dreadnought's top rigging, boys were fighting sail and wind, and praying for their lives.

By the time we had furled the topsails, Bill was blue

beside me, and I had to prise his icy fingers from the yard, and help him down the ratlines. He was slow, and in the cold gale I was freezing fast, yet when we'd come only halfway down, he stopped, and began talking to his dead mama. I screamed into his pale face that if he didn't keep going, he'd kill us both. He smiled. And then he let go. I tried desperately to hold him, yet he slipped from my numb fingers. I heard the dull thud as he hit the deck. Then, as my own strength left me, strong hands grabbed me and swung me down to the deck, saving my sorry life.

Pete told me later that the sailors had leapt up the ratlines as soon as they saw us in trouble, and what had seemed an eternity was over in moments. I blamed myself then for not hanging onto my friend a second longer. The First Mate picked me up, and heaved me below, out of the way of the great seas that were washing over the deck. I crawled to my kennel, and lay there, shaking with the Demons that urged me to follow my friend overboard.

I heard the Captain bellow for all sails and yardarms down, and ignored him. Soon after the lookout screamed. "Land! Land ho! Three leagues to leeward." Terror sent us all running, and we threw out all the storm anchors we had, the waves beating us towards the cliffs, the winds howling through our empty shrouds.. Towards morning, the wind eased and came around, and we were safe.

Then the Boatswain tied a cannon ball around Bill's thin white ankle, and with a short prayer from the Captain, he was tipped into the cold gray sea. My mind broke, and I thought to leap after him and save him, yet the First Mate's sudden grip on my shoulder held me. I knew then that he too had seen a comrade go over a corpse, and wondered if Bill's death was a burden on his conscience, as well as on my own. The men who'd bared their heads in the icy wind gave me awkward nods of sympathy, for they too had little in the world, and they valued a mate above all. Even the Captain tried to convey, in gruff, halting phrases, his awareness of Bill Search's death, and my loss.

I stood all my watches in the tops as lookout, my eye on the exact rung of the ratlines where I'd let my friend slip. Pete found me there, and talking gaily of how brave Bill had been, he produced a flask of rum with a flourish, and insisted on my drinking it in token of a wake. Knowing how much he loved the stuff, I had to thank him and drink it. It burned through my frozen soul, and then I wept for my friend's senseless death, and my own useless life. The next day, Old Tom found me secluded in a corner of the cable tier, and told me that as half the ship's boys perished every year, I was no more guilty of their deaths than the wind.

Storms set in until the end of June, and we sheltered off Harwich, our squadron re-provisioning and gathering the convoy for the Baltic. Pete, burning with ambition now he'd made able seaman and earned fourteen shillings a month, complained that the battles were over for the season, and so were the chances of promotion.

The Gunner had us practice our drills while we waited for the merchant ships, and flattered me by having me show my skill with the rapier again. A few of the boys sneered at me for pretending to be a gentleman, yet I merely shrugged and said I was simply so quick with it, it seemed a pity to lay it aside, and they could only agree with me.

In mid-July, we weighed with our squadron, and made our way down to Yarmouth to convoy the trade towards the Baltic. We were approaching the Dogger bank when squalls came blowing up from the south, forcing our Fleet to turn their bows into the wind, to ride it out, The seas swelled until the Dreadnought seemed but a cork tossed upon them, the great waves as high as our mainmast and smashing in through ports and hatchways. We manned the pumps day and night, no one spared this duty but the Officers. Yet even when the torture of a whole watch of continual pumping was over, it was impossible to sleep, for fear that she'd broach and sink. And she leaked to soak us all, even the Captain, beds, blankets, and belongings. The Cook was unable to keep the fire going, we ate cold peas and raw fish, and while the healthy sickened, the sick died.

As soon as the gale slackened and the Fleet had gathered, we made for the Baltic again, though Old Tom swore the wind had not finished with us yet, and was but coming round. Days later we sighted the south coast of Norway, and rounded the Skaw of Jutland into the welcome calm of the Kattegat. Hearing from a fishing smack that there were two French men o' war sheltering in the Swedish port of Gothenburg, our squadron made plans to take them. Yet icy gales swept down upon us again, pushing us south despite our bare poles. I was taking the Captain his dinner, when I heard the lookout: "Captain! Rocks dead ahead!" We heaved all our anchors over, and prayed they'd hold us, yet as the sun rose on a hard, grey morning, we found ourselves on the edge of the Needles, with not another ship in sight. The Chaplain led us all in a hurried morning prayer, and the wind died, and then changed. Blessing God, the pressed men set to the capstan to haul up the anchors. The best bow anchor had snagged so badly, that the Captain saw nothing for it but to bear the shame and cut her away, for if the wind changed again, we were lost.

We gathered our scattered Fleet, and the wind finally dropped as we drifted past the great port of Kobenhavn. We anchored off Halsingborg, the merchant ships continuing through the Strait, into the Baltic Sea, our guard duty done. The Captain sent the First Mate ashore to scout about for a storm anchor, then, as the weather promised fine, he ordered the wet and stinking Dreadnought to be scrubbed. We opened all the gunports and rigged up wind-sails in the hatchways, brushed the decks with vinegar and sand, sluiced them down and scraped them, drying it all with swabs and firepots. Yet no matter how we swabbed, the ship still leaked, and all would soon be filthy and damp again, causing the cramps and catarrh that plagued sailors. As for the stench! The scurvy was blamed on it, all the ship's refuse being swept into the bilges, to breed pestilence and vermin, and I was glad I did not have to live down there with the rest of

131

the crew.

The next day we moored at Halsingborg to pull aboard a four ton anchor. I gazed my fill at a pretty Swedish fishing village set in the most rugged coastline. The sturdy people suited the place, and I understood the strength of the armies of the Swedish King, and why both the Allies and the French were anxious not to offend that warlord.

Then we were placed on short allowance of all food, so that what had starved four, must now serve six. Our stores were sea-washed and our meat maggoty, yet this was our fare until we returned home. At first I refused it, sharing it between my appreciative messmates. Then hunger won, and I forced it down. We were promised extra pay for being on short allowance, yet sickened at such a rate, that the Navy was relieved of many of the eight shilling debts.

Our squadron sailed north to Gothenburg to search for the French warships, yet squalls struck again, and we pulled our yards and topmasts in, the wind plucking hard at those of us scrambling in the rigging. When the weather dropped, we tried to run our convoy out of Gothenburg, yet were soon chased back in again, leaving the Dragon on a rock in twelve foot of water, waiting for the next high tide to lift her off, our Captain cursing, and our men dying.

In Gothenburg, it rained for nearly two weeks. On the third day, the Captain announced that he was letting all but a skeleton crew go ashore. Our crew scrubbed their working clothes, hanging about bashfully in blankets while their mates dried their trousers over the Cook's fire. Those with shore-going gear donned red Monmouth caps, checked shirts, buckled shoes and bright waistcoats, so all might know them for English tars.

I had the dead sailor's coat , and I craved to go ashore, dreaming of warm stew. As soon as I put a foot on shore, the nauseous fluttering that had plagued my stomach eased, though my head turned about strangely. Our crew headed for the nearest tavern, and though Pete urged me to join them, I told him I'd no intention of wasting my shillings on rum. In

132

truth, drunkenness horrified me, and I feared the sharp eyes of the whores.

I walked about the port in the rain, trying to work up the courage to buy food from foreigners. Finally, made brave by cold and hunger, I pushed into a busy pie shop. The locals dropped into silence as I walked in, and I could think of nought but retreat or bravado, so I gave them my best bow, and wished them an English good day. The woman behind the counter smiled, and I showed her my coins, and she laughed at my miming, and gave me a meat pie and a bowl of hot chocolate. The smells intoxicated me, and I ate my best meal since leaving London.

I was astonished at the lilting strangeness of the speech about me, the outlandish clothes and the odd food. And as the gnawing of my guts left me, I found myself happy to be away from the Dreadnought, a liberty man on leave in a foreign land. Then I ran through the drizzle to the sailors' tavern, to find Captain Mitchell ready to return to the Dreadnought. The Coxswain's crew merrily rowed the replacement skeleton crew out to the ship, and I watched Gothenburg mist over behind us, and thought it beautiful.

The Swedish pie saved me, for 'twas weeks before we set sail with the convoy, and by then our provisions were indeed scanty. The pressed men whispered mutiny, and I prayed to make some sense of all our suffering. We finally set sail, yet even as the thirty-odd merchant ships struggled out to join us, the weather worsened again.

Two weeks later, we were within sight of Yarmouth, still making our way west, the wind blowing hard, when we saw seven ships flying English colours, hulls heeled out of the water, noses into the wind. Knowing that any English ship in that weather would gladly have made port, we chased them, sure they were privateers from Dunkirk. Sir Edward Whittaker sailed with us as Admiral, displacing the Captain from his cabin, and me from my kennel, and creating a vast friction with his disdain for all below him. Ambition stirring him to recklessness, he ordered us to cut our longboat away for greater speed. This we resented, for it endangered all our lives to have no boat to escape wreck in, and still there was no sign of privateers the next day.

We made our way through hard gales to Hollesley Bay, where we landed forty-four sick men, the lack of provisions and the hard seas having done for them. After a few days re-loading with fresh food and beer, we continued south through headwinds, all the crew cursing the Captain for the bad weather. And indeed the ship pitched horribly as the great waves smashed into her, leaving her wallowing in each trough, the wind catching our heavy upperworks, the helmsman fighting to bring her bow back into the wind before the next wave broached us.

With six other men o' war, we made for the lee of Canvey Island, close to the Benfleet tar pits. There we went ashore, crowding around smoky fires in dripping huts. We heeled the ship with the tide, tipping her ungainly bulk first on one side and then the other, repairing the rotten planks, caulking and sealing her with stinking black pitch. We were there until mid-October, helping Old Tom repair the damage that the season of foul weather had inflicted on the Dreadnought.

The Gunner had noted my steadiness under fire at the siege of Ostend, and he asked the Captain to let me make seventh man on the eleventh gun on the orlop deck. The Captain grudgingly gave his consent, and I learned to sponge down the gun, put home the shot gently, and realign the gun, all without fumbling. I learnt to keep the linstock, with its smouldering match, well away from the powder bucket, even when leaping out of the way of the recoiling gun. We learnt to make the canvas and powder cartridges that were pushed up the gun's muzzle, the canvas leaving the gun foul at each discharge, so that we had to worm it out. I learned to fill the touch-hole with priming powder, and to thrust the sharp priming-iron down through it, into the cartridge. I learnt to lay a train of powder along the gun from the touchhole to the base-ring, for if I applied the match

134

directly to the touch-hole, the force of the explosion would blow the linstock from my hand, sending the burning match flying.

I learnt that in heavy weather, the lowest gundeck was never used, as the sea might come washing through the open gunports, wetting the powder. As for aiming, the shot bounded down the barrel so wildly, that I could not see how 'twas possible. As they could only be raised ten degrees, or lowered six, one had to await the rising of the Dreadnought on the waves, and anticipate the movement of the enemy ship. The seven of us learned the complicated dance that resulted in a crescendo of murderous thunder, the Gunner demanding four shots an hour off us. We often fired the ship's guns as salutes when in port, yet even when choking on black smoke, I knew that this was nothing compared to battle, and shuddered to remember that horror.

In the Autumn, a hundred pressed men from Her Majesty's ship the Ruby shambled aboard, already fit to follow those who had sickened and died on the last voyage. On the tenth of October, James Ball of the Swallow was court-martialled for buggery and condemned. They hung him that afternoon from the Ruby's yardarm.

The next day William Brown of the Ruby was tried for desertion, yet cleared, and when I told Pete that a man should not hang for not being as brave as he hoped he was, Pete sneered at me for a mere cabin boy. We fought, the ship's boys urging us on, and though he bloodied my nose, I blacked both his eyes. Then the Boatswain swept down on us, and reluctant to punish such useful workers as Pete and I, he grabbed one of the Chaplain's servants, and beat him in our stead. The injustice of it curdled my guts, yet I was too afraid to speak out, and so added the sin of cowardice to the burden of my soul.

At the end of October, we picked up the East Country Fleet from Hollesley Bay, and sailed with it until squalls blew our foretopsail and staysail overboard. We made for Ireland then, and squalls kept us locked in Gorey harbour to freeze for most of November. The Duke of Marlborough sailed in on his way home from Flanders, and in my martial ardour, I was full of frustration to be at sea when the great fight was in Flanders.

I mentioned it to Old Tom once, and he scowled blackly at me. "Are ye so careless o' yer life, boy, that ye'd leave a steady position aboard one o' Her Majesty's ships, for the hard life of a soldier?" In truth I felt my life had little value, and no future, apart from an abject death. I hung my head, and Old Tom sneered at me. "Aye, yer not brave, yer death-hungry. Damn ye boy, ye'll die young, in some feat o' courage that'll make a hero of ye, and for that I cannot help but curse ye for a fool, fer yer life has but started, and every man suffers 'til he reaches Heaven."

The Fleet guarded Marlborough back to the Downs, where we saluted him with twenty-one guns as he landed. Then we waited days for the easterly wind we needed to get us out of the Downs. Soon after, we chased two privateers, yet lost them.

We convoyed the trade to Sweden again, yet were hit hard by squalls as we came past the Skaw light, and in trying to reach the shelter of Marstrand, we were driven amidst the Paternosters. I was high in the ratlines, screaming directions to the First Mate, rocks to port and starboard, and then dead ahead. The wind howled our deaths, the black rocks glistened evil in the spray, and then we struck. The Dreadnought shuddered with the impact, and then she struck again. And even the hardest men dropped to their knees to pray, for we had not replaced our longboat, and would not survive long in the cold waters of the north.

The First Mate screamed for his watch to man the pumps, and I leapt below to see the rats swarming out of her hold. Sure we'd die that night, I set to it with the others, pumping until I thought I'd already drowned and gone to Hell. Yet the Dreadnought's sturdy timbers held, and with the help of our squadron, the Captain brought us off. When we changed watch, we were already within sight of the lights of Marstrand, and I resolved then to find some other way of life than the sea.

We sailed the convoy out of Marstrand with snow on the decks, and men dying at a terrible rate. I had spent my wage on a thick Swedish stew while in port, and though I still had my health, I was shaking with the constant cold. We were sailing south from Scarborough when we struck on a sand bank, and though we came off with little difficulty, Old Tom muttered of a doomed ship and crossed himself. We were all glad to drop anchor in Yarmouth, where we finally bought a ship's boat. The Second Mate came aboard with a little dog that the sailors made much of. I avoided becoming fond of it, though it had the most engaging nature, sure it would go overboard in the first storm.

Christmas was a miserable affair, with no roast beef or plum porridge for us. A little bit of Irish beef between four boys, that had lain rusting in pickle for two years, with stinking butter all colours of the rainbow, made four mouthfuls for each man that was not sick or dying.

When we went to unmoor, we found that our new bow anchor had snagged so badly that it had to be cut away, and this seemed the final curse on our voyage. Yet further south, the Pilot mistook the channel, and ran over a shoal, there not being more than two feet of water under our keel. Old Tom whispered that we must throw a boy over to appease the sea, and I shuddered and moved away. We got through at high tide, and with a great sense of relief, anchored at Blackstakes in the Chatham River.

The sick men were carried ashore by their mates, and fresh provisions came aboard. We ate fresh pork and peas for the first time in many months, yet when the Captain threw me an apple from his own store, I left a tooth in it. He laughed at my dismay, and told me to eat better to avoid the scurvy. I had to stand hard on my tongue then, to save myself a beating. The next day we took out all the lower guns, and there were few enough sound hands to drag the capstan around. Then we existed on petty warrant victuals, which were worse than when at sea, and many swore they'd carry the Purser before the commissioners, to get the pay he owed us for suffering short rations.

The great ships were sent up the Chatham to Winter, and when we had moored her below the Castle, the Captain finally saw his duty done. He asked me if I'd return in the Spring, and I lied, and assured him I thought of no other post. He wrote me out a ticket for the rest of my wages, and another to keep me clear of the press gang, and then offered me a ride in the ship's boat, back up the Thames to London. I thought he had grown fond of me, yet instead he spent the first afternoon telling me of how I could be of further use.

Since Bill's death, the Captain and the Second Mate had shared a servant betwixt them, the Second Mate considering himself such a fine gentleman, that the two allowed him was not enough. Being but a little boy, this servant could not be entered upon the ship's account without the Captain's consent, and now the Captain expected the greater part of his wages for this favour. The boy was to be paid the day before me, and the Captain ordered me to go into the Pay Office, and answer to the boy's name. I could see no choice but to agree, for I had no other master, and so I went with them to the Navy Office, and wrote down the boy's name instead of my own. The dandified Second Mate was at the gate to meet me, and he and the Captain shared the money, with a shilling for me, and sixpence for the boy. He blubbered that his father would beat him if he brought home nothing more, yet the Second Mate stated airily that he was too young to earn a man's wage, though we all knew he had done a man's work for it. Yet I did not share my shilling with him, and was glad to return the next day, in better clothes, with my hair brushed back, to claim my own meagre wages.

Then full of my adventures, I made my way to Covent Garden to search for Sally. I found her at the Queen's Head Tavern, newly built upon the foundations of old Bedford House. She almost didn't recognise me, so much had I grown, and she hugged me, and waved away my lowly boasts, stating that London had lost any enthusiasm for military affairs, for the war had gone on too long, at too great an expense, for too little reason.

Instead she bragged of having a Dutch merchant besotted with her, and showering her with gold. Yet when we met him that night at the Bedford tavern, he was old, ugly, had little English, and no conversation. Sally saw my disgust, and began laughing at his poor understanding, and refusing to let him touch her. As he was paying, we were soon drunk, and Sally started treating him vilely, throwing bits of bread at him when he wasn't looking, and hanging on my arm in order to make him jealous. Around midnight, he started insisting on her attention, and pulled her into his lap. "Damn you and your broken tongue!", she screamed. "How can I love rotten teeth and stinking fifty?", and she emptied her beer over his head. I burst out laughing to see his face, and he stormed off, leaving us with the bill to pay.

Sally pulled out her purse, and when I saw how much gold she had, I advised her to save what she had, and find some other way of making a living. She threw down enough coins to cover the bill, and swept out, angry again.

The next day, she introduced me to a young black woman called Jenny, who'd been bought as a slave in Barbados, and abandoned in London without a penny. Sally had found her freezing in Saint James Park, and introduced her to her own bawd, and 'though there were enough black whores of both sexes starving in the streets of London, she had taken the bawd's fancy. She was now a slave again, and I could see that it soured her. Yet she had found herself a young Jew who visited her three times a week, including Sundays, for their holy day was on Saturday.

I met him, and he was gentle, not a great drinker, and though he carried a sword, he had no idea what to do with it. He told me his father had sailed from Holland when Dutch King William declared England a haven from the persecution of the Spanish inquisition. The Jews had set up the Bank of England, thus financing the war, and the Tories had vilified them as war-profiteers. Some had grown wealthy, but most lived meagrely in the cities, land denied them, though there were more than four thousand in England.

Sure that I'd not be recognised as the boy who'd killed the Army Officer at the half Moon tavern, I took a room in the Bermudas near my old friend the Army Captain, and helped with tutoring his new pupils in swordsmanship. He knew all the military news, and regaled me with the details of Marlborough's last campaign. After Ostend, Marlborough had taken Menin, with Lord Orkney's infantry taking the counterscarp and the brunt of the battle. Dendermonde had fallen next, yet only because of a freak seven week drought that broke the day after the place was taken, proving to the Allies that God was with them. Yet despite these great successes, the Army was in an uproar of scandal, with Marlborough's favourite, Cadogan, accused of jealously pulling Orkney's regiment back from victory at Ramillies, though Marlborough himself insisted that Orkney had not seen the French cavalry sweeping down upon him.

Sally was so determined to avoid my reproaches, it took me some time to find her alone. Finally, I insisted she meet me at her grandparents' lodgings, and asked her news of my mother. She told me she had not heard of her, but that my aunt had taken a deposition out against her.

Then she told me that my grandmother was dead. On her way back from Christmas Mass, the old lady's yearly foray out of her great house, her carriage had been waylaid by a gang of aristocratic hooligans. They had declared her too old for their usual abuse, and instead had bundled her into an empty beer barrel and rolled her through the streets of Covent Garden. Ashley had scoured the streets looking for her, and had found her at dawn, already dying.

This was enough to disgust me with London entirely, and with the worst of the Winter over, I bid the Army Captain farewell, took the few shillings I'd made teaching swordsmanship, and walked to Wapping. There I bought a

140

small sea chest and a change of clothes, and at the Hermitage Stairs, found a hoy laden with beer going as far as Chatham. We passed men on rafts and dories, unloading ships that were moored together mid-river, and after five days of bad weather, entered the Medway.

I was glad enough to see the Dreadnought's imposing bulk against the grey sky. Surely, I had no other home in the world. I could tell Captain Mitchell was pleased to see me, though he did not say much. I made a formal request then to be made an able seaman, and he coldly refused me, stating that none kept his cabin as well as I did, and if I slacked, I'd taste leather for it. I had the good sense to say nought, yet could not forgive him for denying me my chance of promotion.

Yet when I complained to the ship's boys, Pete's sneered at me for being the Captain's bumboy. I pulled my knife and told him I'd once killed a man for an insult, and that if I heard it again, I'd gladly go overboard tied to his corpse. He sniggered, and Old Tom saved us by slapping Pete with a backhand like a plank.

Chapter 9: King James the Third

We did not set sail with the convoy until early March, and by then I was already sated with the drudgery of ship life. Off Hollesley Bay, we saw a hundred and forty transport ships bound to Ostend and the war, and I thought on all that the Army Captain had told me of life as a soldier. Off Ostend, we chased a privateer, yet lost sight of her when our main topmast came crashing to the deck, shrouds awry. We convoyed the trade back to England without incident, and then stood for the privateer's nest of Dunkirk, where our squadron's boats sailed in close, and counted their shipping. The next day they chased four small French coastal vessels, and took them and their provisions. Pete was involved in this action, and felt it a great injustice when he was not immediately promoted.

I thought there might be more excitement when, at the end of May, Admiral Whetstone hoisted his white flag at the mizzen topmasthead on board the Dreadnought, taking the Captain's cabin for his own, and sending me to sleep with the rats. We sailed with the Fleet for Ireland, and almost immediately, a great storm broke with thunder and lightening and squalls of rain. Just as the sun fell, we saw a Fleet of ships to the east. Sure they were privateers, we saw the merchantmen safe into Gorey, and then made the signal for the Line. As the sun rose the next morning, we had our guns loaded, yet 'twas only a Dutch squadron. We returned to Dunkirk to keep an eye on the privateers, and then made our way back to the Downs.

In mid June, we spied three privateers in the Channel, and took up the chase, and though two of the privateers were captured, the Dreadnought was too slow to see action. Soon after, we spoke with a Scots man o' war, who told us there were fourteen foreign ships north-east of Scotland. In clear weather, we sailed for Fair Isle, where we divided the Fleet, the Dreadnought sailing south. We chased a Fleet of privateers close to taking a small galley, yet they fled when they saw us, and we could not catch them.

Then in early July, in stormy weather, we finally saw battle with privateers, yet though the squadron took five prizes, the Dreadnought sprung her maintopmast again, and Captain Mitchell bore us away rather than risk capture. For me it was the final disappointment. The only possible recompense for our hard life was promotion and bounty money, and I seemed to be denied both.

In Hollesley Bay we heeled the ship, and conducted the court martial for the Boatswain of the Worcester, the charges of sodomy being dismissed for lack of evidence, yet the man disgraced nonetheless. In August we convoyed the Baltic trade to Sweden again, and again ran into storms. In Jutland, we scraped the Dreadnought's sides, pumped the water out of her, and continued with the merchants, back to Gothenburg. There I ate as much as I could afford, knowing that my life depended on finding sustenance other than that of the Navy. Pete spent his money on rum, and his first dose of pox from an old Swedish whore.

Returning to England in September, the squadron chased and lost two privateers. Two days later, we saw thirteen sails, and made the signal for the Line. Yet the next day, when we bore down on them, they again turned out to be Dutch Men o' War. Their Captain brought news of the war, however, and pouring him wine, I heard that the French had broken through to the German states, and that the Austrian empire was too absorbed in its civil war against the Hungarians to help. Our Austrian commander, Prince Eugene, had destroyed the French Fleet in the Mediterranean, yet was being blamed for failing to take some port. The French and Allied armies had sat within a few miles of each other all Summer, without a battle, much to the disgust of the rest of Europe. Both Captains blamed the cowardice of the Dutch Generals. King Charles of Sweden had decided against attacking either Austria or Germany, which would have destroyed the union of the Allies, and had instead marched east into Russia, and been swallowed up by the snow.

The Dreadnought returned home in fair weather, and we moored in the Rowling Ground for repairs. The weather turned foul at the end of September, yet the squadron headed north, making the Shetlands. There a Danish Captain hailed us, and despite the wind, rowed over in a cockleshell of a boat. We hoisted him aboard, and he bowed to our Captain, and told him terrible news. The English squadron that had sunk the French Mediterranean Fleet had struck the Scilly Islands, and seven hundred men were lost, including Admiral Shovell. Captain Mitchell thanked the Dane for his courtesy in bringing us news of the tragedy, and gave him a bottle of his best Madeira.

That evening, while they worked out the dead reckoning and the course, the Captain and the First Mate discussed the implications. "This will give the Whigs the ammunition against the Admiralty that they've been waiting for", the Captain observed gloomily. "They'll drag Prince George's name through the mud, and that of George Churchill. They've already been accused of making their fortunes from the Admiralty, without protecting the Trade."

"If one wasn't the Queen's husband, and the other Marlborough's brother, the embezzlement would be ignored", the First Mate stated flatly. "That we spend not enough time convoying Trade is a foolish accusation, for we are battle ships, and there is a war on. The merchants may be suffering, yet, damn their eyes, they are suffering less than those who are fighting, and would suffer more if the French invade us."

"Aye, they complain of the war, as though we had any choice in the matter. Better to sail for France, and rap the French King's knuckles", and they laughed and toasted damnation to the French.

In late September, we chased five sails to the north-west in squally weather, yet they turned out to belong to the Russian Fleet. Soon after, we saw two sails to the South, yet these were merely Russian flyboats lost from the convoy.

144

Fog descended, and we lay by with our head in the wind, with hardly a glimpse of any of our ships.

Visibility dropped, and Old Tom swore bad weather was coming, and begged the First Mate to double the lines. An hour later, the storm hit us. The Dreadnought's huge bulk heeled out of the water, four of our main shrouds snapped, and the full length of the mainmast went crashing to starboard. The weight of the timber and sails pulled the great hull further over, and water poured in through the gunports, sending the ship's boys shrieking for the upper deck. The Captain stood firm, directing the strongest to cut the mast away and heave it overboard, and the pressed men to man the pumps.

The main yardarm had gone over with the mast, and our spare main topmast too, and yet the seas grew greater every hour. We had our mizzen whole, and with this we kept the Dreadnought's head to the wind and waves, the great rolling swell pushing us south. When the mizzen gave way, the Captain ordered all sail crowded on the foresail, until the foresail shrouds snapped. We were in desperate straits then, yet still with our squadron, and the Montague came close enough for us to take her main topmast, both ships crunching together with the sea. Old Tom set a jury mast once the winds lessened somewhat, and soon had every spar in the ship lashed together and holding sail. Then gales struck again, and we furled our jury sail for fear of losing all.

We limped into Edinburgh in time to fire fifteen guns for Guy Fawkes Day, counting off our rate of fire against every other ship in the harbour. Then we made our repairs as best we could, and headed south, round Saint Abb's Head in hard gales, to the Nore. At midnight, the lookout hollered, and we turned out to see one of the Russian ships in our convoy on fire. She burned in the water, a terrible sight, her men leaping overboard to be picked up by other ship's boats. We all watched as the flaming ship settled in the water, and then sank, smoke billowing out of her. Old Tom muttered a prayer for her soul into the cold Winter wind, and though the

145

Chaplain prated of blasphemy, I saw the Captain cross himself.

We put into Blackstakes in December, and there was much for Captain Mitchell to do, supervising the repairs to his ship. I tended him as carefully as I had ever done, yet when I asked him again if he'd make me an able seaman, he grunted that there were sailors enough, yet few he could tolerate to have about him. I knew then that I would never rise as a sailor, and though I loved the Dreadnought, and admired the Captain, life at sea seemed great periods of starvation broken by terrible fear of drowning, and all of it too far away from the real struggle that was taking place in Flanders.

When I returned to London, I rolled into the Half Moon Tavern in Navy garb, sure none would recognise the murderous lad from two years ago, so tall and broad-shouldered had ship work made me, though in truth I was skinny enough. My old friend the Army Captain was at his usual table, and I bespoke an ale and a pie, and told him that I intended to desert the Navy, to go fighting under Marlborough. He tried earnestly to dissuade me, speaking of the disastrous campaign of the year just gone, of the great slaughter of men, and of the much greater chance of death and maiming. He reminded me of the good position I had, and how lucky I was in my master. I told him that my next birthday would see me turn sixteen, and I would grab whatever opportunity presented itself to enlist, quitting the Navy and saving my life.

He thought for an instant, and asked me if I'd had much sword practice. I answered that I'd been coaching the ship's boys, and he grinned and offered me my old position as assistant tutor, and hinted at making it permanent. "Are you so swamped with students, then?", I asked him.

"Aye, more than I want, for, in truth Mark, I've a love affair with a rich and pretty widow taking up most of my time of late. If she'll marry me, I may expand my small business, perhaps even needing a partner."

"She must be a pearl indeed to have you considering marriage", I teased him.

"I'd have a fondness for her if she wasn't rich", he sighed, "yet since she is, marriage it must be."

"A rich woman doesn't need the security of a marriage, a poor woman does."

"Aye, and a poor man must make a great show in the world if he courts an heiress. Yet they all need love, boy, and a lad as good-looking as yourself..."

"Me?"

"Aye lad, you've the skin of a woman, and the eyes of a poet. If ye dressed well..."

"I'd rather earn my bread with swordsmanship."

"You speak like a virgin", he scoffed, yet when I blushed he kindly forbore teasing me, and renewed his offer of work. We settled terms, and he offered me the use of his bed, since he was not often using it these nights. I laughed, accepted, and wished him luck in bringing the lady to a reasonable settlement.

I asked after Sally, and he directed me to an elegant house in the heart of Covent Garden. My heart sinking, I rapped on the door, and a uniformed flunky showed me into an overly-decorated drawing room, where Sally soon joined me. To my grief, she boasted that she had become a raging success, and was rich enough to keep me ashore if I wanted. Taking sharp aim at the nobility, she had announced that her resemblance to the notorious Lady Salisbury was too marked to be ignored, and claimed to be the Lady's natural daughter. As Sally Salisbury, she had joined the infamous Mother Whybourne, who taught her highborn manners and introduced her to the gentry. The combination of her white-gold beauty and her mocking laugh earned her the attention of the ageing Lord Bentinck. Soon tired of him, she had publicly vowed to follow in Lady Salisbury's footsteps, and befriend only the handsomest and wittiest of men. When the ambitious Viscount Bolingbroke laid himself languidly at her feet, she became the toast of the town, and thus an

147

orange girl was allowed to give the final cachet to the blades of the nobility.

I sat at Sally's dressing table, surrounded by gentlemen and Lords who glared at me while she powdered and preened, and made witty remarks. When I muttered that a few months of glory would be the most she could expect, she laughed at me. "If 'tis a whore I must be, then I'll be the best whore London's ever seen. They'll never forget me." I asked her if she wanted to be infamous for whoring, and she smiled sweetly and told me that I was nought but the pretence of a man, and a liar, while she accepted the farce of being a woman, and would make the best of it.

I could but shrug, and she made the most of her advantage, and asked me to meet her at the Rose Tavern that night. I baulked, demanding to know how she could set foot in that Hellhole. She waved her white hand elegantly, and said that all the wits went there, and they would be expecting her, as she was the wittiest of them all. I cruelly asked if she'd seen Colonel Honeywood lately, and she answered coolly that she mixed with much higher company than that now. She boasted that the ageing Matthew Prior, the poet, wanted to marry her, and I urged her to accept. Calling me a simpleton, she told me she'd be a duchess yet. I resolved to break with her then, and told her that this kind of success was what she had settled for, not what she had dreamed of. She smiled sweetly, and agreed with me, and then I did indeed feel like a churlish oaf, and begged her pardon.

I spent my time going about the taverns and coffee-shops with her, listening to the gossip and intrigue, the rumours and half-truths. In Covent Garden, the Duke of Bedford had finished re-building his estate, and of the fourteen new houses that had replaced the old wall, now called Tavistock Row, all were brothels. The Duke had newly filled the market place with potters, tinsmiths, basket-weavers, cutlers, knife-grinders, coopers and carpenters, as well as the usual fruit, flower and vegetable sellers, and the

148

din and bustle was terrible.

I visited Old Jonas, the coachman at the Lord Blakeney's Head, and he told me that Mordington had been thrown into the Fleet Prison for debt, and had been forced to petition the Queen for release, on the grounds that he was a peer of the realm. Then Peter Dillon had denied him the gambling tables, and he'd disappeared. Mary had been convinced that he'd thrown himself in the river, only to hear weeks later that he'd married the daughter of a respectable clergyman. Mary refused to sue him for bigamy, claiming that her marriage was done in a marriage shop, not a church, and meant nothing in the eyes of God. Her brother was coming down hard on her, first for marrying the ne'er-do-well, and then for not blackmailing him, and Jonas scowled that she'd end it in the Thames for sure, for she had a babe coming. On my way out, I saw her staring from a window, a ghost of the bonny woman she'd once been.

The London gossips were calling our good Queen 'Brandy Nan', for 'twas said she'd taken to drink. Sally said that after seventeen failed pregnancies, she deserved to get as drunk as she wished, and pointed out that no King had ever been abused for sottishness, not even Old King Harry. The Union of Scotland and England had taken place last May, the Scots claiming that their merchants had sold Scotland to the English, in fear of a blockade. They mourned the short-lived Scottish parliament, and sang scurrilous ditties of their Crown being used as a can for Brandy Nan to piss in when she's tipsy.

The Jacobites were openly hoping that their exiled Prince might be restored to the English Crown. Our Queen's sympathy for her Catholic half-brother was well-known, as he stood nearer the throne than she did, being the eldest of James the Second's sons, not the youngest of his daughters. In my heart, I too championed the young man the Whigs called 'The Pretender', and the Jacobites 'James the Third'. He was only four years older than I, and his birth too had been a disaster, leading to accusations of illegitimacy, and triggering Dutch William's invasion, so desperate had the people been to escape Catholic rule.

The Army Captain shook his head to remember old King James fleeing England with his young wife and baby son. Despite his reputation for courage, the King had run again at the Battle of the Boyne two years later, broken-hearted at the betrayal of his beloved daughters, one of them once married to Dutch William, the other now our Queen. Dutch William had lived long enough to declare war on France in the name of England, and Queen Anne had begun her reign with a divided Parliament, and a war-starved country, vowing to rule for her people. Lord Marlborough, already known for his military talents, had gained Anne's friendship by turning on her father, and supporting the Revolution, and 'twas said that he ruled the Queen, while being ruled himself by his beautiful and imposing wife, Sara Churchill.

On ascending to the throne, our Queen had promised to make the German grandchildren of Old King Charles her heirs, as they too were Protestants. Now everyone in London seemed to be plotting the return of the young King over the water, including, it was rumoured, our hard working, brandy-drinking Queen. All prayed that young Jamie would give up his Catholicism for England, yet he insisted on maintaining his faith, his constancy only making him more popular with half the mob, and more hated by the rest. Then rumours flew that he was sailing over, to declare himself King in Scotland, and march on England. Jacobites were arrested all over the country, and the rest rushed off to France, to join the Pretender's court.

On a cold February night, the Army Captain quarreled with his dear lady, and returned to his own rooms, drunk and brotherly, refusing to let me vacate his bed. In the midst of the night, he turned and put his arm about me, and called me sweetheart, before resuming his snores, and I found myself too confounded to sleep. The following morning, he demanded if that harlot Sally had not broken

150

my heart, hugged me, damned all women as cruel sluts, and finally left me to my turmoil.

I had barely begun to see the swamp I was sunk into, when he came storming back, bellowing for me to dress. A soldier had seen me drinking with Sally, and identified me as the lad who'd killed the Officer in the Half Moon Tavern two years ago. "Grab your seachest and run! The constables are waiting at the end of the street, and that dead fool's Regiment has worked up a mob to carry you to Newgate." We slipped out through a reeking gutter, and threading through the alleyways, we ran for Wapping, where I hastily found a passage down river. My head whirling, I embraced my friend in farewell, told him to kiss Sally for me, and sailed away on the tide. In truth I felt it a great relief to be away from him, and knew Sally would say 'twas the truth I was afraid of. Yet I felt sick at heart to return to the Dreadnought, having failed to reform Sally, and what was worse, with no further news of my mother.

The Dreadnought was at Blackstakes, re-provisioning, and taking on great numbers of pressed men to replace those who had died in the last voyage. As I watched them rowed aboard, their faces sullen and angry, I could see nought but walking corpses.

I had eaten well through the Winter, and I felt my own health to be sturdy enough, for I was not so thin and shaky, and my monthly bleeding had started again. My fears of discovery had lessened, and perhaps I had grown careless, yet I was sure that even if one of the crew could see me naked, he'd rub his eyes, and damn the rum, for they already knew me for a brave, hard-working, earnest young man. They sang ballads of girls running off to sea, yet had a sturdy disbelief in the courage of women. They stated flatly that women were bad luck aboard, and Old Tom told a terrible tale of a woman stowaway being tossed into a storm to save a ship. Yet my friend the Army Captain had unwittingly reminded me that I was not a man, though I hardly felt myself to be a woman either. In truth, I felt myself constantly confounded, now that I was in no danger of discovery.

I found the crew agog with rumours of a Jacobite invasion, and as the other ships of our squadron arrived, we were all sure that battle was at hand. I knew that as a lowly cabin boy, I stood no chance of either promotion or bounty money, yet knew better than to appear ungrateful to Captain Mitchell.

The only recompense was that I heard the Navy news first, while serving the squadron's Officers at table, though I remembered to never repeat a word. Vice Admiral Byng had been promoted to Admiral of the Blue the day before his forty-fifth birthday, making him a man without rivals, younger than both those under him. Captain Mitchell toasted the Treasurer, Lord Godolphin, who had insisted on the promotion of this great sailor, despite his low birth. It shocked me that Marlborough had been trying to promote some friend of his own, and they abused him mightily, until Captain Mitchell led the toast for a Naval victory for England.

He nodded to me to leave them to their wine, yet I saw there was something in the wind, and slipped into my dark kennel to listen. What I heard set my heart pounding. The Captain of the Edinburgh announced that Byng's promotion was due to the French Fleet being assembled for the invasion of Scotland, the Pretender to be the figurehead for a march on London. This would cause civil war, forcing the withdrawal of England from the war with France, ensuring the failure of the Allies, and the end of English trade. And the Pretender was already at Dunkirk, embarking thousands of French soldiers onto twenty-six ships.

The Captain of the Edinburgh said that Sir John Jennings, Vice-Admiral of the Red, was soon expected to join us, to assemble our squadron, and meet Byng's Fleet at Portsmouth. Captain Mitchell bemoaned the Dreadnought's foul bottom, and all the Captains nodded sourly. The French would be clean and fast, while we were caught with our ships' hulls thick with a Winter's growth of seaweed.

The next day, Vice-Admiral Jennings rowed out to the Shrewsbury, the sailors' gossip insisting he'd killed a horse to get to us before the Pretender sailed. He immediately ordered the signal for unmooring, and we leapt for the halyards, feeling the urgency of the Officers, the wild rumours pretty close to the truth for once. Pete pestered me for information, and then cursed me for a close-mouthed cur, yet all talked of the Pretender. There were many fervent Jacobites aboard, and though they all prayed for a King in Scotland, none could stomach the thought of French troops on our soil. And, whatever we felt for the young King, all of us feared civil war in England. As we made our way to the Downs to join the Fleet, Old Tom spoke of the ravages of Cromwell's time, of brother fighting brother, of neglected harvests and famine.

By the twenty-fifth of February, our squadron was in the Downs with the great ships of the English Fleet. Two days later, the elderly Vice-Admiral Jennings hoisted his flag on board the Dreadnought, and took over Captain Mitchell's quarters for a great conference of the Flag Officers. All stood as Admiral Byng joined us, a tall man in an abundant brown wig, who looked sternly down his long nose at his colleagues, and yet smiled kindly when I poured him Captain Mitchell's best wine.

During the War Council, Byng spoke of sending Rear Admiral Baker to keep the French Fleet holed up in Dunkirk. Captain Mitchell growled that any seaman worth his salt knew that the Spring northeasters made a permanent blockade impossible.

Jennings nodded. "'Tis the season for westerly storms. We'd be forced miles to leeward, and the French would have the winds to go where they would." Byng mentioned the Admiralty's plan to sink enough ships in Dunkirk harbour to block it up completely, and his Officers shook their heads and declared the channel too deep and too wide. Jennings stated that only continuing westerly winds

153

would keep the French Fleet at Dunkirk, and to this, they all had to agree.

Noting the growing moroseness, Byng declared the campaign as good as won. "The Fleet is gathered, ready to protect England, and out-numbering the French. The only difficulty is in preventing them landing. The need for fresh intelligence of the French is vital." Jennings declared that the small, clean snow that he had sent to scout the Flemish Road the day before had been chased out. Byng then announced that we would immediately proceed to Dunkirk. We weighed anchor that afternoon, in heavy gales, and by midnight we were off Calais. At noon the day after, we heard the guns fired at Graveline as the Pretender passed through the town. Byng took the Ludlow Castle within two miles of Dunkirk, and counted the twenty-seven sail of the French Fleet. The next day, we stood on the back of the Dunkirk sands to prevent their coming out, and to intercept ships from Brest that were carrying French soldiers. The Second Mate was optimistic, stating that if the French did not break out soon, they would have to wait for the next Spring tide. Captain Mitchell reminded him grimly of the variable March winds.

Sure enough, the wind began to rise, and it looked likely to blow hard. Byng sent messages declaring that we would return to the Downs to save the Fleet, leaving a squadron to watch the French, who would be windbound in Dunkirk. When the gale came south-westerly, the Fleet weighed and stood for the Downs, anchoring there in thick, dirty weather on the second of March. The Plymouth squadron finally joined us for another Council of War, and we prepared to sail the next day.

Yet before Byng could give the signal for unmooring, an advice boat sailed in, bringing letters from General Cadogan at Ostend. He requested a squadron to convoy ten battalions of troops, to follow the French ships, land where they landed, and fight them. The Captain of the advice boat also confirmed that the Pretender was still at Dunkirk, though fifteen French battalions were now embarked, and ready to sail for Scotland, under fourteen Scottish Lords.

We sailed with instructions to meet off Dunkirk if the winds permitted, but to make back for the Downs otherwise. In a sou'westerly drizzle, we crowded sail for Dunkirk, and when the Lark reported eleven French ships, our whole force chased them, though they were nought but privateers, and easily escaped us. We anchored off Dover on the night of the sixth, and the blockading squadron reported that the French were still in Dunkirk.

Yet late that night the wind threatened to blow us onto the French coast, and Byng saw no choice but to bear away for Dungeness. As day broke, the Glasgow broke her anchor and lost a maintopmast in the storm. We endured a blast of hailstones, yet the Fleet rode out the worst of it in Rye Bay. At four bells, with the wind blowing north-east, we set the yards and topmasts, and prepared to sail on the flood of the tide, beating to windward if we could. We all knew that Byng must be panic-struck to be so far to leeward, his only hope that the French would not have sailed, over-loaded, in such terrible weather. He gave the signal to weigh in the evening, and we tided it eastward.

At dawn, the great guns of the Bedford blasted her distress. Jennings' pilot had sailed her onto the eastern part of the Ripraps, the long sandbar betwixt Boulogne and Dungeness. Byng, impatient at the delay, sent his three cleanest, fastest vessels ahead, and waited for the flood tide to lift the Bedford clear, her hull thankfully undamaged. Mid-morning, we were all standing at the back of the sands between Calais and Dunkirk, where the Dutch Admiral Van Buren joined us with four Men o' War.

Byng had heard nothing of the French since the sixth, and could only wait impatiently for news. When an advice boat came in from Ostend, he read the letter on deck, and immediately ordered a War Council. This was over by half past four, when we all heard that the French ships had sailed from Dunkirk on the night of the sixth, into the teeth of that storm, and must already be in Scotland. I was convinced that only the courage of the young Pretender could have urged such a desperate enterprise.

Byng announced that Vice-Admiral Baker's squadron and the Dutch men o' war would be sent to convoy Cadogan's troops from Ostend, and the rest of us would stand away north for the Edinburgh road. He gave out the Line of Battle, and days behind the French, we sailed for the Scottish capital, looking for a would-be King. It was miserable work for us, rain and snow icing the decks and freezing the halyards in their blocks. We hugged the coast, and rounded Saint Abb's Head still in bitter westerly gales, then the wind dropped, and we anchored just south of the Isle of May.

As darkness gave way to another grey dawn, the lookout screamed, and there, only four leagues from us, was the French Fleet. The storm had blown them too far north, and they had made the Edinburgh road on the same evening as we had, lying just north of the Isle of May. Now their entire Fleet was getting underway, and I raced aloft with the rest of the ship's boys, desperately crowding sail, for they would soon be upon us.

After the first panic, every man in the English Fleet, tar or Admiral, looked to the Stuart flag flying at the maintopmasthead of the French ship the Mars. It was identical to that flown by our Admiral for Queen Anne. Knowing King Jamie was there, I wondered how I could fire upon him, even as I heaved at our guns. No man would meet another's eye, and the Gunner was grim as thunder, aware that we might throw down our duty, and persuade our mates to mutiny.

Yet as our Fleet lumbered into the Battle Line, the French blithely passed us by. Their attack was a bluff. They had been more interested in weathering the Cape and getting away to the north, than engaging a superior force when over-loaded. By eight of the morning, we were underway, some cursing the French for their cowardice, others admiring their daring, all of us relieved to have been spared slaughter before breakfast.

Byng sent boats to advise the Admiralty and the Commander of Edinburgh of the Pretender's position, and we chased the swifter French ships north. The Dover and the Ludlow Castle were our cleanest vessels, and we watched them overtake us, Captain Mitchell grim at another missed opportunity for promotion, for Captain Haddock of the Ludlow Castle was only twenty-two, just a little older indeed than the Pretender.

During the afternoon, the Dover and the Ludlow passed by the smaller sail of the French Fleet, working handsomely to cut off three ships, including the Salisbury, now French but lately an English man o' war, and still foul on her bottom, and slow. We watched the light fade off Aberdeen that night, and followed the stern lights of our headmost ships. They came up with the Salisbury at two in the morning, and when they fired, she struck her French colours. The Ludlow Castle sank her boat trying to board her, and many men were lost in that cold sea. The Leopard's boat entered men on the Salisbury first, claiming the Prize, and the bounty money.

By dawn the next day, we had lost sight of most of our Fleet. Then at noon, we saw them returning towards Edinburgh, for Byng feared a Jacobite uprising in the Scottish capital. The Shrewsbury and the Advice both had masts disabled, the Dover and the Salisbury prize needed repairs, and our new ship's boat had been crushed under our stern by the greatness of the sea. The captured French troops were distributed throughout the Fleet, dropped into the suffocating stench of the bilges and left there.

Fair weather saw us back in the Forth of Edinburgh with no news of the Pretender. Once they'd re-provisioned, the Dover and the Ludlow Castle were sent to cruise off Buchan Ness, while the Rye and the Squirrel scouted around Aberdeen. We heard that the Londoners had been stirred to a fury by broadsheets claiming that our soft-hearted Queen

157

had asked Byng to let her half-brother go, not wanting him brought a prisoner before her.

The Admiralty ordered us to continue guarding the coast of Scotland, yet we were windbound in the Leith Road for a week, gales pounding us again. We re-distributed provisions, and went on half allowance of beer, which had all the men grumbling. The Purser mixed up beverage, one butt of sour Portuguese wine to three butts of bad water, and this brought on the flux, which killed many a strong man.

At the end of the month, the Dover and the Ludlow Castle sailed in without having caught sight of the French Fleet, both greatly damaged by the storm. Indeed the Dover had sprung all her masts somewhere beyond the Orkney Islands, and was lucky to return at all. The winds moderated over the next few days, and we hoped to be allowed to return to Chatham to re-provision, for we were dying of the flux, the scurvy and the cold.

Old Tom came down with a fit of ague, lying huddled in his hammock, muttering the name of his dead wife, and weeping. There was no fresh food for him, only bad water, hard biscuit, and stinking salt beef. When I dragged the surgeon in to see him after he had been unable to rise for three days, he felt the old man's pulse, asked him how he had slept and the colour of his stool, and gave him some medicines upon the point of a knife which I am convinced did him as much good as a blow to the head.

When he died, there was no church for Thomas Pullen, no passing bell rung for his soul, no digging of the grave and making of the coffin, no family at his burial, no wine and cake and memories. He was stripped of his clothes, wrapped in rotten canvas, and heaved over to feed the fish. The Chaplain muttered a sermon, some men shivering on deck, wishing they could be below, for 'twas freezing cold, and no amount of respect could help Old Tom now. My own health was failing, and every night I dreamed of a cold white corpse falling through the dark depths of the sea, until I knew the death was my own.

158

Two days after Old Tom died, the Admiral took note of our plight, and ordered other ships of the Fleet to aid us with provisions. On the sixth of April, we joined Admiral Baker's squadron, to return our troops to Flanders. We took on a Company of soldiers, the First Foot Guards, Orkney's famous regiment. Then the Admiral hoisted his flag on the Dreadnought, and we sailed from the Forth. When we were abreast of Saint Abb's head, the sun struck the Cheviot Hills, and I gazed my last upon my fair country, without even knowing it.

We sailed east then, the winds light and not with us. I bedded down damp and cold with the redcoats, who complained that their voyage out from Ostend had been Hell itself, ten of the oldest English regiments sleeping on the bare decks in the sleet, with little food, and no liquor. I made friends with Corporal John Deane, who seemed capable of the highest spirits in his attempts to keep heart in his comrades. He was anxious to try for a better distribution of the ship's provisions, for indeed what the fat Purser let them have was hardly worth the eating.

"'Tis damnation afloat boy, I know not how ye bear it. Continual destruction in the foretop, the pox above board, the plague between decks, Hell in the forecastle, and the Devil at the helm. I swear I'll not to sea again, but to get home to Scotland when this bloody war is over."

"I love this ship. We were at the siege of Ostend you know. Yet I have seen more men die on her for lack of food than in battle, and the Purser is as fat as a stuffed goose. I don't think I will ever lose my love of the sea, yet I have had enough of the Navy."

"Then join up with the greatest regiment afoot. Yer a scrawny sort o' lad, yet canny enough. How old are ye?"

"Sixteen Sir."

"Well if ye can find us a drink, we'll steal ye away, won't we Donald, and enlist ye as soon as we get to Ostend."

I could see he was only joking, yet my need to quit the Navy was strong enough for me to take Corporal Deane at his word. Once again, I stole into the Surgeon's cabin, knowing that in his helplessness at having the men dying about him, he would be dead drunk. Wearing my thick coat, I loaded six bottles of rum into the pockets, and scurried back with them to Corporal Deane, praying that none would hear the betraying clink of glass. Trying to keep my theft a secret, Deane sent his friend Donald Macleod around to give each sickening man a drink. Macleod did not touch a drop, and neither did Deane, and when they returned with but one tot left in the bottom of the last bottle, they courteously desired me to finish it.

"To the health of your Regiment, Sirs, and the glory of the Duke of Marlborough. And now I am yours if you'll have me."

"Lad, yer a marvel, and if ye want to desert yer post, we'll manage it somehow. Yet yer thin, for all your breadth of shoulder, and a foot soldier must slog through the mud of Flanders with everything on his back. We have marched across Europe..."

"To Blenheim?"

"Aye, we were at Blenheim, and Ramillies."

"Don't ye forget Schellenberg", Macleod growled, trying to find a comfortable way of laying his thin bones on the deck. "Never forget that shitfight lad, for that was the worst." They spoke of battles and sieges, and boasted of Marlborough as a hero to equal any that had lived in ancient times. Macleod was an old Highlander from the isle of Skye, and Corporal Deane declared him born to penury, fish, porridge, and feuding. His parents had eloped at sixteen and eighteen, and their prodigious family nearly starved during the famine, when the English landlords shipped all Scottish produce to London. Sergeant Macleod had walked away from his family, one of the two hundred thousand beggars that filled Scotland. He had been saved by a recruiting party that was beating up for volunteers to serve in Orkney's Regiment.

We anchored in the Ostend Road a few days later, the

low, flat coast of Flanders before us. Most of the boat crew were ill, so I volunteered to help row the soldiers in, and slipped back into the Captain's cabin for my sponges, my rapier and my mother's Bible. I hesitated over the Captain's battered copy of Dryden's poems, knowing he found him almost impossible to read, and then took that too. Then I dashed down the rope ladder before the rest of the oarsmen, hiding my things as best I could in my thick coat.

As soon as we were ashore, my soldier friends made a diversion by pretending to fight, and I dove under a wagon full of hay. The Coxswain was in a hurry to get back to sea, yet still he counted heads, and found I was missing. He abused the soldiers roundly for having persuaded me to desert, yet my fate had been decided. I would wear a red coat, and march with Marlborough.

PART 3: FLANDERS 1708-1710
Chapter 10: Foot Soldier

Despite the Coxswain's parting curses, the soldiers thought it a great joke when Corporal Deane pulled me out of the hay cart I was hiding in. Then laughing at our sea-shaky knees, we staggered into the nearest tavern, where a glass or two of brandy set us up after the rigours of the voyage. Their foppish Captain then strode in, and Corporal Deane introduced me to him as a willing recruit. He glanced at me, curled his lip, and tossed off a brandy. "Nay Sir, he's not just any filthy brat of a ship's boy, but a lad full o' pluck and resources, and o' good enough family to serve under Marlborough himself." I nodded eagerly, and insisted that I'd be honoured to fight in his Company.

"Of course you would, boy", Deane's Captain murmured, twirling a lock of his long, black wig between his long, white fingers, "yet perhaps a less prestigious regiment would suit you better." He then gave orders for them to march to Ghent, where they would be paid for their time at sea.

I was miserable at this rejection, yet Corporal Deane would not let me stay downhearted. "Most of our Officers are duel-happy fops, half-drunk most o' the time, and completely soused the rest."

"Aye", Donald Macleod growled. "They step on us, and allow the mighty to step on them, ignoring all of a man but his wealth and family. So, it might help if ye got a wee bit scrubbed up in the kitchen. I'll lend ye a clean shirt, and we'll enlist ye with the next Captain who walks in."

"I'd rather be with you."

Corporal Deane looked sheepish. "My Captain has decided yer not for the likes of us, lad. And if I'd thought ye serious back on that rotting old tub, I'd have explained that we're an elite regiment, hand-picked, with an honourable place on the right of the Battle Line. Why, Marlborough himself is enlisted as a Colonel in the First Foot Guards."

Macleod interrupted. "Yer not tall enough, or, by the look of ye, robust enough to be a Grenadier Guard."

"Nay don't think I misled ye into jumping ship", Corporal Deane insisted, when he saw my face. "Ye'll be a soldier yet. Look, here's Captain Gordon o' the Royal Scots. Not the first battalion, but Colonel Hamilton's second. He's a sensible man, and they're not too grand for ye. Ho Captain Gordon, I see ye survived the Hell of the wooden world, death by cold and sea, eh?" A neat, sober man in a simple campaigner's wig nodded politely to him, a great contrast to Deane's own Captain. "We stole away the cabin boy o' the Dreadnought, John Smith, a clever lad, and hot to be a soldier. Will ye take him as a cadet?"

"I won't take him but as a volunteer serving without pay", Captain Gordon replied. "He's had no drill, and his chances of surviving long enough to learn the flintlock are too small for him to be of use to me."

"I learnt to load and fire a musket on board the Dreadnought, Sir, and would not be useless to you, I swear it. I learn quickly, or I'd not have survived two years at sea. As for serving without pay, the Navy has taught me that all God's creatures must eat."

"I'll give ye fourpence a day, take it or leave it."

I was about to accept with gratitude when Donald Macleod growled that I was worth full soldier's pay, or they'd enlist me with someone else. "All the Regiments that sailed out after the Pretender are under-strength, many o' their men now food for fish. It won't be much trouble to find a good place for such an eager, knowing lad as this. And with respect Sir, how can you expect a soldier to survive on four pennies, with the cost of his necessities taking two of those away every payday? Why Sir, he'd be bound to starve, and the bad name your Regiment would get..."

"Enough Corporal Macleod, I'll take him at the full rate, provided ye'll buy me a bottle." The Captain thought their goodwill would not stand the test of a few shillings, so

I pulled out my purse, and with as knowing an air as I could muster, called for a bottle of good brandy for the Captain.

Captain Gordon nodded, told me I'd do, and bidding Corporal Deane goodnight, bade me follow him. I thought it rude of him not to share the bottle with my new friends, yet I wronged him, for we entered a tavern close by, where he introduced me to my own red-coated Company. While they inspected me, Captain Gordon deposited the bottle on his Sergeant's table, and pulled out a chair for me to join them.

The Sergeant, an ugly, drinking fellow, thanked me heartily for the grog, and cursed the Paymaster for leaving the Regiment without a guilder for brandy until we reached Ghent. Captain Gordon made me swear an oath to follow the Colours and not desert, telling me he'd read out the Articles of War once we were in our garrison. He gave me two pounds as bounty money, and amazed at my sudden riches, and taking the Sergeant's hint, I immediately called for another bottle, thinking it wise to win them over at first.

I lit my pipe, and asked if some others of my Company might not join us for a glass, and Captain Gordon shrugged and condemned them as a rough lot, mostly peasants who'd been tricked into enlisting, or petty thieves recruited by their local Justices of the Peace.

He called over a handsome young farmer, who swore that he had been unjustly recruited, consigned to the wars by his Squire, who was after his pretty sweetheart. "The Recruiting Officers grow desperate for men to feed the wars, and now there's no one left to help my old father bring in the harvest. And if I was to try to make my way home to them, I'd be shot as a deserter." Our ugly Sergeant made a game of tormenting him, playing on the Squire's lust and the maid's helplessness, until I thought the angry young farmer would hit him.

Captain Gordon asked if I was not a gentleman's son, and I told them my name was Mark Read, for if the Army was as haughty as it seemed, then 'Smith' was not enough. I assured them that I had been well raised by a good London

164

family, yet a youthful indiscretion had forced me to run away to sea under another name. Two and a half years as a cabin boy had seen me still starving and poor, and the Captain damned the Navy and vowed I'd prosper as a soldier.

I asked them to tell me of Army life, and an eager young Londoner swore 'twas better than most of them had known before, the discipline not too harsh and the food regular. They toasted Marlborough for their bread and beer and regular pay, and I joined them. When the drums beat at nine o'clock, I went with them, up the stairs to our billet, the drunken Sergeant instructing me to sleep in my coat on the floor, and promising to find me a blanket and see me properly kitted out in Ghent.

Just before dawn, a blast of drumming in the street saw me leap up. The young Londoner laughed and assured me 'twas nought but Reveille. About me, men woke and groaned, holding their heads and staggering cursing to their feet. They all wore knee-length shirts, and hauled their trousers on over the top, and I saw this would suit my deception.

By the time the sun was up, we'd messed on my brandy and freshly made biscuit, tidied ourselves, packed our few belongings, and assembled for marching off. Captain Gordon then inspected us, promising the grumbling men their pay in Ghent. He frowned to see me barefoot, and advised me on a steady pace, for we'd be on our feet all day, and he could not allow me to fall behind for fear I'd desert.

Our Company stepped out after the rest, marching to the beat of the drum in easy time, many singing as they marched together. We soon left the town behind, to follow a pretty canal lined with windmills that ran south-east, the countryside remarkably flat. The few farms we passed were mere burnt-out shells, the windmills, and even the trees destroyed. Only when it rained would we sometimes see peasants sowing grain in the fields. I noticed no women, and when I asked the Sergeant, he said they were all in hiding. I told him his leer was cause enough for all the maids of

165

Flanders to flee, and he grinned horribly. We spent the night camped in a field, and the Sergeant took a few men scavenging. They returned with a few scrawny chickens and a tale of a pretty girl they'd given a guilder to.

On the second day I suffered terribly with blisters, yet shuffled along as best I could, allowing the steady drumbeat to blank my thoughts. When I rose on the third day, my blisters had blown out to such an extent that I could not stand on the soles of my feet. The Captain lanced the blisters, and found me a seat on a sutler's cart for that day. The next day, he declared me fit to walk, and at dusk I hobbled to the gates of Ghent in a daze of pain, tired and dusty soldiers all about me.

I found a well-fortified town, peopled with the small, dark-haired Flemish, rather than the sandy-haired, sturdy Dutch. The Flemings scowled to see us come marching in, even the lace-hatted, bustling women in the market place turning their backs upon us. Yet I was too exhausted to care much, the march having been hard on me in my poor condition.

Our quarters were in a grand stone hall, safe behind the fortress walls. We ate at great trestle benches as soon as we came in, messengers having been sent ahead to notify the Company's sutlers. I messed with five men, including our Sergeant, who was already drunk, yet kind enough to have saved me a little brandy for the pain of my feet. The angry young farmer sat with us, and a one-eyed card-sharper, who the Sergeant whispered was intent on deserting. The eager London lad also joined us, and proved so glad to have survived last year's campaign, that he could hardly eat for tales of his own valour. I ate well for the first time in months, the excellent roast meat and abundant fresh vegetables surpassed only by the generous tankards of wine.

Then, while the rest helped clear the tables, Captain Gordon insisted I sit, and called for a bucket of hot water for me to soak my poor feet. One of our sutlers came up with it, and threw in some sweet-smelling flowers, which she swore

166

would help against infection. When the Sergeant brought me another brandy, I had to fight back tears, for I was unused to anything but the harshest treatment. The Sergeant called the London lad and the farmer's son to help me to my billet, and I dossed down in a blanket that had no salt damp, on a mattress that was dry, and best of all, a bed that was motionless, and thanked God to be safe off the Dreadnought.

I woke at dawn to find the swelling in my feet much lessened, though my soles were still raw. Before breakfast, Captain Gordon was ready with salve and bandages, and the London lad and the farmer's son came to help me to breakfast, and then back to my billet. Captain Gordon then came to formally enlist me in the Royal Scots. He read out the Articles of War, which comprised a list of punishments so severe that I was reluctant to sign my name to it. I could be hanged for plundering, shot at the head of the Regiment for desertion, or flogged for assaulting a superior.

Our sottish Sergeant then staggered in with a load of gear, and dumped it on my camp bed. He asked Captain Gordon to sign for my weapons from the armoury, and I took advantage of their absence to slip my filthy old shirt off and my new one on, too fast for anyone to notice the rag that covered my breasts. The coarse linen shirt went to my knees, and the baggy, grey breeches completed the disguise. When I donned the full-skirted scarlet coat, there was a neat round hole just over the heart, a keepsake from its last tenant. I also had two pairs of strong stockings, and stout square-toed shoes only a little too big for me.

The Sergeant then reeled in with a rolled blanket and a cooking pot, and advised me to double the stockings to help against blisters, and to wear my coat inside out when marching, saving the better side for battle. He explained that I'd be given a new coat each year, and could then rip the arms off the old one to make a waistcoat. Yet as I'd missed the dole this year, he advised me to await battle, and take a dead man's coat for a waistcoat, no matter what the colour, for I'd freeze this Winter otherwise. I tied my hair back into a soldier's queue, bound one of my two neckcloths into a neat knot, and donned a three-cornered black hat, the soldiers' tricorne, which made me look quite the part.

As the Sergeant helped me buckle a white cross-belt over my coat, Captain Gordon returned with my weapons. He hung a heavy leather cartridge box from the right side of my belt, a bayonet and sword from my left. Then he handed me a flintlock, the first I had seen, and almost as heavy as a ship's musket. The whole kit must have weighed fifty pounds. When the Sergeant grinned and told me I would also sometimes shoulder a spade, I laughed and asked him how far I was expected to stagger under it all. "Until I call the Halt, you march boy, or you'll be shot for a deserter", the Sergeant scowled.

Captain Gordon explained that we had wagons to help us, yet the Sergeant muttered that as the Officers demanded them for their luxuries, there was little space for our necessities, and that the Army had marched many a man to death.

Captain Gordon ignored him, and told me that the cost of my gear would be taken out of my pay, at the rate of twopence a day. He then ordered the Sergeant to take me through my paces with the flintlock, and left us. The Sergeant then explained that fourpence a day was ample if I patronised our sutler's tent, and didn't drink too much. I wondered how he managed to stay so full of brandy, yet when he hinted at robbing the dead, I began to see how he survived so well on his meagre pay. He also advised me to buy a knapsack for my own possessions, to find a water bottle and put rum in it, and to sew any money I had into my coat.

When the keen young Londoner stepped up and declared me a fine figure of a soldier, I felt as if I'd grown six inches, such was the effect of shoes and a hat, and admiration. Sure I'd made the right step in life, I left most of my gear by my billet, and limped after the Sergeant and the Londoner down to a target range in an outer courtyard, so they could see me fire the flintlock. The Navy was still using loose powder, and I was stumped by the rows of ready-rolled cartridges in their box. The Londoner showed me how to bite the bullet end off, shake the powder into the priming pan, pour the rest down the muzzle, spit the bullet after it, and ram the paper down on it all, using the ramrod from underneath the barrel.

I fired, the recoil sent me over, and the Londoner laughed. "The French still have the old muskets, no cartridges, bayonets that obscure their aim, and slow-matches that go out in the rain. They'll sigh with relief to see you coming." I jumped up and reloaded, the sound of the shot still ringing in my ears, a dense cloud of blue smoke drifting through the courtyard.

"Bloody slow", grunted the Sergeant, as I fired again. "Reload. No boy, don't bother aiming past sixty yards. That only interferes with the smoothness of the Drill. For we fire together, fix bayonets on command, and draw steel on the order. No man acts on his own, and that is our strength. Close up, aim for their shoe buckles, for the recoil kicks the barrels up, and the ricochet off the ground will get him, or the man behind him. And take care of your ramrod, for if it breaks, you'll be unable to fire at all. And keep your flints dry. There are spares in your cartridge box. Now, I'm due at our sutler's to check supplies, and when I come back, I want to see your rate of fire matching this lad's. If not, I'll whack you with me bloody halberd."

The London lad soon coached me to load and fire to the count of twenty, insisting that, French or English, the Infantry suffered the most hurts, the hardest duties, and the lowest pay. "We boast of our new flintlocks, yet one day the French will have them too, as well as our new guns that destroy whole platoons." Then he showed me how to lock the bayonet over the end of my flintlock, and how to re-load without impaling my hand on the bayonet. "Bayonets leave a great hole that blood pours out of, and the old soldier swears they have doubled the dead since Dutch William's wars. We

169

only use them in close fighting, or against the Cavalry."

"How do they help against men on horseback?"

"The front rank plant the butts of their flintlocks into the ground, and slant the bayonets out, while the rear rank fires. 'Tis the only way to keep the bastards off us."

As the Sergeant returned from checking the sutler's brandy, I unsheathed my clumsy sword, a soldier's short hanger, double-edged, with a sharp point, and according to our sot of a sergeant, only good for gathering firewood, reaping corn, and frightening peasants. I asked if any would take offence at me carrying a rapier instead, and he told me that until I was an Officer, I would have to leave it in the care of our Captain, for I could carry nought but necessities when on the march.

That night, Captain Gordon asked me how I liked the life so far. I told him that after the Navy, 'twas Heaven. "I pray to acquit myself well, Sir, and hope that with experience of battle, I'll soon be a Corporal." The soused Sergeant grinned, and Captain Gordon smiled and replied rather dryly that any man who behaved like a gentleman, and had some influence, could soon become an Officer. "I don't know what influence I can count on, Sir. I lost my family's favour when I ran away to sea on account of a duel."

"Any hot-headed nonsense in this Company lad, I'll confiscate yer rapier, and have the Sergeant horsewhip ye."

I blushed. "'Twas an unavoidable affair of honour, Sir. An Army Officer insulted a friend of mine. I do not fight for pleasure, even though I seem to have come into it as a profession."

"Yer lucky to be alive. Did he make a fool of ye?"

"I killed him."

He regarded me more kindly. "If ye wish to rise in the Army, lad, write to yer family, excuse yeself, and tell them yer a soldier with the Royal Scots. For ye could die, one o' thousands over here in Flanders, and they would never know what became o' you. Let them use their

170

influence on yer behalf, for 'tis a desperate slow rise unless ye've money to purchase an Officer's commission."

"Surely if a man distinguishes himself on the battle field..."

The sottish Sergeant laughed. "You'll be hard enough pressed to stay alive, without thinking o' glory, boy. Yet don't fret, I'll see you well rehearsed in the Drill while we wait in Ghent for further orders. We'll keep you from getting killed if we can."

Captain Gordon gave me paper and ink, yet with no family to write to, I resolved to write to Sally, and tell her I was a redcoat, and beg her to keep an eye out for my mother.

We stayed in Ghent for almost a month, and I soon learned the handling of all my arms that comprised our Company Drill. Then I was allowed to join in the Regimental platoon exercises, which manoeuvred six ranks of marching men into three ranks of fighters. I still did not know the orders by drumbeat, yet I thought I could manage by watching the men about me when on the field. I came to know the men of my Company better by working with them, for we were constantly kept busy, standing guard for the garrison, or doing more menial duties, such as mending our regimentals, or cleaning our flintlocks.

The best of the life for me was the constant food, a pint of beer, a pound of meat, and two pounds of bread the standard ration every day. Soon I was stronger than I'd ever been, and knew my monthly bleeding must soon return. Yet I still had an ample supply of sea sponges, and as soldiers never removed their knee-length shirts, and only bathed at the end of the campaign, I thought I could still maintain my disguise, despite sharing a tent with seven men. I'd taken the opportunity to piss at trees through my horn on our long march to Ghent, and my Company took me for a sharp, eager lad, sure to be killed before the end of the campaign.

Towards the latter end of April, our Regiment was abuzz with the news that the Duke of Marlborough had landed at the Hague, having recruited the English army up to

171

seventy thousand men. He ordered us all to meet our Allies in Brussels, and on May the eleventh, I marched with the whole of the English Foot under General Lumley, the men of the Royal Scots singing "The British Grenadiers" with more gusto than any. To be part of that great river of men made me feel ant-like, yet also invincible, a tiny part of an indomitable force.

Two nights later, I stood guard, smoking my pipe and gazing at the myriad lights of the Allied campfires about Brussels, wondering where the Duke of Marlborough lay. Corporal Deane strolled past, arm-in-arm with another soldier, and when I called out to him, he congratulated me on my uniform, and introduced Sergeant Millner to me. The sergeant was most amused to hear how I'd jumped ship to be a soldier, and when I asked his opinion of our strength, he told me that there were over one hundred battalions of Foot, and as many squadrons of Horse and Dragoons on the march, and that behind us lumbered over one hundred cannon, twenty-four mortars and howitzers, and carts carrying nearly fifty pontoons for crossing rivers.

Corporal Deane nodded proudly. "Prince Eugene marches to join us with troops he's gathered from the German states. The French will try to cut us off from him, and from our supplies. They'd rather starve us than risk a battle, though there are over one hundred thousand of them, the largest army ever seen."

"I'm not afraid!"

"Then you're a fool boy." I clapped my hand to my sword hilt. "No, I don't mean to insult you; I mean merely that you've not fought for as many weary years as I have."

Sergeant Millner grinned at my excitement. "We have been fighting so long, we don't know how to stop. The Whigs support the war, since they make their fortunes supplying us so badly, and as they call all Tories 'Jacobites', they will win next month's election."

"We fight to contain the French, to keep them from England!"

"And the Dutch fight to keep Flanders as a barrier against France. Yet the Flemish are Catholics. I'm sure you noticed how the market women scowl as they fleece us. Just last month Antwerp tried to surrender to the French. Brussels, Ghent and Bruges are just waiting to go over."

"Don't listen to the old bottle of physic!", the London lad called out to me. "He'll talk you yellow if you let him. Here, have a swig of brandy, and talk to me of Covent Garden." He'd seen me address a letter to Sally, and was convinced I had a sweetheart, an impression I'd done nothing to allay.

After a few more days marching, we stopped at a village near the great forest of Soignes, to bake bread and rest for a few days. We had just erected our orderly lines of tents, when a horseman came streaking into the camp and flung himself on the arms bell, shouting that our Cavalry had found the entire French Army encamped on the other side of the forest. Even while we hurriedly dressed and armed ourselves, we heard firing, yet were ordered to hold our ground. That night, Captain Gordon returned from drinking with the Officers to declare that the French were marching north for Louvain, attempting to stop Prince Eugene's army from joining us.

The next morning, we decamped in worsening weather, and stood to Assembly in the rain. Captain Gordon announced that Major-General Schulenberg had been sent with a detachment of Cavalry to secure the pass into Louvain, and we were marching to support him. I caught him up on the march, and asked him who this foreigner was, who could hold a pass against the entire French Army. He laughed at me. "Nay lad, don't despise him merely for not being English. Schulenberg started life as a mercenary in the Polish army, and rose fast as a man of dauntless courage and enterprise."

"I wish I was with him then. I'd soon earn my promotion."

"Perhaps, yet he'll take troops of his own choosing,

173

not raw recruits."

Around noon, we stopped by a stone bridge with an old inn on the riverbank, the massive outworks of Brussels dimly visible through the heavy rain. Awaiting our turn to cross, I told the London lad of the Coach and Horses at Brent, while we ate damp bread and sipped our brandy. He fished for information on my friendship with the infamous Sally Salisbury, and I admitted I'd met several high-flyers through her, and the odd noble gull, and so gained his undying respect.

We marched on, and by nightfall, I was exhausted with lifting mud-caked shoes that seemed heavier than the rest of me. Yet we marched on through the night, and through the next morning, many men falling by the wayside. When finally ordered to halt, just before noon, we fell to the ground, and it was some time before we could rouse ourselves to pitch camp. A Cavalry Officer rode by, and when Captain Gordon begged him for news, he told us we were south-east of Louvain, and had cut the French off, barely three leagues short of the pass.

When the rain cleared the next morning, we could see the entire blue mass of the French Army, and I thought we would fight. Yet both armies sat and looked at each other, day after day, week after week, for nearly a month. We waited for Prince Eugene to reach us, with fifteen thousand, instead of the forty thousand men he'd promised. The French waited for thirty thousand men to join them from Alsace, under Berwick.

The London lad told me that Berwick was Marlborough's nephew. Marlborough's sister had been old King James' mistress before he was ousted, and Berwick had been raised in exile with his royal father. He was now a devoted follower of the Catholic Pretender, and fought bravely for the French King, though he never had any luck against his English uncle.

The Duke of Marlborough reviewed us in detachments of ten thousand each day, and I paraded with

174

the Royal Scots, and cheered a tiny, red-coated figure on a white horse. Fat Prince George of Hanover was there too, on his fat horse, and we cheered the man who might one day be our King, though many in our Regiment openly toasted the Pretender.

Towards the end of June, the dull afternoon was broken by the drumming of the Assembly, and Captain Gordon ordered us ready to march. The French had decamped in the night, and were marching on Ghent. We marched back past Brussels at noon the next day, cursing to see the place again so soon. We marched until the Halt was drummed at ten that night, falling on our arms one mile from the French, the old soldiers expecting battle in the morning.

Yet again the French decamped in the night, and were already on the west bank of the Alost River by dawn. Schulenberg was sent off with a detachment to engage them, yet the Frenchmen he chased proved to be a decoy. The French Army had already crossed the Dender, broken all the bridges, and sent large detachments to march on Ghent and Bruges. The next day, they invested Ghent, and though the seven hundred men of our garrison held them off at first, after three days they had no choice but to surrender, and march off with honour. Bruges fell when Ghent did, and as Ghent was the key to the canals of Flanders, our whole Army was suddenly cut off from Ostend, and England.

I was standing guard when Prince Eugene rode into the village of Asche, four days ahead of his promised Cavalry. A Frenchman, he had risen to the top of the Austrian military, only to find himself fighting his own country. He had the reputation of a modest, humane man, yet I thought him a disappointing sight, slouched with fatigue over his horse, his pock-marked cheeks sagging in his pale face. Yet Marlborough embraced him as a brother, and they shut themselves up together for the whole afternoon.

That night, the news was all over camp that our forced march from Soignes to Louvain had been a French trick, to clear their way to Ghent. Yet it was the next day's news, that the elderly Duke of Marlborough had been bled for a feverish despondency, and that his own doctor advised his removal to Brussels, that truly dampened our spirits.

Then the Duke emerged smiling from his tent, with a plan to cut the French army off from France, by crossing the river Scheld and reinforcing Oudenarde. Heartened, we stepped out on a two day march around the Dender to Ath, thankful for the good weather and easy roads. Then we chased the French another ten leagues north, the Duke on horseback to encourage us in our exhaustion. That night we lay on our arms, expecting battle in the morning, the Duke in the field with us, his Officers declaring he was as eager to engage the French as we were.

In the dead of night, two young Scotsmen joined our Company, deserting their posts as guards for the baggage wagons. Captain Gordon looked the other way, and we shared our brandy and bread with them.

We were drummed awake at dawn, to see the steel flashes of the French Army marching off north to hold the Scheld. As we assembled, General Cadogan, Marlborough's handsome favourite, rode up to command us. He declared that the French were already crossing the river, yet at a leisurely pace, and that we must cross before them. We understood what was at stake, and though we had marched fifty miles in two days, we pushed the wagons that held the tin pontoons almost at a run. There were strict orders against anything getting in our way, and we hurled the Officer's baggage wagons off the track, our greedy Sergeant halting briefly to stuff something silver into a knapsack.

By noon we reached the Scheld, to see the French Army only six miles to the east of us, and already partly across the river. Frantic with haste, a man stripped to his skin to swim across with the first rope, and we began laying the boats out beam to beam. The first bridge was completed in half an hour, and Rantzau's Cavalry marched over the wooden planks we'd laid, to defend it.

Our detachment laid five bridges, and when our

entire Horse had crossed, we were given the honour of being the first Infantry to follow them. We drew up as quickly as we could on the other side, wondering if the French were finally ready to give battle, for they had made no attempt to halt our crossing. An Adjutant rode by, and told Captain Gordon that the French Infantry was digging in, taking advantage of the woods, hedges and ditches that broke up the plain. The old soldier muttered that the ground was too broken for Cavalry charges, and despite the work we'd done to get our Horse over, it seemed we would be bearing the brunt of the battle.

At two in the afternoon, with only half our army on the field, Marlborough ordered us to form battle lines. The cannonade started, and I watched great plumes of blue smoke drifting over the battlefield, and then jumped as cannon balls smashed into the ground about us. As the rattle of French musket fire became constant, we were ordered to attack, and my Sergeant roared at me to stay by him. Led only by our Captains and Drummers, we marched through the smoke, straight for a small village, seeking a stronger position to fight from. The French Infantry already posted there must have thought us the entire Allied Army, for they deserted their strong position, to be caught by our Horse. They scattered, and were cut down right before our eyes.

We re-grouped and then marched straight at the blue lines of Frenchmen beyond the smoke, Captain Gordon cursing that we had no Generals to lead us, and none behind to shoot deserters, furious that some lesser Regiment had broken the battle line to march before us, swearing that whoever fired without his express command would be shot.

We advanced as regularly as the broken ground would permit, stepping up as our mates were smashed aside by cannon or felled by a French bullet. Twenty yards from the French, Captain Gordon gave the order to halt, and form platoons, and we reformed as gracefully as if on parade. Then our front rank dropped to one knee and I fired, re-loading as those behind fired in their turn, until, half-stunned

177

by the noise, we lost sight of our foe in the cloud of blue smoke from our flintlocks.

There was a great shout, and a rush of soldiers from our left. We leapt to our feet, and in the thick smoke, I lost my bearings, and found myself no longer with my own platoon. Suddenly I saw men in blue ahead of us, and an Officer called us to re-group. Before we could re-load, the Frenchmen threw away their muskets and took to their heels, our Horse sweeping down upon them, sabres flashing. We finished re-loading, ignoring those screaming and dying about us, my fear so intense, that I fumbled my cartridges with the clumsiness of a nightmare.

Then there was a great shout behind us, and we saw a mass of French Cavalry riding right at us, sabres drawn. We scrambled to form a defensive square, yet those with unloaded muskets wanted to be safely in the middle, not on the outer rank with only a bayonet, and we were soon a frightened rabble. At the last moment, Rantzau's Horse thundered up, and chased them away from us.

"They are wavering!", someone shouted. "Stand together!" We marched steadily forward, through a rain of musket fire, towards the ruins of a thick hedge. Finding Frenchmen desperately trying to re-load behind it, we ran at them. Some were stabbed with bayonets before the rest threw down their muskets. We ran on, and suddenly a Frenchman raised his musket to fire at me, and I shot him dead. And then it was hand-to-hand combat as the French disputed every tree and bush. Terrified, I parried and slashed, fighting for my life, and covered with the blood of those I'd cut down. I relied utterly on the grim-faced men fighting hard with me, and we faced the worst of it together.

Then there were no more of the enemy ahead of us. We cheered, thinking we had won through, then turned to see fresh French reserves marching up, and our entire side faltered. There was a shout, and Lottum's Hanoverians came marching in to support us, as precisely as if on parade, just in time to repulse an overwhelming surge of French Infantry.

Then, without any orders, the whole of our Foot struggled up, and step by step, we pushed back against the greater French numbers, and advanced. Never will I forget the united resolve of those men about me, and how it carried us all forward. We staggered across that plain like some wounded giant of old. And then we saw the French Horse circling to attack.

Prince Eugene launched his entire German Cavalry in a desperate charge to save us. They broke through the French Horse, into infantry fire so deadly, that they were cut to a quarter of their numbers. Yet as the French Cavalry wheeled to attack us again, seventeen English squadrons rode up in perfect order, and we were saved.

Then old General Overkirk charged down the hill behind us, through the enemy fire, his Danish Cavalry pounding after him. They cut off the French Infantry, which broke and fled straight into the sabres of our Horse. I turned my eyes from the slaughter, yet some of our men cheered, and urged our triumphant cavalry to commit further barbarities

As we advanced to take French prisoners, the light was already failing. Visions of the day's killing flashed before my eyes, and I began to shake so I could barely hold my flintlock. When the drum beat the ceasefire at nine, I limped in sudden agony back through the moaning men and screaming horses, asking after my Company.

When I stumbled up to him, Captain Gordon was trying to stem the bleeding from a deep scratch on his arm. He leapt to his feet, thanking God that I was still alive, and called for a dram of brandy to keep me on my feet.

Yet it made no difference, and when I fell to my knees, desperately trying not to weep before them all, Captain Gordon ordered me carried to our sutler's campfire. There he examined my leg, and found a hole where a ball had ripped through my calf. We bound each other's wounds as best we could, and then too exhausted to make camp, we slept on the ground beneath the carts, a soaking rain putting out the campfires and increasing our misery.

And all about us, the screams of men and horses filled the night, and I was not the only one who wept, and dreamed of death.

Chapter 11: General George Macartney

We awoke to rumours and boasts. I gritted my teeth against the agony of my injured leg, and the London lad told me that most of the Frenchmen we'd defeated had escaped into the night; though Prince Eugene had cleverly ordered his Officers to call out the names of famous French Regiments, taking whole battalions prisoner when they rallied in the darkness. Lumley's Horse chased the remnants of the French Foot all that day, taking another thousand prisoners, and killing many more. Yet many escaped by breaking the bridges over the river Lys.

We heard from French deserters that their Princes had countermanded General Vendome's direct order for their Cavalry to advance, declaring the ground too bad, even though Vendome had just ridden over it. The uncertainty this had caused in the French Army had saved us, though it had left Vendome fighting with a pike like a common soldier.

We heard too that Fat Prince George's fat horse had been shot from under him, and he had fled the battlefield on someone else's mount. The Dutch boasted that their young Prince of Orange had charged with General Overkirk's Cavalry, and when his horse was killed, he had picked up his sword and charged the enemy on foot.

We had to clear thousands of corpses from the battlefield so we could pitch our tents, digging vast ditches, one for the French, and one for our own dead. As I threw the spades of earth into their sightless eyes, I found myself weeping, yet none about me said a word of reproach.

That night, Orkney's Royal Scots marched back from chasing the French, and I limped over to their sutler's fire to find John Deane promoted to Sergeant, and busy binding Sergeant Millner's arm, where Kit Welsh had cut out a bullet.

Sergeant Millner supped a brandy, and claimed that we'd smashed the French, killing six thousand, taking nine thousand prisoners, and scattering another fifteen thousand.

"They will still be a hundred thousand strong when Berwick joins them, yet their poor leadership has shattered their morale. Our casualties were but three thousand, and we'll have so many recruits from French deserters and captured mercenaries, we'll hardly notice the loss."

"Aye, 'twas a noble action, from highest to lowest", Sergeant Deane declared. "The French may have cut us off from our supplies, yet we have cut them off from France." I tried to feel that the horror might have been worth it.

Sergeant Millner then explained that France was protected on her northern border by a line of defences that ran for fifty miles, from Dunkirk to Lille. "Marlborough must level these lines before Berwick arrives, and then he'll want one of the fortresses. Yet he's got no cannon, and Vendome won't be willing to let our siege trains through."

The next day, a detachment was sent off under Count Lottum to level the French lines near Warneton. The rest of us decamped and marched after them. When we assembled under the walls of Courtrai a few days later, we heard that the French garrison had fled for Werwick, and that Lottum's men had run upon the works with shovels, and thrown them down. By the time we had marched to Werwick to support him, Lottum's men had already taken it, and we toasted them well that night. Extra pay was offered to demolish the French defences, so I took a spade, and we soon had the lines levelled for several leagues.

This allowed our Cavalry to take war into France for the first time in many years, exposing French provinces to the horror that their Army had been inflicting upon the Dutch. Twenty-five thousand men ravaged the province of Artois, and Berwick's Cavalry was now too decimated to stop them. Those villages that would not provide cheap food, forage, or horses, were left in ashes.

In revenge, the French harried the Flemish peasants around Ghent and Bruges. Then in order to break French communication from Bruges to Nieuport, Marlborough ordered the Governor of Ostend to open the sluices, and the salt sea ruined the land we were fighting over. In truth, I thought the peasants of Flanders must hate both sides.

Berwick was ordered by the French King not to abandon Douai, so he gathered the remnants of his Army into the fortresses of Ypres, Lille and Tournai, unsure which we would attack first. Yet we could take no advantage of our success at Oudenarde without the munitions and supplies which were progressing slowly through canals to Brussels.

Heavy detachments were made to escort the siege train between Vendome's and Berwick's armies, and my Company marched with them. And though our march back to Brussels was hard enough, heaving those wagons through the mud of Flanders was terrible work, especially for the horses. There were a hundred heavy cannon, pulled by twenty horses each, and three and a half thousand munitions wagons, travelling in two columns, each fifteen miles long.

By late July, we were as far south as Soignes, where German troops gave us each a tot of brandy. We rose at dawn the day after, turned the wagons west, and pushed for two days, in a grim struggle that swallowed up most of our complaints. It was on one of those hellish days, after heaving the damned wagons through a swampy plain and over several streams, that I realised I should have joined the Horse, instead of dooming myself to slavery in the Foot.

Once we were over the Scheld, an adjutant rode up and announced that Marlborough wanted Lille, the capital of French Flanders, though our German Guard swore that the immense citadel had never been taken. "Only another twenty miles. A piece of piss!", someone yelled, and we staggered up, and pushed on. At Menin, with rumours of the French Army all about us, we turned the wagons south, cursing the rain and the mud, knowing the whole campaign was lost if the French intercepted us. Our impeccable German Cavalry guard were soon ordered off their horses to fall on their arses in the mud with the rest of us.

We came up to Lille, the town walls surrounded by our Armies, batteries already playing against her double outworks. Fresh men heaved our wagons away as soon as we approached, and we were ordered to pitch camp. When the Assembly was blown, Colonel Hamilton made sure that we were immediately paid for the heavy work we'd undertaken, and thanked us for having saved the campaign.

With my heart set on brandy, I made my way to our sutler's tent, to drink the Colonel's health. There I found Sergeants Deane and Millner, told them my Company had just returned, and invited them to drink with me. Sergeant Deane nodded. "We'd be pleased to, lad. Yet not here. Yer Company will want to celebrate, and we're both quiet fellows. What say we take a stroll to Kit Welsh's tent?"

I feigned good humour, yet had been at some pains to avoid the infamous Irishwoman. Although I was sure that no one would recognise me as the duellist of Covent Garden, I remembered that Colonel Macartney had spoken of drinking at her tent, and was unwilling to face any of his Company. Yet I could think of no excuse against the Sergeants' kind invitation, and so I followed them to their camp.

To my relief, the notorious Irishwoman was busy in the kitchens, and a teasing young Scotswoman waited on us. I ordered three bottles of their best wine, and the Sergeants ordered a feast. I smoked my pipe and described the Hell of the siege train, and then asked the knowing Sergeant Millner for news of Lille.

"Two weeks ago, we were led by the brave young Prince of Orange to surprise Marquet Cloister, just over there." He pointed to a small fort guarding a bridge on the west bank of the Lys. "When they saw us coming, the guards on the bridge took to their heels, and ran the two miles to the gates of Lille like rabbits. We thought we'd pay dearly for the bridge, yet before the garrison could send reinforcements, Sergeant Littler of Godfrey's Grenadiers swam the moat and hacked through the ropes of the drawbridge."

"We're still drinking his health", Sergeant Deane laughed. "Littler had his Colours bestowed on him by the Duke o' Argyle's Regiment." We raised our glasses to a

184

lucky man, whose little talent had seen him rise in the world.

I poured myself another bumper of the excellent wine. "I wish I'd been here, instead of heaving a wagon through half the mud of Flanders."

"Your turn will come, lad", Sergeant Millner assured me. "General Boufflers commands the Lille garrison, and he's a canny old fighting man. That first afternoon, he and his Cavalry paraded out, gasconading as if they'd charge, though their courage failed them." He almost smiled.

"Aye", Sergeant Deane interrupted. "Yet we expected another sortie, and lay on our arms for three nights, praying that Marlborough would be in time to shield us from the oncoming French Army."

Sergeant Millner continued the account. "We all crossed the Lys and blocked up Lille, strongly manned as she is. Eugene and his German troops came up a day later, and now Eugene's drawn up a full duty roster, with the role of each squadron and battalion outlined. The bold young Prince of Orange attacks the north-west side of the city, while the careful Prince Eugene attacks the south-east."

Sergeant Deane broke in again. "Lille is a great way round, and we're lying thin, each Regiment taking up the ground o' two. We've been digging a nine mile double ring of earthworks in the rain, shovelling mud out o' trenches that instantly fill with water. Thousands of peasants are being paid to dig with us, and when we finish the line tomorrow, the French Army won't be able to get in."

"And with the cannon you've dragged up now manning the batteries, the Lille garrison can no longer get out", Sergeant Millner declared.

"There's extra pay for bundling sticks into fascines to fill the great ditches", Sergeant Deane continued. Or ye can have the peasant women teach ye to weave gabions. Yet for a crown, ye can crawl out an' place a gabion at the top of a trench, so the peasant behind ye can fill it with mud, and ye can both stand up. You're quick enough. Ye might end the week alive and rich."

185

"A crown for a basket of mud seems a fair deal to me, and 'tis true I need the funds to buy a horse." I opened the next bottle, and told them of my plan to join the Dragoons.

"Yer selling yeself cheap", Sergeant Deane protested. "The Dragoons are poorly paid and worse treated, no more than peasants on nags. If ye truly know horses, and can bow and scrape like a gentleman's son, then join the Cavalry. Not a top o' the line Regiment, they insist on wealth, yet the Queens would take ye. And as for buying a horse, it could take ye years to save for it. Look for the chance to catch a French horse in battle, or do a little pilfering."

"I feel I shall be lucky, and take a French General prisoner!"

"There'll be none o' the fortune o' battle here, just mud and mines and hand-to-hand fighting", Sergeant Millner declared. "There's fifty battalions in this northern attack alone, ten of us always in the trenches, and it seems more a battle of ants than lions. When 'tis your turn lad, don't run in at their heels if they retreat, for that is when they blow their mines. Let the experienced men search for the mines and nip out the fuses."

"And what of the French Army?", I asked him.

"They have re-crossed the Scheld to cut us off from Brussels."

"You don't seen worried", I commented, pouring us all another glass.

"We're old campaigners, lad", Sergeant Deane declared. "We've seen that the bigger an Army gets, the hungrier it gets, the more commanders it needs, the less anyone knows what's going on, and the more disheartened the men become. We won at Oudenarde because the French commanders were at each other's throats, and because we all know Marlborough won't let us down." He called a toast to our beloved Captain-General, and all those in the tent rose to their feet and raised their glasses.

Kit Welsh herself then bustled up with three roast fowls, three hunks of brown bread, and a bowl of fat corn cobs. She filled our glasses, and sat down next to Sergeant Deane with a tankard of beer, wiping her red and steaming face. "Tell me now Sergeant Deane, with us sittin' here in the open, ready to take their greatest fortress, should the French not be fightin' us?"

"They should, Mistress Welsh, yet that doesn't mean they will." She laughed hard at this, and Sergeant Deane introduced me, and told how he'd found me starving on the Dreadnought, and how eager I was to earn my promotion.

She sternly told me not to be foolish, and get myself killed for nought. "I donned me brother's clothes an' enlisted in '93, to follow me young husband, cruelly pressed by English redcoats into Dutch William's war. I marched with this Regiment for years, an' not one sniff of a promotion did I ever get. I was wounded at Landen under King William, I marched with Marlborough to the Danube, an' fought with the Scots Greys at Schellenberg, an' every time, 'twas an English gentleman's son promoted, not me. After many years, I learned me young husband was already dead. By then, I could no longer think o' quittin' our Regiment."

"How did they discover you a woman?", I asked.

"I was wounded at Ramillies two years ago. Look, ye can see the scar the bullet made across me head. One o' me mates tore me shirt to make a bandage, an' thought he'd gone mad. I'd already secretly married Sergeant Welsh from me own Regiment, an' I told Orkney I'd never leave the Royal Scots, so he let me stay on as Grand Sutler. On condition I wore skirts."

"Aye", Sergeant Deane laughed. "She rules the petty sutlers of each Company, insisting they forage for vegetables to help us against the scurvy, and when funds run out, she steals what she needs to feed us."

"I'm damned if I'd know what to do otherwise."

"Run a tavern", Sergeant Millner suggested, toasting her, and she laughed and poured our glasses full again.

"Your life would be well worth the writing, Mother Welsh", I flattered her.

187

"Yours too, child, I don't doubt it!", she flashed back, and I was suddenly sure she knew my secret. Then I felt like a fool pretending to be a man, when I was not even a boy, and resolved to avoid her in future.

After inspection the next morning, I was sent with the rest to drag artillery up to the batteries, a man sometimes falling with a cry of surprise, picked off by marksmen on the city walls. Yet 'twas the cannon balls screaming over our heads, causing us to cringe into the mud, that I truly feared. The London lad told me that the brave young Prince of Orange had fixed his headquarters so close to the Lille artillery, that when being dressed that morning, a cannon ball had passed over his shoulder and smashed his valets head in, besmearing the Prince with blood and brains. "He has since found a safer abode", the lad grinned, and we all laughed, as the reckless young Prince was a great favourite, especially with his Dutch soldiers.

When Lille was about to be bombarded, Eugene offered the town ladies safe passage. He included Engineer Officers amongst their escort, and they decided on the points of attack. The next day dawned with the pounding of cannon, and after five days of ceaseless bombardment, the moat was almost filled with shattered masonry.

The pounding of cannon had been so constant, that when the French Army came marching up to save Lille, I was relieved to march out to meet them. Yet the French soldiers sheared off, marching hard to circle about us, while we easily kept between them and Lille. The whole mass of us wheeled about to a great plain, perfect for battle, the French soldiers shouting they would rather fling themselves upon us than march another day. To remedy our smaller numbers, Marlborough marched us between two rivers, leaving the French only a narrow front for an attack. Then he refused to tire us with the digging of trenches, and placed Eugene's Cavalry all about us instead. We lay on our arms, and hardened our hearts for fighting at dawn, rumours flying from one campfire to the next, our London lad insisting that

188

Marlborough had a secret deal with his nephew, Berwick, and knew that the French would not attack.

"The French fear us more than we fear them", Captain Gordon stated coolly. "So we don't need to dig trenches." The next day seemed to prove him right, for Berwick's army found itself too hampered by marshes and woods to attack us. The Prince of Burgundy decided that as 'twas the French King's birthday, he would not fight, and instead he showered us with cannonballs, most of which we dug up to sell to our own armoury.

Later that day, the word went around that back at Lille, the besieged Boufflers had taken advantage of a fog to spike some of our guns. It became clear that the gasconading French were keeping us from the siege, and the rumour was that if the town was not taken soon, we would run out of ammunition for the taking of the citadel. Captain Gordon calmly pointed out that Boufflers must have even less powder than us.

The next day, Eugene and his troops returned to the siege, halving our numbers, and we dug trenches and armed batteries all night to strengthen our position. In the morning, the French advanced with three huge Armies, but retreated at dusk, declining the fight. That evening, we heard that our Princes had led fourteen thousand men against the counterscarp of Lille, taking it after a furious struggle that lasted all night. Four great mines had exploded under them, and then the French rained so terrible a fire down upon them, that they could not advance. The Engineers were all killed, the peasants deserted, and we lost three thousand men, as many as at Oudenarde. I prayed that Boufflers would surrender before the first of September, for if it came to a Grand Storm, the men would be let loose on the townsfolk of Lille, and this I did not want to witness.

We were soon camped back at Lille, enduring the cannonballs. I signed up again for setting gabions, and after a hard day in the reeking mud of the trenches, strolled down to a small tributary of the Scheld to wash my hands and face.

I saw Sergeant Deane by his campfire, disputing with his foppish Captain and three over-fine Generals, and hesitated to step out of the shadows. Then the stoutest of the Generals emptied his tankard and slammed it down, and I froze. 'Twas Macartney, the bastard who'd raped me. "I tell you, fool, your Colonel Hamilton told us to meet him here. He lost the wager, and owes us drink and whores!"

"Colonel Hamilton o' the Scots Guards is a whoremonger, indeed", Sergeant Deane agreed. "Ye find yeselves, however, with the Royal Scots, and our Colonel Hamilton is a true gentleman, though he is the other's cousin. He sups tonight with the Duke of Marlborough."

I shrivelled into the horrified child I'd once been, while Macartney refilled his tankard. "Marlborough sets a damned stingy table that's not worth the prating conversation."

"He hails us as his friends, yet he's so old, he wants none to sup with him but his favourites and his damned Chaplain", his friend sneered.

"An' Prince Eugene, a foreigner as well as a bloody fool, is bungling the siege", Macartney declared.

I cringed back into the shadows, while Sergeant Deane scowled and lectured them. "Aye, Lille would be easily taken by those with their heads full o' wine, thinking themselves wiser than the best o' Generals. If cursing and swearing would do, ye'd take Heaven itself by storm, instead o' lookin' to Him who's the giver o' Victory."

Macartney thought Deane referred to the Duke, not thinking of God at all, and lurched to his feet, his face bloated and red under his extravagant wig. Sergeant Deane remained seated, and looked him straight in the eye. "I heartily wish that such coffeehouse warriors may take the place o' many a brave soldier that has been lost", he declared grimly, and Macartney snatched up the Captain's spontoon.

His foppish Captain hastily assured Deane that none who knew Macartney's reputation in Spain could consider him anything but a brave Officer. Deane snorted. "Aye, to have been captured after destroying his Regiment at Almanza must confer some sort o' distinction on a man."

Macartney yanked Sergeant Deane to his feet, and raised the spontoon like a club. Deane's captain protested ineffectually, and the soldiers about them rose helplessly to their feet, frightened of the enraged general. I pulled my knife, and prepared my soul for murder. Then the alarm bell rang, and Macartney threw Sergeant Deane at his captain and stalked off, screaming for an adjutant.

I slumped to the ground, while the men waved down a cavalryman, who reported that three hundred Frenchmen had taken a chateau in front of us, greatly strengthening their position. Old General Webb had then sent General Howes' Fifteenth down a hedge-lined lane, straight into an ambush. Brigadier Temple's Regiment and Webb's Eighth were already marching against the chateau, and we were ordered to join them.

Throughout that march, I kept my mind white as snow, so empty that the wind seemed to whistle through me. We heard that the Frenchmen had retired, and I was glad to see no action that night, unsure if I could have faced it. By the time we marched to rejoin our Army, I knew that only death could save me from madness. And I preferred the death to be Macartney's. The bastard was older now, and must be slower. If I challenged him sober, I'd be offered a beating for my impudence, yet if I found him drunk and insulted him, he'd lose his temper, and witnesses would declare that I'd acted in self defence. The only drawback to this plan was that my rapier was in the possession of Captain Gordon. I would have to steal it back from our Company's wagon, or borrow another.

We spent a week marching after the French army, who broke the bridges and were masters of the Scheld again, cutting us off on all sides, but Ostend. We were running out of provisions and ammunition, our only supplies fifty miles away through hostile and well-fortified French territory.

We marched towards Ostend, and finally halted and

191

set up a strong camp. That night we heard that Prince Eugene had led fifteen thousand men in a determined assault on Lille, and had been wounded under heavy fire, a musket ball grazing his forehead. Marlborough had then undertaken the siege, and to his horror and their shame, he discovered that the Engineer Officers had been at fault in their calculations, erecting their batteries too far from the walls of Lille, and wasting our precious powder to no effect. We heard too that a furious attack by our grenadiers had been repulsed with great loss, and I worried for Sergeant Deane.

Our only consolation was that, as low as our supplies were, those in the citadel at Lille must be desperate. Yet Boufflers managed to get a messenger through our lines, and five nights later, four thousand double-mounted French Dragoons rode up from the Douai road, each extra rider carrying sixty pounds of powder on his back. They wore green boughs in their helmets as though they were Allied troops, and declared they were Germans bringing in French prisoners. They gave the sleepy sentry the correct watchword, and several hundred Frenchmen passed through before the guard heard one of them say in French how easy it had been. He immediately discharged his piece into the thick of them, leaving holes in their powder bags. Half galloped along the road to Lille, yet the rest turned back in disorder, dropping powder bags and scattering powder all over the road. When the next man fired, an enormous blast flung hundreds of men and horses into the air. Yet that night, the garrison at Lille celebrated the delivery of nearly sixty thousand pounds of powder.

Our convoy of supplies from Ostend was now vital, yet Vendome had cut all the dykes between Bruges and Nieuport, laying the country open to the sea again. Marlborough heard that Vendome had sent twenty thousand men to intercept the convoy, and immediately sent the handsome General Cadogan off with his Horse to escort the convoy, with the Earl of Orkney to march at the head of our Regiment as a reinforcement, with eight hundred grenadiers, a German regiment, and General Webb's Eighth. The rest of our Army advanced beyond Menin to support us.

We marched hard through half-swamped roads, almost as far as Ostend. As soon as we met the convoy, we turned the carts south, and began to push. After ten miles, we were almost at the village of Wynendael, when an adjutant galloped past, yelling that the French were at the opening of the plain ahead, behind the forest. The French could have gone around the forest and out-flanked us, yet instead they marched up to meet us through two thick woods, not a thousand yards apart.

Webb immediately ordered us to form for battle on the plain. Then leaving Lottum's Horse in front to take a punishing three hour cannonade, we were ordered to slip into the woods on either side. When the Horse pulled back through the thick smoke, the French took the bait and marched into the trap. When their blue coats filled the space before us, the order was given, and we cut them to pieces. They hardly knew where the volleys were coming from, and retreated, re-formed, and advanced straight into our fire. Some made it to the woods, and it was hand-to-hand fighting until Webb ordered trumpets to sound, as if reinforcements were coming, and the French finally turned and fled.

We remained on the field of battle until late that night, getting our wounded to the carts, and collecting prisoners. I could not find my own Company's sutler, yet I found Kit Welsh. She had Sergeant Millner with her, a great bruise on his head from a musket ball that would have killed him, but for the steel cap in his hat. He told me that though we had been six thousand against twenty thousand, the French had lost four thousand men in that narrow space, and we but a hundred and fifty, though hundreds were wounded. Kit Welsh insisted that General Webb was wounded too, though rumours disagreed as to how seriously. She had caught a fine bay horse, which she sold to Colonel Hamilton the next day for nine pistoles, and I kicked myself for getting no more than an old coat off a dead Frenchman.

Yet we had our convoy through, and when we heaved the carts into the camp at Lille, there was great rejoicing. Eugene immediately resumed the siege, attacking Lille night and day, though at great loss, so stoutly was it defended with mines. Those not blown apart or smothered were scarred by hellish bombs of boiling pitch, tar, oil and brimstone. I found Sergeant Deane being treated at Kit Welsh's tent for a great burn on his back. "The English Grenadiers have scarce six sound men in a Company", he scowled. "We've paid more for Lille than even Namur in King William's war. Christ only knows if 'tis worth it."

To distract him, Kit boasted of how she'd been captured by French soldiers that day, when foraging in an abandoned farmhouse. The soldiers, not realising she was a woman, were quarrelling over the right to her clothes, when she heard their Captain mutter something in Irish. She immediately acclaimed him a cousin, and after an afternoon of drinking and reminiscences, he had remembered meeting her father, and released her.

I spent my time working on the trenches, gruelling work, more from the fear of cannon balls than anything else. Our one-eyed Corporal Taylor worked with me that month, constantly pressing me to lose some of my earnings to him in card play, though I steadily declined the honour. When he shot himself, 'twas revealed that he'd gambled away our Company's pay.

The day after, I was making my way alone through the trenches, flintlock loaded, when I was pinned down by a hail of musket fire from the town. Then suddenly, I spied Macartney sheltering in the trench just ahead of me. He turned his fat back, and I carefully aimed my flintlock, fired, and missed him. When he ducked away without seeing me, I cursed and reloaded, yet the workmen returned before I could fire again, and I was left shaking with fury.

That night, old General Overkirk died, dropping suddenly in our siege headquarters, surrounded by the standards of Oudenarde. The Dutch soldiers loudly lamented the loss of such an experienced and courageous General, and we all drank to his courage, remembering how he had saved us at Oudenarde. Soon after, the muzzles of our cannon pointed over the last of the palisadoes, and to spare the townsfolk of Lille, Boufflers capitulated the town and marched into the citadel.

When Vendome marched his Army to cut us off from Ostend again, great parties of our Horse ravaged the open country of Bois le Duc. We lived better off Artois and Picardie than the French Army did off war-torn Flanders, yet still Marlborough ordered that our bread ration be reduced by a third, and money be given to us instead. There was little enough to spend it on, yet for a month we held our bellies, and proceeded with the digging of trenches between the town and the citadel. Boufflers made small sorties against us every night for a week, yet they suffered great loss, the besieged now weary and careless.

To save their great fortress, the French besieged Brussels. We took advantage of a thick fog to slip over the Scheld on pontoon bridges, and marched all night, without beat of drum, and without opposition. At dawn we ran upon the French entrenchments, and they fled and fell back, reinforcing all the fortresses now open to us.

Winter came down hard upon us then, the nights bitterly cold, and Lille's moat frozen. With the muzzles of our cannon finally over the citadel's palisadoes, Boufflers surrendered Lille, at the cost to us of sixteen thousand men, most blown to pieces.

An hour after Lille was surrendered, we marched for Ghent, furious at the necessity of fighting our way into our Winter headquarters. We were outside the walls within a week, where a hard rain soaked every man in the Army before we could pitch our tents. That night saw a severe frost, and we began to curse the people of Ghent in earnest, shivering in our damp clothes, with no fuel to burn, and poor provisions. Unable to sleep, I stepped out into the bitter wind, and to my surprise, saw the glow of a fire. I roused my

Company, and we found a fire blazing in front of Kit Welsh's tent. Not only had this enterprising woman begged wood from the Officers, she had also found an abandoned vegetable garden behind a deserted brewhouse, and had a hot stew simmering in a massive cauldron.

Yet, despite our thanks, Kit was grim. She later told me she'd seen a cannonball take off the arm of a drummer boy. She had carried him to the Regiment's surgeon, where he laid shivering in her arms until he died. In the morning, we heard that two sentinels had frozen to death at their posts, and we knew that Kit had saved our lives.

We dug trenches under a constant hail of fire from Ghent's castle, before our siege cannon arrived. Then the moats froze again, and we were ready to storm the town, many of the men promising the citizens of Ghent vengeance for all we were suffering. The French soon surrendered, and we marched into Ghent on Christmas Day, having lost four thousand men for the treachery of that town, most dead of cold. That night, a terrible snow storm broke upon us, that must have killed us all had we still been outside the walls, and Sergeant Millner declared that God was on our side. I said He might give the French King the pox if he truly wished to help us. Sergeant Deane declared that our long, tiresome, mischievous campaign was over, leaving us in undisputed control of Flanders, with every likelihood of a favourable peace.

I redeemed my rapier from our Company baggage, and went looking for Macartney, only to find that he had already taken ship for England with Marlborough. Although I had a small stash of coins sewn into my coat, I could not return to England as the Officers did, unless I was part of a recruiting party. I cursed myself again for missing him outside Lille, and promised myself his death as soon as I saw him next.

We soldiers were then left to enjoy the peace of garrison life. I bought a plain suit, hired a room for an afternoon, and enjoyed my end-of-campaign bath in privacy.

Then I scrubbed out my regimentals as best I could, and leaving them to dry in the thin sunshine behind the garrison walls, I joined Sergeant Deane for a pipe of dry tobacco and brandy at Kit Welsh's, the soldiers all scorning to spend money on the sullen townspeople.

I soon made friends with Sergeant Deane's friend Donald Macleod, the old highlander who'd urged me to jump ship and sign up. He took me riding about the countryside, looking for deserters to sign up, and we did well until his friend Sergeant McBain, a drinking, whoring rogue, gambled away our recruiting money. I went back to selling lessons in swordsmanship, and I was glad of my success, for all through the great frost of January, the price of bread doubled, and many peasants perished of hunger in the bitter and unrelenting cold.

We soon heard that Marlborough had sailed for the Hague to open peace talks, most of his Officers and their wives with him. Sally wrote to me that Queen Anne, on receiving the news of Oudenarde, had wept, crying: "Lord, when will all this dreadful bloodshed cease?" To make it worse, Sara Churchill, Marlborough's glamorous wife, had quarrelled publicly with the Queen, threatening their alliance. It seemed that all England was disgusted with the war, declaring Lille not worth the blood. It was a joy to see Spring come, our hopes of peace increased by the desperate plight of France, her treasury exhausted, her peasants starved, her people holding public prayers for peace.

Admiral Leake had taken Minorca, and thus control of the Mediterranean, and I marvelled that in my short life, England could have risen so far. When I was born, Protestant nobles had invited Dutch William to rule us, our own Catholic King James too ready to bow his knee to the French King, as the Stuarts had always done. When I was a child, France was an invincible force, both Flanders and Spain within her grasp. Now she was humbled, and Sergeant Millner declared it a victory for Parliament and Protestantism. Sergeant Deane gave the credit to

Marlborough and his brave redcoats, and we all drank to that.

Yet during the peace negotiations, the Whigs, firmly in control after the elections, insisted that the French King send troops to dethrone his own grandson, who had been crowned King of Spain. King Louis declared that he would rather fight his enemies than his relatives, and appealed to his people to finance yet another campaign. Boufflers sent his plate to the mint, the Spanish Church sent in its silver, and the aristocracy declared it infamous to dine off silver when the King needed it. Then hard famine forced the French peasants into their Army, and they all prepared for one last campaign to defend Paris.

I had fought for the liberation of Europe, not the destruction of France, and I was not the only one who felt that the justice of the war was no longer with us. Sergeant Deane declared that the chance of an honourable peace had been ignored by greedy Whig politicians, who were making their fortunes off this war, and cared not how many of us died for it.

By mid-May, new recruits were arriving daily, and as most of our Officers had returned, I was keeping an eye out for Macartney. Sergeant Deane was now backing my skill with the rapier, and had challenged all duellists in the Infantry on my behalf, so I had been getting a lot of practice, as well as making money. My fourth opponent gave me a good fight, and when he handed over his money and complimented me on my speed, I invited him to join us for a drink and a smoke. We decided on a nearby tavern, and pushed our way through a noisy throng of soldiers, to order brandy off the busy barkeep. I had just poured us all a glass, when Sergeant McBain sat down, raging against the ingratitude shown to the Army. I thought he was talking of Marlborough, but he mentioned Macartney.

My adversary saw my confusion. "Haven't you heard? One o' Marlborough's favourite Generals has been indicted for raping his housekeeper in a drunken fit."

Sergeant Deane pounded the table with his fist. "Not

that braggart of a General I abused outside of Lille? I cannot believe that Marlborough would wish such a man to serve him."

"Nay lads, they're whittling away at Marlborough", Sergeant McBain declared. "The Chief Justice declared it a vexatious suit, and dismissed the charge, yet the bitch housekeeper got the Bishop of London to petition the Queen for her, and women will stick together, damn them!"

"The whore was a parson's widow", my opponent declared. "The worst of the lot, eh! And instead of Her Majesty's thanks for his courage, Macartney got a letter saying she has no more occasion for his service. He's been forced to sell his Regiment. And she didn't consult Marlborough at all."

I exploded. "He should have been strung up from the nearest tree for disgracing the honour of the Army. That drunken bastard has always abused women, and he's only been caught this time because he attacked a lady above reproach."

"Nay lad, the Queen is old and foolish and drinks too much brandy..."

"Take that back or fight me in earnest! How dare you criticize the Queen for drinking when you can't keep your filthy snout out of the grog! How dare you excuse a terrible sin on account of a man's friends! And worst of all, you filthy dog, how dare you call a parson's widow a whore, simply because a foul degenerate has overpowered her!"

"What a bloody mad thing to do! Look the lad's thrown brandy all over me! Very well, you fool, in earnest then!" We stalked out the nearest town gate, duelling being forbidden in the garrison, Sergeant Deane offering himself as my second, and a fair crowd following us. Then the Provost came running, and we scattered, still swearing to spill each other's blood.

I was so angry I was shaking, and Sergeant Deane dragged me off to my quarters. Fearing I must burst with anger, I begged him for a pipe of his fine tobacco, and he ran

199

for it. As soon as the door closed behind him, I fell to my knees and damned God for not correcting my aim at Lille. Then I swore that next time I saw him, Macartney would die by my hand. By the time Sergeant Deane returned, I had recovered my composure, yet that did not stop me from accepting my adversary's written invitation for a meeting.

I met the scoundrel with dawn just showing over the towers of Ghent. Our seconds agreed on the terms of the fight, and instructed us to stop at first blood. It took me two minutes to run him through his sword arm, and to accept his faint apologies. The story was soon all over the garrison, and the gentlemanly Colonel Hamilton threw me a gold coin for upholding our honour.

Chapter 12: Malplaquet

At the latter end of April, the Duke of Marlborough and Prince Eugene stopped in Ghent and I saw the Duke twice, once when I was on guard, and once when he and his entourage rode past me in the street. Even past sixty, he was a good-looking man, with a most convincing air of confidence and an enormous curling wig. He seemed to revel in our acclaim, waving his hat to us with the courtliness of a past age, laughing when my drunken sot of a Sergeant called out: "We'd charge Hell itself with you at our head, Corporal John!"

In the first week of May, Marlborough ordered the Allied Army to assemble at Lille, and we marched south in easy stages, sure we had the French Army on its knees. Yet, as we strode through the devastated countryside, we became appalled by the hard misery of the Flemish peasants, left without seed to sow, or bread to feed themselves. They begged from us on all sides, and many of us halved our rations for the wretches, and then halved them again.

After a week, we filed out upon the plains of Lille to pitch camp, and our tents filled that great arena. I found Sergeant Millner drinking with Kit Welsh, and he declared that we had nearly two hundred battalions of Infantry, over three hundred squadrons of Horse, and over a hundred and thirty cannon and mortars. He thought the French had fewer guns, yet a stronger Horse, and reported them strongly entrenched near Arras, surrounded by woods and marshes.

That evening, our Generals decided against sacrificing us in the swamp of Arras, and marched us south, without beat of drum. Many wagered we were bound for Paris, yet in the middle of the night, we were ordered to turn east, and at dawn, we found the towers of Tournai cathedral before us. At mess that night, our drunken Sergeant toasted Marlborough, for although Tournai's citadel was said to be the strongest ever built, the garrison had only four thousand men, commanded by General Surville. And as we had slipped between Tournai and the French Army, the fortress was now cut off from all succour.

Marlborough decided to conduct the siege himself, and chose my Regiment to make the first attack on the outworks of Tournai. Lord Orkney and his Piper led us forward, and we heaved eight guns towards the moat, setting up the first battery within musket shot of the bridgehead. Orkney rode up and offered the Artillery men a bottle of brandy if they could shoot through the chains of the drawbridge. They all aimed carefully, and the drawbridge crashed down through the billowing smoke.

Colonel Hamilton gave a ferocious yell, and charged over the moat, and we leapt after him. A bullet grazed my cheekbone, and Captain Gordon took one in the arm, and though most of the French guard fled before us, 'twas hand to hand against the bravest. We soon had them out, and the sconce was ours, 'though that scoundrel, Sergeant McBain, had the honour of capturing the French Captain. We were then posted in the sconce as guards, and another detachment was sent in to take the Fort, sword in hand, opening Tournai to our investment.

Then we began the long, hard work of digging trenches in steady rain, working up to our knees in mud, shovelling it up to a parapet of fascines, where it washed steadily back in through the twigs and branches. It was slow work, yet when we had finished, our Army had a strong position between the two arms of the Scheld. Then we heard that the French had blocked the canal north of Oudenarde, to stop our Artillery barges getting through. We were immediately marched off to dig a new channel, and though the duty was hard, the siege could not continue without cannon, so we broke our backs, and had the guns through by the first of July.

We returned to camp in a cold and miserable rain, and I fortified myself with hot rum at Kit Welsh's tent. I asked Sergeant Deane for the news, and he told me that the

Tournai garrison had used the Scheld to flood the moats, astounding our Engineers with their ingenuity. Marlborough had already sent in Grenadiers to attack the town in three places, and they had made their way into the cover before the French could bring their guns to bear. Again breaking with tradition, Marlborough sent us in against the citadel before the fortress had surrendered, stretching the numbers of the thinly-manned garrison. Indeed, the siege progressed so well, that within weeks, Surville ceded the town and marched into the citadel to concentrate his defence, vowing to die in the ruins of Tournai rather than surrender.

Two days later, the battalions that had engaged in the first part of the siege were relieved, and we marched off, glad to be away from the cannonballs and mud, though I had another full purse from carrying gabions. We set up camp upon the plain, foraging what we could from the ravaged land about us, our Scottish sutler still carefully tending Captain Gordon's injured arm to keep him from hospital. In the last week of July, we finally broke camp, and left the empty land about us, following our scouts to fresher fields closer to Arras.

Because of my experience with driving wagons as a farm boy, I was detailed to drive cartloads of hay and corn back to the siege at Tournai. It was pleasant work in the Summer sunshine, and a great relief to me, to be so far from threat of cannonballs.

Captain Gordon ordered me to keep my ears open and report any news, so once back in Tournai I went looking for Sergeant Deane. I ran into Donald Macleod, and he told me that Deane had been badly hurt, and was being tended in Kit Welsh's tent. I found him half drunk, and about the arms, where he had been burnt.

His detachment of Grenadiers had run upon the outworks of the citadel, and when a great party of the besieged had sallied out, the Grenadiers had charged them. The French had immediately turned and fled, only to find Sergeant Deane and a few men blocking their escape. The

Frenchmen had screamed, their terror proof to Sergeant Deane that the sally was a trick, and the outworks were about to be blown. He had bellowed at them all to run, and as they fled the world had roared, and the ground had given way. Many men had to be dug out from the rubble, half-roasted. Sergeant Deane was lucky, only burned upon his arms, having thrown them up to protect his face. To save him from the garrison hospital, Kit Welsh treated them with a salve of her own making, and they did not fester.

I spent a day resting the horses and repairing the carts for the return journey. Upon my arrival back at the siege the day after, I heard Kit Welsh was celebrating, and found her diverting her Company with her latest adventure. "I went to look for me husband in the trenches, and found Lord Cobham instead, urgin' on the Artillerymen by offerin' a guinea to whoever shot down a windmill. Well, I snatched the match out o' the nearest Artilleryman's hand, and clapped it to the touchhole. I was beaten backwards by the blast for me impudence, an' I swear I can still hear it echoin' in me ears. At least I couldn't hear the fury of the Artillery-man who'd aimed the gun, an' missed the guinea. An' as 'twas his guinea that bought us this wine, we owe him a toast!"

Later, as curfew neared, and the men left, she poured me another brandy and told me that soon after she'd earned her gold, Captain Brown had been shot in the leg. "I helped his servants carry him to the Surgeon, who prepared to amputate. The Captain screamed his refusal, and his frightened servants would not hold him down. So I did. 'Twasn't so bad once he'd swooned." She shuddered, and tossed back another drink.

"Truly, 'twas easier fightin' side by side with me husband. We'd always bring each other out o' the worst of it. He's in the thick of it tonight, and I cannot bear it. So sleep here by the fire, and lend me yer sword, in case I find meself in any trouble."

"You've been in enough fights, Mother Welsh, without seeking any more. I feel the same when Sergeant

Deane goes off on some forlorn hope, and I stay behind digging ditches. Yet we all have our duties assigned us, some of it terrible, all of it necessary. Your husband will need a good hot meal when he wins through, and that cannot be easy to provide in this poor country."

"Aye, yer a good child. Yet, I'll borrow yer sword, an' leave ye to keep me fires hot." She threw her dress off, and was wearing trousers and a shirt underneath. She donned the old soldiers' coat she always wore against the cold, and loaded her pistol, and I saw she was indeed determined to seek her husband at the battlefront.

Certain she had seen through my disguise, I shrugged and handed her my sword. She laughed quietly at me, and slipped off into the shadows, leaving me resolved once again to avoid her, and 'twas then I discovered I liked her best.

Throughout July, Tournai became a new horror, an underground war. Our men dug to find the French mines, while the French sapped under them. They met in narrow tunnels and fought with picks and spades in the darkness. Sergeant Deane declared that all those manning the batteries were nervous, many swearing they could hear the tapping of miners beneath them.

Then a townsman of Tournai offered to reveal one of the principal mines of the citadel, if he could have the post of head gaoler when the town was taken. He uncovered a large mine, about to destroy an entire Hanoverian battalion, yet while they were rejoicing at this good fortune, another below it was sprung, and all were entirely lost.

In mid-August, Governor Surville found himself out of food, and proposed to surrender the citadel, if a truce could be extended throughout the Netherlands. Marlborough rejected these terms, and the following day, our batteries assailed the besiegers so furiously that they could not contain the fires that broke out. That night, they blew all the mines they had in one great blast that shook the earth. At dawn the next day, Surville beat the chamade, only to find that Marlborough would allow him no terms but abject surrender, so angry was he at the terrible destruction of his army. Surville then threatened to blow the whole citadel up, and Marlborough promised that if they forced us to fight for it, we'd show them no quarter. After another two days of constant bombardment, the Governor beat the parley to surrender, having lost three thousand men in the siege, while we'd lost more than five and a half thousand, most of them blown to pieces or buried alive.

As soon as the surrender was beaten, Lord Orkney led a great detachment of us south-east, in heavy rain. The Prince of Hesse's detachment followed us on another road, and we marched hard for two days, rumour insisting we were headed for Paris. We had just made camp when the Assembly was blown, and Captain Gordon told us that Hesse's detachment was being threatened by the entire French army. We left our tents and baggage and marched all night, the weather worsening into a downpour. At dawn, we came upon Hesse's forces, yet before our sutler could feed us, Hesse ordered us all closer to Mons. Half dead for want of food and rest, we struggled through the rain and mud, to halt at dusk on the Bellin Hills. France was before us, the campfires of the French Army glittering on the other side of the dark forest below.

Utterly weary, we slept in the mud where we fell, defenceless against the expected French attack. Yet there was no immediate prospect of battle when we woke at dawn. Indeed, our Scottish sutler had found us, and was already cooking up an enormous cauldron of porridge. When Captain Gordon inspected us, he shook his head over the number of men lost or deserted on our weary march, yet stragglers fronted up all day. By the afternoon, our wagons found us, and we unpacked tents and baggage, and pitched camp properly. And then the French let us sleep with the luxury of food in our bellies and a roof over our heads.

We were woken the next morning by a French cannonade that smashed into the Dutch on our left wing. We spent hours dragging cannon up muddy hills, so our Artillery

206

could reply to the French guns, the resulting barrage continuing until evening. In the afternoon, we struck camp, and marched close to the forest pass, noting the dense wood and the heavy French entrenchments.

Expecting battle in the morning, I sat with my Company about a small fire. Our sot of a Sergeant poured his friend Sergeant McBain a tot of brandy, and toasted the French Army as nought but a rabble of ragged Winter recruits, no match for the well-equipped veterans of Oudenarde. Captain Gordon reported that General Villars had marched the French hard to get between us and Paris, and then not trusting their inexperience; he had neglected to attack us when we were weary, and could have been easily defeated. Instead, he had greatly increased the strength of the French position by digging in around Malplaquet, a small village in the thick of the forest.

We slept on our arms, and the cannonade resumed at dawn. Rumours swept the lines that Marlborough was urging an attack, the French entrenchments growing stronger by the hour, while we lost hundreds to their cannon. Yet Eugene insisted on waiting for reinforcements, so we spent the day cutting and bundling sticks into fascines, to fill the swamp between us and the forest.

That night we heard that the Generals had resolved to fight, hoping to end the war at a single stroke, by destroying the French King's last remaining army. We were told that all attacks were to begin at daybreak, the signal to be a salvo from our entire Artillery. We settled about our campfires, rumours of war and peace flying about us, many promising a stiff vengeance for friends blown to pieces at Tournai, others praying that this battle would end it.

'Twas nearly midnight when the London lad shouted that there were horsemen in the woods before us. Fearful of a Cavalry attack in the night, we all stood to look. Then we heard the cry of "Peace! Peace! It is peace!" taken up and repeated, sweeping down the line, and we gaped, then laughed, and then went mad with joy. The horror was over, we had won! With the terrible fear of death lifted, life seemed utterly precious to us, and war an evil madness.

We ran towards the entrenchments that guarded the pass to Malplaquet, and the Frenchmen sprang over their parapets, and ran forward to embrace us. Grown men wept, others exchanged gifts of food and liquor, and swapped uniforms. I found myself arm in arm with a young Frenchman, trying to converse with him, both of us laughing, full of curiosity and goodwill. Then one of their Officers came riding up and screamed at them, and they parted from us in confusion. Yet there was no mistaking the next order, for they moved towards their discarded muskets. We took to our heels and ran, and they sent a full volley after us, wounding many.

Back in our lines, the men about me erupted into fury, swearing vengeance on the traitorous French bastards. I found myself without any heart left for anger, but my courage was gone, and I needed brandy. I slipped away to find Kit Welsh sitting by a small fire next to her cart, and promised that if she could enlighten me as to the night's events, I'd buy us both a bottle. Kit laughed at my gloom, and told me that some French General, in an excess of martial gallantry, had wanted to speak to one of our generals. General Cadogan and the Dutch Princes had met with him in the French defences just before us, and men of both sides had thought that the old French King had finally surrendered. As soon as Villars had heard that Cadogan was viewing his defences, he had sent orders to chase us off, and the French, thinking us spies, had shot at us.

I laughed at the confusion of it, and after another glass, wept at the senselessness of it. For half an hour, war had seemed impossible, and now 'twas peace that could not be had for any price. Kit tried to reason with me, telling me I must sleep, for there was battle in the morning, yet my tormented soul writhed in agony, and I finished the bottle regardless.

By first light of the last day of August, two hundred

thousand God-fearing men were ready to fall remorselessly upon each other. We received a day's bread, which we ate a mouthful of, stowing the rest in our knapsacks for later. Priests then offered prayers at the heads of both Armies, and like a miracle, the sun drew a dense fog from the marsh. Instead of seeing it as a sign from God, our Generals ordered us to draw up. My regiment stayed in the centre as Marlborough's reserves, the cavalry behind us, and the artillery on the hills behind them. Schulenburg's twenty thousand men formed three ranks on our left, and were ordered to force a way through the French entrenchments. The gallant young Prince of Orange formed his thirty battalions into two ranks on our right, to make a lesser attack past the French Artillery.

Captain Gordon nodded to see this, and stated coolly that 'twould be just like Blenheim. "We'll attack their left and right wings until they've no choice but to reinforce them from their centre. Then we'll rush their weakened centre, and take it, allowing our Horse to pass through the forest to attack the French Horse on the other side. If they win, there is nothing between us and Paris. The marshy ground means the burden of the battle will fall on the Foot, as it always does, and we will win it for Marlborough, as we always do."

Just then the drinking, fornicating Sergeant McBain was approached by a hooded peasant with a knapsack. Their squabble ended when the peasant fled, leaving Sergeant McBain holding the knapsack, from which exploded the unmistakeable cry of a baby. Captain Gordon dashed up to him, and the red-faced Sergeant haltingly explained that his Flemish girl had run off, leaving him with the bairn. "A battle is no place for a child! Do something with it!"

"For Christ's sake, I know nothin' o' bairns!"

We laughed at him, though truly the child's cries were piercing, even Marlborough turning in his saddle to stare down at us from his hilltop. In desperation, McBain gave the child some brandy, and when it slept, he slung the knapsack on his back, declaring that his son would be battle-

209

hardened before he woke.

Then, as the fog lifted, the commanders of both sides presented themselves to their soldiers, the French cheering Villars and Boufflers, while we roared for Marlborough and Eugene. And at nine, the grand battery fired the salvo, and the battle began. Eugene marched Schulenburg's troops straight for the French battery in the dense wood, the French firing hard from behind their entrenchments. Almost all the Officers in Schulenburg's first line fell, cannon shot carried off whole ranks of men, yet each gap was immediately filled by those behind, and with Eugene rallying them in person, they continued their steady advance. Yet the fringe of the wood blazed with fire and smoke, and there the first line was brought to a standstill. Then Schulenburg's second and third lines broke on the edge of the wood like a double wave, and bore them all forward, and they poured through the first breach in the French defences.

On our right, the rash young Prince of Orange, spurred on by Eugene's example, led his men forward without orders, straight past a French battery, to attack the French entrenchments. Showers of cannon balls felled most of the Prince's staff and his horse was killed under him, yet still he pressed on. His men followed him with faultless discipline, the grapeshot mowing thousands down like wheat. They made it into the forest, yet the terrible fire from the trenches chased them out again, back into the fire from the French battery. If the Prince of Hesse's Cavalry had not ridden up to stop the French pursuit, the Prince of Orange might have lost his entire force at once. Then, though the ground was strewn with five thousand writhing, screaming men, and despite having his second horse shot from under him, the Prince of Orange seized his Regimental standard, and ran at the French entrenchments. With a ragged cheer, his men charged after him, and again a French counter attack swept them back in disorder, and again the Prince of Hesse saved them.

Meanwhile, on our left, Lottum's troops marched

steadily towards the forest after Eugene, and became the target for a terrible fire from two batteries. Although they withstood this punishment with the utmost fortitude, they were being cut down too quickly to be an effective attack on the woods. That was when Marlborough ordered the Duke of Argyll to lead his brigade to Lottum's support, taking Lord Orkney's two battalions as reinforcements.

Argyll rode up to us and roared, "I require none to go where I refuse to venture!" Then, head high, he spurred his old warhorse forward. And his courage drew us on, for Argyll was always where the action was hottest, and scorned to wear the Officer's breastplate, since we poor soldiers had none. As we followed him over the marshy ground we'd laid with fascines the day before, I too held my head up, and marched to the stately beat of the drum, and prayed that I would not disgrace myself. Then enemy fire smashed into us, and in front of me a man fell, and I stepped up, and then stepped up again as another went down screaming. Through the thick smoke, I glimpsed the edge of the woods, and saw the enemy aiming at us over their entrenchments.

Then Argyll roared, and we charged them, Lottum's troops carried along with us, into the dark shadows of the forest. And there, within a triangle no more than six hundred yards long, thousands of men lay dying, lying thickly one on top of another, writhing amongst the blasted trees and screaming, or limp and gone. Argyll shouted, and with cannon balls tearing branches off the trees about us, we formed up as well as we could, and marched through the enemy fire, straight at the first French parapet. Then Argyll bellowed and ran towards the French, and we charged followed him, bayonets fixed, half sick with fear.

Argyll's brigade had suffered heavily, and Temple's was almost entirely destroyed, yet we made it to the first parapet, and clambered over the pointed branches, to fall mercilessly upon the remaining Frenchmen.

We halted in a ditch of corpses and screaming wounded, and breathing hard, I reloaded my flintlock, and wiped my red blade on a dead man's coat. Men of my Regiment were dropping in about me, few without hurt, though we were so glad to live, that we hardly regarded our wounds. All those with flasks pulled them out and shared their brandy, and then Captain Gordon stood, called us his best and bravest, and commanded us to follow him.

I leapt after him, and we ran through the dark forest to the next parapet, cannon balls whistling past our heads. We leapt into the second ditch, only to find Vain's Second Battalion of Guards plundering the wounded of both sides. Captain Gordon levelled his musket at one man who was about to bayonet a helpless redcoat, and I aped him, my soul aghast at this new horror. "Leave this unholy plunder!" Captain Gordon bellowed. "The battle's just begun, and can still be lost! If we can but drive them from this wood, France is ours!" We re-loaded fast, many with us, and leaving the looters, we ran straight into the fire of the French guns, and over the last parapet. We fired as one, the Artillerymen broke and ran, and we found ourselves alive and in possession of their guns.

Argyll rallied us, miraculously unhurt, though musket balls had peppered his coat and hat. We drew up in good order at the edge of the forest, only now seeing how many men we'd lost. It was then I felt the pain in my brow, and realised I'd been cut. Captain Gordon wiped blood from my eyes and bound my head with a rag torn from a dead man's shirt, declaring the cut not too deep.

Before us on the plain, the surviving French Infantry had drawn up in parade order, well-covered by their Horse. A battery was brought to fire upon us, and Schulenberg ordered all the unwounded men back into the forest to drag up the captured French guns. At Captain Gordon's nod, we joined them, dragging seven light cannon through the woods just in time to keep the French Cavalry from riding down upon our weary men.

Then we took our place in the line again, facing fifty French battalions, all heavily entrenched along a mile of front, not more than two hundred yards before us. "Oh God no, they can't expect us to attack again", I groaned.

My sot of a Sergeant held out his brandy flask. "Not us lot. Totally shattered. Have a swig."

"You don't look too bad."

"Oh I know how to take care o' meself, lad." I eyed his bulging knapsack, and I felt I could kill him too.

Captain Gordon stopped an adjutant, and begged for news. He dropped from his horse, demanded a drink, and told us that while we were in the forest, Villars had indeed emptied his centre to resist our overwhelming attacks on his left and right flanks. Eugene had rallied the Dutch troops, sword in hand, refusing to withdraw even when grazed above the ear by a bullet. Then, when Marlborough ordered the Prince of Orange's brigade to support Eugene, his shattered forces had refused to charge. Their dauntless young Prince had turned his back on them, grabbed their colours, and had run, screaming defiance, at the French entrenchments. He had gone a hundred yards before his men had caught him up, and this time they had entirely overwhelmed the French, and the forest was ours.

Before the battle, Marlborough had sent Withers' twenty squadrons around the forest, and now they cantered onto the plain to protect us from the French Horse. They charged and wheeled their magnificent horses like heroes, their sabres slashing in the sun, yet they were slowly beaten back into the woods by the French Cavalry, their wounded slaughtered before our eyes.

Then the French Artillery pounded our whole front in a terrible cannonade that left scarce a whole man in any platoon. I saw the London lad killed outright, and stumbled back over the fat corpse of my Sergeant, just as a cannon ball whizzed over my head. Ducking down behind his ample bulk, I drank all that was left in his brandy flask and re-loaded. Then Captain Gordon yelled that 'twas better to be killed standing than cowering, and I stood with the Sergeant's knapsack over my shoulder, and fired. The French

213

Infantry had advanced to within twenty yards of us, and just as we faltered, our courage gone, they fired a final volley, and marched off.

We lay where we were for a time, and then, around noon, our Captains assembled us into what remained of our shattered platoons. We ate our remaining bread and re-loaded, rumours flying that Villars, the French General, was badly wounded. And then we saw Marlborough leading our Cavalry from the forest pass, and we all stood to cheer him. Boufflers, now in supreme command of the French, was leading his Cavalry away to cover his Infantry's retreat, yet when he saw the English Horse, he wheeled his own Cavalry and charged them straight past us. Argyll shouted, and we fired upon their flank, and turned them.

Then, with a cry of "God and Corporal John!", Colonel Campbell whipped his great stallion past Marlborough, and led his Grey's thundering into the French Horse, turning their first line and breaking through the second, little Lord Lumley and General Woods hot on their heels. Boufflers' Cavalry wheeled and again we fired upon their flank and turned them, allowing our entire Horse to file out of the woods to protect us.

The two lines of Horsemen clashed and wheeled and charged for over an hour, as we common soldiers stood and cheered. 'Twas a glorious spectacle, and when the French Horse finally retreated, we rejoiced. 'Twas then I decided to leave the hard slavery of the Infantry, and see my next campaign in the gallant Cavalry.

Argyll ordered the Assembly, and we found few unhurt in our Company. The London lad and our sottish Sergeant were both dead, Sergeant McBain and his baby unscratched, Lieutenants Dixon and Stratton badly wounded. I thought then that I'd have the promotion I'd fought for, just as I'd learnt not to want it.

The forest was crawling with shattered men, the battlefields thick with the dead. It was a sight that none who saw it could ever forget. We spent the afternoon piling the

214

wounded into separate carts, the French sent to the nearest French towns, ours billeted upon the local peasants, or sent to our garrison hospitals. Then our baggage carts came up, and we had to clear away the corpses to make camp on the bloody field, too stricken to march anywhere.

That evening, after our sutler had fed us well, many spoke of the glorious Cavalry battle we had witnessed. Captain Gordon reported that our own King Jamie had charged twelve times with the Maison du Roi, until wounded in the arm. The Jacobites in the Royal Scots drank his health, Sergeant McBain boasting that he'd seen him scouting our way before this battle, and been careful not to fire on him. The men laughed at him, implying that he might have been otherwise busy, and asking what he'd done with the baby.

I shook and drank brandy, as I always did in the aftermath of battle, and thought that nothing could justify such horror as I had witnessed. Instead of fighting for glory and Queen Anne, I determined to survive until the end of the campaign, when I would leave the perilous life of a Foot soldier, and join the Horse.

I thought of my dead Sergeant's knapsack, and wondered if there was any brandy or tobacco left to share with my brave Company. I took a lantern to my tent, and poured the contents upon my camp bed. Amongst the stolen gold crosses and empty flasks of rum, I found a small bag. When I opened it, it was full of gold coins, enough to change my fate entirely.

Needing his advice, I found Sergeant Deane at Kit Welsh's tent, glad to find that she was away, still looking for her husband. Sergeant Deane was but lightly hurt, and busy binding Sergeant Millner's wounds, both of them already soused. I immediately bought a bottle, and joined them, and we toasted the glorious dead. Sergeant Millner told me that we had lost perhaps twenty-five thousand, and the French about fifteen thousand. "Forty thousand men!" I was aghast. Never had there been such terrible bloodshed in one battle.

Sergeant Deane declared that we could win the battle

and still lose the war, for with our dauntless courage, we had not destroyed the French Army, but ourselves. "The Dutch have not a hundred men left in any of the thirty battalions that attacked the French entrenchments."

Sergeant Millner winced in pain and drank again. "The French massacred us before their entrenchments, and then retired in good order to a strong position, mostly intact. We were left with the field of battle, yet we have lost a quarter of our Army, and they are still between us and Paris."

Sergeant Deane scowled and drained his tankard. "Before Malplaquet, we were invincible, and sure of a worthwhile peace. It seems we have sacrificed ourselves for nought."

With my soul aghast at all the death I'd seen, all seemed confused and shameful, and not worth the blood. Glory was gone, and I too could only find solace in brandy.

The day after Malplaquet, we fell back to fresher ground, between two streams, where we washed the gore from our hands and faces, shoes and coats. I messed with my Company, and our sutler told us that Kit Welsh had lost another husband. It took days for her to show, and when she did, her settled gloom cleared her tent of all the fellows who'd laughed with her. Despite Colonel Hamilton's denial, she was convinced that Lord Orkney would demand her dismissal as Regimental sutler, and though she would not say why, the rumour was she'd played him some scurvy trick. She stayed away for days at a time, returning with cartloads of brandy that she'd stolen for us from the French, and it was evident her daring had turned to recklessness.

We heard that the French General Villars would live, though he'd lost a leg. Marlborough, grief-struck at the slaughter of so many brave men, made easy terms for the return of the French wounded, asking them only for their parole not to serve again in this campaign. Indeed, the Generals of both sides did all they could, in terms of money and compassion, everyone distressed at the carnage. Amongst the dead, we discovered the corpse of a young

Frenchwoman dressed in French uniform, and buried her with honour.

Then Sergeant Deane told me that just before Malplaquet, Macartney had asked Colonel Hamilton of the Scots Guards to accept him as a volunteer. Hamilton had made him brevet commander of a Regiment, and when their Colonel was wounded, Macartney had been promoted in his place. I resolved then to kill him before I quit the Foot for the Cavalry, for the Scots Guards were always posted close to the Royal Scots, and I would see him every day. I considered challenging and killing him honourably, yet had no rapier handy. A knife in the back or a shot in the dark seemed most likely to succeed, without getting me killed for insubordination. I practised my aim, sharpened my knife, and awaited my opportunity, following him at night, hoping to find him drunk, alone and off guard, yet he was always in company.

Then, at the beginning of September, our entire Army marched to invest Mons, Marlborough needing to prove that we had won at Malplaquet. We spent a couple of days bundling fascines, and then marched up to take our turn at the trenches, the rain and mud making the digging tedious. I kept my head down, and made no rash moves, not even volunteering to plant gabions, the gold coins sewn into my coat making that risk now unnecessary.

I planned my promotion to the Cavalry. I knew they liked their riders a little lighter than the average soldier, which suited me, and instead of sharing a tent with sometimes seven men, there might be but two. I was sure that with a good nag, I could match the skill of any Cavalryman. And I could wear my rapier always, and find any excuse to challenge Macartney.

When the siege train arrived from Brussels, we took advantage of the better weather to make two separate attacks on the town. The handsome General Cadogan led my Regiment as part of two battalions in an attack on the south. The French discovered us before we got into cover, and four

217

hundred men fell that night, Cadogan catching a shot in the neck, though he was not killed. The following dawn, the besieged sallied out on their approaches, and we charged them, killing many before they fled. Immediately after, our Artillery began firing against their flankers, dismounting them before nightfall, so we could move even further in.

The rest of my company then heaved all our cannon into batteries, and at dawn on the twentieth of September, all our guns began to pound a breach in the counterscarp of the town. That day and the next, they attacked, taking more of the outworks, and driving the besieged back in when they sallied out against us. It was a week before they tried again, a night attack that was sharply repulsed to their great loss. The next morning, in a heavy downpour, a detachment of our Grenadiers attacked the counterscarp, Sergeant Deane amongst them, and after two hours, they beat the French from the outworks in front of the approaches. At the end of September, more outworks were taken, the work completed a week later, when several fresh batteries were erected against the main wall of the town.

At dawn, fury of our batteries was such that the Governor beat a parley, capitulating on honourable terms, and marching out to the garrison of Maubeuge with honour. They had lost nearly a thousand men, and we had lost twice that, wounds festering fast in the damp, though mine stayed clean and healed well. The French army concentrated to protect Maubeuge, yet Marlborough had already decided that we had suffered enough from the hardships of the siege, the bad weather, and the lack of forage, and the next day, he and Eugene declared that year's campaign in Flanders over.

Chapter 13: Venus and Mars

The Regiments were dismissed to their Winter quarters, and we followed little Lord Lumley towards Brussels, our men heaving the Artillery wagons over the muddy roads, me driving the rest of those wounded in carts.

I spent the first night drinking quietly in Kit Welsh's tent, her sombre widowhood suiting me better than her hard laughter had done. She no longer looked at me long and quizzically, and I no longer feared her sharp-eyed curiosity. I bought us both brandy, and when Captain Gordon walked in, requested a discharge.

"Nay lad, ye'd not leave us! There are ranks above yers empty now. I can promise ye..." he started up as a dour-faced nobleman rode by, amidst a small entourage. "My Lord! My Lord Orkney! Would you witness a proposal I'm making to this soldier? He's been with us two years, and thinks to leave just as his courage has earned him advancement."

Orkney raised a quizzical eyebrow at me. "Your Regiment has been a good home to me, and Captain Gordon deserves the trust of his men", I muttered, staring at the ground. "Yet I have some skill with horses, and the Cavalry is still under-manned after their valiant charges to save us at Malplaquet." Captain Gordon abused the Horse as a drunken mob of debauchees, and praising my steady character, mentioned I carried a Bible.

Orkney smiled at me, and I forbore to mention that I carried it more as a token of my mother's goodness than my own. "The only Troop that deserves such a lad is my friend Lumley's", he told the Captain. "Remind me to mention the lad." I bowed low, and bought Captain Gordon a bottle of brandy so he'd not forget this night, and by the time we reached Brussels, I had an honourable discharge from Orkney's Infantry.

We marched up to Ghent at the end of October, and I

was the first in the door of the Dutch tailor, with a list of measurements I'd made, 'from my English tailor'. I then took a small room at a good inn, settling on a ridiculous price for the next few days, while the Officers were all in town, and a fair price for the months after. The landlord sent me upstairs with a little mouse of a housemaid, who glared at me. I requested a hot bath before the fire in an hour, and she told me they were terribly busy, so I threw her a guilder, and then a few more, until she nodded.

I took myself off for a good dinner, carried a brandy bottle away to the tailor's, and smoked my pipe while his three sons stitched industriously at my new suit. I accepted the tailor's offer of three fine shirts and neckcloths almost new, three pairs of stockings knitted by his wife, and some fine buckled shoes, well worn in, and paid him handsomely.

On the way back to my room, my ragged uniform seemed more louse-ridden and stinking than was bearable. I bolted the door, beat up the fire, and stripped entirely, including my pissing tube. Then I stepped into the hot tub, and scrubbed off the filth of an entire campaign. Then I dried myself as well as I could before the fire, and tried on my new clothes. The usual long shirt and breeches were well made, and the coat fitted across my strong shoulders. I knotted on a neckcloth, pulled on the stockings and shoes, and tied my hair back into a queue.

When I called the girl in to see the transformation, she almost laughed. To keep her smiling, I told her I was not going to spend the Winter trying to make a whore of her, when there were enough already in Ghent. She was soon easier with me, and when I gave her five guilders, and asked her to throw the filthy water into the street, she asked me what she was to do with my old uniform. I suggested that she wash and dry it, so I could sell it, halving the cash with her, and she agreed.

I did the rounds of the taverns, and eventually found Sergeant Deane singing Jacobite songs with the stalwarts of the Scots Regiments. Around midnight, we lit our pipes, and he settled into a quieter mood. I asked him for his advice on joining the Cavalry, and he told me that his uncle had been promoted for his heroism at Malplaquet. "And not before time, either. Little Lord Lumley's always dancing at Marlborough's side, so Lieutenant-Colonel Deane has effectively commanded the Regiment since the year seven. They wouldn't confirm his promotion, as he's a Scotsman, and none too rich. Yet he's got his commission now, and will take whoever he pleases, though you must pay for the privilege. You will like him. A steady, careful man, who would never sacrifice a Regiment in some fit of pride or foolishness."

"I remember Kit Welsh speaking of Lord Lumley too, as a polite and humane man."

"Yet Lumley prides himself on the good breeding of his Officers. You'll have to play the gentleman, and spend more than you ought on clothes and horseflesh."

I decided to attribute a fortune to my dead grandmother and pretend a recent reconciliation, and the next morning I waited on General Lumley, with a short memorial. His Secretary took it, and then returned to tell me that I was to look out for a suitable vacancy under the degree of Captain, and to let him know when I had found it. "His Honour grants you permission to dine with the troopers until then. Here are five pistoles. Please do not expect more."

"I had not expected even this", I told the Secretary's cool sneer. "Please thank His Lordship for me."

He condescended to tell me that I'd find Lumley's Officers at the sign of the Black Bear, close by. After a cold walk, I found the crowded tavern ablaze with light and laughter. An Irish Captain was proposing a toast to Lieutenant-Colonel Deane, barely acknowledged by two English Captains, with a great deal of gold lace about them.

A table of Lieutenants toasted a new comrade, Jim Stalker, who had transferred to their troop after Malplaquet, and I offered to buy them a round to drink the Queen's health. Stalker was soon soused, and confided that he felt it

221

unlucky to be taking Old Stirrop's place.

"How did he die?" I asked.

"Cannonball took his head clean off."

"Now that's what I call a lucky death", I declared, and cajoled Stalker into another glass, and a better mood. After many more loyal toasts, I left the Lieutenants drunk and friendly, and ready to recommend me to their Captains, while I was sure that they were not a troop of debauched fools.

In the morning, I tracked down Kit Welsh, and told her I was looking for a good horse. She knew of a lively roan mare, taken from a French General at Malplaquet, according to the liar selling her. Her gear was shabby, yet I liked the look of her. To find if she was truly battle-hardened, I saddled her, and rode her towards the town guns just before their noon firing. When she barely flinched, I decided I liked her.

I then bought a new black tricorne and jacked leather boots, the heels not too high for walking. When I rode out to the fields frequented by Lumley's men, spurs jingling, I felt as though I'd already embarked upon a different life.

Lumley's Irish Captain recognised me, and nodded, so I bade him good morning and introduced myself. He was Captain Patrick Lisle, and when he asked me if I was looking for a post, I agreed to it, and offered to stand him lunch to discuss the matter.

We dismounted at the Black Bear, gave our horses over to the ostler, and ordered the best wine I'd ever tasted. After a loyal toast, I told Captain Lisle that I'd Lumley's leave to find a post in his Regiment, and that I'd refused an Infantry promotion to join the Horse, and was looking to be Corporal at least. I then hinted at a family quarrel, and a recent, rewarding, reconciliation. Captain Lisle shrugged and explained that everyone was begging for promotion after Malplaquet. "We lost ten troopers, so there are some openings at that rank, yet all above are already filled."

"In truth, Captain, though I like your troop, the

thought of remaining a trooper for an entire campaign dissuades me. Yet if I prove valuable, and a post comes up, I'd not forget your kindness if you considered me for it." I slipped him the silver spurs that had weighed down my dead Sergeant's knapsack, and he courteously accepted the present, promising to consider me for promotion, if I proved valorous. I thanked him and ordered a substantial lunch and another bottle of wine for us.

Then Lieutenant Stalker strode in, hot from hard riding, and greeted me heartily. Yet even as I shook his hand, and asked him to join us, my eyes were caught by the fresh-faced young man who followed him. He seemed aglow with good health and good spirits, and Stalker introduced him as Jan van Laatham, a young Dutchman who'd newly joined the Regiment as a Corporal. He bowed gracefully, tossed his golden hair from his laughing blue eyes, and sat next to me. I insisted that there was enough lunch for us all, and poured them bumpers of good wine. The handsome Dutchman congratulated me for joining the best of all the English Regiments, and we toasted Little Lord Lumley. Throughout the meal, I dazzled myself with my own wit, saying anything to keep Jan laughing, my habitual silence gone.

Captain Lisle was the first to leave us, citing orders, and then Lieutenant Stalker joined a card game. Unwilling to part so soon from my new friend, I took Jan to the stables to admire my roan mare. He showed off his white gelding, and spoke of a pretty canal bank that caught the afternoon sun, and we were soon saddled up and riding out into the cold Winter wind. To take the chill off the horses, we had a good gallop, and then followed the stream to a grove of gray willows that sheltered us. The horses minced down to the icy water, while Jan and I sipped brandy from his flask, and agreed that a Cavalry Regiment under the great Lord Marlborough was the most a man could ask for.

He was unreserved and friendly, and soon told me of his boyhood on his family's farm, raised on tales of dauntless King William, who took the Dutch from a subjugated people, at the mercy of the Spanish inquisition, to a nation of free Protestants. Jan had been just sixteen when his father had enlisted, and eighteen when he had heard of his death. The next morning, he had dug up one of his father's money bags, and despite his mother's tears, and the prospect of a wealthy fiancée, he had ridden off to join the Dutch Horse.

After a hard campaign, he had sought his promotion in the English Cavalry, because he'd wanted to fight under Marlborough. "I thought I would never find advancement, being a Dutchman, yet at Malplaquet I saved a man being dragged along the ground. An English General. We all fought like demons, yet I was the one who became Corporal when Stalker was promoted."

"That was beautiful fighting to watch, the Cavalry at Malplaquet."

"In truth, I hate it. The slashing. Yet this is my land, and I will fight for the right to live a quiet, peaceful life here. When we have won, I will return to my village, and run my father's farm with my family."

"A large family?"

"Oh yes. I have enough cousins to fill a church." I had to laugh, and thinking I was laughing at his excellent English, he threw himself on me, and wrestled me to the ground. It was with a shock that I remembered I was female, and I threw him off me, my heart pounding. I quickly explained that I'd not mocked him, 'twas simply that I was so delighted to meet him. He instantly declared us brothers, we shook hands most cordially, and I blamed the brandy for the glow in my soul.

He drank another sip of brandy against the chill, passed me the flask, and moved closer. "My great-grandfather fled the persecution of Protestants in Hainault, and ended dealing cattle from Laatham to Ghent. My grandfather became rich, but refused to move from the village, sure the immorality of the townsfolk would ruin us, happy enough to live among Catholics. By the time I grew

224

up, our family was half the village, and we'd built our own church. And you?"

I told him what I'd told the others, that I was of good family, and had recently mended a quarrel with my rich grandmother. I told him nothing of my mother, or my strange childhood, or Sally Salisbury. And my deception grated upon me, as it never had before.

That evening I waited on Lumley's secretary, told him my post, gave him a heavy purse and accepted his chilly congratulations. Captain Lisle then formally entered me in his troop, at the rate of two shillings a day. We went to wait on the gruff yet dignified Lieutenant-Colonel Deane, who shook my hand and bid me welcome to the Regiment.

I presented myself for inspection in my civilian clothes the next morning, and Captain Lisle sent me off with Lieutenant Law, an old drinking Trooper, who complained of not having had a promotion in forty years. He gave me a leather cuirass to wear over my shirt, to blunt sword cuts, musket balls and cold winds. The troop's full-skirted scarlet coat with yellow facings was quite new, and a white shoulder belt went over the whole. I tied my neckcloth simply, donned my black tricorne, and though Law scoffed at my Puritan simplicity, I told him 'twas a soldier's fashion.

He then gave me a flintlock to sling over one shoulder, an ammunition pouch for the other, a sword, pistols, and a cylindrical valise for my belongings. When he finally handed me stiff leather gauntlets, I had to laugh. "And how the Hell am I supposed to use firearms with these great gloves on?"

He grinned at me. "Your firearms are not for battle, but for guarding the infantry against desertion. In action, we leave the flintlock in its saddleboot, and the pistols in their holsters, and rely on cold steel. Don't worry, we'll teach ye the business. Now let's go an' see yer horse." We turned for the stables.

"Oh Christ, here's Dodsworth. A mere cornet now. Demoted from adjutant three years ago for cowardice." A mincing fop met us at the door, and insisted on walking to the stables arm-in-arm with me. Yet his horse, a great black stallion, was truly magnificent. Dodsworth told the usual boast of taking it from a French General at Malplaquet, and refusing to part with it, though Lumley himself made a bid.

"If Lumley asked for me dearest girl, I'd hand 'er over", Law muttered reproachfully.

"I've seen your dearest girl, Old Law, and I'd make a friend of any who took her off my hands. Now dear boy, this is the gear you'll need. The saddle is packed front and rear so you can sleep astride, though Law takes a regular tumble, don't you Charlie? Yet this can't be your horse! My dear boy, she's tiny. A mere peasant's nag. She'll kill you. I'll take her off your hands, and sell you a Spanish stallion fit for a King."

My mare had given a friendly toss of the head as I approached. "I like her. She has heart. Yet the gear I'll take. Give me a good price, and you can have the gold in your hand this evening." We argued pleasantly on how many guilders I should part with, and I gained the respect due to a rich man. As I saddled my little horse, a sharp-eyed young Welshman admired her, and introduced himself as Matt Pitt. He'd volunteered four years ago, and though recommended for a cornet by Lumley himself, was still unable to afford his commission.

Pitt challenged Dodsworth and I to a race, which my quick little horse easily won. Then Law ambled up and threw us wooden staves to spar with, Jan and the rest of the troop riding up to watch. From the glint in Law's eye, I thought I might be in for a pummelling. Pitt and Dodsworth both attacked me at once, and I dealt Dodsworth a whack on the head that left me with but one assailant. I parried a sudden flurry of blows from Pitt, then the Welshman left his guard up, I swung hard, and half knocked him from his horse. Jan cheered, the rest laughed, and Law ordered us to pair off. Jan and I parried with our Cavalry swords then, scabbards on.

When Law was satisfied, we rode back to the stables, and tended our beasts, the smells reminding me of the shining days of my childhood. It was growing colder, and Jan warned of snow, so we covered the horses with blankets against the cold, and then, half frozen ourselves, we made for the tavern and ordered mulled wine, hot and spicy.

Captain Lisle joined us and went through their fighting tactics with me. "No hell for leather charges, lad. We hold the line, move at a fast trot, relying on numbers, not speed, for impact. Then we reform fast. I'll get Jan to show you the drill. Stay out o' the wheeling or you'll put us all off. Watch how the pivot men stay still, and the rest fan about him."

"I remember watching the German Horse charge at Oudenarde. And our own Cavalry at Malplaquet."

"And after the charge", Dodsworth added avidly, "the pursuit of the enemy, the rounding up of prisoners, the searching of the dead, the foraging for sweet Dutch fruit...For God's sake, someone fill my glass! To the best life, comrades! Long may the war last!"

We met for inspection the next morning after breakfast, and Captain Lisle asked Jan to take me through the commands, so I could drill with the rest of the troop that afternoon. Jan easily agreed, we rode out together, and I was already unsure if the pleasure of being with him was worth the resulting confusion.

"Now, 'open order' means six feet between the horses, 'close order' means three, and at 'close order from close order', we get ready for a charge, closing up knee to knee, and nose to tail. We start at a walk, and at the command, quicken to a trot. We do not break into a full gallop until only two hundred paces from the enemy. Then we give our horses free rein, and draw swords. The ground must be smooth, or our horses will trip each other. And if you fall under the hooves, you are a dead man. At the last minute, we raise our sabres, slash the air once or twice, and yell, and they run. Rise up in your stirrups and practise that slash

227

again, with more of a sweeping cut from left to right. That is better. And again. Good."

At noon I commenced my duty as a trooper, standing guard in my heeled boots, my mare tied loosely by the bridle to the other horses of the guard. After that came the afternoon's drill, where, stationed between Captain Lisle and Jan, I managed not to disgrace myself.

At the beginning of December, I went to visit the widow Kit Welsh and found her smiling at yet another Welsh Grenadier, a big man called Hugh Jones. The knowing Sergeant Millner was there, making sly jokes on soulful Welsh eyes, and though 'twas only eleven weeks since the death of her second husband, I was not surprised when I received an invitation to their wedding breakfast not a week later.

Apart from Jan, my comrades in the Cavalry turned their noses up at the thought of a camp marriage. "These campaign ladies can't be true to a troop, or even a Company, let alone a man", Dodsworth declared. "When they marry, a soldier lays two swords crossed, the man jumps first, the woman after, the priest saying: 'Jump rogue. Follow whore!'"

Kit Welsh became Kit Jones more soberly than this, some of Orkney's Officers condescending to show the bride their respects, and Colonel Hamilton's wife presenting her with a lovely silk gown. Towards sunset, when the Officers were gone, and we were all well-drunk, the jokes bawdy, and the songs ribald, she dragged me off to help bring more brandy. Filling my arms with clinking bottles, she claimed this was a good man she'd found. "He's neither a drinker, a gambler, nor a whoremonger, and tall enough to match me into the bargain. I hope your luck's as good my dear!" She grinned at my blushing dismay, and I fled the feast soon after.

When I wrote to Sally, Jan assumed I was in love with her, and I did not correct him. At the end of December, I finally received one of her rare but massive epistles, long and witty and full of puns on my sex. Sally had enjoyed great success, first as the mistress of the Duke of Cleveland, and then of the Duke of Richmond, both of them Old King Charles' bastards. She wrote that Richmond, a rake she called Richworld, had protested against her admittance to a company of ladies, citing her infamous character. She had found him at the theatre, and ripped into him for implying that her character could possibly be worse than his. She started on slanderous details of his infamy, and he paid a hundred and fifty pounds just to shut her up, and then threw himself at her pretty feet again. She spurned him for his half-brother, the Duke of Saint Albans, and then began courting the Earl of Cardigan.

She wrote spitefully of rich and powerful men, and her letters were so scandalous, that I feared keeping them. "Our dearest little Queen has been hounded by intrigue all year, though refusing to leave her little cottage at Windsor, and her dying husband. No one noticed Danish George when he was alive, yet apart from his love of a dram and his fat idleness, he never embarrassed our hard-working Queen Nan. Such a pity they had no brats to comfort her now, sick with gout as she is, ill-dressed and brooding.

"During his long death, a chambermaid stole our poor Queen's heart, with such kindnesses as Marlborough's wife could never stoop to. Indeed, they say that once he was dead, Marlborough's Lady arrived, and wrestled a favourite portrait of Fat George from the weeping widow, insisting she grieved too much and declaring she must get rid of her lowly Abigail, and pull herself together. The Lady seems convinced the crown would suit her much better than our dowdy, dutiful Queen, and since Marlborough insisted on being made Captain-General for Life, the mob call him King John. Hah! I knew that would enrage you. Yet those who love their Queen are paying double for bread, and their lives for a war that no one wants. They hate Marlborough's Lady for her ostentation, and will turn her carriage over in the mud for a few shillings.

229

"Abigail got her fool of a brother promoted to a Regiment, despite Marlborough's protests. In revenge, Sara wrote a salacious song detailing the erotic adventures of Abigail and our dear Queen, no less. Oh, the poor woman is surrounded by snakes and vultures! I've been hiring louts to break the heads of any caught singing it. 'Tis fun to be rich.

"Apart from insisting on this unnecessary campaign, the Whigs have shaken us with the sudden withdrawal of that old slander against the Pretender. When he was born, they said he was a common street bastard, stolen into the lying queen's chambers to ensure Catholic rule of our poor nation. Everyone believed it true, because they wanted to believe it. Now everyone knows he's the rightful King, and Jacobites, like Argyll and Webb, are heartened anew. They have attacked Marlborough in the House of Lords for the hard loss of Malplaquet, and plot to end the war. Our Queen declared the Protestant Germans her successors when she took the throne, and now she finds that Jamie is her legitimate brother, and as her father's only son, the rightful King.

"I think your glorious war will come to a ridiculous close. King Louis has told his nobles that unless they sacrifice all their silver, the English will be dining in their chateaux come Summer, so it seems there will be yet another campaign. Marshal D'Artagnan will stand in for Villars, while he recovers from his wound.

"Don't let me hear of you found dead on the battlefield. 'Tis your duty to survive and shake your head at me occasionally. Truly, you are the only man in the world I do not hold in some contempt. You I only laugh at. I'm glad you have joined the Cavalry and are a gentleman again. As soon as the Gods permit your Puritan soul to mix with my wanton one, do come to London so I can see you in your uniform. Fond kisses await you, from your own Sally Salisbury."

Jan and I busied ourselves with drinking, drilling and duelling, and I gained such a reputation for quickness with the rapier, that few would match foils with me. On April the Second, our Officers returned, and our Regiment was immediately drummed to arms to receive our Colonel, leaving me no time to find Macartney.

It was a fresh Spring morning, and the sun lit the yellow satin liveries of the kettle drummer and the trumpeters, and the Regimental colours and standards. Little Lord Lumley was proclaimed by beat of drum as he reviewed each Troop, stopping to admire the useless Cornet Dodsworth on his magnificent stallion. He ordered us furnished with three charges of powder and ball a man, asked us of any grievances, and announced that the General would beat at break of day, and we would ride south for Tournai. When he told Lieutenant Colonel Deane to give the entire Regiment a dram to drink our Queen's health, we bellowed our huzzas, and he grinned at us like a boy.

I was up with Jan before dawn the next morning, helping him check the baggage wagons. Then we tied our valises to our saddles, and at the order, mounted as one. With Lumley on a beautiful grey mare at our head, we took to the fields to guard the marching Infantry against desertion, the Artillery filling the dusty road behind us. Yet soon our spirits palled, the sky leaden and weeping, Winter refusing to make way for Spring.

All Winter, famine had devastated those provinces laid waste by our armies. There were terrible rumours of men being driven to eat one another, and of deserted villages haunted by packs of ferocious children. Now we saw the truth of it, the fields deserted, peasant women openly offering themselves for food for their swell-bellied brats. Against Lumley's orders, we halved our rations, halved them again, and gave away the rest, riding south with empty bellies.

Jan rode beside me, his spirits oppressed, and when I gave him brandy he told me that he was worried for his family. "I've written, and all was well two months past. But since then, I've heard nothing. They thought it was possible

231

they would spend the Winter in Amsterdam with my mother's family. But there are a lot of them, it is a long way, and my uncle is not kind. I will write again, and if I hear nothing by June, I will ask for leave to ride over. They will have left a message."

"I'll go with you and meet your family."

"And my sisters I suppose!"

"And all your cousins."

We made camp near Oudenarde, pitching our tents on mud, our Troop ordered to stand guard over the horses, at the rear of the camp. Matt Pitt stirred our cooking pot over a small fire, and young Lieutenant Stalker passed around a flask of brandy, much to the joy of Old Law. I leaned against a tree stump, admiring Jan's profile against the fire, and despite the rain, I felt I had never been more content. I had gold, a friend, a horse, and brandy. I could envisage no end to my life but a bullet, yet even if I never had more than this, it would be enough.

Then Jan mentioned that he'd miscounted the cots, and we'd be sharing a bed. I could not hide my sudden blush, and as he never doubted me a man, he immediately judged me a Molly. He said nothing, yet the open friendship I had come to rely on was replaced by a careful distance. We curled up top to toe in his small cot that night, and though he soon slept, I lay awake trying not to move, trying not to feel the warmth of him. When Reveille sounded, I was exhausted, and felt myself to be in desperate trouble. Jan politely refused to complain of my restlessness, and all through the day, as we rode past Tournai, he kept me well supplied with brandy, as though I had a fever. Yet again that night I could not sleep, but lay rigidly awake, mocked by the moon.

The next day we rode past a French Regiment, guarding a bridge over the Scheld, and the two Armies shouted insults and pleasantries at each other. Towards nightfall, a sentry at Ourney village directed us to the tavern we were billeted upon, and we stabled our poor horses, and then called for ale and food for ourselves.

At the next table, the Officers of Hartford's Regiment were twitting their Sergeant about his sister, and Dodsworth begged for the tale. The Sergeant explained that his mother had been a Frenchwoman, and his sister had been raised in that country. "When King Louis begged his people to stand between us and Paris, two campaigns past, she enlisted. From shouted exchanges between the Armies today, I realised that the French Regiment we were marching past was hers. Our Major gave me leave to make enquiries after her, and soon afterwards, she jumped over the French breastworks with a bottle of brandy for me.

"Our Officers invited her to drink with them, trying to persuade her to join our Regiment, and boasting of our excellent provisions and better pay. She said French bread was better than English beef, and that if we needed brandy to withstand the cold, the French would do without, and still keep us out of France. At that, we heard a Drum coming over the French breastworks, her stay having created such a jealousy amongst her Company, that a French Officer had come to fetch her back. Our Major insisted on sending an English Drum to accompany her safely back over no man's land."

Cornet Dodsworth snorted his disapproval. "I' faith, all that parade for a harlot of a French spy."

Hartford's Sergeant heard him. "Nay, she's a French Lieutenant, and fought hard for her promotion. 'Twas two years afore they found her out, and her Company was so desperate for soldiers, they kept her secret."

Dodsworth sneered at him still, sure that the Sergeant was too drunk to hurt him. "She's that French Officer's whore. That's why he was so eager to get her back. Of course she'd tell you such lies, otherwise you'd be ashamed to have such a sister."

Jan intervened. "Peasant women are as quick as their men to defend their own soil. They follow their men, as Kit Jones did, or just the beat of the drum, like their brothers."

"Stupid sluts!" Dodsworth spluttered incoherently.

"If you say that again, I will slap you", I said quietly, and both he and Jan stared at me. I turned away, shaking, for despite living as a man for most of my life, I had spoken with my mother's voice. My mask was slipping. I feared then that I had raised the suspicions of the men about me, and that I would be watched so closely that they would see that my morning shave was not a ritual of manhood, but a pretence, and my noted virtue mere incapacity.

The next day, we welcomed the Duke of Marlborough and Prince Eugene with a great deal of pomp and ceremony. That night, with rumours flying that the French were trying to head us off from Douai, we decamped and headed South, guarding our Infantry. A detachment of Germans was sent ahead to the river Deule, and they reached the French fortified line at Vendin bridge by the next morning. Marshal D'Artagnan and twenty thousand Frenchmen then fled the lines that had cost them so much in raising, and our Generals rode through them without drawing a sword. At noon that day, we guarded the bridges as the exhausted soldiers stumbled over the Deule, having marched thirty miles without halt.

Orders came through that we were to pitch camp a further three miles south, and as the soldiers dropped, we took them on our tired horses, or carried them to their baggage wagons. It took our Army until mid-afternoon to reach camp, and there they fell where they found themselves. The next day they staggered on, and at sunset, reached the outskirts of Douai. D'Artagnan's army immediately retreated across the Scarpe, breaking the bridges and making for the safety of Arras. At dawn, we left Eugene and his Germans to begin the siege of Douai, and chased the French for another ten miles, pitching camp on the south bank of the Scarp. D'Artagnan, retreating into war-ravaged land, had no choice but to fall all the way back to the French border at Cambrai, or starve his Army.

At Douai, the Scarpe joined the Deule by way of a canal through the town, making it the key to the waterways of the area. It was a strong town, with a garrison of eight thousand chosen men, commanded by Albergotier, an old and experienced French General. Soldiers and peasants spent four days digging the lines of circumvallation, and then the Army fell back and pitched camp safely within them, and Douai was cut off. The French were using armed galleys to hold the Scheld against our Artillery barges, and Marlborough was forced to bring our siege cannon through on wagons. On the last day of April, our heavy batteries began to pound the walls of Douai. I found Sergeant Deane, who told me that Macartney had sufficiently demeaned himself to work for the Engineers, and had been promoted to Major-General, and made the acting Engineer of the siege. I wished him a cannonball.

All the Horse were ordered into nearby forests to cut and bundle fascines for the siege. My Regiment camped in rich country near Vitry, five miles from Douai, resting our horses after the hard march. Then the trumpets blew. Even as we mounted, the news was shouted that Villars was marching to relieve Douai with a hundred and sixty thousand men. By the time we'd ridden back to Camp, the report was that sixty thousand of his poorly-trained peasants were down with the pestilence, and we could rely on many more to desert before battle.

When Villars marched up on the morning of May the eleventh, he found our army straddling the Scarpe with twenty bridges, easily able to block him, without abandoning the siege. The French marched up to face us in good order, and drew up in line of battle within cannon shot of us, looking better than we had expected. By noon, Villars and a detachment of French Horse had advanced close to the front of our camp, reconnoitring the redoubts our soldiers had hastily thrown up. We galloped over immediately, they retired, and we fell back to stand with Lumley's Horse to the right, enduring the French cannonade, as they endured ours, waiting for the order to attack. Of all the horrors of battle, the whistle of the approaching cannonball was hardest for me to bear, yet my little roan mare stood bravely, and I had brandy to sip.

Towards nightfall, the French withdrew out of cannon range, and we slept on our arms, expecting battle at dawn. The next day both sides called up heavy reinforcements, and we sat watching each other, still expecting battle. The following night, our scouts reported that the Arras garrison had crossed the Scarpe, intending to relieve Douai from the east. We rode to head them off, and the next day, the entire French Army wheeled east after the Arras garrison, with us a league to their north. On the fifteenth, they halted within cannon shot of us again, on the opposite side of the Sanset.

We lay all night on our arms, celebrating Marlborough's sixtieth birthday, toasting his good health with bad brandy. At daybreak, the French circled in towards Douai, and we drew up to face them, most of the siege troops with us now. Again we lay on our arms all night, expecting battle, and again the next day they withdrew. We marched all day, and then guarded the Infantry while they threw up a running trench in our front, and again we all lay on our arms ready for battle in the morning, only to have the French withdraw. We spent that day watching the Artillery haul cannon to a ridge above us, while the Infantry extended their running trench, and the besiegers joined us.

The following dawn, the French advanced, gasconaded, and finally withdrew, Villars more concerned with defending Arras than risking a battle for Douai.

Thanks to the cannonballs, I got a dead man's cot, and no longer had to bed down with Jan. I thought I'd finally be able to sleep, yet instead my dreams deserted me for nightmares of Jan dying. Convinced that death had rejected me, I lost all fear for myself, and rode whenever Jan did, saddling up even when not detailed to go, determined to come between him and the bullets. Too afraid of my rapier to taunt me, the men goaded Jan with sly jokes and jeers, and unable to ignore my intensity, he treated me with more

236

distance.

Heart-sore and confused, I began taking regular comfort in the brandy bottle, and let my horse grow as shaggy and unkempt as I was, sure 'twas only the presence of Captain Lisle that stopped me catching a bullet in the back from the sniggering Dodsworth. The area we foraged in was rich compared to Flanders, and we had money to buy food, guns to take it, and Jan to argue for us, so we did well. Captain Lisle turned a blind eye to pilfering, yet following Marlborough's clearest orders, he allowed no abuse of the peasants.

Jan's presence also controlled the men, who knew he had family to the north. When he finally asked for leave to visit them, Captain Lisle made sure he got a pass. Jan did not ask me again to accompany him, and when he rode away, I felt left without a friend in the world. I knew then that I had trapped myself into all the hardship of a man's life, while gaining none of their freedom.

Then Captain Lisle took a bullet in the leg, and Old Law was brevet-Captain, and in charge of a piquet. He selected Lieutenant Stalker, Cornet Dodsworth, and the English troopers he drank with, and as Jan had improved my Dutch, I was taken along as interpreter. Law had frightened a peasant into declaring that a farm a league to the east of us had a secret cellar of wine and cheese, and now Law declared we'd try it.

As we rode into the yard, the farmhouse door was slammed and bolted from within, leaving an old farmer bowing at us on the step. Sergeant Law ignored him at first, and ambling through the barn, ordered the hay loaded onto the farmer's cart, and his old horse harnessed to pull it. The poor old farmer protested piteously at his loss, and I explained that we had to take what we needed for his country's sake, and began haggling a price with him. Throughout these exchanges in broken Dutch, Law kept demanding the whereabouts of the secret cellar, until frustrated at being ignored, he grabbed the old man and shook him, swearing and waving his pistol about.

I had thought hard on the possibility of a hidden cellar, and knowing where my aunt had secreted her best bottles, I began scuffing the remnants of hay from the floor, the English troopers soon helping me, and even old Law distracted from shaking the old man. Then with a whoop, one of the English troopers pulled at an iron ring set in the floor. The desperate look in the old man's eye convinced me we'd found the family treasure even before I saw the dusty bottles.

I began bargaining a price, but the indignant Sergeant Law grabbed the old man, and began shaking him again, calling him an old thief to keep anything from us. I threw him a bottle of wine, thinking 'twould calm him, but after he knocked the top off and drained it, his eyes narrowed and his mouth hardened, and he kicked the old man out into the yard. There he caught him by the hair and slapped him, and a high wail came from the house.

The hair on the back of my neck rose as the men turned as one, and moved towards the house. Then Dodsworth giggled. "Time for a little female company, eh boys?"

The farmer howled and threw himself at Dodsworth's knees, giving me just enough time. I leapt for the steps, and drew my pistols. "The first man to step up gets a shot in the guts. I'll take my chances with a Court Martial." They stopped, stunned. "We're here for provisions. We found 'em. 'Tis time to pay the old man for what we've taken, and leave these people in peace."

"Out of the way, Molly!" Dodsworth spat. "We know you're not man enough to help pluck a covey of Dutch chickens."

"Stop now, for if you don't, either I'll shoot you or you'll have to shoot me. Then Marlborough will hear of it, and you'll hang, disgraced before the eyes of all."

"You've pulled a pistol on a superior officer", Old Law spluttered. "I can have you court martialled!"

Young Stalker stepped away from them. "To Hell with this! Have we not sisters and sweethearts back home?"

Dodsworth exploded with anger then, cursing us for sodomites and worse, yet the evil spell was broken. I holstered my pistols, walked over to Dodsworth and slapped him, hard. "Ten paces. Neither of us should miss. We'll let God decide between us. Or the Devil, eh Dodsworth?" He faltered, and could not face me, a true coward.

I threw the old farmer a bag of gold coins, and stalked off into the barn, to begin loading the dusty wine bottles and cool cheeses into the straw of the wagon. The English troopers soon followed, and when most of the work was done, I threw everyone a bottle. By the time we rode into camp, they were drunk.

Stalker found me later. "I know you're nought but a Molly, and 'twas no temptation to you, yet I thank you for saving my honour. Christ, I could never have looked me old Ma in the face again."

I looked him in the eye. "I am no Molly. And now I wish I'd stayed in the Infantry. You all disgust me."

This comment was duly reported and exaggerated, and the troop was divided between abusing Dodsworth's cowardice, and abusing me for self-righteously interfering with the well-deserved pleasures of Her Majesty's troopers. We were reviewed by Marlborough himself outside Douai, and I felt no pride at all.

A week later, the French Army made one last attempt to relieve the town. We turned them back, and soon after, Douai surrendered, much to the joy of the Infantry, for the fever from the trenches had killed many.

Jan returned to us grim-faced after a long absence. Begging Captain Lisle's pardon, he explained that he had found his village in ashes, deserted but for one half-mad, starving old man, who told him that a French Troop had descended upon the village, and that Jan's family had stood against them. "My uncles were killed for their cattle. My brothers tried to protect the church full of women and children. The Frenchmen burned the church. There were no survivors. I've lost them all. I should never have left them in these troubled times. I have no one left now. No one."

"You have a friend, Jan. And comrades." Yet his lightness was gone. He never spoke of his loss again, yet carried it rotting in his heart. And the only comfort I had to offer him was the brandy bottle.

In July we marched to invest Bethune, a minor fortress, though strong, which would open the waterways to the west, making Aire and Saint Venant easy to take. The town was well supplied, with flooded ditches, mines, and double outworks on the low side. Despite the stony soil, the Infantry made the most of the hot, dry weather, drained off the water, and the siege began.

Whether foraging or guarding convoys, we spent the Summer fighting off desperate ambushes and sharp skirmishes by the French Horse, who would not stand against us, but retreated quickly once the damage was done. On the thirteenth, a Captain of Eugene's Horse, thinking highly of Jan, invited us all to join a foraging party. Sure that a nearby village might yield something, we rode towards it, ambling down a quiet country lane, shaded by linden and poplar.

I was watching my mare flick flies off her ears, trying to follow the German's conversation with Jan, when a sudden barrage of fire sent us all reeling. As we wheeled and dashed back down the lane, a sharp blow knocked me forwards. Then Jan was holding me upright, our two horses running together, blood streaming from the hot agony of my shoulder. "For God's sake, not the hospital!" I begged him, and then all went black.

I woke in my own cot, in our tent. Jan was sitting with his head in his hands. Confused, I tried to sit up, and nearly swooned. I felt like someone had ripped my arm off, and groaned with the agony of it. Jan looked up. "No. Do not move. I had to cut deep for the bullet. I did not dare call anyone else." He blushed and looked away.

"Does anyone else know?" He shook his head. "Then keep my secret. For at least a little time."

He looked at me, appalled. "You cannot stay a soldier, not now that I find you a woman, and the kind of woman I'd always dreamed of. It all makes sense! I was drawn to you from the start. Your courage..."

"A soldier must be brave. And if I have risked my life all these years, 'tis because I have nothing else to make a shilling with. I forgot I was not a man many years ago."

"I think I reminded you of the truth."

"How is my shoulder?"

"I packed it with mouldy bread and clean cobwebs, as my favourite aunt once showed me."

"Was it an ambush?"

"Yes. They cut us off from Camp, but some troopers of Eugene's Horse heard the volley, and attacked, letting us get you away."

"Thanks for the nursing. A swig of brandy, and I'll be on my feet again."

"I don't even know your name."

"Mark Read."

His eyes flashed. "Do not pretend nothing has changed, when everything has!"

"I am the same person I always was. My shoulder will soon heal."

"I will tell Captain Lisle if you try to ride as a trooper."

"Then I will desert the army, and make for England."

"Then you would be cruel to us both."

"'Tis you who are cruel, forcing me to leave. I have always lived as a man. I know nothing else."

"Now that I know you a woman, it seems I cannot see you as anything else."

"I am Mark Read, a Cavalryman in Lumley's Horse."

"Do not be a fool. There is no such thing as a Cavalrywoman. The peace will come soon. What will you do as a man?"

"Give fencing lessons. I have always survived."

"Why will you not, even now, admit that you are a woman, not a soldier? Why not say you love me. We will both be happy and..."

"Get off me you fool! Christ that hurt. Pass the damned brandy." I took a deep drink, and saw his disapproval. "Jan, I can out-drink you, outfight you, out-ride you, and out-talk you. Why do you then tell me what to do with my life?"

"You do not need to be afraid of me."

"You're mad! Of course I fear you. You refuse to keep my secret. You would slake your little passion, and leave me alone with a child to guarantee my whoredom."

"Now it is you are mad! Did you think I would make a whore of you when it is a wife I need."

"You cannot marry a soldier."

"If you promise to take no risks, I will say nothing. But you must tell me your name, and promise to consider me as a husband."

"On the condition that you never approach me in lust, but treat me as a comrade. At the end of the campaign, I will tell you my decision."

"I swear to abide by this. And your name?"

"Mary. Mary Read."

"This will be the strangest courtship. I must pretend you are a brother, but the thought of seeing you in a dress..."

"I thought you liked me in breeches." He blushed then, and I knew I could not trust his indiscreet eyes. Yet his care of me re-doubled, and I was grateful. In truth, my soul had been starved of affection for so long, that our new intimacy was most welcome to me. I took the earliest opportunity to tell him my true history, and he was all astonishment to think I'd lived a man for so long, without being discovered. Yet the men of our Troop noticed our renewed friendship, and treated us with open contempt. Jan thought it all a great joke, though I warned him he'd catch a bullet in the back.

242

Then rumours swept through the camp that Marlborough was about to resign. The Queen had dismissed Sunderland, his son-in-law, for his Rakehell character, thus announcing to all that she was the head of the English Army, not her Commander. The Whigs were expected to lose the next elections, and everyone knew the Tories would make peace. Bethune surrendered, fever killing more men than cannonballs, and Marlborough immediately split his sick and despondent army between Saint Venant and Aire.

We marched on Aire, many declaring this the last siege of the campaign, and of the war, and I prayed it was so, having had my fill of blood and bravado.

The Prince of Anhault addressed us, calling us his brave Englishmen, and swearing he'd not shave until we'd taken the fortress. Then the siege convoy from Ghent was over-powered by the French, and while we awaited the next, Jan and I made the most of the long Summer afternoons, feeding our horses, and resting. Then the weather worsened, and the trenches flooded, and our men died of fever where they stood.

In Venant, the Prince of Orange attacked the town hard, and Kit Welsh lost her third husband. I attended his simple funeral to find Kit morosely drunk. After the priest had rambled his way to an Amen, she stepped up to the grave, threw in the first handful of earth, and poured in the rest of the brandy intoning: "The Lord giveth, and the Lord taketh away. And damn you for an ungenerous bastard. I only had him a few months. Have you no mercy?" Colonel Hamilton's lady led her away in tears. Venant ceded only four days later, and the cruelty of Fate made me more afraid for Jan, and less willing to repulse him.

The siege of Aire proceeded, despite the rain and the fever, and there was a rash of minor mutinies, the temper of the Army much changed since the glory of Oudenarde. Pestilence and loss of faith in our commanders, had achieved what rank slaughter could not. We were disheartened. Most talked of the peace, and home. Then the

243

Tories won the next election by a landslide, and 'twas Marlborough who supported Macartney's successful run for Minister of Parliament.

I was drinking his damnation, when Jan burst into our tent. "I have news of Macartney. He, Brigadier Meredith and Colonel Honeywood have been ordered to leave the Army. They put up an effigy of Harley, the new Prime Minister, and shot at it, drinking damnation to the new Ministry." We drank a bottle of brandy together, to celebrate, and he kissed me. "Peace is coming. Stay here with me as my wife."

"I do not know if I can be a wife."

"Any idiot can do it. It is much harder being a soldier, I assure you."

"Don't laugh at me."

"Admit that marrying me is the utmost wish of your heart."

"And my utmost fear."

"You are brave, Mary Read. And you love me, as I love you. Promise me that you will marry me when the campaign is over."

"I swear I'll marry no one else. Yet I'll make you a terrible wife, Jan. Surely you deserve someone less at war with herself."

"As long as you will wear a dress, everything will be clear enough."

A month later, Aire finally surrendered, and with Winter upon us, we marched for Ghent. We saw Marlborough ride past us, and Jan blessed him for making no great battles that campaign, and leaving us both alive. He grinned at me, and I could not help smiling back. For my hard years as a soldier were over, and life tasted strangely sweet to me again.

PART 4: BREDA 1712-16
Chapter 14: Wife

While we waited for the sentry to open the gates of Ghent, Jan laughingly insisted on buying me a dress, so he could flirt with his betrothed without covering the Regiment in blushes. My soul was all confusion when faced with the prospect of dressing as a woman again, and the thought of marital intimacy seemed hideous. Yet what choices did I have? I had thought to enjoy the freedom due a man for his hard toil, yet starvation at sea and brutality ashore had curdled my dreams, and I hoped to never see another battlefield. Jan had saved me from despair and an early death, yet 'twas the warmth he brought into my cold, lonely life, that made me wager on being his wife.

He did not understand my trepidation, and declared the joke worthy of an April Fool, anticipating the looks on the faces of our comrades. "We will buy you something fine to wear, and I will have the last laugh for fetching a pretty wife out from under their noses."

We stabled our horses, endured our last Assembly, and then asked a well-dressed whore to recommend a modish Dutch dressmaker, not too expensive. We found a merry, fat Dutchwoman, who refused to invite two Cavalrymen into her back parlour, without her shy apprentice as chaperon. When she refused to believe any of our soldiers' lies about me being a woman, I stripped a little, and confounded them both. Jan then gave them such a romantic tale of my life as a soldier that the Dressmaker wagered she would make a woman of me in an hour.

They sent Jan off to clean himself up with the other soldiers, and retrieve his civilian clothes from the garrison commander. I agreed to the luxury of a hot bath by the fire in the Dressmaker's kitchen, despite the evening chill, for the stench of the campaign had set her nose wrinkling. The apprentice poured a hip bath full of hot water, poked up the fire, and set a screen for me, and I stripped off my man's apparel for what I thought was the last time.

While I scrubbed, she listed a woman's necessities, starting with two working gowns, one for Winter, and one for Summer. She told me she had a green serge that would be sensible for Winter, and showed me a stout calico the same blue as my eyes. Then she suggested black kersey petticoats for Winter, and bright red muslin for Summer, as she had those already made up. She had black boots and a thick black hooded cloak that would keep me warm, and buckled shoes with red heels that fit me well. I needed two calico shifts for under-linen, and she suggested a nightshirt, and hinted at lace, since I was about to be married. When I blushed, she insisted on making it my wedding present, since she'd never stitched a trousseau for a soldier before.

I dried myself with lengths of warm flannel the thoughtful apprentice had set out by the fire, and she passed me a shift and the red petticoat. Then she sat me on a stool close by the fire with a Winter petticoat to hem, and began wrapping my hair to make ringlets.

The Dressmaker came in with a large basket. "Here's something fit to marry in, my dear." She pulled out a deep green velvet dress, and with a flourish, spread it over the table.

"In truth, 'tis lovely, yet we have so little money…"

"An English Officer ordered this for his mistress last season. They fell out before he'd paid for all of it. I only show you because she had the same tall, slender frame as you. And I assure you, I could sell it cheap, for there's not much left to pay."

After what seemed a lifetime in filthy uniforms, I could not resist trying it on, and slipped the green velvet over the shift and the petticoat. The apprentice helped me lace it up, and though the bodice proved a little large, it looked better with some black lace tucked in as a fichu. The Dressmaker, aglow with my successful transformation from filthy soldier to blushing maiden, began haggling a price. I stared into the mirror, trying to accustom myself to my new appearance, sure that in this dress I could fool anyone that I was truly a woman, yet unconvinced myself.

As the apprentice finished unwrapping my hair, Jan knocked at the door, and let himself into the front room. The Dressmaker led me out to him, and 'twas the light in his eyes that convinced me I was indeed a woman, and not a silly lad masquerading in his sister's clothes. He insisted on buying the dazzling green velvet dress, as well as my other necessities, and we thanked the Dressmaker for her assistance. She laughed and hugged me and wished us well, and then 'twas time to face the rest of the world.

By the time we reached the Bear tavern, my soul was quaking, and my face so pale, that Jan promised me a brandy if I did not swoon. We strolled in arm-in-arm, to find most of our Troop discussing the past campaign, and drinking hard. When he saw me, Dodsworth leapt to his feet and pulled out a chair, congratulating Jan on his taste. He then proceeded to ogle me so rudely, that Jan rattled his sabre, and the rest looked around. Dodsworth demanded a proper introduction, and when I asked him if he did not recognize his old comrade, his total consternation cheered me considerably.

Jan then raised his glass. "Gentlemen, may I present my betrothed, the brave and beautiful Mary Read, late of Lumley's Horse." When I asked them to the wedding, they were so utterly confounded, we both had to laugh. Then they erupted with questions, demands and congratulations, and I saw their relief at not having a couple of blatant sodomites in the troop. They made a great noise about my courage, and Jan praised my virtue, and the story of two troopers marrying swept through Ghent faster than fire.

Soon Captain Gordon was sitting before me, aghast, and then Kit Jones, chuckling that she'd known all along. Yet 'twas Sergeant Deane who was most astounded, telling Jan of the scrawny boy he'd found aboard the Dreadnought, and how I'd kept his Company alive with stolen brandy. Finally, even our Officers heard of it, and Lieutenant-Colonel Deane

247

came to shake our hands and ask our plans. Jan had to admit he'd not thought beyond our discharges from the Army, and the Lieutenant-Colonel promised us a little towards house-keeping.

Jan wanted us to be married in a Church, under the eyes of God, yet it would have meant publishing the bans for three successive Sundays, and he declared that we'd waited long enough. I was so sure that I'd make a terrible wife that I rushed at it headlong, in a mad charge at what I feared most. Captain Lisle bribed the Regimental Chaplain to perform the ceremony the next afternoon, and I asked Sergeant Deane and Kit Jones to stand by me.

As a woman, I could no longer bed down at the barracks, and Kit offered me a share in her lodgings until the wedding. She had taken two rooms at an inn over-looking a canal, and there we saw the dawn in, sipping on Ghent's best brandy, supping on cold chicken and warm bread from the bakery, and comparing our adventures. I slept until noon, when she woke me to prepare for my wedding, as merry as a jackdaw and just as loud, despite my sore head. Indeed, I had not seen her so happy since the funeral of her last husband, and she insisted on presenting me with a fine gold chain as a token of our comradeship in hard times.

When Kit and I approached the garrison chapel the next afternoon, I was again in my green velvet dress, shaking hard, and ready to flee even my beloved Jan. Inside the chapel, there was a great crowd, and their staring and whispering unnerved me further. Captain Gordon took my arm to walk me down the aisle, and laughed. "Rather charge a trench o' Frenchmen, would ye girl? Never seen ye so cowardly!"

I laughed too, and we made it down the aisle of the church, to where Jan was waiting. When I took his arm, and looked into his happy face, I started to breathe again. We sat down in chairs garlanded with greenery in the Dutch manner, and after a short and stern sermon, the priest told Jan to put the ring on my finger. He kissed me, Kit threw rice over us, to bless us with children, and the soldiers about us cheered in true military fashion.

Then I saw that all our Officers had done us the honour of coming to see us married. Little Lord Lumley was the first to kiss me, and congratulate Jan, assuring us of our honourable discharges. Then Lieutenant-Colonel Deane stated that, as fellow soldiers, he hoped we'd accept a small present. I felt the heavy weight of the purse, and thanked him with all my heart, for it would make a great difference to our immediate prospects.

We made a merry procession to the Bear, where Kit toasted us, wishing me longer use of my new husband than she'd had with any of hers. Then the men toasted Jan and Mary van Laatham, making much of Jan's perceptiveness, and the jokes grew ribald. He insisted on my modesty, and told them that he'd never have guessed, but for me being wounded in that ambush. I drowned my nervousness in brandy, Jan sang our wedding song, and the bawdiness increased as the night wore on. Towards midnight, Jan winked and nodded at the door, and we edged towards it, and out into the cold night. A roar announced that they'd missed us, and we ran hand-in-hand, laughing down the street. Some of the men gave chase, yet we raced for our new lodgings, and left them singing bawdy songs in the street.

Our laughter lasted as long as it took to climb the stairs to our room, and then not even all the brandy I had drunk could quell my nervousness. Jan shook his head. "You have nothing to fear from me. I shall not touch you until you ask me." He helped me change into my new nightdress, and I slipped between the two feather bags that made up the bed, the room cold despite the fire. Then Jan stripped, the firelight flickering on his white skin, and his beauty caught my breath. He slipped into our bed, so ardent and laughing, that I forgot my own fears and allowed his passion to inflame my own.

I was well-rewarded for my trust, and that night, we

used our bodies to bind our souls together, so that by the time the sun came creeping through the mist to announce another day, we felt truly married, united and indivisible. I found that being female had its compensations, the first time in nineteen years I'd thought so, and it seemed that I'd dropped some terrible burden from my soul. Released, my spirit soared, and Jan was delighted to see me so happy.

I only wished that my mother could know how well my life had turned out. Jan also missed his lost family. We spoke of what to do next, and he talked of his father's old friend in Breda. "He once offered me a partnership in his brewery. Of course I am not rich enough now to buy it, and I never really wanted to marry his daughter, but, with his help we might lease a small tavern."

"In Breda?"

"You'll like it. A pretty town with a large garrison, well-defended, with busy markets, and storks in the sycamore trees behind the church. The gallant young Prince of Orange has his castle there, and goes hawking in the park."

"It does seem right for two troopers in search of employment. We might as well ride that way after breakfast. There is no point to spending our gold here."

He suggested that we ride to the nearest small town, and take a canal boat to Antwerp, and then another north to Breda. "You will like the canal boats. They are comfortable and cheap, and full of all sorts of people. The boatman, who rides the great horse that pulls the barge, is always a hard-headed ruffian with a sharp knife in his pocket, and a gay girl aboard to flirt with the passengers."

Jan then insisted on carrying all our gold in a bag under his shirt, and although I pointed out that no one would attack two soldiers, he made a great point of us travelling as civilians. We breakfasted with our friends, told them to look for us in Breda, and rode off into our new life, our pistols primed against highwaymen. I began the day in my Winter dress and cloak, riding uncomfortably side-saddle, but by noon had donned trousers under my skirts to ride astride, despite Jan's protests.

As the grey afternoon descended upon us, we were forced to ride close by Jan's burnt out village, and his laughter died. Dusk crept upon us as we neared Lokeren, and the drizzle turned to solid rain.

We stopped at the nearest tavern, tending our horses ourselves in their stable before we stepped out of the freezing cold, and into the crowded, smoky warmth of their public room. Jan gave our coats to the skivvy to dry by the fire, and ordered a Hutsepot, the national dish that every family ate every Sunday.

A big, broad-shouldered woman brought out the pot on a wooden trencher, took one look at my handsome young husband, and nearly dropped it.

"Jan!"

"Blessed God! Lotte!", and they were in each other's arms, the Amazon almost lifting my slender Jan off the ground. They exchanged explanations in Dutch, speaking too quickly for me to follow them, and then Jan turned to me. "Mary, this is my mother's youngest sister. She married a town man, and escaped the massacre."

She hugged me too. "My dear Jan, my favourite nephew! I am so glad you have married. You must work hard now at making our family bigger!", and she laughed at my blushes.

"But how long have you worked in this low place?", Jan asked her.

"I've been doing the rough work in the kitchen this past year. I was lucky. Many starved."

"We are taking the boat for Breda, to ask old Amelsvoort for a lease on a tavern. If it works out, I'll send for you Lotte."

She hugged him again. "You can catch the boat to Antwerp tonight, if you are on the quay in an hour. Now eat your food, you both look cold and hungry."

The boat showed up precisely on time, and we tied

our horses to the barge horse, Jan promising the boatman something for keeping an eye on them. The passengers were a mixed lot, mostly merchants, soldiers, and whores. They were a merry crowd, and gossiped, sang songs, and argued over religion and politics, with more goodwill than I'd thought possible.

Then at ten o'clock, a gaunt man in a black coat exhorted us all to sobriety and blessed sleep, and at the request of a respectable Dutch matron, he led us all in prayers. Jan told me he was a predicant, not an English priest, but a God-fearing man from a poor family, who the Church council had set as a shepherd over his community. "They are highly valued for their care of the godly poor, and their disdain of the godless rich. At worst, they can be humourless bigots, at best they remind us that life is fleeting, and death a home-coming." I told him my life had been exile, and he was my homecoming, and he kissed me in front of them all.

I was so stiff from riding, I thought I could never get comfortable with the thirty other passengers on the floor. Yet in truth, I was exhausted, and I soon let the pleasant rocking of the barge lull me to sleep. Soon after we awoke, we docked in Antwerp, and there we took lodgings for the day, feeling the need of a big bed.

Before I could stop him, Jan joked with the manageress, telling her we were two soldiers on our honeymoon. When I explained, she beamed at us, and showed us her best room. Upon leaving, she presented us with a large hamper of bread, cheese, herring and wine, and as we had indeed forgotten to pack any necessities for the rest of our journey, we thanked her earnestly.

We soon found the Breda boat, and the bold young boatman agreed to lead our horses, yet refused to care for them, standing by his right to rest when he could, and spurning a handful of silver for his precious liberty. Jan shrugged and said that he'd have to tend them himself, and the boatman winked and said Jan might as well care for his own poor beast too, then. Jan laughed, and I was struck by this Dutch ease between rich and poor.

At dawn, we were roused by the boatman's furious argument with a lock keeper, the sun and the mist making a silvery bower of the tree-lined canal. We breakfasted with a fat Dordrecht merchant, who boasted of the fresh beauty of the girls of his town, and swore his own wife was the prettiest of them all. He toasted a windmill as we passed it, calling it by name, and I was surprised when Jan joined in. Then he pointed out a gang of windmills to me, each raising the water from a ditch by a foot, until it drained into our canal. "God made the world, but the Dutchman made Holland", the merchant announced. "No laughing, young Englishwoman! We've fought the sea for eight hundred years. We still talk of the flood of 1421 that drowned one hundred thousand people, and made Dordrecht an island."

"But if the Dutchman made Holland, 'twas the dykes made the Dutchman", Jan insisted. "They are only sand sown with grass, Mary. They need constant maintenance by the peasants, so each village is responsible for its dykes. Local drainage boards are now legal authorities, and working for the common good is still the Dutchman's notion of power."

I told them I'd already noted the sturdy independence of the Dutch, and praised them for being prepared to flood their hard-won fields against the French. "We've had thirty years of peace for a hundred and fifty years of war", the merchant sighed. "Before the French it was the Spaniards and their Inquisition. Thousands of Luther's followers were burnt in the town squares, entire towns were slaughtered."

"Prince William the Silent led our grandfathers against them", Jan explained proudly. "He persuaded the peasants to cut the dykes for twenty-two miles, leaving Leyden an island. When famine forced the mob to protest, the Burghermaster offered them his own flesh to eat, rather than surrender. William sailed barges of bread and herring down the flood only days later.

"Spain emptied her treasury trying to conquer us, until the garrisons here mutinied for their pay. Then the Spanish King sent his brother, Don John of Austria, to quell us. He sacked Antwerp, murdering eight thousand people in three days, and the southern provinces surrendered to Spain.

"But the Northerners formed the United Provinces, the first independent Protestant Republic, and continued to sail their sloops against Spanish warships, in great feats of courage and seamanship. The Spanish King placed a huge reward on William's life, but that merry man refused to guard himself from his people. In 1582 he was nearly killed, and then two years later, the assassin's knife struck home, and we lost him.

"Then the Spanish King died, and we flourished, using Flanders as a buffer against the avaricious French. When they finally invaded in 1672, our Burghermasters turned immediately to William's grandson, and we made him our war-leader. You English made him your King when he married the English Princess Mary, and chased out her father. You English like your Kings, and revolutions. We admire our Princes of Orange, but we never make them Kings. We prefer to be represented by fat town burghers, who are corrupt if not closely watched."

That afternoon I donned breeches under my skirt, and took my mare for a gallop. The boatman laughed, and I think he must have said something rude to Jan, for he took a dislike to the impudent rascal, and asked me to forgo my daily exercise, or learn to ride sideways.

"I'd wager my hat I ride better than any man aboard", I objected. "And I'd certainly not neglect my mare. She saved my life too many times for that. Remember when I took a ball in the shoulder?"

"It was me who saved you, and me you married, not your horse. So you are now a Dutchman's wife, and they do not wear breeches and ride like soldiers."

"If you wanted a Dutch wife, why did you marry me?"

"Because you are the other half of my heart."

"I don't mind living as a woman, Jan, but an English horsewoman."

"The good housewives of Breda will be terrified of this female centaur I bring them. But they will expect you to be foreign, and the English are known to be mad for horses."

"I will brazen it out."

The next morning the sun made a determined attempt against the drizzle, and Breda's spire stood gold against the leaden sky. As we drew slowly closer, steeples and the sails of windmills appeared over the sodden green fields, and by noon we could see all the moats and fortifications of a strong town. It took the rest of the afternoon to work our way north, sliding under bridges, through locks, and past guards, to Breda's main gate, where two squat, octagonal towers dominated the inner wall of the little harbour. Jan pointed past them, to a low, elegant building, just visible through the bare trees, the castle of the Princes of Orange.

We tipped the boatman, and led our horses through the bustling harbour, past the reeking fish market, with baskets of great sea fish laid out on the cobbles, and stalls laden with herring. Dusk was gathering, and we were still rich with the gold from our Troop, so we led our horses to the first respectable inn, De Arent, on the corner of the Oat Market, in the shadow of the great church. We found every surface in the little inn polished to a rich shine, and the inn-keeper, a respectable war-widow, assured me that her meat was fresh, and her sheets clean.

Jan was anxious to talk to his father's friend, and establish our future, so we left our tired horses to the ostler, tidied ourselves as best we could, and set out for a brisk walk through the cold dusk. The dying sun was suddenly smothered with cloud, and Jan whistled for a skinny lad to go before us with a flaming torch. In the dancing light, Breda seemed the prettiest of Dutch towns, with her circling canals, humped bridges and overhanging lindens. The tall buildings had elaborately stepped and curved gables, and the

255

stately homes, their walls tarred against the damp, glistened black in the light of our torch. A flurry of rain drove into us, and throwing the boy a coin, Jan and I ran up the steps of an imposing mansion, where Jan rapped smartly on the green paint with a great silver door-knocker.

A maid opened the door, gasped to see Jan, and shouted for her master. She urged us into a high, white room, with heavy, dark furniture, yet Jan insisted we stay on the mat, for our shoes were filthy. Then a large, hearty Dutchman strode in from the back room, resplendent in a brocade dressing gown. He clasped Jan's hands, and shot off a volley of questions. Jan then introduced me formally to Johannes van Amelsvoort as his wife, and Mijnheer could not hide his surprise. Neither could his stout, red-cheeked wife, though she bade us both a kind welcome, fetching slippers for us herself, being most anxious for the mud on our shoes, and whisking off my sodden cloak.

Mijnheer ushered us from the cold grandeur of the front room, to a cosy back parlour, and there a pretty young woman started to her feet and running to Jan, kissed him freely. He laughed and called her his old playmate, and I understood that this was the girl he had nearly married. Isabella's mother disliked the girl's fervent kisses nearly as much as I did, and she sent her off to mull wine for us, while the servant resumed spinning in a corner of the room. Mijnvrouw placed a warm shawl over my shoulders, and insisted I rest my feet on a hot brick wrapped in flannel, while Mijnheer demanded news of his family from Jan. He received a doleful look and a quick shake of the head in reply, and I explained in my halting Dutch, that we had lost all but Lotte.

"Ah that Lotte", sighed the good Dutchwoman, shaking her head a little. "To marry so unwisely..."

"She is a widow now, and she will join us here, once I am established", Jan replied firmly.

Isabella returned with hot, spiced wine. As she handed me my glass, she asked me how I had met Jan, and though I tried to keep my explanation simple, they seemed to find my life astonishing. Smoothing back her golden curls, Isabella raised her eyes to Jan, and insisted that she could never have lived as a man. He could only agree with her, and I felt their amazement that Jan had married a tall, dark, skinny foreigner, instead of this golden Dutch girl. Indeed, I could barely believe it myself.

Mijnheer insisted that we stay for dinner, and Jan happily accepted. Mijnvrouw bustled off to see if it was ready, her servant accompanying her more out of interest than duty. Isabella set the sturdy table, removing the finely embroidered table cloth, and stacking plates, knives, goblets and napkins into the centre. Then the mistress and servant appeared with trays of steaming food in fine dishes, trenchers of hot bread, and jugs of warm beer. We stood while Mijnheer presided over prayers, and then each of us found a chair, the servant taking hers at the bottom of the table. I remembered the studied distance between my 'grandmother' and her devoted Ashley, and decided I liked this easy familiarity.

I knew the Dutch habit of serving the leftovers from the midday dinner for supper, and had not expected much, yet there was hot meat broth, hashed meat and cabbage, and abundant cheese, bread and butter. It seemed that Mijnvrouw had cooked everything, as the undeniable duty of the Dutch housewife, which was a shame, because she had no understanding of flavour. I was also surprised to find an old rag inside my immaculate napkin, and smiled at this unexpected practicality.

We hardly spoke through the meal but to praise the food, Isabella rarely taking her eyes off Jan, and ignoring me entirely. When the maid cleared the table, Jan asked Mijnvrouw if he might smoke his soldier's pipe, and she scolded him for taking up such a filthy habit, her husband grinning broadly. "My wife has sacrificed a tiny downstairs room to this crime. Let us go and smoke our pipes in peace." I stood, Jan raised an eyebrow, and I realised that good

257

Dutchwomen did not smoke tobacco. Yet I needed my pipe to bolster my waning courage, so I ignored the stares of the women, the one so conventional, the other so hostile, and followed the chuckling Dutchman down the stairs.

As Mijnheer passed his tobacco jar, I realised my husband was angry with me, yet feeling I'd been womanly enough for one day, I packed my pipe regardless. Mijnheer asked me how long I'd been a soldier, and I told him three years.

"Then you'll always like your pipe", he smiled.

"I was a sailor for two years before that, and we smoked to keep hunger down, if we could afford it. Yet a sailor's tobacco is always damp, a soldier's is often so, and I've never smoked anything as fine as this."

He preened himself a little, and Jan warmed him further by complimenting him on his excellent beer. "Ah yes, that was a good barrel. We are a popular brewery, and if the guilds would let me brew more than once a week, I could make enough to get all the soldiers in town drunk, and still have enough to trade with other towns." Mijnheer then gave us a brief account of the iniquities of the town officials. "I've opened three taverns in Breda", he sighed, "and when they run out of beer, I must buy someone else's leftovers, rather than brew again. But Dutchmen like quality in their beer, not just quantity."

Jan then asked him to look out for some small business we might invest our gold in. Mijnheer crinkled his broad brow in thought, hummed a little, and told Jan that there was something, indeed something that needed a friend he could trust. "And someone who'll trust me", he winked. "The guilds are trying to limit the number of taverns for each brewery, but an 'independent' tavern can serve what it will, and demand more supplies. You would sell none but my beer, and I would arrange a cheap rent. Come and see me at noon tomorrow, and I'll let you know. You may have arrived just in time. I'm thinking of a run-down place by the Old Cloister, which is full of soldiers. With your military

258

backgrounds..." and he bowed to me and smiled, "you could be what we are looking for. Now, let us return to the ladies."

'Twas then that I understood that it was not just the smoking I had erred in, but in going off with the men after dinner, instead of staying with the women. I wanted to laugh, yet Jan was still annoyed with me, so I swallowed it. We entered the cosy parlour, to find that Isabella had arranged herself in a low chair by the dim, peat fire. She threw Jan a soft look, picked up her guitar and began a French love song, the flames burnishing her hair to gold, her eyes raised to Jan at the plaintive ending.

Mijnvrouw brusquely ordered her off for more hot wine, but Jan leapt to his feet, declaring that we had passed a hard day, and must leave them early. Mijnvrouw kissed us, and then Mijnheer, and Isabella took the opportunity to salute Jan firmly on the lips. I felt my heart grow hard against her child's game, for I had none but Jan in the world, and could not compete with such a practised female as this.

Chapter 15: The Three Horseshoes

The next day, we rose late, breakfasted on cheese and bread and beer, and then walked up Guesthouse Street, to wait on Mijnheer van Amelsvoort in his office at the Three Horseshoes Brewery. The rich smell of steaming hops filled the street, and we found Mijnheer in deep dispute with his foreman, three nodding workmen sitting in on the discussion. When he saw us, Mijnheer waved the men away, and invited us to sit with him at the taproom over the road, next to the old Blacksmith's shop that had long ago given the brewery its name.

With another tankard of foaming ale in front of us, Jan explained that as half the money was mine, I wanted to hear of its investment. Mijnheer nodded, and stated that the truth of his offer was to go no further than us. "It is not much, but it is the best I can do at such short notice. It involves Old Joost Nijnens, a very respectable Calvinist burgher, who runs the orphanage here. He has always been a clever man, with a great deal of respect for a stuiver. Though it is not known to many, Old Joost has the lease on the old tavern I was telling you about on the Nonenveld, next to the military barracks, and it has helped make his fortune. But the present manager drinks more than he sells, and they are looking for someone they can trust to take over. I don't know how familiar you are with taverns..."

"I was raised in one", I pointed out. "And Jan's Aunt Lotte was working in one last time we saw her."

Jan looked less pleased, and declared that if Mijnheer would make him a partner in a tavern, he'd hire his own manager. I was about to object that a tavern needed proper attention to prosper, yet van Amelsvoort was already shaking his head. "If something else comes up, you will be the first to know, but no one with any sense would sell even part of a tavern with so many soldiers about. No, all Nijnens wants is a discrete manager who will not cheat him."

"If he is not interested in a partner, I am not interested in making him rich," Jan stated flatly. "I have English gold to invest..."

"You are only known here as a lad who broke an engagement to run off to war", Mijnheer chided him. "No, you don't need to excuse yourself to me. But I tell you, you will not find anyone willing to make you such an offer, unless you are family."

"Both you and Mijnheer Nijnens need someone you can trust. You have no other candidate, and you have been lucky in finding me. No, Mijnheer, I am not a wealthy man, but I am rich enough to turn down such an offer. I will invest my gold in my own place. I don't mind adding to Nijnen's wealth, but I must keep an eye to my own interests. I'm sure if you introduced us, I could make him see that a half share in a tavern run by me, is better than a full share in a tavern embezzled by some hired hand."

Mijnheer shrugged. "I could take you to meet him this evening, but I cannot think...Still, it can do no harm. But if you try to charm him, as you have me, you will find him as sour as old vinegar. To him, you must make it sound like money."

"I would like to have a look at the place before I see him. Can you not ask him to meet me there tonight?"

"On the Nonenveld? Breda would be set by the ear! No, a man like him would never be seen in such a place. Better I bring you to meet him this evening, outside his own house. Most Dutchmen hate to talk business once the day is done, but he'll listen if he thinks he'll win by it. Only one thing," the Dutchman added, turning to me. "He will not be interested in making your acquaintance, Mijnvrouw van Laatham. If you insisted on accompanying us, he would be rude to you. Then your husband would take offence, and ruin his slim chances."

"I do not know if I can go into partnership with someone who would insult my wife!", Jan declared loftily.

"Old Joost would offend Saint Peter at the gates of

Heaven", Mijnheer insisted. "The predicant is always preaching tolerance to him. He is especially hard on women, probably because none has ever regarded him with favour. You must know, Mijnvrouw van Laatham, that our children choose their own spouses. I serenaded my wife when she was a pretty slip of a girl, and she convinced her father I was respectable. That was enough, and will be enough for my own daughter. But Old Joost had to buy his wife, and she's the scold of the town. No, it is better to marry for love, as you children have done, for marriage must endure a lifetime. Here we have very few unhappy unions, and only the nobles to provide us with the occasional scandal."

"And me", I smiled. "So I will be helpful, and stay away." Mijnheer kindly invited me to visit with his women while the men talked business. I refused as politely as I could, though he protested that I would be lonely by myself. I insisted on spending my evening with my toes on a foot warmer, darning stockings. Jan swallowed his laughter, and Mijnheer let his foreman hurry him away, he and Jan promising to meet at dusk.

We finished the tankards Mijnheer had pressed on us, and arm-in-arm, made our way to the Nonenveld. Jan asked if I could really stoop to such a low living. "'Tis good enough for me, who has lived so hard already", I told him. "Yet you evidently don't like it."

"When he thought to have me for a son-in-law, van Amelsvort offered me half of all he had. I find the littleness of this offer insulting."

"'Tis no crime to save a partnership for a son-in-law, and keep your money in your own family. I'm sure he is helping us as much as he can afford to."

"He would never have offered me work in a tavern if I'd married his daughter."

"You didn't marry her. Or her brewery. You married me, and a small bag of gold. So since you are not a poor man, and will not starve, what have you to complain of?"

"This low life, that you seem so used to."

"You'll have to get used to it too. Unless you poison me, and marry Isabella."

"What a stupid thing to say...", he began, and then saw I was joking. "I'm sorry. I'm disappointed that his friendship for me seems directly related to my fortune."

"He was your father's friend, and your father is dead. And you did turn down his minx of a daughter. And he is our only friend here, and this our only chance..."

We strode past the Old Guesthouse, the poor of the town huddled about its elegantly carved doorway, and there I gave a silver piece to a weeping woman with a thin babe. She blessed me, Jan squeezed my hand, and I sent a prayer to the spire of the cathedral, gold against a silver sky, that such a fate would never be mine. We turned south along the canal, and found the poorer section of town, the boy pointing out the spire of Saint Joost's, where the destitute were buried.

"That is the same name as Mijnheer Nijnens..."

Jan nodded. "Joost is the Saint of epidemics. When the pestilence comes, that simple little church is filled with flowers and candles."

"London was a terrible city for sickness until the great fire cleaned it. Yet every time the Spring rains sent the gutters over-flowing, the poor beggars left over from Winter would take the ague and die."

"Our towns are so damp, that when an epidemic takes hold, people of all sorts are lost."

We passed the Old Cloister, a red-brick building with an imposing roof, much more suited to a military barracks than the nunnery it had once been. Men in different uniforms sauntered arm-in-arm through the great doorway, and there were many Cavalrymen riding in the adjoining field, a wide square with an avenue of bare lime trees ending abruptly at Breda's wall. Beyond the lime trees, we saw a low, wooden building with the Three Horseshoes sign above the door. It had none of the thatched charm of Aunt Susan's Coach and Horses, but leaned drunkenly against itself, many of its

263

filthy windows panes broken, and the unpainted door hanging askew.

As we stooped to enter the low doorway, our eyes were immediately assailed by thick smoke from a peat fire on the floor, as in a peasant's house. This gave but little light, enough to make out a handful of soldiers smoking pipes over their small beer. None of them were Officers, or even Cavalry, and they looked too poor to pay the rent of the place. An old man scowled at us, and at Jan's polite request, banged half-full tankards of beer on the table before us. One sip convinced us he'd watered it down, and the lone, haggard whore agreed that he was a dreadful cheat.

Jan asked her if it was more lively at night, and she shook her head mournfully. Unable to understand Jan's continued good humour, I glared about me and spat on the floor. "Christ Jan, think of coming to this cold, dark, miserable place at night!"

The whore wandered over to the soldiers, and I scowled again. "You see, 'tis nought but a filthy trap for fleecing the men of their pay."

"I agree. And that is why we will buy half of it cheap. We will spend some money improving it, and attract a better crowd. I will do a deal with Mijnheer Nijnens tonight, and then do the rounds of the taverns, looking for a musician to drag in all those soldiers across the way. Someone with a following."

I looked about me in scorn. "Anything we did would improve the place. Yet is it worth it?"

"We are sitting on a gold mine. Old Joost knows it too, I would say, but he is too respectable to take it up directly. We will buy in cheap, get Lotte to help us, and make our fortunes."

I still had my doubts, yet I allowed Jan to talk me out of them, happy to see him so optimistic. Unwilling to risk our lives by eating in such a place, we stepped out into a cold wind, and made our way back to the centre of Breda. There we found a warm, merry inn on the Grote Markt,

264

ordered fish pastries, and enjoyed the piping of some musicians by the fire. Food was expensive, as I had noticed before in the Netherlands, yet I still found it surprisingly tasteless, and told Jan to keep his ears open for a good cook.

"Do not forget Lotte."

"She could do the traditional Dutch fare, yet in truth, I was thinking of offering other food too. Better spiced, perhaps."

"Lotte married a Frenchman. She cooks very well."

"Is that some kind of family scandal?"

"Yes. Before the French war began..."

"Oh, I didn't mean the Frenchman, I meant that she could cook. After all, a respectable Dutchwoman..."

Jan laughed and kissed me, and then it was time for him to meet the man our future depended on. All day I had thought of dressing as a man, and going along to help with the bargaining, yet I had no doubt that my history was already being related to an incredulous Mijnheer Nijnens. I had to trust Jan to make what he could in the deal, and when he had not returned by eight o' clock, I told myself that a long interview with Nijnens must mean success.

Feeling our future to be secure, I went downstairs to the front room of the inn for company and a simple supper of haricot beans, turnips, a fried egg, and a fine tankard of Three Horseshoes ale. A very friendly Dutch matron from the next table, slightly red-faced from beer, leant over and ordered me to join her and her dear husband. We shared a jug between us most agreeably, me leaping over questions of my background, to ask details of the Three Horseshoes on the Nonenveld. By ten o'clock, I knew that the Nonenveld was a den of iniquity, that it would take a Saint to reform it, that she would pray for my success, and if it was ever respectable enough, she would come and down a tankard with me.

She was a merry, garrulous person in her cups, and I soon knew all about her many pregnancies and miscarriages, her children, dead and alive, and her delight in hearing she was finally to be a grandmother. "There was many a time I wept at not adding more soul's to God's treasury on Earth. Yet I have sent so many little cherubs to flutter about his throne…" She wept, and her silent husband hugged her, hauled her to her feet, and together they lurched out the door.

And then it occurred to me, almost as a revelation, that I too could be a mother. Indeed, by now I could be with child. I thought of Jan holding our baby, and my heart overflowed with joy. The one shadow on my happiness was not knowing where my own mother was, and having no way of finding her.

'Twas only when the town clock boomed the hours, and I heard the watchman's rattle, that I remembered the curfew. Sure that Jan was drinking with Mijnheer van Amelsvoort, I disdained worry, and took myself off to bed, leaving the smiling inn-keeper to wipe her tables and bank the peat fire. Jan would either wake up in a cold cell if the Watch found him, or groaning over Mijnheer's leather lounge in the debris of the morning. The thought of Isabella seeing him pale and retching gave me some satisfaction.

When I woke, the morning was well advanced, and 'twas then I thought something might be amiss. I had the inn-keeper write a note to van Amelsvoort in proper Dutch, and she sent a boy around with it. By the time I'd eaten my breakfast, the boy was back. Amelsvoort had not seen Jan since they'd drunk a tankard together early the night before. The inn-keeper patted my shoulder and told me the Watch probably had him, and as soon as he'd sobered up, he'd send me a note.

Yet my relief when he walked in soon after was immense. He was pale, shame-faced and holding his head. "My God, Mary, forgive me! I had such a strange night! I meant to get back to you, but forgot the curfew. The tavern keeper let me sleep on a bench. My God, my head!"

I ordered him some small beer, and demanded news of the deal he'd made with Joost Nijners. "The place is ours. I have negotiated a half-share for us that still leaves us some

266

gold. Old Joost will take half the profits, but we pay no rent. If anyone asks, we own the whole place. And I found us a singer. Lots of soldiers' songs, and popular enough to bring a big crowd with her."

"Just as long as it wasn't her who kept you out last night", I joked, and laughed at his blushing denial.

As soon as his head cleared, Jan dispatched a letter to Lotte. Then we returned to the Nonenveld, where Jan gave the surly barkeep his marching orders. He cursed us for taking his place from him, swearing he'd have justice from Old Joost, and Jan grabbed him by the throat, pushing him up against the wall. "Mijnheer Nijnens does not speak with those who embezzle his profits. Nevertheless, he remembered your pitiful hide, and asked me to give you this purse. If you bother him at all, I will take my rapier and make a beer fountain of you. I think leaving town might be the best answer." The man scowled, examined the purse, spat, retreated up the back stairs to bundle his things together, and still cursing, rolled unsteadily out the slanting door.

'Twas then we took a good look at our new home, my first since the kennel aboard the Dreadnought. A door led from the dark front room to the reeking kitchen, where a narrow stair twisted up to the attic that would be our bedroom. I sent Jan out to buy sand, scrubbers and pails, there being none in the place, and I did not yet know all the Dutch words. I cancelled our expensive room at the inn, fetched our bags and horses, and then went to the market for provisions. Jan returned with two frail street urchins, who would help with the scrubbing if we fed them and let them sleep by the fire.

Four days later, Lotte finally arrived, her hands flying to her face in horror at the state of the kitchen, despite all our hard work. Together, we whitewashed the outside and inside walls, re-painted the door bright red, and mended the window panes, and I felt we were soon friends. Before I could have thought it possible, Lotte had the kitchen stocked

267

and shining, copper pans glowing over spotless benches, and a Hutsepot bubbling on top of the peat firepot. She slept in a camp bed by her kitchen fire, partly for warmth, yet mostly because she thought that our urchins would steal her spoons.

Jan found a stonemason, and together they set a proper chimney into the wall of the main room. This took most of our remaining funds, yet with Winter coming, we knew it would be worth it. On the afternoon of our opening night, I re-hung the freshly painted Three Horseshoes sign, just as three Dutch Cavalryman passed, and when Jan told them we were opening with Erica de Jong, Breda's own nightingale, they promised to come.

Erica turned out to be an exquisitely beautiful pink and gold doll, the dark shadows below her enormous blue eyes hinting at a very bruised innocence. She fluttered her eyelashes at Jan and I disliked her instantly, yet a throng of gathering soldiers soon demanded all her attention. When the place was full, she called for another tankard, drained it to the dregs, and leapt on top of a table, lifting her skirts to her pretty knees. She started with a fast one, and though I could hardly follow the words, the chorus was all about drinking, and the men were draining their tankards faster than we could keep them full.

Later in the evening, Erica grew maudlin, and swapped beer songs for sad ballads of love and loss. A drunken tear rolled down her cheek sometime past midnight, and I knew it was her own story she sang, and forgave her for the enraptured men about her, including my sentimental husband.

Jan enjoyed the life more than he'd expected, the sociability suiting him. I found the boastful drunks tiresome, and wondered whether I could raise a child in such a place. As both Jan and I had served with Lumley's Queens, the English Officers made a great fuss of us, and soon there was a constant stream of them drinking to Marlborough, and bringing us news of the war. Garbled versions of our romance could be heard in every tavern in Breda, and every day someone turned up to ask if I really did march after Argyll, straight into the Hell of Malplaquet.

One day, 'twas Daniel Defoe, the political pamphleteer, who stopped by to meet me. He was staying at the Prins Cardinaal, the elegant white inn on the corner of the Kasteelplein, yet he dined with us, while we told him our adventures. He was a witty, dry little man, different when he laughed, which was often that night. I told him too of Kit Jones, and he told us he'd be interested in hearing her story at first hand. I asked him if he knew of Sally Salisbury, and he said all knew of her, for she was the greatest whore in London.

Sometimes I could persuade Jan to saddle his gelding, and ride south through the burgher's gardens with me, to camp in the great forest for the afternoon. These were magic days, when the sun shone balmy and golden across the bright green fields, only to be lost in the cool depths of the old forest. Jan and I had a favourite stream, where we would bask in the sun amongst the poppies and drink a bottle of wine, his head drowsy in my lap, while I prayed for his child. Indeed, Lotte was convinced that this was the next duty on my schedule, most of the dumpy Dutch matrons with child after only weeks of marriage.

Erica sang for us every Friday, and we made more on that one night than all the rest. The soldiers she brought in congratulated us on making such a cosy nook for them, and as we were the closest tavern to the barracks, English and Dutch Officers were soon coming regularly for Lotte's food.

Lotte proved invaluable. She was cautious enough to balance Jan's optimism, a slave for work, and imminently respectable, going so far as to join all the other Dutch matrons in scrubbing our front step every Saturday morning. As soon as she was assured of my affection for Jan, she opened her heart to me, and we would discuss the most intimate subjects with a frank good humour that I found most attractive. Unlike the English, who quarrelled over every issue, the Dutch seemed to think no idea worth

269

disturbing the peace for, and this I put down to their greater experience of war. Indeed, when another bad Winter saw the peasants still suffering, and a virulent camp fever desolating entire towns, they seemed in the right of it.

We heard all the military gossip in our tavern, that Marlborough had ridden into London to see his Queen at the end of the last campaign, old now, his health ruined by the Flanders war. Despite his humble approach, the mob had recognised the great Duke, and had clamoured about him in such numbers, that he had been forced to stop at a friend's house, fearing that such a mob would follow him to Saint James and alarm the Queen. He fell at her feet later that day, referred to their long friendship, and begged her to leave his wife her Offices. Queen Anne acknowledged the glory he'd heaped on her and England, yet insisted on her right to choose her own servants. She sent him home for the pleasure of pleading with his wife to resign her posts, and Sarah had flung the gold key onto the floor for him to stoop for.

"It takes scolds like that to send a man happily off to war for forty years", Erica sneered, before beginning another drinking song, and she afterwards insisted on crediting Marlborough's virago of a wife, Sarah Churchill, with all his military enthusiasm.

Understanding that he had lost the Queen's favour, the Tories immediately accused Marlborough of profiting from the war, and his friends dropped from him. Yet the Tories had to keep their election promise, and voted six million pounds for the earnest prosecution of the Flanders war. More important, Queen Anne sent a letter to the Dutch Army supporting Marlborough, despite the changes in her Ministry, and ordered Argyll and his Jacobite Officers dispersed to the Spanish front.

In March, the French made a move towards Douai before the Allies had taken the field. Marlborough sent Cadogan to hold the plains of Lille, and strengthened the garrisons along the Scarpe. Now only Arras and Cambrai stood in the way of the Allied advance into France, and when Marlborough took the field at the beginning of May, something in me still wished to be marching with them. At Douai they faced ninety miles of fortifications that ran from Arleux to Bouchain, dug by French peasants all Winter, and defended by ninety thousand Frenchmen. Both armies had trouble with forage in the devastated countryside, and there were early skirmishes between their Cavalries.

Prince Eugene joined the Allies by mid-May, yet a sudden attack of smallpox unexpectedly carried off his master, the Emperor Joseph of Austria. This upset all plans, for if the Emperor's younger brother Charles inherited that throne, and was voted Emperor of the Holy Roman Empire by the German Princes, he would be powerful enough, without the Allies fighting to make him King Carlos of Spain as well. The whole War of the Spanish Succession had been aimed at stopping one man from ruling too much of Europe, and now there could be no balance of power, even if the Allies won. And for this confusion, we had neglected the chance of peace in 1709. For this, forty thousand had died at Malplaquet. Then rumours swept through the taverns that the Tories were secretly negotiating with France to cede Spain.

Feeling the cohesion of the Allies crumble, the French rejected peace, and immediately sent a massive detachment to invade Germany. Prince Eugene and the whole of the Imperial forces were ordered to march after them, the Dutch insisted on stronger garrisons, and Marlborough was left begging on all sides for troops. The entire burden of the war now fell on him and ninety thousand men, all of them muddy and cold in the incessant Spring rains.

They sat still until the beginning of June, when Marlborough marched them six leagues to the plains of Lens. So intense was the Summer heat, that many fell, and some died. We heard that one corpse, buried but slightly, recovered and dug his way out, much to the horror of his Regiment.

271

In July, a great fog covered a hundred French squadrons from Arras, who crept past the watch, and in amongst the tents of the Allied Infantry. The alarm was raised, and the Infantry turned out of their tents in their shirts, and seizing arms from their bells, drove the French Horsemen towards the walls of Douai just as the fog lifted, exposing them to the fury of the town's guns. Then they found that these Frenchmen had foully attacked the sutlers in the rear of the Allied Camp, hacking out their tongues and cutting their throats while they slept. I feared then for Kit Jones, and wished she still had a husband to look out for her.

Soon after, Cadogan made a detachment of Grenadiers from the Royal Scots, including Sergeant Deane, and they stormed the fortified post at Arleux, surprising the enemy in the night, and driving them out. Yet when the French made a determined attempt to re-capture Arleux, the garrison of British Grenadiers was utterly defeated. My old Regiment of Colonel Hamilton's was so shattered, that they were garrisoned in Ghent for the rest of the campaign.

Kit Jones was thus free to visit me and tell me the news. I was glad to see her, for now that the campaign had started, we only had Breda's small garrison to entertain. Jan enjoyed playing host too much to abandon his post behind the bar, Lotte never stopped scrubbing and cooking, and I had nothing to do but finish the sturdy lean-to I'd constructed for our stables, for I made the care of the horses my special concern. As a riding companion, Kit was doubly welcome, bouncing like a ball on the back of her big horse, taking ditches and canals at a flying gallop, and laughing too much to notice the stares of the Dutch shopkeepers. She enjoyed the life of the tavern, and earned Lotte's grudging respect by throwing out a foul-mouthed drunk. I also liked her open scorn for the sluttish Erica, who still flirted with every man she saw, including my husband. Kit seemed to understand me, so similar had our lives been, and I found that the loss of her last husband had softened her bravado. She seemed less ready to boast of battles, and reflected often on what she would do when the peace came.

The King of Prussia was the curse of our tavern at the time, demanding the hereditary southern estates of Orange, in direct contradiction to old King William's will. At the beginning of every campaign, he sent twenty thousand men to serve under Prince Anhalt, and the English soldiers argued that the needs of the war negated the rights of the Prince of Orange. Yet the Dutch loved their Prince, and argued vehemently for him.

Soon after Kit came to visit, we returned from a hard gallop to hear the direful tolling of Breda's bells. When we saw all the sails of the windmills stopped at the same angle, we knew it was a national disaster, and thinking only of the frail Marlborough, we both clapped spurs to our mounts, and raced for the town gates. As we rode up and dismounted, we found the sentries agape with shock, one old man wiping tears from his craggy face. It seemed the Prince of Orange had been called to the Hague to discuss the impasse with the King of Prussia. In crossing the Rhine by Moerdyke, a squall had capsized his small boat, and he had drowned at just twenty-four years of age.

The entire town plunged into mourning for him. Everyone stayed late in the taverns drinking, or in the churches lighting candles. Soon after, we heard that the claims of his widow and daughter had been entirely ignored, and their estates granted to the Prussian King.

At the beginning of August, we were expecting news of a terrible slaughter in the taking of the heavily fortified town of Arras. Indeed Kit insisted that if Marlborough attempted to take the place by storm, then he had lost his mind. We heard of him galloping along the lines to reconnoitre, often close enough to be saluted by the enemy's cannon. Villars was draining his garrisons to man the front, and Marlborough sent orders to the Governor of Douai to send any spare troops to march with all expedition to join the Allies. Yet when the Commander of the Douai detachment opened his sealed orders later that night, he found they were expected to march in two hours, in the opposite direction.

As night fell, with both armies expecting a terrible battle at dawn, orders circulated amongst the Allies to take the beating of the Tattoo for the General. Instead of blowing their lights out, they struck their tents, and loaded their luggage, and at half past ten, they were on the march in the moonlight, following after the Artillery that had already been secretly sent eastwards. The Infantry realised their canny Duke was up to something, and they would not all die, gallantly attacking Arras in the morning. So they marched hard, their spirits high, despite a sudden rain.

At dawn, they caught up with the Artillery at the Scarpe, and found pontoon bridges laid for them, and Cadogan's Cavalry ready to guard their crossing. Three loud huzzas swept through them, and once they'd crossed, Marlborough sent Officers down each exhausted column of men, stating simply that "My Lord Duke wishes the Infantry to step out." And they did. As the day lightened, they saw the blue coats of the French moving on the other side of the marshy Sensee, trying to cut them off. Our Infantry marched forty miles in sixteen hours without halt, and though many died, and many deserted, half made it. Villars, hurrying ahead with twenty squadrons to dispute the Allied passing of the stream, found Marlborough already over, and was nearly captured before he would believe that the Allies were again in France.

Then we heard that the French Horse had been let loose to pillage Brabant. Jan and I went to a special service at Saint Joost's, where we lit candles in the small, white-washed church. The predicant gave us a beautiful sermon on love in the midst of hate, and when Jan said he found it difficult to believe that God could condone the murder of innocent civilians, the predicant told him not to blame God for the excesses of men. I had rarely attended Church, seeking my soul's peace in the forests, away from people, yet I began to go between services, to light a candle for my lost mother, who didn't even know I was married.

Marlborough took Bouchain within weeks, and wanted to immediately invest Quesnoi, and spend the Winter right on the French border. Louis would be unable to pay the cost of subsisting his entire army, and France would be forced to a treaty. Yet the Dutch would not provide the immense supplies that would be needed, so Marlborough dismissed his Army, and Breda was immediately flooded with soldiers. The Winter was cold and rainy, and we heard of renewed outbreaks of fever in the devastated lands to the south.

Chapter 16: Betrayal

At the beginning of January, the English Queen created twelve new peers to stack Parliament against Marlborough, and allow the Tories to accuse him of peculation of Army funds. Then the returning English Officers claimed that Queen Anne had dismissed him. I received a letter from Sally, full of fervent congratulations and scurrilous jokes on my marriage, and boasting of her assured place in the boudoirs of Henry Saint John, the Secretary of State, who was now paying dearly for her favours. She confirmed the terrible rumour. Despite ten successful campaigns against the mighty French, Marlborough had now no protection against his enemies. The Duke of Ormonde had been given the Captain-Generalcy of the armies, and command of Sergeant Deane's beloved First Foot Guards. When the French King heard the news, he laughed and ordered his Army to march early.

The scurrilous Jonathon Swift was immediately paid by Henry Saint John to write "The Conduct of the Allies", which insisted that England owed them no loyalty, and had indeed been soundly abused by the timid and greedy Dutch. Jan paled with anger to hear of this, and insisted that the Dutch had kept double the number of troops on the field, and had repeatedly called for an end to the war in 1709, when the English had refused to make peace without Spain.

When I told Corporal Bishop the news, he went pink, and then climbed onto a chair, called for quiet, and declaimed:

"God and a soldier men alike adore,
When at the brink of Danger, not before.
The Danger past, alike are both requited:
God is forgot, and the brave soldier slighted."

I poured him beer all night for that effort, and made

him write it down.

Sally wrote that Prince Eugene had insisted on visiting England to plead for Marlborough. Strafford, the English Ambassador, tried to delay him at the Hague by involving him in the peace talks, at which the French treated the Allies like conquered states. Eugene said he had much to say about the coming campaign, yet not before the English ambassador, for he was not sure if he was an Englishman or a Frenchman.

Then the Austrian Imperial Minister had gone on the attack. "I put it to Lord Strafford that a Treaty has already been signed between Great Britain and France. I can tell him the day and the hour on which it was signed. I can tell him the room, how many candles there were burning, how many seals there were on the document, what was the colour of the wax, and of the threads whereby the sheets were bound together." Strafford, purple with embarrassment, was left with nothing to say.

After a hard week at sea, Eugene had sailed into Harwich, and such a warm welcome from the mob that it was almost impossible for him to land. Yet when Eugene saw Queen Anne, she was aloof, and told him to deal with her ministers. Henry Saint John, now Viscount Bolingbroke, had schemed to prevent Eugene from attending a banquet given in his honour by the City of London. Yet when Eugene and Marlborough went to the play together, the rabble in the gallery rose as one and gave them three loud huzzas. Sally wrote that Eugene had looked stunned, though Marlborough had assured him 'twas as good a salute as a volley of cannon.

She wrote too that Harley, now Earl of Oxford, gave Eugene a dinner, and toasted him as the greatest general in the world. Eugene replied: "If it be true, I owe it to your Lordship." It took some moments for the drunken Tory Prime Minister to understand this reference to his stripping of Marlborough. Walpole, Marlborough's accountant, was thrown in the Tower, yet though the Tories ransacked his accounts looking for proof of profit, Marlborough proved to have been orderly in a lavish age, and none of the charges could be proven.

In February, my old Infantry Regiment was made part of a detachment that crept into Arras, to set fire to the French magazines, and burn the town. They were seen by French priests, who begged Albermarle's mercy for the townspeople. He demanded that they cede the town to him, and the mighty fortress the entire Allied Infantry had feared, surrendered without a fight.

Then Breda was abuzz with the news of the sinister deaths of the three French dauphins, apparently from smallpox, though the whole of Europe thought the Duc d'Orleans had poisoned them. That left the Allied candidate for the Spanish throne, not only a contender for the Austrian Empire, yet also within one sick child of the French throne. The Allies, who had united to curb the imperialism of the French, were now without a reason to fight, unless it was to create another empire to disturb the balance of power in Europe.

In April, Ormonde was at the Hague, outwardly enthusiastic for war, yet stunned to find that the Allies had made Prince Eugene their Commander-in-Chief. Albermarle was sent with a strong detachment to take Arleux, the rest of the Army following, only to find that the French had heard the plan, and had emptied their garrisons to hold the pass. Eugene withdrew to Douai, while Ormonde joined the English at Tournai, the two armies unable to unite, as the entire area had been stripped of forage in the last campaign.

The Allies besieged Quesnoi, the English providing the covering army. Yet Villars had been told that Ormonde would never move against him, and did not even bother entrenching, though only a league away. When Ormonde refused to attack the French, Eugene demanded to know what he was about, and unable to disguise his embarrassment, Ormonde insisted on waiting for the next post from England. Eugene forced him into a compromise, and a few English Regiments were allowed to help in the siege, yet rumours of a separate English peace flew through Flanders.

By June, the general accusation of English traitors raised questions in Parliament. Oxford admitted that the British troops were confined to sieges, and would not take part in battles, as though besiegers must not often turn to repel a relieving force. Yet he insisted that there was no separate peace, as this would be foolish, villainous, and knavish.

One of his underlings, Swallow Poulett, then diverted the attention of Parliament by sneering at "a certain General who led troops to the slaughter, to cause a great deal of Officers to be knocked on the head, to fill his pockets by disposing of their commissions." In reply, Marlborough sent a challenge through his friend Lord Mohun, a friend of that bastard Macartney, and infamous for once stabbing an unarmed man over the affections of an actress. Lady Poulett told the Queen of her husband's terror of meeting the elderly Marlborough in a duel, and she set sentries outside the Poulett's door to protect them.

On July the first, the Allies stormed the counterscarp of Quesnoi and took it, and soon after the town ceded. The Allies immediately turned to encircle Landrecies. Fagel had just marched off with all the Allied Horse, when Ormonde told Eugene his orders were to withdraw the English troops, and the troops in English pay. When Eugene protested, Ormonde offered to stay with the Allies, if he would abandon the siege of Landrecies. Eugene replied that he would be glad if the English would march off, they being now only a burden to the Allies.

Ormonde expected to take forty thousand men with him, leaving Eugene hopelessly out-numbered, yet it soon became clear that the foreign troops in English pay would not desert the Allies. When Ormonde told their Generals to prepare to march, they replied that they could not separate from Prince Eugene without direct orders from their respective Princes. Prince Anhalt replied politely that he had joined Eugene at his King's instructions. The Prince of Hesse-Cassel was more direct. "Hessian troops desire nothing more ardently than to march, provided it be against the French."

Though only twelve thousand English troops were to march off, this still left Eugene with a demoralised Army, each soldier certain that Ormonde had meant to ensure the Allied defeat. Sergeant Millner later told us that the English set up a separate camp, neither Army permitted to speak to the other, the Allied soldiers looking very dejectedly upon their old comrades, the English doubling the guard over their Artillery in case the Allies were tempted to take the guns they needed. On the sixth of July, the English finally marched north, towards Ghent. As they marched away, the Allied army turned their backs on them in complete silence.

'Twas more than they could stand, and when they reached camp that night, the redcoats broke rank, smashed their flintlocks, tore their hair, and cursed the Queen's Ministry for their terrible ordeal. Grenadiers that had faced the fire of Malplaquet unflinching, wept with rage and grief, their cause and their courage both a mockery.

Near Bouchain, they were drawn up at the head of the encampments, and finally told of the cessation of arms. This was followed with French Officers riding over from Cambrai to buy the spare British horses. On their march to Ghent, Dutch garrisons refused to open the gates to them, though some took pity on the troops, and passed provisions over the walls, though they demanded the money first. At Bouchain, Douai and Tournai, the British were refused entry, despite the blood they had shed to take those places from the French. Dunkirk had been a prize of the secret negotiations, and now Orkney marched to man the garrison there. Ormonde kept the rest of the British at Dronghen until the end of the Allied campaign, and many thought 'twas to threaten their old comrades.

On the sixth of June, the terms of the English peace were finally presented to Parliament. Marlborough pointed out that England had pursued peace in direct contradiction to Her Majesty's engagements with the Allies, and that this betrayal sullied the triumphs and glories of her reign, and would render the English name odious to all other nations. Strafford then implied that Marlborough had maintained a secret correspondence with the Dutch, persuading them that a strong English party would help them carry on the war. Earl Cowper chuckled that, according to our laws, it could never be suggested as a crime to hold correspondence with our Allies, where it could be seen as a hard matter to justify treating clandestinely with the enemy.

Still, the stacked Parliament passed the Treaty, though twenty-four formal protests were made against it, including Marlborough, Godolphin, the duellist Mohun, and Cowper. The majority ordered this protest expunged from the Journals of the House, yet the protesters defied Parliament and had it published. Marlborough's enemies then fell upon him. That liar Swift wrote that at Malplaquet, ravens and dogs had fed on the wounded, and that thousands might have been saved if Marlborough had not embezzled the hospital funds.

The Allies still had immense supplies for undertaking a siege, and only a slight numerical disadvantage. Eugene persisted with the siege of Landrecies, though this was no longer a surprise move. He left the French garrisons of Valenciennes and Maubeuge in his rear, extending his fragile lines of communication to sixty miles, and scattering his Army from Landrecies to Tournai. Then he denuded the Allied garrisons to provide a new covering army.

Six days after Landrecies was invested, the French feinted an advance, and then marched all night to attack Albemarle at Denain, which was vital to Eugene's lines of communication. Faced with the entire French Army, Albemarle ordered his men to retreat back across the lone Scheld Bridge, Ormonde having taken all the pontoon bridges with him. Albermarle's garrison was caught between the river and the French, and when the French attacked, whole battalions were pushed into the water, Generals on horses dragged down by drowning men. Unable to succour them, Eugene could only weep on the opposite bank. One thousand men were killed in the first attack, one thousand five hundred were drowned, and two thousand five hundred surrendered, including Albemarle. The Scheld was so blocked up with corpses that the French had to dive for them before they could get their boats up the river.

Eugene was forced to abandon Landrecies, and his cannon, while Villars invested Marchiennes, taking it at the end of July, and all the Allied supplies with it. In August, Villars besieged Douai, the superb fortress that had cost the Allies fifteen thousand men in 1710. It was so lightly garrisoned, that it surrendered within weeks, though Eugene marched up to defend it. Eugene then marched his Army to defend Tournai, and then abandoned that fortress too. He marched them back to move his Artillery from Quesnoi, to find the French had already laid siege to that town, as well as encircling Bouchain. Eugene gathered the Allies about Mons, yet Quesnoi was taken by the beginning of October, and Bouchain in eight days. Forty thousand men, over a third of the Allies forces, surrendered with these fortresses.

In three months, Prince Eugene lost more than had been gained in the last three years of war. Many blamed the Prince, yet he was inexperienced in master-minding an entire campaign, and comparing him with the veteran Marlborough was unjust. Yet I too drank hard and demanded from Jan the reason why I spilled my blood, and that of so many Frenchmen? For what my dauntless courage and triumph over the terror of death? I thought it had been for the safety of Europe, yet now I felt it had been for nought but the pride of England's ministers. The despair of the English redcoats, marching away from their Allies at the bid of a dishonourable coward, was the despair of men whose lives had been suddenly made meaningless.

The English camp at Dronghen seethed with indiscipline, and with nought but quarter-guard duty to occupy them, they were ripe for trouble. When Villars gave permission for the English troops to forage in the fertile fields of France, they were outraged that Ormonde had asked leave of their old enemy.

Then we heard that six hundred English soldiers had run mad in Molain. The inhabitants had barricaded the town against them, so the troopers had forced four hundred people into the church, and burned it. Then they plundered the town, abusing the civilians terribly, and leaving Molain afire. Horrified outcries were raised against the English camp, yet neither Ormonde nor Villars paid any attention to them.

At the beginning of October, with Eugene's Army in total disarray, Ormonde finally withdrew the English troops from Dronghen. He sent the Dragoons to take Bruges, and the remainder to garrison Ghent, thus assuring English control of the Allied convoys by the Scheld and the Lys. Sergeant Millner rode north to visit us soon after, and told us all the horrors of that year. He was as precise as ever, yet his hair had gone grey, and he told me he was broken-hearted to see the Regiment he loved so abused.

Later that year, there was a near mutiny over bad bread in Ghent, something that could never have happened under the careful Marlborough. Then rumours flew through Ghent that Ormonde would disband them without their back pay, and three thousand men of the Infantry seized arms, refusing to let their despised Captain-General leave. Ormonde immediately promised to pay the Cavalry what was owed them, and they surrounded the mutineers with cannon, and forced their surrender. The ten ring-leaders were immediately tried and executed, and Ormond sailed for England, where Parliament voted thanks for his services in the past campaign. Soon after, Eugene broke up the devastated Allied camp at Mons.

The coming Winter saw our tavern full of Dutch soldiers, who cursed the English for continuing the war, and then betraying them. I was drinking hard, and arguing bitterly for justice for the brave British soldiers, and contempt for our ministers, who had lost all our victories in an ignominious peace that justified none of the slaughter.

Then, late in November, I had a hurried letter from Sally. Macartney had foully murdered the Jacobite Duke of Hamilton in a notorious duel that involved my own Colonel Hamilton of the Royal Scots. Swift was insisting that it had been a Whig plot to stop the great Scots nobleman from taking up his post as Ambassador to France. He described Macartney as a bravo kept by Lord Mohun, both of them Marlborough's friends.

Mohun had nominally challenged the Duke of Hamilton over a property dispute, naming Macartney as his second. Then they spent the night in a notorious bagnio in Long Acre, and met the Duke in Hyde Park at dawn on a Sunday. Mohun had declared that the seconds were not in the fight, yet Macartney had argued otherwise, and the Duke, indicating Colonel Hamilton, said: "There is my friend. He will take a share in my dance." The two pairs had then attacked each other, their rapiers flashing in the light of the rising sun. The elderly Duke fought like a lion, and soon gave Mohun a mortal wound. Yet, when he stooped over the dying Mohun, Mohun shortened his grip on his sword, and with one last vindictive blow, stabbed the Duke of Hamilton through the heart.

Macartney wounded Colonel Hamilton in the foot, yet ceded when the Colonel disarmed him. When they saw the Duke reel away from the fallen Mohun, they ran to them, Colonel Hamilton holding his dying Duke against a tree, and calling for help. Macartney snatched up Mohun's rapier, gave the Duke another murderous thrust through the body, and ran off.

Colonel Hamilton tried to get the Duke to the cake house by the ring, yet the life had already left him, and he bled his last there on the grass. The Colonel then took the corpse home in a coach, sending word to wake the newly widowed Duchess, and then he went looking for Macartney. Sally wrote that medical evidence proved it was Mohun's dying blow that killed the Duke, yet our Queen had offered five hundred pounds for Macartney's apprehension. The widowed Duchess had offered a thousand for his murder.

"Macartney is said to be hiding in Holland", Sally wrote, "while the Whigs do their best to discredit Colonel Hamilton's evidence. Lord Chesterfield has declared Macartney capable of the worst, yet holds him guiltless of such ungentlemanly behaviour. I think Macartney loved Mohun more than most people knew. I had a terrible dream of him entering your tavern, and you challenging him..."

That afternoon, I donned trousers, and strolled down to the Pasbaan, where the garrison's best duellists showed their paces. I found an old Dutch Officer I liked to spar with, for though I was much quicker, he had flowing footwork, and some admirable tricks. Eventually, I disarmed him, and someone laughed. I threw down a guilder and challenged the fool, and though he was slow on his feet, his friend gave me a better bout. I thanked them for the exercise, and told them to find someone who might give me a run for my money.

The fool glowered, and I knew that if Macartney came to Breda, he would hear of the infamous Mary Read. I hoped he would not be able to resist the chance of humiliating a woman duellist, and thought that if Colonel Hamilton had indeed bested him, then Macartney was slowing up, while I had never been faster.

In April, the Allied peace was finally concluded at Utrecht, and many found the terms outrageous. The Allies asked Prince Philip to cede the throne of Spain, if he ever came to inherit France, yet he amazed all Europe by choosing to keep the country he had won with his sword, as well as the fierce love of the Spanish people. The Allies then abandoned the Catalans to slaughter, the whole Spanish front a disaster.

France gave the English Hudson Bay, Newfoundland, and Nova Scotia in Canada; Saint Kitts in the Caribbean; and Minorca and Gibraltar, which meant English domination of the Mediterranean. Oxford, the Tory Prime Minister, also demanded a share of the Spanish slave trade, and made massive profits shipping African slaves to the New World.

The French recovered the fortresses of Lisle, Aire, Bethune, and Saint Venant, all of which had cost the Allies much blood. Flanders became the property of the Emperor of Austria, and the Dutch Republic manned garrisons against an exhausted France. The French agreed to recognise George of Hanover as the Protestant successor to England, and to expel the Pretender, who was then exiled anew to Lorraine, where he still refused to change religion in return for the English throne.

The end of the war meant an end to our immense popularity as a tavern. Some Dutch soldiers from the garrison still came to see Erica sing, yet I was heartily sick of their bitter abuse of my brave comrades. Neither could I take Lotte's devotion to domesticity seriously. Instead I longed for a child, both as proof of my love for Jan, and to give my life some purpose.

In March, I received a badly penned letter from Kit at the Queens Head in Charing Cross. She wrote that she'd married again, this time to a publican named Ross. She had begged both Marlborough and Argyll for an allowance, on the grounds that she'd served in the Duke of Orkney's Regiment for twelve years, yet they had not helped her, and she'd ended by petitioning the Queen, who'd granted her a shilling a day for life. She too blamed the politicians' squabbles for wasting our victories, and said it was as though her husbands had all been basely murdered, instead of dying bravely for a just cause.

I had a letter off Sally that boasted of a drunken riot at Mother Whybourne's, in which Sally was arrested with Lord Northington's son, the Earls of Scarborough and Ossory, Lady Marsham, a French Baron, and Beau Buckingham. Sally was sent to Bridewell, yet the Judge sent a message to the gaoler that she was not to be punished, and she was now one of the Duke of Buckingham's harem. With the war over, her father had turned up again, glad she was supporting Jenny, and happy to take an allowance himself, though he had still abused her for a harlot.

One cold, windy Friday evening, I was helping Lotte ready the tavern, while Jan fetched Erica. Colonel Kane came in with the news that the Duke of Marlborough had decided to flee England, before Parliament began. "Forced to fly the country by a set of profligate rogues", the good Colonel growled into his beer. "The drunkard and the womaniser have insinuated themselves into the favour of our weak Queen..."

"No Sir", I interrupted. "I'll not have you abusing that good, hard-working woman. She always wanted peace, and she should have insisted on it in the year nine, despite the Whig politicians. Marlborough will have to wait until George of Hanover is King of England, to be in favour again, yet the Queen is sickly, and it cannot be long before he can settle in his own home."

"The Devil's in it if she lasts the Winter", someone sneered from the door, and I did not need the cold shudder down my back to know 'twas Macartney.

I turned, my fingers on the hilt of my rapier, to find him indeed older and fatter. I did not waste the opportunity for a challenge. "In this house, the Queen is honoured as much as Marlborough, and you will speak of her with respect. You are George Macartney, are you not? The rapist and murderer?" The few soldiers in the tavern stiffened. "I was a soldier once, and found it abhorrent that such a monstrosity as yourself could be entrusted with the command of honest English soldiers. This latest assassination of the Duke of Hamilton is only one outrage amongst many. I give you warning that I intend to spill your filthy blood."

Macartney laughed, as arrogant as ever. "I don't fight women."

"Only unarmed girls, parson's widows, and country virgins, I know." I drew, and the sound of cold steel rasped my senses like a caress. The soldiers fled from the confined space, and I hoped the good Colonel was not running for the Watch. "You will fight me now, Macartney, unless you fear to. They would laugh to hear that you'd run away. They will laugh harder to hear a woman has killed you. You who have ruined the lives of so many."

Something crossed his face then, and fearing it was recognition, I cast about desperately for something that would utterly enrage him, and remembered Mohun. "You killed Mohun too with your stupid and dangerous friendship. He'd never have challenged Hamilton unless he was pushed into it. "'Tis only old Hamilton", you told him, and then dragged him off to the bagnio for a full night of frolic." He went red, then purple, and I knew I had him. Then Jan walked in, Erica on his arm.

"Is this vicious bitch your wife, Mijnheer?"

"If you do not leave, she will kill you. Go now."

"George! Darling! Did you come to hear me sing? What are you doing, Mary? Calm her down Jan!"

In Dutch, I told her: "He raped me when I was still a child", and she and Lotte gaped at me.

Jan shook his head. "Vengeance will solve nothing..."

"He is such a foul piece of work. The Earth will be a much cleaner place without him."

Erica threw herself on Macartney. "Now George you mustn't. You're a naughty boy, always hurting people and not noticing, the way a child pulls the wings off butterflies."

"Piss off, whore. I'm going to give this bitch a lesson she needs. Swords are for gentlemen not..."

"English bully!", Jan suddenly roared. "Give me your sword, Mary!"

"Hah! A man after all, though you do let your wife wear the trousers!"

"Let me be Jan! This is my fight. For God's sake get out of the way."

Macartney was already circling for the attack, when Jan snatched at the hilt of my rapier. We struggled for it, and then Erica was dragging at Jan's arm. "Nee my darling Jan,

288

don't get killed for your shrew of a wife. George, I amused you once. Remember that and let him be."

"What! The virago's husband is the whore's lover?" Macartney dropped his guard and started to laugh. One look at Jan's face proved his guilt, and I dropped the struggle for my sword. For an instant I thought Macartney had struck me when my back was turned, so sharp was the pain through my heart. Jan, Erica and Lotte all started talking then, the women dropping into Dutch in their excitement, Jan pleading earnestly with me. With one last look at him, I turned for the door and fled, Macartney's laughter following me down the street.

I ran until I could run no more, and found myself freezing in an alleyway. I stripped off the full skirt I wore over my trousers, and threw it around my shoulders to make a cloak. Then I tied my hair back, and with my hand on the hilt of my rapier, stepped into a smoky gin shop. No one gave me a second glance, and I found a dark corner, took a gulp of the foul stuff they sold, and counted the coins I had left. 'Twas not a lot to start a new life on. It amazed me that I had been a woman this morning, and was now a man again. I nursed a cold anger against Jan, both for stopping me from killing Macartney, and for betraying me with a woman as weak and corrupt as Erica. It made Jan seem not worth striving for, our marriage a sham, even more ridiculous than my own existence.

I remembered Macartney's laughter and poured myself another glass. By the tolling of the curfew, I was sodden with the foul brew. I could not face Jan, knowing that if he said the wrong word, I would kill him, so I took my cue from another drunk, and refused to leave. The barkeep shrugged, bolted the door, banked the fire, and lay down next to it. I put my head down on the filthy table, and listened to the two of them snoring through the dark hours, while my soul raged in Hell. When the Watch called midnight, I was halfway through another bottle, and when they passed by again at four, I had finished the bottle.

289

Needing to see the sun rise, I let myself out into the clear night air, and staggered up the stairs of the town walls, the sentries keeping a lax watch now the war was over. It was so cold I could not stop shivering. Then the sky to the east became awash with a light so pure, that life itself seemed filth. I wanted to drop into the moat and drown. Anything else would be torture.

Yet I made my way back to the Three Horseshoes, and waited behind a lime tree until I saw Jan and Lotte come out, he heading one way, she another. I lifted the latch on the back door, and climbed to the loft to pack my trunk. I packed some of Jan's clothes, and left our wedding ring, and the gold chain Kit had given me in exchange. I found a few guilders in Lotte's jar, and was halfway through writing a note, so she did not blame our urchins, when I looked up to find Jan standing in silent misery by the door.

Immediately, he began fervent protests that he was not Erica's lover, well once, but only once, when he had first come to Breda, and had got drunk with van Amelsvoort. I remembered the night I had waited up for him at the inn. "She asked me many a time after, but I refused on your account. Many times she threatened to tell you, and many times I thought I must tell you myself. It was such a stupid little thing, but I knew you would take it hard, and..."

"Why did you think you had the right to stop me killing Macartney? You are not fit to look me in the eye, let alone rule me."

"I beg you Mary, scold me, ruin my name, and hers too if you want. Take a lover, make me a laughing stock, do anything but leave me over that low tramp."

"You have already lost me. Abusing her won't help."

"And this old garb of yours? Would you punish yourself for my foolishness?"

"It is you who has made anything else impossible. If you had told me the truth, you would not have stopped me killing the bastard who first abused my innocence. Now you who I loved more than any other, have done me even worse

290

hurt than he did. Through weakness. My love has disappeared with my respect. The only thing I don't understand, is why then this pain?"

Lotte found us, and scolding him fiercely, she chased him away, threw her arms about me, and burst into tears. When we had both recovered, she found a bottle of our best brandy, and we proceeded to drink it all. She insisted that, as it was Jan who had wronged me, he must find his own bed, and she would make a bed in her kitchen for me now, so I could sleep by the fire while he cleared his things out. Light-headed from fatigue, liquor, and grief, 'twas the promise of sleep that beguiled me. She kept insisting that I stay with her, that I could work the afternoon shift while Jan took the night shift. Half aswoon, I agreed to stay on condition that Jan never approached me. She told me he was desperate enough to agree to any terms.

In the end I stayed because Jan kept to his promise, and never came near me. When we had to speak, he treated me with desperate politeness, and plagued me only with letters, in which he swore his undying love, and begged me to forgive him. Erica no longer sang at the Three Horseshoes on Friday nights, and, with all of Breda knowing the scandal, our Dutch soldiers deserted us. When anyone did enter our warm, dark tavern in the afternoons, they found me snarling over a bottle of brandy, and soon left. Jan did better business at night, yet old Joost Nijnens still complained of the drop in profits. Lotte could not stop slaving, though there was none to eat the food she cooked. My heart was utterly frozen, and I could not care.

In December, we heard that Queen Anne's gout had turned to gangrene, and that the Jacobites were preparing to restore the exiled James, rather than accept the Protestant Hanovers. Civil war threatened England again, and the aged Marlborough accepted Prince George's commission as Commander-in-Chief. Argyll, bitter after his time in Spain, insisted that the Tories were arming the Scottish clans, and that those loyal to the Succession were being purged from the Army. When he wrote Marlborough a sincere letter of reconciliation, Orkney accused him of inciting his beloved Scots Greys to follow the Pretender, and Argyll was removed from their command. The Queen declared the wrangling Parliament prorogued at the beginning of July, and Marlborough felt safe enough to return home.

Sally wrote to grieve with me over my miserable marriage, though she pleaded with me not to take the whore so seriously, as no one else ever did. She tried to cheer me by laughing at the dissolute Bolingbroke's fall from grace. He had tried to take control of the Tories by identifying himself with the Church of England, calling for an end to tolerance for Dissenters in political life. Furious with this betrayal, Oxford attacked him before the Queen at the next Cabinet, calling him a rogue and a thief, and promising to denounce him before Parliament, even at cost to himself. This violent scene caused the Queen to relapse, the gout moved towards her brain, and she lay dying.

For a vital two days, Bolingbroke wavered, without the courage to use his plenary powers to bring over the Pretender, as he had promised. Perhaps the prospect of a Civil War between Marlborough's veterans and the Scots Highlanders deterred him. "I thought of you, Mary, and wondered which side would you fight on?", Sally wrote. "You've always had a softness for young Jamie, as every Englishwoman has, and none here wants fat George for a King. Yet Jamie's love for the French stands hard against him in my heart."

Bolingbroke missed his chance. Our devoted Queen had always urged her ministers to ignore factions and serve their country, yet though she had worked remorselessly, and sacrificed her friends, it took her death to accomplish such unity, and that only for a short time. She rallied long enough to pass the white staff to Lord Shrewsbury on the thirtieth of July, instructing him to use it for the good of her people. She died two nights later, alone, but for a crowd of politicians who sighed with relief to know she was gone.

Marlborough sailed in the day after to a royal welcome, the people cheering him from Chatham to London, hundreds of gentlemen riding as his escort, and Grenadiers turning out to salute him. The new Ministry, appointed in his absence by King George of Hanover, sent Bolingbroke a curt dismissal, and rifled his private papers. Oxford then betrayed Bolingbroke with details of his peculations.

"In mid-September", Sally wrote, "George the First stepped ashore at Greenwich, a coarse, miserly German martinet, with two incredibly ugly mistresses, one skinny and one fat; and a son who he hates like the plague." Sally then swore she'd lain with the Prince of Wales, and found him more inclined to laugh with her than bed her. Richmond, once again a favourite, claimed that she was a good enough whore for a Garter, and her reply, that whores and bastards were always lucky, was quoted throughout London, for 'twas not often that a Duke laughed when reminded of his illegitimacy.

As that momentous year drew to a close, I wanted to be in England again, and suggested to Jan that he give me what money he could from the business, and agree to a separation. He insisted that the tavern was losing so much, that he could not spare me a guilder. I erupted in hatred, Lotte stopped me from hurting him, and brought us to some reconciliation. He agreed to put aside a few stuivers each day from our proceeds, so that if I still wanted to go at the end of Winter, I should have something in hand. This was on condition that I stop drinking so much of the profits, that I stop scowling at customers, and that I wear skirts. This latter submission I made only because Lotte begged me, saying that in such a small town, I stood out as a strange eccentric. I told her it was not small towns, it was small heads that were the problem.

Becoming more involved in the business, I made better friends with Jan, and saw that the fervent youth I'd fallen in love with was gone, and only a rather plump, good-natured Dutch tavern-keeper remained. I made better friends

293

with Lotte too, who benefited by the thaw in my soul to point out my injustice to Jan. "You thought he was perfect, but he's always been much too easily ruled by pretty women. He had to run away from Isabella, he was so afraid she'd bully him into marriage. I dare say Erica threw herself on him that night, and made his life Hell ever after. And you have never asked yourself just why he was afraid to tell you."

"This is rubbish, Lotte."

"Perhaps. But you're not perfect either, my dear Mary. You carry anger in your soul like a permanent blight. It is no wonder you never conceived a child."

"Thank God! I am still free, and can go where I will."

"And yet you have stayed this long."

"Sally wrote me that Macartney has been acquitted of murder by the new Ministry. He's free, rich and powerful, and if I returned to England, I'd still have to kill him. Besides, over there I have only one friend who I cannot respect, and a missing mother. Though that is more than I have here."

"Perhaps. Perhaps not. You cannot have what you will not take."

Spring brought the New Year, and in England, Jacobite uprisings. Sally wrote that King George had already planned his escape to Holland, and swore that London was Jamie's. Marlborough had dropped Bolingbroke a hint of his imminent arrest, and the fool had panicked and fled the country for the Pretender's court, thus admitting by his fear what his enemies could never have proved. The Duke of Ormond's plans were then discovered, and he fled after Bolingbroke. Hundreds of Jacobite nobles were then arrested, sending the rest flocking to the Pretender.

The whole of Europe was waiting for him to sail, when the news of the French King's death rocked us all. A sickly boy-king was named Louis the Fifteenth, yet the Duc D'Orleans was Regent, and as he wanted good relations with England, Jamie's twelve ships of French soldiers and arms were immediately unloaded.

Yet war with Scotland could not be stopped. Both the English and the Scots ran away at the Battle of Sheriffmuir, and the Scots failed to push into England at Preston. When Lord Mar sent for Prince Jamie, he sailed for Scotland with Spanish help. Though his main Fleet was scattered by a storm, yet a small contingent made straight for the Firth of Forth, and Jamie landed just before Christmas, to be instantly proclaimed King of Scotland. He spent forty-five days there, mostly as a fugitive, complaining to Lord Mar: "Instead of bringing me to my Crown, you've brought me to my Grave."

My regular wage was slowly filling my purse, and I planned to leave and march under Marlborough, though Jan begged me to stay longer, the military activity bringing us more customers. I refused, and when Jan started buying drinks for pretty coquettes, Lotte shrugged and told me my hard heart had ruined our only chance of making a family. I thought to return to England, and report the death of Mary Read, so Jan could marry again.

Yet before I could leave, Jamie abandoned Scotland, the Highlanders fled back to their mountains, and the rebellion was over. Nearly a hundred Scotsmen were hung, drawn and quartered, and hundreds more sent to the Caribbean as slaves. Of those sent to the scaffold, only two were Lords. King Jamie found a home in Italy, where he soon married, and many prayed that he bring no more Catholic Stuarts into the world to plague us.

Spring was late, the Summer seemed to last mere weeks, and then the Autumn rains came down hard upon us, sending epidemics raging in the war-torn towns of Flanders. I had almost saved enough to leave Breda, when Lotte fell ill of a putrid fever. Plague doctors had been recruited, and our tavern was immediately closed down. As we were both needed to nurse Lotte, this hardly seemed to matter, until Old Joost sent a testy note demanding his proceeds.

Despite the virulence of the fever, Lotte struggled

back to beg for our reconciliation. She lasted two weeks, wasting away before our eyes, and in that time, Jan never let her see him weep, urging her to hold hard to life, and stay with him. I saw so much tenderness in his love for her, that my own heart warmed towards him. When the predicant came to begin the prayers for the dying, Lotte smiled one last time, and passed away. I closed her eyes, Jan turned our mirror to the wall, and when the church bell tolled that evening, her coffin joined those in the long train of corpses waiting to be buried in Saint Joost's cemetery.

I offered Jan the money I had saved to pay for her funeral, and when he burst into tears, I could do nought but hold him, and beg his forgiveness for my intransigence. Yet when I kissed his forehead, his brow was already burning. I held his hot and clammy hand as they filled Lotte's grave, and prayed that it was not too late for us. Yet by the time we returned to the Three Horseshoes, he was already too ill to stand.

I sent our urchins to find a physician, and prayed as I never had before. By nightfall, Jan was delirious. By midnight, when the exhausted physician finally came, he was raving. The physician could only shrug his shoulders, and declare that Jan was young and strong, and might make it. His eyes avoided mine even as he offered his hollow reassurances. I did not have the four stuivers to pay him, and fearing I might receive no assistance in the coming ordeal, I gave him Kit's golden chain and my wedding ring, and begged him to come when he could. Then I sent one of the boys to beg assistance from Mijnheer van Amelsvoort. Yet from him, no assistance came.

When the physician came back on the third day, he shook his head. I left Jan in the care of our urchins and ran to Saint Joost's to pray. There I was but one of many, all of us lighting candles with trembling fingers, on our knees to beg God for someone we needed. I abased myself utterly, vowing to repent of my pride, anything to not be left alone in this cold, hard world. And all about me people wept and made similar vows, and I knew in my heart that we prayed in vain.

Towards dawn, Jan became conscious of me, and we wept together, our tears and vows of love mingling with the evil sweat of the fever, and our fear. He swore he could never leave me, not if I loved him. He was not ready. Each day the flesh fell from his bones, yet still he would not surrender, and the fever made a battleground of him, shaking him with tremors and convulsions, until his mind was touched, and he knew me not.

Days later, at dawn, a small bird perched on our windowsill and sang. Jan looked at me and smiled, and I fell on my knees by his side, sure he had recovered. It took me some time to see he was gone. The physician found me still sitting with him that afternoon, holding his cold hand, staring at everything I had lost. When I turned my dry eyes to him, he saw no one behind them. Fearing madness, he forced me to help lay out Jan's corpse. This broke me, as he had meant it to, and I thought I would never have done weeping. There was no money, and we buried him behind Saint Joost's, in the cemetery for suicides and destitutes. The church bells rung soft and low, and I swore to God that He would never hear another prayer from me.

I was just turned twenty-four, a widow, childless, and poor. Old Joost sent me a demand to visit him, and told me that Jan had agreed to pay a minimum sum a week, even if there were no proceeds from the tavern. The debt had mounted, and though I begged for time to pay it, he refused. I asked him to buy me out for what Jan and I had put in, and he said that with the war over, the tavern was not worth so much, and offered me the sum of my debt to him. I refused, and told him I was his partner, whether he liked it or not, and he smiled coldly, and told me that the agreement had been an informal one between himself, and Jan, who was dead. I sought help from van Amelsvoort, who'd been the witness, yet when he shrugged and prevaricated, I realised that as a woman and a foreigner, I could not enforce my rights.

I considered returning to England and Sally, yet knew that her whoring would soon disgust me, and I feared meeting Macartney. Instead I sold what I could, and dressed as a man, I rode my mare for Ypres, where I enlisted with the garrison there. I found them easily fooled as to my sex, yet the long grey Winter and my remorse weighed heavily on my soul, and I could not stay.

Thinking again of England, I resigned from the Regiment, and headed for Ostend, and that was where I met a particularly eloquent First Mate, and let his descriptions of the warm beauty of the Caribbean persuade me to sea again.

PART 5: THE CARIBBEAN 1717
Chapter 17: Sam Bellamy

I stood aboard the crowded pirate sloop, my seachest on my shoulder, half-starved and scurvied, my thoughts running on the life that had led me to this desperate choice.

Then I recalled the desperate plight of my old Dutch mates. I found Captain Bellamy directing the stowing of the stolen cargo, and when I explained my concerns, he shook his head. "I swear by the Devil, we're low in provisions ourselves. Ho, Paul!" The handsome, yellow-eyed mulatto, who'd so terrified the Dutch Captain, stepped up to us. "Paul Williams is Quartermaster, and cares for the rights of each man aboard, and that includes provisions. What say ye, mate, can we spare those sorry Dutchmen some water and biscuit?

"We're on quarter rations already Sam. I'd hoped to find more aboard the Dutchman. I'll ask the men." He turned to the busy crew, and shouted "Parlez!", and they left the Dutch barge, and came up from below, gathering about us. "You know how low on provisions we are. Yet those Dutchmen have nothing. I say we spare them a barrel of water and the last of that stale biscuit. What do you say?"

"I say they're in a bad way, from no fault o' their own", Bellamy called out. "We've all suffered from lack o' water at sea. I beg ye to be merciful." The 'ayes' had it, and Bellamy ordered a cask of water and some biscuit to be dropped aboard the Dutch merchantman.

Then, still shaky, I followed Williams below, into the large stern cabin of the pirate sloop. It smelled rank, the pirates following the Navy custom of relieving themselves in any convenient corner during foul weather. The mulatto showed me where to stow my chest and hang my hammock, explaining that most of the men slept on deck under the stars. He told me to hang my rapier from a nail above my chest, for none went armed when aboard, unless in battle.

Back on deck, Bellamy was calling for men to man

the sails. "Ho, Carty, time for us to cast off", he called to a huge old Viking with the strawberry nose of a drinker, and I helped him unloose the grappling hooks that held us to the Dutchman. Others raised a jib, and as we drifted gently away, I shook to think how close death had come to taking me again. 'Never again', I vowed to myself. 'No more tyrants!'

In the lightest breeze, the sloop slipped easily through the darkness towards the stern light of the pirate schooner. Yet even before we could make out her dark shape, we could hear curses rolling out over the waves. They seemed to surprise no one but myself.

"You Irish bastard! You leave me sitting here all night awaiting you, with no provisions, and not even a messenger to say whether we win or no!"

"Success Captain LeBoose!", Bellamy yelled back. "Gold, goods, and wine." The pirates brought the sloop to nestle gently against the schooner's bulk, and I was impressed again at their seamanship. Carty dropped three crates of wine onto the Frenchman's deck. "That's enough to keep you happily drunk 'til Saba", Bellamy grinned. "We'll split the loot there."

"I do not like to divide the goods later, and I wanted the Dutch trader!"

"She was an unseaworthy pig", Williams spat, his yellow eyes reflecting gold in the torchlight.

Bellamy laughed. "We'll not cheat ye of a single coin, LeBoose. We've sworn it, and our word means somethin' to us, even if it means little to you. Forget not that we took the tub, ready for battle, while you stood by, as ye generally do." He ignored the resulting French tirade. "We must make the most o' the night, for there's a man o' war cruisin' these parts. Push us away Carty. Set a course south-east for Saba, Paul."

We slipped into the night, the Frenchman's curses rolling after us, our crew grumbling bitterly. "I say that after Saba, we lose the useless French bastards", Williams declared from his post at the wheel.

"Let them help us take a decent ship, eh Paul",

Bellamy countered. The men talked of it, as they had evidently talked of it before, yet 'twas clear our sloop was heavily over-manned.

A huge, silent Indian hauled a cauldron of hot fish chowder into our midst, and Bellamy invited me to mess with himself, Paul Williams and Patrick Carty. Carty handed me a bowl from a basket, and the prospect of food nearly undid me. "Now lad, easy does it, just a sip to start, then some bread so it stays down. And water. Don't touch the stuff meself, yet we've no beer, and the wine will overset ye entirely."

"Another Irishman", I noted awkwardly.

"Aye, we're easily talked into this game. Me four brothers are still at sea, and none of us slavin' for any master. Not that you English dogs left us any choice but the sea after Limerick."

"In truth, the Irish have good reason to hate the English lords who have so cruelly treated them. I am thankful then I am no lord."

Carty laughed heartily. "Sam says we are all Lords of the Sea, yet a skinnier, more woeful, beardless, shambling stick of a man..."

The pirates feasting about me laughed with him, though there were many younger than me. They were less ferocious with the soot washed from their faces, though some had not bothered. Many were truly Africans, and they seemed more fearsome to me than the brigands I had so willingly joined. I stared at the great welts that covered the back of a huge black man sitting close to me, until I looked up to see his glare.

"A King in his own land, that one", Bellamy murmured. "I know not the full tale, yet it seems he was tricked and sold into slavery by his own uncle. Paul makes great sport o' takin' slavers and releasin' the cargo. These have been with us for months now, signed up as brothers, learnin' the ropes, ready to claim their own vessel, and sail for home. That big one will be their Captain, that tall, skinny

301

wight is learnin' all he can o' navigation."

"We are all exiles then. Truly I wish them luck."

"Aye", Carty nodded. "That Dutch Captain o' yours will swear a deposition 'gainst ye for joining us, an' yer head's fer the noose if ye head fer home, lad. Never forget it."

We slipped through the quiet sea, and though my guts tortured me, I found myself strangely at peace. I watched Williams check the course and relinquish the helm to the sailor who brought him a bottle of wine, no need for any master's orders here. 'Twas then I understood their skill. The sloop was theirs, their work was their own, and freedom from fear of the lash left them with their own judgement.

Then Williams turned and stalked towards me, pulling an oilskin packet from inside his shirt, and picking up a lantern. "These are our Articles. You must sign to be one of our Company." He spread four pages of thick parchment out on deck, close to the lantern. "Can you read or do you want me to..."

"I can read." The Articles impressed me with their good sense. I had the right to help myself to food and drink, as I wanted, unless the Company voted for rationing. If I lost a limb or an eye, I'd be liberally compensated. The Ship's Council included the voice of every man aboard, and any man could call parlez, but when chasing or being chased, when the Captain's word was law. Their crimes included cowardice in battle; stealing from the Company; taking any flame below, where the gunpowder was stored; bringing on boys or women for amusement; or raping any prudent woman found aboard a prize. The punishment for any crime was being made Prince of an Island, the size and comfort of the island being up to the Company to decide. "I'm surprised", I told Williams, "especially about the women."

"If it's crumpet you want, there's plenty in port, cheap enough. It's a conviction of the Nassau Council that we are in business here at sea."

"I'm not interested…that is, I'm surprised to see

Justice here, when I have not found it anywhere else in the world. And what is the Nassau Council?"

"You vote for Captain and Quartermaster, and when in Nassau, they form the Council. Some don't bother, though Sam here can always be counted on to stick his oar in."

Bellamy shrugged. "If by raisin' his hand, a man may stop injustice, then 'tis a crime for him to sit still, at least so Henry Jennings says. Now lad, say not that ye've never heard o' the great Captain Henry Jennings! The year before last, when I was first out on the account with Ben Hornigold, Jennings rescued a drownin' Spanish sailor. His men would have thrown him back to the sea as a Papist, yet the Welshman said nay, and was well-rewarded for his kind heart. The Spaniard told Jennings that the entire Spanish treasure Fleet had been wrecked by the last hurricane, leavin' bodies and gold litterin' the beaches o' Florida. Hornigold convinced us to join Jennings and five hundred buccaneers, on a raid of the Spanish salvage camp. We were all made rich by it, and outlaws, for the war with Spain was two years over. Yet Jennings knew o' Captain Mission's old pirate base on Providence, where our sloops can sail freely in, yet the men o' war go aground. Aye, by the Devil, Jennings is a canny man."

Carty growled. "Aye, canny enough for a Welshman. Yet his nonsense o' not takin' English ships would have seen us starve, for most o' the trade is English."

"And as Ben Hornigold always follows Henry Jennings, he insisted that we spare the English Trade", Bellamy explained. "For days we argued, then we voted him down as Captain. His men claimed our schooner, and last we saw, he was headed for Providence, leavin' us no choice but LeBoose's company."

"Aye, damn his eyes for it!", snarled Paul Williams. "Once a man takes to the sea, he must hold true to his comrades, or we'll all hang. King George has given his Navy and his Governors new powers to hang us all, not just Captains and Quartermasters, but every man aboard."

"Aye lad", Bellamy grinned. "We're o'er the line now, free Princes at war with the unjust world, and we have only each other to stand fast with. And that is all we need."

I committed their few rules to memory, then followed Williams in an oath that made my blood run cold, swearing to uphold the freedom of the Brethren of the Sea, and binding myself by all my remaining honour to these sea robbers. Then Williams handed me a quill, drew his fish knife, sliced the base of my thumb, and sucked just enough blood into the quill for me to sign my name amongst the crosses and thumb prints.

Then he called for a bottle of wine, and the pirates lying about gave a cheer as I drank. I passed the bottle to Williams, who wished me luck and called me brother, and then Carty drank to my good health. When Bellamy called for a toast to their new comrade, they all cheered me again, more bottles open now, and my heart warmed to be so welcome, so long had I been alone and friendless in the world. Carty advised me against too much wine, yet I could not hide my growing swoon. Shaking his head at my miserable spirit, he easily picked me up and heaved me lightly to my feet. Then, with surprising gentleness, he helped me below, into the stinking stern cabin and my hammock.

Fever took me then, as the oaths and songs of the celebrating pirates thundered above me. In my weakened state it sounded like the revels of demons, and my soul quaked in fear. Towards dawn, the carousing ceased, and I fell into a sleep as deep as the sea herself. When I finally woke, it was to stinking darkness, and the splash of water against the hull of the sloop. I staggered up and out of the cabin, and found myself in the midst of a glorious sunset, a sweetly scented island drifting past our port side.

The pirates were crowded on deck, most winding up fishing lines in the fading light. They looked like ordinary sailors, dressed in cast off Navy garb, as I was, baggy canvas trousers, ragged blue and white checked shirts to the knee, red Monmouth caps and sagging tricornes. Some, like Bellamy, indulged in ribbons, feathers and lace, yet since their suits were stained from rough living, I thought them merely thumbing their noses at the Sumptuary Laws. Most of the crew wore the price of their funerals in solid gold earrings, and there was an abundance of rough tattoos. I guessed them to be mostly deserters from the Navy, as I once was, or from captured merchantmen, as I now was.

Bellamy saw me then. "Aye, half starved to death, then on his feet in two days. I knew he was a man o' spirit!"

"Two days!"

"Aye, ravin' an' sweatin' in a terrible fever. Carty took ye some water." He thrust a loaf of bread and a bottle of wine at me, and I was suddenly ravenous. "To port lies Saba, and LeBoose is off our stern."

Saba was an outline of jungle, with one huge, spreading tree standing out clearly against the red tropic glow. Williams called out that we were tacking in, and needed soundings, as the tide was low. A few men rose to drop the mainsail, and we ghosted in under the goose wings of a jib, Carty swinging the lead and bellowing the soundings. Williams lined us up carefully between the tree and a rock on shore, and then ordered the anchor away. It went over with a rattle and a splash, and we turned then to watch LeBoose's schooner come alongside.

Yet before the two pirate vessels were lashed together, LeBoose had leapt aboard, followed by most of his crew. The French pirate was a swaggering, mincing fop, with more feathers in his hat than manners, and he immediately demanded to see the gold taken from the Dutch ship.

Paul Williams narrowed his eyes and stepped in front of him, his hand on the hilt of a low-slung rapier. "Damn your eyes, LeBoose! You're an ill-tempered snake on your own ship. On this vessel, mind your tongue or lose it." LeBoose snarled and went for his sword, and with cat-like quickness, Williams flicked his steel loose, and under LeBoose's chin.

"Ho now boys, no need for fightin'," Bellamy calmed them. "Sheathe yer swash Paul, 'tis clear 'gainst the Articles. LeBoose is anxious to get to business, so he can get to the wine. He does not mean to display the manners of a cheap whore, eager for her fee. And ye've no need to fear we've cheated ye LeBoose. Though if ye fear it, yer free to sail off once we've divided the booty."

LeBoose covered his relief at not having to fight Williams with a ferocious sneer, and stalked off to examine the Dutch goods being hauled on deck. Under his directions, the cargo and the gold was halved, for it seemed there was an equal number of men on the much bigger schooner, most of them Frenchmen. Then LeBoose complained that he was low on food, and Bellamy suggested that they repair to Saint Thomas to sell the goods, and re-provision. The pirates then swarmed ashore in over-loaded dories, to build a fire on the beach, and get drunk again. I was astounded to see two of our crew strip and dive overboard to swim in. Carty told me that all the island-born could swim like fish, yet we agreed that so much water must thin the blood and make a man susceptible to ague.

"Better an ague than a damned Frenchman", Carty scowled, and the rest of our crew growled an agreement that boded ill for the feast. When I was finally ashore, my knees ashake with the joy of it, I saw Carty give one of LeBoose's crew a massive swipe to the head. Brawling amongst the Brethren when aboard was forbidden by the Articles, yet duels ashore were not, and a fight was soon arranged between the giant Irishman and the quicker Frenchman. They would each have one pistol to fire at twenty paces, and a cutlass if they missed, the fight to stop at first blood.

At Bellamy's signal, they fired their pistols, and both shots went astray. Cursing horribly, the two combatants then raised their cutlasses and charged. With the clash of steel ringing through the still night, Carty's strength drove his cutlass through the Frenchman's guard, and slashed his arm. Williams then stepped between them, and the fight was over.

All cheered, LeBoose's crew enjoying the fight as much as ours, the spilt blood easing the tension. While our silent Indian pulled out his medicine pouch and attended to the pale Frenchman, tubs containing all the fish caught that day were placed around the fire for us each to skewer and grill. Bellamy passed around bottles of wine and baskets of stale bread. Given our numbers, there was little enough to eat, and both crews were soon drunk.

I was just thanking the Lord that there would be no more violence, when Bellamy whipped some pages from his breast pocket, and to my astonishment, he and two of the other men took turns to read out a satire in verse that Bellamy had written on the old French King. It was foul, scurrilous and amusing, especially as I saw that the darts were aimed at the arrogant LeBoose. He could only attempt to laugh, as no self-respecting pirate could be seen to defend monarchy, and he did not want to claim these sallies for himself. Our crew grew merrier, while the Frenchmen grew more sullen, most choosing to return to their schooner to sleep.

Then 'twas evident that among the discarded laws of the Navy, were those against sodomy. The pirates wandered off into the night in drunken pairs, Captain Bellamy and Paul Williams amongst the first. Not all the men were so inclined, yet all accepted that this was so, without a raised eyebrow. I stayed close to the fire, afeared that some drunken pirate might take a fancy to me, despite my haggard scrawniness.

Carty and his mates were quietly comparing the corruption of the different colonial Governors. One mentioned a rumour that the King planned to pay them so much money, that they would be rich enough without trading with us. A cool breeze blew in from the sea, and soon I was calm, and then asleep.

I woke at first light, stiff from the chill of the damp sand and afire with the bites of tiny sand-flies, pirates snoring all about me. There was nothing for breakfast but

307

hard bread and the dregs of the wine, and my pipe.

Once I'd scavenged what I could, I made my way around the headland to the next beach, seeking some privacy for my ablutions. I found great spreading trees, full of squawking parrots of fantastic colours, and beyond the white sand of low tide, warm blue water that tempted me to wade in and wash more than hands and face. I saw fish so brilliantly beautiful that they rivalled the birds, and a great eel with vicious teeth that held its ground in the sharp coral and warned me off. It was a world intoxicating to the eye, yet dangerous, and I was glad to find my way back to my comrades.

Carty was already up, despite the quantities of wine he'd consumed the night before. He waded into the sea, splashed himself vigorously, belched, farted, and swore when he found there was no wine left. I pointed to a bottle half buried in the sand, and he beamed like a baby. After his first swig, he sat and watched me scraping soap off my face with a sharp sword, the closest I could come to a shave. "Yer an outlaw now lad, and can forget the niceties if ye wish."

"I'd be laughed at for the wispiest beard in the Caribbean, though the fashion suits Bellamy well enough."

"Ye were a gennulman once."

"Every London fop with a sword and a wig thinks he's a gentleman. My father was a sailor."

"Ye got some learnin' though."

"And then ran away to sea. There I found life too near death, and deserted for Marlborough's Army. There I found that there are worse things than death." I took a stick of charcoal from the fire, and blackened my face against the heat of the rising sun.

Carty chuckled. "Aye, ye look right fearsome, and not quite the puny wreck that staggered aboard a few days ago. 'Tis the life for a man, this."

"'Tis not my choice of a life. I've seen too much fighting as a soldier to want more. Yet it seems to me your Company understands well the art of bluff."

308

"Yet if it comes to a fight, show no mercy Mark Read. For none will show you any."

"I know. The world belongs to the man with his pistol primed and sword drawn."

"Aye lad. The world is like that."

"Yet something keeps whispering 'peace' in my ear. I don't think I'll be with you for more than one cruise."

"Many have said the same, havin' gone on the account out o' necessity. Yet 'tis a grand life."

I nodded. "Aye, the freedom of it is as heady as new wine. In the Old World, a man gets used to the threat of the lash, and thinks himself scum too easily. And in the New World, I hear any man with money is a Lord."

"A King, lad. A man with money is a King, in a land where most are so poor, they'd sell their sisters for a hunk o' bread."

The pirates were stirring about us, cursing the sun, nursing their sore heads, growling like bears when they found there was no more wine. There was no argument when Bellamy suggested we make for Saint Thomas, taking any ship along the way in hope of provisions.

We slipped out of the cove on a thin breeze, the sea like glass, the reef clear below us. Paul Williams, amused by my fascination, pointed out finger, brain and star corals, flaming with scarlet, yellow, and rose. Yellow fans of lace grew next to purple staghorn, and pink twigs danced with wispy yellow sea feathers. I saw blue sponges, black and spiny sea urchins, golden sea stars and a spiny lobster spotted with scarlet. Flocks of vivid parrot fish, yellow tails, and angel fish flew through this undersea world, preyed on by vicious barracuda. And then we were in open ocean, leaving the treacherous beauty of the reefs behind us.

Bellamy roared that his best pistols were promised to the lookout who sighted us a prize. "No prey, no pay", Paul Williams yelled, and I dreaded the first call of 'Sail!', knowing I would soon have to prove my worth to these hardened adventurers. I eyed them askance, yet most were

309

busy untangling fishing lines, hoping for breakfast. Others mended nets and patched sails. Only the rasping of the whetstone, and the sly jokes as they lined up to sharpen their cutlasses, showed that they expected battle. I considered that a rapier is for killing, not threatening, and asked Bellamy for a pistol. He told me to see Paul Williams, who readily agreed to lend me one of his.

I had just finished cleaning and loading it, when a boy yelled: "Sail! Two sails to starboard!" Fishing lines were rolled in, hammocks down, faces were blackened, and pistols primed. Soon we could make out a brigantine and a sloop.

"I swear by the Devil, we'll take a prize today!", Bellamy shouted, and the pirates about me filled the air with cries of bravado. And even my soul began to sing a battle song, for 'tis a glorious thing to throw life itself into the dicing cup. Never are the senses so alive.

Then Carty yelled: "Her colours! Devil take it, 'tis a man o' war we're chasin'!" Bellamy laughed and ordered all guns primed and ready. Swivel guns were loaded with pebbles, and baskets of grenadoes were placed near smoking slowmatches. I saw Carty loading our sloop's gun with shot, and my old training saw me leaping to help him, ramming the oakum on top of his cartridge, and after he'd rolled the ball in, tamping another wad down. There was a tarred fireball in a bucket, and he roared that we'd only use that if the fight grew desperate, as 'twould set her sails alight, and ruin her for us.

LeBoose's schooner soon chased the merchant sloop away. "May the Devil damn the lubberly son of a French whore," Williams swore. "He's got the guns, yet he's chasing the prize, and leaving us to take on the warship alone."

Yet Bellamy laughed from his perch in the rigging. "Unfurl our true colours! We'll push them up against the Saba bank, and she must cede, or wreck!" Then we all saw the dark shadow in the blue of the sea, and grasped his plan. The man o' war was much deeper in draught than our little sloop, and so slow and cumbersome, she must have a bottom afoul with weeds. She would not be able to avoid both us, and the reef. "Prime the guns and reef the mainsail. All hands to starboard! Ready the grapnels and prepare to board!"

I poured the trail of gunpowder, while Carty strained to lever the muzzle up, then Bellamy shouted at us to fire, and I put the torch to the powder. The blast broke a rope, and sent the gun recoiling at Carty, who leapt out of the way. The ball whistled over the bows of the warship, as she was trying to tack away from the bank. They had not even primed their cannon, and had no choice but to raise the white flag.

Then we flooded up and over the sides of the great ship, cursing and swearing, to find her crew assembled on deck. Bellamy gracefully accepted the Navy Captain's proffered sword, and soon half the scurvied Navy crew were in their smallest boat, rowing for shore, and the rest were being welcomed by us as brothers. Bellamy called for a vote, and was soon Captain of His Majesty's ship the Sultana. Paul Williams, his yellow eyes agleam, was then voted Captain of our sloop.

When LeBoose sailed up with the merchant sloop under his command, he screamed with fury to find Bellamy already Captain of the warship, and demanded her for himself. Carty and I caught a wink from Bellamy, and Carty pulled me below, and down to the gun deck. When we saw the hull of LeBoose's schooner through a gunport, we finished the priming of that gun.

Above, Bellamy was trying to negotiate his way out of the standoff, insisting that we had won the ship alone, and that LeBoose had the merchantman after all. The Frenchman's curses rained down on us all, and Bellamy coldly suggested that since each crew had two vessels under their command, they had better part the Company, rather than risk a battle over spoil. The Frenchman hesitated just long enough for Bellamy to nod at our gun, primed for a broadside, the muzzle only a few feet from the Frenchman's

311

hull. LeBoose cursed Bellamy most foully then, and Bellamy grinned and offered to meet him with cold steel in Nassau.

Once the Frenchman was away, we raided the warship's meagre supplies, and all feasted. Then we set about separating into two crews, and choosing Quartermasters. I stayed with Bellamy on the Sultana, preferring the good-humoured Irishman to the angry mulatto. Bellamy's crew voted the earnest Richard Connor to represent them, and he set to work, signing up the new hands. Then Carty demanded the post of ship's Gunner, and insisted that I be Gunner's Mate, for with the greater firepower of the Sultana, we'd need two gun crews. In my joy at our success, and my relief at having to do no murder, I accepted my new appointment with pride. Then the Sultana's store of wine was discovered, and we toasted each other in bottles of fine Canary.

The men were pleased with the size and firepower of the Sultana, yet grumbled over her foul bottom, Williams sailing rings around us in his sloop. Yet our luck held, for the next day a trading ship ceded to us without a shot being fired. She was bound from Ireland loaded with salt beef, cheeses, flour and cages of chickens, and we were very hungry. Finding her leaky and awash, we let her Captain keep her. Most of her crew joined us, for they'd been pumping her continually since leaving Ireland, praying she'd make port.

We celebrated with a great feast on the poop deck of the Sultana, after which our contented Company swore they'd go whither Bellamy wished. He suggested the rich hunting grounds of the Windward Passage, between Cuba and Hispaniola, and our two vessels set north-west courses, the wind steady to starboard. Towards noon, Williams tacked into a narrow passage between two small islands, their reefs stretching around us like laced skirts. The first, Crooked Island, was so covered with fragrant trees and flowers that it scented the wind. Long Island was a mere stretch of sand in a shallow sea. Then the lookout bellowed, "Sail!"

When Bellamy turned from his spyglass, I saw his eyes alight. "She's a true Queen o' the Seas, lads, a frigate, and fast. She'll outrun us if we let her." He bellowed at Paul Williams to cut her off, while we blocked this end of the channel. "Don't raise yer colours 'til ye've passed her, or ye'll take her broadside. Then scare her into comin' about. We'll raise the Navy's ensigns, and she'll sail straight into our arms."

Her Captain could not have realised the danger of the pretty sloop racing past him, Williams giving a jaunty salute, all his men crowded below, out of sight. Then the sloop came about, guns levelled, drums rolling, and King Death fluttering from the mainmast. The frigate jibed smartly, and headed back towards us. We had raised the Navy ensigns, yet not fast enough to allay her Captain's suspicions, and as we moved to cut her off, she tacked away. Carty swore, yet Bellamy replied that there was no hurry, we were sailing the only Navy ship in the area, and the lovely frigate was trapped.

We harried her for three hours, our vessels tacking in the steady breeze as in a chess game, the frigate determined to fire upon us, while we were determined to take her, not sink her, though we occasionally fired a careful gun as a warning. Finally, off the eastern end of Long Island, her Captain had to choose between ripping her bottom out or surrendering, and he struck her colours.

We were not slow with the grapnels, and swung aboard to find the abashed crew assembled, their muskets at their feet. Bellamy bowed to her young Captain, who stood with his hat under his arm, his sword unbuckled, and his nose in the air. "I am Captain Prince of the Whydah", he snapped. "You have out-sailed me, and I cede my sword and my ship. I only ask that you show mercy to all aboard, including my female passengers."

"Yer a great and subtle sailor, and if ye'd known the waters as well as we, we'd never have trapped ye", Bellamy flattered him. "'Twill go well with ye, that ye offered us no battle, for then we'd have hoisted the bloody flag, and yer mother would have wept fer yer early demise. As it is, yer lives are yer own, though yer property is not. I'd appreciate ye requestin' yer passengers to assemble above decks with all their valuables upon 'em, Death the sentence for any who hides so much as a piece of eight from us. From yeself, I require an inventory o' the cargo." Captain Prince, jaw rigid, nodded curtly at his First Mate, and then stood with his eyes on the horizon.

The Whydah was loaded with sugar, indigo, Jesuits bark for the ague, and enough provisions for a comfortable journey to London. It looked like a good haul to me, yet Bellamy was not satisfied. "I swear by the Devil, yer hidin' somethin' from me, Captain Prince. No man makes such a spirited defence as that for sugar. I thought a ravishin' dove amongst the women...yet these are a pack o' hens. Yer half-sick to lose such a fine ship to a band o' ruffians, and ye might lose yer post. Yet she's not yer vessel, and ye'll rise again. So, Sirrah, yer hidin' somethin'. 'Whydah' is another way o' sayin' 'Ouidah', is it not? And Ouidah is the busiest slave port in Africa". Bellamy did not see Paul Williams turn, his hand on his rapier. "From the stink below, I'd say ye've been usin' this lovely ship as a slaver, and ye've hidden the profits from us. This is the deal. I count to ten, and ye disclose yer gold, or I let me men loose among the ladies."

He leered at the now hysterical women, and 'twas only their terror that stopped me from laughing at the joke, for it seemed to be the pirates who were least interested in women who ogled them the most. Poor Captain Prince, implored on all sides, was white-faced when he reached inside his shirt, and handed Bellamy a parchment.

Bellamy scanned it and bellowed that we were rich, and we all cheered. "We'll now relieve ye o' this fine vessel, Captain, to use in the more honourable trade o' rovin'." Captain Prince could not conceal a sneer, and Bellamy's eyes flashed. "Aye Sir, rovin' is a man seekin' his own way in this hard world. Slavery is the work o' the Devil." He turned to find Williams ready for the young Captain's blood, all the black men behind him. "Nay Paul, we've already offered quarter, and they accepted. 'Twould be foul to kill him now, and none would ever cede to us again."

Williams began a furious argument with Bellamy, and Carty winked at me, and collared the Boatswain. With the help of two mates, we broke into the Captain's cabin, found two locked chests, and hauled them on deck. Williams was still demanding justice against the proud young Captain, so we dropped the chests before him, and Carty smashed the locks and flung back the lids. The sun set the gold aglow, and the pirates gave no more thought to vengeance.

Bellamy quickly told Captain Prince that he was free to depart with his passengers in his ship's boat. With all possible dignity, Captain Prince told Bellamy that his boat had been lost under tow, and coldly demanded one of our own. Bellamy scratched his head and confessed he had no boat large enough to hold them all, as the Sultana's was mostly rotted through. Then he shrugged. "The Sultana is filthy bottomed and slow, and too deep in draught to enter Nassau harbour. I say we let Captain Prince return her to the Navy, sayin' we don't want their old barge. What say ye lads?" Bellamy's careless generosity and the insult to the Navy appealed to the pirates, who affected to scorn the wealth they helped themselves to, and the vote was soon carried.

Captain Prince saw his passengers and crew safely onto the Sultana, yet when he went to clamber over the gunwales, Bellamy whisked off the young Captain's hat, and into it poured a handful of the Whydah's gold, telling him it was in compensation for the loss of his command. Captain Prince scowled, yet kept the gold, the guffaws of the pirates seeing him away, his Boatswain and two experienced sailors staying with us.

The Sultana was soon left far behind as we sped south, still heading for the Windward Passage. The pirates were immensely proud of their new flagship, for she was

315

large for her draught, well appointed, and carried eighteen great guns. They began stripping her for action immediately, raising her gunwales for extra protection, and removing any unnecessary cabins, to make a space we could all use in foul weather. One party set about destroying the over-fine Captain's cabin, the gilt mirrors and velvet hangings going overboard before I could argue the prices they might fetch us, so much did they hate the trappings of power. Carty and I inspected the guns, and called for volunteers to train as a gun crew. Before the afternoon was over, we had checked the powder for damp and rolled fresh cartridges.

Off Petit Goave, we took another English vessel, loaded with sugar and indigo, and with enough provisions to supply us with another feast. Bellamy hardly needed to give this crew a stirring account of life as a freebooter, as the Captain was vicious, and the crew utterly dejected. They all came with us, from the cabin boy to the First Mate, leaving the Captain to sail his own ship.

I helped an old seadog over our gunwales, and he grumbled that life at sea had done for him. "Half the men dead, and the rest unpaid to prevent desertion", he muttered. "Now that the war is won, we sailors are left to starve or slave. Aye, 'tis the pirate life for me. Better a merry jig to end me days than misery such as that!"

After feasting and signing on the new men, we conferred on our route, many feeling we had won enough to end the cruise. Carty suggested that we sail straight for Saint Thomas, and sell our loot to Governor Esmit, taking anything we found in our path. The new men, still atremble from the force of the oaths they had just made, were the happiest to hear it, for they might be rich without raising a sword. In light breezes, we sped eastwards, following the jungled coast of French Hispaniola. Then we skirted Puerto Rico, flying the red and gold colours of Castille to deceive any of the Spanish Governor's guarda del costas. Bellamy explained that these swift sloops were filled with the worst scum of the Caribbean, who were paid well for their depredations against English settlements.

We reached Saint Thomas in the late afternoon of the next day, a small, pretty island owned by Denmark, a minor power at best. We slipped into the wide harbour of Charlotte Amalie, tying up at a bustling wharf, where trading houses abutted the docks. If I had imagined that the pirates would sneak in, cowed by all this gentility, I was much mistaken. All opened their sea chests and spruced themselves up in stolen finery, and Bellamy, dressed like a Lord, went to call upon the Governor.

Carty said that the infamous pirate Blackbeard truly ruled here, for he had built a tower on the island, when his foul temper had seen him no longer welcome in Nassau. Rumour had it he had taken a slip of a girl as his fourteenth wife, the rest not long surviving the rages his pox threw him into. He shot at their feet to make them dance, whored them to his crew, and if they asked after his wealth, he locked them in to starve with it.

Carty soon had us busy hoisting merchandise out of the holds of our vessels, and onto the dock. Paul Williams hauled out a crate of Canary, both to moisten the throats of the merchants gathering about us, and to keep up the spirits of those working. As the sun roasted us, Bellamy turned auctioneer, trumpeting our goods and charming the buyers. Williams took each successful bidder by the elbow, and relieving him of his purse, dropped it into a chest, the warm chink of gold setting us all agrin.

It might have been the heat and the fine Canary, yet for the first time in my life, I felt free of care. For as a known pirate, I could never return to England, to find my mother and reform Sally. I had to leave those burdens behind me. A new life awaited me in the New World, and for the first time, it would be on my own terms, for I would be rich.

When Bellamy had sold the last of our goods, the chests of money were heaved back aboard the Whydah, and Carty called parlez. "I say we return to Nassau, to divide our shares and drink with our mates", he bellowed.

"Afeared Blackbeard will sail in?", Bellamy teased him.

"Aye, Devil take it, for I talked Hornigold into splitting from the mad bastard, and you stood against him in the Nassau Council."

"Fer Christ's sake, a little beer and a night ashore..." one man pleaded.

"With a whore!", another agreed.

Bellamy shrugged. "Wait 'till Nassau, and it won't cost us Carty's life, eh mates?"

"A vote", Richard Connor insisted, and within the hour, we had re-provisioned both the sloop and the frigate, and were headed out to sea. A warm breeze sent us skimming through the dark waves, and then the moon rose, and we slept on deck, covering our eyes against moon fever.

Carty shook me awake to stand the dogwatch, and told me to hold the course until dawn, when I must keep a close eye out for the Navidad bank. Then he lay down close by the helm, and was soon snoring with the rest. I spun the hourglass, checked the compass against the chart, and took the wheel, alone and at peace in the warm, tropic night, the Whydah holding true to her course like the lady she was.

As the sky began to lighten to the east, the wind strengthened and veered a little to the south-east. I made out William's sloop just ahead, under light sail, left the helm to keep itself, and woke Bellamy. Soon after, Williams fired a gun as a signal, crowded sail, and changed tack, angling more northwards. Bellamy roused two other men, and as the sun boiled up orange out of the sea, we re-set the sails, and followed the sloop.

It took us three days to make the Bahamas, tacking through the Berry Islands in sunshine and light winds, until we saw the substantial island of Providence. Our Company cheered to see the shallow channel between Hog Island and Long Key that led into Nassau Harbour,. I joined them, and it did not seem strange to me that I should hope to find a haven there. I anticipated the richness of my share, and felt that piracy had taught me something of freedom. And in truth, the comradeship of these brigands had been like mulled wine in Winter, warm and rich and welcome. Yet I was most thankful 'twas over, and I was rich, with no more deaths upon my conscience. I felt the hard, black stone that was my soul break open, and something wan and pale begin to grow. Hope perhaps.

Chapter 18: Anne Bonny

The Nassau channel was shallow and not easy to navigate, especially with the light fading. We followed William's sloop, tacking the Whydah through the narrow passage with all eyes on the shoals. 'Twas easy to see the difficulties a man o' war would face coming in here, even at full tide.

'Twas only when we had tied up to the creaking, rotting wharf, that I had liberty to wipe the sweat off my brow, and examine the infamous port of Nassau. The rosy sunset showed a broad sweep of white beach, crowned by a low ridge of forested hills. A scattering of shanties, a few larger buildings, and a ruined fort, seemed to comprise the town. The harbour was crowded with vessels, mostly the swift island sloops, though there were frigates in full battle array, while others were mere hulks rotting in the shallows. At that late hour, men were leaving their work, rigging sloops and careening prizes, and dories full of sailors rowed from ship to shore.

Carty noted the pirate Captains who had already anchored. "Oliver LeBoose will be in for certain. Aye, there's his schooner. Thomas Coclyn has moored by Edward England's sloop. That's Burgess's fine frigate over there. Ashore is Christopher Winter arm-in-arm with Jim Fife. An' the fop swaggerin' up to them is Johnny Martel, a right cruel bastard, and not altogether welcome here."

Our first business was to divide the loot. Torches were lit, a sail was spread on the sagging dock, and our Quartermasters and their mates hauled three locked chests out of the Whydah, and two from the sloop. With great solemnity, our two Captains unlocked them, and threw back the lids, and we all cheered to see the gold and silver gleaming in the light of the smoking torches. Yet when they tipped the treasure into one vast pile on the patched canvas, we were suddenly silent.

Then the Quartermasters unrolled the Articles, and Connor counted the men, and called for claims for compensation for injuries to be heard. Then they began dividing the gold into one hundred and seven equal piles, each representing one share, the Captains and Quartermasters to receive a share and a half. It took a long time, as the coins were from many countries, and of different values, yet the pirates waited patiently, passing around bottles of rum and swiping at the bothersome mosquitoes. At last Connor was satisfied, and Williams and Bellamy threw dice to see which Captain would choose first. Then it was the turn of the Quartermasters, and then each man chose his share, in the order of signing on.

When it finally came to my turn, I chose a small bag of gold doubloons to buy my piece of the New World, and a large purse of silver to supply my immediate needs. The gold I tied securely around my neck, the silver went into my pocket. Then Bellamy praised us for a grand Company, the best to ever sail the Caribbean Sea, and urged us to sign up with him and Williams for the next successful cruise. Only Richard Connor and I climbed back aboard the Whydah to retrieve our seachests, the rest choosing to stay in the Company.

Then under the rising moon, our entire Company, including the Africans from William's crew, followed Bellamy to his favourite tavern. The main street of Nassau smelled rotten after the clean sea, and I wondered to find myself in a town of masterless men, known only for their lawless deeds. A bedraggled harlot winked at me, a fight broke out behind us, and I held firmly to the seachest on my shoulder.

Bellamy, arm-in-arm with Paul Williams, led us towards a greying wooden building that stood silver in the moonlight, at the far end of the street. It looked at the mercy of the next strong wind, yet the door stood open, and someone was playing a fiddle fast and loud. Bellamy tipped his hat to an old sea dog by the door. "Good cheer Governor

Sawney, I'll send you out a drink", and the old man grinned toothlessly, and took another shaky swig from a bottle of rum.

We pushed into the crowded tavern, dimly lit by smoking candles and dirty lanterns, assailed by the stink of stale beer and spilt rum. The fat tavern keeper leapt to his feet when he saw Bellamy, and bowing and scraping, led us through the mass of drunken men and laughing women to throng about a large table. Bellamy threw down a small purse and ordered rum for us all and a bottle for the Governor.

"You've been lucky, Captain Bellamy".

"And now I am thirsty, Cullimore."

Snubbed, the landlord nodded curtly at a filthy wreck of a woman who staggered up with trays of rum, until every man had his dram. Bellamy threw the fiddle player a coin, and he played Irish jigs for the rest of the night. The rum warmed my heart, and I toyed with the notion of signing on again, if only for the comradeship, for I had been a long time alone.

The rovers about us were a mixed lot, mostly English, Irish and Scots, with some Dutch and Frenchmen. The late wars would have seen them fighting against each other, yet, as Bellamy boasted, now 'twas the Brethren making war on the rest of the world for their Freedom. To satisfy my curiosity, he explained that Governor Sawney was the oldest pirate on the island, and respected for beginning the first pirate haven on Nassau with Captain Mission, full thirty years before.

Then the talking hushed, and all eyes went to the door. A dark man with a martial eye had stepped into the room, one hand on his sword hilt, waiting until his eyes adjusted to the dim light, nodding at acquaintances to cover his caution. "'Tis Jennings", Carty muttered at me. "He who led our Buccaneer Fleet to take the Spanish salvage, he who brought us here, and taught us to rule ourselves in the way o' Captain Mission. A brave man and honourable, Mark Read."

Bellamy had stood, and beckoning with a bottle, caught Jennings' eye. He nodded and moved towards us through the crowd, acknowledging many greetings, a lion in a den of wolves. Though a Captain, he dressed simply, wearing his grey-streaked hair tied back in military fashion. He was older than I had expected, and though broad of shoulder, still a small man next to Carty. When he congratulated Bellamy on our cruise, I heard a strong Welsh lilt. "LeBoose was in three days ago, furious with you, don't ye know? Is it true you fell out over a Navy man o' war?"

"We fell out o'er every prize with that French fop who calls himself a rover. Yet 'twas one o' my satires that did it, a nasty description o' the King o' France, aimed at the Frenchman. We'll read it later."

"Hornigold is here too, and not counting himself a friend of yours either. He's in the right of it in not taking English ships, my friend, not if you want to trade with English Governors."

"I'm at war with the world, my dear Henry. I've just captured one o' King George's warships, with nought but a one-gun sloop, and returned it soon after as an ill-sailing pig. I say all trade is fair game, and the English trade is the richest."

"Times are a-changing Sam. We must change with them. Most have noticed the trade falling off, the cargoes less, the ships leakier, isn't it true? They say war makes pirates, and peace hangs them. It is time to pause for reflection."

"Nothin' lasts forever, my dear Henry. If the trade falls off here, we'll make for the East Indies and raid the Spice Islands. Or make for Africa and make life Hell for the slavers."

"It is easy to see you love the life, Sam. Yet I have had my fill of fighting for my bread. I've made my stake, and wish to spend it on more than watered ale in this curse of a town. Perhaps I'll trade on my own account. Perhaps I'll buy a plantation in Jamaica and a charming wife."

323

He had not seen the young redhead arrive at his elbow. "You must follow Captain Morgan and marry the Governor's daughter", she told him sweetly, "and let her make a fool of you."

"Anne, cariad! Sit and drink with us. Sam and I are debating the trade."

"And your coming marriage?" She raised her tankard in mock congratulations. I wondered how she dared be so bold, for though she was dressed in little better than rags, she held herself like a Duchess. She was pretty enough, with magnificent red hair and green eyes. Yet though she had to be all of sixteen, there was something child-like about her, not innocence, possibly carelessness. Perhaps 'twas this that reminded me of the sharp-tongued, golden-haired young whore I'd once loved like a sister.

I looked up to find Jennings' jealous eye upon me, and feeling that my life was in my hands, I made haste to introduce myself. "I am Mark Read, Sir. I've been on the account with Captain Bellamy since he saved me from certain death at the hands of a tyrant captain. Yet now I find myself with a large enough stake to leave the life, and 'tis peace that I dream of."

"I knew you for a coward", Williams scowled, already half soused. "A pirate when it suits you, and now you're rich, a man of conscience."

"I am no coward. I killed my first man at sixteen to save a woman's honour."

"Women have no honour", the mulatto sneered at me. "No more than Puritan hypocrites."

I was rising to face death, my hand on the hilt of my rapier, yet the redhead forestalled me. She blazed up to Williams, her face flushed with fury. "Aye, honour's a privilege that men keep for themselves! If a woman gets too high and mighty, she's beaten into submission, or worse. If she seeks redress, she's laughed at, and told she had no honour to lose. But not me, Paul Williams." Her anger would have been laughable but for the fish knife in her hand

and the pirates moving out of her way.

"You think I'd fight a woman", Williams snarled.

"Aye, that's right, back down you stinking coward", she taunted him. "For if I cut you, they'll laugh, and if you cut me, they'll despise you. If I were a man, I'd be one o' the Brethren, and a comrade. But as a woman, I'm nothing more than a pretty harlot, no matter what courage I have."

"And a grand pirate you'd make, Annie bach", Jennings soothed her, pouring her another drink.

She sheathed her knife. "I sailed from Charles Town to Port Royal, and then to Nassau, and none but my fool of a husband knew I was aught but a swaggering boy."

"You'd make a better pirate than a wife, at any rate", Williams scoffed, feeling safer.

"If I had a better husband, I'd be a better wife", Anne retorted. "That he can't keep me is one matter. That he expects me to keep him by working on my back, is another."

"Snap your pretty fingers, and I'll run him through for you", Jennings offered. "Or buy someone a drink to have it done. He's disliked, and you'd make a fine widow."

"I'd do it myself, but a woman who kills her husband is still burnt for treason, and I have a horror of burning. No, I'll have my revenge on all who scorn me, by escaping this rat hole, and making my fortune."

Bellamy raised an eyebrow. "Ye'd look well in silk and pearls. Yet I know of only one way for a woman to be rich."

"You mean that a whore needs a wealthy lover. Yet I'm no whore, though I do rely upon the kindness o' my friends." She smiled sweetly at Jennings who bowed gallantly.

"And though you're no whore, you'd be rich", Williams sneered again.

"I've a good head for business, and I've run a plantation before now. I know a profit when I see one. And I know that the larger the stake, the bigger the profit. I'll raise a stake somehow, and make my fortune, while you boast o' freedom and catch the pox!"

There was a bellow of laughter, and a balding, stocky, bearded pirate picked Anne up and hugged her. "Still holding yer head high, me girl! Give the bastards Hell! Don't let her challenge ye to a duel with pistols, young Williams. She was a crack shot even before she met me."

Jennings was smiling. "Hands off her, Ben Hornigold. Drink with us, and help me persuade Bellamy and Williams to forego the English trade."

Hornigold shrugged and Bellamy pulled him out a chair. "Now Ben, we're old mates, and I hope there's no grudge against us for partin' Company. 'Twas a shame, yet we disagreed, and the vote went against ye."

"Aye, ye charmed yer way to Captain on that one", Hornigold growled. "Let's see if ye can hold it more than a month or two." Yet he sat and accepted a rum.

"Damn him to Hell!", Anne cursed. "Here's my fool o' a husband come to wheedle his evening pipe. I'll bid you all good night and slip out." She took the liberty of saluting both Jennings and Hornigold, kisses that they both accepted gallantly.

Yet as she pushed her way through the crowd, a young man grabbed her elbow. He was thin and pale, his handsome features spoiled by bad health. She shoved him away from her, trying for the door, yet he grabbed her again, and she whirled, and shoved him to the floor. "Damn you for a fool, why do you clutch at me? I'll neither beg nor whore for your damned opium. You've been no husband to me James Bonny, and I am no longer wife to you, yet you hound me every day. I swear one day I'll kill you, partly from vengeance, but mostly from disgust."

She pushed her way outside, and Bonny scrambled to his feet, all eyes upon him. "She's my wife", he announced feebly. "I married her. She should share with her own husband. Any other woman would." Even Cullimore was sneering at him, and he finally accepted that there was no comfort for him there, and the broken wreck of a man

326

staggered after his wild young wife.

Wanting to move away from the hot-tempered Paul Williams, I sauntered over to the bar, where a quiet young man invited me to share a bottle in the night breeze on the veranda. The stars shone clear over Hog Island, and Bill Lewis pointed out Venus, blazing blue on the horizon. I asked him how he'd come to piracy, and he shook his head, took a swig of rum, and then suddenly laughed. "I went to sea as an island lad, sailing a stolen French corvette under Captain Bannister. I'll never forget that bastard. Me and another boy were found privately engaged, and the dog triced us to the corvette's mizzen peak, and sailed into Port Royal with us hanging there. I left his service, and as I'd always a good ear for the many tongues of men, including the Mosquito Indians, I took berth as supercargo and interpreter on a Jamaican merchantman.

"We were captured by Spaniards on our third cruise, and taken to Havana as slaves. After days chained to a log in the blazing heat, scraping away at their roads, me and six others killed our guard, took a canoa, and then captured a Spanish piragua from the harbour. Two Spaniards joined us, and the nine of us took a turtling sloop. Enough of the turtler's crew joined to make us dangerous, and successful.

"We came across a beautiful Bermudan brigantine of ten guns. I knew her Captain Tucker, and sent him a letter offering to buy the brigantine off him for ten thousand pieces of eight. Tucker showed the letter to the other Bermuda Captains in his Fleet, and begged fifty men of them, so he could fight. The others declined and when we saw them making sail, we attacked the Fleet in our turtle boat, with nought but muskets. All ran but Tucker and his friend Captain Dill. Dill opened fire with his two ship's guns, firing away hot and heavy, until one of the guns over-heated and burst, killing three crew, and wounding almost all aboard with flying shrapnel. Tucker called on the other Captains to send Dill reinforcements, and attacked us with a terrible broadside, but his fellow Bermudians sailed off, the cowards!"

"Those were men of peace, in the trade for profit, not honour."

Lewis snorted. "There's not a bean of honour to share amongst 'em. On one ship we took, the Captain dropped the sails before we'd hauled up the Jolly Roger. I berated the knave for such an easy surrender, telling him he'd betrayed the trust of the owners, and the fool wept and prayed so hard for his unthreatened life, that I could stand it no longer, and beat him with the end of a rope. He instantly told me there was money on board, and in my fury with his cowardice, I beat him harder."

I couldn't help but laugh. "The poor man couldn't please you no matter what he did. What a Devil he must have thought you, and him being so obliging!"

"He think me a Devil? You should have heard Captain Bannister curse when I hung him from his own yard-arm." He laughed again, and I hastily bid him good night.

I hauled my seachest over the road to the dosshouse, where the poxed whores cost a fortune if you were drunk enough to use them. I insisted on a cheaper bed, and was shown to a room full of sleeping bodies and a mat. Though the whores were expensive, the bedbugs were free and liberally provided, and I slept but fitfully, the gold about my neck also too grave a concern for ease.

I woke at dawn, and stepped out onto the sagging dosshouse veranda, to see Anne Bonny dancing down the dusty street towards me. I doffed my cap and bowed, and she fanned herself with her ragged palmetto hat, and smiled. "So Mark Read, up early to defend female honour?"

"My own was also involved."

"You're not like the general run o' men here. Come with me and breakfast with Ma Davies. Fresh fish and yams, and she doesn't grovel like that fool Cully. Her husband was lost two years ago in a hurricane, leaving her with a brood of half-grown children to raise. She sends her boys roaming the island after wild produce, while she and her pretty daughters cook and serve it. They are good people. I don't take everyone there."

I bowed and declared myself to be on my best behaviour, and we strolled arm-in-arm through the Hellhole that was Nassau. The town consisted of a disappointing scatter of warped huts disintegrating under the pressure of the sun, a few tents on the beach, and flies swarming over everything. Anne said the listless islanders scraped a living from the careless generosity of the pirates, and what little the island could provide, yet it seemed to me that they built nothing, planted nothing, and dug no fresh latrines.

The pirates emerged slowly into the day, staggering from brothels and taverns, covering their eyes and cursing the harsh light. Others came rowing in from the ships that crowded the harbour, their night watches over, seeking the bad rum and the pox-ridden women that had amused their comrades the night before. Though most were dressed in old canvas and rags, as I was, they could not be mistaken for islanders, as they carried themselves so proudly, and all walked with their hands on the hilts of their swords.

There were many Africans, their skins any colour from black to copper, and though most walked free, one followed a pirate master. Anne insisted that most of the Brethren abhorred the trade as much as any Quaker, and that if they had slaves, they were from traders in payment for gambling debts, and soon freed. She said that most of the black men in Nassau were traders from Eleuthera, where Governor Bennett had allowed the most rebellious of his Bermudan slaves to settle, rather than hang them.

We walked along the beach, and the sun rose higher in the fierce blue sky, striking off the white sand to dazzle my eyes. The sea breeze died, the heat grew even more fierce, and I was glad to reach a large tent set in a grove of palms. A thin, straw-haired girl was grilling fish over a green wood barbecue in the buccaneer manner. She looked up at us and called for her ma, and a thin woman as brown and cracked as old leather stepped out to greet us.

"Good morning Ma", Anne smiled and curtseyed. "I've brought Mark Read to breakfast with you. He believes in the honour of women, and looks for a life other than pirating." We sat down on woven mats in the shade, and Ma Davies gave us plates of fried fish and flat bread. She was a pious woman, in the Puritan fashion of her youth, yet generous with her food. There were bananas, figs and watermelons heaped in woven baskets, and a great bowl of yam steamed with china root.

When I had eaten my fill, and pulled out my pipe, Anne ordered the youngest boy up a palm tree, to cut down a frond. Then, with another boy doing somersaults in the sand to amuse us, Anne bent the tip of the palm frond into a circle, and began deftly weaving it. Then she lopped the circle of green from the rest of the frond with the boy's cutlass, pushed the circle into a bowl shape, and presented me with a hat similar to the ragged one she wore.

"Now you can join me by the sea, without danger from the sun. I know a quiet cove where we can sit with our feet in the water, and talk o' London." I threw down some silver, and we strolled along the beach, away from Nassau. The sea sparkled turquoise in the shallows, and Anne pulled her skirts up, exposing her legs, and splashed through the gentle waves. We made our way around rocks that would be sea-covered in a few hours, to a small cove she called her own, and there we sat in the dappled shade of a spreading tree, tiny fish darting about the rock pools at our feet. A flock of scolding parrots of brilliant colours flew into the tree above us, and it struck me then, that apart from the desolation of Nassau, Providence Island was beautiful.

I talked to her of London until the afternoon wore into evening, and she hung on every word. Yet tales of wits in coffee houses, orange girls who became actresses, and Lords who gambled away their fortunes, seemed unreal in this Paradise. "It's my dream to see London", she sighed.

"Aye, leave this place before you're starved into

330

whoring, despite your good intentions."

"And how do I get the money to leave without whoring? It's a point that confounds me still."

"Can you not ask your father?"

"I would not be governed by him. He disowned me."

"Your mother?"

"Dead. He barely knew I was alive until I defied him. He was too busy grieving for her to see me. And when he did, it was all rum and Hellfire. O' course she wasn't his wife, my mother I mean. She'd been his servant back in Ireland. His true wife accused my mother o' being a thief, in revenge for the harlotry that got her pregnant with me. My father bribed the constable, and left with us for the New World once I was born."

"Surely he would be happy to see you again, to know you are well. After all, he raised you."

"I was raised by our slave women."

"By Heathens? Yet who taught you your Scriptures, who schooled you?"

Anne shrugged and looked away. "Our field hands were men from the coast o' Guinea, stolen by the Arabs, and sold in Ouidah to the English. On the voyage over, they were chained together in the dark hold o' a ship for months, with bad food and stinking water. One in three died. I've seen those ships unloading their cargo o' wretches in Charles Town, Mark, and I swear to you that no fortune made can justify such cruelty. O' those that survived the voyage, many died from childish diseases like chicken pox and measles. The planters call it seasoning. I think they died because they were without hope. They knew their own country was too far away. And their own people. Yet the survivors married our Indian house slaves, and every full moon, they would drum and dance and laugh and keep their spirits strong. That taught me something."

"I thought to see Indians here."

"They were driven from these isles within a generation o' the Spaniards first coming here. Most were

331

taken as slaves, and died o' their cages, as birds will. They say that a hundred years ago, the Spaniards stole the last woman away, and as they sailed off, she dived overboard to drown, rather than live a slave. I've always hoped she could swim."

"And those that raised you?"

"Cherokee women raided from the inland forests. Their men were shot dead the night they were enslaved, their villages burned, and their old lives lost. So they took our African field hands as husbands, and showed them how to live in the New World. How to grow mulberries, potatoes, plums, snake root, how to make cornbread and succotash and hominy. They were tall and clean and proud. Each woman made her own house, and if she found she had chosen the wrong man, she put his pipe and clothes outside, and he had to find somewhere else to sleep. Their children taught me to whip tops and spin hoops and shoot arrows and make cat's cradles. They all laughed at me if I was childish. They did not know how to read."

"And that was where you learned to fight with a knife, like a savage."

"And to use my fists. When I was fourteen, the son of a neighbouring planter would have lain with me against my will. I beat him so badly, he lay in bed for months. But it was an old Cherokee wanderer who taught me to shoot as though my life depended on it. My father employed him to hunt for us, and paid him with whiskey. Mostly he kept his will to live strong and whole, but during the dark o' every moon, he wallowed in misery and drink, bewailing his lost people. He told me of entire towns that had never seen a white man, wiped out by whooping cough, smallpox, influenza and malaria, the diseases of Europe and Africa. He mourned the life o' the Cherokee warrior, his lost prestige, and the lost strength o' his men.

"When I was almost thirteen, the planters who ran Charles Town ignored their own constitution, which states that the highest amongst us cannot oppress the meanest, and

332

led by John Barnwell, they raided the Tuscarora Indians to the north o' us for slaves. Many Yamasee warriors accompanied this expedition, and they were so much the better woodsmen, and so contemptuous of the cowardice of the colonists, that great ill-feeling arose in both camps. The expedition failed, the Tuscaroras forced Barnwell to parlez, and the Yamasee were furious. Two years later, the Florida Spanish incited the Yamasee to rebel against terrible abuse from our traders, and there was war.

"Soon after, our old Cherokee warrior did not come back from a hunting trip. Without asking permission, I took my father's best horse, and went looking for him, riding through the thick Carolina forest dressed as a boy. I followed the track and asked everyone I came to. His killer was a white man who had not been long in the colonies, and did not know the difference between Yamasee and Cherokee. He had shot him in the back. He boasted to me o' his courage. I found the body lying between the woods and a farmer's field. He was already part earth. I sang the song the women had taught me for his soul, and mourned him.

"When I returned, my father beat me for leaving without his permission, and I ran away to Charles Town, dressed as a boy again. There I sold my father's horse, and lived on the waterfront, amongst the sailors and traders and whores. I liked those people. They made the most o' life and laughed when they could. The women were kind when they thought me a boy, they laughed when they found out I wasn't, and soon betrayed me for my father's reward. He came to Belle's and called me a whore." She laughed a little. "Me with my hair tied up, dressed in boys clothes.

"He dragged me home and this time, when he came at me with the whip, I was ready. I clapped a loaded pistol to his head, and told him I hated him, and that if I had ever had a father, it was the dead old Cherokee hunter. He wept then, and we came to some understanding. I saw that his fury was his fear o' losing me, he saw that I had to be free. Then I stopped our bully o' an overseer from whipping one o' our

333

women for insolence, and had him dismissed. I took over the running o' the plantation then, riding astride my horse in trousers, a scandal to the Charles Town ladies. And he found me a tutor who taught me enough o' reading and writing to make me useful, before my father found us in my bedroom together, and threw him out.

"When my father began talking o' marriage, I'd not think o' it at first. If he'd brought anyone to visit who was not old and fat and graceless, my life would've been very different. We argued again when I rejected a man o' some property, and again I ran away.

"And that was when I met James Bonny. He'd just deserted from the Navy, and saved me from being pressed onto a merchant ship. I took him to meet Belle, and we drank together, more than I was used to. Belle whispered to him that I was female, and he made the most of it that night. In the morning she told him I was rich, and he asked me to marry him. He was handsome before the opium took him, and I only knew worse men to judge him against. He talked o' us running away to North Carolina together, and returning to confront my father, a married couple. I thought it an amusing revenge, and let him persuade me.

"When we returned, I'd been away a month, and my father had given me up for lost. He was drunk, and instead o' being grateful to see me, he attacked me with his walking stick. James defended me, and suddenly they were fighting, rolling in the dust like mad dogs. There was no chance o' reconciliation then, so James and I returned to Charles Town, and were happy enough until my money ran out. Then we decided to turn pirate, and come here.

"But after his first voyage, the Brethren scorned my husband for a coward. The poorer we became, the more he needed drink, and then opium. When he thought to turn pimp to get it, he was lucky I did not kill him. I have survived with the help o' my friends, but I know there is no future here for me. And I know enough o' life to make my own way. I'll go to London, and make my fortune. If I was a man, I'd make my stake as you did. The Brethren are the only way for a poor man to be free."

"You could always make hats."

She threw her head back and laughed, and then suddenly bent to kiss me. I jerked backwards, and she looked at me in astonishment, and then anger.

"What kind o' man are you, Mark Read?"

"My own kind."

"I thought we could be friends, without secrets between us."

"I was a soldier during the last war, and married into the Netherlands. My spouse died of fever. I have not yet recovered from the loss. I may never do so."

There was a long silence, and when I glanced up, her green eyes were narrowed, looking at me with frank speculation. "You've pretended to be my friend, and now you're not honest with me."

"If I'd wanted to tell you more, I would have done. Since I haven't, keep your questions to yourself."

"Do you think I'd mock you? I know you're in your own exile, standing away from the crowd, not wanting to be over-noticed. It is more than modesty. It is a wish to not be looked at."

"This is not your business. Leave it alone."

"You shouldn't be too difficult to figure out. Definitely not a sodomite. Bellamy has already seen that. So, just not interested in me? You'd be the first. Heartbroken? Possibly. Could I see you with a wife? No. Not at all."

I leapt to my feet, and my anger found words. "You are all vanity Anne Bonny. You wish all men at your feet because your own father did not love you. You only pester me like this because you see my indifference as a challenge."

"Hah, that's not true! I say you're a liar. You never had a wife!"

"I said 'twas none of your business. Our brief acquaintance is over."

335

"Liar. You said you had a wife, and you lied. Williams was right, you're a Puritan hypocrite!

"I didn't say I had a wife. I said I was married!"

She stopped then, and looked at me, and I could see she knew.

"You're not a man. A woman then?"

"As much as you are. God damn your impertinent soul. I should kill you now."

"I can keep a secret. Truly. But I need to hear all about it. I thought you a good-looking boy, only a little older than me. But a woman..."

"I'm twenty-six."

"Your name."

"My mother first called me Mary."

"How did this come to be?"

"I'll make my story the price of your silence, and if you betray me, I'll kill you."

"No one would believe me anyway, Mary Read. But you must tell me everything, and right from the beginning."

Chapter 19: Theft

I spent the night telling her of my beginnings on the banks of the Brent River, and of the end of my childhood in the taverns of Covent Garden. I had spoken of this so seldom in my life, that the tale-telling gripped my soul, and shook tears from me throughout that dark night. I spoke of the loss of my mother, of my grandmother's death, and Sally's betrayal of herself, while Anne Bonny smoked my pipe, stoked the fire, and listened.

When she finally laid her hand gently on my shoulder, I looked up, startled, to see her red hair blowing in the sea breeze, the Caribbean sunrise crimson about us. It had been so long since I'd allowed myself to dwell on my past, that I'd become lost in an indulgence of memory and emotion. I felt shaken to the depths of my soul, and resolved to think on my childhood no more, for 'twould endanger my disguise. I asked myself why I had trusted this foolish wench, and shuddered to think of Bellamy's laughter, and Paul William's revenge.

Anne sighed and stood. "I'd not believe any of it, if you were not sitting here before me. Come. I must return to Nassau. Henry will be anxious. You must tell me more o' your life, Mary."

"I shall speak of it no more, and if you do..."

"Keep your threats to yourself. I'll keep your secret. On that you have my word. I could even help you."

"What help could you possibly be to me?"

"You have money enough, but you need to get off this stinking isle."

"For all it lacks in soft English charm, I think I could live happily here, quiet and peaceful and free. I'd spend little of my money..."

"Nassau is the most expensive town in the Caribbean. I'm not saying you'd thrown your money away on whores", she grinned, "but even eating is costly. I'll make an arrangement with Ma Davies for you, if you wish."

I left her and walked away from Nassau, needing solitude, looking for a camp of my own. I walked along the shore for some time before I noted a huge fig tree dominating a small headland that jutted into the sea. When I came close to it, I saw a steady trickle of water falling down the low cliff, and hauled myself up the rocks. Following the rivulet, I pushed my way through the thick undergrowth, to the roots of the massive fig tree. There a level clearing under the tree made an ideal site for my camp, both secret and sheltered, yet with a fine view of the open sea. A mere lean-to would be adequate to ensure my privacy, as no one could approach through the bushes without alerting me.

I had solved one major concern, yet the pirate gold still hung heavy about my neck, and I needed to hide it. I continued to follow the rivulet, climbing up into the shadows of the thick, vine-covered forest, careful not to lose my way. In the half-light, I stumbled more than once before I came to a rocky hill, deep in the forest, from which the rivulet trickled. To one side was a strangely forked tree, and beneath it, a large stone. With a great effort, I heaved this aside, scraped a hole in the sandy soil, and laid my purse of gold in it. When I rolled the rock back, it looked entirely undisturbed, and I was sure I had the perfect cache.

With a lighter heart, I returned to the fig tree, and found an easier path down to the beach. I then returned to Nassau, reclaimed my sea chest from the brothel, and carried it back to the fig tree. I then ate lunch with Ma Davies, who told me where to pay an exorbitant amount for a patched strip of canvas, and made me a present of a small copper pot she insisted she did not need. I returned to Nassau and bought provisions at the small market by the dock, including rum, tobacco, and coffee beans, and staggered back under the entire load, for I wanted my whereabouts to remain secret.

The canvas went over a horizontal branch, with the corners pegged down, and my hammock strung up underneath. I built a small camp fire nearby, hoping the smoke would help against the mosquitoes, and hung my food from a branch where no beasts could get it. My few belongings I left safe in my seachest, which would protect them from the worst of the weather.

I returned to Ma Davies for supper, well satisfied with my day's work, to find her glaring at Patrick Carty. He leapt to his feet, clapped me on the back, and handed me an open rum bottle. "Read, good to see ye. Anne Bonny said ye'd be here. Well, we sail on the morning tide, lad. I've come to ask ye, on behalf o' Bellamy an' all yer old mates, to change yer mind an' sail with us. They've all signed up again, and new hands too, yet we could use a Gunner as handy as yeself."

I declined as kindly as I could, and when the old pirate shrugged and bade me farewell, I shook him by the hand and wished him fair winds. As we watched them go, Ma Davies raised an eyebrow at me.

"I meant what I said, Ma. One cruise was enough. In truth, I fear to go back on the account. I have had enough of death. I will live quietly for a time, and carefully consider my next step."

"Will you find a wife and begin a family?" She could not help glancing at her oldest girl, who suddenly blushed, and became busy cleaning fish.

"No. That I know I will not do."

The birds woke me in my own camp early the next morning, and it seemed I had at last found Paradise. In happy solitude, I smoked my pipe and made up the fire, my eyes filled with the early morning sparkle of the sea. For my first breakfast, I brewed some fine coffee, and cooked flat bread wrapped in leaves in the ashes of the fire. When I washed my face in the rivulet, I found myself singing, so content was I, and so carefree.

I then strode back to Nassau, wanting to wave my old mates away. Carty was right, only Richard Connor, Bellamy's quiet Quartermaster, remained behind to try his hand at honest business. The rest blasted a salute as they sailed out, and despite my own good intentions, my heart wished them every success.

I settled into a happy life then, the gentle rains of May making a garden of my camp, which was filled with strange and beautiful flowers, birds and butterflies. I ventured into the stench of Nassau every few days, to buy provisions, drink an ale and catch the news at Cully's tavern. Walking into that putrid stench of a town, I always wondered why man must defile Paradise, and was ever glad to leave. Yet I knew Nassau was too lawless to protect any gains I might make, and talked to all I could of farming on the American Main, for England was barred to me.

I could never enter Nassau without finding Anne Bonny at my elbow, and now she knew my secret, I found her truly disconcerting, and knew not how to speak to her. To add to my confusion, I often saw Henry Jennings looking at us with a jealous eye, and Anne's husband kept demanding payment from me for her 'friendship'.

June came, with great towering thunderheads split by bolts of lightning, the rain so heavy, each drop could fill a bucket. James Bonny began spending gold doubloons freely in the taverns and brothels of Nassau, Anne insisting he must have rolled a drunk for it. I would often look up from an animated conversation with her, to find his dull, opiated eyes upon me, and a sneer distorting his lips. The last thing I wanted to do was kill her mad husband, yet I was so sure of his hatred, that I considered getting a dog to keep watch on my camp.

Then I ran out of silver again, and resolving once more to leave before my gold was entirely spent, I thought to allow myself one more doubloon. I followed the rivulet to the forked tree, and heaved back the rock. My bag of gold was gone. My mind left me for a short time, and I scrabbled desperately around in the dirt, unwilling to believe I was once again left with nothing. Then I thought of James Bonny, and when I found Anne at Ma Davies' camp, she agreed with me that he must be the thief.

"I'll kill him, if he doesn't return it", I vowed.

Ma Davies pursed her lips and shook her head.
"Don't be a fool. Your gold may have been stolen by Anne's
husband, or by anyone who knew you'd done well with
Bellamy, and watched you for a time. Killing that idiot will
not help you. And he will certainly not tell you where the
gold is, unless you torture him. Nay, cheer up, Mark Read.
The Good Lord has you well in hand. That gold was ill got,
and the longer you enjoyed your idle life, the sooner you'd
find yourself back on the account. You said you'd left piracy
for your soul's sake, and now God is trying you. Not so hard
as he tried Job, but hard enough considering how humble a
man you are."

"I'd not go pirating again, yet to be stuck on Nassau
with no money!"

"You think you'll starve? If you walk in the way of
the Lord, he'll provide."

"'Tis also said, God helps those who help
themselves."

"Aye, I knew you for a sensible man. My customers
are bored with fish, and I do not trust my boys with our old
musket. There are wild cattle roaming the inland forests.
Bring me some beef, and I'll feed you, and pay you enough
to keep you honest."

I thanked her, and asked her to keep any payment
locked away for me, for I trusted her entirely. She smiled
and asked me to go to church with her before I left.

"Church? Here?"

"'Tis no more than a tent on top of the hill, where the
old church was. The Spaniards burnt it down when I was a
girl. Yet 'tis sacred ground, still."

"I thought to head off this afternoon."

"You must end your feud with God sometime, Mark
Read."

"Perhaps. Yet not today."

I packed up my camp in a light drizzle of warm rain,

and bid Ma Davies' farewell. Then, at her suggestion, I took her two boys with me, partly as apprentices, yet mostly because they knew the island so well. Harry was twelve and eager, and John fourteen and shy. They were the healthiest of the island children, though scrawny enough, and were both wild to shoot the forbidden musket.

They showed me ancient Indian paths that led straight into the dripping green depths of the forest, where tall pine trees, mahogany and cedar, were so thickly covered with flowering vines, that the light was dimmed. The rain fell steadily through the canopy of leaves in thick drops on our necks, and after a time we ignored the leeches that fastened onto our feet, for there were too many of them. The sudden flash of a Yellow Throat, and the darting jewels of humming birds relieved the oppression, yet the monotonous, unceasing shrill of the insects warned me I was in another world. The boys told me what they could of the place as we walked through mud and rain, eating strange fruit that we found.

It was the afternoon of the second day, and the rain had abated somewhat, when we found hoof prints in the mud where two tracks intersected. We followed them to a thin stream in the hills, and crept through the underbrush, downwind all the way, to find a scrawny herd of wild cattle nervously drinking. I picked out a young bull, and shot it through the shoulder to the heart. The boys whooped as the rest of the herd tore off down the trail, happy as boys usually are at loud noises and the stink of blood. Then we butchered the animal, salted the meat, and packed it into a sack made of its own hide. Slinging a stick through the bundle, we carried it back to Nassau by dawn of the next day.

Ma Davies was well pleased with our success, until I suggested that we could double our take if the boys had muskets too. Though their mother shook her head at the waste of ammunition, I gave the boys lessons in aiming and firing the musket, until they finally hit the mark. Ma Davies sighed, unlocked her strongbox, and counted out enough money for two more muskets, powder and shot. Anne made a deal for us with the quiet Bill Lewis that afternoon, and we returned to the forest the next morning.

Three days later, we found and stalked the same herd, and all three of us fired on my command. I killed a beast, John brought one down and quickly slit its throat, and Harry was badly bruised in the shoulder from his musket's recoil. With two beasts at our disposal, I cut six rough circles from one hide, scraped the muck off, and bound them about our ankles to make rough moccasins for our feet. The other hide was used to carry back the meat, John capering in his triumph, his mother pleased with us.

We hunted in the forest for three months, the rain ceasing, the heat growing intense and suffocating. With never a breeze penetrating the thick forest canopy, the nights were almost unbearable, and every evening a different creature tried to share my hammock. Harry and John pestered me for stories of piracy much more than their Ma would have approved of, so I told them of the Navy and the Army as well. We ate everything we could find, the boys catching birds with cunning spring traps, and shooting agouti and utia, the fruit-eating rodents that were delicious when roasted. The hills were full of fireflies, and we saw many lizards, geckos, and iguanas, and Harry made a pet of a chameleon.

I saw Anne briefly at Ma Davies, and she once did me the favour of keeping guard at her small cove, while I stripped and scrubbed a month's worth of butchery into the sea. I felt I trusted the frivolous flirt less, and knowing she'd be hard pressed to keep something so interesting to herself, I often wondered when she would betray me, and stayed away from Nassau.

In truth I preferred exploring the dense forests of Providence with Harry and John. We climbed the blue hills that cut across the island, separating two large, brackish lakes that were encircled by mangroves, and full of flamingos and spoonbills. We walked through the quiet pine

343

forest on the western shore, where the trees were huge, and the boys showed me the cave where their family had hidden from the Spaniards. We explored the low, swampy south coast, and the rocky eastern end, and I soon felt I knew the island as well as the boys did.

Yet I earned but little, and soon felt myself to be one of God's jokes, doing filthy work in a sweltering forest, with no company but inquisitive boys, and no way out but piracy. Then, in September, we staggered back loaded with meat, to be met by an elated Ma Davies. There were rumours that the King had given up expecting his corrupt Navy to defeat us, and offered us all a Royal Pardon.

As soon as she mentioned the Pardon, hope filled me. Quickly splashing the worst of the butchery off into the sea, I made my way back to Nassau, and went straight to Cully's to hear the news. There was no one there I knew, and the pirates were so hostile over the Pardon, that I drank my ale and smoked my pipe outside on the veranda.

A scrawny, dried up old rover with a sour face and only one arm joined me, and wheedled some of the last of my tobacco for his own pipe. I lit it for him from a strand of hempen cord that lay smouldering in a pot by my foot, and he accepted this politeness with a low growl.

"Is Mistress Bonny still in Nassau", I asked him.

"Jennings' whore?", the old man sneered. "Careful lad, he's a jealous one."

"He's a friend of mine, as is his lady."

"Then you must be of a particularly diplomatic disposition", a cool voice claimed from the door of the tavern. "The jade has indiscreet eyes, and every man in Nassau is trying to catch them." A darkly handsome young man pulled a rickety chair out onto the veranda and dropped into it, his long legs stretched in front of him. He was very brown, and wore his black hair curled about a massive gold earring. His clothes were as well-kept as his weapons, and I took him for a rakehell with an opinion on each of the local harlots.

344

"Jennings has nothing to fear from me, yet you certainly sound interested enough to inspire jealousy."

"She seems content with Jennings," the young man sighed, "and I doubt she'd spurn a man such as he is for just another rover. I must look to my promotion."

"Whores should not be so proud", the sour-faced old man scowled, spitting into the dust.

"As Ben Hornigold chased Judge Walker out of Nassau for calling her that, you'd be well advised to let the word rest", the younger man advised the older one, his fingers caressing the silver hilt of his sword. "'Tis well known she has no price, though she does favour none but wealthy captains."

"No one in their right minds would poach a girl Jennings was interested in", the sour old man growled. "He's killed for less."

"Jennings does not kill unless 'tis business", the young man stated coolly. "Though, as an honourable man, he would not hesitate to kill any scum that blackened a friend's reputation."

"He's as foolish as the rest of ye", the old man snarled. "What about the night he threw down five hundred pieces of eight to see a Port Royal whore strip."

The young rover laughed. "Aye, that was a mad night. He'd wagered Blackbeard that the mark on Brass Betty's arse was a heart that beat for him alone. Blackbeard swore 'twas a fish, and the joke was, there wasn't a mark at all. They'd both got the wrong whore."

"Five hundred pieces of eight!", hissed the old man, "when those who have slaved all their lives cannot feed their hungry families!"

"Take no notice of his bad temper", the handsome young man advised me. "Master Harwood is the best pilot in the Bahamas, and sails with whom he pleases. Though I'll not sail with the sour old bastard again until he can tell me a joke filthy enough to make me laugh." He stood and reset his tricorne on his long black hair with all the care of a

London beau. "And here comes our fire-haired beauty ."

Anne was arm-in-arm with Jennings, and I was surprised when he smiled at the young rover. "Jack Rackam! It is good to see you. A profitable cruise, isn't it true? They say Cully's excellent brandy is down to you."

"Too profitable to swap for this Pardon of yours Henry. Let's take a table, and I'll get the first bottle, and you can attempt to justify it to me. Please join us, Mistress Bonny. It seems an age since I last saw your smile." Anne simpered, Jennings frowned, and I followed them into Cully's, eager to hear all Jennings could say of the Pardon.

When I saw how Cully fawned over the young rover, I realised he must be very successful indeed. Yet Rackam ignored the fat tavern keeper, winking instead at the ragged crone filling tankards from barrels behind the bar. When she grinned back at him, I saw she was not much older than me.

"You're a dangerous man if you can crack a smile from the likes o' Peg", Cully flattered him.

"I'm a dangerous man, Cully", Rackam agreed coldly. "But only to those bastards who anger me with injustice. Bring me four bottles of your best brandy, and let me hear no more of your inability to pay those who work for you." Cully paled, Peg cackled, and Rackam threw her a coin.

Then nodding to the roughest men, and touching his hat to the worst women, he led me through the crowd. "Be a mate, and let me have the seat next to the fiery redhead", he murmured. "I'll meet you with cold steel otherwise." I could only hope he was joking, for he moved with all the grace of a hunting cat, and I knew him for another duellist.

Anne Bonny was watching him too, and as their eyes met, hers flashed green in the darkness of the tavern. Jennings stood to clasp hands with Rackam, and then pulled out a chair next to himself. It was a courtesy that Rackam did not dare rebuff, and neither did he show a hint of disappointment when I sat next to Anne. She smiled at me, yet she could not take her eyes off him.

Cully had followed us with an armful of bottles, and

a stack of glasses. "Pour it out man! Mistress Bonny, you must taste some of this fine French brandy we stole yesterday. Henry, here's to your good fortune. Captain Vane will soon be in to talk to you on this Pardon. We touched bottom coming in over the sand-bar a little too early in the tide, and he's waiting to see if she leaks."

"The Lark is an uncommon pretty sloop, even for one of John Haman's making. A pity Charles Vane cares less for the men who sail under him, than the ship they sail in. I hear you've got your work cut out as his Quartermaster, caught between the rights of the men and his hard pride, isn't it true? You should sail with me, Jack. I treat every man with respect."

"I know you for a most civil man, Henry, and I'm flattered you think so well of me, but my loyalty is to Captain Vane. 'Tis true he's a hard man, and cannot suffer a fool, but he's master of his craft, and I've still much to learn from him."

"Aye, a tricksy bastard, we all know that. Yet his arrogance makes him mean."

"Captain Vane cares little for the opinions of most men, but I know he cares for yours, Henry. If you wish to speak with him of his arrogance, he'll be here soon enough."

"I admire your loyalty, Jack, but do not risk another fight between us. One of us will die the next time, and that should not be taken lightly. Besides, there is enough cause for dispute between the Brethren over this Pardon. Hornigold sailed under a flag of truce to hear the deal from Captain Durrell of the Swift."

"The Pardon is nought but a poxy trick to take the Bahamas from us," Rackam scowled. "They know they will lose if they attack us openly, so they seek to divide us."

"What is the deal?" I asked Jennings quietly.

"The Admiralty will forget any crime committed at sea against any ship of any country. We get signed certificates from a Governor or Navy commander. We may take our fortunes, keep our ships, and go where we will, free men."

"Free!" Rackam snorted. "Once they've drunk their profits from the last cruise, most will be back begging for work from tyrants. Many will mutiny at the cruel treatment, and hang. Nay, Henry, think on! This is an attempt to halve our numbers without firing a shot, and thus 'tis a betrayal of the Brethren to even consider it. Though you led us here, perhaps Nassau is no longer home for you."

"Aye, I led you here, and most of you are rich thanks to me, isn't it true? Do you think I would sail out now, leaving you all high and dry, unable to see the storm sweeping down upon you? The King wants the money from his colonies, and we are in the way."

"And I'd rather fight them than surrender."

"Aye", Anne agreed fiercely. "The Brethren are in a position o' strength as long as we hold Nassau. Without it, we are nothing."

Jack grinned at her and raised his glass. "Here's to the Brethren, who trust neither Kings nor Pardons, and who won't hand Nassau back just for the asking. Besides, Captain Vane is looking for crew to man the Lark, the fastest sloop in Nassau harbour." Many heads turned, and the noise rose as the pirates discussed the Pardon, and the successful but unpopular Charles Vane.

Jennings was still smiling. "You must love the life, Jack. Yet I am older, and I have had my fill of it."

"Think deeper Henry. Don't forget Captain Mission. Every man is born free, and if we must make war on the world to defend that freedom, we will. We know the value of freedom, for most of us have lived without it. You can easily retire and be comfortable, but there are a thousand men who have no choice in the matter. We will stand firm, and hold Nassau against any enemy."

"Bravo Jack!", murmured a voice from the shadows. A tall, angular man stepped into a pool of light that streamed from a hole in the roof. He was as lean as Jennings was solid, his face yellow from the ague and close-shaved, his eyes the coldest blue I have ever seen. He dressed in black, wore his fair hair long and tied back, and stood with his hand on his sword hilt.

Jennings did not look the least discomforted by his arrival. "Charles Vane, you snake. You should not listen in the shadows if you do not want to hear yourself spoken ill of. Cullimore! Pour more of that brandy, and fast. Here's a dangerous man with a killing thirst."

Cullimore moved quickly, and Vane slid into an empty seat across from Jennings. "So Henry, you want us to take the Pardon. You pride yourself in being a careful man. You should not be so trusting."

"They want us out of the trade, and will do anything to get rid of us, isn't it true?"

"You never took English ships, and never committed any crime but theft. They should find you easy to pardon. Most of us have long depositions filed against us for the games we play when we are too bored, too hot, and some tortured crew demand revenge on their Captain. I have more to fear from the Admiralty courts than you."

"They are too eager to see us gone, to quibble over a few merchant captains made to run the gauntlet of their own crews. If we do not take this Pardon, their next step will be less merciful."

"The timing of this is not convenient to me. As you know, I am signing on new crew for my next cruise. If you speak for the King, I must speak against you."

That was when Hornigold strode in. "Me darlin' girl, drinkin' with the Devil himself. An' he doesn't even like women. Or is it that handsome fool Rackam ye've got yer eye on? Ah Henry, don't tell me the chit isn't bored with ye yet! Now sweetheart, give yer old friend a taste o' yer sweet lips, an' make me young again." Anne saluted the burly pirate, and it amused me to see Jennings indifferent, and Rackam jealous.

"Vane, have ye heard o' this Pardon? We're all going to make a fortune trading as honest men."

349

"And I will steal it from you", Vane insisted coolly. "Now, my mates are thirsty, and look to me for rum. Gentlemen, another time. Mistress Anne, I beg your indulgence, but I must take Jack with me." Rackam bowed gallantly to Anne, yet his mouth was hard, and we could see he liked Vane's ill manners as little as anyone.

"Cully!" Hornigold bellowed. "Bring ale. I can't talk with a dry throat. We'll debate this business now, and open the brandy bottles after." All heads turned to watch the flamboyant ruffian drain his tankard and slam it to the table. "I see it this way, lads. Goin' out upon the account was a way for an honest man to take the riches of a dishonest one, for how else did he get rich but by cheatin' the poor, eh? They hate us, not only because we boldly live by our own laws, but because we have destroyed the trade. There were riches once. 'Tis all scraps and sharp dealing now. We scrape away at this miserable existence, longing for our homes and sweethearts, afraid o' the rope. And now the English Governors no longer buy from us. Yet what do they need? Traders! We can take the Pardon, keep our ships, and still share profits as we have always done. And if any of our old comrades in arms think to take it, we'll fight. There. I think I've said all I wish. Vane, 'tis your turn."

Vane stood and looked about him, catching each man's eye, waiting for the talk to die down. "In the world outside Nassau, there are two types of men. The few rich masters and the many slaves. We have all suffered in that world. We have all found refuge here. We rule ourselves, and have done well." There was a rolling murmur of agreement. "Outside Nassau, they know nothing of this. Once we become part of it again, we will lose all our freedom, all our rights, and be but dogs again. Merchants will believe Hornigold owns the ships he commands, because that is how it is in their world. They will not know he is only voted Captain because of his courage. And there are no laws to protect the rights of his crew. You can leave him, yet you can't take your share of the ship with you. And

Ben Hornigold has an appetite for profit that will see him do well in that world. He is already rich. The Pardon will make him fat."

"You Hellsnake!", Hornigold bellowed, his hand on his sword. "I'm a truer friend to the Brethren than you are, Charles Vane!"

Vane ignored him. "The Bahamas control all the shipping in the Caribbean. To get from Europe to the English colonies to the north, and the Spanish colonies to the south, all must run our gauntlet. That is why this place was selected as a pirate base by Captain Mission, why Jennings returned here, and why King George wants it now. It is because force has failed him that he is now using guile. Yet if we combine our strength, then nothing can stop us. We could raid any city, hold any colony to ransom, and have a permanent Fleet waiting for the Spanish treasure ships. Then let the whole world fear the pirates of Nassau!"

"And let the whole world fear Charles Vane", Jennings interrupted, standing in his turn. "For if the Brethren combine into one Fleet, then someone must lead it, isn't it true? And who else would be arrogant enough to dream of being our Pirate King? You betray yourself Vane. You want power, and you care little for anyone's rights or freedom. All would work to make you rich, and you'd never go out on the account again, but wait for the profits of other men's work to pour into your lap. Then we would have a tyrant to rule us, like, and no rights at all."

Jennings sat, his hand on his sword, and his eyes on Vane. Vane appeared to take the insult well, shaking his head and looking mournful, yet 'twas easy to see that few trusted him. I felt that the pirates could be led either way, and wished for an instant to urge them against Vane, yet I hesitated to draw attention to myself.

Then Rackam stood, and the crowd hushed again. "You know me as a man with little ambition past the next prize", he began.

"Or the next doxy", someone yelled. There was

laughter at Rackam's easy grin, and the tension eased.

"I see the Pardon as something to be used by each man as it suits him", he began again, and I saw Vane stiffen, expecting betrayal. "If a man wants to end his roving days, and has money to retire on, as Jennings and Hornigold do, then what could be more timely? But if a man has nothing when he takes the Pardon, then he is a dog who will endure being beaten for a scrap and a place by the fire. As sailors, we were at the mercy of our greedy Captains, cheated out of our pitiful wages, despised for the hardest work. We risked our lives every day, until a storm swallowed us, or the boom caught us on the head, or an ague in a foreign clime, far from home. And if we rebelled, even at the cruellest usage, we swung for it. After the free life we have now lived, who could live like that again? And if you sign the Pardon, then mutiny, they will have proof that you are a relapsed pirate, and you'll hang all the faster for your honesty.

"The small profits from trading, shared amongst us, will hardly keep us all in pocket. So I say, we stay on the account until we all have enough put by to make better lives for ourselves. Those that can afford to, should retire now, and leave the rest of the trade to us who need it. And let us remember that, Pardon or no, we are sworn brothers here in Nassau. So let there be no squabble, but let each man take the Pardon when he feels it convenient. And for those who need a little more convenience", he flipped a gold coin into the air, "sign on with our Company tomorrow at the stone tavern."

Then Anne Bonny tossed her flaming hair, Rackam missed the falling coin, and when it hit the floor, Peg's filthy brat snatched it up, and ran out with it. Rackam laughed, the tavern laughing with him, and he raised his glass and toasted: "The Brethren of the Sea!", and that brought us all to our feet, unified again.

As day wore into night, a few more men rose to make speeches, yet neither side seemed to prevail. At our table, Jennings mulled over who might sail in with the

Pardon. He thought Captain Durrell of the Swift might be brave enough, yet Hornigold disagreed. "They'll either come in force, an' risk a fight, or they'll send someone they don't care about, certain we'll kill him and steal his ship."

"There will be a new Governor in Jamaica soon, and he will be empowered to pardon us", Jennings mused. "Yet if we sailed in, and they decided to hang us after all, we'd all be helpless like"

"A delicate problem", Anne agreed. "We'd weep to hear o' you hanged, when we'd imagined you free, married to the Governor's daughter, and living in luxury."

I think I was the sole wight in Nassau who stayed sober that night. Towards midnight, Vane and Jennings exchanged bottles of rum and toasted each other, and the pirates cheered them. Yet, soused with brandy, Rackam could no longer keep his eyes off Anne Bonny. As Jennings scowl grew blacker, she plied him with rum to keep him sweet, yet it still looked like ending in an ugly brawl. When his head finally sagged, I hauled the handsome young rover over to the dosshouse to sleep. I let him drop to a filthy mat, and as he fell, he grabbed my shirt, and pulled my face down close to his. "God damn me, but I'll have her", he muttered, "even if I have to fight Jennings for her."

"If she wants you, no doubt she'll manage it so she can have you. Now sleep." And like an obedient child, he closed his eyes and blacked out.

Chapter 20: The Pardon

I made my way back to Ma Davies' camp, and told her of the Pardon. She was pleased, and feasted her two boys and I right royally for two days, before we went back into the forest. There, we endured another month of storms, each one taking days to build to a terrible intensity of heat, and then breaking with extraordinary displays of lightening, and buckets of rain.

Yet they were nothing when compared with the hurricane that assailed us in early October. I thought that between the roaring waves and the pounding rain, Providence would be washed into the sea. The three of us sat huddled in a shallow cave, the boys stoically silent, their arms about each other, while torrents of water flooded in upon us. Towards nightfall, the screaming wind changed direction, sheltering us somewhat. When another of John's valiant attempts to light a fire was doused, I swore ferociously. "At least we are safe on land", John reminded me. "We should think of all those souls out upon that Hell of a Sea, and be thankful." He muttered a quick prayer for all those at sea that night, and I remembered that their father had lately died in such a storm, and bowed my head and prayed with him.

Towards the end of October, we staggered into Ma Davies camp under another load of beef. She had her daughters take it into Nassau immediately, for the heat allowed no delay. When I had splashed the worst of the gore into the sea, she fed me, packed my pipe with her best Virginian tobacco, and with concern in her eyes, prepared me for bad news. Sam Bellamy's Fleet had been wrecked in that last hurricane, off Cape Cod. The sailor who brought the news to Cully's had reported sixty-two men dead on Poachy beach. A few surviving pirates had been unable to resist the gold being washed up on the beach with the corpses, and were caught, and taken to Boston for trial. The Indian cook had been released, as savages were regarded as children, and thus beyond stern judgement. Ma Davies said that Cotton Mather, the hardest of the Salem priests, had himself prepared the captured pirates' souls for death. I could only hope that Sam Bellamy and Patrick Carty had been among those saved from the sea, with time to repent their sins and prepare themselves.

In November, a cool north-east wind cleared the storms away, and hunting became more comfortable, though tracking was not so easy. Still thinking on the Pardon, I made my way to Cully's one night at the beginning of December, to find the talk was of Blackbeard. "He used to put even Spaniards ashore before burnin' their ships", Hornigold was protesting. "He was a great one for bluster, yet not cruel. I can only think the pox has rotted his brain."

Captain Martel played with the French lace on his cuffs. "We have always been the hope of the poor sailor and the terror of the cruel Captain, yet this..."

"It reflects on all of us, isn't it true?", Jennings fumed. "Ah, Read, good to see you. Have you heard the news? Blackbeard has been sweating merchant Captains half to death."

Hornigold scowled. "I thank God I'll leave the life with me conscience still me own. I'm no Saint, nay don't you laugh Martel! I'm no Saint I say, yet I've never fallen into the pit of Evil, an' taken to killin' for pleasure."

Jennings shuddered. "Stop there, Ben. Let us hear no more on that, like. We have all seen it. The wars we have endured make room for the worst sort to do what they wish. Yet men have always had the choice to go straight, or go to Hell. Blackbeard has chosen the last. He terrifies his own crew with his madness, insisting that the Devil sails with them, and many say they've seen him aboard, isn't it true? A pox on Him, and on this talk of murder. Cully, give me a rum! By Christ, I feel as cold as a ghost ..."

And then the massive form of Patrick Carty stepped through the door, and we all gaped, frozen with fear. He gave a loud guffaw, clapped Jennings on the back, and then we were all pummelling him, asking him if he was alive or dead, demanding to know why the fishes did not have him. He knocked back a huge dram of rum, laughing at how white our faces had been, when we thought him a ghost, and drowned with Sam Bellamy.

We sobered then, and watched him swallow another dram, the memory of that charming Irish pirate heavy in all our hearts. "I was on the Whydah when she struck", Carty muttered. "A murderous bastard called Fitzgerald piloted us onto the rocks off Cape Cod. I was thrown over to drown with Sam Bellamy, and am alive by the merest chance. Only eight men made it off the Whydah, and none off Williams' ship.

"Aye, The Devil sailed with us on that voyage, make no mistake. Yet we began the cruise with one hundred and thirty men on our two vessels, an' sailed out o' here thinkin' ourselves invincible. We had only been a few days out, an' had just sighted the Virginia Capes, when the clouds that constantly stream south began to spiral, an' a great storm boiled from the sea. Williams shouted for us to make for the open ocean, there bein' no safe haven nearby. We had not his speed, an' had barely battened the hatches and reefed the sails when the first blast nearly overset us. Bellamy ordered all but me below, an' together we held the wheel, and fought to keep her from broachin'. By the first morn, the sails were gone, an' she ran like a mad thing under bare poles.

"Bellamy had lashed the two of us to the binnacle, an' that saved our lives, for just on dawn, a great wave curled up to meet our mast-top. When it crashed down upon us, the Whydah groaned, and her mainmast crashed to starboard. We cut it away, and then the mizzen fell on us, and we cut that away too. The men had been pumpin' in watches all night, yet now Bellamy called for relief, an' the Indian took the wheel. Then a wave like the end o' the world lifted up over the Whydah, an' broke hard upon us, stavin' in the taffrail, an' sweepin' me and the Indian straight over the

356

bow. Bellamy hauled us back from the nets, and the Indian grabbed the wheel and righted us just in the nick o' time. That Hell lasted another three days and nights, and none slept or ate or ceased prayin'.

"Then just as suddenly as it came upon us, the wind died. We were in a sorry state, yet soon made enough repairs to keep our rendezvous for Block Island. There we cruised back and forth, Bellamy in a fever o' worry for Paul Williams in his little sloop. On the tenth day, something died in our gallant Captain, an' I swear I saw him pray. The next dawn, the sloop came sailin' in, Williams waving from the bowsprit, and Bellamy wept with joy an' forgot whatever bargain he'd made with God. If only we'd heeded that first warnin', they'd still be alive." He knocked back another dram, and all those crowded about him sighed and drank too.

"We met Vane cruisin' the Virginia coast, an' joined him. He spent weeks tryin' to get Bellamy's support for some mad scheme to have himself voted Pirate King. We cruised past Rhode Island, and back to Carolina, and though we took three ships, one of 'em put a broadside through William's pretty sloop. He picked out a pretty snow, fast an' well-laden with rum, and though Vane wanted his favourite to have it, we voted Williams her Captain.

"We thought we were in luck again, yet 'twas not so. Bellamy an' that scamp of a player had put their heads together, an' written 'The Royal Pirate', a play in rhyme that they were most proud of, full o' slander on the ambitious pride o' Charles Vane. We were becalmed for an afternoon, so Bellamy had the Fleet lashed together, an' staged the play on the quarterdeck o' the Whydah. Our Company was soon helpless with laughter, an' Vane white with fury.

"Yet, just as Alexander the Great, played with a right swagger by Bellamy, was sentencin' the pirate to death, Williams' Gunner staggered above deck, after a three day binge on rum and opium. Alexander intoned: 'Knowst thou that Death attends thy mighty crimes, and thou shalt hang tomorrow morn betimes'. Thinkin' the play to be in earnest,

357

an' his messmate in danger, the Gunner dropped below, and ran for the snow's gunroom. He grabbed a grenadoe, declarin' to his drunken comrades that they were about to hang honest Jack Spinckes, but by God, they should not hang him, for he'd clear the Whydah's decks. Half-persuaded by his fury, his comrades snatched up their cutlasses and ran after him, an' the fool of a Gunner had threw the grenadoe amongst the actors, breaking Jack Spinckes' leg. One of his mates attacked Bellamy, who fought back an' killed him. The rest of us threw ourselves on top o' the fools, bearin' them by main force to the decks. The Gunner an' his two surviving comrades were thrown in irons, an' we held a court martial the next day. We voted to forgive 'em, yet we gave 'em no more opium in their rum, an' we heard no more o' that play. Vane sailed away the next morn'.

"Aye, you can grin, Martel, yet we felt the Devil was laughin' at us, an' despite our success, many spoke o' returnin' to Nassau, to see if Vane had spoken truth o' the Pardon. Then we took a pretty sloop off Cape Cod, laden with wine, an' Bellamy persuaded her whole crew to join us in the rovin' life, for their Captain was a tyrant. The wine was good, the new sloop quick an' lively, an' our Company had never been so strong. Yet we needed to careen both the Whydah and William's snow, so we headed north, and made for a bend in the Machias River that Williams knew of.

"There we anchored, set the forced men to buildin' huts, raised a breastwork, an' dug embrasures for the cannon on either side o' the river. I dug our powder into the earth, an' roofed it, an' then Bellamy felt secure enough to careen the ships, startin' with the snow. We tied her to two trees on the riverbank, an' hove her down with the tide. With all of us hard at it, it didn't take long to scrape off the barnacles and weed, and cover her with tar and arsenic. This was no boot toppin', but a thorough job, Williams wantin' his snow to spin in the water. We scoured her bilges of all the filth that had been half-blindin' the men whenever they went below, an' then started on the Whydah. 'Twas a pleasant few weeks, lads. The Africans hunted game in the deep forest, an' we ate as hard as we worked. At night, we sat about the fires talking o' the Pardon, an' what it might mean for us, though Bellamy spoke hard against it.

"With our vessels clean an' fast, we only wanted provisions. We cruised to Fortune Bay in Newfoundland, an' took fishing vessels off the Banks, the miserable fish-splitters always happy to join us, for they are paid next to nothing, and end up drowning in debt to those they work for. Aye, they make grand pirates, those Newfoundland lads do. We scuttled two death traps o' ships, setting their Captains afloat in leaky boats, with our curse upon 'em for endangering their men.

"We were congratulatin' ourselves on our change o' luck, when we spied a sail off the isle o' Saint Paul. The Devil must have split his sides laughing that day, for we attacked a French corvette o' thirty-six guns, full o' soldiers for Quebec. She waited without colours until we were close, and then swung about and gave us a broadside straight into the Whydah's bow. Bellamy shouted that the Whydah was done for, and we needed the corvette, and Devil take her, she was a ship worth fightin' for. He led our attack on her, an' then we saw how many men they had aboard, an' had to hack our way back aboard the Whydah. In two hours o' hard fightin', the Frenchmen boarded twice, an' twice we repelled 'em, an' 'twas Bellamy who finally cut us away. We fled into the night, the corvette still chasin' us, with hardly a man whole, sixteen near death, an' twenty four dead.

"With the Whydah still carrying shot in her hull, we staggered down the coast, back towards Newfoundland, prayin' for fair weather, for we were done for if it stormed. The Indian stitched our wounds, while Bellamy, cursin' the Devil an' his poor judgement, farewelled our mates, their corpses litterin' our wake. To cheer Bellamy, our player swore he'd write a new play on the courage o' the Brethren, who thought nothin' of attackin' one o' King Louis' warships, that jester laughin' at our sorry Captain despite the ball in his knee.

"We met the fishin' Fleet at Placenta Bay, and spotted the Mary Anne, a likely-looking Irish pink. We raised the Jolly Roger, ordered her Captain to strike her colours, fired a shot o'er her bows, and she surrendered. It turned out she was a whaler, outbound from Nantucket to New York, and full o' provisions. We put seven well-armed men aboard to crew her, and Bellamy sent her crew back to the Whydah under guard, offering to put 'em close to shore in a boat come morn.

"As night fell, the weather grew thick. The Mary Anne had orders to steer nor-nor-west after the Whydah's stern light, yet the fog suddenly came down heavy, an' we knew we were near the shallows off Cape Cod. There was but little wind, yet the sea was rollin', an' Bellamy chose to let the Mary Anne go first, her havin' the least men aboard, the lightest draught and the best pilot for these waters. Most o' the men were below, out o' the cold. I trusted neither the fog, nor the pilot. Neither did Paul Williams. He wanted to lay to, knowin' we were close to land, an' just before dawn, he came up in his snow, nervous as a cat, cursin' the fog. Bellamy hollered at him to stop worryin' an' threw him a bottle of wine he'd had from the Mary Anne. Williams lifted it to his lips, an' then dropped it, screamin': "Land! Land ho! The bastard has beached us!"

"We tried to wear, yet there was not enough wind, and before we could come about, the lovely Whydah smashed into the rocks. I was thrown into the water with Sam Bellamy, men screamin' all about us as the breakers hurled 'em into the rocks, dragged 'em back and hurled 'em into the rocks again. An' the Whydah screamed too as the bottom was ripped out of her. I thought my time had come, yet a spar came my way, and I grabbed it and hung on for my life.

"Then I looked up to see Williams at the tiller o' the snow, heading her straight in after the Whydah, shouting for Sam. His African crew jumped him, the snow struck the rocks, an' he dived overboard to try to save his mate.

"There was a break in the fog, and through a gap in the reef I glimpsed the shore. I kicked for it hard, shoutin' to those about me to follow. When I crawled ashore, 'twas already littered with the corpses o' the dead, many of 'em the Africans o' Paul William's crew. For though eight of us made it off the Whydah, none made it off the snow. An' just as dawn was breakin', Bellamy and Williams were washed ashore, locked in each other's arms.

"As the sun rose, I could see the Mary Anne, carefully beached just opposite Slut's Bush Island. I knew then that Fitzgerald, the pilot of the Mary Ann, had deliberately led us aground, and knowing he would be back for the gold that was washin' up with the corpses, I begged the eight survivors to stand by me, and lay in wait for him. Yet they could not resist the lure o' the gold in the sea, and when Fitzgerald and his crew returned to the wreck with some local men, they seized the fools as pirates. I saw then that my revenge must wait. Yet not for too long. Fitzgerald must meet Bellamy in Hell."

The tavern was full by the time Patrick Carty finished his story, and every man there was silent. I could only think of Paul Williams, a man I had never liked, diving overboard to die with the gallant Sam Bellamy. Overwhelmed, I stood, bowed my head, and muttered the sailor's prayer for those dead at sea, all silent about me.

I knew how close I had come to sailing on that fatal voyage with Bellamy, and now convinced I would never go out upon the account again, I returned to hunting. Yet, though needing the money more than ever, I now resented the labour and the hardship, wanting nothing but my Pardon and my Freedom. My young companions still talked of going out on the account, and I swore that their honest mother would see it as a betrayal, and they were not to think of it.

My chagrin was terrible when I stepped into Cully's nearly a month later, to find I had missed an extraordinary display of courage, as well as the Pardon. Governor Bennett had sent his only son to sail straight into Nassau Harbour, with no Navy escort, to inform us that the Pardon was on offer in Bermuda. He must have been a courageous stripling, for he had come ashore unarmed, alone, asking for Captain Jennings. When Jennings and Hornigold and a hundred and fifty men had then sailed north with him, it had caused a great divide amongst the Brethren. Charles Vane talked of betrayal, yet there were many who spoke of the end of a long exile.

I was there when Jennings and Hornigold sailed back into Nassau a week later. The rovers left the taverns to crowd about the waterfront. I joined them, thinking Jennings might need my sword, for the mood of the pirates was explosive. Jennings moored the Bathsheba close in, and yelled to the crowd that he needed a drink, and would meet all that wished to hear of the Pardon at Cully's. The stinking tavern was instantly full of men, some angered, some hopeful, yet all intent on hearing him, so his life was safe for the moment.

We all watched Jennings swallow a tot of rum. "Well lads, I have taken the King's Pardon under oath, and am no longer out on the account, like."

"Then you are no longer one o' the Brethren, and should not have returned to Nassau", Martel stated bluntly.

"I felt obliged to report on our excellent treatment at the hands of the Governor of Bermuda. A little shocked at the success of his venture, he may have been, yet he remained courteous, despite our overwhelming numbers. We have kept our profits, and may go as free men where we will."

"I am a free man because I insist upon it, not because some King's puppy gives me leave", Vane sneered. "You shouldn't have come back, Henry."

"I will fight for my right to speak for the Pardon, my dear Charles. Besides, there is more news, isn't it true? The King has appointed a new Governor for the Bahamas. He is on his way."

Martel rose and doffed his be-feathered hat. "Outside of Nassau, there will always be some fat bastard who expects a man to tug the forelock, it doesn't matter how rich you are, Henry, or how honest. Here we are but rogues, yet we respect no man who hasn't earned his name..."

"Then you will have no trouble with the new Governor of Nassau", Jennings noted dryly. "Have you not heard of Captain Woodes Rogers?"

I gasped, and suddenly all eyes were on me. I steadied myself, and explained. "Woodes Rogers commanded the cruise that took the Spanish galleon back in 1711. The richest prize taken since the days of good Queen Bess. Nearly two hundred thousand pounds. Yet as a Commander, 'twas his attack on Guiaquil that showed his mettle. He had taken the town, and was about to destroy it, when the town's Governor informed him the ransom was raised. Despite his brother's death, he refused to sacrifice the town and its people to his vengeance, nor would he risk his men in an unnecessary battle.

"Aye, he looks after his own. When he began his famous cruise, he guaranteed every sailor ten pounds each, and when they began to fall sick of the scurvy, he spent months on the Galapagos nursing them back to health. Then he kept them at sea for months awaiting the Spanish Treasure Fleet, his men restless almost to mutiny. He took a Spanish ship off Saint Lucas, the rapidity and precision of the English guns winning the day, and it was during that action that he was shot in the face. He gave his orders in writing, refusing to leave the deck until the battle was won.

"He is a man of God, and refused to throw his Spanish prisoners overboard, even though rations were short. And in his gratitude, one of the prisoners told him of the Manila galleon, a Spanish treasure ship loaded with two hundred thousand pounds of gold. He found and took that ship, despite being shot in the ankle, and again he refused to abandon the battle. Yet I dare say he thought the pain worth

363

the profit. He made a fortune from it, and his reputation. He wrote a book of the voyage, that is how I know of him. He is a brave man, of strong principal, almost a Quaker, and not to be bought."

Jack Rackam stepped up. "If we fight for Nassau against this Governor, whose side will you be on, Henry?"

"I have the interests of the Brethren at heart. The Pardon is timely and just. Your men don't want to rot here. They want to go home, isn't it true? Charles Vane wants to keep you as his own subjects, just as the King does, for his own power."

I found Anne next to me in the crowded tavern. "Mark, I'm so sorry I couldn't find you when they sailed. I looked everywhere."

We made for the door, Jennings' jealous eyes upon us. "And next time, I'll not be deep in the forest, tracking after nervous cattle. The Pardon must come to Nassau soon, and I have enough put by to live on for a month, so I'll be at my camp. And if you hear of anyone else sailing to Bermuda for the Pardon, I don't have enough saved to buy my passage, yet I could work it."

"If I had any funds at all, I would lend you the fare. Though I must protest at the epidemic of honesty that has swept through Nassau, I can see you are no pirate."

"Doesn't Henry Jennings give you anything? In truth, you could use a new dress."

"Henry is generous, yet, as I am his friend not his whore, I draw the line at him buying me dinner."

I thought her pride almost absurd. "You must see there's nothing in Nassau for you. You must leave before fate intervenes to make it impossible."

"Worry is a luxury I cannot afford. I'm young and strong, and have survived a great deal already. And how can I leave without being someone's whore? Why can I not live free, and work for my pennies, as you do?"

"There is nothing to stop you, but your love of idleness, and your lust for handsome men."

364

She glared at me, then threw her head back and laughed. "It's true I'm willing enough, yet indeed, I'm no whore. Most men can't tell the difference."

"In truth, you amuse me. Most women insist on their virtue, and would sell themselves as soon as fart. You insist you're a harlot, and yet I've trusted you with the truth about myself, instead of cutting your throat. What a strange woman you are."

"Me, what about you! When I am with you, I keep forgetting your secret, which is for the best, considering where we are. Yet I often lie awake at night, and consider your strange life. One day, you must tell me more of your story."

"And you must tell me how you have survived here with no money."

"It's mostly due to the kindness of Ma Davies. See those bushes behind that shack? Wild chickens roost there, and we may find eggs to take to her. Or a scrawny chicken if you're fast enough to catch one. Go quietly." We crept into the dusty bushes, and had soon filled our hats with warm eggs, though the hens carefully kept their distance.

We were working our way past a derelict shack that backed onto the ruined fort, when a boot came flying out of a doorway, followed by a painfully thin, wild-eyed boy, and torrents of screeched abuse. The boy stopped running when he saw us, and made an attempt to compose himself, yet when the next tirade started, he began to weep, his tears making tracks down his dirty face. Anne stopped and laid her arm over his shoulders. "What's angered him now, Georgie? I thought that having the Pardon come, and the Governor here soon, would have sweetened his temper."

"Captain Bennett of Bermuda did not come to pay his respects, Mis'ess Bonny, an' he feels slighted. I am abused now morn to night, and I cannot stand it. I swear one day I'll smother the old bastard with one of his own pillows!"

"Your patience with him is wonderful, dear. Who else

would do for him what you do? Can you not threaten to leave him again? He must know how much he needs you."

"If I hint at going, his rages get worse, an' he makes himself really ill. An' he does pay me regular, an' my Ma gets nothin' else..."

"Shall I go in to him?"

"Oh, if you would, Mis'ess Bonny! He's always quieter when you speak to him."

Anne turned and shrugged. "Do you mind waiting just a little longer for breakfast? Mister Graves is officially the Collector of His Majesty's Customs, for which he still gets paid a small stipend, though he collects nothing. When the last Governor failed us, Mister Graves appointed himself Governor, in opposition to Old Governor Sawney, who the pirates still honour. Ma Davies says the heat has disturbed the old man's brain. He insists on all formalities, despite being bedridden. If George had not the patience of a saint, he'd starve. Still, we can't have him torture the boy, and if George leaves, no one else will care for him, not for what he pays. Let me see if I can quiet him a little."

A cracked, querulous voice called from the shack: "George, damn you boy, get back here now, and bring that boot!" George sniffed, picked up the boot, and we followed him into the shack, the stench of illness almost overpowering us.

"We've come to visit you, Governor Graves", Anne announced as she entered.

I saw an emaciated old man in a filthy shirt heave himself up in a pigsty of a bed. George, fetch a chair you dolt! How are you my dear, how is your health in this terrible place?"

"I'm as stout as ever, Governor. It's you we are concerned for. I didn't hesitate to invite a dear friend of mine to meet you. This is Mark Read, lately o' London."

"I am delighted to meet any friend of yours, my dear. Sir, I am honoured to make your acquaintance. Surely we met at Covent Garden the other night?"

366

"I was often at Covent Garden, yet I have not been recently", I told him truthfully, shocked by the extent of his madness.

"Mistress Anne said you are one of the Reads. Is that the Reads of Surrey?"

"My family is of Bristol, Sir. We are sailors."

He raised an eyebrow and turned to Anne. "Colourful, to be sure, my dear. How is your health?"

"I am well. And you Sir?" She gave me a desperate look, yet I was of little use, relieved to have the old man's mad eyes off me.

"Oh, this island will hold my bones soon, make no mistake of that. And yet, I have a day or two left to me, I hope and pray. Make yourself comfortable, my dear. Some tea?"

George began shaking his head, his face screwed up in anguish, and Anne hastened to say that she'd already had tea. Then the old man noticed me again.

"Good afternoon Sir, are you Captain Bennett of Bermuda?"

"No, Sir. Captain Bennett has left for home, after bringing us news of the Pardon."

"Do please extend an invitation to the good Captain to dine with me when it pleases him", the old man insisted. "I keep an informal residence, and I expect the Governor's son is a gentleman."

"'Tis not only gentlemen who are worth meeting, Sir, and not all the baseborn are churls", I objected, ignoring the finger that Anne dug sharply into my ribs.

"These revolutionary notions! I have no time for them. A gentleman is a gentleman because his father was one."

Anne was glaring at me, and the old man's lower lip was beginning to tremble, so I contented myself by saying piously: "We are all children of God, Sir".

"Amen", the old man whispered, and pursed his lips profoundly.

"You look tired Governor, perhaps we should leave you to rest", Anne suggested.

The old man roused himself, and thanked her profusely for her visit, yet he refused to look at me. When we were outside, Anne shook her head. "Now George will have to work twice as hard to keep him reasonable."

"George has chosen his own cross to bear. And that old bastard can't see that his servant is more of a gentleman than he is."

"George is too timid to go pirating. The old man pays him almost enough, and he can't live much longer. Every year he spends here takes ten off his life, and he gets madder with every moon."

"You enjoy being treated like a fine lady, don't you?"

"I love it. He talks o' the gossip of London o' forty years ago, and it fascinates me. How I would love to have been a mistress o' the second King Charles, like Nell Gwynn. I would have made myself a Duchess, and my sons would have been Dukes!"

"There is a King on the throne of England now."

"But he's fat and dull, and being his mistress would be a chore indeed."

"Then you'll have to be content with being a Pirate Queen," I teased her. "Or the Governor's lady."

"Governors are a sorry lot according to Ma Davies. I doubt if this one will be much better."

We made our way to the edge of the stinking township, carrying warm eggs carefully in our hats. When we came to the Davies' shack, we dropped all the eggs into a pot of boiling water, and while they cooked, Anne told Ma Davies that we had been to visit mad old Governor Graves, and they sighed over the life of poor George Bendall.

After breakfast, Ma asked me how much of my silver had survived the high price of Nassau's ale, and I told her I'd enough to keep me a little longer about Nassau, for I was anxious to take the Pardon. She grinned. "The boys are ready to go out hunting again. Yet if you are looking for steady work, I have a little task I need help with, not too far from Nassau."

And so I lived frugally for a time, planting farina for Ma Davies in a swamp on the south coast. She explained that these weeds would be small trees in two years, when she would harvest their roots, press out the poisonous juice, and grind them for flour. I thought the bread she made with it tasted like sawdust, yet there was no wheat in these hot countries, and the pirates liked it.

My poverty was the excuse I needed to avoid Cully's, and Anne Bonny. She had started drinking openly with Jack Rackam, and yet she made no move to break from Jennings, a delicate balancing act, and not one to my taste. They both looked at her with hunger in their eyes, and I was sure she'd undo herself between them. One night, I told her she was a fool. "Rackam may be handsome, Anne, yet he is a committed pirate, while Jennings has taken the Pardon."

"Henry will leave me in Nassau and look for a respectable wife", Anne answered me coolly. "Jack Rackam is a man o' spirit, and will be Captain soon enough."

"The time of the Brethren is over."

"They can never take Nassau from us."

"These men don't want Nassau."

"They have no choice."

"'Tis the same choice, stay straight or go to the Devil!"

The silly chit took umbrage at that, and called me a preaching hypocrite. I avoided her for a time, living alone at my camp, and working hard for Ma Davies, who kept my coins saved up for me.

In February, when I'd been in Nassau a full year, I woke one morning in the middle of a squall, my face wet where the water dripped steadily through my canvas shelter. Chilled to the bone, I glared at my sodden fireplace, cursed the drizzle, and pulled on my jacket. Then feeling the few coins in my pocket, I decided I might as well have a rum to warm me at Cully's, and see if there was any news of the

Pardon. I combed my fingers through my hair, tied it back, scratched my new mosquito bites and then ran past Ma Davies camp, down the beach, and through the mud of Nassau, to the tavern.

The place was almost deserted, and disregarding my hunger, I asked Peg to warm a rum for me against the chill. Some rovers drifted in to join the few that had been up all night, old men who couldn't start the day without a rum to warm them, and young men happily discussing the night's debaucheries over an ale. I sipped on my rum, watching the rain drip steadily through the roof to collect in leaking buckets, none of which were disturbed from the natural process of overflowing. This was no tragedy, however, since there were enough holes in the floor for the water to escape through, and this had to be the first wash it had undergone since the last rain. I thought of how I could reverse all this sloth in an afternoon, if Cullimore would hire me, yet shook my head to think of working for that leery Devil.

Peg's filthy, silent brat was washing dirty tankards in the overflowing buckets, and I wondered who'd fathered it, and hoped 'twas not Cullimore's. I could not tell if 'twas male or female, and when I tried asking Peg, she just shrugged and ignored me.

I was warmed and comfortable, and considering a dash back to Ma Davies for my breakfast, when a bulky, red-faced sailor came in, dripping water from his tarred canvas cape, his short sandy hair spiked from the rain. He demanded to see Cullimore, and when Peg shrugged, he thrust his big head through a doorway that led upstairs, and shouted for him. Cullimore descended in moments, and the burly sailor ordered him to find Henry Jennings.

Cullimore winced. "'Tis more than my life is worth to disturb him", he muttered, avoiding the sailor's eyes.

"By the four winds, our lives are at stake!", he bellowed back. "There's one of His Majesty's warships lying off Harbour Island, not two hours sail away. I need Jennings, or Hornigold, even Vane..." The tavern was paying him all

370

the attention he wanted, yet none could help him, and he started to show all the signs of exploding.

"I think perhaps I can help you", I offered quietly. "I know where Jack Rackam sleeps, and he will wake Vane if 'tis urgent."

"'Tis urgent enough for me to sail in over those reefs, with the wind ripping me sails to shreds! Where lies Rackam?"

"I'll show you."

The rain had increased to a deluge, and the sailor had the courtesy to try and cover me with his cape as we dashed through the mud to the dosshouse. I knocked at the door of Rackam's grimy room, yet the sailor barged past me, to find him thankfully alone, yet sleeping like a dead man. The sailor gave him a shake, and bellowed "Warship!" into his ear, and Rackam was instantly awake, buckling on his sword, thrusting pistols into the belt, and his feet into boots.

"Auger, you saw her?"

"Aye. An' it seems King George's Navy has finally seen sense. She's no square-rigger, but a frigate, an' shallow draughted. She could sail straight in with a pilot who knows the harbour. She's probably still riding out the squall. Anyone trying to sail in here last night without knowing every reef and shoal would have come to grief."

"You did well, mate. I'll find Vane, and meet you at Cully's."

"An' Jennings?"

"I know where he lies. I'll fetch him after I've roused Vane. Come on Mark."

We ran to a ramshackle house behind the main street, the whole structure about to collapse into the mud from the pounding of the rain. Rackam stood under one of the windows, and shouted: "Vane! Charles Vane! 'Tis Jack Rackam. Stir yeself smartly, for there's a Navy warship off Harbour Island!" Vane was instantly at the window, dressing himself and demanding details. He finally ordered us to meet him at Cully's.

"Auger wanted me to tell Jennings too. He lodges above the Coopers. I won't be long."

A handsome, golden-haired young man stuck his head out into the rain, and wiped his face with his shirt. He saw me watching, and stepped suddenly back into the room. I'd have thought nothing of it, if Jack had not turned on me.

"That was none of your business."

"I can hold my tongue."

"I know. Yet pretty Tom Brown is Vane's secret, as he's no fighter, and would be an easy target for any wanting to hurt Vane. Now, let's find Anne. Uh, I mean Jennings."

We were wet to the skin by the time we arrived among the barrels and staves that littered the coopers yard. We bellowed, and when Jennings stuck his head out a window, we told him to meet us at Cully's tavern.

We ran back to Cully's to find a knot of pirates hotly debating whether 'twas the King's Pardon or the King's Justice we were about to face. We had not finished a dram before Jennings joined us. "If she's sheltering from the storm, then she won't be in until it clears", he pointed out. "And anyone going near them will be forced to pilot them in, like."

Martel fronted up to him, hand on sword hilt. "And you Henry, do you stand for or against us?"

"If King George's Navy is foolish enough to attack us with but one ship, you will hardly need me, isn't it true? Yet, as a favour to you all, I will raise the red flag on the Bathsheba and load her guns. After all, the Bathsheba is the best ship in the harbour, and your sloop is fouled and slow."

Vane yawned. "Wet through for nothing. I'm back to bed with a rum to ward off the ague. I was to sign up men for the Lark today, yet that too can wait for the sun."

"The Lark is moored the furthest out", Rackam worried. "She's undermanned, and may be taken as a known pirate vessel."

"Well, 'tis your watch, and there are enough men aboard to sail her out. Perhaps you'd better hurry. They won't stay once they see that warship."

Rackam frowned. "It's more likely they'll have closed the hatches, opened the rum bottles, and started a card game. They won't look up until George Featherstone has won all their shares again. Unless they're captured. I'd better go out. Is the longboat on the beach?"

"No, only the canoa, though there's canvas in the bilges you can use against the rain. Take the Lark around to Bushes Key, and keep her in close. Ah, Mister Harwood, a bottle of rum and a place in the ship's Company for you, if you help re-moor the Lark." The one-armed, sour old seadog pretended to think on it, then snatched up a bottle of rum with his remaining hand, and hurried after Rackam, who was already running for the beach.

Only moments after, Anne came flying in, a wet shawl over her head, her dress sticking to her legs.

"We have decided that the alarm is over until the weather turns", Jennings reassured her, taking her arm.

"Aye, I tore sail to get here in this storm for nought", Auger complained.

"Nay man, we'll be ready for them on the morrow", Hornigold soothed him. "Well-warned is well-armed, and for that we all thank ye heartily. Now, let me get ye drunk, and ye can tell me all yer adventures." There was a rumble of assent from the pirates, and a bottle was uncorked.

Vane decided to see if the old fort could be of any use in defending the town, and his men went with him. The tavern emptied, as the rovers left to prepare for war, and Anne Bonny and I were left alone.

"Jack Rackam should be here."

"He has Vane's orders to sail the Lark away from the harbour."

"So he sails the Lark 'gainst a warship, while Vane stays warm in bed with his favourite."

"He meant to run, not fight. She's undermanned."

Then he's a fool to row out to her without more crew. The Lark is a notorious pirate ship." I poured her a rum to

373

calm her, and we spent the rest of that long, wet day together, while she worried about Jack Rackam. The storm was over by sunset, and we ate a dismal meal in Ma Davies' dripping tent. The sky was red under the purple storm clouds, and Ma declared that the next day would bring fine weather, and the warship. We bedded down where we were, damp and anxious and wakeful.

When the Navy frigate slipped into Nassau Harbour at dawn the next morning, the whole town was waiting on the shore, and pirate flags flew from every masthead. The townsfolk looked to Richard Connor with his spyglass, and he announced she was His Majesty's ship the Phoenix, that her lower tier of guns were out, and there were armed men on deck. It took her until ten o'clock to pick her way carefully amongst the shoals to a mooring, and then after a great deal of bustling about, her longboat was launched, a white flag of truce flying from the masthead.

There was confusion until Jennings rowed in from the Bathsheba, some declaring they should blow the frigate out of the water. "We don't even know why they are here", Jennings noted calmly. "They may have news for us, don't ye know. Her Commander will be in the longboat."

Instead, the longboat carried only a very nervous young Lieutenant standing bravely in the prow, and six hardened sailors, who looked more our sort than his. The lad acquitted himself well, leaping to the shore as the longboat beached, and bowing gracefully to the ragged crowd. "Greetings from Captain Pearce of His Majesty's ship the Phoenix", he stated boldly. "Governor Bennett of Bermuda sends His Majesty's Royal Proclamation of the Act of Grace, by which all those who have committed robbery at sea, against ships of England and her allies, may be pardoned, if you will swear loyalty to His Majesty King George the First, and take oaths to leave the repre...reprehensible life that must otherwise end at the gallows."

"Bravely done, lad, and welcome, like. I am Captain Jennings, this is Captain Hornigold. We sailed into Bermuda a month ago to take the Pardon from Governor Bennett. You need not fear those disposed to stay on the account. You came courteously under a flag of truce, and the Brethren respect courage, isn't it true?"

The young Lieutenant regained some of his colour, and happily followed the two Captains to Cully's to talk of the Pardon. Hundreds of pirates pushed into the tavern after them, and seeing Vane and his men among them, I thought there might be a fight. I decided then to breakfast with Ma Davies', and find out about the Pardon later, knowing I'd take it on any terms.

Ma Davies grinned to see me. "Aye, a Navy ship in the harbour. They'll pay any price for beef."

"Ah God, more mud and leeches! Yet if I'm to be free, I'll need every penny. I'll take the Pardon first, and leave with the boys directly after."

We heard the boom of a ship's gun late in the afternoon, and hurried back to Nassau for the news. We found drunken men wheeling down the street, shouting and weeping for home. Salutes from ship's guns were fired indiscriminately, and I hoped that no drunken Gunner would load in shot after the powder, and accidentally blow the Navy frigate out of the water.

'Twas high tide, and the Navy sailors were at their oars, awaiting the young Lieutenant. I saw him come down the beach, arm in arm with Henry Jennings, who whispered earnestly in his ear before helping him into the longboat, and shoving him off. Fires were lit on the beach, and the rovers sat around them drinking hard. When Jennings told me that the Pardons would be issued the next morning, I too felt a great relief.

We were just finishing the rum bottle, when a sailor yelled: "Look! Look there! The Phoenix is making sail." Her mainsail had indeed bellied out, and she began to make her stately way out of the harbour. "They are leaving and taking the Pardon with them!", someone cried, and a doleful wail swept along the waterfront.

375

Vane laughed long and loud. "Nay, 'tis too much. They get you on your knees with repentance, and then sail away. 'Tis like a teasing virgin demanding marriage, and eloping with a tinker." He laughed again, and the handsome Tom Brown took one look at the crowd, and hauled his captain away.

Hornigold was frowning. "Why the Devil would they do that? Their anchors are holdin', the winds light, and the Lieutenant has nothin' but good news to report."

Jennings shrugged. "Captain Pearce is a coward, isn't it true, sending that boy in his place? He may fear Vane's treachery. Without doubt, they'll be back tomorrow." I wondered then if Jennings had whispered a warning in the boy Lieutenant's ear.

He invited me to drink at his lodgings, rather than risk a fight with Vane's crew at Cully's, for they knew I sought the Pardon. Anne was pleased to see me, and poured brandy until we were all sodden with it. Jennings' head dropped first, and she told me then that she was sick with worry for Rackam. I slept on their floor, and woke with a bad head early the next morning, two pirate ships firing their guns to waken the town.

We all stumbled up and ran for the shore, to watch the Phoenix sail back into the harbour. Then we saw the Lark in her wake, and understood that she had been captured. Vane came storming up, the rest of his crew with him, and tore the spyglass from Richard Connor. When the Lark anchored just behind the Phoenix, he went white with fury. "The sons of whores! Those are not my men aboard the Lark. They have stolen her, and they will regret their impudence. And if they have harmed any of my Company, I will burn their frigate in the water, and all aboard her, I swear it!"

"Not so hasty", Jennings intervened. "Let us not make threats until we know what in Hell is happening, like. I will sail out and speak to the Captain, before he hangs anyone. Pardoned I've been, and he can't hang me."

"I'm with ye", Hornigold insisted. "The Captain's

bound to have fine wine and dry tobacco."

"I'm with you, too", Vane snapped. "His Majesty's Navy will know what to expect if my vessel and crew are not returned to me."

"We would be better off without you, don't you know?", Jennings declared. "The Captain of the Phoenix is evidently a greater fool than we feared. If you turn up making threats, he may sail us all off to Jamaica for a hanging. Nay, come if you will, but come claiming to be a wronged man, captain of a sloop coming in for the Pardon, like. They can have no proof otherwise, though it is clear someone in Nassau has a grudge against you. Think on though. If you claim to be wanting the Pardon, you might have to take it."

"And use it after to wipe my arse with. Do ye think I'd stop at perjury to get the Lark back? Now, there are three of us. We need four to balance the oars." They looked around, and everyone avoided their eyes. Sailing on the strength of a promised Pardon, to meet a fool of a Navy Captain, did not appeal to many.

"I'll go", Anne Bonny stated, pale but determined. "I can handle oars, and they have no reason to hang me."

"No, stay here and wait for us", I insisted. "The Navy has no respect for women."

Vane shrugged, Hornigold beamed, and Jennings clapped me on the back. "Glad to have ye with us, Read. We'll take the Bathsheba's longboat."

Thomas Brown stepped forward. "The Phoenix can't leave until the tide is high again. I'll get an armed sloop ready to attack if she tries to leave with you. If you're kept as prisoners, we'll storm her tonight."

Vane clapped his friend on the shoulder, and I wondered again at the devotion that the ill-favoured, mean-spirited pirate could inspire in handsome young men. "One other thing, Tom. Some bastard betrayed the Lark. One of the Brethren. Find out who."

Hornigold pushed out the longboat, and I bailed,

while Jennings and Vane readied her sail. At the last minute, Anne waded out brandishing a bottle of rum. Pushing it into my hands, she leaned forward and whispered: "Bring Jack back to me, Mary. I beg you." Then it struck me that jealousy was another motive for betraying the Lark, and wondered again what Jennings had whispered in the young Lieutenant's ear, and if he regretted it now.

Hornigold hauled himself aboard, Jennings hoisted the sail, Vane swung the tiller, and we were soon skimming across the harbour. The longboat was an elegant design, made by the famous John Haman of Harbour Island, who had been the first in the Caribbean to perfect the winged sail and the long bow. The Captains drank rum and talked of the swiftest of his sloops, including the Lark, until we neared the dark hull of the Navy frigate. Then we hoisted a flag of truce made from Hornigold's enormous white shirt, and though my heart was thumping, their ribald jokes kept me laughing. We were within six lengths of the frigate before we dropped the sail and took to the oars. Their lookout finally spotted us, and called out to know our business.

"We come to enquire why it seems fitting to Captain Pearce to offer us the Pardon one day, and take one of our sloops the next", Jennings bellowed back.

A tall, thin figure with an enormous white wig, and masses of gold braid on his coat, came to the rail. "I am Captain Pearce of His Majesty's ship the Phoenix", he announced, looking down his great nose at us. "Governor Bennett of Bermuda begged me to come in here, with the King's Pardon. My Lieutenant was informed yesterday that the Lark sloop intended to go out upon the account, and was even today to sign men on as pirates. I will make an example of her crew. They will be taken to the Court of Admiralty in Jamaica."

"I am Captain of the Lark", Vane shouted. "Captain Jennings, Captain Hornigold and I have been the King's strongest supporters. They have already been pardoned by Governor Bennett. Yet your move against my sloop is enough to make all the Brethren doubt your fair intentions. You have been misled by lies, you have angered the Brethren, and you have put your own career at risk for being so easily gulled."

"If the Lark was for the King, why was it hiding away from Nassau harbour? And why did she make off as we approached, nearly escaping us? No, we will keep both sloop and crew, and they can explain themselves to a Judge."

"I sent a pilot to bring the Lark back to town. They were at Bushes Key for careening. You must have noticed her bottom foul with weed. And as for them fleeing upon sight of you, you must know that you are the smallest ship to fly the King's flag in these parts. They probably thought you Spaniards with false colours. And even if they did think you the King's men, we are not yet pardoned, and must still fear the rope you are so eager to hang us with. Perhaps we could come aboard and clear these misunderstandings to everyone's satisfaction."

Captain Pearce, thoroughly confused by Vane's lies, shrugged and nodded brusquely to a sailor to drop a rope ladder for us. "Do we come unarmed", Jennings called up. "'Tis the custom to leave swords behind, isn't it true?"

"Do as you wish. You will be watched too closely to use them."

"Then I'll keep mine", Hornigold bellowed. "I feel naked with no steel about me." He pulled his white shirt over his hairy barrel of a chest, and adjusted his sword and pistols.

Jennings gripped my shoulder and muttered: "Read, I trust this arrogant King's coxcomb not at all. We three captains will go aboard well-armed, and then separate, so his crew is obliged to split to watch us. Take this knife, get through a gunport if you can, and free our comrades from this death ship. They may have to swim for it, yet that is better than dancing on air in Jamaica, isn't it true? Sorry I am to give you the hardest part, yet you are the best of us for something quiet like this. Will you do it?"

379

I swallowed my fear, nodded, and hung his sheathed knife on it's leather thong around my neck. Vane and I held the ladder while Jennings followed Hornigold aboard, and I then held it for Vane, who went up swift as a snake. I heard the voices of the pirate Captains move to different parts of the ship, and quickly arranged the unfurled sail, dressing it in my hat to fool any careless look.

Then I reached up, and found the lowest gunport open. With a quick prayer, I swung myself in, and on top of a gun. I hid next to it, gagging at the rancid stink of the ship. There were voices from the Gunner's room, and I crept closer, my heart in my mouth.

"We cannot hold out against all the pirates o' Nassau", one voice was complaining. "The Captain stirred them up for nought but his own hope of another promotion, though who was fool enough to give him the last, God knows."

"If he hangs a few, he'll put the fear o' God into the rest", another voice growled.

"We're here to bring the Pardon, not fight a war with 'em all. An' those we took yesterday seemed civil enough, an' claimed to be for the King loud enough. An' if so, then they've been long enough without a bucket o' water. I'll prime my pistol first, in case they're restive."

"Damn ye for befriending vermin, Gilmore."

I crept after the kind sailor, and as we headed towards the stern, picked up a heavy belaying pin. He filled a bucket from a barrel, and stopped outside a bolted door to prime his pistol. Praying his skull was tough enough to survive the blow, I took a deep breath, and smashed him over the head. There was a rush against the door, and when I flung it open, the pirates gaped at me, Rackam and Noah Harwood among them.

"Quickly. Captain Pearce wants to hang you all in Jamaica. Vane, Hornigold and Jennings are playing for time up above. The Lark is moored astern, and her canoa and longboat are tied to her still."

I led them to the nearest gunport, gave Rackam the

knife, and ran back to the gunport I had used before. I was soon back in Jennings' longboat, watching the pirates thrash towards the Lark, some nearly sinking, some swimming well and helping the one-armed Noah Harwood. They soon cut the canoa's cable, and holding her gunwales, they kicked her back towards Nassau.

I was delighted at this success, yet nervous of the commotion that would soon follow, and wondered whether Jennings had swapped their deaths for our own. Soon after, Hornigold stuck his head over the gunwales of the Navy ship, and I gave him the nod, and pointed to the canoa, now nearly swamped by wet men rowing for their lives. He grinned and saluted me.

Soon after, Captain Pearce screeched: "Search the ship!", and stuck his head over the gunwales to check the longboat.

"You lying dog!", I heard Vane curse him. "You've thrown them to the sharks. The Brethren will have your throats for this!"

"There they are, halfway to Nassau", a sailor pointed out.

"They escaped with your help!", Captain Pearce accused the pirate Captains.

"Nay man, we have been well watched, isn't it true?", Jennings protested. "And our deal still stands as far as I am concerned."

"Aye", Vane grinned. "Follow Governor Bennett in granting Pardons in Nassau tomorrow."

"Tomorrow be damned!", Pearce swore. "Do you think I trust the word of a pirate? You'll take your oath now, or sail to Jamaica to hang."

"With my men safe, I do feel better disposed towards the King", Vane answered him smoothly. "Yet we have not discussed the return of my vessel."

"Your vessel be damned!", Pearce exploded. "I know you for the most wanted man in the Caribbean, Charles Vane, and I'd get more credit for hanging you than pardoning you.

This Act of Grace is not as popular with the Navy as you imagine."

"Aye, for without pirates, the Navy won't be able to keep a quarter of every cargo they convoy", Hornigold chuckled.

"The Lark is mine", Vane insisted. "If you keep her, then you are as much a pirate as any in Nassau."

"I'll not be insulted on my own ship", Pearce shrieked, and both men went for their swords.

Jennings thrust himself between them, while Hornigold chuckled. "Come now Charles, you've been pinin' so long for the Pardon. Swallow your pride and take the oath, e'en though 'tis from this nincompoop. If we find he has maltreated your men, he'll not escape us. If he thinks he can keep the Lark, let him try." Then he shouted down at me. "Mark Read, will you take the King's Pardon?"

"With all my heart", I shouted back. I clambered up in time to see the confusion in the young Navy Captain's face. He had not expected the Pirate Captain to concern himself with anyone as lowly as me.

We were escorted to the Captain's cabin by sailors bristling with loaded muskets, and ushered inside. I had forgotten that a place could be so fine when there were servants to keep it so, the cleanliness belying the stench below decks. I studied a painting of a pretty young gentlewoman playing with a kitten, and thought it a timely reminder of what lay outside Nassau. If I left, I would have the same old struggle to stay alive, bending the knee to whoever would pay for my services. Still, if I wanted the Pardon, then I would have to be polite to this arrogant, foolish man, merely because his breeding had earned him an important post, despite his young arrogance.

Yet Hornigold had other ideas. "A fine thing it is, to be a gentleman, an' count yeself higher, because of all those that are lower."

The Navy Captain blustered, less sure of himself now that he was shut up alone with three notorious pirates, all heavily armed by his permission.

Jennings took up the attack. "I can see you cowering in here when the storm hits, the men slaving through the gale, your brave young Lieutenant, no doubt, at the helm."

"That's enough", Vane snapped. "Read and I would be pardoned of our piracies. 'Tis time this little game was over."

"Then I will take your oaths of loyalty to the King." Pearce rummaged in a great sea chest, and produced a Bible. Charles Vane and I put our hands on it, and duly promised to be honest men, loyal to the King, and pirates no more. Pearce signed and dated two pieces of parchment, and printed our names on them. Then he handed them over to us with the ink still wet, strode to his cabin door, and flung it open. His relief at finding his own armed men waiting there made him brave again. "Now get off my ship."

Vane smiled, shark-like and dangerous. "I will have the Lark back, so watch her like a hawk. I called you a thief when I was still a pirate. Now that I'm an honest man, I make no retractions."

"Get off my ship!", screamed the harassed Navy Captain, and with Hornigold's mocking thanks for his hospitality, we clambered overboard, and made our way back to Nassau.

PART 6: NASSAU 1718
Chapter 21: Hunters

Anne was waiting on the shore of Nassau harbour, with Jack Rackam, Noah Harwood, and the others we had rescued. They all helped heave the longboat ashore, and then hauled Jennings, Hornigold, Vane and I off to Cully's tavern. Many rums were then poured for me, and many friendships pledged, with many slaps on the back. I laughed when they spoke of my courage, for I was no hero compared to the Pirate Captains.

"You snivelling dogs!", Vane suddenly snarled from a corner, where he was drinking rum with pretty Tom Brown. "You congratulate yourselves for your lives, and forget that those bastards had every intention of taking them from you. I have met Captain Pearce, and know him for a coward, as well as a thief. I will take back the Lark, and have my revenge."

"Then I am with you!", Rackam declared. "That bastard would have hung us all!"

Vane eyed the other pirate Captains contemptuously. "And will you not aid me in recovering my stolen sloop? Jennings, Hornigold? Will you allow that coward to boast of how he humbled us?"

Jennings laughed. "The craftiest bastard to ever enter this Hellhole of a town, you are. What help could ye need from me to get the Lark back? How long it will take you is the only point to wager on."

"I accept the wager. By the end of next month I will have the Lark back, and Captain Pearce will run from the Caribbean with his tail between his legs. I will also find out who betrayed the Lark. The Pardon will die with him."

Henry Jennings was suddenly sober. "Though they did not trust us enough to send anyone but that fool, Pearce, I'm still committed to the Pardon. If you allow each man of the Brethren the right to choose his own fate, I will also seek to find who betrayed you."

"You no longer have the right to speak for the Brethren, not until you use your Pardon to light your pipe with. And as for the betrayal of the Lark, your jealousy of Jack Rackam..."

Without warning, Jennings threw his whole weight at Vane. The rickety table collapsed under them and they crashed to the floor, pirates leaping out of the way. Jennings rose with his hands locked around Vane's gullet. "You snake! Betray the Brethren for a woman, would I?"

Immediately Vane's crew drew steel. Jack cursed and knocked the cutlasses aside. "You are fools to fight like this. Even that idiot Pearce can get us at each other's throats. And Henry, I swear I haven't touched Anne Bonny..."

Jennings loosened his hands, and Vane catapulted to his feet, sword out. Jennings also drew steel. "I cannot abide Nassau with you here, Charles Vane. And yet I find myself not willing to leave."

Rackam kept his place between them. "Calm yourselves! Charles, Henry, I beg you. This is no time for personal animosities. We can only keep Nassau if we hold fast to the code of the Brethren, pardoned man or not."

Vane stepped back a pace. "We have already fought with cutlasses and pistols, Henry. Let us now fight for the soul of Nassau. I swear that in a month, this town will still be a pirate haven, strong against the King and his Governor. You do your best to make them honest. You can find me at the stone tavern by the water when you wish to concede defeat."

He stalked to the door, his crew with him. Yet before he stepped out into the sunlight, he turned and called out to me. "Mark Read! Your heart is here at Cully's with these cowards. Nevertheless, today you put me in your debt. You may remind me of that debt at any time." I nodded somewhat feebly, cowed to think of such a dangerous man owing me anything.

Rackam followed his Captain, yet at the door he

turned, and his eyes found Anne Bonny. She dropped her eyes to the floor, and he spun on his heel and stalked off. Yet when Jennings put his arm about her, she flushed as red as her hair, grabbed a rum bottle, and with the whole tavern watching, she took my hand, and pulled me out the door after her.

"Come with me to get my gear from the Coopers. I'm through with Henry Jennings. I have some pride, after all. How dare he be so insulted for my sake? No, he'd never betray the Brethren for a mere woman, damn him to Hell!"

"So you'll follow Jack Rackam?"

"While he sails with Vane, there is no place for me in his life. Vane hates me."

"He is not fond of any woman..."

"He's as jealous as Jennings is. Oh Mark, you must be blind. Vane and Jack were mates as buccaneers. He resents Jack's stubborn preference for females."

"You could rely upon Ma Davies."

"She has enough children to feed without wasting charity on me. No, I need to earn my own living. She said that with the Phoenix here, she'll need more meat. The traders are too expensive for the Navy, and if Vane blockades the island, they won't even have that. I'm a good shot and a fair tracker. Tell her you need me as a hunting partner."

I hesitated, knowing what the rovers would think. Yet I admired the young chit's independence, and did not want to destroy her frail hope. "For my part, I agree, yet as I work for Ma Davies, you must also ask her."

"She'll say no. I'm nothing but a wayward girl in her eyes. I need you to stand by me, to persuade her to accept me as an extra hand at a busy time. It is my only chance."

"She supplies my musket, ammunition and supplies."

"I have a matching pair o' pistols I could sell for a musket. I'm loath to part with them as I stole them from my father, and they are all I have to remember the old bastard by. But I'll sell them if you'll stand by me."

386

"The truth is, the cattle we have been hunting are scattered and wary now, and not breeding as fast as I had hoped. Her boys are skilled with their muskets now, and soon they may not need me at all."

"There are wild pigs in the lowlands, too fierce for Ma Davies' boys to hunt. And the old Cherokee who taught me to shoot, also taught me to smoke meat, keeping it better than salt does, without the cost, and with a better taste." She moved closer, and whispered into my ear. "You know this is my only chance. Please, Mary. Help me."

"You've hunted wild pig?"

"I hunted with the old Cherokee all through my youth, to keep our plantation in meat. He had none to teach but me, since the plantation boys were not allowed to roam, and the girls were sold on."

"Then we are in business, and Nassau in meat."

She laughed and tossed her red hair. "And I am free, and the sots at Cully's can gossip over some other harlot."

"And I wonder who will kill me for it, Rackam or Jennings."

"Oh yes, you'd be more than compromised. And you'd not want to strip and prove your innocence the easiest way. I know! I'll tell Henry I'm sailing home to my father, and avoid Nassau for a time."

Anne went down to the market by the dock, and managed to sell her father's matching pistols for a fair price to Captain Holford, who had always admired them. As the pardoned men had most of their possessions for sale, in an attempt to fund their passages home, she then bought a new flintlock cheap from Ned Ward, claiming it was a gift for her father, ensuring many heard her 'plans' for returning to Carolina. I bargained hard with Noah Harwood for dry powder, and Anne declared that she bought her shot off only one man in Nassau, and that was Patrick Carty, who cast his own.

'Twas already sunset, so I left her looking for the giant Irishman, and made my way back to Ma Davies' camp.

387

When I told her of my new hunting partner, she was entirely dubious. I explained that Anne had been taught to hunt as a child, that she claimed to be a good shot, and that she had her own flintlock and ammunition, and would be little additional expense. Ma Davies shook her head, and I insisted that I had not lost my head over the chit, and was not trying to mix business with pleasure, and told her of our plan to track the more dangerous wild pigs. Seeing Ma still against it, I declared that Anne was intent on escaping the attentions of the Brethren, and had to earn her passage home. She was still shaking her head when Anne ran up, dressed in an old shirt and trousers, her flintlock and a small bundle her only possessions. She threw herself at Ma Davies feet, thanking her for a chance to make her own way in the world, and the old woman suddenly smiled, and blessed her.

When Anne declared that she wished the Brethren to believe she had already sailed for Carolina, Ma Davies called all her children over, and they crossed their hearts, and swore secrecy. Anne wanted to leave immediately, yet Ma Davies insisted on being sure of the Navy contract first, so we agreed to wait until the following afternoon.

Despite the rain, Anne rose early the next day to farewell Henry Jennings, telling him she was returning to her father. She was enraged when he believed her, and when he asked her tenderly if she was not with child, she answered him so haughtily, that I shook my head when she told me of it. When I wondered why she had to constantly offend the most powerful men in Nassau, she only shook her head and laughed at me, unable to believe they could have any power over her.

Ma Davies returned just before noon, to report that the Phoenix had sailed in as promised, despite the weather. Captain Pearce had rowed ashore with a large number of armed men, to find hundreds of rovers waiting on the beach in the rain for their Pardons. Jennings had suggested Cully's tavern, and there Pearce had read out the entire Act of Grace, something he had not bothered with when pardoning me.

Jennings had done his best to smooth matters between the arrogance of the Navy, and the keen pride of the surrendering Brethren, helped by Captain Pearce's determination to keep the matter as brief as possible.

Then Pearce had demanded the names of all the merchant captains who had traded illegally with the pirates. Jennings had immediately insisted that those in the harbour had only come into Nassau once the Act of Grace was published. Pearce had then called Jennings a liar, and swore he had a right to requisition the cargo of every ship in the harbour. Jennings had quietly pointed out that if Pearce stole all their goods, there would never be another trader foolish enough to sail into Nassau, and that the town would starve.

Ma Davies had stepped in then, suggesting that she be the Navy's sutler in Nassau. Captain Pearce, unable to deal with such mundane matters, had told her to speak to the boy Lieutenant, and he had agreed to her supplying a beast a day for at least a week.

The next morning, despite the continuing rain, we set off into the forest, the boys with us. The brushwood and pine reminded Anne of South Carolina, and she described the dense forests of fir, cedar, beech, ash, and elm that covered the inland plain. She spoke of great chestnut and walnut trees that the settlers harvested by cutting whole trees down. She described the great rivers winding through the forest to the marshes of the low country, thick with ducks, geese, turkeys, pigeons, and partridges. I saw that Anne loved the place she'd been young in, as I loved the green valley of the Brent River, and I attempted to persuade her against London, for I knew how little that filthy, cut-throat city would suit her independent spirit.

After a day's march through hard rain, we climbed up to a low rise, where the boys knew of an over-hanging rock, which would shelter us from the worst of the weather. With the help of a little gunpowder, Anne made a blazing fire and a warm supper.

We found cattle tracks in the mud early the next

morning, and spent another day following them back along the trail. On my count, we fired together, and were all successful. Harry and I hit our beasts in the chest, John hit his in the shoulder, and Anne shot her beast through the eye. When I commended her on her luck, she merely shrugged.

The boys and I butchered and salted the meat, the most we had ever killed at one time. Anne cut strips from the hides, and used these to roughly stitch the hides together into strong sacks. With these slung onto long poles, we struggled back towards Nassau through rain and mud, heavily laden.

As soon as we laid the meat down at Ma Davies' camp, Anne insisted on the boys promising her again, on their honour, never to betray her continuing presence on Providence to the Brethren. They vowed solemnly, already smitten with her blazing presence, and she took what food she needed, and ran for my camp.

I sat under Ma Davies' shelter, and she feasted the boys and I right royally on turtle meat, pineapples and sweet potatoes. She reported that the pirates were surrendering in droves, every day a boatload rowing out to be pardoned by Captain Pearce. She told us that the heavy gales we had endured in the jungle had dragged the Phoenix's anchor, and driven her aground. Yet Captain Pearce had behaved so high-handedly, that not even Jennings would help get him off, and, wholly vulnerable to attack, he had been forced to wait for the tide.

Ma Davies also told us that pretty Tom Brown had heard of his father dying in Bermuda, and stolen away in a trading sloop, leaving Vane demanding news of him from every Bermudan sailor. Worse, Ben Hornigold had mocked Vane for losing his wager over the Lark, and the next day, his ship burned in the water, only the quick action of the Brethren saving all those who leapt overboard, unable to swim. Vane had furiously denied the resulting accusations, insisting that as Hornigold had helped to save his crew from Captain Pearce, he'd never play him such a scurvy trick. Ma Davies said Vane had taken to eating opium and cursing them all, swearing he was going out upon the account, despite having no vessel to sail in.

Before we left, Ma Davies took me aside, on the excuse of replenishing my camp's supplies of flour and coffee. "I have kept an eye out for Anne for some time now, and I've never known her without a paramour."

I made haste to inform her that Anne and I were friends and business partners, no more than that. She raised a sceptical eyebrow. "Neither of us wish it to be more than that", I insisted.

She shrugged and smiled crookedly. "If she really has decided to earn her own hard living, and 'tis true that you're no more than friends, then I believe you have saved that particular Magdalene."

"She is no saint, and no whore either. And though 'tis well she can earn her own bread for now, it will not come to much. The herds are thin and scanty, and if we over-hunt them, they will disappear altogether. Still, they should keep us going for a couple of months."

"Could they be trapped? I could ask any price for milk and butter, and as for cheese...And the meat would not be so tough if they were penned. It might be best to wait for the Governor to get here, since we might need his protection to stop any herd from being stolen."

"Is there news of the Governor?"

"Aye. Captain Pearce mentioned that he's due in July, before the hurricane season."

"His arrival will surely be good for business."

"I've sent my girls to the other side of the island for more salt to properly tan the hides."

"I claim no share in whatever profit they make. Neither will Anne."

"I thank you, and I will pray for you."

"We will go out hunting again tomorrow, to make the most of the time the Phoenix is here."

I wished her farewell, and then walked back along the beach, grieving for my own lost mother. For Ma Davies' piety had suddenly reminded me of her, and I could only pray that she had found a safe haven somewhere in this hard world. I wondered then if the New World could be a home for me. I might do better returning to the fresh green fields of England to search for her, now that I was pardoned.

As I reached my old camp, the rain eased, the clouds parted and the new moon shone out above us. Exhausted from our hard time in the forest, Anne and I soon rolled into our hammocks. We woke at dawn, covered with biting flies and reeking from yesterday's butchery. With the sun flaming over Hog Island, we took turns to strip, and wade into the sea, scrubbing the filth off with handfuls of sand, while the other watched for intruders.

As I scrubbed blood from my clothes, it struck me that I was taking risks I'd never taken before. I was forgetting to shave every morning, and expecting the boys not to notice that I grew no beard, and bathing only miles from Nassau, when discovery would have been disastrous to me. I wondered if Anne's friendship would prove to be my downfall, undermining my solitary strength, reminding me that I was not what I appeared to be.

Soon after, the Davies boys found us, and we trudged back into the dense heat of the jungle, and the constant thrum of innumerable insects. We tracked a small herd to a watering hole, and all crawled downwind, until we were close enough to choose our marks. I counted down, and we shot as one, the blast sending parrots screaming through the trees, and the herd tearing off down the path. Only two beasts were left behind, as Harry and I had missed. John dispatched his wounded cow immediately. Anne had once again shot a heifer straight through the eye.

"That was an impossible shot", I told her severely, slapping at the mosquitoes that descended upon me. "You can't be that good." Again, she merely shrugged.

With only two beasts to deal with, the butchery was soon over, and Anne suggested we leave the boys, and try for pork. She was adamant in declaring this hunting too dangerous for the boys, as she didn't trust their growing rivalry, and the boars were fierce. As we were not too far from their camp, we left them to the hard work of getting the meat back to their mother.

Then Anne and I followed a trail over gently rolling hills, pushing through thick forest to marshier ground that surrounded a swamp. In the late afternoon, Anne pointed out the tracks of pigs, and we followed them to a thick wallow of mud. She insisted they were creatures of territory and habit, and we could take them easily when they returned for their afternoon wallow on the morrow. She showed me the track of an enormous boar, and insisted we kill him first, for otherwise he would return and attack us when our backs were turned.

We set up camp for the night, set a smoky fire, and tied our hammocks high above the leeches. My fears that our solitude would throw us too close together were entirely unfounded, as we were more reserved than we had ever been. Anne talked of the necessity of making enough money to leave Nassau, before she ended up like the whores she scorned, yet she did not speak of Jack Rackam. I spoke of making enough to head home to England, to find my mother, yet I would not speak of my past.

We rested until the afternoon of the next day, and then chose our positions, lying along the over-hanging branches of a great jungle tree, directly above the pigs' wallow. When the thick heat and the mosquitoes seemed no longer bearable, the pigs finally filed down the track, a huge boar with curling tusks leading the way. I chose the largest sow without young, Anne counted down, and both our shots hit their marks, Anne's going straight through the boar's eye to the brain. As we commenced our butchery, I accused her of witchcraft, and she mockingly agreed with me. She then showed me how to construct an Indian trapeze, a triangle of wood lashed together with vines that allowed us to drag a great weight on one post along the narrow jungle path. We spent two hard days hauling the meat back to Ma Davies'

393

camp, arriving just before lunch.

After we'd splashed most of the gore off ourselves into the sea, I declared a few days rest, and proposed a visit to Nassau to buy more ammunition. I waxed lyrical on how good the first sip of Cully's ale would taste, and Anne spat at the sand. "I've drunk enough o' that watered-down dog's piss to last me a lifetime. I'll stay at your camp and make the most o' this freedom."

"You want to make the most of earning just enough to live, existing in the jungle like a savage, covered with blood…"

"I've been content this past week. I have indeed felt more free than when I lived in Nassau with Jennings, or in Carolina with my father. You can bring me back the town gossip, and a bottle of rum. And if you can find one cheap enough, do buy me another shirt. This is in tatters."

She walked off down the beach towards my camp, leaving me reclining under Ma Davies shelter, enjoying my pipe. The girls began smoking the pork over a greenwood boucan, and when Ma Davies returned, we ate a stew of pork and mango. She then showed me her accounts, and I asked her to keep our earnings safe, allowing me only enough to buy more powder and an ale. She insisted on paying for our powder, so pleased was she with our venture, and gave me a small bag of silver for our necessities. I told her Anne was playing hermit, and she nodded happily and said 'twas a sign she was searching her soul.

"If you insist, Ma, yet please don't suggest it to Anne."

The boys accompanied me into Nassau, and I made straight for Cully's, where the bulky, freckled John Auger remembered me from the morning of the Phoenix. He bought us a tankard each, and with the boys doing their best to look like men, we sat in the shade of the veranda. The sun shone bright for the first time in many days, steam rising from the mud of the road, and I asked for the news, explaining how long we'd been in the jungle.

"Well, there's a crowd of us pardoned men now, all looking for something to do with ourselves. Many have already left for home."

"That was good advice of Rackam's, for each man to take the Pardon with more than a few pieces of eight in his pocket. What will you do?"

"I'll find a trader who needs a good Captain." Just then the Phoenix sent her guns booming out across the water. "Their Gunner was found dead yesterday. Stabbed, an' with his throat cut for good measure. All suspect Vane, yet the Gunner had such a foul mouth for the Brethren, that most would've done it for a dram of rum."

I remembered the arrogant Gunner on the Phoenix and shrugged. "Is Vane still at the stone tavern? Have he and Jennings made up their quarrel yet?"

"Hell will freeze over first. Vane works hard at keeping his men from taking the Pardon, an' insists he's sailing out upon the account soon, 'though he still has no ship. He's been sending Rackam to seduce away the Phoenix's crew, not too hard a task given the fool those poor bastards sail under. Hornigold called Pearce 'a boy in too big a wig', to his face, an' he went so purple with rage, we thought he'd have a fit.

"An' did you hear the news of Tom Brown? A trader came in two days ago, declaring a man of that name accused of piracy in Bermuda. Vane is tearing his hair out, an' threatening to lead an expedition, and reduce the settlement there to rubble."

"Then he's raving."

"Don't underestimate Charles Vane", Auger advised me seriously. "If I was the Governor of Bermuda, I'd be taking damned good care of pretty Tom Brown!"

"Is there any news of our Governor's arrival?"

"Just that he's due in July, though by the four winds, many think us civilized enough. Those two young daughters of Ma Davies are the toasts of the town now that Anne Bonny has sailed. Seems there's a fashion for virgins an' marriage now we've reformed.

"These are their brothers, John and Harry. We've run out of powder, and need a bag of flints. Shall we try for them at the market then, lads?"

"Ma Davies boys, eh? There'd be no beef in Nassau but for her. An' don't worry about yer sisters. They have so many admirers that any who laid a rude hand upon 'em would lose it."

We walked down to the dock together, to find Ma Davies' daughters selling their baskets of meat, fruit and vegetables, rovers crowded about them, despite their high prices. The eldest was Sarah, a quiet, competent girl of fifteen, with her mother's self-assurance. The youngest, Rachel, was only thirteen, and could communicate only in whispers to her sister, or in flurries of giggles. Neither of them were beauties, yet they were the best Nassau had to offer, and their proud innocence was a great improvement on the desperate charms of the Nassau prostitutes.

A handsome young man with long fair hair and an Irish lilt threw an arm over Auger's shoulders. "Ahoy Auger, admirin' me darlin' yet again? How are ye, sweetheart? Do sell me one o' those mangoes, now. Ah, look at that sweet ripeness, such a waste on a bad man like meself, eh?" Sarah blushed, and I recognized the light in her eyes.

"Dennis Carty, ye young dog, are ye pardoned yet? Read, this is me new trading partner. Read sailed with Bellamy, and yer brother Patrick, an' rescued Vane's crew from the Phoenix. Now he hunts with these lads, brothers to the girl ye keep leering at. They need to buy dry powder."

"Holford's got powder. An' no talk o' leerin', I beg ye. 'Tis love that has me by the throat, an' I'll stand no rivals."

"Then you'd better speak to the girl's mother", I suggested dryly. "She's to church with them tomorrow morning."

"Church, eh? A hardened sinner like me could do with some prayin', and 'twould help persuade the lady to see me as a true son-in-law. An' so ye sailed with me brother

396

Patrick?"

"On my first cruise. He tended me when I was fevered and starving, and I was never happier to see any man rise from the dead. You must have heard of the loss of Sam Bellamy and all his Fleet."

"Aye, a great loss, that. Patrick would sail with none other. When I first thought him drowned, I wept that he'd spoken o' the Pardon, and made one cruise too many. Then as soon as I'd taken the oath for his sake, who comes up and abuses me for a turncoat, but him? And now he gathers with the rest o' Nassau, to marvel at the beauty o' me darlin' Sarah."

"Is he mad?", I asked Auger, smiling in spite of myself.

"We are all a bit moony just now. 'Tis the new freedom. We've had offers of marriage flying all week. Lucky there's no priest..."

"Are his intentions honourable, or do I warn Ma Davies?"

"Oh, please don't say anythin' to Ma", Sarah objected. "She's worried enough about us bein' here, an' he means no harm."

"I'll say nothing if he accompanies you all to church tomorrow."

"I'll be there!", Dennis Carty declared, adding to Sarah's blushes.

I asked Auger to introduce me to Captain Holford, for we still required powder. "Aye, Holford's equipped like a small army. That's him over there in the bright red waistcoat. Holford! How was yer cruise?"

"The worst yet. We spent too long in the lowlands of Virginia, and went down bad with fever. Five dead. That and no luck on the account have made honest men of us."

"I want ye to meet Mark Read, who rescued the crew of the Lark."

"Anne Bonny's friend, aint ye? A sad day when that pretty doxy left Nassau for home."

I examined Holford's powder, which he had stacked in small tubs, next to a fine display of artillery. The boys handled muskets and flintlocks with shining eyes, while we haggled. I ended up spending more of Ma Davies' silver than I had thought to, yet Holford threw in flints for nothing, so in the end we agreed.

I also found a sailor selling old clothes, and bought a sturdy shirt for Anne, as well as two out-of-shape tricornes to replace our ragged palmetto hats. I looked longingly at some mouldy books, yet could not justify paying the absurd prices demanded for them.

The wind then started blowing hard, making it unpleasant to linger on the waterfront. For Anne's sake, I thought to seek Jack Rackam while in town, and asked Auger if he was still drinking at the stone tavern.

Auger agreed that he was. "Yet I wouldn't recommend any place ruled by Charles Vane for a quiet ale. Rackam is always welcome at Cully's. Send one of the boys with a message, and meet him there."

"I'm not afraid of Vane. He still owes me for the Lark. Yet I don't think you boys should come with me to such a lawless place. Take our powder back to your mother's camp before the rain comes."

"We'll show Anne...", Harry enthused, and then he remembered his oath, and clapped his hand over his mouth. None seemed to have heard, yet I glared at him, bade them all farewell, and strode off for the pirate tavern.

I found Rackam staring moodily into a tankard of ale, two whores trying hard to amuse him. He waved them away, pleased to see me, and his first question was of Anne. "She left for Carolina weeks ago, and is certain to be with her father by now", I lied.

"She didn't even say farewell. I wish she'd given me the chance to speak to her before she left. Indeed, if I knew her direction, I'd seek her out. We go out upon the account any day now. Perhaps I'll make one last addition to my fortune, and leave the life. If only I knew what she wanted.

398

If you hear anything of her at all, even after the Governor gets in, leave a message with Old Peg at Cully's. I rely on her."

I made the required promise, and hoped that one day they would have a chance to declare themselves to each other, instead of to me. We drank a tankard together, Jack distracted and sad. When Charles Vane came in, I bought a bottle of rum, and made my farewells. I left Nassau, the full moon rising to light my path, and felt I had made the right choice in turning my back on the Brethren, despite my hard life as a hunter.

I called out when I came near the campsite, and was surprised to find fish grilling on the open fire, and no one near. For an instant I felt a touch of fear for her, left here alone. Then I heard a noise in the bushes, and glancing over my shoulder, felt my jaw drop. Anne stood, arms akimbo, feet planted wide, her hair cropped into a ragged mess. She was grinning with delight at my face, and looked for all the world like someone's scapegrace son.

"Your beautiful hair!"

"I cut it myself with a fish-knife and no mirror! Now, tell me the news o' Nassau."

I told her all that I had heard, and she listened carefully, especially to news of Jack Rackam. "I wish him success", she said quietly. "Yet I'm in no hurry to see him. The freedom o' this life in the forest is more than anything I've known before."

"Aye, the freedom of mosquitoes and leeches. A grand life." I uncorked the bottle of rum and passed it to her.

"You've never known what it is to be obliged to be charming. I prefer to do what I have to, and make no excuses for it. And I'll get out o' this pigsty of a town, even if I have to swim to bloody England!"

"I'm convinced that you can make what you want of your life, as long as you are certain of what you want."

"Are you certain o' what you want? It seems strange to me that your greatest concern is to appear to be what you are not. Being a woman is hard, but it's better than being neuter, and it seems to me that that is what you are, neither male nor female."

"I chose the freedom that men take for granted, not being able to restrict myself to the narrow confines women live in. Yet I was lucky that my masquerade started so young, and I was bred to breeches. None ever guessed I was aught but a ragged scrap of a lad, even when I sailed in the Queen's Navy."

"Tell me o' that time."

"You know I dislike speaking of my past."

"You dislike conceding that you're really female, something I've learned to appreciate, despite the dangers. Now, tell me how you lived as a sailor."

"Those were hard times, fighting for Good Queen Anne. I was lucky to survive. I'd not recall them merely for your amusement."

"Not for my amusement. For my instruction. I feel that your life has many lessons for me."

"I doubt that my strange and twisted life can teach you anything."

"You are wrong. There is much I would learn from you. And as I am your only friend, tell me o' your life as a sailor, Mary Read."

Chapter 22: Adam Cormac

I told Anne of my life as a sailor in Queen Anne's Navy, of sailing against Ostend and the Pretender, of the death of Bill Search, of the loss of old Noah Harwood, and of Sally Pridden's bitter determination to be a whore. The rum bottle was empty and the new moon had long since set when I was startled out of my reverie by some beast screeching in the forest behind us. The fire was low, and I was glad Anne could not see my tears in the darkness.

"Don't stop there! You must tell me the rest o' the story. You said you marched as a soldier..."

"I have talked enough. In truth, speaking of all this confounds me."

"I swear you can trust me to tell no one."

"And I have no choice but to trust you, since I like you too much to murder you in cold blood."

"I've been hatching a plan since you spoke to me o' your childhood. You must tutor me in the finer details o' your deception, so I can sail with the Brethren. I've always been one o' them at heart."

"Don't be a fool, Anne! I was raised to be a boy. I am tall and thin and small-breasted. I'm broad of shoulder from a lifetime of hard work. You look like a woman, speak like one, walk like one, and flirt if there is a man within eyesight, even if 'tis only me."

"I sailed as a man to get here. It's not so hard, to swear and swagger. I know I can do it. And I've already hacked off my hair."

"Listen to me, girl! Sailing with the Brethren is needlessly dangerous. Vane is the only pirate Captain still successful, and he'll drop you overboard if he finds you aboard his ship. And he'll believe that Jack Rackam brought you aboard for his own pleasure, and maroon him on a spit of sand."

"And so I must be as convincing as you are! I'll make

myself a horn like yours to piss through, and those sea sponges are always washing up on the beaches here..."

"Remember how I fared with fate, Anne. Here I am, a known thief, and yet as poor as ever."

"I won't slave for pennies as you do! And I'll make my stake without whoring for it, and leave this dusty town. And you will help me, Mary Read. For I'll try it without your help, you know that. And it will be just one cruise."

I saw she was adamant. Perhaps I would have refused, but for the fate of Sally Pridden. I could not bear to see this proud young woman humbled, as she had been.

"'Tis true Vane would take you to be rid of the debt he owes me. Yet Jack Rackam would be sure to recognise you."

"Jack knows me as a big-breasted redhead with promising eyes. I'll pretend to be my own younger brother to cover the resemblance. The one person I must avoid is my husband. He's seen me dressed as a man before. But he's terrified o' Vane, and never goes near the stone tavern."

"And what of the Davies boys? They've seen you in trousers. They would certainly recognize you."

"I may have to take them into my confidence. It will be safer than saying nothing, and meeting them on the street when I'm Adam Cormac."

"Adam Cormac?"

"My father's name. The name I'd have worn if I'd been born a boy."

"I thought you hated your father."

"If I'd been a son rather than a daughter...He always wanted a son. And I look so much like my mother. It must have been hard having me as a constant reminder o' what he'd lost. Now, help me bind my breasts. I will begin my life as a man now, with no one to watch me but you, and you must tell me when I give myself away. I've also brought leather and needles, so I can make a pissing horn like yours."

"I will help you as much as I can. Yet we will test

your disguise before we send you to sea with pirates. You must spend the entire afternoon in the stone tavern with Vane's crew, including Jack Rackam, without being discovered. And now you can discover how uncomfortable it is to have your breasts constantly bound in this tropic heat."

Having gained her point, Anne slept for what was left of that night, while my own thoughts roamed restlessly through my past, filling me with loss. I mourned for my mother and Sally, knowing how slim my chances were of ever seeing them again.

Then Anne laughed in her sleep, and I wondered if I had found a true friend. Her youth I held against her, for she was impulsive and careless, yet she had courage and spirit, and if a month at sea as a man did not teach her prudence, nothing would.

The Davies boys arrived at dawn, amused to see Anne's raggedly cropped head, and all admiration when she announced she was in training to be a pirate. They swore on their lives to keep their mouths shut, even to their own mother, and I insisted that we begin her training by calling her 'Adam', and treating her like one of us.

The boys showed us an old Indian trail that led into the green half-light of the dense pine forests, where yellow snakes slithered out from under our feet, hummingbirds flitted about like living jewels, and mosquitoes sang constantly about our ears. We had to tramp almost a week through the low, gently rolling hills, and our supplies had nearly run out, before we came to fresh cattle tracks. We crept up on them soon after, and John whispered that he recognised the lead bull. This worried me, for it meant there were even fewer herds on the island than I had hoped. All four of us then fired on my signal, and two heifers went down.

As we fell on the dying beasts, 'Adam' chided Harry for his impatience, and told him that his aim would never improve if he didn't calm himself before killing. I asked if she had any hints to improve my marksmanship, and she

403

said I should squeeze the trigger more gently, and not be so afraid of the recoil of my old musket.

We sent the boys back to Nassau with the meat, and then 'Adam' and I continued into the depths of the jungle, after the wild pigs. They came at noon to the same waterhole, and 'Adam' shot a great sow, while I missed entirely. We cleaned the sow, cut off the best meat, and made a trapeze to haul it back.

Emerging from the dense jungle to the clean salt smell of the open sea, we were lucky to find a great swathe of sea sponges left stranded by the high tide. Unwilling to let Ma Davies into her secret, Anne elected to collect as many as she could, and meet me at my camp. I fetched the Davies boys to help haul the meat around the shore for the girls to smoke, and returned to my camp by nightfall, the boys with me.

At dawn the next day, we made our way into the forest again, and we stalked the nervous cattle for a week before we could catch them downwind. Our success was complete when we crept up on them, and at 'Adam's' signal, all four of us killed together.

'Twas a hard haul back, and when we finally had the meat at Ma Davies camp, I decided on an ale at Cully's. I returned to find Anne at my camp, and she kept watch while I washed off the worst of the butchery in the gentle sea. Once my clothes were half-dry, I made my way back along the white beach, and into the putrid stench of Nassau.

I found Patrick Carty and John Auger drinking ale in the smoky darkness of Cully's tavern. Patrick kindly bought me a tankard, and congratulated me on my hunting venture. "First salted beef, now smoked pork. In God's name, I was well sick o' fish!"

"'Twas Ma Davies' scheme. Her boys know the forest, and I taught them to shoot."

"She's a shrewd woman, that one."

"The women in that family are the canniest in the Caribbean", a merry Irish lilt informed me, and handsome

Dennis Carty sat next to his brother, pulling Sarah Davies onto his knee. I frowned to see the girl on such familiar terms with the rovers, yet Dennis laughed at me. "Ye know me darlin' Sarah. Ye might not know that she's even cannier than her Ma. For in exchange for her sweet smiles, I've pledged meself, body an' soul, an' agreed to marry her when the Governor comes in."

Auger shook his head in mock sadness. "Ye'd think that with all the wicked harlots on this isle, Dennis might have left this angel alone, an' yet he speaks as though she has the best of the bargain."

Patrick Carty hugged his brother, and kissed the girl, while Dennis laughed. "Get yer hands off me sweetheart, Patrick. Her Ma insists on a true weddin'. We've no priest, so we'll have to wait for the Governor. And we'll be married where the Spaniards burned down the old church, on consecrated ground."

"And they'll name their first boy after me", Auger boasted.

"An' ye won't have long to wait", Dennis crowed, flinging his arms about Sarah. And although she blushed at this public announcement of her pregnancy, she was so aglow with love for her handsome man and their coming child, that a vicious envy of the girl suddenly swamped me. I looked away, to find Patrick eyeing me strangely. Ben Hornigold joined us, and insisted on buying rum to toast the young couple. I added my congratulations to those of the rovers, telling Dennis that these blessings were his because he'd chosen the honest life.

"Aye, an' because David Soward has made Auger master o' the Mary, an' Auger has made me First Mate, to keep us both honest. Ah, to be no longer rovin' the Spanish Main with me brothers, desperate and dangerous", Dennis sighed, teasing Sarah.

"We can always glory in Vane's adventures", Auger grinned.

"Is he out on the account again?"

405

Patrick grinned. "Ye haven't heard? A couple o' weeks ago. Vane, Rackam and ten others stole a pettiauger from the beach..."

"My pettiauger!", Hornigold reminded him bitterly. "The only boat the bastard left me after burnin' me ship!"

Patrick shook his head. "I never thought that was Vane. Not after what you did for him over the Lark. Anyway, Vane sailed her west to Andros Island, and snoopin' about, found a Jamaican trader moored for the night at Freshwater Creek. They went straight up an' over her sides, an' the sloop was theirs before the poor old Captain woke. Vane kept him for better knowledge o' the sloop, promisin' to give her back when he stole a faster vessel."

"'Twas neatly done", I commented.

"Aye, yet the next morn', Vane sailed her secretly into this harbour, moorin' on the other side of Potter's Key, where Captain Pearce couldn't see him. Rackam sailed the pettiauger in secretly that night, beachin' in front o' Vane's tavern, where he spoke so sweetly o' the free life to those who'd refused to surrender, that over twenty men joined Vane's Company. Hornigold's pettiauger an' most o' the longboats an' dories of Nassau were left at Potter's Key for the sloop's crew to row back to Nassau in. Vane gave one sailor a warnin' for Captain Pearce, promisin' him death if he stayed in the Bahamas, and darin' him to try and keep the Lark.

"Pearce immediately called all the traders in the harbour to him, yet the next day, Vane took another Jamaican sloop comin' in from the east, removed her cargo, an' cursin' her for another ill-sailin' pig o' a boat, declined keepin' her. Her Captain complained to Pearce, who sent a manned pinnace to surprise the pirates. Yet Vane was keeping a careful watch, an' the Navy men ran with smallshot up their arses. Pearce then came stormin' in here, red o' face an' foul of temper, an' ordered Jennings to attack Vane, in the name o' King George." Patrick grinned again, while the rest of the company chuckled.

406

"Jennings had already grown tired o' that man's arrogance, an' he pointed out that he was in the middle o' an ale, that Vane would have a well-fortified battery set up on Potter's Key by now, an' that he had no desire to be killed doing work that the Navy was too frightened of."

"He called him a coward?"

"A lily-livered, lubberly, son of a whore, as I remember", Hornigold chortled, and when the men around the table laughed, he took over the story. "The arrogant young fool swept Jennings' tankard to the floor, and they drew on each other, Pearce, a loaded pistol; Jennings, his sword. Half the men in the room drew steel with Jennings, and Pearce went out backwards, fear in his face, every man in the tavern abusin' him for his cowardice.

"The following morn', Pearce demanded an eighth o' the merchandise carried by any merchantman that wished to be in his convoy. After he had loaded the Phoenix, he escorted them out o' the harbour, an' they immediately came across Vane chasin' a sloop off Harbour Island. Vane sheered off, knowin' the Phoenix could both out-sail and out-gun his stolen sloop. The lucky trader he had been chasin' joined the convoy, sailin' with the Phoenix until she saw them all safely past the Bahamas at sunset, headed north for New York.

Patrick Carty poured Hornigold another ale, and took over the story. "Pearce had sent the Lark out weeks ago, under some o' his own men, with a cargo to trade at Saint Augustine's. Three days after seein' him sheer off, Pearce watched Vane sail the Lark back into Nassau harbour, guns loaded, a red flag flying at her masthead, no quarter offered. Pearce must have pissed himself with fear, for the Lark can out-sail the Phoenix. So Pearce hauled anchor an' abandoned Nassau to Vane. Vane then declared himself Governor, an' has been swaggerin' up and down the town, settlin' old scores, drunk on his own arrogance.

"When he sailed out on the account again, he left Holford's sloop burnin' in the water, and Jennings' Bathsheba adrift on the rocks of Hog Island. Yet he did not forget to leave the Jamaican sloop with her old Captain, as he had promised. Soon after, he took John Cockram's sloop, leavin' our old mate marooned on Crooked Island when he refused to join 'em, makin' mock o' Rackam's plea for brotherhood between those pardoned, and those still out on the account.

"After Vane sailed, Pearce stole back into Nassau with a convoy o' merchant ships. He spent the next few days moored by the old dock, havin' his men scrub down the Phoenix, trying to exert what authority he had left, while they deserted or died o' fever."

"I heard nothing of any fever."

"The old churchyard is full of new graves", Sarah said quietly. "Those of us raised here hardly suffer, but the Navy's sailors die like flies. An' old Governor Sawney was buried by the Brethren not three days ago, though 'twas not fever that took him, but the rum."

Hornigold took another swallow of ale and continued with the story. "Vane knew he had Pearce runnin', so he just sailed in with his next prize, the John and Elizabeth, and anchored her in the middle o' the harbour, red flag flying. Pearce did nothin'. The followin' day, Rackam and a boat-load o' rovers rowed merrily in for shore leave, and Pearce contented himself with firin' on them from a safe distance. Rackam came visiting here, drank a couple o' bottles o' rum with us, happy to hear Jennings had managed to float the Bathsheba off the rocks. He says Vane is mad with anger at our surrender, an' swears we all deserve his vengeance.

"Vane re-named the John and Elizabeth, callin' her the Ranger, after his first ship. He appointed Robert Deal, his new favourite, as her Captain, without asking his crew for a vote. Rackam, as his Quartermaster, is furious, caught between Vane's arrogance and the anger o' his men.

"Yet Vane celebrated that night at the stone tavern, an' when he rowed out o' Nassau the next morn', he had seventy-five more men with him, enough to make his Fleet the Navy's nemesis in these waters. That afternoon, two incomin' traders sailed straight into Vane's hands, and Pearce did nothin' more than fire off a few guns. The followin' day, the pirate Fleet sailed, Vane loudly promisin' Pearce that the Phoenix would burn in the water.

"'Twas only three days after, that the Phoenix's carpenter accidentally tipped over his bucket o' boilin' pitch in the forecastle, and the fire was only just contained. Though he could prove nothin' against him, Pearce had the man whipped. And now his crew hates him for keepin' them dying o' fever in the Bahamas, while he makes himself rich from the convoys.

"The next day, he gathered some merchantmen together, and went to sail out, yet his pilot left him grounded on a shoal. None o' us would help him, an' he had to wait for the tide to lift him off. Those must've been anxious hours for him, for if Vane had returned, he could've had all those vessels for the askin'. We were tempted to take 'em ourselves, an' debated it all that afternoon, yet decided that not even Pearce's idiocy and Vane's darin' could get us back on the account."

Auger sighed, and I guessed that Jennings had been hard pressed to talk them out of it. I could imagine how hard the reformed men were finding it on Providence, with few merchantmen taking them on as crew, and their money spent. I guessed that Jennings was buying most of them their beer.

Hornigold continued: "As soon as Pearce sailed out, Vane sailed in lookin' for him, an' he is still peacockin' about, attractin' more o' the pardoned men back to him, declarin' there will be no Governor in Nassau but himself."

"He's in town now? And Rackam?"

"Aye, Handsome Jack's in too."

"I must speak with him urgently. Gentlemen, I bid you good day. Sarah, Dennis, congratulations again."

With the arrogant Charles Vane so very successful, I wished to stay away from the pirate tavern, yet I had to speak with Jack. I saw Peg's filthy brat playing cats cradles in the sun on the veranda, handed over a coin, and gave a simple message, asking Jack to meet me at the small cove

409

past Ma Davies' camp.

I made my way quickly along the shore, waving to Ma Davies as I ran past, wondering if she knew Sarah was pregnant, and if she blamed the chit. I found 'Adam' waiting for me at our camp, and when I said Jack was meeting me at her old cove, she ran back with me, and hid in the bushes behind the rock pool.

Almost immediately, Jack arrived, looking wildly about him. "Peg's child said a woman was waiting for me..." he began.

I thought coldly of Peg's filthy brat, and knew it was not at all fooled by appearances. I wondered if Peg knew too, and if I would have to bribe her to keep her mouth shut. For an instant, I believed that remembering my past had changed something in the way I walked or talked, yet I covered my confusion as best I could and lied. "I asked you to meet me here, and called you Anne's friend. I must have confused the brat."

"She's not here?" His disappointment was so keen, I wondered that Anne could be so hard-hearted as to stay hidden.

"Her young brother turned up just after Anne sailed for Carolina. He had heard she was here, and came looking for her. He's a brave lad, much like her in looks and temper, and wants to join you on the account. I'd call in that favour Vane owes me..."

"Vane is convinced that Tom Brown will hang, and talks wildly of raiding Bermuda. I'm afraid of bloody retribution..."

"Which any must take part in who sail with him."

"I am the only one who dares to risk his anger. And the men's distrust of him grows daily. There was no vote taken for the Captain of the John and Elizabeth."

"I heard it from Hornigold."

"Yet Vane's scheme was brilliant. The Captain of the John and Elizabeth, Benjamin Bill, had been abusing the pardoned men, insisting that if traders signed on sailors from

410

the Bahamas, they risked mutiny. Captain Pearce liked him so much, he assigned Bill three Navy sailors to replace those of his crew dead of fever. Then he asked Bill to make a trading voyage on his behalf, to sell some of the merchandise he had collected from his convoys. Yet Robert Hudson, a Phoenix deserter now sailing with us, betrayed the venture, and told Vane they were sailing through Saint Augustine to Charles Town.

"Vane had carefully plotted the re-taking of the Lark, wanting her un-harmed, and full of Pearce's cargo. We paid her crew well to hand her over without a fight, and join us. The same day we took the Lark back, we found the John and Elizabeth two leagues off Abaco Island, and went over her side in the middle of the night, knives at the throats of the ship's watch before they could scream. We found wine aboard, and once drunk, decided to keep her. Vane re-named her the Ranger, after our first ship, and we christened her liberally with Captain Bill's wine.

"We were sailing her back to Nassau when Robert Hudson spotted Gilmore, a prisoner in the hold of the Ranger. He was the Phoenix's Boatswain, and the man you hit on the head with a belaying pin, when freeing us from the Phoenix. Hudson clapped a pistol to Gilmore's head, and swore he'd blow his brains out for sending him out on the Phoenix's mainyard in a storm, when he was nought but an untried seaman, pressed the day before at Liverpool, and half-dead of seasickness.

"Vane has always been a stickler for his word, and he refused to let Hudson kill Gilmore, since Gilmore had surrendered with the rest, on promise of his life. Insisting that the quarrel wait to be settled in Nassau, he kept Gilmore close by him until they moored here. Then a duel was fought on the beach, Hudson drew first blood, and Vane stepped in and declared the matter finished. Then he sent the bleeding Gilmore into Nassau with me, as well as any other man who would not join us.

"I know you have no love for Charles Vane, yet he

411

lives his life by his own code, and in his own way, is a man of honour. He swore he'd out-face Pearce and re-take the Lark. And he protected Gilmore, and returned a Jamaican Captain his ill-sailing trader."

"He is not without honour, Jack. Yet he appointed Robert Deal as Captain of the Ranger, and your crew is furious."

"It's true he is so arrogant, he cannot see they will vote him down soon. And then I shall have my own ship, and the pick of the men. Yet in truth it will be a sad day for me."

"What did he ever do to earn your affection in the first place?"

Jack scowled and looked away, and then shrugged. "I was but a boy when he found me. I had deserted from a merchant vessel in Port Royal, after her Captain whipped me half to death." He pulled his shirt up, and though I had seen stripes before, I'd rarely seen scars like these. "I had nothing but the rags I swam off in, and starvation and fever had me too near death to even beg for sustenance. I lay in the gutter between two Port Royal taverns, where Vane saw some scurvy seadog kick me out of his way. He lost his temper, insulted the bastard, fought and killed him. Then he threw a whore a doubloon to care for me, and I was carried to a room and left to die quietly in a corner, glad of the luxury. But Vane remembered me, and when he found that the whore was neglecting me, he took me aboard the Ranger, and cared for me himself. He saved my life, and we were comrades from that time on.

"He had been privateering for Queen Anne against the French and the Spanish. When the war ended, and his prize money was spent, he took trusted men from his old crew into the Bay of Campeche as logwood cutters. After a year, they were chased out by Spaniards, and took up hunting the wild cattle on the Mosquito Coast. There were small bands of rovers throughout that wilderness, hated by the Indians, who would kill a lone man on sight. They

412

learned to stick together, and made oaths and pacts that bound them into Companies. Everything they had they shared, and every decision was voted on. They must have been hard years, yet Vane and his mates were always happy to recall them. Gunpowder was like gold to them, and they became crack shots. To hit a coin spinning in the air was nothing for one of the Baymen.

"Some of the Companies raided Indian villages, others small Spanish settlements, taking food, guns, gunpowder and women. At least Vane left the women alone. Then the Captain of a merchant ship tried to cheat them, Vane killed him, and kept his ship, renaming her the Ranger. He saved my life soon after. Soon we had a Fleet raiding up and down the Spanish main. And when Jennings wanted a hand to take the Spanish treasure, he called us in. He told us of Captain Mission, and that we weren't the first men to try and live masterless and free. We sailed here with money, ships, and a life we could not surrender.

"Through all of it, Charles Vane and I were mates. I saved his life as often as he saved mine. And when I recall his care of me in Port Royal, I wonder that I can even think of leaving him."

"Yet he has changed, Jack. He is not the same man you first met. His arrogance has made him think he is your master. He treats his men not like equals, but vassals, and he controls his crew through fear. He is now worse than the man who kicked you when you lay dying. No, don't shake your head. You know 'tis true."

"You still don't understand, Mark. When they were Baymen, they lived as they had to, and relied on each other. Vane was one of those who saw his mates as more than brothers. But as rovers, we sailed into ports where whores could be bought for a piece of eight and an ale. And when many of us preferred them, Vane resented us for it. His comrades insisted on keeping their affections private, and then hidden, and Vane's pride soured on him. The men he now favours are those who are utterly loyal to him, and the

Brethren mean less to him than his favourites."

"You are a good man, Jack Rackam, and I am proud to know you. I will pray that you will soon sail under your own conscience."

"You are a strange man to talk of praying for pirates", he laughed. "Will you stay in Nassau now you are pardoned?"

"I would like to meet the new Governor. I have heard great things of Captain Woodes Rogers. If he found me useful, I would like to work for him. I write a fair hand. Perhaps he will need a clerk."

"That puts you and I on contrary sides of the Admiralty courts."

"We are friends, nonetheless, I swear it. If I can, in good conscience, help you, I will get word to Mistress Peg."

"And if you hear anything of...her." He turned away, his heart in his eyes. Then he had himself in hand again. "We are careening our Fleet. That will take some weeks. Our Company is large, and Vane won't take on an untried boy now. When we come back from the next cruise, we might have more vessels to man, or, worse luck, gaps in our Company. Bring Anne's brother to us then. If I like him, I'll speak for him." He clapped me on the shoulder and strode back towards Nassau.

Then 'Adam' was standing by me, looking after him, and despite the ragged hair, ragged clothes, and dirt, I could clearly see the woman in her. We returned to our camp to continue hunting in the morning, and I was resolved that Jack should not see 'Adam' until all the woman had gone, and only a bold young rover remained.

We walked out of that jungle more than a month later, in baggy canvas trousers, long calico shirts and leather jerkins made from badly cured cow hide. Anne had become a dangerous rascal, with a cock-sure swagger, mouth grim and eyes level, carrying her flintlock as though 'twas her best friend. I did my best to persuade her to forgo the risks of piracy, yet her dreams were grand, and she would not be

414

dissuaded.

Then I reminded her of the test she had to face, an afternoon with Vane and Rackam at the stone tavern, and she laughed and agreed. We did not look like anyone's idea of women, and sure that if we convinced them at first, they'd never doubt her afterwards, we stayed filthy, using the butchery as part of our disguise.

I had sickened of the life of a hunter, and as I had saved enough silver, I resolved to stay at my camp and await the coming of Governor Rogers. We left Ma Davies with the meat, took all the silver we had earned, and strode into Nassau in the late afternoon.

'Adam' was eager to buy back her father's pistols, and when she found Holford, was pleased he still had them. Holford accepted her as Anne Bonny's young brother, and sold her the pistols for much more than he had paid Anne for them. We could say nothing of the cheat, however, without exposing 'Adam', even though it cost her most of her silver.

Then we made for the stone tavern, to find Jack at a back table, half a bottle of rum before him, yawning at the doxy on his knee. When he saw us, he gave her a push, and she flounced off upstairs, giving 'Adam' the eye as she passed. Jack clapped me on the shoulder and shook hands with 'Adam', not seeming to notice any untoward resemblance. He poured us both a rum, Vane joined us, and when I asked after the success of their cruise, Jack grinned and saluted him with his glass.

"No one in the Caribbean can stand against the Lark and the Ranger. We did well, though there was bad luck at the beginning. The fever took some of our recruits, and we didn't leave until the second week of April. I looked for you then, thinking this lad might join us, but Ma Davies said you'd not be out o' that jungle for weeks."

"We had to press a couple of blacks from Eleuthera to make up the numbers", Vane drawled.

Jack's jaw tightened, yet he continued the tale. "A couple of days into the cruise, we took a trading sloop from

Bermuda. Their Negro deckhand joined us willingly enough, but there was nothing else aboard. Three hours later, we took another Bermudan ship, the Diamond, off Rum Key. We took three hundred pieces of eight off her. A good haul."

"Tell them of Nat Catling, Jack", Vane drawled, and all the good humour left the handsome rover. Vane shrugged, his cold blue eyes as hard as ice, and took up the story himself. "The Diamond was a Bermudan ship, so I asked news of my mate, Tom Brown. Mister Catling had the bad manners to wish him hung, so I put a noose about his neck, and hauled him up to give him a taste of it. He danced beautifully, yet Jack here has such a soft heart, he begged me for the scurvy dog's life. Then as soon as he hit the deck, the fool cursed us again. Featherstone slapped him with the flat of his sword, and when Catling began to weep for fear of his life, Jack stopped the fun again. We ended up cutting away their mast and bowsprit, and started a fire that most likely scuttled her."

Jack's mouth was a grim line, yet he continued his account of their adventures. "We holed up on Crooked Island, it being well-protected from the season's storms. The men voted in Yeats as Captain of the Ranger, Robert Deal to be his Quartermaster." Vane scowled at him, yet Jack avoided his eyes.

"We were drinking afterwards, when Deal spotted a pretty sloop, the Betty, sailing in. We upped anchor, and as she came in, unfurled just enough sail to cut her off, hauled up the Jolly Roger, fired a shot over her bows, and she struck her colours without a fight. We found only provisions aboard, and let her go. Then we caught the wind to Whale Key, where we took the Samuel, another Bermudan ship, the Penzance, and a Jamaican trader. A good day's work."

"Don't forget that we made the Bermudan crew beg for their lives", Vane sneered.

Jack ignored him. "A few days later, we took the Fortune off Crooked Island. They too struck as soon as they saw our flag, and her Captain was polite enough to show us where he had stowed seven casks of liquor. We sailed back here, and sold the liquor to Nat Taylor, who keeps this tavern. We cruised back to Exuma, took another Bermudan sloop..."

"And beat them", Vane interjected again. The tension between the two men was suddenly razor-sharp and I could see that Vane could not understand Jack's refusal to torture poor sailors for Tom Brown's sake.

Jack threw back another dram of rum, and again continued his story. "The Bermudans had no money or cargo. We met at Stocking Island to distribute our small plunder, and then voted ourselves satisfied with the cruise, and deserving of a few days shore leave. We came here, and I looked for you, but we soon put to sea again. We went back to Crooked Island, had no luck for a week, and then came across a Spanish sloop beating to windward. 'Twas laden with enough royales to gladden the hearts of all the new men. But her Captain insulted us, and we burnt his ship, putting all her men in their longboat..."

"Because Jack here told our Company 'twould be bad luck to let them all burn with her", Vane sneered. "Sailors are so superstitious."

"Then we went by Saint Christopher and Anguilla, took a brigantine and a sloop, with nothing more than provisions from both, and voted again that the cruise was over, and it was time to return to Providence and spend our royales..."

"And wait for the Governor". Vane raised his glass. "Here's damnation to him, and to the King, and to all the higher powers."

I had already emptied my tankard, so did not have to drink the toast, yet 'Adam' joined in with gusto. "If you are signing up more men, I'd be proud to sail with you, Captain Vane. I'm a crack shot, and can swing a cutlass."

"If you've half your sister's spirit, you'll make a grand pirate", Jack grinned.

"Yet we have little need for untried boys", Vane objected.

417

"I have hunted with this lad for months now", I stated firmly. "He is the best shot I have ever seen. And he has a brave heart and a ready laugh, even amidst the mud and leeches. I'd have talked him away from you if I could. Even I can see he was born to be a rover. And 'twould even things between us, Captain Vane."

"Perhaps the men will vote to sign him on for half a share."

"Half a share!", 'Adam' objected. "There are many companies sailing out before the Governor comes, and they'd be pleased to take me for a full share."

I sat, stunned at the chit's impertinence, having lectured her constantly on the virtues of keeping her mouth shut. Yet Vane laughed.

"You must not think I ask it out o' foolishness. It's because I know my own worth. I may be the youngest here, and may be the least experienced at sea, but I'll stake my skill with a pistol against any in the Company, including you, Captain Vane."

"Just because you've practised hitting targets at home, you conceited brat, don't think that qualifies you to challenge me", Vane hissed. "I must accept, yet shoot well boy, or I'll have you beaten for your impudence. Jack, load your pistols for me. We'll shoot with two pistols each, into that door there. The man who can place his shots closest, wins. Nat, do tell your lad to see that no one walks in at the wrong moment."

'Adam' winked at me, and I glared back as she began loading her father's pistols. The pirates cleared the way, and Captain Vane stood to go first. He shot off one pistol, aimed very carefully at the bullet hole in the door, and fired again. The holes were scarcely an inch apart, and the pirates cheered.

'Adam' stood then, and bracing herself with her feet well apart, she calmly drew both pistols at once. Raising them both above her head, she drew them down together, and without seeming to aim, fired them both. There was only

418

one hole made in the door. The pirates jeered and surged forwards to look, yet she pushed through them, and with the point of her fish knife, dug out first one bullet, and then the other, from the same hole.

There was an instant of silence, and then the pirates went wild, and I nearly fell where I stood. Another impossible shot. Even Vane was visibly impressed.

"'Tis true you're all more experienced than me in battle at sea", 'Adam' spoke, and I wondered why she could not simply keep silent. "Yet you'll never see me miss my mark, shirk hard work, or hold back from a fight. If you do, throw me out of your Company with nothing. If I prove useful, give me a full share."

Most of the men cried "Aye, lad, you're in!", yet there were discontented voices, and of these, George Featherstone's was the loudest. Jack nodded at him, and he stood to speak, the vicious scar down his face red with his anger. "The lad talks and shoots well, but to kill a man with blood underfoot in a stormy sea takes more than bravado. And what if we decide against him? He'd tell the whole Caribbean that we'd cheated him. I started as a lad on half a share, and I don't see why he's too proud."

"George, ye can't shoot like that, even now", Jack protested. "I say he's in, and I draw up the Articles now. All in favour say "Aye!"

The 'ayes' had it, and I left them to their business, not liking Vane's cold blue eyes upon me. I returned to my camp that night, and the next I saw 'Adam', she and Jack were working on the rigging of a prize. They waved to me, and 'twas evident that Jack liked the lad, and was enjoying showing him the ropes.

My next task was to find out what Old Peg knew of me, and what she might do about it. I found her one morning alone on Cully's veranda, yet she was so taciturn and suspicious, that without asking a direct question, I could not get more than a word from her. In the end, I thought her too exhausted to care what I was, and insisting I was a friend of

419

Jack Rackam's, I gave her a few pieces of silver, and left her and her brat to their resentful silence, convinced they would never say one word more than necessary to anyone on any subject.

Vane's good fortune was handsomely capped when a small Jamaican trader sailed in, pretty Tom Brown waving his hat gaily from the bowsprit. He told the pirates he had stayed peacefully by his father's bedside, until the old man died. Then hearing that Vane believed him captured, and was ready to burn Bermuda for his sake, he had taken passage on the first trader sailing south, and come to rejoin the Brethren.

Vane, happier than I had ever seen him, strode into Cully's tavern, to offer Jennings a truce. There was to be a celebration at the stone tavern, and all were invited. I thought to go too, as it would be my last chance to see 'Adam' before she sailed with them on the morning tide.

The pirate's carousal was an uproar from dusk till dawn, all of us reeling with music, dance and drink. Vane mockingly toasted his handsome lover for his skill in evading the Admiralty court, and before he knew what was happening, Jack had thrown an old tarpaulin over his Captain's shoulders for a robe, with a bunch of palm leaves for a wig, and declared him a Judge of the Admiralty. Jack then loosely bound Tom's hands behind him, appointed himself counsel to plead, and Featherstone the Prosecutor. Others stood by with bottles of rum as signs of Office, willing to supply any but the prisoner with a drink. The rest of us sat at their feet as the jury.

Featherstone began with the charges. "An' it please yer worship, an' you gentlemen o' the jury...", we all cheered. "Here's a man who is not a man, but a dog, Sir, and who ought to hang this very day, for committing piracy on the high seas, and refusing to lie with his betters, despite being offered a bottle o' rum to do it. An' you know My Lord, that a man who won't be bought ought to hang, for what is the use o' being high born and rich, if the poor will not sell themselves to ye cheap? I say hang him, and hang him

420

high!"

Vane glared down at Tom Brown with all the haughtiness he could command, and the jury broke into guffaws. "You there, you damned ill-looking dog of a fellow, what have you to say for yourself? Why should you not be choked on a rope, and your maggoty corpse gibbeted for the gulls to feed on?"

"I'm not guilty, My Lord."

"Not guilty! Not guilty! Take that back you cur, or I shall have you hanged immediately! How can a dog like you live without committing a single crime against man or God? You are poor are you not?"

"I am Sir, and the sole support of my beloved parents, Sir. But the ship I worked on was taken by one Charles Vane, Sir, as great a rogue as ever sailed, a notorious pirate, Sir, with a terrible taste for men, Sir, and he forced me Your Honour."

The pirates were rolling with laughter. "He forced you to refuse the learned Prosecutor?"

"No Sir. He forced me to go a rovin', and make enough money to feed me beloved parents."

Featherstone leapt up. "There! He admits his guilt, and shows no repentance. I say hang him now, before he can speak more o' this Devilry, or half the men here will be out on the account before dawn."

"Aye, he's a cur, a rascal, a rogue!", Vane ranted. "The gentlemen of the jury have two ticks of the clock to find him guilty, and if they trifle with this court, they will stand in the dock, accused of abetting piracy, for which the sentence will also be death."

"Hang him!", we all shouted.

"Please My Lord", Rackam began, "should we not consider..."

"Consider? Consider! He is tried by the law, not by consideration, you lying rogue. How many villains could we hang if we took time for consideration?"

"But Sir", Rackam persisted, "the man is innocent."

"Innocent? Innocent! If he was innocent, he wouldn't be standing in a courtroom, on trial for his life! He has kept bad company, and will endanger any man he comes near with tales of theft, courage, blood and treasure. And the young must be content with nothing, especially if they are as ill-favoured as this ugly rogue. Well, Sir, is there any reason why sentence of death should not be passed upon you?"

"Aye Sir, I am indeed innocent. 'Twould be a crime to hang me."

"And do you think I'd stop at crime to serve the law? And do you think I've sat here for nothing, hungry for my beef and porter? And do you think that all these good people should be deprived of seeing you dance, when they've waited so patiently, and by the look of them, could do with a reminder to stay in low service to their betters? I sentence you to dance, you filth! Music!"

A merry jig was struck up on a fiddle, drums and tambourines, and Tom kicked up his heels and danced wildly, sending sand flying. He threw his ropes off, and held himself by the throat, sticking his tongue out. Then we were all dancing.

Someone yelled:

"Fifteen men on a dead man's chest".
We bellowed back: "Yo ho ho and a bottle of rum!"
"Drink and the Devil have done for the rest."
"Yo ho ho and a bottle of rum!"

Vane's Fleet sailed that morning, and returned only two days later, with a French brigantine of twenty-two guns, laden with sugar, indigo, brandy, claret, white wine, and other goods. 'Adam' ran around to my camp, and hugging me, showed me a purse full of gold. "Featherstone insisted on having the cocky new hand as Gunner's boy. And after our attack on the brigantine, he told Jack I was worth a full share." I interrupted her boasting, to point out that she'd made her stake in one cruise of only two days, and could now give up the life.

"Oh no! I'm going along with Jack's plan. We'll take as much booty as possible until the Governor arrives, and then take the Pardon. Those that refuse to surrender will sail with Vane, 'round the Horn for the coast of Brazil, where wealthy merchants will pay high prices for their share o' the cargo." I attempted to curb her youthful zeal and her high expectations of wealth, yet she laughed at my caution, and pointed out that she could stop being a pirate whenever she wished, just by changing clothes, and need not worry about the Pardon.

"I helped you become a pirate because you needed to begin an independent life for yourself. If you stay with Vane, you will be corrupted with the sins of theft and murder and greed. Will you sell your soul for your freedom, Anne Bonny? You promised me once that you would always be honest with yourself."

"My soul is my own business, and no concern o' yours. I am suited to the roving life. You can't reveal my sex without risk o' revealing your own, Mary Read, so do not ever think o' betraying me. I will be what I wish to be, and will not be dictated to by a mealy-mouthed Puritan..." I turned and walked away before she could say any more to anger me, and I did not see her before she sailed the next morning.

Vane's Company soon returned with the Drake sloop, taken between Providence and Harbour Island. They found a considerable sum of money aboard, and kept her, though there was grumbling when Vane once again made Robert Deal her master without taking a vote. 'Adam' was furious, sure that the Company would have voted for Jack if given the chance. They took the Ulster next, which was loaded with timber from Andros Island. Vane dumped the timber in Nassau, much to the delight of the islanders, who immediately quarrelled over it. Ma Davies wanted a church, Cully wanted to repair his tavern, and those in shanties clamoured for houses.

Vane put seventy casks of sugar from the French brigantine into the Ulster, and moored her with the rest of his Fleet. With one ship for those taking the Pardon, and one for those staying on the account, the entire Company was content. On the next cruise, the pirates took the Eagle sloop, and filled her with sugar too.

While still in Nassau harbour, the Lancaster and the Dove, owned by Neal Walker and William Harris sailed in, expecting to find the Governor, and Vane took them also. Neal Walker was the brother of the ex-Chief Justice, who Hornigold had chased out for insulting Anne, and he blustered and fumed a great deal before giving up his ship, and vowed that there would be justice once the Governor came.

One stinking hot afternoon, I allowed a black loneliness to drive me to the pirate tavern. Glad to see me, Jack clapped me on the back, shielding me from Vane's scowls. Then 'Adam' threw herself on me, begging me to accept a rum, and I knew then that the bold harlot was the only friend I had in the world, the only one who knew me for what I was. I resolved to pray for her safety, even if I had to make my truce with God, as Ma Davies had once said I would.

We had barely had time to exchange greetings, when Peg's brat came flying in, to whisper in Jack's ear. He leapt from his seat, and turned to Vane. "It's the Governor", he announced crisply. "His Fleet is hove to just outside the harbour."

Vane grinned like a shark scenting blood. "Then each man chooses this day to be free or slave, to stand with the Brethren, or betray us."

Chapter 23: The Governor

Vane considered the Governor's arrival a moment longer, raised an elegant eyebrow at me, and asked if I still had my Certificate of Pardon. I nodded, and he asked if I wished to make the Governor's acquaintance. I agreed to serve him, and he called for paper and ink from Nat Taylor. All the pirates gathered about as Jack carefully wrote out the letter he dictated.

'To His Excellency, the Governor of Providence: Your Excellency may please to understand that we are willing to accept His Majesty's most gracious Pardon on the following terms: That you will suffer us to dispose of all our goods now in our possession, likewise, to act as we think fit with everything belonging to us, as His Majesty's Act of Grace specifies. If Your Excellency shall please to comply with this, we shall, with all readiness, accept of His Majesty's Act of Grace. If not, we are obliged to stand on our own defence. So conclude, your humble servant, Charles Vane and Company.'

Jack pondered it. "You've spoken well for those, like me, who wish to surrender, and I thank you for it. This will allay the Governor's fear of an attack. Yet it gives him time to blockade the harbour, if he decides against all of us." Vane thought an instant, and taking the pen, scrawled: 'We await a speedy answer', at the bottom of the page.

I thought it impolite, yet agreed to deliver it, anxious to ensure the Pardon for those who wanted it, and eager to meet the man who would decide my fate.

I raced back to my camp, snatched my certificate from its place in my mother's Bible, and ran back to the waterfront. There I saw Henry Jennings in the midst of an anxious crowd, and explained my mission to him. He asked me to report to him at Cully's once I had any news, and borrowed a dory for me. I raised its small sail, and with the murmured good wishes of the crowd, Henry pushed me off.

While skimming across the harbour in a gentle breeze to meet Nassau's new Governor, I was all optimism. Yet the sight of the Fleet of warships at anchor sent a shiver up my spine, and I remembered the ruthless cold that often went with power, and prayed I would be treated with the courtesy normally accorded to messengers. There were three ships, the Delicia, the Rose and the Milford, and two sloops, the Buck and the Shark, both shallow enough to sail straight in. I thought then that the new Governor was no fool, and made for the Delicia, the grandest, as the most likely to have him aboard.

I was almost there before the lookout hailed me, a short sturdy man who obligingly dropped a rope ladder over the side. I tied the dory to it and scrambled up. When I saw his dented sword, sober suit and out-of-curl wig, I guessed him to be an Officer, and when I saw the terrible scars on the right side of his face, I knew he had fought hard for his promotions. Yet before I could speak, he hushed me urgently, indicating the decks crowded with sleeping soldiers and sailors. From this vantage point, I saw that the other ships were equally crowded, though with civilians and cattle.

"We had a hard voyage, with gales all the way. None slept last night, so I told them all to rest now. Are you from Nassau?"

"I am, Sir. I have a message for the Governor."

"Hand it over then. I'm Captain...uh, Governor Rogers."

I could not mask my surprise, and he smiled, twisting the scars on his face. Relieved to find no over-fine lordling, I snatched my hat off, and made him my best bow. "Mark Read at your service, Sir. I was pardoned by Captain Pearce of the Phoenix, and have lived honestly since, though on friendly terms with some who have remained on the account. Many of the Brethren found it impossible to surrender to Captain Pearce, Sir, he managing the business with so much cowardice, arrogance and disrespect for the independent pride of the Brethren. Yet they know of you Sir, of your courage, and your great deeds, and would be honoured to surrender to you, providing only that the Act of Grace is respected. I bring you a letter from the Pirate Captain Charles Vane, who also took the Pardon from Captain Pearce. He is keen to ensure the rights of those seeking the Pardon. It is rough in tone, yet I beg you to read it in a spirit of forgiveness, and so spare the wretched people of these isles a battle that you cannot win."

Rogers read the letter carefully, looked me over, and shook a man awake. "'Hoy, Boatswain! Ask the Fleet Captains to meet me in my cabin at their earliest convenience." He limped away, and I remembered reading of him taking a shot in the ankle in a battle for a Spanish galleon, and refusing to leave the deck. He then ushered me into a cabin of such spartan neatness, that I knew him for a simple, hard-working man, who might make Nassau a place of peace, as well as a place of law. While we waited for the others to come, he quietly asked me to tell him of the Brethren.

"When I first came to Providence, early last year, there were well over a thousand pirates, Sir. Most of them are decent fellows at heart, forced into the life by starvation and ill treatment, as I was myself. Captain Jennings is the best of them, and has great influence with the Brethren, being the man who led them here in the first place. 'Twas Jennings who persuaded hundreds of the Brethren to follow him to Bermuda for the Pardon.

"Then Captain Pearce sailed in, and though he was treated with all due respect by the Brethren, he nearly wrecked everything by the theft of a sloop, the Lark, from Charles Vane. Vane told him he'd made a mistake, and that his crew was eager for the Pardon, and indeed he and I took it together. Yet Pearce kept the sloop for his own trade, and though Vane recovered it, many of the Brethren were outraged, and decided to wait until you came, so that their surrender would be less humiliating.

"They hold the town Sir, as most of the reformed

men have left Nassau for home or to seek employment. Others, including Captain Jennings, remained to meet you, hoping that they could be of use in the new colony. Captain Jennings believes you will need traders, and is still intent on persuading his old comrades that the days of pirating are over. Vane is also convinced that this time has come, and sends me to beg you to do him the honour of pardoning his men. I beg you Sir, let the worst of them sail away, the best will stay, and Nassau will be yours without a drop of blood shed."

The sombre little man was not fooled. "I see little of begging in this letter. He seems most concerned that he be allowed to keep his plunder. You know that if repentance is sincere, then the fruits of the crime must be renounced. The vessels must be returned to their rightful owners."

"Yet the Act of Grace allows for the Brethren to keep their ships, which I believe encourages them to become the traders that we need so badly. The new Governor of Jamaica, Governor Lawes, as well as Governor Bennett, have not expected the reformed pirates to renounce all they have. And Sir, you must see that if even some become traders, then the pirate forces are divided and pitted against each other, to their ultimate loss. Only the Brethren can fight the Brethren, Sir. I mean no disrespect when I say they are the greatest sailors I've ever seen, and I was a sailor with the English Navy."

"Governor Bennett tells me Vane has been more active since taking the Pardon, and that Bermuda's traders live in fear of him, for he commits atrocities on ordinary sailors. How many prizes has he?"

"He has a well-armed, well-provisioned Fleet that could hold Nassau until Hell freezes over. No Sir, I make no threats on their behalf. Yet I beg you to understand their situation, as well as your own. Do not judge them by your own strict standards. They were miserable outcasts, left to starve by those they fought for. They were tempted beyond themselves Sir. 'Tis easy to tempt a desperate man.

"And please Sir, I beg you in the name of mercy to remember the simple people of the Bahamas. There are about thirty families on Providence alone, people who have prayed to live once more under English Law. And the reformed men are anxious to meet the man their lives depend on. Your generosity could do everything towards persuading the rest of them that there is a well-tempered mercy in Government. Captain Vane is not greedy Sir, he merely wishes to ensure a future for all those who have sailed under his command, that does not include slavery and maggoty biscuit. You know the hard life of a sailor, Sir. I'm sure you understand."

"I understand they are lucky to have you plead for them. You speak well lad, yet I'll not let this Vane fellow get away with breaking his oath to the King."

"Then I must tell everyone to prepare for war. Those seeking a Pardon will desert Captain Jennings, who has tried so hard to keep them as honest as himself. They will swell Vane's numbers, and hold the town, and you will never be Governor of the Bahamas. I have friends amongst them all Sir, pirates, pardoned men and islanders, and none will think this your choice the right one."

"Not so fast away, Mister Read. Nay, fear not, I'd not hold you against your will, yet I have much to ask you. And here are my Officers. Gentlemen, I would like you to meet Mark Read of Providence. Mister Read, this is Captain Gale of the Delicia." An arrogant fop looked down his nose at me, making no attempt to return my bow. "Captain Chamberlen of the Shark". This shrewder gentlemen condescended to nod, understanding my usefulness. "Captain Whitney of His Majesty's warship the Rose". I bowed to a scowling, red-faced bully, who kept his hand on his sword hilt. "And Mister Fairfax". A bright-faced young man smiled and bowed gracefully, as though attempting to atone for the rudeness of the other gentlemen. "And this is Mister Thomas Walker, who was Chief Justice here, before threats to his family meant he had to leave." He glared at me, and the rest

429

of the introductions flew over my head, so anxious was I to warn Ben Hornigold that his old enemy had returned. Governor Rogers sat at his desk, and regarded me kindly. "Do you know anything of farming, Mister Read?"

"Yes Sir, I was raised on farms. There are pockets of fertile soil, and the interior is well-wooded and well-watered. Yet the people are dispirited, too used to their labour being destroyed by Spanish raids. And to clear the land without oxen and plough..."

"We have those", Mister Fairfax enthused. "And hundreds of settlers from Europe. We will have a thriving colony within a year."

His enthusiasm lightened my own doubts, and I could not help smiling back at him. "I hope you are right, Sir. For the sake of the honest people of Providence."

Thomas Walker snorted with derision. "This is not the only island of the Bahamas which is inhabited", he pointed out. "We need not keep this pirate haunt as our main settlement."

"The other islands are indeed inhabited, Sir. Mister Walker lives on Abaco, I believe, and the people on Eleuthera and Harbour Island are said to support themselves. Yet this is the only harbour that will admit a ship of any size, if she is carefully guided through the narrow channel at high tide."

"Is the fort well-armed."

"There are only the ruins of a fort, and there are no guns there now. The Brethren fight at sea, and they are ready for you. I beg you again Sir, let Vane go and spare yourself a terrible battle you cannot win. 'Tis not too late to change your mind."

Governor Rogers explained what I had told them of the pirates, and Captain Gale immediately accused them of arrogance in expecting anything more than Pardons from His Majesty's Government. Though I once again stated that the King's Act of Grace allowed them their ships, no one listened. I rose then, bowed to the new Governor and his men, and bid them farewell. Captain Whitney's sword was immediately at my throat, and I stood, my fists clenched, feeling like a fool to have trusted them at all.

"Damn it man, drop that sword!", Governor Rogers snapped.

"We need a pilot, and this man knows the way in", Captain Whitney objected.

"I could never pilot a ship as large as this", I protested. "You would go aground and be left at a terrible disadvantage against the Brethren."

Governor Rogers stepped forward. "And I have given him my word that he would not be kept against his wishes. Sheathe your sword, Sir!" Captain Whitney reluctantly dropped his sword, yet did not sheathe it. Captain Gale was also scowling at the Governor, and verging on mutiny.

Thomas Walker glowered at me. "If you were an honest man, you would not be seeking the favour of pirates."

"That is a harsh judgement Sir. I have my Certificate of Pardon, signed by Captain Pearce, and am no longer a pirate, having no love of a violent life. Whether I am now honest, I will leave to the Governor to decide. Now, if you please, Sir, I will bid you farewell, and inform Captain Vane of your decision against him. I will then inform Captain Jennings that you come for war. He knows the harbour well enough to guide you in, and may be able to persuade you to let Vane go, where I cannot."

"You have strange loyalties, Mister Read", Rogers commented drily. "Make your way back, and tell Charles Vane that I have enough soldiers aboard to take Nassau by force. And make sure you send us that pilot."

"With respect, Sir, I will tell the Brethren that your soldiers don't look strong enough to take tea. Yet I swear I will not fail you as to the pilot." I bowed to the Governor and the pleasant Mister Fairfax, ignoring the scowls of the rest, and climbed back into my little boat.

Dusk had brought the land breeze, and I tacked to and fro in Nassau harbour, dismal with failure. The waterfront was crowded by the time I made the beach, and I clambered out, utterly despondent. Henry Jennings was waiting for me too, and when I told him of the Governor's decision, he groaned. "'Tis war then. The reformed men against their old comrades. Hell and damnation!"

When I told him the Governor's Fleet needed a pilot, he assured me he would find one. Then he was busy sending out messengers to call in all those who would stand by the Governor, so I bid him farewell, and with a heavy heart, made my way back to the stone tavern to tell the pirates the news.

Vane erupted in a terrifying fury, swearing he'd hold Nassau against them all, and sent his best men to ready his Fleet. Jack cursed, his dreams of being pardoned and rich now over. I felt it treachery in me to stay and hear their plans, when I was not one of them, and bade them farewell and fair winds. I clasped 'Adam's' hand, questioning her hard with my eyes, yet she would not look at me, and I had no choice but to leave her.

Then there was a scream from the waterfront. "Here they come!" The whole town dashed down to the beach, to watch the Rose man o' war edging in between Hog Island and Silver Key, the Shark sloop slipping in after her.

Vane sped down the rotting dock and flung himself aboard the Lark, sailing out with only the few men who'd managed to scramble aboard after him. Jack and his mates rowed furiously for the Ranger, yet the Lark did not wait for them. Instead she raced towards the Rose, turning broadside at the last minute to fire all her guns high, cutting the warship's rigging to pieces with chain shot. The Rose did not manage to score a single hit on the pirate sloop, and the Shark stood uselessly by. Completely disabled, the Rose had to anchor, thus blocking the entrance to the harbour.

The furious Captain Whitney was forced to send his Lieutenant in a longboat to the Lark to beg for mercy, and the pirates kept him for hours, swearing they would die under the Jolly Roger rather than surrender, and urging the young Lieutenant to join them for a wild life on the high seas. Whitney fired his guns as night was falling, signalling his Lieutenant to return, and though Vane returned the volley, he scorned to keep the lad as a hostage, and released him, dead drunk.

Vane then sailed back to organise his Fleet, and kept his men busy loading and unloading their ships, preparing some to sail out with their loot, lightening others for battle. Only Vane himself seemed cool in that feverish heat, truly a man made for war. I hung about the docks in a sweat of impatience, frightened for Anne Bonny, and hoping to catch her eye.

At about ten o'clock at night, Vane ordered his men to prime the port guns on the French brigantine, and then ordered all but Jack and George Featherstone to disembark. They cast off and hoisted the brigantine's foresail, drifting down upon the Rose in the darkness. I could not understand what they were about, until a hundred yards from the Rose, fire blossomed from the brigantine's hold, lighting the dark harbour. As the fireship drifted towards the stricken Navy vessel, we saw Jack and George Featherstone, silhouetted by flame, leap overboard. Then, all at once, the brigantine's guns blasted into the Rose at close range. We could hear the screams of the Navy sailors clear across the water, and I was not the only one whispering a prayer for them, their choice to burn or drown. Then Captain Chamberlen in the Shark sloop came close enough to throw the Rose a cable. With aching slowness, he towed the great ship out of the fireship's path, and out of the harbour.

Charles Vane then strutted along the harbour, triumphant at having chased them out, and we knew that the Navy would not venture in again that night. At Cully's, Henry Jennings urged the pardoned men to make a stand for their Governor, yet most swore they'd not fight their old mates for any King's man. Jennings thought Vane had won, yet his spies reported that those of Vane's men who had planned to be pardoned and rich, were baulking at the prospect of going back on the account. Hearing this, I prayed that Jack would have the sense to leave the life, and that 'Adam' might follow him.

All through that long hot night, Vane's men trickled away from him. Some hid in the bushes, afraid both of Vane's vengeance and the Navy soldiers. Many joined us at Cully's, swearing they'd rather live under a Governor, than endure Charles Vane as their Pirate King. Some cursed God for taking Sam Bellamy from them, and I wondered what would have happened if the charming Irishman had been here to lead us all against King George's Navy.

In the darkest hour of the night, Vane realised he had lost the followers he needed to hold Nassau, and chose to run. His committed comrades then loaded the Lark with plunder and provisions and ammunition from their Fleet.

I sat with the islanders and the pardoned men on the beach, all of us huddled around small fires, anxious to see what would come with the dawn, some eagerly discussing the coming war, many laying wagers on the outcome.

As the sun rose over Hog Island, Henry Jennings gave the men he most trusted a dram of rum, and asked us to prime our pistols. Then we all sat watching the sun turn the scattered clouds into a triumph of red and gold, the sea wind picked up, and once again I silently questioned the foolishness of men, who could quarrel and die in the midst of nature's generous beauty.

Then young Harry Davies came running up from the dock, swearing that Vane had just forced old Noah Harwood. "Captain Vane swore he'd drop him on Catt Island once he'd got them through, but Mister Harwood refused to be his pilot, so Captain Vane clapped a pistol to his head..."

Jennings knelt in the sand by the excited boy, and grasped his shoulders. "Through? Through where, boy?" Harry turned and pointed to the thin channel between Hog Island and Potter's Key. We could all see the rocks. "Then God save them", Jennings muttered. "If they go aground, the Navy will blast them to pieces, so they will."

434

As the Navy ships crept in, we watched all sails hoisted on the Lark, King Death fluttering to her mizzentop, and the English cross of Saint George flying from the mainmast. Firing one last parting shot at the Governor, Vane loosed her mainsheet, and when his flying jib filled, the Lark sped through the dangerous eastern passage under full sail, and loaded to the gunwales. We cheered to see it, partly for their dauntless courage, yet also because we would not now have to fight them.

The Buck sloop gave chase, and the Shark followed, yet both Captains jibed sharply when they saw the rocks lining the shallow channel. We mocked them for lacking the courage of pirates, yet in truth, there were never men who could sail a ship like the Brethren o' the Sea.

Across the water, we could clearly hear Ben Hornigold on the Delicia, damning the Navy sailors for land-loving gutter-rats, and bellowing for soundings. Then we heard him roar, the Delicia turned, and with great stateliness, ran up onto a sandbank. Then the Milford followed her, their masts slowly tilting across the dawn sky, completely helpless until the tide came high enough to lift them off. Those watching were either amused or horrified, and many shook their heads and swore we should have fought them.

The Delicia launched a dory, and as it came skimming straight for us, Jennings told the crowd that he'd take it as a personal insult if any hindered the landing of the Governor. I did not think the Governor would be so rash, and was relieved to hear Hornigold's bellow: "Ahoy! Who holds the town?"

"Ahoy, Ben Hornigold! All is well!" Young Mister Fairfax was with him, and he cheered and raised the flag of Saint George on the dory's masthead. This was the signal for longboats full of sailors and soldiers to pull away from the Navy ships for the shore. And thus, despite the skilled courage of the pirates, and the clumsy cowardice of the Navy, we surrendered Nassau with barely a shot fired.

I returned to Cully's with Jennings, praying to find Anne in skirts, on Jack's arm, both of them looking for the Pardon. They were not there, and I knew then they had stayed out on the account with the vicious Charles Vane. And although dread for their fate filled my heart, there was also pride, in that there were some rovers who would not surrender so easily, and one of them was my bold young friend, Anne Bonny.

Then Ben Hornigold came in with young Mister Fairfax, who he introduced to Henry Jennings. Jennings demanded to know why the Navy ships had run aground, and the young Englishman laughed. "At dawn this morning, Captain Thomas Walker, who makes such a noise about having once been Chief Justice here, stumbled up on deck, saw Captain Hornigold at the wheel, and went for his sword. The Governor stepped between them, yet Walker refused to believe Captain Hornigold pardoned, and then threatened to hang him anyway. I thought he must drop dead of an apoplexy when the Governor insisted he was our pilot.

"Captain Hornigold protested that he had indeed chased the pompous fool out of Nassau for insulting a pretty friend of his. Walker, seeking an easy revenge, then repeated the insult. Captain Hornigold bellowed like a bull, the Governor leapt for his sword arm before he could draw steel, and in the scuffle, the helmsman was left without a guide. The shock of the Delicia running aground threw us all to the deck. Captain Hornigold then sheathed his sword, apologising for letting Walker make him forget his business, hoping that the Governor was satisfied that he had offered his services with the best of intentions. Governor Rogers grudgingly forgave him, amazed that any man would endanger a ship to defend the honour of the fair sex. Just as Captain Hornigold was promising to get boats to pull the Delicia off the sand at high tide, the Milford sailed trustingly in behind us and stuck too."

"And my offer to guide them in came to nought", Ben Hornigold scowled.

436

"Governor Rogers trusted you not to kill him when he grabbed your cutlass. And he knows 'twas Walker who was truly responsible for grounding the ships, and that he must in future be more polite about the ladies you admire. A toast, gentlemen. Here's to beautiful women with soft hearts! Let us hope there is at least one here for me!" Jennings poured the young man another shot of rum, and asked him his opinion of Rogers, and I could see he liked the good-humoured, bright young Englishman too.

"Governor Rogers will transform this dung heap. No offence gentlemen, yet I don't know how you stood it so long. The stench of those hides rotting on the waterfront! The dispiritedness of the people! The general decay! Oh yes, I have high hopes for Nassau under the new Governor. He is a man that you will find easy to respect. He is a fair man, of sober Protestant stock, his father a Bristol sea Captain. He has no time for the ladies, yet he respects the man he knows to be loyal."

I resolved then to stay in trousers, and try to prove myself useful to the new Governor.

"He'll have everyone here bustling in a week", young Mister Fairfax continued. "Houses built, ground cleared for plantations, crops sown. And that is where you gentlemen come in, trading the wealth of the Bahamas to England and her colonies. Yes, better days are ahead. Yet if you prefer, you can discuss it with the Governor yourselves, since Captains Jennings and Hornigold are invited to join him for luncheon aboard the Delicia today."

I was anxious to see what the canny Henry Jennings made of our Governor, and despite my fatigue, I returned to Cully's after a hurried lunch with Ma Davies. Ben Hornigold decried the meal as the worst he had ever eaten, yet boasted that the Governor had appointed him Captain of Vane's prize sloop, the Ranger. "He knows what it is for a man like me to be without a vessel", Hornigold beamed. "And when he heard that the bastard had burnt my ship, he said 'twas only justice. In return, I am to keep an eye out for Vane. A trader

437

came in with a message from him, swearing he will burn Nassau about our ears, since the Governor was rude enough to send sloops after him, instead of answering his letter."

"Vane will never return to a place that has so humbled him", Jennings insisted. "Mister Fairfax, you must continue to assure the Governor that all is safe for him ashore."

Mister Fairfax bowed gracefully. "He has announced that he will row ashore tomorrow morning to read the proclamation of himself as Governor. When you know him better, you will understand that when he sets his course, he holds to it. Do not doubt him gentlemen. Courage he has in abundance."

That night, I went to eat with Ma Davies, full of news and hope for our new colony. Sarah leaned against the handsome Dennis Carty, and spoke hopefully of her wedding, and we all toasted their happiness. Ma Davies and I sat by the fire and talked of the possibilities of a dairy, and I promised to introduce her to the Governor, so she could ask for his protection for such a scheme. "He will be the making of us all", I enthused.

Ma Davies shook her head. "A Governor is no guarantee of peace, young Mark. We have had many here over the years, and there was not one fit to clean Henry Jennings' boots. In 1686, over thirty years ago, my parents escaped the cesspool that was Jamaica, to live a godly life under the Reverend Thomas Bridges, a conventicle preacher, and a great man. I was the first babe born here, and I am their only living child.

"Our men elected Reverend Bridges to be our Moderator. Thinking that this smacked of independence from England, and lack of respect for the King, the Governor of Jamaica ordered us to return, citing fear of the Spaniards as a reason to annex the Bahamas to Jamaica. Reverend Bridges refused to leave, and was elected Moderator again the year after. Then settlers came from Bermuda, and we built the first fort against the Spaniards.

Every Sunday began with the good Reverend firing one of the great guns to summon everyone to church, and there were few who dared stay away.

"We had buccaneers here even then, and they were wilder than Jennings' privateers, though Captain Mission did his best to control them. They kept to their side o' the bay, paid big taxes for the right to stay, and funded our small colony. The following year, Bridges was confirmed as Governor by the King, and we thought all was well.

"But nine months later, Colonel Cadwaller Jones arrived in Nassau, declared himself the new Governor, and showed us his commission from the King to prove it. He was a greedy snake, thinking he could find every man's price. Captain Mission sailed away for Madagascar then, stating that he'd do no business with such a scoundrel. John Graves, who is old and mad now, was a handsome young man then, and a great friend of my father. He deserted Reverend Bridges to become Governor Jones' agent, doing all his dirty work for him, much to my father's grief.

"My father tried to insist that we continue with our General Assembly, but the Governor had his son aim his ship's guns at the meeting house. For this, some hot-heads threw Governor Jones in prison, and the men elected our own Mister Ashley to replace him. Ashley charged Jones with high treason, and Mister Bulkley was to prosecute him. Graves, unwilling to fall from power with his master, rescued Jones, who rallied the merchants behind him, promising no taxes. Bulkley was imprisoned in irons for four hundred and eighty-five days, while Graves went to England to explain his version of what had happened to the Proprietors. Graves returned with Jones confirmed as Governor, and put Bulkley on trial. Bulkley escaped before six buccaneers, two drunks, and a sodomite could condemn him. He returned to England, to seek justice. We heard that he ended quite mad.

"But because of his complaints, Jones was sacked, and Nicholas Trott, a Bermudan merchant, came out to govern us. He had been given the post as compensation for a spoiled load of tobacco, and he saw it as a mere business venture. Yet, under his industrious leadership, Nassau thrived. We built a hundred and sixty houses, sunk wells, and lived as a prosperous village, our church spire rising over us, and God in our hearts. We had Fort Nassau built within three years, manned it with twenty-eight guns, and felt safe from the Spaniards, for a time. Yes, Governor Trott was a man of energy and determination, but he too was greedy. Captain Avery was made to pay a thousand pounds to land here, and none of that money went to pay for our church or our fort. They came out of our taxes. The Lords Proprietors eventually dismissed Trott for his blatant association with the pirates, and then sent us Webb, who was even worse.

"John Graves survived the change as Collector of Customs, and was only too happy to help Governor Webb line his own pockets, by charging us excessive quit rents and taxes. Webb encouraged our young men in smuggling, wrecking and piracy, taking a part of each man's spoil for his own fortune. A young mulatto, Read Elding, lived here then. He was the son of a plantation owner and a slave, a graceful, handsome man, the first I ever thought so, God help me. He was a smuggler, selling cheap English goods to neighbouring colonies, and he had a reputation as a clever seaman by the time Governor Webb turned up. Webb appointed him to catch a pirate named Kelly, but Elding lost control of his crew, and they took a merchant ship instead. Eventually Webb too was dismissed by the King, and when he left here, he was captured by pirates, and the thousands of pounds that he had stolen were taken from him. We held a thanksgiving service to celebrate God's justice. When Webb was sacked, Thomas Walker declared himself Governor, on the strength of an out-of-date commission as an Admiralty Judge. Elding took up pirate hunting seriously at his behest, and brought five pirates in. Four were hung from that great tree next to the stone tavern.

440

"In 1701, Governor Haskett arrived. He was a tyrant. He abused our only Church Minister, levied illegal taxes, and starved every penny out of us. Once he stole an entire shipload of corn, so he could sell it to us at double the price. He took whole cargos of claret and brandy, until traders stopped coming in with it, and men would take to the sea as the only way of getting a drink. In his last year, he took to imprisoning men for piracy, whether they were guilty or not, and auctioning their lives to their friends.

"A woman called Tabitha Elfroad ran Nassau's best brothel then. She was a London whore, transported to the colonies, and she was a sophisticated, beautiful woman, God save her. I washed her floors, though she laughed at me nearly every day for a pretty fool, and begged me to be one of her own girls. I was not so pure as to love scrubbing floors, but both of us were in love with Read Elding, and at that place, he followed her upstairs nearly every day, his soul in his eyes, her laughing back at him. Since I wanted him, and couldn't have him, I scrubbed the floors of his mistress's house to punish myself for my shame.

"Then the Governor arrested Elding for his first piracy, committed years before. Mistress Elfroad tried to buy him back, but the Governor demanded her diamond ring, rumoured to have been a gift from the King, and then her finest jewels, a silver tankard that took his fancy, gold plate...and then her favours. When Elding was released, she invited the whole island to a great party, and when everyone was drunk, she described in detail the ludicrous, puffing, puny efforts of the Governor the previous night. We all laughed, while he went purple with fury, and then she announced that she was closing her house, and would not open again until our tyrant of a Governor was pulled down.

"The next day, Governor Haskett turned on Mister Graves, calling him a pitiful dog and abusing him in front of the whole town, for he too had laughed at Tabitha's satire. Our young Mister Lightwood tried to reason with him, but the Governor swore murder, and drew his sword. Mister

Lightwood could not draw his own, that being treason, but he fought the Governor for his, and broke it over his knee. We all went mad to see it, and John Warren, who had been elected the Speaker of the Assembly, seized Judge Thomas Walker, who had been allowing all this to go on, and then went looking for Governor Haskett. Warren and Haskett struggled over a loaded pistol, and when it went off, Warren broke Haskett's head with the pistol butt. Ellis Lightwood was elected President by public tribunal, and he threw both Haskett and Warren in jail, Haskett in irons. Then Haskett was put into a ketch and sent to New York. His family was left behind, cowering in the woods. His wife died badly. I won't tell you of that. 'Tis a terrible thing when women pay for the crimes of their men.

"The Proprietors showed surprising sense, and allowed Lightwood to be our acting Governor. Then they showed their usual lack of sense, and appointed a man called Birch instead. In 1703, everyone in the Caribbean was anxiously awaiting the first blow of the war with France and Spain. We knew that the Spaniards had sworn to wipe out Nassau, before all the pirates turned privateer against them.

"I was sixteen, I had been married a year, my first babe but a few months old. My husband was out fishing and saw them coming, and he raced back into Nassau to warn us. We took food and hid in caves west of here, but the Spaniards stayed two weeks, and ah God, we nearly starved. They took hundreds for slaves, even Governor Lightwood. The fort was destroyed, the Church burnt, the town razed. They left us nothing. Nothing. And once they realised this, the traders did not bother coming in.

"Then we found out what hunger truly was. My first babe almost died when my milk dried up, and I fed her on coconut milk. Both my parents wasted away before my eyes. I dropped my second child before time, and lost him. When my husband fell ill of a terrible fever, I climbed to the top of the ridge where our church had been, dropped to my knees, and demanded God's mercy. But none came.

"On the first day of 1704, Governor Birch arrived. He had expected us to be a thriving settlement that he could rake for every penny. Instead he took one look at us, almost naked, and thin like starving dogs, and he sailed out and left us to govern ourselves. The Spaniards came back the next year, and again the year after. John Graves wrote to the Lords Proprietors after the last raid, and begged them to help us. They appointed another Governor, the Queen appointed someone else, and he never came. Most of our surviving two hundred families were scattered through the islands, living in palmetto huts, ready to run to the woods at the first sight of a ship, wilder than the Indians who had once lived here.

"When the war was finally over, nearly ten years later, the privateers turned pirate again, and a few came here. We welcomed them, and they fed us, and we grew stronger. For the first time, I watched my children thrive. My husband helped John Haman build the small, quick sloops you see in the harbour, and we began to claw our way back up to what we are now. We thanked God on our knees every day that we had survived those hard times. And then my husband was caught at sea by a hurricane, and never came back." She looked deep into my eyes. "I lost my faith then, for a time. But it grew again, as I watched his children grow.

"Thomas Walker was still at war with the Brethren. He arrested some pirates and sent them under guard to Jamaica, but they escaped on the way. Then he had his old appointment as a Judge of the Admiralty confirmed by the Queen, and it went to his head. He armed a sloop, and hunted them himself, killing as many as he could. He turned back a Spanish invasion too, with his small Fleet. He has an inflexible will, which in danger is his strength, but it makes him foolish otherwise.

"Captain Cockram married a girl on Harbour Island, and Henry Jennings visited him there. When Jennings took the Spanish gold a year later, he remembered this harbour, and brought two hundred wealthy men to live here. Walker was suddenly out-numbered, but he barely noticed, and went around insulting everyone until Hornigold threatened to kill him. Then Walker left for Abaco, his family with him. His brother, Neal Walker, sails in sometimes to trade, and helps the family survive there. They live as poor as the rest of us. His son Charles is about the age of my oldest boy.

"You met Mister Graves in his shack on the other side of Cully's, did you not. And found him half-mad and half-starving, I've no doubt. Though he has not collected any tax for the King for years now, he still receives a small salary as His Majesty's Collector of Customs, enough to keep poor young George Bendall starving as his servant, though the boy has a sick mother to support."

"Yes, Anne took me to meet him, and I thought him entirely crazed. Now I see why. Yet your life has been as hard as his. I honour you Ma, for you have worked hard to feed your children, raised them in the sight of God, and will prosper again, now the Governor is here, for nothing else would be just."

"Look not for justice from a Governor, my dear Mark. 'Tis only to be gleaned from the hearts of those who have suffered injustice, and yet commit none."

"This is such a man, I stake my life on it. If it was any lesser man, I'd be heading for England now. As it is, I hope to prosper here, working for a man I can truly respect."

The next morning dawned with drizzling showers, yet the whole town turned out to watch the Governor come in. The vessels in the harbour were festooned with the flags of all nations hanging damp in the rain, the islanders waved and cheered, and salutes from the Navy ships and the traders deafened us. After the Governor, the Navy sailors rowed in the settlers, and they seemed as thin and ragged and dour as the islanders that met them. The Governor's soldiers, mostly pensioners from the Chelsea Hospital, made an unimpressive attempt to form a guard, and were completely over-shadowed by the hand-picked guard of honour that Jennings had selected, for he too feared assassination.

Governor Rogers stepped ashore, very sprightly and

good-humoured, his tatty brown wig further ruined by the rain. The great guns boomed a ragged salute, the townspeople cried: "God bless the Governor!", and "God save the King!", while his Officers prowled about, hands on the hilts of loaded pistols, utterly distrusting us. Rogers cleared his throat to let us know he was about to make his first speech, and Hornigold hushed the crowd.

"Good citizens of Nassau, I claim the Bahama Islands in the name of King George of England, Ireland and Scotland. I have a Commission from the King to govern in his name, with the laws of England uniting and protecting all men. I wish now to proceed to His Majesty's fort, where I will read my Commission, as well as the Act of Grace, for I will pardon any still wanted for acts of piracy."

Jennings showed him the path west to the fort, a small hill of rubble and crumbling defences. It was easy to see Roger's disappointment, yet he scrambled up onto the wet rampart, and surveyed the crowd. "This fort is now in possession of the King, and held by me for your protection", he declared solemnly, his sharp eyes almost daring us to laugh. "The King has appointed me your Governor, and I will do my best to make this colony flourish. I demand respect for the Law, the Church, myself, and my Officers, and in return, you will be regarded as loyal citizens of Great Britain.

"I will take the strongest building in Nassau as my office and residence, and anyone can come and speak to me there, on any morning but the Sabbath. I will appoint a Council of six of your men, along with six of mine, who will administer the colony, under my supervision. You will find me honest and industrious. I hope to find you the same. Now I will read out my Commission, and then the Act of Grace, and take oaths of loyalty to the King from any who wishes the Pardon."

He began to read, and I slipped quietly away, looking for Nat Taylor. I found him twisting his hat in his hands, the rain dripping dismally down his face. "Mister Taylor, I can

445

see we have had the same thought. Your stone tavern is the only dwelling in Nassau that could withstand an attack. 'Tis close to the fort, and right on the waterfront."

"When I was a lad, I helped my father build it", Taylor mourned. "No doubt the Governor will hear that pirates drank there, and blame me for it, yet you know I am a better man than Cullimore."

"You must take advantage of your position, Mister Taylor. You must volunteer the tavern. Say Vane wanted a sturdy place too. It will need a thorough scrubbing to remove the stench of the pirates. I'll get Mistress Peg from Cully's."

"Her! She'd not stir even to see the Governor!"

"Yet she'd do anything to get away from Cully. Surely you'd not deny her the chance."

I found Peg sitting dispirited on Cully's veranda, and I did not have to say much to convince her to take her child and her meagre possessions, and leave John Cullimore's employ. I hoped that by doing her this favour, she might feel she owed me some discretion, yet in truth she seemed as little interested in me as in anyone else. I was only worried at putting Jack's informer in the Governor's household. She, her child, and Nat Taylor's lad, all set to with a will to clean the stone tavern. On my advice, Taylor left all the liquor in the cellar, for I knew the Navy Captains would buy it at any price.

When we returned to the fort, the Governor was shaking hands with the last of the pardoned men, and I saw Ma Davies waiting to speak to him. I bowed, and he nodded happily, telling me he'd pardoned nearly three hundred men that morning. "Then Vane has no support left in Nassau, and you have the Bahamas without bloodshed, much to my astonishment. Indeed Sir, in their desertion of such a strong position, you can see the clearest proof that these men want nothing more than to end their exiles, and peacefully return to their families.

"Your next problem would be provisions for all you

446

brought with you, would it not? Please let me introduce you to the Davies family. They know what the island can provide, and they are honest and hard-working."

Rogers nodded. "I intend to govern Nassau with a Council. Anyone of good sense and good character would be most useful, though I must insist on those who have had little dealings with the pirates over the years..."

"Then Mother Davies will suit you."

He laughed. "A woman on the Council? They may be useful, but they have their...limitations, shall we say. Yet, I will certainly speak to the good lady if she has provisions."

I led him up to Ma Davies, who bobbed a curtsey. "God bless you, Governor", she said quietly, her eyes level, and Rogers looked a little less dubious.

"Mister Read has been most insistent that I meet you, Madam."

"I wish to speak with you on three counts, Sir. Firstly, you will need food from the island. Second, I need protection for a dairy. Thirdly, and most dear to my heart, I wish you to marry my oldest girl to the man who loves her. They have been awaiting your arrival for some months."

"We must speak of the business in detail. Yet let the marriage be soon. Meet with me as soon as I have my offices arranged."

I smiled. "Excuse me, Sir, but I may be able to help you with that problem, too." I called Nat Taylor over, and he shuffled up, his face bright red. Muttering "God Save you, Sir", he thrust a great brass key, newly polished, into the Governor's hand, and retreated.

I grabbed his arm. "You mentioned your need of a strong residence, Sir. There is only one house in Nassau that would suit you. It belongs to this man, who built it with his father."

The Governor looked at him kindly, and Nat Taylor found his tongue. "I ran the place as a tavern, and Vane needed a sturdy place too. But I never liked those braggarts. I am a quiet man, and think only of my boy, who's all that the cruel sea has left me."

"You might buy the liquor in the cellar off him, Sir. You could sell it immediately to your Captains, who always need it for their men. And if you need someone to keep the place for you, he has a woman who works for him who holds her tongue uncommonly well."

He looked me over, a twinkle in his eyes. "And what do you get out of it, Mister Read?"

"I would serve you, Sir. I write a fair hand, I can keep my mouth shut, and I am honest."

"You have already been of some service, though you over-estimated Vane. Shall I explain my next problem?"

"If I can help, I will."

"Many of the settlers who came from Europe with me are ill, and greatly in need of accommodation on land. They have begged me to find somewhere for them, until they are strong enough to start building. Yet where can they stay in this derelict place?"

"The dosshouse looks like it will fall over, yet 'tis sturdy enough. 'Tis filthy and full of bugs, and of course, Nassau's doxies..."

"My settlers would be more uncomfortable with whores than vermin. Any lewd women will be sent to Jamaica on the next ship." He said it loudly enough, and instantly the news swept Nassau, that the whores who had cheered him so loudly that morning, were to be unceremoniously dumped in Port Royal. Nat looked as if he wished to say something for the men who would not stay without the company of women, yet he did not dare.

The Governor took Nat Taylor's arm, and I left them in earnest conversation, and went for an ale at Cully's. Jennings was there, buying drinks for the newly pardoned men, letting them know that Hornigold had been awarded the Ranger, and that our generous Governor wanted traders. "Vane might try to blockade Nassau, as he did with Pearce", Jennings noted. "We will have to keep our crews large, our vessels well-armed, and sail in convoys. We can still share

448

the profits, and prosper."

Then Auger came shouldering through the crowd. "Jennings, this new Governor has some useless fart demanding to board me vessel, and help himself to me cargo."

Young Mister Fairfax groaned. "Richard Turnley is a tactless fool. The Governor has the right to a very small percentage of every cargo as port tax. He has put all his fortune into this venture, and must make his money back, as all the Governors do."

"He has no right to take without paying. I told his dog to get off my sloop, and he tells me marshal law is declared, and he'll have me locked up. Edward England has already slipped out."

"Turnley is only the chief pilot, and has no right to threaten you with arrest, martial law or no. And the Governor will act fairly by you, as that is his way. I will go immediately to speak to him of Turnley's foolishness. Captain Jennings, Captain Hornigold, I look forward to your company this evening", and with a graceful bow and a flourish of his feathered hat, he left us.

We had not time to drink a dram, when shouts and screams suddenly filled the street. We dashed outside, to find the Palatine settlers besieging the dosshouse. Although a few of the older settlers called for peace, insults were hurled, and shutters slammed and bolted. A few of the younger men put their shoulders to the rickety door, yet were easily dispersed by a couple of well-aimed chamber pots. Some of the men then made a determined run at the door, and kicked it open. Yet they were dispirited and in poor condition, while the whores were fighting for all they had in the world, and they easily held the place with a few nasty household implements, while we cheered them on.

Then the Governor marched up with his Officers and soldiers, furious to have Ma Davies' fine lunch interrupted by the insistence of poxy women to a roof over their heads. Fairfax spoke urgently against sending the soldiers in, and I

449

pointed out that the dosshouse was large enough for them to share. Over-hearing this, a tired old man stepped up, and in highly-accented English, insisted that there be no fighting. "They are just poor girls, hardened by poverty and bad usage. I will speak with them."

The soldiers loading their muskets must have been a keen inducement to the whores to hear reason, and when the old man called his grey-haired wife over, she soon persuaded them to let the settlers have most of the building. Before the afternoon was over, the Palatine women had scrubbed the entire building with buckets of seawater, and the men had fixed the holes in the roof.

Later that evening, the sailors, settlers, whores and soldiers, were all crowded about Nassau, toasting each other. At Cully's, young Mister Fairfax sat with me and poured me a tot of rum. "Well, Mark Read, if you want employment, the Governor wants a scribe. You will have to be at his elbow all day, yet though he is dour, you are serious, so you should suit. And as every man on this isle has a plan for making money, you will be kept busy noting them. Some talk of raking salt, as we're closer to the Newfoundland fisheries than Salturtega. And the governor wants an experienced man from Bermuda to hunt the whales as they come past each year. He thinks our first crops must be cotton and sugar, for they pay the best, yet he also wants to try oranges and pineapples. He will allot one hundred and twenty square feet of land to anyone who'll clear it, and plant it."

Hornigold snorted. "I'm no farmer. The Brethren are men o' the sea."

"We need both traders and farmers, yet more of the latter, so there is something to trade", Fairfax explained smoothly.

"I'll not dig for the Governor unless I'm paid cash", Auger scowled.

Fairfax shrugged. "Cash is something the Governor does not have excess of. He invested all of his fortune, and his credit, in this venture."

Jennings raised an eyebrow. "Then it is fortunate he brought so many Palatines with him. They will work for nought but promises, isn't it true? We will be idle until the crops are grown, if we stay. Perhaps it is time to seek cargo elsewhere."

"Excuse me please, Mister Fairfax, you were speaking of farming."

"Ah, Mister Dupuis, have you met Captains Jennings and Hornigold? Abraham Dupuis, gentlemen, and his wife Susannah. 'Twas they who ended the siege of the dosshouse this morning."

"Do any of these gentlemen know of farming in this clime?" I told him that I'd only experience of farming in England, and the rest none at all. "That is a pity. We brought many European seeds with us, but we also hope to grow figs, bananas and papayas."

"And melons, yams and cucumbers", Susannah added.

"And coffee. There is a lot of money in coffee now", a younger man chimed in. Olives, limes and plums were all mentioned with enthusiasm, and our heads were filled with images of abundance. I pointed out that there was a great deal of hard labour ahead of them, and they smiled, sure of their ability to conquer the land. Even the Brethren, with their sailor's contempt for tillers of the soil, had to admire their determination. I remember grey-haired Susannah Dupuis, flushed and smiling in the tropic heat, while Jennings made a speech of welcome, and the Brethren toasted the settlers in rum, and wished them luck.

With joy in my heart, I drank more than usual, and bought a bottle of rum to take back to my camp. Then Peg's brat was at my elbow, handing me a lock of red hair, and muttering: "Your place, now." Taking the bottle, I ran along the beach, past Ma Davies shack. Next to my path up the cliff, there was a dinghy pulled up on the sand, and a dark figure sitting by a small fire.

451

She stood as I ran up, and sure she'd repented of piracy, I embraced her, while she laughed and demanded the rum. "Tell me o' Nassau? Does it truly have a Governor? Then damn them all for fools and cowards. When I saw them all turn from us that night, I swore I'd put no more faith in the courage o' men!"

"For God's sake, Anne! They chose to follow the Governor because they did not trust Vane."

"Because they feared a fight they were not sure of winning! Cowards all!" When she'd drunk, she assured me of the efficacy of my training, and the success of her disguise, and explained that she had rowed in as a spy, on Vane's account.

"Then you're still a pirate?"

"Certainly. Else I'd have donned a dress and met you at Cully's. No one would suspect me. But come, our time is short. They will meet me just off the harbour at dawn. And I didn't risk hanging to argue with you. I need to be me again, talking with you, even for just one night. 'Tis exhausting keeping a constant guard on what I do and say. Now, for the sake of our friendship, pass back that rum bottle." She took a long swallow and grinned. "Piracy has given me greater respect for you. I've thought much on what you said o' your years as a sailor. I'd gladly miss sleep to hear o' your time as a soldier."

"You think it but a small price to pay for the risk you've taken, coming in here. Yet those were terrible years that left me drowning in blood, and half mad. I do not want to remember."

"I could learn from your hard experience, Mary. I know you have much to teach me."

"And you are dear to me, Anne Bonny, even though you are a foolish scamp of a girl." I stared into the flickering flames, and let the tropic heat and whining mosquitoes fade from my mind. I told her of my time as an eager lad in a red coat, brave and foolish, marching for Marlborough with my brave friend Sergeant Deane, the dour Macleod, and the

452

knowing Captain Millner. I told her of joining the Cavalry and riding with Captain Lisle, the vain Cornet Dodsworth, and lawless Lieutenant Law. I told her of how I fell in love with my own Corporal Jan van Laatham, when he was a golden, handsome, smiling youth.

PART 7: THE CARIBBEAN 1718
Chapter 24: The Colony

As I ended the story of my years as a soldier, the dawning tropic sun etched Hog Island with gold, and the birds began a screaming cacophony behind us. I felt my past heavy upon me then, my present life a mere shadow of the horror of those times. And ah God, to remember Jan so young and eager, and me happily expecting to bear him our child!

Anne was poking thoughtfully at the dying fire. Seeing I had finished, she sighed and roused herself. "A strange life, bloody and terrible. And did you marry your sweet Dutch Cavalryman? And live as a woman?"

"I did, God help me. No, don't ask me to remember it all. My years as a wife were even harder on me than my time as a soldier. I don't have the heart for it, and you don't have the time. The tide is full and if anyone sees you, you're in danger. Unless you want me to fetch you a dress."

"And leave Vane's Fleet out there waiting to be caught? Besides, my dear Mary, piracy suits me much better than you had hoped. Even Charles Vane gives young Adam Cormac the occasional nod of approval. But I'll be back when I've made my fortune, to hear the rest o' your story."

"Only if you don't get caught. Your disguise gives you a chance, no more than that. And not even that much if the Devil recognises you for one of his own. Now off with you, before one of the Governor's men sees me with such a disreputable lad as yourself." We dragged her dory down to the gently foaming waves, and she embraced me before she clambered in. I pushed her off, watching until her small sail was lost in the glare of the rising sun.

Then, with my head still whirling with battle and blood, I made yet another small, reluctant step back towards my old Faith, and prayed for God to guard her, thief as she was, for in truth she was my only friend in this cold, hard

454

world. In return for protecting my friend, I offered Him my honest life, toiling in the cause of our new Colony.

With my soul greatly lightened, I returned to Nassau. The Palatine settlers were already abroad, inspecting the soil for house and garden sites, digging fresh latrines, and planting young fruit trees in the old pits. Their cheerful greetings and sturdy optimism raised my spirits further. When I arrived at the Governor's house, he ignored the scorn of his Captains, and invited me to join him and his Officers for breakfast. He began discussing the future of Nassau with me, as though my opinion was worth considering, and then asked for a sample of my hand-writing. I fetched pen, ink and paper, and as elegantly as I could, I wrote: 'Governor Woodes Rogers, Governor of the Bahama Isles, by the Grace of God and King George.' He nodded, and asked me to keep his notes, and I felt as though my luck had changed, any my life was, for once, on the right course.

We all walked out with the Governor after lunch, to find that Ma Davies had roused the island women, and they and their children were sweeping Nassau clean of refuse, young Harry devising a plank between two poles to push the worst of it down the beach. Jennings offered a doubloon to the man who could dig the deepest hole in three hours, and new latrines sprung up all over Nassau. At the Governor's insistence, these were covered to keep flies out, and the air improved immediately. That night, Jennings paid Ma Davies to feast the workers, and we all sat around bonfires on the beach, and toasted the unity of Nassau, heartened by what we had achieved.

Yet before the week was out, young Sara Davies came to see me, concerned that the fever that had distressed us before the Governor's arrival was now cutting a grim swathe through the newcomers. By the end of the following week, settlers, soldiers and sailors alike had succumbed to the bloody flux, suffering excruciating pains in their bowels, loins and back, and rising fifteen times a night to shit blood. There were so many ill in the crowded dosshouse and on the

455

Navy ships, that Rogers feared a general contagion. I suggested we keep them on the beach, and dig latrines in the sand below the tide-line, so the sea could clear away the worst of the filth.

To make them shelters, the Governor demanded all the spare sails off the Navy ships. When their Captains refused, the Governor rose to his feet, fury blazing in his eyes, and swore he would write a letter to Sir William Whetstone, commander-in-chief of the Navy in the West Indies, and his own father-in-law, charging them with mutiny, unless they obeyed him. By the end of the day, their sails were makeshift tents lining the shore.

And 'twas the tough old whores who cared for the dying, lifting them gently to the latrines when they could no longer walk, and bringing them water and what little food they could stomach. I knew they must still be carrying on their old trade, since they must eat, yet I asked the Governor if their kindness did not justify them as worthwhile citizens. He sneered, and I reminded him that a repentant sinner was more acceptable to the Lord than someone who had never sinned, and that they too could be set to work for the Colony. He sniffed with disgust, yet said nothing more of them being shipped to Jamaica, contenting himself with simply never acknowledging their existence.

We buried the children first. Then the old and frail. Abraham Dupuis mourned his beloved wife Susannah, and then wasted away to nothing. The heat and humidity rose with every day, and every night, someone's mad delirium would fade into a querulous murmur, and then into the final silence. By the end of that sultry, suffocating month, we had nearly a hundred people suffering, and twenty dead.

The Governor did all he could for his suffering people, despite having all his Officers ill, and taking the fever badly himself. He blamed the epidemic on the stench of the rotting hides that the Davies girls had left on the dock a month ago, hoping to trade them. An unexpected shower had caused them to putrefy, and the Governor insisted that they were infecting the air, and bullied Nat Taylor into shoving the rotting mess into the high tide with a long pole. I took the fever only mildly, being in good health to begin with, and with Ma Davies to nurse me, I soon recovered.

Towards the end of August, when the fever was at its worst, a merchant trader from Jamaica sailed in with Mistress Kate Pritchard aboard. She introduced herself to the Governor as a well-connected, wealthy London widow, looking for investments for her money, and enjoying the adventurous life of the Caribbean. In truth, she was a merry, energetic woman, with strong opinions, and imprudently loud in her support for the Pretender, now that his cause was well lost. Though she dressed soberly, she was attractive in a big-bosomed, fair-haired, over-painted way, and though virtuous, she openly sighed after another husband. By her own admission she was fatally addicted to romance, and hinted that every man she had ever met was dying for her favours. She flirted with all the Officers who were still on their feet, and the best of the reformed men, and they all flattered her outrageously. Yet she offended Governor Rogers by referring to Governor Lawes of Jamaica as 'that sweet man', and bragging that his superiors, the Lords of Trade and Plantations, were among her conquests. She constantly boasted of her connections with the First Quality of London, including Mister Cardonnel, the Proprietor of the Bahamas.

Whilst flirting with the Navy Officers and the reformed rovers at Cully's, she met young Sara Davies, who told her of those dying on the beach of Nassau. Without regard for her own health or social position, Mistress Pritchard immediately took her own supply of quinoa bark down to the makeshift hospital. When she saw the extent of the suffering, she tucked up her lace sleeves, and worked with the whores to help those who needed it the most. And she was there every day after, toiling from dawn to dusk, showing the greatness of her heart in her care of the Palatine women and children, doing her utmost to keep them alive, and weeping bitterly when they died. Despite warnings from the Officers, she did not succumb at all to the fever, declaring stoutly that such things never touched her.

Mistress Pritchard also took it upon herself to sponsor the marriage of Sara Davies and Dennis Carty, urging the Governor to take their union seriously, and waste no time in formalising it. He did not bother to hide his scorn for the big-bellied Sara, yet I too thought it blind of him to make so little of a pirate marrying for love, instead of making a whore of the woman he fancied. Amid the horror of the epidemic, there could be no true festivities, yet Mistress Pritchard gave Sara a pretty blue dress to wear, and made her a crown of scented white flowers.

When the young bride walked towards us over the greensward where the church had once been, the brilliance of the sea and sky were nothing to the radiant beauty of her happiness. She caught at the breath of even the hardest amongst us, and all sincerely wished her luck. Dennis Carty was jubilant, acclaiming the Colony a success, and planning his first voyage with the solid John Auger. His massive brother Patrick wished him the best of the honest life, and then got horribly drunk, staggering about the streets of Nassau, weeping for Sam Bellamy.

Every night Cully's was plagued with rumours of Vane returning in force to attack us, every vessel he took being instructed to come in to Nassau and frighten the Governor. Henry Jennings swore he'd been too humiliated to ever return, yet Ben Hornigold still careened and cleaned the Ranger, so he'd be ready to defend Nassau against him.

Captain Chamberlen of the Shark, who preferred to eat his dinner apart from the rabble of Nassau, stalked into the Governor's house one morning, and declared he was leaving. Given the rate at which his sailors were dying, and the money to be made convoying merchant ships, it came as no surprise to me. Yet Rogers refused to hear of it, and reminding Captain Chamberlen of Vane's threats to burn Nassau about our ears, insisted he stay, or else face a formal accusation of desertion. Captain Chamberlen bowed coldly, returned to his sloop, re-provisioned, and without further consultation, he sailed out a fortnight later.

The next day, two gentlemen by the names of Buck and Gohier sauntered into the Governor's house as though they owned it, to demand the first payment on their investment. They were the Governor's avaricious creditors, Mister Buck exceedingly fat, Mister Gohier exceedingly thin, and they had sailed in from Jamaica, where they had been safely waiting on news of the new Colony. The Governor explained that he had to create industries on the island before there would be trade enough to pay the port tax that would be his primary income. He tried to persuade them to invest further in the enterprises we had been considering, and when they refused, the Governor declared he would not use the small tax that had already accumulated to pay their interest, but would invest it into encouraging trade, and pay them their first return in three months.

Because of this, mere weeks after he had engaged my services, he admitted that he could not pay me in coin. Instead I accepted notes of credit, also redeemable in three months, and an offer to eat all my meals at his table. Knowing that war with Spain was looming, and that this would further stop trade, I saw this as a gamble. Yet I felt confident in the Governor and his Colony, and preferred taking promissory notes from him, to joining Harry and John hunting in the forest. I agreed to serve him faithfully, on the condition that he would order me a new suit on his own credit, so I no longer disgraced his table with my rags. In truth, I felt the Governor's struggle to be a noble one, and though some of his Officers sneered at me, yet I thought there were some who trusted me, and thought me useful.

All of the Governor's plans were set back by the contagion, few of his settlers surviving the fever. His Fleet had stopped at many other colonies on his way to the Bahamas, and he had invited many to join him, particularly the thousand poor but industrious people on the defenceless, barren island of Anguilla. Yet, none would come when they heard of the epidemic that raged on Providence, not even when Captain Chamberlen stopped by Anguilla to talk to them.

Then one night the Governor visited Cully's to down a cool ale with his creditors, and, ill himself, complained bitterly of the fever proving hardest on those he had brought with him. These careless words were deeply resented by the islanders and rovers, for we saw clearly that the Bahamas had no future without us. The islanders soon found that he had no money to help them, and shook their heads as he limped down Nassau's dusty street, half-delirious in the midday heat, afire with his dream of a Colony worth governing. He gave himself entirely to this vision, expecting as much zeal from those he governed, and in this he was disappointed.

He encouraged his surviving settlers to take on the hard work of clearing the jungle for crops, though Ma Davies insisted that the soil about Nassau was poor, and would only support tropic plants. He promised a hundred and twenty square feet inside the town, if anyone would build a house on it within a month, yet amidst the illness and heat, with no materials, no money, and with the hurricane season almost upon us, few took up his offer. He extended it to four months, and Ma Davies and Sara claimed land and put up thatched palmetto cottages, teaching their skills to some of the surviving Palatines. The rovers put up simple shelters, cleared a patch of land big enough to grow a few yams, and then went fishing or turtling, away from the fevered Governor and his arrogant Officers. Soon he was complaining that none of the islanders had the industry of his dying settlers, and that the rovers would not work at all.

Henry Jennings had asked his trusted friend, Captain John Cockram, for a copy of his chart of the Bahamas. Cockram had lived his youth a rover, yet he'd given it up many years before, to devote himself to his pretty wife and family. Now captain of the small settlement of Harbour

Island, he had high hopes of the new Governor. Like Jennings, he was an older man, though still handsome, with the dignified bearing that comes from an independent life. He had a piercing blue stare, an abundance of grey in his long, sandy hair, and though now a man of peace, he walked with his hand on his sword hilt.

Cockram was also a skilled sextant man, and had been collecting small maps of favourite harbours and sketches of perilous reefs from many captains and navigators for many years, to combine them into one comprehensive chart. Yet when he presented his unique and invaluable chart to the Council, the Governor, disappointed at the few deep harbours, did not bother to hide his suspicions that Cockram was lying, and keeping his favourite cove to himself. Cockram merely raised an eyebrow, bowed, and made to roll up the chart. The Governor then had to quickly retract his contempt in order to keep it. Yet he never regained Cockram's respect.

Yet I could have forgiven Governor Rogers some of this inflexibility, if I had thought his heart sound. Thinking himself safe amongst his men, he spoke sneeringly of all women. He never mentioned his wife, but to imply that he had been pleased to leave England for her sake, though we all knew that marriage had earned him his first promotion. When he declared a man o' war the best place for him, as there could be no petticoats aboard, his men agreed heartily. Yet they were all secretly angered when he criticised the popular Kate Pritchard. He also assumed that all the island women were whores, since they had lived here with pirates, and treated them with marked disrespect.

When Ma Davies approached him with her scheme to trap wild cattle, and begin a dairy, he informed her that he'd never met a woman with a head for business, and advised her to marry. Shocked, she demanded to know why he offered such unwanted advice to a Godly woman, who had survived the death of her beloved husband, and ran the only successful enterprise on the island, apart from the tavern. The Governor snorted his disbelief in her good sense, and declared her prices for beef extortionate. She was in the midst of explaining that it would be cheaper to breed cattle than to hunt the few left on Nassau, when the Governor interrupted her, and insisted on paying a top price of sixpence a pound. Ma Davies declared that this would barely cover the price of ammunition, and when he accused her of cheating him, she spat on the floor, turned on her heel, and left. The remaining cattle on Providence were soon hunted down, the Governor had to buy beef for his sailors and soldiers from merchantmen at ridiculous prices, and even his table was no longer so well laden.

The Governor's fears for his Colony were further increased by the might of the declining Spanish Empire. Furious that they could not keep the New World from being whittled away by French, English, Dutch, and Portuguese settlers, the Spanish Governors had begun hiring the worst scum of the Caribbean to harass vulnerable settlements. One intensely hot afternoon, we sat on the veranda of the stone house, hoping for a breeze, me reading from my notes as the Governor mopped the fever from his brow. A blow on the door downstairs announced Ben Hornigold, who swept Nat Taylor aside, and bellowed for us to come quick to Cully's tavern.

The Governor limped over as fast as he could, Hornigold explaining that Bill Dewick had just come in with three other sailors from the Jamaican sloop the Edward and William, after a narrow escape from Spanish pirates. We found them quenching enormous sea-thirsts, yet Dewick was willing enough to talk to the Governor.

"We were workin' hard with four other sloops, salvagin' Spanish wrecks on the Florida coast, divin' off the beach for gold," he began. "In July, we sighted four Spanish vessels at the mouth o' the harbour, and our Gunner fired a shot to bring 'em to, not knowin' if we could trust 'em or no. Well, they landed about a hundred and thirty armed men on the shore, and when their brigantine fired at our Fleet, they attacked our salvage crew. One man was killed, and six wounded, but despite their greater numbers, we fought hard to beat 'em back and make it to our ships, knowin' our fate otherwise. In the end, the Spaniards returned aboard their brigantine, and stood away to sea. We worked for a few more days to stow aboard what we'd found, then thinkin' they might come back with reinforcements, we upped anchor and stood for home, Captain Singer eager to report the attack to Governor Lawes.

"We returned to the same harbour just a few days ago, with twenty more men, all ready to work, hungry for more o' the gold we'd seen lyin' about on the sea floor. Well, the Spaniards found us again, a bigger Fleet this time, with two English prizes already taken. We flew a flag o' truce, and they sent us a message that there was a storm brewin', and swore that if allowed to enter the harbour, they would not harass us. We gave the signal of agreement, they came in and moored, and after a time we went back to work.

"When we were hard at it, they sent a canoa to surprise our sloop, the Gunner surrendering without a shot, the bastard. Not content with all the plate and money we'd salvaged, the thieving Spanish dogs declared us slaves for the Spanish Alcada. They made us prisoners in our own hold, and put a dozen of their own men aboard to crew our sloop. Then with five guarda del costas about us, we sailed for Cuba, sure that our lives were as good as over. But foul weather swept down upon us, and in the fury of the storm, we smashed open a loose companionway, overpowered the Papist dogs, cut their throats, and threw them to the sharks. The guarda del costas were scattered by the winds and so we made our way here. We'd be building roads on Cuba now, but for that storm."

The Governor's anxiety over Dewick's report increased his fever, yet he still asked me to convene the Council. The Councilmen groaned when he told them that Spain was astir again, and we must look to our defence. It was clear to all of us that the Spaniards would attack the

463

Bahamas again, preventing the rovers from turning privateer, and cutting off all trade from Europe.

"There can't be more than a hundred and fifty inhabitants in the whole of the Bahamas who can be relied upon to fight for us", the Governor complained.

"Many of the reformed men will return to Nassau to wait out the hurricane season", I pointed out. "They know how vicious the Spanish raids are, and their martial skills are considerable. You can trust Captain Jennings and Ben Hornigold to rally them."

"No offence, Mister Read, yet once a man has chosen the Devil, he will always turn that way again. Men like Jennings and Hornigold may have talent, yet by the evil choices they have made, they have lost any chance of taking their place next to respectable men." I sat there, my head bowed, wondering why he could not see the pain his words caused me.

"Yet, if we appointed our own men as Officers to command them…", Mister Fairfax suggested.

"Gentlemen", I tried again, "please understand that there is no one like the Brethren for independence. Let them choose their most trusted and experienced men to lead them as they always do."

"Nonsense, Mister Read, I need them loyal to me, not each other. I require three companies of militia. I will choose my own Officers, and those who sign up will behave as soldiers, or face a soldier's discipline."

Dennis Carty, reluctant to sail away from his pregnant wife, signed up as a soldier. He complained that the Officers refused to treat the rovers with any respect, and that the rovers refused to respect their Officers. "We decide what is needful, and call for volunteers. They think we need an order to piss. They won't see that an attack can only come at high tide, insist we stand guard all night, and kick us if they find us sleeping." When a man was found drunk at his post, the Governor confiscated his arms, and he laughed, and went fishing. The next time one of the Officers found a man

464

sleeping, they insisted he pay a fine. He declared he had no money, and they confined him on the Delicia, which was now a guardship. Most of the militia downed arms and deserted that day.

Dennis Carty was then promoted to Ensign, yet though he did his best to keep his men awake on guard duty, he could never remember a salute, and was incapable of saying 'Sir' as though he meant it. Captain Thomas Walker, the Brethren's old enemy, had replaced his brother William, dead of fever, on the Council. He used his position to speak hard against the reformed men, urging the Governor to distrust them, and warning always of treachery. The Governor soon promoted him to Assistant Chief Justice, and the autocratic old man swaggered about as though he was Governor himself. He passed by Dennis Carty one afternoon, and when Dennis merely returned that gentleman's nod, Captain Walker stamped off to inform the Governor that Dennis had refused him a salute. Despite my pleas, the Governor immediately sent a soldier to relieve Dennis of his duty. He came storming in, the Governor surprised to find he cared at all about losing his post, yet refusing to reverse his arbitrary decision. He thus lost one of his best men, and made enemies of all who valued the charming Irishman.

Then, on the first of September, three of Vane's Company crept into Nassau for the pardon. Old Noah Harwood was with them, and when the Governor accepted his claim that Vane had forced him, Harwood reciprocated with the news that the pirates were expected off Abaco. The combined threat of Papists and pirates convinced the Governor that he urgently needed the fort in good repair, though he complained bitterly that the rovers would not work unless paid. I tried to explain that the Brethren would fight the Spaniards at sea, and saw no use in slaving on any fort.

Then, instead of agreeing to chase Vane, the bad tempered Captain Whitney of the Rose announced he was sailing out. Sure that the fort would soon be stronger, the

465

Governor threatened Captain Whitney with an accusation of desertion if he did not stay another three weeks. Then a sudden relapse saw the Governor very ill, and though no work was started on the fort, Captain Whitney sailed out two weeks later.

We were then left without a man o' war, apart from the Delicia guardship, foul with weeds and slow. Henry Jennings insisted she would be of little use against any enemy, yet the Governor refused his offer to careen her, sure that Jennings would inform Vane when we were defenceless. Yet despite her uselessness, it cost him a great deal to keep the Delicia, as he had to buy all the food for her crew from traders, with greatly discounted notes of credit from his financiers.

When Captain Whitney sailed, the Governor sent a letter home begging his superiors to allocate him Captain Chamberlen and the Shark, to guard the important trade of the area. Neither this letter, nor any other that he wrote to ask help of his Government, was ever answered.

The Governor was so afraid that the fever would leave him without soldiers that he wrote to Governor Hunter in New York, and begged for forty men from his garrison. Then, as his fever increased, he feared that this letter had miscarried, and wrote another to Governor Lawes of Jamaica, begging twenty or thirty men from him. When the rains came in cataracts in early October, and the heat abated, those soldiers who had survived the fever recovered somewhat. Then he thought better of his pleas, for he could not afford to feed any more soldiers, and wrote again to New York, saying that if they were not already on their way, to send only twenty-five men. Then he wrote to Governor Lawes, asking him to keep his men, though the sneering Captain Gale insisted that neither Governor would send their soldiers to die of fever in the Bahamas. The Governor even pounced upon a trader's news of an imminent Indian war in Carolina, presuming that her colonists would flee to us. "Gad, how disappointed they'd be", Captain Gale sneered.

The day after the Rose sailed away, Captain Powers sailed into Nassau in a canoa, complaining that he'd been robbed by Charles Vane, who'd taken both his ship, the Emperor, and Captain King's ship, the Neptune, in a determined attack off Charles Town. Vane had then sailed them to Green Turtle Key, off Abaco, where he'd plundered them at his leisure, wishing the Captains a good voyage home as he sailed out.

Ben Hornigold and Captain Cockram then requested the Council give them privateering commissions against Vane. Thomas Walker declared they could not be trusted, and would join Vane on the account, and Hornigold clapped his hand to his cutlass. Cockram restrained him, and insisted that if they had wanted to join Vane, they could have sailed out without the Governor's permission. Despite Thomas Walker's ravings, the Governor then signed both commissions, promising the Captains a small percentage of any cargo they recovered. Hornigold offered me the post of Gunner, yet I turned him down, declaring myself too busy with the Governor. I told him later, over a quiet bottle, that in truth, I feared to meet old friends in battle. He admitted that many of the old rovers felt the same, and that 'twas lucky that Vane had made himself so unpopular, many blaming his lordly airs when 'Governor' for the fall of Nassau.

Soon after Hornigold sailed out, Thomas Bowlin of the trading sloop the Dolphin sailed in, demanding that something be done to put the fear of God into the damned Spaniards. The Dolphin had left Nassau in June to trade with an old Spanish gentleman of Porto Prince, in Cuba. She had been attacked by a Spanish guarda del costa, and Bowlin and five others had been forced to act as pilots for them. The Spaniards had raided the logwood cutters of Andros Island, and then sailed for Providence, wanting more intelligence of our Governor. They had spied pirate vessels in our harbour, and returned to Porto Prince to report this to the Alcada. Their friend the Spanish trader had then insisted on selling

Bowlin a pettiauger for thirty-eight pieces of eight, keeping an English lad as hostage for the money. The Alcada allowed them to sail away, on condition that they delivered a message from him, declaring that the English were all pirates, and refusing to recognise the Governor of Providence.

Then one bastion of the main fort, the most important, since it guarded the sea, simply fell down one afternoon, having only a cracked wall for its foundation. The Governor not only wanted this fort repaired, he insisted on having another built to guard the rocky channel that Vane had escaped through, though no Spaniard would have chanced it.

He questioned Nat Taylor, and ordered him to set up a kiln to burn coral, to make the lime needed for mortar. Then he demanded further credit from Buck and Gohier to pay the workers one piece of eight a day. Yet the rovers worked with little industry in that killing heat, and only for long enough to buy rum and women.

The only man on Providence who really knew stonework was George Hooper, the first mate on the Delicia. He was a solid, surly man, with little to say apart from snarled orders. He treated Nat Taylor with contempt, and would let fly with his fists at any man he thought shirking, though he never laboured himself. 'Twas a measure of our differences, that the Governor thought he was the most valuable man he had, admiring his command and vigour, while the rest of us hated him.

The Governor soon lost what little patience he possessed with the rovers, and towards the end of September, he ordered every man up at dawn, every day for ten days, to work either on the main fort under George Hooper, or on the eastward battery under Nat Taylor. Rogers thought it was the promise of free food and drink that persuaded them, yet in truth it was because he pitched in himself, despite his fever, and insisted that his Officers also soil their hands, their sweat and curses lightening our hard labour. Nat Taylor and George Hooper were soon included in the Council, despite the objections of Captain Gale of the Delicia, that neither were gentlemen.

Though the work stagnated at the main fort, the smaller eastern redoubt, where Nat Taylor directed the men, rose stone by stone, and was soon finished. Then we began the hard work of hauling the great guns from the Delicia guardship up onto the ramparts, work that took us many weeks, and used up all the Governor's remaining credit.

As the work on the forts finally got under way, the Governor succumbed to a fever that left him entirely prostrated, despite his immense strength of will. Mistress Pritchard was the only one of us with the backbone to insist that he take to his bed, and when he raged at her for her impudence, she asked him why he wanted to die in Nassau. When he finally gave way, he made a great fuss of refusing to have whores tend him, until Mistress Pritchard declared she would nurse him herself. He cursed all women to the depths of Hell then, yet was too ill to do anything but suffer her firm and gentle ministrations. He was a bad patient, yet she paid no attention to his complaints, and forced him to eat her soups and drink the bitter quinoa bark that she hoped would save his life. She wanted him cooled by bathing, and when he insisted on his modesty, she laughed, and reminding him that she was a respectable widow, asked Nat Taylor to perform the task.

She was often alone upstairs with the Governor in his room, and I would hear him abusing her feebly, while she called him a baby, which infuriated him. Yet, over the long course of his illness, he did come to rely on her good nature, and would fret if she was late, or if she did not spend as much time with him as the day before. I prayed that her good nature would soften him a little, and it seemed to me that by the time the fever left him, he was more tender with her. Then, when he was again on his feet, he stood on his dignity with Kate Pritchard, and though evidently hurt by it, she pretended not to care, and was as loud and flirtatious as ever.

She had carefully invested small sums with those she trusted, both in produce and trade, relying on Jennings' judgement of a man's character, and Hornigold's assessment of the enterprise. She was particularly helpful with the financiers, Buck and Gohier, who were slowly gaining more control over the Colony, as the Governor became more obligated to them. Whenever they complained of their lack of capital return, Mistress Kate insisted that the Bahamas would prove a worthwhile investment, and offered to buy them out. Without this, they would have been even more pressing with demands for repayment and higher rates of interest. As it was, the Governor was plagued by them.

When ill, the Governor left the quiet, industrious, Robert Beauchamp, as head of the Council. He had sailed in as first Lieutenant of the Governor's Militia, then when most of his soldiers died, he was appointed Secretary General of the islands. On the Council, Mister Salter died of fever, and Colonel Christopher Gale, the guardship Captain's brother, replaced him. Since he had done legal work in North Carolina, the Governor also made Colonel Gale our Chief Justice, the townspeople glad enough that Thomas Walker was not given his old post back.

Mister Fairfax was also on the Council. Rogers had tried to appoint the light-hearted young man as Deputy to the bed-ridden Mister Graves, who was still, nominally, His Majesty's Collector of Customs. Fairfax had refused the position, declaring the old man too petulant to work with. Yet, not wanting to be idle, and wanting to be paid, Fairfax proposed that he keep a small fee from the port tax he collected, letting Mister Graves keep his salary for the short time he had left in the world.

He came into Cully's shortly after, called for a good bottle of brandy, and declared that, as he was a trained Judge of the Admiralty, the Governor had asked him to formalise an Admiralty Court. "I'm so glad you took the Pardon, gentlemen. For God's sake stick to it. 'Twould give me no pleasure to hang any of you. So drink another dram and

470

pledge me the honest life!"

Thomas Walker proposed an Assembly for all the Bahama Islands, based on their populace. The Governor decided on fifteen Providence men, two for Eleuthera, where there were about fifty families, two for Harbour Island, where there were about sixty families, and one for Abaco, which was less well-inhabited. Then he declared that he could not find fifteen men on Providence that he trusted, and this was a great source of ill-feeling between him and us, and another good plan delayed. He did appoint Deputy Governors to the other islands in the Bahamas, however, and asked them to form militias of their able-bodied men. Following Captain Cockram's directions, the men of Harbour Island completed two small forts at the entrance to their cove, and the Governor gave them powder and shot for their trouble.

Thomas Walker was counting the weeks since Hornigold and Cockram sailed out, and by insisting that they had betrayed their Pardons, he did much damage to the remaining patience of the rovers. Many were now back out on the account, having had their fill of the honest life. Those that could not escape, and the few of us still dedicated to the growing colony, kept working on our defences. We built a palmetto hut inside the main fort as a guard house for the garrison. We cleared all the brush and scrub within gunshot of the fort, and when the Governor was again on his feet, we began the palisado around it. Every male on the island, between eighteen and sixty years of age, was ordered by the Council to bring ten straight sticks of wood nine feet long and four inches in diameter within ten days, or pay ten royales to the Governor. The keepers of the punch houses that had proliferated in Nassau, selling bad liquor to the soldiers and sailors, were to send in forty sticks, or pay forty royales. The rovers called this unpaid work 'slavery', cursed the Governor, and went out turtling, or drifted back into piracy.

The back-sliding of the reformed men proved to the

Governor that he had been right about us all along. He could not see that it was his poor opinion of us that sapped our support. He spoke well of Jennings and Hornigold, yet it was with regret, as though their few years of piracy had ruined them. When I explained that there were no people like the rovers of Nassau for independence, and that they would stand him in good stead if he would respect them for men of action and character, he ignored me. He called the pride of the Brethren a constant curse on his Government, and Nassau was divided into the few who ruled, and the rest of us.

Chapter 25: Mutiny

The colony had only survived its first few expensive months, when the two London merchants, Buck and Gohier, chose to begrudge the Governor any more credit. Insisting they would ruin him unless he repaid them somehow, they demanded the old dosshouse, to turn back into a brothel. The Governor refused Mistress Pritchard's assistance, preferring to swallow his principles rather than his pride. And with this defeat, something broke in the man. He struggled on stubbornly, yet without any real hope of making a Colony from the wreck of Nassau.

Never an elegant dresser, he began to entirely neglect his appearance, so that when strangers sailed in, they looked askance to meet him. Yet 'twas the drink that undid him, for once the wine in Nat Taylor's cellars was gone, he descended upon Cully's, talking loudly and with little judgement, and further offending those he could have relied on. He raved incessantly of the simple life aboard a man o' war, with no women, and the lash for any that disobeyed him.

He seemed incapable of seeing beyond a man's circumstances to his character, and flatterers gathered about him, while honest men stood aside. Richard Turnley, his chief pilot on the Delicia, a thin, sly man, reported drunken conversations to him, and good men would be snubbed because Judas Turnley had spoken ill of them. Finding the Governor impossible to please, even Jennings talked of sailing for Jamaica and I was sure that it was only Mistress Pritchard's promising eyes that kept him with us. The surviving Palatines complained bitterly that none of the pledges made to them in Europe had been kept, and the old islanders stated bluntly that they had lived better under pirate rule.

Captain Thomas Walker also drank at Cully's with the Governor, counting the weeks since Hornigold and Cockram had sailed to attack Vane, and insisting they had reneged on their Pardons. He was so loud in declaring that none of us could be trusted, that even the Governor saw he'd get his throat cut some dark night. When a Barbados merchant offered to carry a cargo for the Governor, he was quick to ask Captain Walker to go along as supercargo, stressing the trust of the position, and how much he depended on a successful trade. Captain Walker preened himself on the appointment, and took his son Charlie as his assistant. Charlie was a sturdy lad of fifteen years, who had come with his father from a quiet family life in Abaco, to find him hated for his mania against the Brethren. Yet the rovers encouraged the boy to hang about the rotting docks, for he was a quiet, modest lad, and they had already noted his skill with his father's sloop.

When Thomas Walker sailed, only Captain Gale of the Delicia was left to talk openly against the Brethren, though he was never seen at Cully's. After another two weeks of Turnley's insinuations, the Governor was ready to believe that Hornigold and Cockram had indeed betrayed him. By then, many of us were wondering if something had indeed gone wrong, perhaps a battle between the pirates and the reformed men, that had left Vane the victor and our mates dead.

Then, one fine afternoon towards the end of September, with massive white clouds towering to Heaven, there was a salute from a ship's gun, and a reply from the Delicia. The whole town rushed to the waterfront to watch Hornigold and Cockram sail triumphantly in, a prize at their tail, Hornigold waving his hat from the bowsprit. He met the Governor on the sand, and saluting smartly, reported that he had exact news of Vane, and that as the Governor's turtling sloop had joined the pirates, he'd brought it back. I thought the Governor would embrace the burly sea Captain, he was so delighted. Hornigold winked then, and the wicked old rover declared he'd had the great pleasure of being able to rescue his old friend, Captain Thomas Walker, from certain death at the hands of the Brethren.

Later at Cully's, Walker staggered in with his son supporting him, only to have Hornigold insist on a comfortable chair for him, assuring him constantly, with a twinkle in his eye, that he need not thank him for the rescue, or feel obligated to repay him in any way for saving his life, and that of his son. The rovers openly chuckled at Walker's mortification, and we drank to the health of the Governor's privateers.

Hornigold explained that he and Captain Cockram had spent weeks watching Vane's Company strip the merchant ships they had captured off Charles Town. As the pirates were too numerous to challenge, they had spied on them instead, and found that many regretted following Vane, and talked openly of coming in for the Pardon.

Then Nicholas Woodall had sailed in with the Governor's turtling sloop, and a Barbados merchantman he'd captured just off Providence, with Thomas Walker aboard. He had with him fifty men, ammunition, and loud complaints of the hard life in Nassau under the new Governor. Vane, delighted to see him, had offered him first share of the loot if he'd join them, and Woodall had agreed, strengthening Vane's Fleet considerably.

As night fell, the pirates lit torches and drank to their new friends. Woodall, soon drunk as a lord, informed Vane that Thomas Walker was a prisoner on board his turtling sloop, and Vane had demanded pirate justice for their old enemy. They voted to hang Walker the next morning, no man calling for mercy, and then dragged him ashore to inform him of his fate. His young son was with him, and he fell to his knees in the sand, and begging hard for the life of his father, turned them against this cruelty.

The Pirate Fleet sailed soon after, leaving all their prisoners marooned on Green Turtle Key, with little in the way of water or provisions. Yet Hornigold and Cockram slipped after them, and as Woodall in the turtling sloop was the slowest, they waited until Vane was out of sight, and then easily cut him off, and brought him in.

The Governor clapped Woodall in irons on the Delicia, insisting he must hang, and only then did Ben Hornigold understand the consequences of his success. He blustered, insisting on the damage to his reputation with the Brethren, and the Governor did not have the good sense to repress his sneer. Hornigold declared that if this was his reward for his loyalty, then the Governor should use Thomas Walker to do his dirty work. The Governor took umbrage, and John Cockram had to step in and calm them both down.

Governor Rogers took me with him to write notes of his interview with Woodall. I could see the turtler was a simple man, and reminded the Governor that he had refused to go on the account with Vane, when the Governor first came in. Governor Rogers told him that unless he could provide substantial information against Vane, he would send him to England to hang. The frightened turtler told us all he knew.

"I swear yer 'Onour, I 'ad no idea I'd ever run across 'im again. When we begged for the sloop to go out for turtles, we 'ad no other plan. Then we spied Vane 'oled up in Green Turtle Key, two prizes with 'im, and not enough food for any man. We 'ad no choice but to give 'em what we 'ad, and 'e insisted on payin' us, and when they 'ad a party, we got kind o' roped in. Ye know 'ow it is when ye see old friends ye didn't think to ever see again this side o' the grave. They were doin' well back on the account, and we...Well things 'ave not been easy 'ere, as I told 'em. 'E said no 'ard feelin's, an' asked us to join 'im, and the crew voted 'aye', though o' course, mostly 'twas from fear o' Vane, and we would o' thought it over when we were clear of 'im.

"'E told us they'd 'eaded up to Carolina, an' taken a small sloop from Antigua, then one from Curacao. That was all right, but Vane an' Yeats fell out over a large brigantine full o' slaves from Africa. Vane wanted the brigantine, an' put the slaves on the Lark with Yeats, where there was no room for 'em. Well, Yeats was that angered at Vane's 'igh-'andedness, 'e slipped 'is cable a few days later, an' made off with the Lark an' the slaves, sailin' over a sandbar to escape, Vane firin' a broadside after 'is old mate.

"Vane took two ships comin' out o' Charles Town, both bound for England an' crammed with goods. They struck their colours as soon as 'e caught 'em, an 'e took 'em all to Green Turtle Key. Captain King o' the Neptune went down bad with fever then, an 'is crew spoke up for 'im, sayin' 'e was a good man, ever sparin' o' the lash an' generous with the rum, an' Vane let 'im keep 'is own cabin an' did 'im no 'arm. Vane wanted to plunder the vessels an' let 'em go, but the Company voted to keep the Emperor, though she needed careening, as did the rest o' their Fleet.

That took four weeks, durin' which we sailed in. They loaded me sloop with goods from the Neptune an' voted to maroon all who would not join us, scuttlin' the Neptune an' breakin' her boats. 'Tis true we took Walker's boy with us, thinkin' it a good joke to turn 'im into one of us, as 'e's a fine lad who knows these waters well, an' we didn't like to think of 'im starvin'. But afore we could get out o' the channel, Ben 'Ornigold shows up, an' though we made 'im chase us, 'e caught us soon enough. 'Ornigold says 'e got in afore us, an' watched it all. Ye can check all I say with 'im. I'm tellin' ye the truth, Guvnor.

"But ye'd better send help fast to those poor bastards marooned on Green Turtle Key, for Vane left 'em no provisions but rice an' water, an' Captain King was dyin'. I know I've bin a fool, Guvnor, but ye don't 'ave to 'ang me for that. 'Tis no easy life on Providence for any man now, an' ye might as well keep me 'ere an' work me 'ard, for I'd 'ate that more'n death."

The Governor's face was a shard of stone, utterly without compassion. "You attacked the Barbados merchantman that I had loaded with the produce of Nassau, hoping to sustain this settlement. You threatened the life of our brave Captain Walker. Although I do not have the power to try you and hang you, I will be sending you, your Quartermaster, and your Gunner to England for trial, with written depositions against you that will leave little room for mercy."

As soon as Woodall's fate was known, Ben Hornigold's popularity vanished. The old rovers growled against him for turning on his own kind, though none had the courage to reproach him directly, for it would have meant a duel. Ben had too much wounded pride to defend himself to anyone but Jennings, who shrugged and told him that he could not be half the Governor's man, it was all or nothing. This gave me food for thought, for I had seen the extent of the Governor's mercy, and felt he would have as little compassion for me.

With the reformed men back in favour, the Governor offered Henry Jennings a privateer's commission. He refused, though he took advantage of the Governor's good humour, and advised him to defend Nassau's trade routes with sloops of old rovers, thus dividing the Brethren against themselves. He also recommended that the Governor extend the Pardon past September, so that dissatisfied pirates could still leave the life, and this the Governor agreed to consider.

That night I returned to my camp, and sat by my fire, unable to eat, questioning my loyalty to Governor Woodes Rogers. I considered his inability to pay me, his notes of credit against his financiers now quite worthless. I considered his growing lack of respect for my opinion, his open contempt for women, and his incapacity to listen to those of low standing. I considered his slovenliness, his indiscriminate drinking, and his sycophants. By dawn, I had decided to look for other employment.

Reluctant to face him, I stopped to speak with Ma Davies, and was late at my post for the first time. Captain Gale sneered at my haggard appearance, and muttered something to Turnley, yet Governor Rogers was too intent on plans to salvage the Neptune and rescue the marooned men, to notice me. Captain Powers was airing his doubts that Captains Hornigold and Cockram could be trusted with the salvage, and seeing an opportunity to be free of Nassau for a time, I offered to go as the Governor's supercargo, to list everything recovered. Captain Gale sneered again, yet Governor Rogers nodded, and I was free to offer my services to Ben Hornigold.

I found him at Cully's, where I asked him to sign me on, and he was glad to, telling me straight that many had sworn they'd never sail under him again for what had happened to Nick Woodall. "Yet 'twas plain enough that Woodall met them by arrangement. The ammunition alone proves he meant to turn pirate. The taking of the Governor's trader..."

"I think so too, yet I think Governor Rogers should have warned you that he'd hang any pirate you caught."

"Aye, he allows no man honour but himself."

"And favours none of us with his respect, not Jennings, not Cockram, not even Ma Davies. I would like to do that good woman a favour, in return for the breakfast she gave me this morning. Her boys, Harry and John, are mad for the sea, and would make fine ship's boys. I've hunted with them, and they're excellent shots, and spirited lads, and would be of service to you."

"Aye, if their Ma will allow it. I was going to ask her to provision us. Walk that way with me. We should be just in time for lunch." Ma Davies readily agreed to both our proposals, needing cash like everyone else in Nassau, though she took me aside privately and begged me to keep an eye out for her boys. Hornigold and Cockram signed their crews on that afternoon, all of us grumbling to be working for the Governor's wages, not shares of the salvage.

We set sail only hours later, the tide then at the full, Harry and John delighted to be at sea at last. I was relieved to be under no orders but those of the forthright, good-humoured Ben Hornigold, refreshed to feel the sea breeze in my face, our graceful sloop running to a clear horizon. I saw then that the vision of a prosperous Colony had kept me chained to Nassau, and her inadequate Governor, and I resolved then to ask for my wages upon my return, and to quit his service with a few coins in my pocket.

We sailed past Abaco, and crept into Green Turtle Key, keeping a good lookout for Vane's Company. We found no pirates, only the ailing Captain King directing work on the Neptune, trying to get her sea-worthy again. Vane's shot had merely dented her strong hull of English oak, and she was far from scuttled, and well worth salvaging. We were anxious to hear that Vane had been in again since Hornigold had taken Woodall, and all of us were thankful to have missed battle with his Fleet. Seeing their repairs to the Neptune, Vane had threatened to burn the ship with Captain King in her, if he ever touched her again. Yet with their provisions nearly gone, they had seen little choice in the matter. Captain King reported himself somewhat recovered, yet two of his crew were now raving with fever, and Captain Cockram carefully dosed them with his wife's quinoa bark tea. We gave them as much beer and bread as they wanted, and those that were strong enough showed us the goods still in the Neptune that were worth salvaging. We worked hard with block and tackle through two days of blistering heat, loading our sloops quickly with rice, rigging and sails, fearing that Vane would show again, and we would have to fight.

On the first night, sitting about a fire on the shore, Ben Hornigold asked Captain King what he thought of Woodall. King declared that his meeting with Vane was no accident, and that it was Woodall who had talked hardest against the Pardon, and against sparing Thomas Walker. I wondered if Anne and Jack, their pockets full of loot, might not have been ready to come in, but for Woodall's furious speech against the Governor. Three men from Charles Town, who had been sailing for England aboard the Neptune to escape the Indian war, swore they would stand as witnesses against Woodall, and make sure he swung.

We sailed back to Providence, and on Cockram's advice, the arrogant stone mason, George Hooper, paid the Governor seventy pounds of Jamaican money for the salvage of the Neptune. Yet despite having the cash, the Governor refused to pay us the wages we'd agreed on, and instead gave us more worthless notes of credit upon his financiers. Though the others protested loudly, I held my tongue for want of my dinner, resolving to quietly enquire after new employment elsewhere, so I could still eat at his table.

Hooper needed a vessel to help with the salvage of the Neptune, so the Governor lent him an old sloop left behind by Vane. Hooper renamed her the Willing Mind, yet the penny-pinching fool refused to give her a bottle of rum for her christening, and refused to pay experienced sailors. Instead the Governor loaned him a Company of Militia, and Hooper hired a few local lads, including Ma Davies' boys, who would sail for any wages.

I saw the Davies boys on their return, swaggering like experienced sailors now, and they told me that the salvage had gone well at first. Hooper had supervised the loading of the last scraps of the Neptune's water-logged cargo into the Willing Mind. He then had them throw out the Neptune's ballast, and when he had patched her slightly damaged hull, and pumped her dry, she had lifted with the tide. Hooper then decided she could be sailed, and had her jury-rigged for the small crossing to Nassau harbour.

Yet his miserliness was his undoing, for in refusing to hire a pilot, Hooper sailed the Willing Mind onto a sandbar. Still declining everyone's advice, he unloaded her salvaged cargo and tried to heave her upright with the tide. Instead, he snapped her keel. When the Governor ordered a warrant of survey upon the stricken sloop, his carpenter declared that with her backbone broken, she was nought but timber.

The rugged John Auger had watched the sloop's destruction, and when Hooper finally rowed away from her in disgust, letting the tide swamp her, Auger was the first man aboard to claim salvage. At low tide, he and his Company tore the Willing Mind to pieces by the light of the

481

full moon, collecting the wood and the fittings, and loading them into Auger's sloop, the Mary. The Governor was furious to lose a perfectly good ship for the sake of the damaged Neptune, yet instead of blaming George Hooper for her loss, he sent a curt note to Auger, demanding the return of his timber. Auger stood by his right to salvage what another man had left to the sea, and refused. Young Mister Fairfax, who was trained in Admiralty Law, told Rogers he did not have the right to deny salvage, throwing the Governor into a rage that reminded me of old Mister Grave's petulance.

I made my way to Cully's, and told Auger that he'd made a bad bargain, trading wood for the Governor's good opinion. He stood on his rights, claiming to be as good a man as Governor Rogers, who was nought but a parasite on the work of poorer men. I saw Richard Turnley sneak off, ready to pour his spite into the Governor's ear, and hurrying after him, found the Governor already convinced that Auger had conspired with Hooper against him, though I told him the two men could not stand each other. The Governor railed against untrustworthy subordinates, muttering about the damned heat, and drinking tots of rum to keep his fever low. I quickly returned to Cully's and told Auger to take his sloop away trading for a time, until the Governor regained his sense. Auger clapped me on the shoulder, and thanked me, yet when I asked him for a place in his crew, he muttered some excuse, and refused. In truth, he saw me as the Governor's man, and did not trust me, and, ashamed, I did not press him.

Another message came in on a fishing sloop from Vane, threatening to attack Nassau with the help of Captain Stede Bonnet. We knew that the gentlemanly Bonnet had sold his Barbados plantation to pay for his first pirate ship, in order to escape his shrew of a wife. Yet he had the Devil's luck, and fell in with Blackbeard, the worst bully in the Caribbean. They did well, yet with his ship full of the Fleet's treasure, Blackbeard had deliberately run the rest of his ships aground at Topsail Inlet, marooning all but his best men, and absconding with the loot. He used the treasure to buy his Pardon from the corrupt Governor Eden of North Carolina, where he settled. The poxed madman married again, and whored the poor girl to his crew when he grew tired of her. As well as terrifying the local planters, and assaulting their wives and daughters, he also continued his piracies, which the corrupt Governor Eden condemned as legal salvages, for a share of the profits.

We did not have a Governor as bad as that. Governor Rogers was simply too convinced that the reform of Nassau could only be carried out his way. He wanted to use those he found on Nassau, yet did not value any apart from his few surviving Officers, or at least those with whom he had not yet quarrelled. Young Mister Fairfax kept a strict eye on what goods came in and out of Nassau, taking a small cut both ways as port tax for Governor Rogers, and 'twas this that brought the stubborn John Auger into new conflict with the Governor. Auger, following my advice to get out from under the Governor's nose, had signed on a crew to cut and trade hardwood. They had spent weeks sailing the Bahamas looking for tall trees growing close to the shore, cutting them down, splitting them laboriously into timber, and loading it all into the Mary. Dennis Carty was with him, hoping that trading would prove more profitable than the military life, for he was now a father. The timid George Bendall had lost his sick mother to the fever, and he now chose to leave the petulant Mister Graves for a new life at sea.

When they returned to Nassau, the Mary sitting low in the water with their hard-won timber, Auger's men strode into Cully's, proud of themselves, each sure of his share in the profits. Auger had assigned guard shifts to each man of the crew, taking the first himself so that he could get gloriously drunk afterwards. George Bendall took the next shift, and it was he who met Mister Fairfax when he rowed out to assess the Mary's cargo. The port tax he asked for was not excessive, yet when Auger received George's message later that night, the stocky, forthright sailor exploded in rage. He had no cash, and he refused to see why the Governor had a right to any of the wood he and his men had worked so hard for. I tried to calm him, pointing out that the Governor was only trying to make the Colony pay for itself, yet Auger, red-faced with fury, clenched his fists and accused the Governor of wanting the salvage back from the Willing Mind, and using this as an excuse to raid his vessel. "He's just sitting on his arse, raking it in from the sweat of working men, needing to save himself from his own poor investment."

Auger's stubbornness proved a rallying point for the traders, and the next day, none would pay the port tax. Fairfax ran around charming the Captains, convincing many that the Governor was only doing what he had a right to do, especially considering how much he was in debt for the Colony. Yet Auger would not be swayed, and made no secret of it, and the Governor talked of imprisoning him aboard the Delicia. Convinced that this would cause a riot, Mister Fairfax spent a long evening drinking with Auger at Cully's, and exerting his considerable charm. The next morning, he announced that, as Auger would be taking a load of salt and coconuts to trade for meat on behalf of the Governor, he could defer paying the tax until he returned with the profits from his journey. Auger snorted and said nothing, yet the compromise was enough to calm the Governor, and ease the tension in Nassau.

Dennis Carty talked to other traders of sailing in convoy to Puerto Principe, in Cuba. Vane had stolen the Lancaster sloop from Neal Walker before the Governor came, and the Walkers had reclaimed it through the council before Neal Walkers death. Now Thomas Walker made Captain Greenaway her master at sea, and invested in a load of produce. Captains Greenaway and White agreed to go with the Mary, yet asked for another man each, since they were short-handed. Dennis promised himself to Captain

White's schooner, the Bachelor's Adventure, and sent the young George Bendall to help aboard the Lancaster.

Governor Rogers then sent James Kerr, a quiet, steady man, once midshipman on the Rose, onto Auger's ship as supercargo, to look after his trade. Auger concluded that the Governor wanted Kerr on the Mary to keep an eye on his wood, to be sure of his cut of the profits. When Kerr brought Richard Turnley aboard to act as his clerk, Auger was convinced there was a conspiracy afoot, and growled at being forced to keep company with spies. When he saw I'd heard him, he gave me a ferocious scowl for being another of the Governor's dogs.

Then, on the fourth of October, Sara Carty, her newborn babe in her arms, waved her handsome husband away from the waterfront. From the rolling deck of the Bachelor's Adventure, Dennis kissed his hands to her and shouted that he loved her more than his life, the water carrying his cry over the bay, men looking up from their work to smile at his foolishness.

Yet the freedom of the open sea soon unleashed the resentment amongst the rovers on the trading ships, and talk of mutiny swept through them. The most adamant was Phineas Bunce, the Quartermaster of the Bachelor's Adventure, who openly regretted leaving Vane's Company for the Pardon, and now called for them all to go back on the account, taking Captain White's schooner with him. When Bunce began his rebellious speeches, Dennis declined joining them, citing his little family as his reason. So Bunce lied, insisting that John Auger was set on piracy, and was relying on his friend to help take the schooner.

Two days after setting out for Cuba, the small Fleet anchored for the night at Green Key, a small isle twenty-five leagues south-east of Providence. It was well known for the pigs that ran wild upon it, feeding on the tropical cabbage and palms. Some of the men, in need of meat and diversion, went hunting in the thick bush and brought back a huge sow, which they butchered and divided amongst the three vessels.

485

After supper, the three Captains met on Auger's sloop to agree on the course south to Cuba. James Kerr, prompted by the frightened Turnley, tried to insist that there be no delay, and that they take advantage of the winds, and sail that night, yet Auger was past listening to him.

"I am Master aboard the Mary, Jim Kerr, and ye'll keep yer mouth shut on anything but tallying the cargo. Is that clear? Now, Captain Greenaway, I think it foolish to sail up to those shoals at night. If we set sail towards midnight, we'll come to dangerous waters with the sun well up, and I can pilot us safely through." Captains Greenaway and White agreed with his plan, and rowed off to drink together on the Bachelor's Adventure. Auger tried to sleep, for he had been up half the night. Half an hour later, John Hipps, the Lancaster's old boatswain, rowed out looking for Greenaway, and woke Auger to warn him of the wild mood of the men. Auger, his mood foul, stamped his way aft for a pipe of tobacco, cursing them all.

At about five o'clock, Bunce came aboard the Mary with the glum Dennis Carty. Dennis immediately stepped aft, to secure the ship's munitions, thinking this was Auger's plan. Bunce distracted those on deck by demanding a drink, and Auger muttered that Kerr, the Governor's dog, was in charge of supplies. Mister Kerr asked Turnley to fetch the beer, and kept polishing the silver cutlass he had found diving off Florida. Bunce snatched it off him, admiring it fulsomely, and then began swinging it about his head, flourishing it too close to Kerr's head. "Ah, the murders I could have committed with this as a rover", he boasted. "It sings for the blood o' cowards, it does. That was the life, eh Auger? The true life for a real man." Auger growled at him to stow it. Bunce then smacked the flat of the sword into Kerr's back, frightening him. Turnley, returning with the beer, cried at him to take care what he did, for Mister Kerr would not take such usage.

"Why ye stinkin', grovellin' dog, what would ye know o' real men, ye arse-licking son of a whore? This is

486

almost the old life over again, eh Auger? To walk the decks of a quick ship, and feel her ready to pounce and plunder. To answer to no man but yerself and yer mates. That is the life for a free man."

"For the sake of my sore head, would ye stow it!" Auger growled again.

"Aye me old mate, I see the way it is. Yer as tame a pirate as Hornigold. Ye may snarl at yer master, but he rules ye, and ye know it." Then he felt the sharp edge of the cutlass, and grinned. "I only know this, John Auger. The Mary is a lovely ship and fast, and rates a better life than trader for a leech like Rogers. I swear, she almost deserves me for a Captain."

"By the four winds, I'll see you in Hell first", Auger snarled, his hands in fists. "Dave Soward entrusted me as her Master, and ye'll not take her or her cargo from me and the men who worked for it."

Auger's crew, woken by the quarrel, gathered about their Captain, and Bunce, out-numbered, laughed at Auger, and throwing down the cutlass, clapped him on the back. "Nay man, I'd not take her. But I'd help meself to those other two vessels, and have ye sail with me, rovin' the Caribbean like in the old days. All the men are sick o' livin' like dogs under an over-proud Governor. An' don't tell me ye don't hate the bastard, John Auger. Don't tell me ye don't wish you were yer own master again. I know ye, once ye've had enough, ye can be pushed no further. We've Bill Cunningham, Blackbeard's old Gunner, ready to captain the Lancaster, and he has talked her crew into seein' it our way. Dennis Carty has seen to the Bachelor's Adventure, and he's standin' guard over this ship's guns right now."

"Are ye asking me to join yer Company, or telling me in yer own damned roundabout way that ye'll have the Mary whether I join or no?"

"Come man, I want ye as a comrade, and yer men with ye. Between these vessels alone, there's enough to set every man up for a year. All we have to do is take 'em. Will ye join us, Auger? Will ye be a free man again?"

"Damn ye to Hell, and the Governor too. But yer right to say that I've thought o' my freedom afore this. I've sworn not to return to Nassau to lick that bastard's boots. But to go on the account again..."

"He don't respect men like you, only arse-lickers like Turnley, who was unwise to sail with us on this voyage. Keeping an eye on us, the little bastard. And who the Hell does Kerr think he is, lording it over us? Hey you, Kerr, bring me a bottle of beer you dog! Hear that Auger, a pun by my life!"

Kerr sent the frightened Turnley for another beer, and attempted to remonstrate with Auger. "You are angry with the Governor now, yet don't let that tempt you to do what will get you hung..."

Dennis Carty's voice rang out from the main cabin, where the arms were kept, singing a popular song: "Did ye not promise me that ye would marry me?"

"That I will, for I am Parson", Bunce sang back, and Auger realised it was a signal. Then Bunce snatched the cutlass from the deck and cut Kerr hard across the back, so that he fell, screaming. "Carty's got the main cabin, the mutiny is on!" Bunce cried. "Tell me now, John Auger, are ye with us or no?"

"Aye, I'm with ye Bunce, if Dennis is. We'll show the bastards they can't step on us. We'll turn all those who won't join us ashore, keep the Fleet, and run for Saint Thomas. The Governor there will buy all we have, and we can continue as a Company, or disband, as each man wants. What say ye men, will ye sail with us on the account? Will ye be free again, and keep the work of yer own hands?" His crew cheered, and the Mary was won.

John Hipps, the Lancaster's elderly Boatswain, had rowed over to the Bachelor's Adventure to tell Captain Greenaway of his fears of the men. He got him alone by asking for a wee pipe o' tobacco, and then quietly reported Mister Kerr as having a mind to sail that evening, not giving the men the night to talk mutiny. Greenaway decided to return to the Mary to speak to Kerr, yet just as he made for the gunwales, John Auger, Phineas Bunce, Dennis Carty, and many others came over the side. Greenaway immediately demanded of Bunce, his Quartermaster, where he had been, and told him to ready the ship for sailing. Bunce asked him to walk down into his cabin, and fearing that Bunce would kill the old sea Captain, Auger felt the first pang of conscience, and pulled Dennis Carty aside.

Before he could speak, Dennis turned on him. "Damn yer soul John Auger, ye should've warned me what was afoot, and I'd have stayed back with Sara and the babe. This is no work for me now, with my family to care for."

"Nay Dennis, I heard yer signal to Bunce, an' thought you were in it. I had already resolved to never sail into Nassau again, but I had not thought o' this."

"Bunce told me ye'd planned to mutiny in Nassau, and I only went along with it for yer sake, knowin' yer anger with the Governor."

"I'd never choose that mad bastard Bunce as a mate."

"Well, 'tis too late to stop it now. Where is he?"

"Below with Greenaway."

"Damn him, he'll murder the old man. I'll go below and stop it."

"Ye were not always so afeared o' blood, Dennis."

"I was not before a man who had helped bring his own child into this world. I would not now be party to murder, as well as theft. An' Bunce hates that old man for reasons o' his own."

"Don't blame Bunce for all of this. 'Twas my fury with Rogers that has dragged you into it. Yet when we're rich on Saint Thomas, we'll send for your wife and babe, and settle on some isle with all our loot. Until then, stand by me, old friend."

"Ye've a stubbornness in you John Auger...Yet this is down to Bunce. Ah God, I should have found some way o' leavin' the Bachelor's Adventure and speakin' to ye earlier.

489

Not that we could've stopped it. Yet serve under Bunce, I will not. Ye must talk to the men and persuade them to vote ye Captain o' the Fleet."

Dennis dropped below and found Captain Greenaway in his cabin, cursing Bunce furiously, and refusing to go out on the account with him. Bunce raised his pistol to strike the old man, so Dennis aimed his own pistol at Greenaway's breast, and told him that if he spoke another word, he was as good as dead. Greenaway realised it was all over then, and slumped into his chair, yet Bunce could not resist striking the old man hard over the head with his pistol butt.

"Damn yer soul, Bunce!" Dennis snapped. "We'll vote and see who ought to be strikers amongst us. For now, keep yer blows to yeself." He hauled Bunce out of the cabin and shut the door. "How stand the other ships?"

Bunce grinned. "Ye can rest easy. The men o' the Mary are with us, and those o' this vessel, an' the schooner. We're out on the account again, Carty, an' our own masters!"

"Don't be too sure o' yeself Bunce. We've too few men to make a Company. Half the crew are boys who've never known the rovin' life, an' young Morris is so fevered he can barely understand what he's agreed to. This was an ill-timed venture, rash an' badly planned, an' if I'd not believed Auger in it from the start, I'd never have joined. Now he tells me that I was in before he was, and that makes you a damned liar!"

"We'll recruit in Saint Thomas and be on the high seas again, with a cool ale when we wish it. Come man, don't be so down on me. An' you Hipps, what are you hanging about here for, looking so haughty."

The old sailor's voice shook. "I'll not have anything to do with it. I won't go out on the account, do ye hear me! I've taken my pardon, I've had good work 'til now, and I've a good name. I won't go with you, and that's flat!"

"Ah, who needs an old fool? Ye can rest in Greenaway's cabin, an' be marooned on Green Key with the

490

rest o' the cowards. Hey Cunningham! All is well down here! The Lancaster is ours, as well as the rest. 'Tis time to draw up the Articles and sign up the Company. Carty, throw Hipps in with Greenaway an' stand guard here. Ye can trust to Auger to see that all is done as ye'd wish."

Dennis thrust Hipps inside with Captain Greenaway, and sat outside the cabin door with a loaded pistol. Greenaway was sitting back comfortably, a handkerchief to his head wound, a bottle of rum at hand. He raised a surly eye to see his old Boatswain. "Here to gloat are ye, Hipps? Happy to see yer old Captain down, are ye. And that bastard Bunce is in charge is he? That makes my life worth nought."

"I'm not with 'em Captain Greenaway. How could ye think I would be? When last I sailed with Thomas Bowling to Cuba two months back, I heard talk of mutiny, an' I told him, and he talked the men out of it. Ye were at Cully's when he declared he owed the safety of his vessel to me alone. I'd not go along with that mischief, nor will I be part o' this. I'm not much, but I'm an honest man now, an' will stay so, God willin'. Yet they've gone to sign the Articles on the Mary, and have left only Dennis Carty as guard. Neither of us are bound, and together we should be able to jump him, throw him overboard, an' sail out of here."

Greenaway snorted. "We're unarmed, and I'll lay money Carty isn't. We're two old men, and he's a strapping big bastard. No, 'tis best to lie quiet and wait and see what they do. If they propose to murder me, then I'll fight. If 'tis no more than marooning on Green Key...Here, have a slug of rum, Hipps. We'd best make the most of a good dram. It may be the last we ever see."

An hour later, when Captain White had also been reduced to a prisoner on his own ship, by his own crew, Carty stuck his head into the cabin. "The Jolly Roger flies from all the Fleet, yet we'll act well by you, rest assured o' that."

The two men in the cabin heard a small boat bump into the side of their vessel, and a short time later, John

491

Auger poked his head through the doorway. "Ahoy Captain Greenaway. I've been voted Captain o' this Company, and will have you rowed ashore now. We'll leave you provisions and the yawl from the Bachelor's Adventure to sail back to Nassau in, if ye'll swear on yer honour not to leave here until the day after we sail. Will ye swear it?"

"I will."

"Come now. Carty will row you in."

As they came up on deck, a young man approached them. "I can't go on the account either, Captain Greenaway. I thought I was the only one to not like it. But I'll stand with you, if you'll excuse me for not speakin' sooner."

Greenaway looked at Auger. "Ye'll surely not press unwilling men. This is Nat Taylor's son, young John Taylor, who served us many an ale at the stone tavern before he became the Governor's servant. He's a good boy, and will be of little use to you."

Auger shrugged, unhappy to lose another hand, yet with Dennis Carty's eyes on him, unwilling to press the lad. As the sunset blazed about them, they all dropped into the Lancaster's longboat, and Dennis Carty rowed to the Mary for more of the unwilling men. They were greeted by drunken sailors cheering Auger and piracy, and cursing the King and the Governor. Dennis could not find it in himself to join the oaths and boastings of the rest of the pirates, and instead he carefully helped the wounded James Kerr into the longboat.

Tom Rich, John Cox, and Tom Petty had all refused to go pirating, and were being mocked by the rest of the Mary's crew. Turnley had been forced to strip, and the pirates were in shrieks of laughter at the way his skinny fingers tried to cover his skinnier privates. As Auger came aboard, Bunce grabbed the terrified Turnley, and yelled for a rope about the yardarm. Before Bunce could whip the men into a hanging frenzy, Auger had wrenched Turnley from Bunce, and dropped him into Carty's longboat, roaring at Bunce to stop giving orders damn him, for they were all free

492

men now.

Bunce then aimed a loaded pistol at Old John Hipps, and motioned him up on deck. "We need someone who knows the Lancaster. Ye'll stay with us old man."

"No, I won't join ye! I am honest! Captain Greenaway, don't let 'em force me!"

Bunce laughed. "Shut yer squalling, old fool. Ye'll come with us or I'll maroon ye on the next key with no provisions at all, an' you can tell the wind how honest ye might be for the wee bit o' life ye'd have left. I'm sure we could find a bit o' sand with not even a palm tree to give ye shade. An' how long do ye think ye'd last in the midday heat, eh? Ye'd burn before ye died old man. Ye wouldn't last a day. Now, out o' that boat."

The old man turned to Captain Greenaway in tears. "I must go. I've no choice. Yet I swear I'll desert him at the first opportunity. I depend upon ye to clear me name to the Governor an' me family." The dour Captain Greenaway surprised them all by saying what he could to comfort the old sailor.

Then Bunce turned to Tom Petty. "We're short-handed. You'll come with us too, or 'twill be your bones the sea-birds peck."

"No Sir, I have a family Sir..."

"Get up here you bastard..."

Dennis Carty could no longer contain himself. "Yer a fool, Bunce. 'Tis no use taking unwilling men on the account. Just when ye need 'em, they'll turn on ye. We need the old man to help us sail the Lancaster, yet if ye try and force Tom Petty, I'll leave the Company. Choose, Bunce. Him or me. Who do ye think will prove the most useful?"

"Damn yer eyes Carty! Would ye betray the Company already?

"Yer not the Company, Bunce, God curse ye."

Just then the weak-witted George Bendall rolled up, already drunk on the ale he had found in Kerr's cabin. "Yer fools not to join us", he crowed. "I wish I'd begun the life

493

sooner, for I think it a truly pleasant one. Masterless and free is the only way to live. You know, I always thought myself a weakling, bullied by that terrible, mad old man. I once had a strong inclination to smother him as he lay feeble in his bed, and I wish now I'd done it." He placed his arm over Bunce's shoulders, breathing brotherly affection and ale.

"Get off me, ye drunken fool!" Bunce snapped, drunk himself, and he slapped the boy hard to the deck.

Bendall scrambled to his feet, glaring at the bigger man. "Beat me again, and I too will desert ye at the first opportunity", he hissed, his face pale and his eyes glaring. "I'm a free man now, Bunce, and I'll not be kicked around by anyone, not even you."

"This is an ill beginnin' for a Company", Dennis groaned. "There is no honour o' free men here. I'm off to get the unwillin' men from the Bachelor's Adventure."

"Hang on there, Carty", Bunce protested. "Yer forgetting that Greenaway is a Bermudian, an' can swim like a fish. He might return aboard an' cut our throats, or make some other mischief. I say we confine him 'til we're ready to sail."

Greenaway insisted that his swimming could not harm them, yet Bunce motioned the old sea Captain up the ladder, determined to keep him as their navigator.

Thinking the old man too well respected to be at risk, Dennis shoved off before Bunce took a fancy to any more of the honest men. Mister Kerr screamed when a splash from the oar sent seawater over his cut back, and Dennis told Turnley to find sea salt and rub it well into the wound before binding it, or else 'twould fester.

"Don't tell me what to do, ye stinking pirate!", Turnley cursed him.

Dennis scowled. "Auger risked his command to save yer miserable wee life. I'd watch yer mouth, Turnley, for God knows most o' the men here hate yer guts." Dennis then collected Captain White, Ben Hutchins and David Meredith from the Bachelor's Adventure, and the night almost upon

494

them, he rowed them to the strip of sand and low bushes that was Green Key. Young John Taylor remonstrated with Dennis, begging him to change his mind for Sara's sake.

With night rapidly falling, Dennis kept rowing strongly for the shore, and grimly shook his head. "I've begun this, and my Pardon is revoked for my part in takin' those vessels. Even if I changed coats now, I'd hang by an Admiralty Court. Yet we'll sail under Auger, not Bunce, and I'll leave the Company as soon as I can. Now, Tom Petty, you have a wife and three children, and you must have some idea of how I feel at being tricked into this. Will ye please speak to me darlin' wife, and explain that 'twas not from want o' love for her that I've done this. Tell her I'm sorry for my foolishness, and for the great trouble I've brought on her and the babe. Tell her I'll send for her as soon as I can, and that I'll go down on my knees every day to beg her forgiveness."

Chapter 26: The Trial

The next morning, Dennis Carty rowed Captain Greenaway into Green Key, the old sea Captain still stern against the persuasions of the mutineers, though he'd been forced to reveal the hiding place of his gold. He'd made a bargain of it, begging clothes for Turnley, and food for the marooned men, though Bunce had argued that dogs should ask for nought. Ashore, Dennis inspected Mister Kerr's wound, and bound it tightly with clean cloth ripped from his own shirt. Tom Petty helped him, still begging him to leave the pirates for his family's sake.

Then the yawl from the Bachelor's Adventure sailed in, bringing two pirates to hunt for more wild pig. One of them, George Rounsivell, was a young sailor of good family from Dorset, who had been rescued from the Neptune. And although weeks with Charles Vane's Company had left him so enamoured of the pirate life, that he'd willingly joined the mutineers, one night of drunken mayhem aboard the Bachelor's Adventure had truly frightened him. When Tom Petty remonstrated with him too, the lad shook his head, and said they would kill him if he tried to desert them now.

Bill Lewis, a middle-aged prize fighter, also repented his decision to join the pirates. He explained that he'd been pressed aboard a merchant schooner at Liverpool, and had jumped ship in Nassau to escape his Captain. "I'd give me right arm to be out o' this business, and back at Cully's with a bottle o' ale. Yet 'tis too late now. We're on the account, and must fight for our next drop, since all aboard went down our throats last night."

The mutineers spent the day emptying Greenaway's less seaworthy sloop, loading his cargo into their two other vessels, and finding his wine in the process. In the afternoon, the two hunters returned with a sow, and were begged by the marooned men for food. Young Rounsivell gave them his tinderbox, so they'd have fire, and Lewis hacked off a leg of the sow for them, and told them to wait for nightfall, so Bunce saw no smoke.

As the sun set, old Captain Greenaway stripped and swam out to his sloop, to see what else the mutineers had left them. Seeing him aboard, Auger and some drunken mates rowed over to try again to persuade him to join them. When he proved stubborn, Bunce bid him keep his sloop, and rowed off. Greenaway spent the night aboard his vessel, and in the morning searched her from bow to stern. The mutineers had left her old mainsail, a foresail, four small pieces of Irish beef in an old barrel, twenty biscuits, and a broken bucket.

Greatly cheered at the prospect of being able to sail back to Nassau, Greenaway swam back to shore to tell the marooned men the good news. Then Bunce rowed in with a boatload of pirates and six bottles of wine, and biscuits. They talked, drank, and offered the marooned men a mug of wine apiece and a biscuit. Then Bunce raised his glass to piracy, and when the recalcitrants refused to join him in his toast, he beat the mugs from their hands, cursed them for cowards and fools, and ordered his men back aboard.

Towards noon, Ben Hutchins sailed his turtling sloop into the harbour, looking for a safe convoy to Cuba, and was instantly taken, the mutineers delighted to have one of Haman's fast sloops in their Fleet. Hutchins refused to join them at first, yet gave in for fear of marooning, and to keep command of his lovely vessel.

The next morning, John Auger rowed the marooned men out to Greenaway's sloop, and helped them jury rig the sails, making Greenaway swear that he'd wait one day after the pirates sailed. Then Bunce came aboard in a drunken fury, Dennis close behind him. Demanding to know what Auger was about, Bunce snatched his cutlass and cut the sails to pieces, threatening to kill all of them if they sailed without his permission. Auger rounded on him in a fury, and Carty distracted them both by insisting that the mutineers were ready to sail. He and Auger leapt into one boat and rowed to the Mary, and Bunce took the other, laughing at the marooned men, stranded a mile off shore on a vessel without sails.

Once the mutineers had sailed, Captain Greenaway set the marooned men to searching the sloop, and they found an old hatchet, marlinspikes and other tools, enough to cut old cable into rope yarns for mending the sails. The wounded Mister Kerr made a fishing line from bent nails, while the rest lashed three spars into a raft. On this they all paddled back to the island, to live on wild cabbage, berries, and prickly pears, the wounded Mister Kerr fortunate with his fishing. They agreed to stock the abandoned sloop, and for five days they gathered what provisions the isle afforded, and paddled water out to the rain barrel on the sloop, one tedious bucketful at a time.

On the fifth day, when Greenaway proposed sailing, young John Taylor pointed out that the mutineers would not be merciful if they caught them at sea. Old Captain Greenaway laughed, and heaving at the anchor, invited the marooned men to stay or go with him as they liked. They fell to, heaved the anchor aboard, raised their patched sails, and Captain White set a course for Nassau.

They had only been at sea for a matter of hours, when Tom Petty spied three sails on the horizon. Sure that the mutineers were returning, Captain Greenaway lowered his sloop's sails, and hoped that in the vastness of the sea, they would not be seen. Yet the mutineers bore down upon them, and Greenaway saw no recourse but to hoist sail and race back to Green Key, the mutineers firing roundshot after them. They fled ashore on their raft, took to the bushes and hid. The mutineers pursued them ashore, yet unable to find them, contented themselves with cutting away the sloop's mast and bowsprit, and scuttling her. Bunce then came ashore, firing his pistols, and bellowing into the bushes that as far as he was concerned, they could rot there.

With their tinderbox ruined by seawater, the marooned men were left with no fire, no fishing lines, and

498

nothing to hunt with. They subsisted on shellfish, berries, and roots for eight days, and when they saw the mutineers sailing in again, did not even have the spirit left to run. Yet instead of Bunce, 'twas John Auger who rowed in. He had insisted the mutineers return with food and wine for the marooned men, and he promised Captain Greenaway beef and biscuit for three days if he would come and unload it from the Mary.

Yet when Bunce saw what was afoot, he exploded with rage and compelled the old Captain ashore again with nothing. George Redding, who was forced when the mutineers took Hutchin's turtler, rowed ashore that afternoon with a few pirates to go hunting, and he managed to slip Turnley his tinderbox.

After three days, Auger came ashore with Bunce, and asked again if any of the marooned men would change their coats. When they refused, Bunce set a loaded pistol to Greenaway's head, and forced him and Captain White into his ship's boat. The mutineers then set sail for Long Island, leaving the marooned men to eat crabs and snakes for fourteen days.

When the mutineers next returned, the marooned men hid from them, but later regretted it, for ample provisions were left on the beach for them, including thirty pounds of flour, a bushel of salt, twelve knives, two bottles of gunpowder, bullets, small shot, two muskets, a good axe, and the three hunting dogs from the turtler. Turnley took the dogs after wild pig, while the rest built a shelter from the sun. A few days later, the mutineers returned, and Bunce burnt the hut they'd built. Auger ordered Bunce back aboard the schooner as watch, and when Turnley returned with a hog, he and Dennis and several others dined with the marooned men, leaving them a bottle of rum.

Then, with John Auger still in shaky command of the mutineers, they sailed south. It was almost dark by the time they came up to Long Island, where they spotted three ships. Thinking they were Bermudans in for salt, and easy pickings,

499

they sent the turtling sloop in, her hold loaded with mutineers, and Bunce calling greetings from the bowsprit. Yet when the turtling sloop fired a warning shot over them, the three ships attacked, a volley of small shot from their swivel guns blasting into the turtling sloop. When the smoke cleared, many of the mutineers lay in screaming agony, Bunce amongst the wounded. The mutineers had attacked a Fleet of Spanish guarda del costas, crewed by privateers of the worst sort, and captained by the notorious Irishman, Turn Joe.

The privateers boarded the turtler, cutlasses swinging, and the mutineers broke under the onslaught, and wounded or not, leapt overboard to swim for Long Island, Bunce amongst them. Then the mutineers' second sloop sailed in, hearing the volley, and sure that Bunce must be secure of his prize. The privateers let her come, and when the mutineers tried to board, they were met by a volley of shot that dropped them to the decks. The third sloop followed the second in, and they surrendered just as quickly, the sails crashing to the decks, and the dead and wounded going overboard to feed the sharks.

The score of men who'd swum for Long Island saw the privateers rowing in the next morning, and terrified, the forced men offered to join the mutineers, to fight their mutual enemy. Dennis Carty insisted on a parlez, yet Turn Joe professed himself shocked at his tale of mutiny and marooning, and willing to do the English mutineers a bad turn for attacking his Fleet, he gave the forced men a launch and provisions to sail for the Bahamas. Only Thomas and Matthew Betty, George Redding and Ben Hutchins were well enough to sail, though Turn Joe insisted they take the wounded who had survived the swim ashore, rather than leave them to die, including Bunce.

As the small launch of forced men and wounded mutineers set sail for Nassau, Turn Joe inspected those remaining, looking for crew. He chose Dowling, a young Irishman, and when the lad refused, ordered him to strip naked. Then at gunpoint, he forced several other mutineers to join him, and sailed away with all the vessels, leaving the mutineers marooned.

The forced men in the launch made it to Providence within two days, Bunce making a full confession before dying of his wounds. Captain Cockram was immediately sent to rescue the honest men marooned at Green Key, and Turnley insisted on accompanying Ben Hornigold to arrest the mutineers marooned on Long Island. The ten surviving mutineers rejoiced to see Hornigold's sloop sail in, and they instantly surrendered when Hornigold told them they had the Governor's promise of mercy, and filed shamefaced down the beach into the longboats. They were rowed out to the Endeavour, where they were clapped in irons and confined under guard. They sailed back into Nassau on November the fifteenth, the whole town turning out on Hornigold's salute to watch them rowed in, Dennis unable to meet his brother Patrick's eyes, his guards pushing away the weeping Sara.

John Auger, Dennis Carty, the foolish George Bendall, Cunningham the Gunner, the old Boatswain John Hipps, young George Rounsivell, William Lewis the prize-fighter, the fevered Tom Morris, Bill Ling and Bill Dowling were all that remained of the unlucky mutineers. They were confined under heavy guard in Fort Nassau, the same fort, Dennis noted, that many of them had helped build. They were allowed no visitors that the Governor did not personally approve of. I asked him for permission to read them my mother's Bible, for I knew too much of him to expect mercy, and thought they would need every assistance to repent their sins and shrive their souls for the afterlife. Sara begged the Governor on her knees for permission to see her husband, and he grudgingly gave it, complaining after that women were always ready to use their weaknesses against the strengths of men.

Governor Rogers had no power to hold a Vice-Admiralty court, yet he resolved to exert his authority on Nassau, and break the spirit of those he governed. He spent many long weeks in discussion with Thomas Walker, Captain Gale and young Mister Fairfax, insisting he had the right to stretch the law, speaking of the expense and uncertainty of sending all the mutineers and witnesses to England for trial. Thomas Walker claimed that the Act of Grace gave the Governor enough power, and Captain Gale insisted that 'twas the duty of the Governor to try them and hang them. And though young Mister Fairfax pointed out that one did not necessarily follow the other, the choice of an executioner was also made.

That night, Cully's was deserted, the old rovers preferring to lie around fires on the beach, sharing rum bottles under the last of the moon. Some cursed Hornigold for taking their old comrades captive, others raved of storming the fort and releasing them, though they stopped when I stepped into the light. I told them of what Dennis Carty had said of Bunce pistol-whipping old Captain Greenaway, forcing unwilling men, and leaving the rest to starve. Some scowled to hear it, yet Henry Jennings stated flatly that there was no honour of the Brethren in any of it.

When I saw Dennis the next day, he complained that Hornigold had promised them mercy in the Governor's name. I told him that they were to have the mercy of a trial, rather than be summarily hanged, as Thomas Walker had urged. Then I advised him to look to his defence, for the Governor insisted that the people of Nassau would see Justice done. "Aye, the people of Nassau will see the full force o' the Governor's power", Dennis muttered. "For that man knows nothin' o' Justice. Yet say nought to me darlin' Sarah. We will beg for our lives, and she shall hope for mercy to the end."

While the Governor debated the law with Walker and Fairfax, the mutineers called for witnesses as to their good character and intentions. The men they had marooned were urged to speak for them, and I asked Mister Kerr to stand up for Dennis, reminding him of the kindness he had received at that man's hands when wounded by Bunce.

502

On the ninth of December, the trial of the Nassau mutineers began in the fort's guardhouse, the Governor still afraid of an uprising. The popular Mister Fairfax was Judge, and to assist him, the Governor appointed the quiet Mister Beauchamp, Thomas Walker, Captain Gale, Nat Taylor, and Captains Burgess and Courant, both reformed pirates. Mister Fairfax's insistence on these last two I thought brilliant. Rovers had captured the mutineers, and rovers would try them for their cruel treatment of their old mates. The reformed men would have to consider this case as more than just the Governor against the Brethren.

Captain Walker opened the trial, addressing the people first, his pomposity evidence of how much he was enjoying himself. "Some of these men have received His Majesty's most gracious Pardon for former offences and acts of robbery and piracy, and have taken Oaths of allegiance to King George." He looked at the mutineers with utter scorn. "Lawful employment had been bestowed to divert you from your former unlawful courses of life, and to enable and support you in just and lawful ways of living. Yet, not having the fear of God before your eyes, nor any regard to your oaths of allegiance taken to your Sovereign, nor to the performance of loyalty, truth and justice, but being instigated and deluded by the Devil to return to your former unlawful and evil course of robbery and piracy, you stand here accused of treachery, mutiny, felony and piracy."

All the men claimed to be not guilty of seizing five hundred pounds worth of vessels and cargo, knowing they would hang immediately otherwise. Then evidence from the marooned men was heard, with Mister Kerr and Captain Greenaway blaming the dead Phineas Bunce for the mutiny. Tom Petty told how Dennis Carty had stopped Bunce from forcing him too, and they described the reluctance of many of the mutineers, Hipps being clearly shown as a forced man.

The court took a break over lunch, and at three o'clock, the prisoners were allowed to speak for themselves, all of them aware that they held their lives in their hands.

503

Auger simply stated that he had not known of Bunce's design beforehand, and I knew that he made so little a defence because he had already condemned himself for leading his crew into this tragedy. Cunningham, Blackbeard's old gunner, claimed that Bunce had threatened to maroon him. Hipps insisted that he had been forced, and Kerr and Greenaway spoke for him, as well as Captain Bowling, who was indebted to Hipps for stopping a mutiny on his own vessel.

Mister Kerr spoke of the kindnesses Dennis Carty had done him, and Tom Petty spoke of his reluctance to join the pirates, and of his concern for his wife and child. Hearing this, all looked to Sarah, her babe in her arms, tears rolling down her face. Dennis tried to speak then, yet his voice broke, and he buried his face in his hands.

The next day, the prisoners were allowed to plead for themselves for the last time. John Auger said nothing, Cunningham said nothing new, and Morris claimed that his fever had left him unable to think clearly. Hipps made a spirited defence, and again men stepped forward to testify for him, and I thought it likely that the stricken old man would be allowed to live. Dennis Carty insisted that when Hornigold had come for them at Long Key, he had persuaded the mutineers to trust to the Governor's mercy. Young Dowling told them how he had refused to join Turn Joe and the Spanish pirates. Turnley confirmed hearing the well-bred George Rounsivell regret his decision to mutiny. Then he spoke against George Bendall, citing the boy's boast of having once wanted to smother old Mister Graves, thus sealing the lad's fate. 'Twas evident to all that Turnley was enjoying this revenge after his humiliation at the hands of the mutineers.

The court was adjourned until four o'clock, and the prisoners were remanded to another hut. When they were again brought before the court, there was a terrible desperation in their eyes. The judges voted all but Hipps as guilty. Fairfax stood and made a small speech, stressing that the decisions had been made on the evidence put before the court. He called out the names of the guilty men, and asked them if they knew of any reason why sentence of Death should not be pronounced, and avoiding their eyes, announced: "It is adjudged that you be carried to the prison from whence you came and from thence to the place of execution, where you are to be hanged by the necks 'til you be dead, dead, dead, and God have mercy on your souls."

The execution was appointed for ten o'clock on Friday, and at this Auger came to himself. "Governor, be merciful! Give us but a little time to prepare for death. We are steeped in sin, and I'd not die unready."

The Governor stood then, and I prayed that he would find some kindness in his soul. He could not. "You have been given since November the fifteenth to think of your crimes, and the court has favoured you in allowing you so long a defence, taking up the time which the affairs of the settlement required in working on the fortifications, besides the fatigue thereby occasioned to the whole garrison, in providing the necessary guards set over you through want of a gaol. The garrison has been much lessened by sickness, and you know I am obliged to employ all the people to assist in mounting the great guns and finishing the present works, as I expect war with Spain. With Nassau destitute of all relief from any man of war, I am indispensably obliged for the welfare of the settlement to give you no longer time."

Dazed, the prisoners followed young Mister Fairfax back to their hut. He declared they could send for anyone they wished to pray with. "For God's sake man," Dennis Carty groaned, "let me see me wife."

"I'm here", Sara called, pushing through the guard, their child in her arms. "We'll pray for a reprieve. It's our only hope. I'll not leave you 'til then."

"This is a grievous business", Fairfax exclaimed. "I do not believe that any of you should hope for mercy. Hipps has been freed, and the Governor does not want to seem soft."

"Aye, I can well imagine that!" Auger snorted. "I am going to my maker, that is certain. I would thank you to stay with us until Friday, Mark Read. You are a godly man, and may be of some comfort to us, there being no priest on this damned isle to prepare us."

I stayed with them all the rest of that week, and it seemed to me that Providence had never been so beautiful. The sultry weather cleared to cool breezes, and the nights were resplendent with stars. The condemned men were allowed few visitors, for many old rovers spoke boldly of insurrection. Dennis urged his brother Patrick to do more than talk, and reminded him that the Governor was but one man, while the Brethren were many. He put a bold face on his fear, yet in his open affection for his wife and child, I could see his certainty that he would hang. He let Sara talk desperately of Mister Kerr's recommendations for mercy, yet he ordered a new suit to die in.

John Auger wept sorely at his conviction that he had been the damnation, not only of himself, but of Dennis, Sara, their child, the men who had died in the attack of the Spanish privateers, and those condemned to the gallows. He was adamant that if he had decided against Bunce, few would have gone back on the account. "I was angry at the Governor, and my judgement was soured. What a dangerous fool I have been." Dennis assured his friend that they had all made that decision for themselves, and Auger seemed a little easier afterwards. He told me of his childhood on the London docks, of how he was the best shipmaster in Jamaican waters before he took to piracy, and of how much he regretted returning to it.

Cunningham, Blackbeard's gunner, behaved penitently too, and since he was not hoping for a reprieve, I had to believe that dour, dark man sincere. He had no faith that God's mercy could extend so far as forgiving him the terrible crimes he had been party to with Blackbeard, and when he told me the worst of them, I was sickened. He promised Auger that when he met Phineas Bunce in Hell, he would avenge them all.

Bill Ling, a quiet man who had nevertheless urged on the mutiny with Bunce, was also truly penitent, and prayed heartily to be forgiven his sins, especially that of sottishness. He blamed drink for most of the mistakes he had made in his life, and swore that wine would never pass his lips again.

On Friday morning, each of the prisoners was called in private to see the Governor, who was convinced that there was a conspiracy to save them from the rope. At ten o'clock, the prisoners were released of their irons, Dennis donned his new clothes, adorned at the neck, wrists and cap with long blue ribbons, and young Tom Morris donned his suit trimmed with red. Mister Robenson, the provost marshal for the day, then pinioned them all, and with guards to assist him, led them to the top of the ramparts fronting the sea, where the militia stood ready to guard them. Apart from the soldiers, about a hundred people stood watching, most of them old comrades.

Auger neither washed, shaved nor shifted his old clothes when carried along to be executed. When he had a small glass of wine given to him on ramparts, he raised it towards the Governor, and drank it with wishes for the good success of the Bahama Islands. Tom Morris, coming behind him, stated loudly: "Aye, we have had a good Governor but a harsh one", yet his voice broke and he could say no more. George Bendall could not believe that death was upon him, and glared sullenly about him, saying no more than he had done all week.

Then Dennis stepped onto the ramparts, and looking cheerfully about him, greeted various old friends in the crowd, including his brother Patrick. "I knew the time when there was many brave fellows on this island that would not suffer me to die like a dog", he challenged them. When none leapt forward to save him, he shrugged. "I see too much power over yer heads for ye to practise anything. Yet I ask all here to see that me innocent wife and child do not suffer. I'll see ye in Hell if ye let 'em starve." He then pulled off his

507

shoes, and kicked them over the parapet, and grinned. "I promised me wife not to die with me shoes on."

At the request of Auger, Cunningham and Ling, several prayers and psalms were read out, in which we all joined for about three quarters of an hour, the time telling heaviest on those who remained impenitent, though Dennis kept a brave face on it, staring at the gallows at the foot of the ramparts, and the black flag hoisted thereon. When the Governor sent a message for them all to get on with it, the condemned men were led up the ladder onto a stage supported by three barrels, and the hangman fastened the cords about their necks as dexterously as if he had been a servitor at Tybourn.

Bill Dowling, the young Irishman, began talking lewdly to the women and cursing the Governor freely. William Lewis, the prize fighter, scorned to show fear, yet heartily desired liquor to drink with his fellow sufferers on stage, and with many of the standers by. At this, Bill Ling upbraided him, and told him that water was more suitable to them at that time. Tom Morris fluttered his red ribbons, and stated: "I might have been a greater plague to these islands and now I wish I had been."

The Governor ordered the marshal to make ready, and then, with all the prisoners expecting the launch, he ordered George Rounsivell to be untied and brought off the stage. There was muttering at this, despite the awed delight on the boy's face. He was only eighteen, and all knew he came from good family in Dorset, yet we felt that the Governor had only reprieved him for his birth, when there were more penitent men about him.

Then Sara Davies fell to her knees and begged the Governor to spare her husband, and when Ma Davies knelt beside her in the dust, I too dropped to my knees, and called for mercy. Yet the Governor had never liked the merry Irishman, and simply nodded curtly at the executioner to proceed.

The barrels holding up the platform were hauled

away, the stage fell, and the eight men swung off, jerking and dancing in mid-air as the ropes strangled them, their piss and shit befouling the air. Sara howled and swooned into her mother's arms, and I stood and berated the Governor for his hard heart, cursing him to hear her wild cry every night until his own Death.

PART 8: THE CARIBBEAN 1719
Chapter 27: Captain Jack Rackam

Although I told myself that there was no sense in it, the death of Dennis Carty forever severed me from Governor Rogers. I quit his service the next day, telling him coldly that his lack of care for any but his own class had estranged us; that instead of uniting us, he had defeated us. I asked for payment for my months of service, and for my work on the salvage of the Neptune, and he loftily informed me he was awaiting funds from England. I told him that both of us knew no funds were coming, and if he gave me nothing, I must thieve or starve. His sneer proved he thought me a pirate still, and I cursed him for a cantankerous fool, and wished upon him the same choice he had left me.

I entreated the rovers at Cully's for work, yet none was prepared to sign on a hand who might be the Governor's spy. Kate Pritchard stood me an ale, and tried to convince me to sail for Hornigold or Cockram, yet I could not bring myself to hunt my old mates. Henry Jennings thought he might need men when he sailed for Jamaica, yet when Kate lowered her eyelashes at him, I knew he would stay. The first pangs of hunger sent me down the beach to Ma Davies to beg.

I found that family greatly suffering from Dennis Carty's death. The young widow was in a grief so black it edged madness, her mother praying for her soul, young Rachel tending the squalling babe. Yet even amidst such trials as these, they still found room in their hearts for me. Ma Davies earnestly persuaded me against going out on the account, as so many had done, and helped me to a bowl of fish soup and a crust of bread.

Then the red-nosed Patrick Carty rolled in, almost sober, and bearing a sack of flour. Cursing Governor Rogers, he declared himself Sarah's brother, and her babe's uncle. Then he helped himself to soup and bread, sat next to me, and asked coldly after the Governor. I explained that I'd left that thankless service with nothing in my pockets, and only wished I'd done it sooner. Patrick nodded at that, tried to speak, and instead great tears rolled down his crag of a face. Ma Davies went to him, whispering words of comfort, assuring him that he was part of her family now, and that together, they would survive their great loss.

Young Harry slouched in, a different youth from the capering boy who had amused Anne and I only a year and a half ago. He asked me if there was any likelihood of cattle being left in the forests, and I agreed to go with him and John in search of them. The boys were greatly affected by the execution, sullen and angry. Away from their Ma, their spoke of going pirating, and I spoke hard against it, asking what their mother and sisters and baby nephew would do if they were hung. For a week we scoured the island, following the forest paths, the clear days and nights persisting. When the winds increased from the north, threatening rain, we returned forlorn and hungry to the Davies' camp, having seen not a single track.

That night, I woke in the darkness, the sea pounding the shore. I could still hear my mother's voice calling my name, her dear face clear in my dream. Shuddering, I prayed 'twas not her ghost that had called me, and fumbled for my rum flask. The rum warmed my heart, yet my bones were chilled, and when I saw the silhouette of Ma Davies by her small fire, I joined her.

As first light appeared over Hog Island, I caught myself insisting to Ma Davies that I must return to England and search for my lost mother, distressed that the chances of finding her were so miserably small. When I looked up, she was regarding me so strangely, I felt I must have given myself away. And in truth, I longed then for the freedom of Anne Bonny's company.

John Davies came scowling into his Ma's camp soon after, swearing that the damned Spaniards had taken another Nassau trader, all the crew now slaves in Cuba, including young Charlie Walker. Harry started up at this news, and cursing the Spaniards most foully, despite his mother's objections, he ran to find further news of his friend. He returned by nightfall to tell us that Thomas Walker was pleading with Governor Rogers to let him organise a raid on Cuba, to liberate his son. The Governor was insisting that he did not have the strength to defend the Bahamas, let alone attack Havana, and all feared a Spanish raid.

Soon after, John reported that Sir George Byng, the same Admiral I had sailed under in the Navy, had destroyed half of Spain's Fleet off Cape Passaro in Sicily. We knew then that war with Spain would follow, and that we were too close to Cuba to be safe. In December, the war of the Quadruple Alliance was formally declared, with Austria, France, the Netherlands and England taking sides against Spain. The Spanish King Philip ordered that all places ever owned or claimed by Spain must be re-taken, and this included the Bahamas.

Though the Brethren armed their ships, Governor Rogers insisted on completing his fortifications. By terrifying his financiers with the brutal prospect of a Spanish raid, he convinced them to give him yet more credit. Then, instead of using this money to pay us what we were owed, he did a deal with some of the local merchants, paying off his debts if they would supply him with poor food and cheap ale. This he offered us for our work, and many were glad enough of the sustenance, and signed up. Yet, though we knew 'twould be hard, when Rogers set the scowling George Hooper over us, his constant abuse made it slavery.

Governor Rogers drank at Cully's every night, complaining bitterly of his lack of support from the Lords of Trade and Plantations. He was still writing impassioned pleas for reinforcements, pointing out the strategic importance of the islands, and the way they dominated shipping in the area. Still he received no reply from his Government, and no one could pay his mounting debts.

Then he relapsed with fever, and in his weakened

state, most thought 'twas his last week on Earth. We heard from those building his great house above the bay, that Thomas Walker was planning to rule Nassau upon the Governor's death, and many of the Brethren resolved to sail. Yet Roger's miserable life was once again saved by Mistress Pritchard's careful nursing. When he recovered, he insisted on showing himself to his people, and took the lady's arm to limp as far as Cully's tavern for a rum. I was drinking quietly with Henry Jennings, when she led the tottering Governor to our table. Jennings ordered a bottle of wine, and though many had been happily predicting his death, they still came up to congratulate Rogers on his recovery.

Rogers was unusually expansive, though soon fatigued by the noise, and Mistress Pritchard began to insist that he return to his bed. Then Ben Hornigold rolled in, clapped Jennings on the back, and nodding drunkenly to the rest of us, dropped into the chair by Kate Pritchard. He grabbed her hand and calling her his darlin' girl, he insisted on his right to kiss her fingers. She laughed, called him a charming rogue and slapped his hand with her fan. Jennings then warned Hornigold off, and kissing the lady's hand himself, vowed he was her dog, to do with as she willed.

Mistress Pritchard was enjoying these attentions, yet the Governor's face was like thunder. Thinking the fever was coming on him again, I leant over and quietly asked if he would take my arm back to his bed. Mistress Pritchard heard, and was all fuss and concern, insisting that his eyes were too bright. Yet he shook his head, and took a long swallow of ale to cool himself. William Fairfax then joined us, and when that gallant young man was also given excess of Kate Pritchard's smiles, our scarred and balding old Governor looked at her with hatred. Suddenly I understood 'twas jealousy that inflamed him, and disliking this evil brew of fever and anger, I tried again to get him away. He shook me off and swallowed another rum, and though I tried to catch Mister Fairfax's eye, he was too busy complimenting the lady on having all of Nassau at her feet.

513

In the midst of this merriment, Governor Rogers stood and made Mistress Pritchard a shaky bow. Then he advised her, as an old friend, to leave Nassau as soon as possible, since under the new laws, whores could be stocked and whipped. It took us all a moment to grasp his meaning, and then we all stood, the old rovers going for their swords, young Mister Fairfax demanding an apology for the lady. She then proved her breeding, and gathering together what was left of her dignity, she quietly suggested that he was disordered by fever, and had forgotten that she had lately saved his life. Governor Rogers sneered again, and knowing that whatever he said next would see Hornigold's sword through his heart, I grabbed one of his arms, jerked him roughly away from the table, and propelled him towards the door.

He lost his temper, yet in his weakness could do nothing against me, and I pushed him down the street, calling him a Puritan hypocrite who ran his colony off the proceeds of a whorehouse. I reminded him that no prostitute had ever been stocked on Nassau, despite their open soliciting, and that the use of such a threat to a lady was a terrible insult. I bashed on the door of his house until Nat Taylor opened it, the Governor raving of whipping, imprisonment, and ducking stools, and quoting the Bible's severest passages against harlots. I ordered Nat Taylor to lock him in his room, for if Jennings or Hornigold saw him again that night, he was dead.

The next day, Mistress Pritchard sent Jennings, hand on his sword hilt, to demand an apology from the Governor. He erupted with fury, and ordered Captain Gale to imprison the lady for three days on the Delicia, ostensibly for her Jacobite sympathies. The proud Captain Gale refused at first, yet even he quailed under the onslaught of the Governor's mad rage, and saw he had no choice. Afraid of Jennings and Hornigold, he marched into Cully's with six armed soldiers, bowed to the lady, and with all possible courtesy, invited her to visit him aboard the Delicia.

514

Jennings and Hornigold drew steel, the soldiers raised their muskets, and to avoid a battle her friends could not win, Mistress Pritchard declared she'd be delighted to spend a few days with such an old friend. She strolled down to the guardship on Captain Gale's arm, her head high, as though the soldiers were her guard of honour. Captain Gale gave over his quarters, and offered her every luxury he could command, partly to spite Governor Rogers, partly because he liked her for herself, and partly because he feared her influence.

When she was released, Jennings was waiting for her, in his best suit, his hat newly feathered. With his best bow, he invited her on a cruise aboard the Bathsheba, to seek the protection of her old friend, Governor Lawes of Jamaica. She agreed, and Jennings immediately rowed her out, sending for her maid and her gear, determined the lady would face no further insult.

When he lost Henry Jennings, the Governor lost the only man who could still hold the old rovers in check, and many more abandoned the honest life, and sailed away on the account. He also lost the support of all those who resented his hypocrisy, including Captain Gale and Mister Fairfax.

Kate Pritchard wrote to Rogers, threatening to take passage for England, to use her connections to avenge his insult. Yet she soon wrote again, excusing his rudeness on account of his fever, and offering him her services as an intermediary with her 'dear friend' Governor Lawes. Fairfax told me that Rogers ripped her letter to pieces, cursing her still. Then, fearing for his reputation in London, he wrote to his friend Steele, defending himself from anything she might say by insulting her first.

'Twas not long after, that Captain Cockram sailed in, with news of Blackbeard's final battle. We crowded around the old rover on Cully's veranda, lightening dancing over the hills, the air sultry and promising rain, while he quenched his thirst, his eyes alight with his story. He reminded us that

Blackbeard had betrayed his Company and the gentleman pirate Stede Bonnet, running all but his treasure ship aground, and making off with his Company's loot to buy his pardon from Governor Eden of North Carolina.

The citizens of North Carolina, horrified by Blackbeard's atrocities, and in despair of their own Governor, had appealed to the upright Governor Spotswood of Virginia for help. They were able to give him exact information on Blackbeard's fortification of Ocracoke inlet, which was a constant threat to Virginia shipping.

Governor Spotswood then fitted out two sloops as privateers, the Lyme and the Pearl, with a Company of fifty-four marines, commanded by Lieutenant Maynard of the Navy. As an incentive, Maynard reminded his men of the bounty offered on pirates, including one hundred pounds of gold for Blackbeard's head. Although Governor Eden warned Blackbeard of the impending attack, he sneered at anything the Navy might do, refusing to believe the Devil could let him down.

At dawn on the twentieth of November, Captain Maynard sailed up to the Ocracoke inlet, to find the tide low. He sent his ship's boat in as scout, yet the pirates were keeping watch, and they fired a sudden broadside that destroyed her crew. Leaving the Pearl to guard the only escape to the sea, Captain Maynard then hoisted his colours on the Lyme, and attacked. Blackbeard, realising he was out-gunned, cut his cable, and promptly ran aground in the river's shallows. Then Maynard too ran aground, both crews heaving ballast overboard to take advantage of the turning tide, Blackbeard bellowing that if he got off first, there would be no quarter shown. Maynard, realising with horror that the Lyme was firmly stuck, hid his privateers below. When the tide finally lifted Blackbeard's sloop, he immediately attacked the Lyme with a blast of grenadoes. When the smoke lifted, the Lyme's deserted decks convinced him he had already won the fight, and the pirates swung aboard. Then the privateers attacked from below, fighting

516

furiously at close quarters, battling for their lives.

When the smoke cleared again, Blackbeard and Maynard were face-to-face, both with loaded pistols. They fired, and though Blackbeard winged Maynard, the pirate took a bullet at point blank range. Yet this only seemed to enrage the mad giant, and he swung his cutlass, breaking Maynard's sword off at the hilt, and slicing into his fingers. Blackbeard had his blade raised for the kill, when a Navy sailor slashed him in the neck. Pumping blood, and attacked from all sides, Blackbeard fought on, taking six bullets and more than twenty sword cuts. When he finally fell, his crew lost heart, and cried for quarter, with only fifteen of them left alive, and none of them unwounded. The privateers lost ten men, with twenty wounded. Maynard found Governor Eden's warning letter on Blackbeard's sloop, and sailed victorious into Virginia harbour with Blackbeard's grisly head dangling from his bowsprit.

Patrick Carty nodded his big red nose at the end of the story and spat into the dust. "Tell me Cockram, did the sailor who sliced Blackbeard's throat get his hundred pounds, or did Maynard collect it all, despite owing the man his life."

Cockram admitted that none even knew the sailor's name, and Carty growled that 'twas the way o' the world, to reward a poor man's courage so generously. Featherstone noted that the Colonial Governors had finally learned that two well-armed sloops were better than a man o' war in these waters, and wondered if they would all be sailing in fleets now.

We heard later that six of Blackbeard's men were seized in North Carolina, including Israel Hands. To make his men fear him, Blackbeard had blown this man's leg off during a card game, and now Hands turned King's evidence, and was the only one not to hang. When Governor Eden heard of Blackbeard's death, he seized all the pirate treasure for himself, yet a Government enquiry saw him replaced not long after.

By mid-December, rumours of plots to overthrow

Governor Rogers began to circulate, though I believe 'twas nothing more than the wistful mouthings of a few drunken rovers. Richard Turnley told the Governor that the Brethren would kill him and restore pirate rule, and that his own militia was privy to the plot. Three men were then arrested and taken to the Delicia, where they were flogged so hard their blood ran through the scuppers, sharks making it dangerous for those rowing back to town afterwards. One of the men flogged was, like many of us, a veteran of the Dutch wars, and he died of this flogging just before Christmas. The Governor made a great deal of noise about his mercy in not hanging them, yet we all knew that Mister Fairfax would have insisted upon a trial, and that Turnley's evidence would not hold.

A few days after the flogging, Turnley's shack was burned to the ground, none raising a hand to save it. On Turnley's advice, Governor Rogers arrested a man for it, and with Captain Gale now confirmed as our Chief Justice, he conducted a summary trial, and hanged the man. The majority of the townspeople stayed away from that hanging, a sign of great discontent with their Government. I told Mister Fairfax that we had a tyrant for a Governor, worse than Vane could ever have been, for Vane would never have been allowed such power. Mister Fairfax warned me not to speak my mind aloud, for fear of Turnley's whisper. Yet Governor Rogers cared nothing for our hatred, terrified as he was of the coming Spanish invasion.

I found work on Thomas Walker's grand house, which was fast rising on its small hill above the town. Then Misters Buck and Gohier decided to build their own mansions from the profits of the dosshouse, though they chose to build on the shore, close to the fort. I also worked for no wages on a tiny steepled church on the eastern fringes of the town.

Then the Council announced that a new street would be made through the middle of the town, behind Front Street, necessitating the rearranging of lots. In practice, this meant

518

that Sarah, Ma Davies, and the last twelve Palatine settlers lost the land they had cleared and planted, in return for one of the Governor's useless chits. Hearing rumours of a rebellion amongst the surviving Palatines, the Governor insisted they swear oaths of allegiance to King George and to himself personally, which they deeply resented.

Christmas was a miserable affair, Governor Rogers refusing to allow a bonfire on the beach, in case the Spaniards guided themselves in by it. He also insisted that every citizen attend church, where he railed against us for idleness and dishonesty, until Ma Davies could stand it no longer. She stood and declared that on the Lord's Day, 'twas blasphemy for a whoremonger to take the pulpit, and was heartily cheered by all. Noting the fury on the Governor's face as he stormed out, I feared that she too was doomed.

That night, the news in Cully's was of the capture of the gentleman-pirate, Stede Bonnet. After Blackbeard had run him aground and absconded with their loot, Bonnet had sold his ships for salvage, and had also bought a Pardon from the corrupt Governor Eden. He settled in North Carolina, the combination of his gentlemanly manners and notoriety making him a great favourite with the ladies. Yet the lure of the old life had proved too much for him, and he had turned pirate again, cruising northward between Virginia and Philadelphia, where he took two prizes, keeping the vessels and forcing their crews. He met up with Charles Vane for a time, and sailed with his Fleet, and then when his own sloop became leaky, he returned to the Cape Fear River to careen.

He stayed over-long, and when news of his presence reached Charles Town, ship owners demanded that Governor Johnson act against Bonnet, before he blockaded them in. The renowned Colonel Rhett approached the Governor, and promised that with two armed sloops and sufficient men, he would bring Bonnet in, just as Maynard had brought in Blackbeard. Then a small Antiguan vessel sailed in, complaining of having been plundered by Vane, and in

519

looking for him, Rhett found Captain Bonnet and his two prizes moored in the shallow Cape Fear River.

The tide was low and night falling, and almost immediately, Rhett ran both of his sloops aground. Captain Bonnet sent his three ships' boats to take what he thought were two defenceless merchant vessels, and to his horror, his pirates rowed into a hail of small shot. The next morning, he tried to sail out into the open sea to fight, yet all three of his vessels ran aground within cannon range of Rhett's sloop. Rhett pounded the pirate sloops for five hours, and his sloop was the first to break free when the tide turned. He immediately attacked Bonnet's flagship, and as soon as he boarded, Bonnet surrendered.

Rhett had lost but twelve men, the pirates seven, though many of the pirates were badly wounded. Rhett carried them all back to Charles Town, where the pirate crew was imprisoned in the watchhouse. However, the provost-marshal had known Stede Bonnet when he was a gentleman on Barbados, and was allowed to keep the pirate Captain as his guest. Bonnet politely requested the company of his First Mate to await trial with him, and with two guards assigned to watch them, the pirates gave their word of honour that they would not attempt escape.

Yet soon after, they stole a small boat and sailed north, the reward for Bonnet's capture jumping to seven hundred pounds. They sailed straight into foul weather, and were driven back south onto Sullivan Island, near Charles Town. Without food, Bonnet was forced to approach a canoa to beg for provisions, and was recognised. Rhett went after him again, Bonnet's First Mate was killed in the skirmish, and Bonnet was taken alive into Charles Town in chains.

Two days later, Bonnet's crew went to the gallows, their Governor keen to hang them before they could die of their wounds. Despite Bonnet's fair dealings, their Governor abused them as brutes and beasts of prey, and their Attorney General insisted they preyed upon all mankind, their own species and fellow creatures without distinction. In truth,

Blackbeard's cruel madness had done us no favours, and we were all judged alike. Other falsehoods and exaggerations were spread by sermons, pamphlets and newspapers, creating a lie that legitimised our ruthless extermination.

Then it was Bonnet's turn for the scaffold, women weeping and handing him posies of flowers, and pleading with the Governor for mercy. Yet as the rope went round his neck, Bonnet's resolution failed him. Sailors had crowded the rigging of all the ships in Charles Town harbour, many of them once rovers, and their disgust with the sorry spectacle that Bonnet made of himself all but ended the reputation of the Brethren for courage.

On New Years Day, a dozen men stole a merchant sloop from Nassau harbour, and went out on the account under Edward England, an Irishman who had once been marooned by his crew for being too humane to a merchant Captain. Captain Moody, hearing of our Governor's harshness to his old mates, then plagued the shipping of the Bahamas, so that no one could sail in. Then we heard he'd joined Charles Vane, and that their pirate Fleet was planning to attack Nassau and hang the Governor.

In January, Pearce Wright and Tom Bradley told Governor Rogers that they expected Captain Condent to sail in for the Pardon with two heavily armed warships. Rogers grumbled that he would be forced to receive him, as Condent had so many friends in Nassau, yet was glad enough at the prospect of some protection for Nassau. Then we heard that Condent had taken a valuable prize, and surrendered it to the Governor of Reunion, in return for the Pardon. Rogers was furious, and had Wright and Bradley arrested for corresponding with a known pirate, and imprisoned them on the Delicia to await trial. That night the shore was crowded with rovers openly talking rebellion. Captain Gale, Mister Fairfax and Mister Beauchamp begged the Governor to back down, insisting that the four of them could not hold Nassau alone. The Governor then released the two rovers, claiming they were too expensive to keep, when

521

in truth, we all knew that they would have cost him his life.

He started drinking hard at Cully's every day, surrounded by toadies and informers, complaining bitterly that he had no way to repay his debts in England, and that, though he had put down the pirates, the colony had ruined him. The rovers refused to drink in the same tavern as the Governor, and instead bought bottles of rum from a den on the shore, and drank by small fires on the beach.

James Bonny then sailed back into Nassau, having spent all my stolen gold. When he approached me, asking after Anne, I claimed she was long gone, and living with her father. Bonny was soon fast friends with Turnley, and through him, the Governor, who bought them both rum, and listened hard to their whispered insinuations of mutinous pirates and rebellious settlers.

Soon after, I found myself at dawn on the shore by Cully's, morose and hungry and drinking away the last of my silver with Ben Hornigold. We watched a periauger sail in and beach, and when Hornigold went to give them a hand and hear the news, his great bellow filled the bay. He staggered up the beach, carrying a filthy, salty, wild-eyed skeleton of a man in his arms, and ordered me to fetch Nat Taylor to Cully's, for this was his missing brother Richard. I ran for the Governor's residence, and at the news, Nat Taylor sped for Cully's, the Governor limping after him.

Recognizing a man half-dead of the sea thirst, Hornigold had poured Richard Taylor an ale, and we entered as the poor man drained it to the dregs. The sight of his brother proved too much for him, however, and he burst into tears, Nat patting him helplessly on the back, begging Governor Rogers to excuse his weakness.

"Think nothing of it, Mister Taylor. When he is ready, we will hear his story. Cully, fetch him more ale and some bread."

Richard Taylor wiped his eyes. "'Twas last July, Sir. I signed on as crew on the Elizabeth and Mary sloop, loading salt on Exuma. The night after we anchored, we were boarded and taken by Spanish privateers on three periaugas from Baracoa."

"Baracoa is on the east tip of Cuba", Nat Taylor explained to Rogers. "And a periauga is a great canoe that sails faster than most ships."

Richard Taylor took another long drink. "The first periauga was the Postillion, captained by an Irishman, Richard Holland. The second, the Mary Ann, was captained by a Spanish mulatto called Josephus, who was Quartermaster to the whole Company. The third was called the Gran Diablo, and captained by a Frenchman, an' 'twas well-named, believe me Sir! There were about fifty men by my count, mostly Spanish, Irish and French, damned Papists! Most of my mates were sent back to Cuba, prisoners aboard their own sloop, to be slaves for the Alcada, that's the Spanish Governor, Sir.

"Three of us were kept by the Spanish privateers as pilots, and for months we cruised the Exumas with them, while they starved and abused us. When they took no prizes, they sailed back to Cuba to re-provision, and I there heard the Alcada is signing up the worst bastards in the Caribbean to sail for him as privateers, offering to pay them handsomely for raids on the Bahamas.

"Last week they landed at Catt Island. 'Twas awful Nat. I could never have believed that men could be so evil, and I was a buccaneer when a boy. They murdered all the men who didn't flee, shooting one man in front of his wife, and then her young son. Then they raped all the women, from grandmothers to little girls. When they invited us to join them, we fled into the bushes.

"Yet eight Bermudan pirates who came in for provisions were more easily persuaded. After three days of slaughter, they loaded Curtis' sloop with everything from slaves down to the meanest household objects. It wasn't done just for gain, Sir, but to destroy the settlement. They kept six poor women with them. As the Bermudan pirates know these waters so well, they no longer needed us, so

523

Holland gave us his periauger, and told us to sail in with a message for you, Sir. He says that the new Alcada has orders from King Philip of Spain to destroy all the English settlements in the Bahamas, and Nassau is next."

"Excuse me Mister Taylor", I interrupted. "Do you know old Noah Harwood? After he was pressed by Vane, he returned to his family on Catt Island."

"Then he and his sons are murdered, his wife and daughters raped and stolen, his house and crops destroyed", Richard Taylor wept, his head in his hands. I remembered how much the irascible old sea dog had loved his family, and hoped they had somehow been spared.

On the tenth of February, Crab Island, between Puerto Rico and Saint Thomas, was also attacked. Because of its position and fertility, it had long been a source of dispute with Spain, who had already wiped out an English colony there when William of Orange became King of England. Only last year, forty settlers and twenty slaves from drought-struck Anguilla had attempted to re-establish the place under Abraham Howell, their Deputy. They had been attacked by a man o' war and six sloops carrying hundreds of men. Some of the settlers were killed, yet most were carried off to Puerto Rico as slaves, including the women and children.

And it seemed as though Governor Rogers would go mad with waiting for the Spaniards to attack us. He ordered Ben Hornigold to equip the Endeavour as a privateer against the Spaniards, yet the canny old rover refused the expense of supporting a large crew, assuring the Governor that all would rally to his call if the Spaniards came. Indeed, when old Noah Harwood sailed in, lamenting the slaughter of Catt Island, and wishing he had died with his family, I knew all the rovers would fight. Yet Governor Rogers insulted the Brethren loudly and publicly, and Hornigold sailed away on a trading voyage, under-manned, his old popularity gone. Indeed, few of his old mates would even drink with him, many declaring that Henry Jennings had used the insult to

Kate Pritchard to abandon his old comrade.

That month, we heard of Captain Worley, who escaped slavery in New York as an indentured servant, sailing out with eight others in a leaky dinghy, with nothing more than dried tongue, hard biscuits, water, six muskets and ammunition. They sailed one hundred and fifty miles down the coast to the Delaware River, where they rowed up to Newcastle and took a shallop, rousing the whole coast against them. Still in only a small, open boat, and made desperate by thirst and hunger, they then seized a trading sloop, re-named her the Black Robin, and successfully cruised the coast. When Captain Pearce in the Phoenix chased them our way, they took another sloop, and then a brigantine, using the captured guns to arm the Black Robin.

Soon after, we heard that a Navy Fleet that had been sent out after Captain Moody, found Worley cruising off Charles Town. There was a pitched battle within sight of Charles Town harbour, sailors climbing the rigging of their ships to watch. The pirates were overwhelmed, and dozens of men were slaughtered. Yet worse, all twenty-two survivors were hanged the next day, after a mockery of a trial, before they could die of their wounds.

These severities, and the dwindling trade in the Caribbean, drove the surviving Brethren into greater cruelties, though nothing like the calumnies that were spread by the pamphleteers to discredit them. The pirates now fought for little more than provisions, and always forced men to join them. And once the hurricane season was over, more of the old rovers forgot their oaths and their honest intentions, and with hope of little else, went back on the account. Only some, like Henry Jennings and Ben Hornigold, made a small living from the Caribbean trade.

Then in March, we heard that Jennings had been imprisoned in Jamaica, unable to pay restitution to an old Frenchman for a cargo that he had once stolen. As their Governor had ignored the terms of his Pardon, Hornigold pleaded with Governor Rogers to intervene, yet he would not, and Hornigold himself was too nervous to go anywhere near Jamaica.

All of April and May, I worked hard on starvation wages, either readying the fort for battle with the Spaniards, or building for Thomas Walker. When not working, I haunted the waterfront, asking the captain of each ship that came in if he'd sign me on, though no one wanted one of the rebellious rovers of Nassau aboard as crew. I felt that my life had drifted away from me, and confounded, I became despondent. I had searched all my life for a safe harbour, and had instead spent years fighting desperately for mere survival. I began to doubt that the struggle was worth it, arguing with the ghost of my mother, waking in tears for the loss of my husband, sure now I would never have a child of my own. I was glad of the company of the Davies family, yet as they were struggling hard to feed themselves, I only joined them when I could catch a fish to take with me.

In the middle of May, when everything looked bleak to me, I was sitting over a smoky fire grilling fish, when a finely dressed couple came strolling down the shore to the Davies' cove. I started when I recognised Anne Bonny, distrusting my own eyes, for not only was she wearing a dress, abruptly belying my last image of her, it was of the finest green silk, fashionably cut, and showing her curves to considerable advantage. Emeralds from the Spanish Main dripped from her neck and ears, her red hair was curled under an enormous straw hat, and she was beautiful, and laughing. Jack Rackam was equally as fine, in a feathered tricorne, new boots, and a suit made entirely of scarlet calico and lace. "We stole all the material from an English trader", he exclaimed gleefully, "and had a seamstress in Jamaica make it up for us."

"In Jamaica?" I repeated, dazzled.

"Aye, where Anne posed as a fine lady, and met a charming widow called Kate, who knew just how much to pay the right man to agree that Henry Jennings should go free. She sends you her best wishes, as he does."

526

"Are you pirates still? Have you not taken the Pardon? You must hide, yet in truth, your clothes!"

Anne hugged me, laughing at my fear. "Fret not, Mark Read. Jack comes in for the Pardon from the Governor. We have made our fortune, and now we return to spend it." I saw Rackam's jealous eye upon me, for there was open affection in her voice, and I knew then my own secret was still safe. "You taught me well", she grinned. "None of the crew ever suspected me, even though Anne reappeared as Adam disappeared. I sailed over here with them, and played the lady, and didn't touch a sheet or a sail. Featherstone is here..."

"And Vane?"

"Vane is off on his own account, and has been since November, when Jack was voted Captain. Oh Mark, don't tell me you didn't hear tales o' Captain Jack Rackam? We were sure he would be famed throughout the Caribbean by now."

"How did Jack guess you were Anne?"

Rackam laughed. "Her bold young brother put my hand inside his shirt one hot night and kissed me. It didn't take me too long to figure it out."

I shook my head. "I knew she would not be able to keep herself off you. What was it, an irresistible combination of ale and moonlight?"

Anne laughed, and I knew I had guessed close. "We had a party with Captain Moody on the beach o' some key at Christmas. What a night! Anyway, Jack was very nobly keeping watch aboard so that his men could carouse. Some of them started eyeing me off, and I said I'd take the Captain out some rum and relieve him o' the watch. They grinned, and agreed that he might be lonely. It was a hot night, with the moon full, and the tide high. You know how it is...But you should have seen him jump when I kissed him!"

Rackam laughed. "I had thought for months that the lad fancied me, and even went as far as telling him how much I thought of his glorious sister. But I never came close

527

to guessing that he was other than a bloodthirsty boy, quick to take offence and draw steel, and hot in a close fight. Even now my mind quivers trying to place them inside one body. But once I knew her secret, I also knew it was only a matter of time before I gave it away. My preferences are too well known for the men to ignore my lust for the lad. Then Anne told me she was carrying my child..."

"You're pregnant?"

"Yes, isn't it marvellous? Oh don't worry, it's months away yet. Don't you think I'll make a terrible mother? You must be the godfather, so the child is not raised an utter heathen."

"I must get my breath back first. I'm overcome."

"It's too hot to think out in this sun", she laughed. "Come, let's to Cully's for an ale, and you can tell me all about your awful time here under the Governor. Oh yes, we've heard it all from Kate. The whole Caribbean knows."

"We can't go to Cully's! We need to be a little careful until Jack is pardoned. And you need to keep your secret Anne, in case you ever need it again."

"Oh Mark! I have no intention of putting off this pretty dress. I'm rich! Yet, if I do spend it all, I might go back on the account, whether Jack will come with me or no."

Jack laughed. "Lets ask Ma Davies for shade and lunch. We can talk frankly here without being overheard."

I called to Ma Davies, and her family all came out to welcome them, Jack enjoying their amazement, Anne curtseying to her old acquaintances, as regal as a Duchess, and as vain as a London harlot. It was a treat to see the embittered old woman smile so upon seeing them, yet her first words too concerned their safety.

"If yer not pardoned, Jack Rackam, yer foolish to walk about so open. Ye must sail off to Bermuda if ye want it as easy as that. Ye can't buy it here, ye have to beg for it. Anne my dear, 'tis a sight ye are for these old eyes."

"Jack has been very bold, and very careful. Now he's

going to combine his money with mine, and live a wealthy man off the investments we shall make. And I'm to have a baby."

"Yet you are still married to..."

"No one will suppose it's his! He will look like Jack. A bonny black-haired boy."

"No, a lovely girl with red hair and green eyes." They laughed into each other's faces with such delight that Ma Davies and I had to smile at each other.

"You'll lunch here with me. The boys found a turtle laying last night, so we have eggs and meat."

"I haven't had a decent feed since the last time I ate with you, Ma. And I want to thank you now for the care you took o' me when I was poor. You'll not find me one o' those who forgets old friends."

"God bless ye child, ye were such a wild young thing. An' I'll be glad to help ye deliver yer babe. Childbirth holds no secrets for me."

I was too worried about Jack's danger to eat comfortably. "Before lunch is ready, I'll run and tell the Governor that you are here and awaiting his pleasure as to the Pardon. Before someone else tells him he has a notorious pirate strutting about Nassau, dressed as fine as a Lord, only more colourful."

"This suit is cool and light, Mark Read, and keeps me in better temper than those who wear old sailcloth like you."

"Yet when we go to see the Governor, I will lend you something old and uncomfortable of mine."

Jack started to object, yet Anne poked him with her finger in the ribs. "Mark is right. I can't have you hung. I was grieved to hear o' your loss, Sarah. It was a terrible thing to happen, and you with your babe in your arms. You wouldn't put me through that, would you Jack? You know it would kill me. Now Mark, tell the Governor that Jack is very sorry, and won't do it again, and come back as soon as you can."

I raced back to Nassau, despite the heat, to paint Jack

as a saddened, repentant man, praying for his soul to be cleansed of his sins, and hoping to use his brigantine against the Spaniards. The Governor sighed and drummed his fingers on the table, yet said he would meet Jack that evening. I ran back to the beach, part of me still not convinced that they had really returned, that I had a friend again.

They were seated on a mat of palm leaves, the turtle steaks smelling sweet, and the eggs hard-boiled. I told Jack that if he could pretend to be repentant before the Governor that evening, the Pardon was his, and Anne hugged him and smiled upon me with such happiness that I had to laugh. Jack grabbed an egg, and finding it too hot, dropped it and swore.

"Serves ye right", Ma Davies snapped. "All things have their time, and now 'tis best to thank the Lord for his bounty." Jack shot an appealing glance at Anne, and she winked at him and bowed her head. "We thank ye Lord that ye have seen fit to keep our young friends safe throughout their trials. Please help 'em understand the need for a true repentance o' their crimes, and help us all to recognise our sins and avoid 'em. I pray also for the life o' the child in Anne's belly. May it grow strong, and be the best o' both its parents, an' keep 'em straight. Ye've been good to us Lord, and we thank ye for it. Amen."

For a while we were too busy eating to talk. Ma Davies ate little, and that quickly, and was the first to start speaking again. "Ye must be careful o' the Governor, Anne. Yer husband has his ear, and if he speaks against ye, he may do ye both damage."

"I no longer think o' him as my husband."

"That doesn't mean yer not married to him. He still has the right to call ye whore, and take yer money. An' the Governor is his friend."

"If the Governor were my friend..."

"He don't like women."

"So Kate told me. I suppose I'll have to pay James off.

If we catch him drunk with empty pockets, he'll take anything. We should go and pay our respects to the Governor now, I expect. Then we can go to Cully's, find some old friends, and drink an ale. Here's a guinea for the finest cook in the Caribbean, Ma. We'll see you again tomorrow at noon, to talk o' business, if you'd give us the favour o' your counsel."

It was on our way back to Nassau, well out of earshot of Ma Davies, that I sat down in the shade of a large fig tree, and demanded an account of their adventures after the taking of the Neptune and Emperor.

Jack grinned and began the tale. "After the loss of Nassau, Vane grew meaner, Deal the only man whose opinion he cared for, and me caught between him and a surly crew. After careening our Fleet at Green Turtle Key, and looting our two prizes, we cruised the Crooked Island Passage. Windward of Jamaica, we took a brigantine, and found Hosea Tisdell aboard, a Jamaican tavern keeper who remembered us from our privateering days. We kept him with us while we cruised between Cape Meise on Cuba and Cape Nicholas on Hispaniola."

Anne interrupted. "We were over-manned, and when I sounded out the men, I found them willing to vote Jack as the Captain o' the next ship we took. Then I spied another brigantine, and when we attacked, she raised the colours o' the French Navy. Vane called off the chase as soon as she fired at us, declaring it would be too much fight for no cargo."

"I argued that with our Fleet, we could take her easily", Jack fumed. "Yet Vane had guessed that I intended to split the Company, and he stood by his right to decide all when chasing or being chased. That was enough for me. I was enraged that he could make captains of his favourites without considering the will of the Company, and then quote the Articles when they suited him."

Anne interrupted again. "That night I spoke to all the best men, and told them Jack would challenge Vane, if they'd support him."

Jack grinned and continued the tale. "In the early morning calm, I called a meeting of the Fleet, despite Vane's objections, and we roped together in mid-ocean. I spoke of all that was in my heart, of how Vane and I were sworn brothers. Of how his cruelty had soured my respect for him, even Tom Brown horrified at what had been done to Bermudan sailors in his name. I spoke of how his arrogance had rotted our friendship entirely, and betrayed the strength of the Brethren of Nassau. I swore that under my lead, they would be true comrades, and asked the men if they would have me as Captain of the Fleet.

"When they voted me in, Vane was sulphurous with anger, his followers standing with their hands on their cutlasses. I then asked Vane if he would remain with the Fleet or quit us, and he chose to leave. I asked the Fleet to vote him a vessel, and though Vane at first insisted that he keep his brigantine, I declared he had not enough men to sail her, and asked for a vote on leaving him the sloop. 'Twas carried, and Vane sailed off with Deal and fifteen others, and a third of the provisions and ammunition."

"He must have hated you."

"He put a good face on it at the end. The best of the men came with me, including George Featherstone, our Gunner. I told them this was my greatest honour, and they could trust me to make their fortunes. We had a lucky start for our new Company, and took a well-laden sloop on her way to Jamaica. We needed three days to loot her, and then returned the vessel to her master, and let Hosea Tisdell go with her.

"It was close to Christmas when we ran into Tom Moody, and had that feast, and I found that 'Adam' was Anne. Soon after, we took a ship laden with Newgate convicts, bound for slavery on the plantations, and had all the new hands we needed. I thought of keeping the ship, though she was under-gunned, and considered marooning her Captain, who had treated the convicts cruelly, especially the women. But a British man o' war hove in sight, and we sailed away.

"We took two more vessels, but found little cargo worth keeping. Truly, I've seen that Ben Hornigold is right, and the best years on the account are over. We must be strong enough to attack convoys, and the Navy ships that guard them; or subsist without honour upon the small traders of the Caribbean, who cannot afford the Navy's services. I was also afraid that the men would see that 'Adam' was female, and maroon us both. Then a turtling sloop from Jamaica came in to our mooring at Princes Island, and told us that because of the war with Spain, the amnesty for pirates had been extended on Nassau.

"I spoke for dividing our Company between those who'd stay on the account, and those who'd turn trader. I declared that we could begin a new life, without fear for our necks, as every man's share would make him rich. A third of them decided to follow me, the rest elected Tom Brown their Captain. He declared the sloops the best for the pirate life, and the Company voted me the brigantine for a trader, swearing they would never attack us. She's in the harbour now, and I must show her to you, Read, for she's a lovely vessel."

Anne took up the tale. "Jack thought to take the Pardon in Jamaica, yet the turtler told us o' Jennings being jailed there. I laughed to hear o' it, Henry taking the Pardon so honestly, and persuading so many of the Brethren to follow him. Yet we sailed into Port Royal, relying on the annual fair to bring many unfamiliar faces to Kingston, and taking the precaution o' disguising ourselves as a merchantman, with a new name painted on the ship, and English colours."

Jack laughed. "I went to present myself to the Governor, as all ship's masters must, having drawn up the ship's papers myself. Young 'Adam' declared he was leaving the Company, and when I returned aboard that night with Anne on my arm, the men swore that she'd just missed her little brother. She asked so many fond questions of him, they were all convinced. Indeed what else could they think? That the cocky rascal and this glorious creature could be the same? A man's imagination cannot stretch so far."

Anne laughed too. "I met Mistress Kate petitioning the Governor, and she knew who to bribe. With a little of our money to augment her own, Henry was soon released, and mighty grateful he was to the friends that stood by him. Kate told us that you were alive and well, Mark, and that there was money to be made here for any man who could stand the prig of a Governor, so we sailed on the next tide."

"And is it really the honest life for you now? Have you had your fill of being the terror of the Caribbean?"

Jack sighed. "It was always more than a business to me. But the best days of the Brethren are over, and I have Anne and our child to think of. We have more than enough to make a good beginning, and Nassau is desperate enough to pay our prices. We will rely on the honest piracy of sharp dealing to make us rich, eh Anne? Yet first, I must clear things with Governor Rogers."

Jack looked a different man in my old canvas suit, and was charmingly penitent to the Governor, sighing sadly over his lawlessness, and claiming his crew was eager to fight the Spaniards. The Governor finally condescended to sign his Certificate, promising to pardon his crew the next morning, and after a final lecture on the evils of theft, we were allowed to go and get drunk.

Anne had taken the best lodgings in town, and there we stopped, so Jack could change back into his finery. Then we all went to Cully's to celebrate, and there was a general uproar at the sight of my two friends. Jack's crew were drinking hard, the rovers from the beach carousing with them. I was warmly welcomed by the scar-faced George Featherstone, who thanked me for giving him such a gunner as young Adam Cormac. When Governor Rogers came in, he had to look twice before he recognised Jack in his red calico suit, and then he glared at me. I hardly cared. I had

534

worked faithfully for him, and he had not even paid my wages. Jack bowed to the Governor, and offered to buy him a drink, yet Rogers did not deign to hear him.

Jack turned to find Hornigold behind him, and instantly, his hand went to the hilt of his sword. Anne insisted on a truce, and I helped Hornigold excuse himself for hunting his old mates. We then followed the rovers, who quit Cully's when the Governor came in, stumbling down to the beach with a couple of rum bottles, talking of the old days, and drinking hard. And for once, I got as drunk as any of them, relieved to be amongst friends.

Chapter 28: The Raid

I woke on the beach at dawn, my head pounding in the cruel sun, and staggered into Cully's for small beer. Patrick Carty looked up from a card game to tell me that Jack had already paid the Governor for Pardons for his men, and we were all to meet at Ma Davies' camp for lunch.

We found most of Jack's crew eating pan bread and fish, and discussing the Caribbean trade. George Featherstone raised an eyebrow to see Carty and I, and insisted that we all had to buy a share in our first cargo. When Patrick and I stated that we'd like to join them, yet had but a fraction of the cash, Anne backed me, and Ma Davies stood by Patrick. She also asked for her son John to be taken on as a shareholder, and I was glad to speak up for the lad. We then discussed trade, cargoes, and prices, and with Noah Harwood's help, soon worked out a route that would see us rich. We planned to buy our first cargo of hardwood at Andros Island, and to sell it at Catt Island, where the survivors were already re-building their settlement.

The next day, I waited on the Governor, and informed him of our plans, offering to carry any cargo that he might like to venture with us on our first cruise. He barely looked up from signing papers, and his sneer made it clear that he trusted me no longer, and was glad to be rid of me. I left him with his fears and worries, a man broken in health and patience.

I was surprised when James Bonny followed me, and asked if he could buy me a drink. I glared at him. "I assume you wish to cut yourself a slice of Anne's prosperity. I'll bring her to Cully's at sunset, to save you troubling her."

James Bonny was horrified when Rackam's entire crew stalked into Cully's that night, armed to the teeth.

"James, how stout you look," Jack hissed. "Not smoking quite so much? Being Rogers' spy evidently suits you. You remember my wife, of course?"

"With all respect Captain Rackam, she is not your wife, but mine."

"My dear James, after trying to sell her, I'd have thought you too wise to claim it. And even though Anne has tried to forgive you, my temper is not so easy. Once I thought I'd slit your gullet for it. Now, what was it you wanted to see her about?"

"Nothing Captain Rackam. Merely to enquire after her health. I have a friendly interest in her, nothing more, I swear it."

"Is that not sweet of him Anne, my love? And we thought he'd be stupid enough to try and extort money from us, and I would have to kill him after all. We misjudged you, James. Oh by the way, was it you who informed the young Lieutenant of the Phoenix that the Lark was at Bushes Key? I always thought it must have been you."

"And what of the gold I earned in Bellamy's Company", I hissed. "You stole it from me, you bastard!"

Bonny desperately denied it all, and Jack shook his head, smiling nastily. "Well, you can go now. We don't really want to drink with you. We'll be back at sea soon, so our paths shouldn't cross that often." He grovelled and left us, and Jack congratulated himself on a job well done. Anne was less sanguine, insisting that her husband had a combination of greed and stupidity that boggled the mind. I suggested that Jack ask Peg, who was still a servant at the Governor's residence, to keep her ears open for anything concerning us.

That night, our Company gathered to draw up the Articles, and we all signed: Jack Rackam as Captain, Patrick Carty as Quartermaster, old Noah Harwood as navigator, George Featherstone as Gunner, John Davies, me, and six more of Jack's old crew. Anne signed too, as a full shareholder, and as she had the most experience from her days running her father's plantation, she also offered to keep our accounts.

We set sail with the tide late that night, Noah

Harwood guiding us out of the harbour under the full moon, and setting the course for Andros Island. In the morning, Anne stepped out of the hold, dressed in her baggy old canvas trousers, her red curls under a bandanna, declaring herself a stowaway. Jack gaped, and I shook my head in horror, for as soon as we returned, the news would sweep Nassau that she had sailed as a pirate.

"Blast my eyes!", George Featherstone gasped. "Adam?"

"Aye, it's your old comrade, George. You must all pardon me for dressing as a boy, and deceiving you. You know I was faithful to the Oaths I took to our Company, that I kept the Articles, and was never laggard in battle. I'm hoping you'll laugh and keep your mouths shut, if you can keep such a good story to yourselves. My neck depends upon it, for you can imagine the Governor's rage if he hears o' my exploits."

Jack exploded then, demanding to know what she was about, to be sailing on so risky a venture when she was carrying their child in her belly. Yet she stood her ground. "Come Jack, you didn't expect me to sit on my arse in Nassau, while you sailed about the Caribbean having all the adventures. I've invested my share, and you need me aboard as your supercargo, tallying the goods and keeping the accounts. And George needs me as his powder monkey, don't you George?"

Featherstone guffawed, calling her the bravest lad he'd ever met, yet old Noah Harwood spat venom, insisting that a woman aboard was the worst possible luck. The rest turned on Jack, demanding to know why he'd thought fit to beak the Articles, and bring a woman into Vane's Company.

"I swear to you, I didn't know until Tom Moody's Christmas party. And I thought it no joke. I made sure we disbanded soon after."

"Aye, and it was good luck I brought you, not bad", Anne insisted. "John Davies, I've no need to ask for your support. You've been true to me since we hunted together.

538

Mark Read, you know my worth from those same months in the jungle. I sailed with the rest o' you for a year, and you counted me your brother, for I earned all your praises. Will you not shrug your shoulders and give me a chance to prove myself as able as ever?"

Featherstone's good humoured tales of her courage as a powder monkey soon balanced the severe reproofs of Noah Harwood, though in truth, it was her relation to Jack that made them give way to her at first. Yet as the days past, and we all shifted sail together, the men soon lapsed into treating her like the lad they'd sailed with, though Harwood still insisted we'd catch a hurricane.

With the hardwood from Andros Island, we bought Catt Island's excess of salt, and sailed for Hispaniola, where we traded salt for sugar. We continued from one island to the next, our cargo growing with every transaction, and ended with a month sailing south through the Leeward Islands. 'Twas the season for storms, and we guessed that there would be few traders, and fewer pirates. After a day's steady sailing, we would moor at another pretty harbour for the night, often docking just as the great thunderclouds above us spilled over. We stayed a few days in each harbour to bargain, setting off at dawn, often in squally weather.

Whenever we docked at a town, Anne would take lodgings for her and Jack, and change into a dress. Yet as soon as she came aboard again, she changed into her baggy canvas trousers, and dropped her refined manners for her usual impertinence. I was worried that having seen one man turn female, they'd be looking for another, yet they never doubted me.

We sailed as far south as Port o' Spain in Trinidad, on the advice that there were always willing gentlemen keeping an eye out for a sail. Sure enough, as dawn filled the east, a smart sloop flying the red and gold colours of Castille met us, and though we feared them as privateers at first, they proved courteous enough. Indeed, we traded almost all we had left with them, and it was so hurried, and so much to our advantage, that I had to conclude that these black-dressed, dark-faced Spanish gentlemen were risking their necks as smugglers.

Not wanting the risk of trading along the Spanish Main, as our two countries were still at war, we turned north-west, and made a long leg for Jamaica, Noah Harwood navigating us so well through the squalls, that we sailed straight into Kingston harbour. There we bought quantities of goods from England, and rum. Frightened of pirates now, for we had a small chest of money, and sat heavy in the water with our cargo, we tacked through the Windward Passage, and along the north-west coast of Cuba. There we ran before a Spanish guarda del costa for two days, Jack resisting Noah's urges to jettison the cargo, glad that the Spanish sloops were so befouled that they sailed slower than our laden brigantine.

To avoid pirates, we risked the lee shore of the Florida Strait, despite the threat of more storms. On the first day, we saw four sail, yet they stood away from us, and we were not threatened again. The anxiety of the merchant trader taught Jack some sympathy for his past victims, and I reminded the Company of Hornigold's claim, that the Brethren kept their honour by preying on the overly rich, not the poor and desperate. Featherstone flipped a coin and wished for a Spanish galleon, and we all sighed over his golden vision.

We sailed north for Carolina then, and docked amid the bustle of Charles Town. Though cattle and pigs roamed the broad streets that ran to the fort, the town had a remarkably genteel air, and Anne declared it much changed since she had left only a few years ago. The town walls were all pulled down, the number of slaves vastly increased, and elegant houses with large windows and little balconies had replaced the dark and narrow huts.

Anne dragged us off to the whorehouse to meet Belle, a fat, over-rouged, wicked old woman, who was delighted to see Anne in fine silks, on the arm of a man as handsome as

Jack. Belle explained that the increasing trade in rice and blue dye had seen the town prosper, yet a small number of rich planters still controlled the town, most of them her faithful clients. After a few rums, I begged Anne to send for her father, so he could meet Jack, and see her prosperous and happy. She indignantly refused, claiming they could never forgive each other their mutual injuries. I pointed out that the old forgave much more easily than the young, and that he might be sick or dying, yet I still could not persuade her.

Noah Harwood sneered to find himself in a bordello, while young John Davies could do little but stare and blush. An elegant mulatta sat close by him and took his hand, and he was almost overcome by her smiles. She teasingly asked him his age, and when he started up, and declared that today was his sixteenth birthday, Jack poured the shy young man a large glass of punch, and we all toasted his health. Belle soon persuaded us to club together to buy him the whore, and the beautiful mulatta lead him off for the night, the boy stumbling in her wake like the captive of an Amazonian Queen. The red-nosed Patrick Carty soon disappeared upstairs with a merry black whore, and Featherstone struck up an intense flirtation with a quiet Yorkshire lass, who regarded him with soulful eyes, and kissed his great scar with exquisite tenderness.

Yet Noah Harwood, Anne, Jack and I, stuck to business, and pouring a second bowl of punch for Belle's other patrons, we boasted of the cargo we'd be auctioning the next day to the planters about us. The next morning, our heads aching from the punch, we set up our booth on the dock. By noon, a fair crowd had gathered, the rum went around, and Jack sold our cargo for good money. Anne spent the afternoon aboard with her account books, and that evening, she showed how we had doubled our investment since Nassau. We then agreed to invest half of our money in another cargo, and to divide the remainder as profit amongst us.

Once we'd loaded our new cargo to trade in the

Bahamas, we divided our shares, and I paid Anne back for her investment in my share, though it left me with little enough. Anne then insisted she needed a new dress, and we strolled about Charles Town looking for a seamstress. Under the sign of the needle, Anne found Annie Fulworth, a plump, motherly woman, who had been fond of Anne when she was a wild young girl. After they shed tears on each other's shoulders, Anne asked her what she did in Charles Town, trying to scrape a meagre living by her needle, and Mis'ess Fulworth misted up with tears again. "The Indian war ruined him. He started to drink. Yet everyone drinks! It was only when the new babe came that he started gambling. He lost us everything. The slaves, the house, the plantation. All those years of hard labour. All my dead babies. Then he shot himself. And all I can say, love, is that a just God would have struck him down two years ago, and left me a rich widow, with three children. I've none but my youngest spared me. Look, he's sleeping in here." At the back of her dark shop, a pale child slept in the sweat of fever. "He's all I have left. He has my dead husband's eyes."

When Anne confided her pregnancy, Mis'ess Fulworth wept again, and Anne quickly offered her the care of her coming babe. "You'll have milk enough for another, and for the first time in my life, I feel I might need help." The poor woman was happy to pack her materials into a basket, and run out on her back-rent, insisting she could sew well enough aboard ship. We sailed with the wind, despite Mis'ess Fulworth's sudden terror of hurricanes, sharks and pirates, and I could only shrug at Noah Harwood's constant complaints of women at sea.

Ma Davies welcomed us safe back in Nassau, and at the news of our good fortune, she celebrated by cooking us a feast. Anne offered her the choice of taking her investment in money or goods, and the wise old woman chose to take the first pick of our cargo, though she declared she needed a storehouse. We spent the week erecting a strong shelter from wood that Harry had stolen, Anne showing us how to thatch the roof with Indian grass, and Ma Davies soon had a locked strongroom, with a wide veranda as her kitchen.

Jack paid our port tax, and offered the rest of our cargo to the Governor at a reasonable rate. Yet when Rogers could only offer us a note of credit, Jack refused him, and sold it instead to James Gohier, who intended to sell it back to the Governor at a vast profit.

With the return of the intense heat, Rogers relapsed into fever again, and without Mistress Pritchard to insist he take to his bed, he roamed the muddy streets of Nassau, drinking rum and raving of the coming Spaniards. He announced that all the survivors of Catt Island must move to our unproductive hovel of a town, for fear they'd be used as pilots against us, and we laughed at him for thinking he could forcibly remove the stubborn Catt Islanders.

Before our cruise, Captain South had taken the Pardon, and turned privateer for the Governor, sharing the command of Hornigold's Endeavour. He now sailed in with real news of the Spaniards plans to invade us, which he had from young Charlie Walker.

Months ago, he and Captain Porter had chased a sloop off Porto Maria, on Cuba, only to be hailed by Captain Leigh Ashworth, who declared himself a privateer of Jamaica. South declared himself from Providence, and Ashworth had immediately opened fire on him, cutting the Endeavour's sails to ribbons. South demanded why she fired, yet the Jamaican sloop fired again, this time at Captain Porter. With his canvas in tatters, South had no choice but to comply with Ashworth's orders to lower his mainsail, though he was still being fired upon, seven men now wounded.

When Captain Ashworth clambered aboard the Endeavour from his dory, Captain South flung his privateers' commission in his face, demanding reparation. Ashworth claimed he had thought them Nassau pirates, and with profuse apologies to both Captains, agreed to their demands for compensation. He then saw them safe into Porto Scrivano, where they made repairs and watered, the

543

Captains amicably discussing terms.

They then proceeded to threaten the shipping of Havana together, and were cruising off Cuba, when South's lookout spotted a small dory. To their surprise, they found Charlie Walker and two other young fellows lying in the bilges, half dead of thirst. The boys had escaped from Havana to bring intelligence of the Spaniards fitting out warships to attack Providence, yet contrary winds had driven them back. Ashworth had refused to sail for Nassau in case the Governor forced him to stay and defend us from the Spaniards, and instead he'd declared that he'd have Charlie Walker as a pilot, to see him safe back to Jamaica. When South objected, Ashworth cocked a loaded pistol at the boy's head. Half the men aboard went for their swords, and Ashworth's Gunner leapt for their swivel gun.

Young Charlie protested that they need not fight over him, if Ashworth would swear to release him in Jamaica, and pay him well for his services. Ashworth agreed, and Charlie reminded them all of the Spanish threat to the Bahamas, begging South to sail with all speed to warn the Governor, and his family on Abaco. At the last moment, Ashworth clapped his pistol to the head of a free black sailor, declaring that Negroes must live as slaves to ensure the continued wealth of the Caribbean. The sailor begged South to tell his people on Eleuthera what had happened, so they could send a petition to the Governor protesting his capture.

When Thomas Walker heard of his son's vile treatment, he immediately took ship for Jamaica to horsewhip Captain Ashworth, and fetch his boy back home. Yet, only days after he sailed out, Captain Courant found Charlie and the black sailor afloat in Captain Ashworth's dory. Ashworth's harsh treatment of Charlie had convinced him he was a slave again, and they had stolen the dory soon after they were taken. Walker sailed back from Jamaica to find his son already recovering from his ordeal, and though Charlie insisted 'twas the Negro who'd saved his life, Walker preferred to thank Peter Courant, despite his past as a pirate.

Charlie reported that the Alcada had one thousand men mustered in Havana, and five hundred more expected from Trinidad, all to attack Providence in two galleys, two brigantines, and nine sloops. The Governor placed an embargo on all ships leaving Providence, but the Samuel, which he sent back to London with more letters begging for help. Mister Beauchamp, who had sickened while commanding the garrison, and had hoped to leave Nassau before the fever killed him, tried to insist upon a passage on the Samuel, yet the Governor would not hear of it. He would not let our Company sail either, and so we stayed in Nassau, living on our share of our profits, until Jack prayed that the Spaniards would attack.

Since Hornigold's success against Vane and Auger, Rogers had kept five sloops as privateers, raiding the Spanish salvage camps on the Florida coast, which provided him with a valuable source of coin. At the end of May, George Hooper sailed in with two prizes and seventy-five Spanish prisoners, plus demands for bounty money. The Governor could not afford to feed them, so the prisoners were put to work finishing Thomas Walker's house, and then those of the Governor's financiers, on condition that they fed them. Now the scrawny Spaniards roamed Nassau like dogs, shunned by the townspeople, the island children throwing stones at them.

Soon after Peter Courant sailed in with Charlie Walker, Courant's wife, Susannah, arrived from Harbour Island, complaining that she and her newborn babe had been abandoned to the charity of friends. When she found her husband living with one of the dosshouse women, Susannah brought a petition to the Governor, demanding that Courant make her proper allowance. The Governor was too fevered to see her, yet the polite Mister Beauchamp requested her to address the next Council. She stayed with Ma Davies, fretting for the babe she'd left with friends on Harbour Island, and cursing her miserly husband.

At the Council, Peter Courant stoutly denied that she

was his wife at all, until Nat Taylor swore they had been living together for six or seven years. Then Courant accused her of being delivered of a black bastard. She protested, declaring that her friend Mistress Saunders could either bring the child, or send her husband, John Saunders, to testify for her. At this, Courant declared that he'd had a gutful of them poking their noses into his private business, and he'd damn the Governor's embargo, and sail for New York, rather than submit to it. To clear his character, he proposed to provide for his wife and son, if they would sail with him.

Susannah declared that he would throw her and the babe overboard as soon as they were out of the harbour. The Governor argued that as her husband had generously offered to take her back, she could expect no maintenance from the Council, for fear of encouraging unwed mothers to beg charity from them. Susannah insisted she'd not asked for charity, but for maintenance in her own home by her own husband, for his own child, yet the Governor waved her pleas aside, mopping the fever from his face. Mister Fairfax then assured Susannah that he'd write a Certificate for the Governor of New York, recommending justice in case her husband ever tried anything of the kind again. She bluntly told the Council that her husband would simply heave the Certificate over with her and the babe, and declined sailing with him.

Then the Governor washed his hands of her, calling her a troublesome woman, of little account, who had cost him a valuable ally in the coming battle with the Spaniards. She protested her own value, as a mother if not as a human creature with a soul, yet he was above listening to her. She was left with no choice but to whore herself at the dosshouse, sending money and goods back to the Saunders on Harbour Island, to pay for the maintenance of her child. Governor Rogers, assuming she'd always been a whore, felt vindicated at the news.

Anne, her pregnancy heavy upon her, cursed to hear

of Susannah's humiliation. Ma Davies sighed and agreed that the bearing of a beloved child could leave a woman at the mercy of the hard world.

"Aye", Patrick Carty growled. "And we must slip the Governor's embargo and keep trading. Otherwise Nassau will have no food, and we'll have spent all our profits, and be forced back on the account, so he can say we were always pirates."

The success of Bartholemew Roberts cheered us all. The tall Welshman had joined Howell Davis in January, and when Davis was killed only weeks later, he was voted Captain of the Fleet. Bound for Africa, they found a Portuguese Fleet, and Black Bart sailed straight into it, guns blazing. He took the Sagrada Familia, a forty-gun warship, and a hundred and fifty prisoners, his Company earning fifty thousand pounds for their courage. Then in June, Black Bart sailed a small sloop crewed with sixty men into Trepanny harbour, in Newfoundland, and took all twenty-two vessels.

In August, just at the beginning of the hurricane season, Captains Thomas Porter, Henry White, and John Cockram brought a Spanish prize loaded with cocoa into Nassau. She was legally condemned, and the ship's Company received their share of her goods, since there was no cash available. Mister Fairfax pointed out that the tavern keepers would impose on the men, forcing them to pay for their liquor with the valuable cocoa, and so Governor Rogers fixed the rate of sale, and the men did well out of it.

Jack laughed at this legal piracy, noting that the Governor had demanded a large cut of the profits in port tax, and then asked the Governor for permission for us to go out as privateers, hunting pirates and Spaniards. We all knew this was a mere ruse, as we did not have the numbers for war, and so we continued trading secretly, smuggling goods in and out of Ma Davies' storeroom. Despite his open contempt for us, Rogers ignored our dealings, glad of the provisions coming into Nassau. With Anne's careful book keeping, Noah Harwood's knowledge of the sea, Jack's sharp bargaining, and Featherstone's well-primed guns, our Company thrived, each cruise adding a little to our profits, so that the next cruise entailed an even bigger stake, and bigger profits. When in Nassau, our brigantine was moored where we could see her, with a watch kept on her every night, and young Harry Davies guarding the storeroom with his old musket while we were away.

Horrified by his son's account of the atrocities on Cuba, Thomas Walker spent October trying to negotiate a trade of fifty of our weakest Spanish prisoners for Englishmen who were still slaves in Havana. Though the rovers for once agreed with their enemy, few Captains would lend their ships for such an enterprise, not trusting the Spaniards to respect their flags of truce.

Then His Majesty's ship the Flamborough sailed into Nassau, cataracts of rain ensuring no one noticed until she blasted a salute to our little fort. The Governor limped to the shore after everyone else, declaring that the Lords of Trade and Plantations must have provided this protection for Nassau. Yet when Captain John Hildesley was rowed ashore, to bow frigidly to our scruffy Governor, 'twas trade he enquired after. Rogers insisted that his embargo applied to Hildesley's ship, and the Navy Captain, caring nothing for this dirty, angry little man or the fate of Nassau, declared he'd not lose a penny of convoy fees for all our lives.

Captain Gale thought he'd take advantage of the Flamborough's presence, and slip over to North Carolina to settle some private affairs. Yet that night at Cully's, a dispute broke out between the sailors of the Delicia and the Flamborough, which ended with Hildesley detaining three of Gale's men for calling him a profiteer. When Captain Gale icily demanded their release, Hildesley refused, and despite the Governor's opposition, he had two of the men whipped that afternoon.

Captain Hildesley and his Officers soon found that no one in Nassau would sell them food, and when they strode into Cully's that evening, to complain to the Governor, the scowling Cully rudely refused to serve them. When Governor Rogers declared that he could not help them either, young Jonathon Coram laughed. Hildesley turned on the young sailor, and Coram abused him foully, for whipping two men for telling the truth.

Hildesley then ordered his Officers to march the lad off to the Flamborough, though young Mister Fairfax stood in his way, protesting that Coram was subject to the laws of the land, not the martial law of the Navy. Fairfax was pushed aside, and Coram marched off. The next day, Hildesley announced that the young sailor would suffer the torture of being whipped from ship to ship. The whole of Nassau again bordered on mutiny, the Governor ordered Hildesley to let Coram be judged by the Council, yet Hildesley refused, and kept the luckless Coram rotting in irons on the Flamborough.

In November, the Governor's creditors finally refused the Governor's bills, and he was left without means to feed his men, let alone pay them. Mister Fairfax gave him six hundred pieces of eight from the King's customs, and that at least paid the garrison's wages. Then it was only our smuggling that supported the Government that had overthrown us. Again Rogers petitioned the Lords of Trade and Plantations in England, yet he received no account of what should be done to save the Colony.

On December the fifth, a boy sailed in from Harbour Island to declare that they were at war with privateers from New York. Some days before, the privateers had sailed in looking for provisions. Though well behaved at first, once they were drunk, they had begun harassing the women. When repulsed, they had endeavoured to set fire to the settlement, and the inhabitants had then united under the leadership of Captain Cockram, and attacked them. They wounded many of the villains, and retreated in good order to the garrison they had built, where they held off the privateer attack.

Our Governor sent Captains Porter and White to their aid, yet when they arrived at Harbour Island, the privateers had already sailed away, leaving the settlement a smoking ruin. Yet the inhabitants were so proud of the forts they had built, and the courage with which they had defended themselves, that I thought they had gained, rather than lost in the conflict.

Then Susannah Courant heard that her baby boy had been caught up in the battle, and was badly burned. She instantly took passage on a sloop bound for Harbour Island, yet her child died before she arrived. She returned soon after, declaring that if she had been with her little boy, he would never have been abandoned to the fire. She took all the money she had saved, and spent it on bad rum. Her body washed up with the tide the next morn', and they found rocks in her pockets. Anne laid the death of Susannah and her child at the feet of our Governor, though Jack insisted that Peter Courant was truly the villain, for abandoning them in the first place.

On the sixteenth of December, the Flamborough man o' war sailed, leaving the Bahamas unprotected, save for the rotting Delicia. Governor Rogers condemned our Christmas merriment, and swore the Spaniards would come in by the light of our fires, yet Jack bought drinks for all, and the hugely pregnant Anne danced wildly to a fiddle around the bonfire. It seemed to me that all of Nassau now knew that she sailed as crew on our brigantine, and most knew she'd sailed with Vane dressed as a boy. I trembled to think of James Bonny hearing of it and telling our Governor.

Three nights after Christmas, Anne finally went into labour, Ma Davies her midwife, and Annie Fulworth helping. Though I longed to comfort Anne in her ordeal, I had to stay outside with Jack and the menfolk, and 'twas almost enough to make me drop my disguise, to hear her scream, and be so useless. Indeed, 'twas only by reminding myself that I had never seen a child born, and would be of no use to Ma Davies or Anne, that I stayed sitting in the sand with Jack.

Towards dawn, Anne's screams filled the bay, and I broke my hard resolve and prayed openly for God's mercy,

Jack weeping on his knees beside me. When I saw his anguish, I swore to him that God could not be so cruel as to take her, and he wiped his eyes. "I have always had an eye for a pretty woman, but she was the first to touch my heart. And now, with her dying in there, my soul is wrenched apart, and I know I could not live without her."

"Then swear to me you'll put your new family before everything."

"I swear it. I'll put them before everything else."

As the sun spilled over the horizon, Anne gave one last screech, and the weak mewing of a babe sounded after. We heard Ma Davies praise the Lord, and then she emerged from the hut and placed Jack's black-haired daughter in his arms. Tears streamed down his face, and when he started assuring her that he would be the best of fathers, I left him before he saw my own. I went in to find Anne lying deflated and exhausted on a grass mat. I kissed her hand, and she opened her eyes, smiled weakly, and demanded a dram of rum. Despite Mis'ess Fulworth's protests, I sent Harry for a bottle, and soon Jack and her comrades had gathered about, full of hearty congratulations, admiration for the babe, and toasts for her future. And in truth the babe was so vulnerable in her new life that she tore at my heart, reawakening my old regret at having no child of my own.

It took Anne more than a week to recover from her ordeal, declaring that if she had known beforehand what it was like to bear a child, she would have stayed a virgin. She moaned of the child screaming every few hours for milk, so that she could not sleep, Mis'ess Fulworth with not yet enough milk for both babes. A week after, none would have known the bedraggled drab, querulously complaining of the heat and the flies, for the gallant Anne Bonny. Yet when I teased her, she surprised me entirely by bursting into tears. Mis'ess Fulworth just laughed and hugged her, insisting that her daughter would soon sleep through the night. "I'll throttle her else", Anne warned us peevishly, and then laughed weakly, yet enough to reassure us.

Soon Annie Fulworth was nursing both, though her own child was a languid, pale thing compared to Anne's bright and bouncing babe. Once she could sleep at night, Anne again accompanied Jack to Cully's every evening, and soon began to be more herself. She insisted that if the babe had kept Jack awake for a month, he would not think her such an angel, yet Jack doted on his daughter, much to the amusement of his old comrades at Cully's. They gathered about the wee scrap of womanhood, as Hornigold called her, Noah Harwood grumpy because Jack refused to let him dandle his precious girl.

Then Mis'ess Fulworth's child died, and, in her grief, she took Anne's babe as her own. Anne was glad of the help, as she was still doing the accounts, doling out a meagre portion of our smuggling profits to live on, saving most towards the next cargo. Yet when Jack suggested that we continue trading, leaving her in Nassau with the babe, she suggested that if he was so possessed by the child, he must stay behind as her nurse, while she captained the brigantine. And so we sailed with Mistress Fulworth and the babe aboard, and the crew askance, though Featherstone declared we had a clean hull, and could outrun most trouble. And indeed his accuracy with our guns saved us from more than one skirmish with pirates on that voyage. Before the week was out, Noah Harwood was claiming the authority of a grandfather in all matters to do with the babe, the child seeing his first smile since the destruction of his family on Catt Island.

Our Company prospered, and though we were not rich, we were on our way to being so, though Rogers resented our happy independence. In January, the Governor had not enough to feed the sailors of the Delicia, let alone his Militia, and he had no cash left. Then a French smuggler came in, his ship waiting outside the harbour, loaded with stores, and happy to trade. The Governor had no choice, yet, instead of being open about the necessity for this compromise, he tried to cover it up, as though anything could be kept secret on Providence.

Only days later, a fishing boat sailed in, her Captain shouting that there was a Spanish Fleet headed our way. We had been waiting for the attack for so long, the Spaniards preferring to attack the wealthy English settlements on the American mainland, that it was almost a relief. Luckily, we had almost double the number of rovers in Nassau than a year ago, many of the men from the outer isles of the Bahamas in for the trade. The Flamborough had just anchored, and the Governor ordered Hildesley to stay, and reaffirmed his embargo on any ship leaving the harbour. Hildesley protested that he was not obliged to help defend the colony, yet the Governor threatened to accuse him of desertion in the face of the enemy, and he reluctantly agreed to help keep the Spaniards off us.

The Governor scurried about madly, so sure we'd desert him, that he impounded the sails and rudders of all the local craft. Ignoring him, Mister Beauchamp and Ben Hornigold quickly agreed to divide their forces, the Governor's privateers, the Delicia, and the militia to defend Nassau, while the rest of the rovers would hold the few landing places around Providence. Jack asked our Company if we would take our brigantine out against the Spaniards, and when we all agreed, he strode into Cully's, calling for volunteers armed with muskets and flintlocks to man the gunwales. He also needed more guns, and many traders moored up against us, and we spent all day hauling our cargo out onto the dock, and the great guns in. I spent the day with Featherstone and Anne in her cabin, rolling cartridges of powder for the guns, and priming all the muskets we could lay our hands on.

The next morning, one thousand, three hundred Spanish privateers attacked Providence from the north, in three warships and eight sloops. We had five hundred men prepared to stand hard against them, revenge for Catt Island in every man's heart. At noon, they anchored off Nassau harbour, and a brigantine and a sloop sailed in to block the eastern channel.

Jack skimmed up the ratlines and addressed us. "Though we have the numbers hard against us, don't forget that these are but dogs, who prefer to fight women and children. They expect an easy victory, yet they've come against the Brethren today! We'll make a feint for the Spanish brigantine, then come about fast to give their sloop a broadside. George, aim low with your starboard guns, so she wallows. The brigantine will be unable to fire her port guns, without hitting her, and we'll take the sloop, and then swing board the brigantine using grapnels. I want our best marksmen in the crows nest, to take out their Officers. John Davies, jump into Cockram's sloop before he sails, and tell him we need a broadside into the brigantine's starboard guns. Tell him we'll meet him aboard! Cast off the mooring lines. Noah, take your course straight to the brigantine's bow!"

Featherstone and Carty and I were still priming the last of our starboard guns, when we found Anne helping us, in trousers again. Though Carty growled, Featherstone grinned and dubbed her his powder monkey, and I thought Jack would kill him for it after. Captain Hildesley hung back, leaving us to sail straight for the Spaniards, and though my mouth was dry with fear, my soul sang its old battle song.

Harwood spun us to port at the last possible moment, catching the sloop unaware, and we let off a broadside that destroyed her. Our men then raked her decks with smallshot and her men went down screaming. We prepared to board, the sloop's commander already striking her colours, when Harry Davies screamed that Hildesley had run the Flamborough aground.

We turned to see the Spanish Flagship closing in on the Flamborough, and Jack instantly called for Noah to get between them. Leaving Captains Cockram, Porter and White to conquer the Spanish brigantine with their quick sloops, Jack ordered the guns re-loaded, and we bore down fast upon the Spanish man o' war.

Then she swung about, and fired at us, and an

554

unlucky cannon ball took out our mainmast. While we floundered in the wreckage, a Spanish sloop came close enough to toss grenadoes, and shrapnel hit almost every man aboard. Young Harry was killed outright, the amazement on his face with me still. I took a splinter deep in my leg, yet hardly noticed, for our brigantine had begun to burn. Carty and Featherstone lowered our boat, and Cockram came alongside in his sloop so we could pile in those badly wounded.

Jack refused to leave his ship, raving like a madman that we could save her, even as she burned about us. We only got him away because Anne was there to scream at him. As we rowed away, Jack wept to see her sink, wreathed in flame and smoke, and we wept with him, for our trading venture was now in ruins.

Chapter 29: Turnley

I spent the night lying helpless in Ma Davies' shack, trying to comfort that old woman for the loss of her youngest son, both of us tended by Sarah, the children hushed by Mis'ess Fulworth. I knew that my mates were fighting for all our lives, that the fate of Nassau hung in the balance, and my uselessness irked me terribly.

In his desperation, Governor Rogers had promised all the black slaves of Nassau their freedom, if they proved themselves in the Militia. That night, the Spaniards attempted several landings, two black men driving off an attack on the eastern foreshore, firing so hotly at the oncoming boats, that the Spaniards thought them an entire Company, and stood to sea again.

The rovers, under Hornigold's command, turned back the main Spanish force from the west coast, fighting so fiercely, that by morning, five rovers lay dead, many more were wounded, and eleven Spaniards lay bleeding into the white sand.

Rogers refused at first to acknowledge our victory, insisting that the Spaniards would return. Yet Hornigold swore they'd never be back, and the rovers lit bonfires and celebrated, despite the Governor's ravings. I wondered if, in his heart of hearts, he had hoped to die in the defence of his bastard Colony, proving to the Lords of Trade that they had abandoned him. Now he would have to continue his grim struggle to make English citizens of the rabble of Nassau, and we had already soured his taste for Government.

Rogers made a great fuss of the two courageous Negro sentries, granting them a present of money to begin their new lives with. Yet he was not at all concerned at our loss of ships and men. Although he had officially commissioned Jack as a privateer, he refused to compensate us for saving the Flamborough and losing our brigantine, stating flatly that our vessel had been stolen, and he should never have pardoned Jack Rackam.

Instead, he presented Ben Hornigold with his own silver pistols, and the entire credit for the loyalty of the rovers. Embarrassed, Hornigold praised us mightily for standing by our Pardons, and Rogers sneered, turned on his heel, and walked off. We muttered mutiny, for without us the prig would have had no Colony to govern, and James Bonny hurried after him to report yet another plot.

I was not the only one who believed that Rogers secretly gloated at our downfall. To make up for his disdain, we did our fallen comrades full honours, digging their graves deep into the sandy soil of Providence, firing a salute over each corpse as it was lowered in, with a friend to recount each man's courage, not neglecting his exploits when on the account.

'Twas Rogers' contempt for us that finally turned me altogether against him. He had arrived, a successful ship's Captain, sure he could impose his own order upon us. Yet his vision of the Colony had grown in England, and had never been something of Providence. His human flaws had been magnified by his complete power over us, and his virtues had fallen away from him. And once again, only tyranny had flourished in the poor soil of Providence.

He began to talk for the first time of leaving Nassau, to personally plead his debts with the Lords of Trade and Plantations. We all prayed that he would not make Thomas Walker his proxy, many hinting that the quiet Mister Beauchamp or the popular Mister Fairfax would be best for us. Yet, though unknown to any of us at that time, and without informing Rogers, or replying to any of his letters, the Crown had already dismissed Rogers, and appointed us another Governor.

Soon after the Spanish attack, Captain Vernon sailed in, and he and Captain Hildesley agreed to take the Flamborough and Vernon's sloop to blockade Havana. This they did, yet the first vessel they captured insisted that the war with Spain was already over. Indeed, it was over even before the attack on Nassau began.

Our trading Company floundered without our brigantine. We sold what was left of our cargo to traders, and shared out the profits amongst us, and had at least immediate means of sustenance. Our men dispersed themselves amongst the various trading enterprises of Nassau, yet many sailed for a miserly wage instead of a share in the profits. Hornigold offered Jack, George Featherstone, Patrick Carty, Noah Harwood and I, positions on his privateering sloop, working for shares, yet only old Noah agreed, the rest of us unable to hunt our old comrades if they turned pirate. With little money in Nassau, few traders came in, and those that did demanded exorbitant prices to cover the Governor's port tax.

Captain Gale of the Delicia had always refused to acknowledge any of the rabble of Nassau as his equal, including our low-born Governor. Yet since Rogers had traded with the French smugglers, Gale's sneer had grown constant, and now he traded with smugglers himself, feeding his crew with goods 'bought out of Nassau', and making his profit. Rogers came to hear of it, yet when challenged, Captain Gale denied it all. Rogers set out to prove him a liar, and when Turnley whispered that the Delicia had sent a ship's boat to rendezvous with a trader outside the harbour one night, Rogers stood guard with a detachment of his militia at the easternmost bastion. He heard a boat coming through the passage, and although he had Tom Ochold challenge it up to twenty times, there was no answer. The Governor then ordered Ochold to fire his musket, and call again. When there was still no reply, Ochold fired once more, and the call floated over the water: "Stop firing. We're men of the Delicia." The Governor called to the boat to come ashore, yet it wisely rowed with all haste back to the guardship.

Lieutenant Howell was sent out to the Delicia to order Captain Gale ashore, yet Gale sent him back with the message that he would row in the next morning. Rogers then called for the marshal, and had him draw up a warrant to fetch Captain Gale ashore. The marshal returned to report that Captain Gale had heard the warrant read, yet refused to come in that night, and as he had his loaded pistols in a chair at his side, the marshal had declined using force.

The Governor sent Howell out a third time, with twelve armed men, to find Captain Gale and his men armed and waiting for them on deck. Then Rogers rowed up in a canoa, in a towering rage. Upon sighting Captain Gale at the entrance to the quarterdeck, he sprang after him, ordering him to surrender. Gale drew a loaded pistol, and Rogers grabbed for the barrel, the two men struggling for possession of it, until the men of the garrison forced the pistol from Gale's hand.

They carried the Navy Captain ashore, Gale raging at the Governor's scum for laying hands on him. Rogers accused him of raising a mutiny against him among the men of the Delicia, and left him all night in close confinement. The next morning, Gale was forced to give security for his good behaviour to the Council, and to swear an oath of loyalty to Rogers, personally. The rovers sneered at him for surrendering, sure that for a similar offence, they would have hung, though Rogers still had no authority from the King to apply the death sentence.

Rogers was now extremely reduced, and completely unable to support himself and his garrison. All those that relied on him were thin to emaciation, their clothing rotting on them, their health destroyed. He had no news of any of his bills being paid at home, and now that he could no longer support his followers, they deserted him. He spent days moaning into his beer of how he had trifled away his health and credit to no purpose, insisting that he would leave his post with the character of an honest man who had done his duty. Turnley and Bonny stood by him in all this mewling, agreeing with all he said, gleaning the last dregs of the Governor's favour.

Then a week of bad weather settled down upon us,

and those of Jack's Company sat despondent about Ma Davies' fire. Jack finished his scanty lunch, and declared that he saw no choice but to sail under Hornigold. Anne glared at him. "Ben Hornigold has made his own choices, Jack, but that one wasn't honourable. He is a friend of mine, and it pains me to say it, but it's true. You moan about not letting me and the babe starve, but if you use me as an excuse to hunt your former comrades, I'll leave you. I've never starved, though I've been hungry. And I'd rather be hungry than shamed."

Jack hugged her and the babe to his breast, setting the child squalling, and Anne scolding, while he demanded of us whether she was not the best woman in the world, as good a partner to him in adversity as in affluence.

"Dammit, ye should make an 'onest woman out o' the little pirate", Harwood chuckled, and Mis'ess Fulworth cheered.

"I'm already married, though to one o' the most worthless men in the entire Caribbean", Anne reminded us.

"And one of the most easily bought", Jack pointed out. "Read, you'd like to see her my woman, all right and tight, how much have you left?" We pooled the last of our coins into a bribe big enough to offer James Bonny, and ensure his separation from Anne. Bonny agreed to our price, yet in looking for men to witness the deed of separation, was foolish enough to ask Turnley. That rat now saw Bonny as a rival for the Governor's small favour, and knowing he would be well rewarded, he informed Rogers that Bonny, once a deserter from the Royal Navy, was unlawfully selling his wife to Jack Rackam.

We had gathered to celebrate at Cully's, drinking flat beer on credit, when the Governor strode in, demanding of Jack whether 'twas true. Anne rose, arms akimbo and fire in her eyes, and stated bluntly that 'twas no one's business but her own. When Rogers exploded into a foul-mouthed denunciation of whores. Anne drew herself back, as if from some pestilence. "I'm a free woman, the only one in the

Caribbean perhaps, but here I am. I'll give myself to the man I love, for as long as I like, and never again to the fool I married as a child. None of that can shame me."

"And what of your bastard?" Rogers demanded. "Any man in Nassau could have fathered that."

"Aye, try to make Jack fight you, and then hang him for mutiny. That's the way of a true coward, to use his power against his own people. You hate women for your own evil thoughts of us. You think it's your ugly scars that keep us away from you, but it's your rotten soul. Nothing grows there but bitter fruit, and you cannot see that the harvest is of your own sowing. Hate breeds hate, and because you can only despise us, we cannot love you. Kate Pritchard..."

Rogers roared then that all whores should be stripped and publicly whipped, and when he saw her shock, he screamed that Jack would be made to wield the lash. Jack laughed then, knowing that nothing could make him, sure now that Rogers was mad. Yet Anne heaved her babe at Mis'ess Fulworth, drew her father's pistol, and began loading it. She told the Governor that he had no right to call her whore, when he ran Nassau on the proceeds of the dosshouse across the road. Then she asked him if 'twas because his wife had turned from him after his jaw was shot away that he was impotent.

From the Governor's face, I knew this for one of Kate Pritchard's giggled confidences. Yet Anne was only stalling until she had her pistol primed, and was only calm because she had not thought beyond shooting our Governor. She had forgotten Jack, her child, everything, and her cool fury made Rogers look like a child with a tantrum. Yet I knew that if she killed him, she would hang. I caught Jack's eye, he nodded, and we leapt upon her suddenly, and pinioned her arms. She fought against us with blind anger, almost silently, until we wrested the gun from her. Then she stalked away from the tavern to a dripping rum shop on the beach, Featherstone, Carty, and young John following.

The news of the uproar at Cully's soon swept through

Nassau, and one by one, all our Company traipsed through the rain to join us. Jack paid off the scrawny crone that ran the place, and she dug up all her bottles for us, and scurried off. We sat crowded under her strip of canvas, and Jack comforted Anne by telling her that Rogers was scum, and not worth the life of the only free woman in the world, a woman he loved more than his life.

"Ah God," I muttered. "'Tis too much. Rogers makes the most of the loss of our brigantine, lost by our own courage in the defence of his Colony, and would now grind us completely underfoot."

"Not me!" Anne stated grimly. "I'll not stop in Nassau with his threat hanging over me. You should have let me kill him. Now we will have to leave."

"We do not have enough money to leave honestly", I pointed out.

At this, Jack turned to John Davies. "This is desperate talk, and I'd not have you in this, lad, for your mother's sake. You're the only son she has left."

"I'm one of this Company!"

"It's your own choice", Jack soothed him. "But any venture of ours is bound to break your mother's heart. Know that, and think hard." Young John left us then, wandering off miserably into the rain, for he had been happy with us, rich and free, for a time.

George Featherstone flipped a coin. "I'm for cutting Turnley's throat, and the Governor's, and Tom Walker's, while we're at it." I thought he was joking, yet Anne didn't.

"The time for murder is gone. None o' us are capable of it in cold blood. You should not have stopped me."

'Twas evident to us all then, that there was nothing for it but to return to our old trade. Patrick Carty suggested it first, Jack swore we'd be free again, and George Featherstone surprised us by pulling out their old and tattered Jolly Roger, a skull over crossed swords, that he'd kept hidden all through our months as honest traders. Jack passed the rum around, and toasted our future on the high seas.

Then Jack began explaining to Anne his plans to leave her and the babe with friends of his in Cuba. She laughed, and though she agreed she had to leave the child safe with Mistress Fulworth, she insisted she would not be left behind. Featherstone laughed and claimed her for his powder monkey, and though Jack glared, Carty waxed lyric on her courage when under fire from the Spaniards. I shrugged at the protests of the rest of the Company, arguing that although our Articles stated 'twas a crime to bring a doxy aboard, Anne was a different matter, being a proven comrade.

Yet the Company protested, Noah Harwood calling her disguise when with Vane a scurvy trick, convinced that women did not belong at sea. Anne merely nodded towards the outer harbour, and we saw John Haman skimming towards us in the sweetest sloop he'd ever built. As soon as we saw her, we all wanted her. She was only about forty ton, and would be quick to attack, and faster to run.

Anne stood and announced briskly that she would take the sloop, and that any who'd stoop to sail with her, were welcome to join her Company. She ran along the shore through the drizzle, and from where we sat, we watched her meet John Haman as he landed in his dory. He was a vain man, and always flirted with Anne whenever he sailed in to buy provisions for his large family, or to sell his latest vessel. She immediately told him of Rogers' foul treatment of her, condemning any who'd stop a woman having the man she wanted. Later, she told us that he almost burst, the blood rushed through him so hard.

She teased him like this for three days, until the poor man could hardly think for lust. Then, when we were sure the night would be dark and rainy, she exclaimed at the beauty of his vessel, and Haman immediately invited her out for a visit. Anne demurred, stating that people would gossip if she rowed out with him, her smile suggesting they might have very good reason to talk. With his eyes on her half-exposed breasts, he suggested that she meet him on board that night. She said Jack would kill him if they were not perfectly discreet, and Haman swore he'd be alone on the sloop at the turn of the tide that night, and her reputation would be safe in his hands. She giggled, declaring she hoped she wouldn't be too safe, and had to jump back as he went to grab her.

The weather set in so hard, that Jack swore that not even John Haman would be vain enough to expect her to keep her appointment. Yet Featherstone returned from Cully's to report that Haman had been dropping large hints of his good luck all night, and had just headed off for his sloop, carrying four bottles of wine. Anne laughed at the foolishness of men, and our entire Company stole down to the beach, and piled into a longboat, hiding under tarpaulins, Anne's babe in a drunken stupor in Mis'ess Fulworth's arms. Anne then sailed us out, and as she nudged the bow of the longboat into the sloop, she dropped the sail over us all.

Haman was on deck instantly, bowing and smiling, ready to help her aboard, and then down into the cabin. There she pointed a loaded pistol at his head, threatened to blow his brains out if he uttered a sound, and screamed like a seagull. The rest of us then swarmed aboard, Featherstone gagging Haman and pinioning his arms. Men leapt to heave in the cable, Patrick Carty and I hauled up the mainsail, and we slipped off down the harbour, past the fort, towards the guardship. A sentry on the Delicia hailed us, and Jack answered that he was John Haman, and that the blustering winds had parted his cable. When we reached the harbour mouth, we dropped Haman into the longboat, so he could sail back to Nassau, with insults to deliver from Anne to the Governor. Then with Harwood guiding us past the shoals, we sailed out into the open ocean, pirates again, and free.

Anne instantly demanded the right to be in our Company, and the vote was carried in her favour, much to Noah Harwood's disgust. "Don't worry Noah, we'll leave the babe with Mis'ess Fulworth in Cuba, and I'll dress in trousers as usual."

"And we've so few hands aboard, we'll need her", Featherstone insisted. "I wish Haman had been quicker at loading in those stores for his family. We're low on provisions."

Anne laughed. "John Davies apologised to me yesterday, saying the only work he could find was fishing with Turnley. I know which key they are moored at. They'll have provisions enough." We came upon Turnley's sloop the next morning, to find that Turnley had gone ashore with his boy, hunting wild hogs. Anne and Jack rowed ashore to find him, Jack carrying a horsewhip, and though I thought them wrong to revenge themselves on Rogers' lackey, I had little compassion for Turnley.

While they were gone, we loaded the fishing boat's provisions into Haman's sloop, and talked to Turnley's crew. John Davies was wild to come with us, declaring his contempt for Governor Rogers since his threat to whip Anne, and his hatred of Turnley, who had used him ill, knowing him a friend of ours. Of the six men on the fishing sloop, John's enthusiasm infected three. Richard Connor, my old Quartermaster on the Whydah, was most welcome, and John Howell was an old experienced rover. We sadly had to refuse David Soward, despite his experience, for he was still lame from the battle against the Spaniards. I argued against accepting John Davies into our Company, citing what we owed his mother, yet he insisted, and Patrick Carty spoke for the lad doing what he wished with his life.

Anne and Jack soon rowed back, Anne in a furious rage. They had waded through the crashing surf, their loaded muskets held over their heads, yet though they had searched for Turnley, he had stayed well hidden.

Jack's mood lifted when he found himself with provisions and three more men, and a new longboat. We then decided to vote in our Officers and draw up our Articles. Jack was voted Captain unanimously, George Featherstone was voted Master of Haman's sloop, since he knew the rig best, and the quiet Richard Connor was voted our Quartermaster, being already knowledgeable of Turnley's provisions. The new men raised their eyebrows to see Anne voting, and when she went to sign the Articles, John Howell asked Rackam if he was serious. Anne stated calmly that as it was she who had stolen Haman's sloop, they could take her or swim. Jack spoke of her sailing under Vane, Featherstone of her courage as a powder monkey, John of her accuracy with muskets, I of her stalwart character, and Patrick Carty of our few hands. She insisted that Jack would show her no favour, promised that she would not give them orders in his name, and swore they would not spoon about the ship, but remember that they were in business together. Richard Connor suggested we put it to the vote, the 'ayes' had it, and she signed the Articles in her own name.

Then we put the men who would not sail with us into their own dory to sail for Nassau. We towed Turnley's leaky vessel into deep water, and scuttled her, leaving Turnley marooned, for his men would not risk broaching the dory in the surf to fetch him away. Then Jack set a course for Cuba, muttering that he had a good source of provisions there, and truly, the presence of Mis'ess Fulworth and the babe added nothing to our martial spirit. Our course meant a risk of guarda del costas, yet we were all anxious to get rid of our passengers.

That night we sailed as far as the Berry Isles, where we moored off a pretty cove, to rest, share our provisions, and wait for dawn. The turtles were coming in, and despite Rackam's jealous eye, Anne insisted that she and I row ashore to capture a dozen for their eggs and sweet meat. We worked hard, until we had enough bound in rope to keep us for a week. Then she lit a fire, threw some turtle steaks onto the coals, and demanded the story of my marriage. I refused, yet she begged me to comply, stating she was half dead of curiosity to hear my history completed. I was still reluctant, and warned her that the tale of my marriage was a grim one, with none of the greatness of battle to flavour it. "And it seems as though it happened to a different person", I tried to explain. "And that if I speak of it, the suffering will be mine again."

"I thought you'd be happy with your young Cavalryman."

"'Twas he who convinced me that I could never be a woman."

She laughed. "It would drive old Noah mad if he knew he had three women aboard. Four counting the babe. Come Mary, you know I have never uttered a word to any, not even Jack, not even to curb his jealousy o' you."

PART 9: THE CARIBBEAN 1720-21
Chapter 30: Pirates

It took all night to tell her of my disastrous marriage, of my false hope and foolish trust, of my inability to bear us a child. I remembered my preparation for Maccartney's murder, and my continuing failure to kill him. My heart heavy with the loss of my young husband, and bitter with the taste of betrayal, I looked away from our smoking fire, and saw our pirate sloop riding easily at anchor, the Berry Isles lit by the rising sun, and wiped my eyes.

Anne sighed, her red hair alight in the blazing dawn. "And that First Mate persuaded you aboard a Dutch trader..."

"A pig of a boat, with a tyrant for a Captain."

"And Sam Bellamy saved you."

"By making a pirate of me."

"And now we're roving together. Somehow, it seems fate that you and I should have met."

"I should have returned to England to search for my mother."

"You would only have found her grave. At least, as a rover, you have lived free."

"How can a life of confusion and suffering be called freedom? I look at my life as I have told it to you, and I see a string of failures. I wonder why I ever thought trousers meant liberty, when I've worn them most of my life, and still cannot be who I am. No, 'tis you who know freedom. Every time you set your fists on your hips and raise your voice in objection, I rejoice. There is nothing in the world that can stop you from taking what you want."

She grinned at me, and then a sudden gust set her red curls dancing in the morning breeze. "A hurricane would do it. If we hadn't been forced to flee that bastard of a Governor, I'd never have sailed at the start o' the storm season. Yet Jack said his friends on Cuba are sheltered enough to survive a big blow."

"Yet how could he have friends on Cuba? How could they survive amidst the Spaniards?"

"I can't get a word out o' him. And all those in our Company ask the same question."

The men woke, and we soon put to sea, our eyes keen for a prize. We were still skirting the Berry Isles, when we came across a small trader, and took it, Anne first aboard. We found nought but provisions, yet these were most welcome. Jack insisted we were so low on hands, we must force two likely sailors to come with us, though Anne, Carty and I objected to forcing any man against his conscience. Yet we were out-voted by our Company, Jack swearing that a good prize would reconcile the forced men to piracy soon enough.

'Twas only when the redheaded 'lad' appeared on deck with a babe that the new men noticed Anne. Featherstone told them her history, yet they still thought her nothing more than Jack's harlot. Anne merely shrugged, sure they'd change their minds if they lived long enough to see her fight. Jack assured them he was taking the child to a safe haven, though he said nothing of Anne joining the trembling Mis'ess Fulworth ashore. Indeed poor Annie Fulworth hardly left the small cabin where Anne, Jack and their babe also slept.

Before we passed the Berry Isles, we took another small fishing boat, Anne the first to board again. We found some provisions, and hidden under the nets, wine enough to give each man a tankard. Anne found a bottle of bad brandy under the Captain's bed, and made hipsy on deck under the stars, and we all got merrily drunk. Jack cried up the pirate life, merry and free, hoping to persuade the forced men to join us. George Featherstone raised a toast to a Spanish treasure ship, and we all cheered.

Anne shook her head. "But while we dream o' such prizes, we're living off poor fishermen."

"We will soon be strong enough to attack the Navy convoys," Richard Connor insisted.

"Aye, we must take another fast sloop, or join up with a Pirate Fleet", Jack declared. "We need but a little luck, and some resolution, and our fortunes will be made."

"A pity Haman hadn't loaded his ammunition", George Featherstone growled. "The fishermen had none. We've only enough left to supply our best marksmen."

Jack proposed a drill, Featherstone raised a target, and Anne stunned us all with her eye for the mark. Under her guidance, young John hit the bull's eye twice, Featherstone but once. He then collected together all our arms, and according to the skill of the man, handed out our pistols, muskets and flintlocks.

Featherstone then declared Tom Earl the worst shot, and he had to help him mix the powder in a great barrel on deck. Featherstone carefully tipped five pounds of saltpetre into one pound of willow charcoal, and one of sulphur, then carefully moistened it with water distilled from orange rinds, until it was blue. When it was dry, they poured it into hollow iron shells, to make grenadoes, and then added more saltpetre to make gunpowder.

While I rolled fuses, he checked our captured guns most carefully, dropping smoking wood down the stoppered muzzle, and looked for leaking smoke. In the glare of the afternoon sun, he insisted on looking inside them all for honey-combing, and told me that when still a powder monkey, he'd seen a gun explode, and that was how he got that great scar across his handsome face and lost two mates.

Once in the Florida Strait, we turned south, the current and the wind against us. Yet Haman's bird-winged sloop held her nose close to the wind, skimming easily over the waves, and dancing about when we tacked. At noon, we sailed close by the shore of Florida, and saw Indians in canoes making signs at us. Anne said they had provisions to trade, and we could safely approach, though Noah Harwood muttered of cannibals, and primed a musket. They were the first Indians I had ever seen, and I stayed at Anne's side while she gestured to them with her hands. They were well-grown, handsome people, their straight hair blue-black and long, their eyes alert for trouble. Both men and women were naked but for bunches of straw over their privy members, though their faces and breasts were painted with red and yellow stars and branches. The women lowered their eyes modestly before the lewd stares of the pirates, yet held their ground when bargaining with Anne.

They offered to trade three canoas of live turtles, fruit, corn and green vegetables, for three muskets, and powder. Featherstone protested that we needed every musket, and we should take what we wanted from the Indians, unarmed as they were. Anne glared at him, and showed them Carty's beautifully etched Spanish knife, which greatly impressed the imposing warrior in the first canoe. The prospect of fresh food had us soon agreed on one musket, ample powder, and Carty's knife. As soon as the bargain was complete, the Indians made off, trusting us too little to accept Anne's invitation to come aboard and view the sloop.

We feasted, and then Jack steered us into the deep Bahama Channel, where we wove in and out of the scattering of islands that run along the northern back of Cuba. Late the next day, we came to one isle nestled in close to the mainland, and he called us into Council. "There are old mates amongst you, and strangers we have forced to join us", he stated coldly. "But, if there was any choice in it, I'd show none of you this place. I must leave the babe and Mis'ess Fulworth with my family, and so I must show you the entrance to their settlement. But you'll swear by the Articles you have signed, never to speak of this place, and all swords against the man who brings trouble to those who live there."

We swore it easily enough, sure we were protecting an English settlement from Spaniards. Then Jack set the sloop straight for the beach, and called for reefed sails. It wasn't until we were almost in the rocks that we saw the channel, and Jack slipped us in with inches to spare, as cool as if he'd risked it every day of his life. The channel opened into a small, sheltered lagoon, completely hidden from those at sea. Jack steered us towards a large, flat rock, which formed a convenient landing, and there we dropped sails and anchors.

Then a Spanish voice rang out from behind a palisade, the meaning clear when we saw the three swivel guns aimed straight at us. We all froze but for Jack, who leapt ashore and declared himself in flowing Spanish. Anne and I stared at each other, still not guessing, until a rugged, moustachioed old man stepped out, and Jack ran into his arms. Three younger men appeared, laden with cutlasses and pistols, and pounded him on the back while he laughed with them.

Then Jack gestured towards us, and when they nodded, he invited us ashore. Despite Noah Harwood's muttered insistence that 'twas a Papist trap, Anne leapt ashore with her babe in her arms. Jack made a grand introduction of it, and the old man bowed like a grandee, and then grabbed the infant, and boosted her up into the sun. He was rewarded with a great smile, for she was used to being dandled by strange men, and then the old Spaniard embraced her, while talking to Anne in floods of incomprehensible Spanish.

With some trepidation, we left our arms aboard, and followed Anne and Jack, past the hard-eyed young men with their muskets, and around the rock palisade. To our surprise, there was a village nestled in the jungle. The old man bowed, and was only half way through making us a long welcome, when an ancient lady screamed and hurled herself weeping at Jack. When Anne handed her the babe, she went down on her knees in the sand, kissing the child's face, and muttering earnest thanks to her God. Jack told Anne she was the child's great-grandmother.

We were all amazed to see Jack a Spaniard, and Noah Harwood could not, in good conscience, waste such an opportunity for rudeness.

"So Rackam, yer a Papist dog after all", he growled.

"The old man is my father, those are my brothers, and these are their families. My mother died of fever long ago. She was an Englishwoman, the sole survivor of a wreck just off the coast. My father risked his life to save her from the sea. When she died, I quarrelled with my father and ran away on a trading sloop."

"It seems they've forgiven you", Anne grinned, and we all laughed.

The Spaniards killed the fatted calf, brought out fine wine, and made so much of the babe that I could see we would have no trouble leaving her with them. We stayed a week, yet when our provisions were gone, Jack insisted we were too many for his family to feed. He suggested we leave on the next tide, and we agreed.

Then he tried to persuade Anne to stay with her child, and she coldly refused, reminding him that she had taken our sloop single-handed, and swearing that we'd all be back on the beach in Nassau but for her. In great confusion, he begged her to let the men vote upon her again, a woman being so contentious on a pirate ship.

"She has signed the Articles, and cannot leave until the cruise is over", I noted calmly.

"And I need her help with the guns", Featherstone added. Patrick Carty glowered down his strawberry nose at Jack, and said 'twas unjust to put her on trial more than once.

Anne spoke of her great relief to leave her babe safe with Annie Fulworth and Jack's family, yet when it came to their parting, she wept hard, and made her friend swear to keep her child alive until she returned. Mis'ess Fulworth had agreed to stay on condition that Anne and Jack help her open a small shop in Kingston when they were rich. She had already begun to learn a little Spanish, and seemed to get on well with the old lady.

The tide was high, and we were making our last farewells, when a smoke signal went up from the headland. Jack's father grabbed his arm and hissed: "Misericordia! Guarda del costa!" A sloop flying Spanish colours came

573

nosing into the channel, the English sloop following her evidently a prize. Though she blocked our escape, Jack ordered us all aboard immediately, and sent me to search Haman's lockers for the red and gold colours of Castille, to use as a decoy. I heard him call out a few words in Spanish, and then a great blast rocked our sloop in the water, and sent a thousand seabirds reeling into the sky.

Despite the frightened curses of our Company, we had not been hit. The guarda del costa could only use her forward gun, our narrow stern her only target, and we were half-covered by the curve of the channel. Yet, as the sun started its quick descent, the Spanish privateers wrapped a rope around a palm tree and began warping their sloop further in. Before they could improve their aim, the light faded, yet we were trapped like rabbits. Come the morning, we would be blasted out of the water.

In a fever of apprehension, we discussed every plan, Carty hot to attack the privateers in the night, Featherstone sure we could make our way around the shore, and take some other vessel. Only Noah Harwood growled that we must jump ashore, and make our stand with Jack's family. "I'll not bring more trouble on my own people", Jack snapped, and Richard Connor insisted we stand by our oaths.

In all that time, Anne lay idly across the tiller, looking back at the lights on the Spanish sloop. I wondered at her calm, and then she looked up with a grin on her face, and I knew she had a plan. She stood, winked at her anxious mates, and asked Noah Harwood how long we had before the moon went down. Then cheerfully noting our few numbers, and fewer provisions, she declared it good that we'd not amassed a fortune, for then we'd have to leave it. We gathered about her, confused, and she laughed and pointed to the Spaniard's English prize, which they'd moored further out in the bay.

As quietly as we could, we hauled our longboat to the sloop's side, and packed it with our remaining provisions, arms and ammunition. In the dead of night, we rowed up to the Spanish sloop, our oars muffled with rags. Young John Davies then stripped, slipped silently into the water, and gently pushed us past the guarda del costa, her guard standing with his back to us, and none daring to breathe.

And then we rowed hard for the English sloop, scaled her sides, our knives between our teeth, and fell on the Spanish guards, cutting their throats before they could call out. Jack found and gagged their cabin boy, insisting we needed him alive. Then we slipped the sloop's cable, raised the foresail, and let the land breeze push us quietly out to sea. Then we dropped the cabin boy into the sloop's dory, Jack explaining that we would have attacked the Spanish settlement we'd found, and murdered them all, if the guarda del costa had not sailed in. Hoping that this was enough to protect our friends from accusations of smuggling with English pirates, and thinking that Haman's lovely sloop would be ample compensation for their inconvenience, we set all sails on our much humbler vessel, and headed for the open sea.

There was great rejoicing then, and Anne was congratulated on her cunning. Half-laughing, she put her fists on her hips and glared about her. "So, I'm good enough after all, am I? Well, after stealing Haman's sloop, and now this one, I should hope so! Yet a full share in the profits is no longer enough for me. I demand an unquestioned place in this Company, and I'll fight any man who goes back on his word!" They could only clap her on the back and praise her ingenuity, George Featherstone recalling her courage under fire while sailing with Vane, and defending Nassau against the Spanish raid. Jack reflected on the battle we must have fought with the Spanish privateers, and swore we would all have perished or ended slaves, but for Anne. Only Noah Harwood scowled and predicted ill-luck for any vessel sailing with a woman aboard.

Our stolen English sloop was a poor swap for Haman's, being leaky, foul-bottomed, and tending to wallow. We were not in any strength to do aught but run at low game,

575

and though Tom Earl and Ben Wright protested, we voted to force new hands at every opportunity, and to try for better vessels. 'Twas evident to us all that the Caribbean trade was proving thin, and we talked of sailing for the East Indies, or Madagascar. Although Noah Harwood was an artist at navigating in Caribbean waters, he was an incorrigible dead reckoner, and would have nothing to do with longitude. To sail for Africa, we needed a sextant man as navigator. Until then, we voted to hunt north of Cuba, Harwood set our course, and young John Davies took the helm.

I had just thrown a fishing line over, when Jack sat down next to me and borrowed my pipe. "Now Mark Read, you taught her to disguise herself, and you've always supported her as a rover. But by the Devil, she's still a woman with a babe! Tell me why she can't be content with that like any other woman would be, and leave the cruising to us? If we sign on any of the old Brethren, I'll be the laughing stock of the Caribbean."

"If you wanted a tame woman, you should never have chosen Anne Bonny. She's not like any other, Jack, and if you can't see that's why you love her, then you're a fool. As for what anyone else thinks, if our Company accepts her, 'tis done; and if we're mocked for it, she'll fight them." He grinned, then frowned, and I knew jealousy had him by the throat again. "Anne and I are friends Jack, nothing more. I swear I'm no threat to you." He nodded brusquely, clapped me on the shoulder, and strode back to Anne, and I wondered then that none of them thought to look harder at me.

For all of August, we lay behind tropic isles, our masts hidden by palm trees, and strained our eyes at the blinding sea. Tar boiled from the sloop's seams, and the beer went flat, and though we took several small craft, yet there was no great booty, and few men we cared to sail with.

At the beginning of September, we voted to look for old comrades in home waters, and Harwood set course for the Bahamas. Desperate for provisions, we took seven fishing boats within two leagues of Harbour Island, one after the other, and though they greatly protested, Jack insisted we take their nets too. At that, some more men came with us, yet this petty piracy wore away at all our spirits.

We raided throughout the Bahamas all that month, still hoping for a better vessel, and more of our old comrades. Towards the end of September, young John spied the sails of two Nassau sloops off Harbour Island, and though outnumbered, we saw no choice but to attack. They ran for land, yet were so foul with weed, that even our cumbersome vessel easily caught up with them. We fired over their bows as they entered a small bay, and they struck their colours and ceded without a fight.

The slowest was one of the Governor's privateers, and that we scuttled. The other was an island-made sloop, and though badly fouled, we were happy to trade her for our English sloop. When given the choice, few hands proved unwilling to join us, many complaining bitterly of the Governor, who was about to sail for London to plead his case. We sailed off with lighter hearts, a faster ship, greater numbers, some provisions and bigger guns. Jack was keen to careen and clean the vessel, and George Featherstone had me hard at work re-furbishing our humble armoury.

Anne had boarded first, a knife between her teeth, and cocked pistols in each hand, her red curls wrapped in a black bandanna. The new men were stunned when they saw her a woman, and aghast to find her name signed on our Articles. Although Featherstone insisted she was a confirmed comrade, they continued to grumble, until Anne swore she'd have to kill one of them.

Chapter 31: Tom Deane

Expecting Rogers to send his Fleet out against us, we wound our way south, back towards Hispaniola. On the first of October, we saw two sails off Turtle Island, and hauled up the Jolly Roger. One struck her colours immediately, and when we sent a shot over the other's bow, she struck too. This was captained by Jim Dobbin, a native of Philadelphia, and an old mate of Jack's, long pardoned. He cursed our gallant Jack most foully at first, yet a bottle of brandy soon put a new face on the matter, and rather than lose his pretty sloop, and his living, he joined us. The other sloop's Captain stood firm against us, and lost his sloop and his cargo, which was rich enough to prove a strong inducement to most of his poor sailors.

Jack poured Dobbin another glass, and explained our plans to sail for richer trade in African waters, bemoaning our lack of a sextant man.

"My navigator's clever enough", Dobbin mused, but he's in the longboat with the unwilling men."

"What! Won't he join us? Which one is he?" Dobbin pointed out a well-made, fair-haired, handsome man, passing his seachest over the gunwales to his mates in the dory. Jack immediately strolled over, and all charm, insisted we needed him for a navigator.

I was struck with the calm sincerity of the man's refusal. "I've chosen against ye. The life of a sea robber is not for me."

"Come man, we need your skill with a sextant, not your life. Join us willingly, teach one of us to find longitude, so we can seek the Africa trade, and ensure our liberty."

"Ye speak of liberty, but threaten to enslave me. I said I've chosen against ye."

Jack lost his small store of patience then, and levelled his loaded pistol at the man. "You'll stay aboard my ship!"

I saw that the navigator had one eye on the distant shore, and remembered that the island-born could swim. When he took a step towards the gunwales, I stepped between him and the sea, and told him that the roving life was not so bad that he must leap overboard to save himself.

He looked hard at me. "If the choice is between the Devil and the deep blue sea..." he muttered.

"Nay, you'll be put ashore if you don't like the life, and your mates will report that we forced you."

"My name's Tom Deane. I look to ye to stand by what ye've said, Captain Rackam. I'll show ye how to get this sloop to Africa and back, and ye must put me ashore when ye see I'll never be one of ye."

Jack grinned and clapped him on the shoulder. "Aye, I swear it, Tom. Mark Read here has a clear head. Teach him the use o' those ocean instruments, and we'll put you ashore directly."

He set his seachest down, and Jack passed him a bottle of brandy. Not trusting the resolution I saw in his handsome face, I told him how I had been taken by Sam Bellamy, and, despite my fears of bloody hands, had made myself rich enough to be honest.

"But here ye be, a pirate still."

I explained how my money had been stolen, how hard I had lived waiting for the Governor, and how he had forced us back to sea. "In truth, I look to leave the life as soon as I have anything in my pockets."

"God keep me from hunger, lest I steal", he scoffed. "I've never wanted riches at another man's expense."

"I have been too hungry too often in this life to deserve that sneer. I know piracy is a bad choice, yet 'tis a hard world. We share all we take, and that is more than the world would ever share with us."

He shook his head. "To threaten a man with death and steal from him is not the life for an honest man. Aye, I can see yer of the same mind as me. In truth, ye dislike it."

"I understand you wish to do no evil, yet with three

sloops, and all these hands, most will cede to us without a fight. Captain Rackam is a good man, and will not make a sport of terror. You'll see little to disturb your sleep."

"Ye reassure me somewhat. I thought my conscience no longer my own. I can only hope yer a quick study."

"I always have been. You realise we'll probably be keeping your instruments. I'll ask Captain Rackam to reimburse you for your loss." We drank to that understanding, and when the dinner bell rang, I made sure we were messmates.

Richard Connor called for the new men to sign the Articles, yet when Dobbin saw Anne's signature right at the top, he questioned her right to be in the Company, many of the new hands also protesting against her. Jack stood firmly by her, though this undermined his chance of being voted Captain of the Fleet, and though they disliked it, they finally agreed to sign.

That night, one of the new men, a great brute of a fellow they called Hog, grabbed Anne's breasts. When she drew her fish-knife to kill him, 'twas the unassuming Richard Connor who levelled loaded pistols at them both, and insisted that there would be no quarrels aboard.

Anne insisted on her right to a duel ashore, and though Hog sneered at the idea of fighting a woman, Connor agreed with Anne. When Anne chose pistols, Featherstone laughed and called Hog a dead man. The brute then apologised for frightening Rackam's whore, declaring he thought the Brethren shared everything. Anne smiled sweetly, a sure sign she was still murderous, and told him that she'd kill any who questioned her rights aboard.

Then Jack called a Council, and we voted to sail for a hidden cove that Dobbin knew of on the north coast of Hispaniola, to careen our prizes and drink our fill. I took my first lesson in longitude the next morning, and found Tom a clear enough teacher. As each day passed, my understanding of navigation grew, as did my competency with his instruments and complex calculations.

And as each day passed, I came to know him better, and like him more. He was well read and thoughtful, and he wavered not at all from his honest intentions. I soon saw that there was a great attraction between our natures, something I'd not acknowledged since I had been overwhelmed by my feelings for pretty Jan van Laathem. I earnestly reminded myself that my sex could not be questioned while still aboard a pirate ship, yet when I avoided him, he sought me out. And there was Anne always before me, a mother, a pirate, and happily in love with our Captain. I wondered if telling her of my marriage had been a mistake, reminding me that I was female despite myself.

We dropped anchor two days later, and Tom, not wanting to get drunk with the pirates, said he'd camp further down the coast and catch turtles to augment our supplies. I asked if he'd mind my company, and Jack grinned, now certain I was an embarrassed sodomite, and suggested I be Tom's guard. That night, around our own small fire, I assured Tom that Jack was wrong, and he shrugged, yet became easier with me. I asked him of his life in Jamaica, and he spoke of that green and mountainous island with such love, that I had to ask him why he chose the sea.

"Now that's a good question, and one my family must still be wondering on. My father is a wealthy planter, but would never see that it's only because our slaves get nothing that we prosper. I once laughed with children who have grown into the terrible burden that our race has placed on theirs. I see the hate in their eyes, and I know they would gladly kill their old playfellow for this injustice. My father calls me milksop for caring at all, and I'm sure I'm the only man on Jamaica who thinks it wrong to profit by the misery of others."

"Yet when you inherit..."

He shrugged. "I never will. I quarrelled with my father a couple of months past over Governor Lawes' new plan for wiping out the Maroons. The runaways. When the Spanish abandoned Jamaica to the English fifty years back,

581

they left their slaves behind. To defend their freedom, the blacks built a fort called Nanny Town on Liberty Hill, in the great blue mountains of the north-east. Liberty Hill was always a beacon to runaway slaves, and there are thousands now living there. They hold their land in common, grow their own food, and make rum from sugar to secretly trade for muskets with the Jewish shopkeepers of Kingston. The Jamaica Militia has often been sent against the Maroons, yet as it's made up of indentured white servants, little better than slaves themselves, they feel no inducement to risk their lives, and run whenever they hear the drums of Nanny Town.

"Then two months ago, Governor Lawes made a contract with King Jeremy of the Mosquito Coast. Fifty of his Indians will hunt the Maroons with blowpipes for six months. They'll get eight pieces of silver for every black head they bring back, male, female, old or young. And more for the leader, Cudjoe.

"My father was talking of the necessity of destroying Nanny Town, and I stupidly replied that liberty was the birthright of every man, no matter what his colour. He declared that God created the black man to slave in the white man's fields, because they are far beneath us. I laughed. Ye've never seen my father. He was a great man once, when I was a boy. But the rum has turned him into a fat sot. And worse, I've seen the way he pushes his slaves down, making the most of the power he has. A man should not have to speak evil of his own father, but I tell ye in confidence that he's fathered more brown bastards than any man in the islands, and most of them on girls young enough to be my sisters.

"My conscience stirred against the injustice of it too early in my youth, and my father enjoyed his own cruelty too much to spare baiting me. By the time I reached manhood, our ways were set against each other. And that hot afternoon, I suggested that his noble blood could surely redeem his own children from slaving in his fields. I recommended making them house servants, and paying

582

them.

"He swore he'd not leave his plantation to any man stupid enough to pay for any labour he could get free. It was when he attempted to use the Bible to justify his cruel use of these people that I found I'd had sufficient of his blindness. I did not want to quarrel with him further, and concluded that a parting was necessary. And yet when I came to look for a post as supercargo, or secretary to some lordling, I found my reputation as a trouble-making Quaker had preceded me, thanks to him."

"And so to sea, and piracy! And who inherits? Some smug younger brother?"

"My father's tragedy is that his favourite son died, and I lived. The only children my father has left are the brown ones he's always refused to acknowledge as his own."

"There is some justice there. Yet not for you."

"Oh I have no complaints. I have tugged the forelock to that bully all my youth, and now, when I should be coming into my tainted inheritance, I find myself free. And it would have been a lonely struggle to make the plantation pay, as no white woman would have chosen to live with a fool like me, without slaves, and shunned by white society. I would've ended up alone and mad in the jungle, fathering more bastards than my father." He raised his glass. "Ah, for a good-hearted, clear-sighted woman, who would not disdain to live simply. Perhaps if I could find a good place on a northern plantation, I might find a wife."

Within me, a flame flickered to life. I fixed my attention on the stars and told myself to risk nothing. Then a turtle heaved itself ashore, and we remembered our business. Tom insisted on waiting until it had laid its eggs, and then we turned it on its back, and bound its flippers with vines. Within a short time, we had five, and so we butchered one of them, wrapped the meat in banana leaves, and set it on the coals to cook. As more turtles lumbered ashore, we were soon busy, and we did not lie down to sleep until late that night, when we had bound more than fifty live turtles,

583

enough to feed us for weeks.

I woke to a rosy dawn, to find I had been dreaming of my lost husband. I sat up and wiped my tears away, and caught myself watching Tom Deane's face as he slept. To distract myself from my over-full heart, I strode back to the bay our sloops were moored in, the low tide making it easy for me.

I found my comrades with sore heads and worse tempers, apart from Anne who greeted me merrily. I told her we had a good haul of turtles, and needed help to get them back. Though Jack glared at us, she helped me push a dory back through the shallow water to fetch them.

When we were out of earshot of the men, I tried to speak to her of Tom Deane, yet she laughed and declared I must drop my disguise and fall at his feet. And though I insisted this would not become me, she entertained herself at my expense until we had pushed the dory around to the next bay.

We found Tom butchering turtles for the pirates' breakfast. Anne hacked down palm fronds and began weaving baskets to carry the steaks in, while Tom and I loaded live turtles into the dory. When we had finished, the sun was high, and we knew our mates would be hungry. We washed our hands and faces in the cool sea, and Tom insisted on hauling the dory back immediately, for the sharks would scent the turtle blood, and be over the reef as soon as the tide was high enough.

When he had gone, Anne told me that Rackam was still jealous, watching her like a hawk whenever she spoke to me, unsure whether I was a sodomite or not. "He believes I favour you, and that one day I'll do to him what I did to Jennings. And though you're but a pretty woman, you're a handsome man. Such soulful eyes."

"I wish Tom Deane thought so." She laughed and hugged me, and that was when Jack Rackam stepped out of the bushes, his pistol aimed at my heart, and his face like thunder.

584

Anne yelped and ran at him, and he brushed her aside. "Quiet harlot. This is what you've brought us to." He tossed a loaded pistol at my feet. "We fight here Mark Read, and I'll kill you, though I owe you my life, and that of my best mates."

"'Tis clear against the Articles", I reminded him. "We are sworn brothers."

"It's clear against my inclination, but I'll kill you anyway."

I could see he was half mad with rage, and might shoot either of us out of hand. So I did the only thing I could. I removed my shirt, and began unwrapping my breasts. They were not as convincing as Anne's would have been, yet they were enough. His jaw and his pistol dropped, he could only stare and stammer, while Anne laughed, and I blushed.

Then he dropped to his knees, and begged Anne's forgiveness for his dark thoughts of her. She made a great scene of it, reminding him that he'd called the mother of his child a harlot, insisting he'd be happier with someone more demure. He protested, swore his undying love for her, and pleaded the madness of jealousy. "I knew that your friendship with Mark, with..."

"Mary", Anne helped him.

"That you had secrets together...the Devil only knows what. I thought that if Mark had wanted you..."

"If Mark was a man, I'd hate him as a Puritan", she declared. "But she's a woman, and a brave and true friend. She has been sailor, soldier, and pirate, and I am the only one who ever guessed she was not what she seemed."

Jack laughed, shook his head, and then bowed, flourishing his generously be-feathered hat. "Now I understand what you meant about Tom Deane. So he is the lucky man, eh? He'll be getting the surprise of his life!"

"I haven't told him. I don't know how."

"Say nothing, woman, just strip. It's most convincing."

"Nay, I won't be laughed at by you Jack Rackam..."

"Don't tease her Jack. She's touchy as Hell about being born one o' the inferior sex. But, if she'd been born a man, she'd now be a sodomite, and how she'd have justified that to her disapproving God..."

Anne and Jack laughed at me while I dressed myself, confusion playing havoc with my mind. They wanted to be alone, so I returned to my comrades, to find them busy careening Jim Dobbin's sloop. Tom greeted me with a grin, and I joined him scraping the thick growth from the sloop's hull, all hands busy under George Featherstone's expert direction, eager to finish before the tide came in.

That day and the next I found it hard to be anywhere but at Tom's side, and often wished that he would do or say something to give me a disgust for him. Yet all he did was done well, and the way he remained himself, without antagonising the Brethren, showed his good judgement.

We finished careening Dobbin's sloop on our second morning, and that afternoon, I started drinking with the others, trying to drown my growing confusion. Jack and Dobbin started a discussion of where we should head next, and when Jamaica seemed the favourite choice, Tom asked if he could be set ashore there, as promised, for he'd soon have taught me all he knew of navigation.

Realising the Brethren had no more use for him, Hog sneered then, and began abusing Tom as a lily-livered coward.

"It was when they signed ye on, they lost all chance of me", Tom answered him.

"Let him be", Carty growled at Hog, yet the blustering braggart went for his cutlass.

"I'm Quartermaster", Richard Connor declared firmly, standing between them. "I say that even though Tom Deane won't join us, his work has earned him a fair fight, according to our rules. Hell, 'tis his turtle we're eating."

"Turtles be damned!" Hog scowled, brandishing his cutlass. "He looks down upon us as sneak thieves, and I say he's a gutless dog, too weak-kneed to join us!"

"It takes more courage to stand alone", Tom noted coolly.

"Then fight me you yellow coward!" Tom spun and slapped him so hard across the face, the fat brute went flying into the sand. Half stunned, he picked up his cutlass, and instantly, a dozen weapons were at Tom's disposal. Yet Tom was no duellist, neither with pistols nor steel.

Anne was pale, her fists clenched, and only Jack kept his head. "It's too hot to enjoy a good fight now. I say we wait for sundown to see ye dance for us all." Hog, too fat a man to enjoy the heat, soon gave way to his mates' calls to postpone the fight for a few hours, on condition that it be to the death, for Tom was no one to the Brethren.

Tom nodded grimly and stalked over to me. "Well Mark, you're the swordsman. What can you teach me before sundown?"

I spoke of lunges, blocks, and counterthrusts, and offered to show him. We made our way over the rocks to the cove where we had caught the turtles, and sparred for a time. Yet he declared it indeed too hot, and that with but a few hours left him, he'd rather spend the time seeking the peace in his soul. I told him I'd bring him some food, and left him.

And I walked away from Tom Deane, knowing that if I let Hog kill him, all the light he had brought into my life would fade. And I could not bear the prospect of being so alone again. By the time I'd walked over the headland and re-joined the pirates, I'd decided to intercede. I loosened my rapier, and wandered over to where the worst of the men were huddled over a rum bottle. When Hog spat at my feet, I kicked sand in his face, and the fat fool staggered up, brandishing his cutlass.

And despite all that Richard Connor could shout of the Articles, I drew steel, and we faced each other, the pirates crowded around, urging us on. With the white beach blazing in the heat, I circled to keep the sun in his eyes, everyone moving absurdly slow, but me. Without waiting to take my measure, Hog attacked with slashing cutlass. I leapt

587

aside at the last moment, thrust out my foot, and over he went. Enraged, he leapt up and charged again, and I lunged. He avoided my blade with more agility than I'd expected, and slashed my fighting arm. Anne screamed, and I glimpsed Jack holding her. Before Hog could overpower me with his greater strength, I feinted, and leapt back even as he lunged. And then I ran him through the heart. He stared at me, amazed, and dropped with a thud.

I stood for an endless moment, chilled to the core with this cold-blooded murder, and it was all I could do to keep on my feet. And then Jack was clapping me on the back, cursing Hog for breaking the Articles, and attacking a comrade. And then Anne was hugging me, weeping and laughing, and calling me 'Mary'.

I watched my comrades' faces drop as they caught my name. Jack started to laugh, and Patrick Carty joined him, declaring, to my astonishment, that he'd known all along. Of the men who'd known me longest, only Noah Harwood damned me for a fraud. George Featherstone chuckled and reminded him that I'd saved them all from the Phoenix.

The rest exploded in emphatic denial of me as a comrade, most stating that one woman was bad enough, but two...they'd be knee-deep in petticoats yet! Captain Dobbin seemed convinced that some particularly insulting joke had been played on him, and that Jack had known all along. Jack yelled for quiet, and when most ignored him, Richard Connor surprised us all by letting off his pistol in a great blast that silenced us all.

"Right, I'm Quartermaster, and I'll sort this out." He turned to me, and there was a twinkle in his eyes that belied his serious mien. "You've signed the Articles in a false name. That I don't like, yet many do it. If Jack has brought you secretly to sea for his own pleasure, we'll maroon you both."

I had to smile. "I don't think I can hold a candle against Anne. And I'll tell you all now that Jack didn't find out until two days ago. As for deceiving you, the only lie I ever told was my name. I did sail for Queen Anne, and march for Marlborough."

"'Taint possible!" Noah sneered.

"Don't blame yourselves for not guessing. I've lived twenty-eight years in this world, and few of them as a woman."

Patrick Carty started to chuckle again, declaring he'd known since he'd nursed me aboard Bellamy's pirate sloop. I demanded to know why he'd said nothing, and he shrugged. "Me whole family fought at the battle o' Limerick, in a last ditch stand o' the Irish 'gainst the English invaders. When me father fell, me mother led us. Seven brothers and me little sister. She re-loaded muskets at first, and when our youngest brother fell, she took up his musket, and killed her share o' Englishmen. A quiet little thing, yet steady under fire. Ye remind me o' her."

He clapped me on the back, and though my friends cheered, the majority of the Company were still glaring, feeling fooled. Captain Dobbin was the angriest of these, and I saw that he'd thought himself off on some great adventure, much too dangerous for mere women. He was like a child on a hot day that had bitten into a rotten apple. "You may think it a laughing matter. I think most of you Providence men knew all along. But I've had enough of sailing with women. They don't belong at sea, and that's an end to it. All those who leave their women ashore can sail with me."

Jack was suddenly alert. "Will you split the Company then Jim? We've all signed the Articles, and none have voted."

"Take your Articles to the Devil, for they declare the sentence to be marooning for those who bring their harlots aboard."

"One is my wife, the other my friend. Say one more slander against either of them, and you'll make me angry."

Richard Connor interrupted. "You may want to leave us, Jim Dobbin, and divide the Company, and take your

589

vessel, yet don't forget that the loot is stored on Jack's sloop. Now, a vote. Each man stand behind his Captain."

They all shuffled about, getting behind either Jack Rackam or Jim Dobbin, and it was easy to see I'd split us in half, and we'd have to work hard to find more men, and another vessel. Jack looked grim, yet he did not hesitate to begin negotiations over the division of loot, provisions, and ammunition.

By late afternoon, the sloops were lashed together in the bay, while men passed chests and barrels across the gunwales. When 'twas done, Jack made a great speech, praising Anne and I as comrades, and boasting that none could match our skill with weapons. Carty raised a toast, Jack suggested one last parting revel, and they all cheered.

I told Jack that I'd make my way over the headland, and let Tom know that Hog was already dead. He flashed his teeth at me, and told me to take a rum bottle with me. "And I'll fetch you a dress", Anne chuckled. "I wish I could be there to see the look on his face."

The tide was full, and I had to scramble high over the headland, the great basket Anne had thrust upon me pulling me off balance. Once over, I took the opportunity to strip in the over-hanging shade of a great tree, and quickly wash Hog's murder from me. Then I donned Anne's faded blue dress, and though 'twas too short, and too wide for me, still it convinced me that I was going to try this adventure again.

I saw Tom fishing from rocks on the other side of the bay, and as he flicked a great silver crescent of fish from the water, I stepped out, walking openly along the beach towards him. With thumping heart and dry mouth, more afraid than I'd ever been charging the line, or boarding a ship, I watched him clean the fish, and then turn and see me. He gaped to see a strange woman on the beach, yet was astounded when he saw 'twas me.

I told him that he was safe, that Hog had attacked me, and I'd killed him hours ago. I explained that Anne's relief had uncovered my secret, and that half the pirates were

590

leaving us, though that might change once they'd drunk enough. He was all amazement, shaking his head, looking hard at me, and shaking his head again.

Then he chuckled, and on that note, I opened the rum bottle Anne had packed. He took a swig, indicated the fish, and invited me to dine with him. "I've spent hours trying to catch something to feed myself, my appetite showing no respect for my last hours. When I killed this poor fish only moments ago, I was thinking of myself being gutted by Hog. And now that I am to live, I've never been so hungry. And as for yer transformation..." He blushed then, and I had to laugh.

"What will ye do now? Will they let ye sail with them still?"

"Jack's determined to keep me, and Featherstone and Carty will back me. Yet, truly, I only went on the account to save my life, and returning to it was not my wish. I've had enough of the life, and my share would give me a small stake in the world."

"What would ye do otherwise?"

"I've reneged on the Pardon, and they'll hang me if they catch me. Perhaps I'd better dress as a woman until far from here. Then I'd buy land somewhere in the colonies, somewhere wild, where the wind is warm. I'd keep no slaves, just a cow and chickens, and grow just enough to feed myself."

"It sounds lonely." He was gazing intently at the fire, avoiding my eyes, and I knew then that anywhere would be lonely without him. Confused, exhausted in truth from the conflicts of the day, I said nothing. He announced that the fish was cooked, and we ate it hot with our fingers, and drank fiery rum.

The sun set before us in a dramatic purple blaze, and though little was said, a deep peace came upon us. Contentment seemed to fill the bay, until the very waves hushed it, and the smoke from our pipes wrote it in spirals for the stars to read.

We sat in quiet companionship until the moon came up, and then 'twas as though we were much too close, or not close enough. Crabs scuttled about us, birds called intermittently, and something screamed from the jungle behind us. Then the perfume of all the flowers rolled down to the shore with the night breeze, gusting the plaguesome mosquitoes out to sea. A shooting star blazed across the diamond scattered sky, and Tom took my hand. "Jump ship in Jamaica with me, Mary. I don't have much, but together we could find a home to call our own, I know it." Happiness filled my heart so that I could not speak. "It's no light fornication I'm offering. It's my hand for life." I grasped his hand and closed the bargain with my lips, before fear could rule me. When he kissed me and called me 'wife', I felt my soul lighten, and prayed God for a little mercy.

Yet I felt I had to tell him I'd been married before, and what misery it had led to. He sighed for my intransigence, and for Jan's death, and declared that Macartney would never have left the Three Horseshoes alive, if he'd been there.

"I have lived too long in the world to expect justice from it. Macartney ended rich and respected, and me..."

"Live just a little longer", he laughed, and then he kissed me again. His delight in me was as great as mine in him, and for the first time in many years, I felt whole and clear, and strangely certain. His caresses smoothed my fears away, and anything else being false, we began our honeymoon before the wedding.

We wandered back to the pirate's bay the next morning, hand-in-hand, and when Jack saw us, and started to laugh, the rest of the pirates gathered around, the jokes growing bawdy at our expense. Tom then astounded them all by announcing our intended marriage, and declaring it our intention to leave them in Jamaica, still with no sextant man. Jack and Anne cheered and Anne suggested that, as Jack was Captain, he marry us directly.

Jack laughed and agreed, and delighted at not

needing to split the Company, the two crews united in their good wishes for our future, and vied with each other in emptying their vessels of provisions for the marriage feast. Anne fussed over me, wishing she had a better dress, and that Annie Fulworth could be there, for she loved weddings. I told her that none of this could have happened but for the lessons I'd learned in freedom from her, and she laughed and hugged me, delighted at the compliment.

At noon, under a great spreading flame tree, Tom took my hand, and before them all, stated firmly: "I, Tom Deane, take ye, Mary Read, to be my wedded wife, in token whereof I hold thy hand."

"I, Mary Read, take you, Tom Deane, to be my wedded husband, in token whereof, I hold thy hand."

The pirates then whooped and cheered, and broke open bottles and casks of wine. Someone sawed a dance out of an old fiddle, and we were soon whirling about the beach, all the pirates insisting on dancing a few steps with me. We sailed that night, Anne and Jack leaving us the sloop's cabin for our honeymoon. From then on, I dressed in women's clothes, and told Tom that I'd stay out of trousers unless we were attacked.

Yet, despite the delight that I took in Tom, and the relief of living a free life as a woman once more, I felt a nagging suspicion that Fate would allow me no more than a taste of happiness. The murder of Hog stayed bloody in my dreams, and I wondered if I'd only won Tom by damning my soul to ever-lasting perdition.

Chapter 32: Capture

The wedding feast left us with little meat, and no flour, though we still had wine. On the lookout for prizes, our sloops cruised the French coast of Hispaniola, and at dusk, Tom Earl spied a fire in a small bay. We sailed in, and found a canoa moored off the beach, and when Featherstone hailed them, two Frenchmen called out that they were but pig hunters, down on their luck. Jack charmed them aboard for a drink, the skinny wight introducing himself as Pierre Cornelian, the fat one Jean Besneck. They woke in the morning with hangovers, far to sea, with Jack telling them they'd make better pirates than hunters."

"But all the meat we had salted..." fat Jean wailed.

"In the canoa, being towed behind us", Jack reassured them, and I had to laugh. They pretended reluctance at being forced for each other's sake, yet I did not think it would be long before they signed the Articles.

That afternoon we sighted two sail, and gave chase. They did not flee, and when we were close enough, we saw the red and gold colours of Castille. Jack cursed and told us to prepare for battle, Featherstone and Carty leapt for the guns, and Anne raised King Death on our mainmast. Tom tried earnestly to dissuade me from battle, yet I was in my old suit with my hair tied back and my pistols primed before the first shot went over our bows. I told him to stay below with the forced men, and ran to port to find all my mates ready for a hard fight against our hated enemy. Featherstone grinned when he saw me, and put me in charge of the swivel gun. Carty chuckled as he helped me lever her muzzle up, declaring I'd just won him a small fortune, for he'd bet Ben Wright his share that I'd take my place in the battle.

"You wagered your share on me?"

"Don't be so astounded. Yer here aint ye!"

Jack ordered a return shot, and Featherstone put one straight through the bow of the nearest Spaniard. By the time we'd re-loaded, the Spaniards had veered off, and we jeered them away.

Patrick Carty clapped me on the back, laughing. "I swear by God yer the best Gunner's mate I've ever sailed with. All that Navy trainin'. Nothin' like it." I laughed and asked him if this was why he had kept my secret so well. "Ye've the right to do what ye wish with yer own life. Ye've always been true to the Brethren. That's enough for me."

The Frenchmen were most relieved when the Spaniards declined the fight. Skinny Pierre took a seat by me on the deck, and opening a bottle of warm wine, he asked me what pleasure I found in the life of a pirate, with the constant danger from fire and sword, and a low death if I was ever taken alive. "Hanging is the price I might have paid", I agreed. "Yet without that fear, every cowardly tyrant now cheating widows and orphans and oppressing those too poor to obtain justice, would turn pirate. The rogues would so infest the seas, that all brave sailors would starve, whether trader or Brethren. No merchant would ever venture out, and the trade would soon not be worth following."

"It's hardly worth the following now", Anne grumbled. "We've little wine left, and we're short on provisions again."

We had just cruised into northern Jamaican waters, when we spied a canoa in Ocho Rios bay, and immediately set our course to intercept it. Her Captain was a middle-aged woman, who cursed us foully from the moment Jack ordered her to lay to. Carty hauled her aboard, and then we emptied her canoa of a season's hard work, enough to last us a month.

She took one look at Anne and I, both in skirts again, and immediately began cursing us for whores, declaring that she'd recognise us anywhere, and would see us hang. Partly to shut her up, and partly in earnest, Anne suggested we drop her overboard, to save her coming against us. Mistress Thomas then stayed quiet until back in her own canoa, when she erupted with curses again.

Soon after, in mid-October, we came upon a

schooner and a sloop just out of Dry Harbour Bay. We fired the swivel gun at the schooner, the Mary, and she immediately surrendered. In her we found fifty rolls of tobacco, and nine bags of pimento, well worth the capture. Her master, Thomas Spenlow of Port Royal in Jamaica, obeyed Jack's order to come aboard, though pleading with us not to beggar him, for he had lost a schooner to pirates only months before. We shut him in the cabin, and then turned our attention to the sloop, the Sarah.

Her men had already abandoned her, and made for shore with all their arms, including a swivel gun. We went in after them at dawn, and got a blast of shot from the bushes for our trouble. Carty, in his great bull's roar, demanded to know what they were about. Thomas Dillon, the Sarah's master, then hailed us, demanding to know what we were about. Featherstone answered that we were English pirates, but he need not be afraid, we would do them no harm, and they should come aboard and drink a glass of punch with us. Realising that they were in an impossible situation, Dillon insisted on our word that they would not be forced, and the lot of them came aboard.

Stripping the prizes took two days, allowing Jack time to cry up the pirate life, another handful of men signing up. Tom Earl spoke with the ten Negro slaves that crewed Spenlow's schooner, and convinced them that they could trust the Brethren to treat them fair and make them rich, and they too signed up. With three sloops full of men, and provisions and cargo to divide, we sailed into a narrow cove of a rocky isle, just off the north-west of Jamaica. We spent the night around a fire, drinking and dancing to a fiddle at first, yet without the necessary liquors for a true revel.

Thomas Spenlow came up to where we lay by the smoking fire, and again begged hard for his schooner. Jack declared her ill-sailing and foul-bottomed, and that we had no time to safely careen her. As we had an ample Fleet, we voted that Spenlow could keep the Mary, and he cheered up. He told us of handsome Tom Brown and John Fenwick taking his schooner, the Neptune, off Hispaniola last June. The pirates had only a small sloop and a handful of men, yet Spenlow's schooner had been foul with weed, and he had seen no choice but to cede. The pirates had found fifty pounds worth of cargo, and ten slaves who they immediately freed. They had kept the Neptune, leaving Spenlow a small boat to get home in.

"I say that considering' how well-armed you were, you ceded pretty fast to us", Jack mocked him. "And to be found in these waters foul with weed, twice!"

"Let me finish. I was still within sight when Commodore Vernon sailed in, on His Majesty's sloop, the Mary. The pirate sloop fled into the night, and Vernon attacked the pirates in my schooner. They fought hard, the freed slaves with them, but your mates were low on ammunition, and soon overwhelmed. Of the survivors, most were wounded, and these Commodore Vernon threw to the sharks."

"That's an act of barbarity that the Brethren would never stoop to", Jack hissed.

"You're forgetting Charles Vane's vendetta against the Bermudans", I reminded him coldly.

Spenlow told us that the surviving pirates were carried to jail in Jamaica. What he didn't tell us was that he was on his way to Jamaica to testify against them.

We feasted ashore that night, and Jack toasted pretty Tom Brown and John Fenwick, his surly friend. When he cursed the Navy for their cruelty, Carty declared it time to leave these waters. Tom and I had been teaching young John Davies the sextant, and though he was apprehensive, we were sure he had the skill to pilot them to the pirate haven on Madagascar.

The next morning, Anne woke, green and swooning, and then staggered away to retch into some bushes. When Jack's alarm gave way to whoops of joy, I understood. "She's with child again", I told Tom, and ran to congratulate her.

Anne was more rueful than pleased, yet the men

were aghast. When she turned down greasy turtle steak for breakfast, one of those who'd joined us from Spenlow's crew asked her how much longer she'd be with us. "Oh I'm only just gone", Anne told him blithely. "When I get too big to fight, I'll go and stay with Jack's family for a time." The men about her growled their disapproval, and even Jack looked dubious. "I'm pregnant, not sick!" Anne protested. "Retching a little in the mornings doesn't mean I can't fight!"

Ben Wright then stood and spoke hard against having women and babes in the midst of battle. The quiet Richard Connor insisted she was a proven comrade, and would leave at the end of the cruise. Jack declared he was to drop me on Jamaica with Tom Deane directly, and would leave Anne with his family on Cuba soon after.

If Anne had held her tongue, Jack might have pulled it off, yet she argued with him bitterly, furious at his compromise, and this public betrayal. Ben Wright then called for a vote to split the Company, and the majority stood behind him. That afternoon, we divided the loot and chose our shares, and they sailed away in the Sarah, as she was clean and fast, though Jack spoke against it to the end. We were left with two sloops, one leaky, the other foul-bottomed, and only twelve loyal men.

Jack suggested we use one sloop for firepower, and the other for boarding, and take another vessel immediately, hoping for more hands, as well as provisions. Jim Dobbin surprised us all by standing with Jack, and we voted him Captain of the slowest vessel, with only Patrick Carty to help him shift her sails and man her guns. All the rest of us went aboard the fastest sloop, with Jack as Captain.

We had only just put to sea, when we rounded the isle to see our old mates in the Sarah, fighting off a Navy sloop. We conferred, Richard Connor calling for a vote on helping our old comrades in the Sarah. "If we had stayed together, we could have fought anyone", Jack stated. "As they have left us so under-handed, we cannot help them."

"The Brethren must hold true to each other", Anne

declared. "If we allow small differences to divide us, we are easily conquered."

"If you'd agreed to leave us, we'd still have a Fleet," Tom Earl snarled.

"You can't blame me for Ben Wright's ambitions to be Captain", Anne argued. "He used me as an excuse to divide the Company and take command." She looked to Jack to back her, and when he looked away, she shook her head, unable to believe that he would not stand by her rights as a comrade.

Our Company continued to abuse her for dividing them, until Richard Connor declared that the vote was on whether we sailed to help our old mates in the Sarah. We chose to hold our course, and bear away.

Over the following days, Jack swore that Anne must accept a life with his family on Cuba, and she declared she would happily leave them another babe to care for, yet refused to rot there, waiting for him to sail in, when she knew he was headed for Africa.

"I would return for you and the children…" Jack promised, and she laughed her disbelief.

I tried to make her see that the men were in the right of it, and that although she was a comrade under the Articles, a woman with child had no place aboard. She called us all traitors, and declared that if she lost the child, she would not regret it, as she had not wanted to be pregnant again so soon. That set Jack's back up, and when Noah Harwood started muttering of family disputes taking up the time of Company business, he glared at the old man, and told Tom and I he would land us off Dry Harbour in two days.

The crew grumbled throughout those two days that Anne should be landed with us, and Jack, still fuming with Anne, begged them to keep her aboard until Cuba.

Soon after, we were rounding Point Negril, the westernmost point of Jamaica, late in the afternoon, looking for a safe mooring before nightfall. In the last of the light, John Davies spied a small periauga crowded with men,

599

rowing hard for the shore. In the morning, we raised a white pendant on our dory and rowed in, yet they stayed hidden in the bushes. We found their periauga loaded with live turtles, and hailed them again, and a voice quavered back, asking who we were. Jack called out that we were Englishmen, and invited them to come aboard, and drink a bowl of punch with us. At first they refused, yet when Jack described the feast we were preparing, ten men came aboard.

They were indentured servants from the plantations of Porto Maria and Dry Harbour, out turtling for their masters. Well-armed with muskets and cutlasses, they stated from the beginning that they would not be forced, though they would dearly love a sip of punch. Jack gave them his word that they were free men, and they laid down their arms, and took up pipes of Spenlow's excellent tobacco. One declared that he liked us never the worse for being pirates, since we were all honest boys and loved our bottles.

Anne and I, in trousers since the splitting of the Company, had barely time to grin at the joke, when a blast out to sea spun us on our heels. Two sloops bearing the King's colours were attacking Dobbin's sloop. Rackam was on his feet immediately, and throwing his tankard overboard, he ordered us to weigh anchor. Tom Earl and I rushed for the chain and began hauling at it, while the rest leapt for the sails.

Yet we were too close to the coast to catch a breeze, and when one of the King's sloops turned into the bay, Jack ordered us to man the oars. He told the turtlers to bear a hand, and when their leader refused, Jack cuffed him to the deck. "Their guns know not the difference between an honest man and a rogue", he snarled. "Row you lousy swabs, or I'll cut your throats and feed you to the sharks!" The next shot convinced them, and we all took to the oars to push our sloop out past the headland.

As the breeze filled our sails, Anne and I leapt for the guns, and most of the turtlers ran below. Then the Navy sloop came within range, and Anne fired and missed. I let fly

600

with the swivel gun, and did some damage to her sails. Then the sloop replied with a broadside that blasted our gunwales, sending splinters flying into our crew. Featherstone was ready with our port guns, yet instead of attacking, Jack turned our sloop to run.

We saw Dobbin's sloop cede, the Jolly Roger fluttering to the deck, and my heart cried out for Patrick Carty. Yet Jack insisted we were undermanned and foul-bottomed, and had no choice but to think of our own lives. Noah muttered that he was thinking of his child in Anne's belly, yet Jack ignored him, and asked Richard Connor to break out a barrel of rum for the wounded men, and to give the rest of us a dram to keep our hearts up.

With the sunset flaming about us, the turtlers ventured up from the bilges, begging us to clear their names if we were captured. Jack declared that night was falling fast, and we'd soon lose the Navy sloop, and the turtlers boldly wished us a fair wind and light heels. Yet the land breeze sprung up, and proved that though we were befouled and slow, the Navy sloop was not.

She came up with us in the darkness, and a voice hailed us, demanding to know who we were. "I'm John Rackam, a merchantman of Cuba", Jack yelled back, hoping for a wind change, or a break in the coast, or anything by which we might escape.

"Strike immediately to the King of England's colours!"

"You attacked so suddenly, we thought you Spaniards!" Jack shouted. "We are privateers against the Spaniards ourselves..."

"Strike your colours and lower your sails!"

"They've caught us", Jack noted calmly. "We don't have the numbers to fight them, and with Anne pregnant..."

Anne cursed, and before any could stop her, she roared out that we would strike no strikes, and fired the swivel gun directly at the oncoming sloop.

They let go a broadside that blasted our bowsprit

away, and then a volley of small shot mowed us down. "Go below!" Jack bellowed through the thick smoke.

"Fight!" Anne screamed. "Fight now, and they'll never take us!"

"Damn you, Anne, we've not the numbers! The fight is over! Now drop below!" He swung down himself, and most followed him. Yet Anne, screaming defiance, ran at the boarders, slicing the ropes from their grappling hooks. My blood up, I shouted and ran with her, George Featherstone turned with us, and the three of us stood together to repel them all. Anne fired her pistol at one man, and dropped another with a swipe of her cutlass, while I pierced an Officer's sword arm with my rapier. Featherstone picked up a fallen cutlass, and began laying about him mightily, shouting for someone to re-load our swivel gun.

I ran to do it, and for a moment, I thought the three of us might prevail, for we were fighting for our lives, and the Navy men hesitated to risk death for their small reward. Anne screamed for our mates to come up and fight, and the Navy men attacked again. Then Featherstone ceded, swords at his throat, and Anne lost her head. Abusing our mates as cowards, she fired her pistol blindly into our hold. I heard their screams, and afraid for Tom, I dropped my rapier and leapt for her before she could fire her second pistol. And then the Navy swords were at our throats. I saw the wild fury still upon her, and sure they would shoot her down like a mad dog, I grabbed her and shook her hard. "Stop now. In truth, 'tis finished. Think of your children."

With a pistol at Anne's head, for she still looked half-mad, their Commander ordered our sails cut down, and our mates up on deck. Jack was first, his head high, and Anne spat on the deck at his feet. Jack bowed to the Navy commander, and offered him his sword, and Captain Barnet then introduced himself, polite enough, though he did not return Jack's bow. He said he was a commissioned privateer for the Jamaican Governor, and had been set on our heels by Dorothy Thomas, the woman in the canoa who had sworn to come against us.

Young John Davies, John Howell, Noah Harwood, Tom Earl, and Richard Connor, all followed Jack on deck. Connor his eyes full of fury for Anne, made the most of being pushed up against her, to curse her for firing at her own mates, for she'd hit one of the forced men. At this my heart lurched for Tom, yet he emerged from the hold unwounded.

Then it struck me. I was a pardoned pirate, caught fighting the King's Navy. I would hang.

Chapter 33: King Death

As soon as Captain Barnet mentioned Dorothy Thomas, Jack stopped protesting that we were nought but privateers against the Spanish. Barnet's partner hove to, Dobbin's sloop a prize behind him, and Jack identified him as Captain Bonnevie, an old rover. Patrick Carty and Jim Dobbin were then ordered aboard, and though Dobbin insisted he was no pirate, but Captain of his own sloop, captured only three weeks ago, Barnet refused to hear him.

Then Barnet ordered his men to throw three badly wounded mates overboard, including the turtler Anne had shot. Then, ignoring our desperate pleas against such cruelty, and the screams of the abandoned men, he gave the order to sail. I knew then that our Government was committed to our destruction, and our lives were almost over.

The twelve surviving members of our Company and the nine turtlers were crowded into our sloop's cramped and stinking cabin, with the hatch nailed down on top of us. I felt for a lanthorn, and asked if any had a tinderbox, and soon we had light. As we had used the cabin as a storeroom, there were provisions enough, yet it was a terrible night, with bitter recriminations against Anne for firing upon her mates. Only Featherstone, who had fought like a lion, could stop her abusing them for cowards. He said it might have been her desire to die fighting, yet the rest of them had the right to die dancing if they willed it.

Anne sneered at that, and swore she'd never surrender. Snatching the lanthorn off me, she inspected the bulkhead, to see if we could smash our way through. Noah abused her for a fool, for our guards would surely hear any noise. "If we try to break out, they'll scuttle her, with all of us still inside."

"There must be opportunities for escape before we see the gaol in Spanish Town", Jack declared. Yet in the morning, we were set ashore at the Davis Cove Garrison, where an entire Company of militia met us. Major Richard James was in charge, and he insisted on us being kept in chains for the long march to the gaol at Spanish Town. We declared my Tom, the Frenchmen, and the turtlers to be forced men, yet Major James declared that a matter for the courts to decide. So we hobbled along together, in leg irons and chains, the dust and flies, thirst and hunger, injustice and humiliation, all a torment.

At Spanish Town gaol, they crowded us into cells, and for the first time since our capture, we were fed. We knew from Spenlow, that we would find handsome Tom Brown and John Fenwick there, yet they had also captured Robert Deal, Vane's old mate. And then Charles Vane himself stepped out of the shadows, bowing gracefully, and as venomous as ever. "This is quite a reunion. First my dearest Tom to torment, and now my old mate Jack, you traitorous bastard. And even Mistress Bonny! Charmed to see you here, my dear!"

John Davies, Patrick Carty, Anne, Tom and I were crowded into a small cell. Anne would speak to none but me and George Featherstone, still spitting at her old comrades for cowards, and they still cursed her for a mad bitch.

We heard that Governor Lawes hailed Captain Barnet as a hero, and gave him two hundred pounds reward, half of which he kept for himself, the rest divided amongst the crew of his two sloops.

Like the other pirates, we then waited for witnesses to come in against us. Captain Spenlow was one, Dorothy Thomas another. Anne blamed our kindness in leaving Mistress Thomas alive, for 'twas she who'd sent news of our whereabouts to the Jamaican Governor, who'd then sent Barnet after us. Noah Harwood insisted 'twas Anne's stubbornness that had split our Company, leaving us short handed, and proving 'twas bad luck to have women aboard.

One by one, our Company was taken for questioning by the Governor's Officers. Though we all declared that Tom, the Frenchmen and the turtlers were forced, and had not signed the Articles, only Tom was freed, as his crew had already put in a deposition against us, declaring him taken against his will.

Though free, he declared he would not leave me, and paid the gaoler to let him stay. When I woke retching the next morning, pale and shaking, Tom forced me to eat a little bread and water. When I could keep nothing in my stomach, he feared that I'd caught some jungle ague.

Anne felt my forehead, swore I wasn't feverish, and burnt some rope under my nose. When the smell set me retching again, she took my hand, tried to smile, and told me I too was with child. I hotly denied it, refusing to hear her, yet I knew the dark of the moon had come and gone, and brought no bleeding. When I wept, Tom took me in his arms, and whispered that the babe would save me, that they could not hang me pregnant. "You have most of nine months", he whispered. "I am free, and will do much to help you. You are my wife, and they will pardon you, if you promise to live honestly."

"If you had influential friends...yet your own father has declared you a trouble- maker. And if I had not been taken fighting... In truth, we know I will bear you a child, and then hang, leaving you a babe to care for." Tom wept then, and I told him I had committed many crimes, and had always known the price. Yet, when he said he'd ride for home, to beg his father for help, I thought the fear of never seeing him again would stop my heart. He swore by his God, his love for me, and his unborn child, that he would come back for me, and I tried hard to believe him.

Anne then called one of the gaolers, exposed her breasts and declared herself female and pregnant. She insisted I was pregnant also, though I refused to strip and prove it. We were put in a separate cell, and when the gaoler's wife came to see us, she was soon convinced we were telling the truth of our sex, though there was no evidence of our pregnancies. She was not unkind, yet she feared us, and Anne's bad temper and my grief did little to

606

reassure her. We were kept separate from the men from then on, in the endmost cell, with a little window looking over a hill. I spent my days looking out for Tom, constantly ill and unable to eat, while Anne blossomed beside me.

In mid-November, our mates were taken from their cells for trial, Vane calling out his earnest wish that they all hang. When the gaoler's wife came to feed us at noon, she said that Mister Bernard, the Court's Commissioner, had been forced to withdraw to attend his dying son, struck down by the fever that was plaguing Jamaica. Yet the court had proceeded, and our mates trooped back, utterly dispirited, only an hour later. Jack had pleaded lack of witnesses to testify that we were not out against the Spanish, and insisted we had never been pirates.

Yet Jim Dobbin, hoping to do a deal for his life, had already provided conclusive evidence against his sworn mates. The two Frenchmen had followed suit, Captains Spenlow and Dillon had settled the matter, and the commissioners had unanimously agreed that all the men before them were guilty of piracy. Sir Nicholas Laws, the Governor, had passed Sentence of Death. They were to hang at Gallows Point at dawn.

That night, the gaoler told Anne that Jack wanted to see her. She sneered, insisting she counted no cowards as friends of hers, and I cursed her pride. "For God's sake Anne, have some mercy! There is little enough of it here. He may not have your desperate courage, yet he always loved you. And if not for you, he'd still be Captain of a Pirate Fleet. See him, tell him you love him, and make his end a little easier."

She shrugged and went with the gaoler then, and I heard her declare: "I'm sorry to see you here Jack, but if you had fought like a man, you'd not have to die like a dog." Vane's laughter completed the cruelty, and I cursed her for her hard and unforgiving heart, declaring that if she had not been aboard, Jack would have fought to the death.

'Twas still dark when our mates were woken and marched from the gaol. Jack stepped out, his head high, and

607

though I begged Anne to make peace between them, she would not. I could only call out after them that it had been an honour to be their comrade, and young John grinned and waved, still not convinced it was the end.

At dawn on the eighteenth of November, church bells rang for the souls of Jack Rackam, George Featherstone, Richard Connor, John Davies, and John Howell. Anne broke then and howled in my arms like the child she was, and I wept for them as for my brothers. It was John Davies' end I regretted most, for I saw our great injustice to his mother, who had always treated us so well, and wished then that I'd spoken harder against the lad signing on.

Jamaica had been plagued with fever for months, and when the ague swept through the gaol, and found me, I knew I had not the strength left to fight it. For the first time, I suggested that Anne write to her father, begging his help. She fired up immediately, and I insisted she think of her babe.

Vane gloated again when Tom Brown and John Fenwick were marched off. They had waited long for Captain Spenlow to return from his trading venture for their trial, and their three remaining comrades had already died of their wounds in the dank heat of the gaol. We heard that the slaves they had freed had been whipped and sold cheap as renegades. An hour after they were marched off, they returned grey-faced, to tell us they were to hang in a week.

Then Vane's old mate, Robert Deal, was tried for the taking of Captain Shattock's Endeavour two years ago, and Captain Rowling's Pearl in December. Shattock complained that Vane had beaten and abused him, and Hosea Tisdell, the Jamaican tavern keeper, declared he had seen the pirates rip up their Pardons when Jack Rackam took over from Vane. Deal was declared guilty, and sentenced to Death, and Vane laughed when he heard it, and toasted him, declaring that Hell would be full of old mates.

Patrick Carty, Tom Earl, James Dobbin, and Noah Harwood were hanged the next day at Kingston Harbour.

Two days later, Tom Brown and John Fenwick were executed. To my horror, Jack Rackam, George Featherstone, and Richard Connor were denied burial, and were gibbeted about Jamaica's coast, Jack's body strung up in chains at Sandy Key outside Port Royal, a warning to all sailors to stay humble, and accept the blows of their masters.

Charles Vane sneered at our misery, and told us that the Brethren had always known that Death was King.

"Only a man could be so stupid", Anne spat at him. "It's life that rules us. Every woman with a man in her arms or a babe in her belly knows that!"

Soon after, Anne and I were told by the gaolers' wife to make ourselves respectable, something Anne declared impossible, making me laugh, despite myself. We were led to a small building near the gaol, where seven clean, dignified, and sneering gentlemen sat uncomfortably in the heat to stare at us. They interrogated me not only about the crimes I had committed, they questioned my very existence. I was feverish again, yet remembering my belly, I made a great effort to save myself and my child. I declared that I abhorred the life of piracy, that I had entered into it only upon compulsion, and that I had intended to quit at the first opportunity. I told them that I was a virtuous woman, and had married one of the forced men, and planned to leave the pirate life for an honest one. I was then accused of firing into our sloop's hold, and I denied this, though I would not accuse Anne of it. To justify what they saw as my unwomanly courage, I felt compelled to give them some of my history, and stated that I had learned to fight on a Navy ship, and seen battle under Marlborough.

"And fought with pirates", another sneered.

"I am with child. So is my friend. That is why we fought."

"'Tis no surprise, surely, that you find yourselves carrying bastards. We have received a letter from Governor Rogers on the subject of Mistress Bonny. He condemns you as an outright whore, madam, and declares that you left your

609

rightful husband to run away with known pirates. Is that true?" They listened to her denials, and her condemnation of the Governor, with more contempt.

After we were led back to our cell, the heat increased, my head spun, and I started to shake. She took my hand, then felt my forehead. "Oh no. Oh Mary, you're much too hot." She called the gaoler's wife, and this rough yet kindly woman brought a bucket of water in a vain attempt to cool me.

We were tried ten days after Jack's death, on the twenty-eighth of November. To my horror, the benches and aisles of the court were crowded with staring men and whispering women, all avid for the details of our lives, and the security of our deaths. Of all the hard days of my life, that was the worst. To stand in front of them and justify my existence seemed false, and I told them the only judge I could admit was God, who understood and forgave all.

We were accused of the same crimes as our comrades, and pleaded not guilty, knowing that otherwise, we would immediately hang. Dorothy Thomas spoke against us first, claiming that we were as active as any man aboard the pirate sloop. Yet it was her emphasis on our unwomanly ways that condemned us in the eyes of the courtroom. She made as much of our cursing and our men's clothes, as our carrying of weapons. I saw then that it was not piracy we were being tried for, but perversity, and the injustice of it stung.

Jean Besneck, the fat Frenchmen, testified against me next, stating that in times of action, there was no person more resolute, more ready to board, and to undertake anything hazardous. Then he repeated what I had said approving hanging, and that raised the murmurs of the crowd. Skinny Pierre testified that Anne handed gunpowder to the men, and that when chasing, we wore men's clothes, and otherwise dressed as women.

Spenlow stated that he had seen Anne Bonny with a gun in her hand, and that we were both ready to do anything aboard. Yet again it seemed that it was his exaggerated

610

descriptions of our cursing and our bloodthirsty natures that condemned us. We would hang not because we were pirates, but because we were unnatural.

We were unanimously convicted, and when brought before them again, and asked why Sentence of Death should not be passed upon us, I pleaded again for my good intentions. I declared that I had always tried to live right, yet in a wrong world, this had not been possible, and I had been driven from my honest course against my will. I told them they should not require us to live as slaves, and then kill us for rebellion.

The judge dismissed my words, and glowered at us. "You, Mary Read and Ann Bonny, are to go from hence to the place from whence you came, and from thence to the place of execution, where you shall both be hanged by the neck 'til you are dead. And God be merciful to both your souls." That was when Anne stepped forward and stated that we were both quick with child. We were then given a respite until the nineteenth of December, when our pregnancies would be more evident.

When we returned to the gaol, Anne tried to cheer me, yet I was aswoon again, and weakness ruled me. The gaoler's wife insisted they would not be barbarous enough to hang women, and did not understand when I explained that they had proved us unwomanly, so that they could hang us.

Tom returned, and though I wept with joy to see him true to me, he was shocked to find me so weak with fever. He told me his father had refused to see him, and though he had made the rounds of all his old friends, hoping for money to help us, he had nothing to show for it but a half dead old horse.

Anne suggested he do the rounds of the Port Royal taverns, and Tom found Henry Jennings, who handed him his purse, and promised to come and see us. He came that night, bringing rum enough for all the prisoners, and we followed Vane in a toast to death and injustice.

"Aye, Captains can murder their men and get away

with it, and poor sailors must suffer the blows", one of the condemned men moaned. "Remember Captain Jayne of Bristol taking months to torture that cabin boy to death, the ship's Company powerless to hinder it."

"A cabin boy!" another snorted. "Remember Captain Floyd on the slaver the Indian Queen. He killed five of his crew, and didn't hang. Mind you, he was tried in Jamaica!"

"Aye", Tom agreed. "And those turtlers will have to face the worst of it, though they did nothing more than come aboard for a drink."

The judges spent a month trying to find evidence against the turtlers, who had come aboard our sloop as Jack's guests. Tom insisted they had committed no act of piracy, and that if they had not readily submitted when Barnet came up, the Navy would have suffered a real battle. They were tried on the twenty-fourth of January, and again the cowardly Frenchmen brought evidence against them, stressing the small help that Jack had forced out of them. The commissioners found themselves divided in their judgement, yet the majority decided that their intent had been piratical and felonious, as Jack Rackam was known to be a notorious pirate.

Sentence of Death was passed against them, the Judge calling them unlucky, yet telling them to bear their sufferings patiently, for if they were innocent, which he very much doubted, their reward would be greater in the next world. John Hanson dropped to his knees, weeping for his wife and babes, and the judge admitted that everybody must own their case very hard. They were left rotting in their cell for another month, and then six were hung, and three reprieved, and the Governor called that 'mercy'. Yet before he could be released, Hosea Tisdell declared Hanson one of Vane's Company. Though he had indeed run with the Brethren for a time, Vane emphatically denied it, and though Tisdell backed down, Hanson's reprieve was withdrawn.

Immediately after came the trial of four sailors of the Abington, who were accused of inciting mutiny on the coast of Guinea. John Whitcomb, Robert Sparkes, William Metring, and William Thorpe were placed in the cell next to us, and described how the Boatswain's cruelty had convinced their mate John Oglesby that he was better dead than alive in such misery. He and his mates had attempted to persuade the rest of the crew to take the schooner for a pirate ship, the third mate had broken the plot to the Captain, and Oglesby was whipped to death before them all. The rest were thrown in irons, yet the Cooper told the Captain that the near mutiny had been the Boatswain's fault. The Boatswain was demoted, and by the time the Abington sailed into Kingston, the prisoners were no longer in irons, and were working well. When they had been in Kingston two days, they asked for their wages, and Captain Smith promptly threw them in gaol. They protested that they no longer had any thought of mutiny, and could have run away at any time, yet the judge berated their Captain for not arresting them as soon as they sailed in. Two were hung for a mutiny that never started, and nothing was said of Oglesby's cruel death.

In January, death was declared the sentence for any contact with pirates, and I saw that now none would trade with them, the time of the Brethren was indeed over. Yet we heard of Captains Corner and Fox, who reneged on their Pardons, and attacked ships off Crooked Island. We heard too of Black Bart burning vessels off Saint Kitts, cannonading His Majesty's fort, and sending word to the Governor that he would burn Sandy Point about his ears to avenge the execution of his mates. Governor Spotswood also received word that Black Bart had vowed to avenge pirates hung in Virginia.

In February, Henry Jennings visited with a letter from Kate Pritchard in London, and she wrote that Woodes Rogers had finally sailed for home to plead for help with his enormous debts. Upon hearing that he'd been replaced as Governor of the Bahamas, his creditors had insisted upon his immediate arrest. Vane laughed long at that, and told

613

Jennings he was forgiven for dividing the Brethren, just for bringing such consoling news. Kate also wrote that Jamie the Rover was raising a son in Italy, and that the Scots had declared young Charlie their rightful Prince, though many called him the Young Pretender, and cursed God for sending another Stuart to plague us.

Captain Pearce of the Phoenix sailed into Kingston Harbour in early March, bringing Alexander Gilmore to testify against Robert Hudson. Gilmore declared Hudson a deserter from the Phoenix, and insisted he was with Vane in the taking of the John and Elizabeth, and had threatened to shoot him. Robert Hudson was then declared guilty, and sentenced to death, and he returned, white-faced, to tell us of the verdict.

Soon after, Gilmore came in to thank Vane for saving his life. "Your thanks can do me no good, unless they can turn into good wine", Vane scoffed. Gilmore sent the gaoler's son out for six bottles of Vane's favourite Madeira, and we all started drinking hard, passing bottles from cell to cell, while Hudson abused Gilmore for hanging him. By midnight, Vane was trying to start a fight between them, and Gilmore rose to go. It was then he recognised John Hanson. When Hanson saw Gilmore staring at him, he tried to face him out, yet the Navy man was certain Hanson had been in Vane's Company. Hanson faced the courts again the next morning, and he too was found guilty, and sentenced to death.

At noon the next day, Anne and I were brought before the same seven men who had first heard us plead for our lives. The gaoler's wife confirmed we were both pregnant, and Anne declared she had a child on Cuba, and a home to return to. I told them my unborn babe was the best possible bond for my future behaviour. I told them I had married an honest man, and had intended leaving the pirate life. Yet Sentence of Death was confirmed against us, only delayed until we were brought to childbed. Tom insisted that we would be reprieved, yet Anne and I thought this impossible, as we had been taken fighting.

614

Then Henry Jennings brought Captain Charles Johnson to visit us. He asked most courteously for our histories, in return for good food and rum. In truth, it seemed he had some sympathy for the Brethren, and I wondered if he was a reformed pirate himself. He claimed he had spoken with the survivors of Bellamy's crew in the Salem gaol, and with Stede Bonnet, and was compiling a true account of the Brethren. Anne was happy to tell him everything of her own life, and I gave him a sketch of my life too, hoping that some truth might survive the lies told of us.

Then it was Charles Vane's turn for trial. They had witnesses to his taking six ships, and Captain Pearce had taken the trouble to sail in, so that he could personally swear to Vane taking the Pardon, proving him a renegade. For months, Vane had lain in the hot darkness, laughing at the rest of us, condemning the Brethren's easy surrender of Nassau. Yet even when he returned from court with the death sentence hard upon him, his bitter courage never wavered. If anything, he seemed relieved that the end was finally at hand.

Yet that night, he called out to us, and demanded to know if young Adam Cormac had really been Anne Bonny in disguise. When she called back that not only was this true, but that he owed the lives of the Lark's crew to a woman, he confessed himself amazed. We bribed the gaoler, and he spent that night drinking rum with us, and for once, he was eager to talk.

"When Jack divided our Company, he left me an ill-sailing, foul-bottomed sloop, and a handful of men. I made Robert Deal our First Mate, and we set sail for the Bay of Honduras, fighting hard for every prize until our numbers grew. We soon had a Fleet and new hands aplenty, and careened on Bonacco Island.

"We cruised for the Bay again, yet were not three days out, when we saw the sun rise through a red and misty sky. Long swells started running in from the south-east, and we agreed that there was a storm coming. Within the hour, the waves were twenty foot high, and the wind was a constant whine in the rigging. We thought it bad, yet an hour later, the waves were mountains, and our Fleet was scattered. Heavy seas carried away our anchors, and then our bowsprit had to be hacked off to stop the jib from dragging us under.

"After two days of desperate pumping, masts and sails gone, she began breaking up underneath us. When I saw the rats jumping overboard, I knew we had to be near land, yet in that Hell of water, we heard the reef before we saw it. Hard men dropped to their knees and prayed for mercy then, yet there was none for any of them. She struck, and was staved to pieces, my mates falling screaming into the sea, grasping at planks and each other for support, the great seas battering them onto the rocks. Then a great wave picked me up to fling me after them, and I commended my soul to the Devil. Moments later, I found myself gashed and bleeding, half-way up the shore. Another wave came to drag me back in, yet I struggled beyond its reach, and listened to my comrades shriek into the howling wind.

"By dawn, the winds had calmed, and I searched the beaches to find not one man alive amidst all those corpses. At first I piled their bodies beyond the reach of the sea, yet when the sea birds and rats came for them, I thought better of it, and left them to the sharks. When the wind died on the second day, I saw that I had indeed been lucky. Though the isle was small and uninhabited, my sloop smashed to pieces, and my comrades drowned, there was a fresh water spring. I thought that, as the isle was within sight of the mainland, I might be visited by Indians in canoes or turtlers. I ate raw crabs and oysters until a dory of poor fishermen sailed in for water. They had no room to take me, yet one man left me his tinderbox, another his knife, and they promised to fetch me on their way back to Jamaica, unless another vessel found me first.

"I thought my luck was the Devil's own when Captain Holford, an old mate of mine, put in for water. I threw myself on his mercy, and the bastard absolutely

616

refused me, sure I would incite his men to take his ship. I protested mightily, and my word is my bond as much as any man's. Holford told me to steal a fishing boat, for he would return in a month, and if he found me, he would carry me to Jamaica for hanging.

"When another ship put in for water, I passed myself off as a shipwrecked sailor, and her captain took me aboard. I then spoke to the most discontented men of who should be captain of the tub, and what we might do with her. Yet, to my utter ruin, this ship fell in with Holford, and the two captains being friends, Holford came aboard to dine, and recognised me. I was put in irons, and brought here, and tomorrow I hang. An ordinary end to an extraordinary life.

"At least I was lucky enough to farewell Jack Rackam. A pity he ever sailed with you, Anne my dear. For he would have fought to the death if you had not been carrying his child. Oh yes, a gallant man, Jack Rackam. I knew him well. Better than you did, my dear. And I loved him better. For I would have forgiven him anything but the sacrifice of his Company for a mad bitch." When Anne saw 'twas true, Vane smiled like a shark to see her distress, his revenge complete.

He was taken away before dawn, with John Hanson still protesting he was no pirate, and Robert Hudson glaring furiously about him, determined not to submit. They were hanged at Gallows Point, and afterwards the corpse of Charles Vane was gibbeted outside Port Royal, along with Jack's.

My pregnancy grew upon me, my belly rounding and my breasts swelling, and yet I grew thinner each day, still unwilling to eat for the nausea that constantly oppressed me. I longed for the sweet red apples of my childhood, yet there were none in Jamaica. I longed for my mother, and knew she must be dead somewhere far away, unmourned by any. Tom begged me to resist death, for the sake of our babe, and I told him I'd rather take my child safe with me, than leave her alone and unprotected in this hard world.

617

Then the fever consumed me and I raved, abusing my mother for making a boy of me, berating Sally for leading me astray and breaking my heart. And Jan for his betrayal. And Macartney most of all. And God for abandoning me.

'Twas morning, a long time later, when my mind cleared. Tom was holding my hand, his handsome face haggard with tears. "What an ignoble end this is", I sighed. "I always learned my lessons too late. I'm only sorry to leave you here alone." Anne was sobbing her heart out. "Don't weep for me. I chose a hard life, and I'm glad 'tis almost over. Yet I fought with the best of them, by land and sea."

As the fever swept over me again, I begged her to escape death, even if it meant writing to her father, and begging his help. She denied me, and I cursed her. "Damn you, Anne Bonny, you always thought 'twas your stubborn pride that kept you strong. Well, you were wrong. 'Twas your courage. Your pride is merely cruel to those you love, like Jack, who'd never have surrendered but for his babe in your belly. Promise me that you will do everything you can to escape, even humbling yourself for your freedom. Write to your father, and tell him he's twice a grandfather. For you were not born to die here, as I was. Be free, Anne. Freedom is all that is worth fighting for." Even when the fever came down hard upon me, I kept insisting that her unborn babe was more important than her pride, and in the end, I persuaded her.

Then fever shook me as the storm shakes the sea. Yet beneath it. I was calm, my cares gone, my babe warm under my ribs. I tried to tell Tom to stop weeping, that all was well, yet I found I could not. And when the world faded and fell away from me, the relief was great.

Epilogue: Anne Bonny

Mary Read died in my arms on the twenty-eighth day o' April, 1721. We buried her and her unborn child in the paupers' section o' Spanish Town's dusty cemetery. Tom Deane's grief was so terrible to witness, I feared his soul would shatter. Needing to get him away from that cesspit of a gaol, I obeyed Mary's last request, and begged him to help me escape.

Indeed, Mary's last words had been like a slap to my face. I resented her hard judgement o' me, but she always spoke the truth. And with her death, something died within me, 'Anne the heedless child', she would say. I saw that it was me who had split our Company by refusing to stand down from battle once I was with child. I had destroyed all those I loved, with never a word o' sorrow for them after, not even for Jack, who had risked and lost everything to protect us. I grieved hard then, and thinking more o' my children, I vowed to stand by them for as long as they should need me.

Tom took my plea for freedom to heart, and sailed soon after to beg my father's help. He found the old sot half dead o' the drink, and maudlin for me. By the time they moored back in Jamaica, Tom had him sober, and together they bribed me out o' gaol. My father's health was wrecked, yet he sailed with us to claim his granddaughter back from Jack's family on Cuba. They were not happy to let her go, but Annie Fulworth insisted on leaving, and as she was the babe's nurse, they had no choice. My father died soon after our return to Carolina, but Annie and Tom were with me for the birth o' my son, Jack.

Not wanting to leave Tom alone, I insisted I needed his help to run the plantation I'd inherited. We made a success o' it, for we earned the loyalty o' our freed slaves, and production doubled. But the local planters hated us, and when we had made enough, we sold out. Tom bought his own place in the north, and shipped our freedmen with him to the New World. Although he asked me to go with him as his friend, I could not resist taking the opportunity to finally sail for England, a rich woman, my two children with me, and Annie Fulworth our companion.

In London, I found Sally Salisbury's great house in Shepherd's Fields, and found her surrounded by Lords. When I told her I had news o' Mary Read, she ordered the Lords out, and when I told her o' Mary's death, she wept like a child. She opened champagne, and we drank damnation to propriety, and to King George's new laws, sure that a more polite world would suit us less, though it would have pleased Mary Read.

Sally declared she'd just ordered the Duke o' Buckingham out o' the house he'd given her, and she showed me all over it, and swore she had eight thousand crowns a year to spend. We became friends, and I was with her that Winter, when she heard o' Buckingham's untimely death, and that he had left her a very rich woman.

I was also with her at the Drury Lane theatre, soon after, when she met pretty Jack Finch, Lord Finch's younger brother. She lost her head with her heart, for though she was rich and successful, her infamous reputation meant he could not marry her. She was plagued by jealousy, even o' his kindness to her young sister, and his casual attentions to me.

I met her at the Three Tuns Tavern in Chandon Street one afternoon, to find her already tipsy and demanding more wine. Jack Finch and her sister Jenny were supposed to meet us at two o'clock, and by four, Sally had drunk herself into a yellow rage. When they finally arrived, and declared they'd been at a play, she picked up a steak knife and stabbed her lover in the ribs.

She was immediately distraught, half aswoon, and begging for forgiveness. Though a surgeon was already staunching the scratch, Finch joked that it would be a pleasure to die by her hand, and sent her to recover at her own house. Yet when her enemies heard the scandal, they sent a Constable to arrest her for attempted murder, and she was taken to Newgate. Despite Finch's pleas for the charges to be withdrawn, she was found guilty, fined a thousand pounds, and sentenced to a year in Newgate gaol.

I visited her in Newgate days later, and she had already succumbed to gaol fever. Jack Finch tried to get her released on grounds o' ill-health, for it was soon evident that she would not live until her release. Sally died almost a skeleton, and six fine gentlemen bore her coffin to rest in Saint Andrews Church in Holborn, Jack Finch weeping all the way.

Sickened with London life, I bought a tavern in the south o' Cornwall, smuggled in the best French brandy, and boasted to the sailors o' my years with the Brethren. General George Macartney stepped in once, a fat, bloated, red-faced braggart, the change in Government having made him very respectable. In Mary's memory, I emptied an Indian poison into his beer that ruined his guts, and he died o' the drink soon after.

I heard that Woodes Rogers was successful in pleading his case to have his debts paid, and when he was re-made Governor o' the Bahamas, I drank to his damnation. He returned in 1739, and with the Brethren gone, claimed credit for finally taming Nassau. That same year, Tom Deane wrote that the Maroons o' Jamaica had forced their Governor into signing a formal peace treaty, recognising their freedom, and granting them one and a half thousand acres o' mountain land. Also in 1739, I saw Kit Ross buried with full military honours at Chelsea Hospital, the first time a woman had ever been accorded such a privilege.

Then the cold, dead Winter made me long for the golden sun o' my own land, as the new fashion for decency and hypocrisy made me long for the freedom o' the Brethren. In the end, I sold my tavern for a handsome profit, and took my children back to the New World, to begin my life again. And though I looked to find new company, I knew in my heart that I could never find a friend as true and as dear to me as that honest pirate, Mary Read.

621